MAGICAL REALIST FICTION

An Anthology

MAGICAL REALIST FICTION

An Anthology

Edited by
David Young and Keith Hollaman

LONGMAN INC.
New York & London

Magical Realist Fiction

Longman Inc., 1560 Broadway, New York, N.Y. 10036
Associated companies, branches, and representatives
throughout the world.

Developmental Editor: Gordon T.R. Anderson
Editorial Supervisor: Thomas Bacher
Interior Designer: Thomas Bacher
Production/Manufacturing: Ferne Y. Kawahara
Composition: Graphicraft Typesetters Ltd.
Printing and Binding: The Alpine Press, Inc.

Library of Congress Cataloging in Publication Data
Main entry under title:

Magical realist fiction.

  1. Fantastic fiction. I. Young, David P.
II. Hollaman, Keith. III. Title: Realist fiction.
PN6071.F25M24 1984   808.83'876   83–19974
ISBN 0–582–28452–X

Printing: 9 8 7 6 5 4 3 2 1 Year: 92 91 90 89 88 87 86 85 84

CONTENTS

ACKNOWLEDGMENTS

"The Nose" by Nikolai Gogol. Translated by Olga Markof-Belaeff. Reprinted by permission of Olga Markof-Belaeff.

"The Porcelain Doll" from *The Kreutzer Sonata and Other Tales* by Leo Tolstoy, translated by Aylmer Maude (1940). Reprinted by permission of Oxford University Press.

"The Wardrobe" by Thomas Mann. Copyright 1936 and renewed 1964 by Alfred A. Knopf, Inc. Reprinted from *Stories of Three Decades*, by Thomas Mann, translated by H.T. Lowe-Porter, by permission of Alfred A. Knopf, Inc.

"The Tale of the Cavalry" by Hugo von Hofmannsthal. Hugo von Hofmannsthal, *Selected Prose*, trans. Mary Hottinger, Tania and James Stern, Bollingen Series 33, Vol. 1. Copyright 1952 by Princeton University Press, © renewed 1980 by Princeton University Press. Excerpt, pp. 321–331, reprinted by permission of Princeton University Press.

"The Death of Chamberlain Brigge" and "The Hand" by Rainer Maria Rilke. Selections are reprinted from *The Notebooks of Malte Laurids Brigge* by Rainer Maria Rilke, translated by M.D. Herter Norton, by permission of W.W. Norton & Company, Inc. Copyright 1949 by W.W. Norton & Company, Inc. Copyright renewed 1977 by M.D. Herter Norton.

"Odour of Chrysanthemums" and "The Blind Man" by D.H. Lawrence. From *The Complete Short Stories of D.H. Lawrence*. Volume II. Copyright 1922 by Thomas Seltzer, Inc. Copyright 1934 by Frieda Lawrence. Copyright renewed 1950 by Frieda Lawrence. Copyright renewed 1962 by Angelo Ravagli and C. Montague Weekley, Executors of the Estate of Frieda Lawrence Ravagli. Reprinted by permission of Viking Penguin Inc. All rights reserved.

"A Country Doctor" and "The Bucket Rider" by Franz Kafka. Reprinted by permission of Schocken Books Inc. from *The Penal Colony* by Franz Kafka (trans. by Willa and Edwin Muir). Copyright © 1948, 1976 by Schocken Books Inc.

"The Sin of Jesus" by Isaac Babel. Reprinted by permission of S.G. Phillips, Inc. from *The Collected Stories of Isaac Babel*. Copyright © 1955 by S.G. Phillips, Inc.

"Lyompa" from *Envy and Other Works* by Yuri Olesha. Translated by Andrew R. MacAndrew. Copyright © 1960 by Andrew R. MacAndrew. Reprinted by permission of Doubleday & Company, Inc.

"The Egyptian Stamp, Chapter One" by Osip Mandelstam, Clarence Brown, ed., *The Prose of Osip Mandelstam*. Copyright © 1965 by Princeton University Press. Selection, pp. 151–55, reprinted by permission of Princeton University Press.

"The Great Frost" by Virginia Woolf. From *Orlando*, copyright 1928 by Virginia Woolf; renewed 1956 by Leonard Woolf. Reprinted by permission of Harcourt Brace Jovanovich, Inc.

"The Street of Crocodiles" by Bruno Schulz. From *The Street of Crocodiles* by Bruno Schulz. Copyright 1963 by C.J. Schulz. Used by permission of Walker & Company.

"The Visit to the Museum" from *A Russian Beauty and Other Stories* by Vladimir Nabokov. Copyright © 1973 by McGraw-Hill International, Inc. Used by permission of Mrs. V. Nabokov and McGraw-Hill Book Company.

"New Islands" from *New Islands and Other Stories* by María Luisa Bombal. Copyright © 1976 by Editorial Orbe, Santiago de Chile. Translation copyright © 1982 by Farrar, Straus and Giroux, Inc. Reprinted by permission of Farrar, Straus and Giroux.

"Views of My Father Weeping" from *City Life* by Donald Barthelme. Copyright © 1969 by Donald Barthelme. Reprinted by permission of Farrar, Straus and Giroux, Inc.

"In the Village" from *Questions of Travel* by Elizabeth Bishop. Copyright © 1953 by Elizabeth Bishop. Reprinted by permission of Farrar, Straus and Giroux, Inc.

"The Smallest Women in the World" by Clarice Lispector. Translation copyright © 1973 by Elizabeth Bishop. Reprinted by permission of Farrar, Straus and Giroux, Inc.

Aura by Carlos Fuentes. Copyright © 1965 by Carlos Fuentes. Reprinted by permission of Farrar, Straus and Giroux, Inc.

INTRODUCTION

THE TERM "magical realism," as applied to fiction, has begun to have a certain currency since the recent award of the Nobel Prize for Literature to Gabriel García Márquez. However, when we first began to compile this collection it was anything but well known. The term had been used in art history to characterize some painters (most notably, Arnold Böcklin and Giorgio di Chirico). Those who have followed the fortunes of South American fiction know that it has been used (in the first instance, perhaps, by Angel Flores in 1954) to characterize the work of Borges and writers who followed him. But its use was controversial, and in 1973, Gregory Rabassa, García Márquez's able translator, felt moved to protest its use because he felt it gave too much credence to "realism" as a norm.

Whatever its limitations—and all such terms have them—we found the term and what it implied extremely useful in defining for ourselves a category of fiction that could be distinguished from traditional realistic and naturalistic fiction on the one hand, and from recognized categories of the fantastic: ghost story, science fiction, gothic novel, and fairy tale. Thus we retained it, both as a working concept for exploring a genre, and as the title for the anthology that eventually resulted from our reading, discussing, and collecting. The recent increase in popularity of the term has made us feel less defensive about our decision to stick with it, but there is also the fact that any other term, such as "fiction of the marvelous," or "fiction of conflicting realities," would be both more cumbersome and less expressive.

One way to understand "magical realism" is as a kind of pleasant joke on "realism," suggesting as it does a new kind of fiction, produced in

1

reaction to the confining assumptions of realism, a hybrid that somehow manages to combine the "truthful" and "verifiable" aspects of realism with the "magical" effects we associate with myth, folktale, tall story, and that being in all of us—our childhood self, perhaps—who loves the spell that narrative casts even when it is perfectly implausible.

A crucial feature of the term, then, lies in its duality. It is a centaur, an easy or uneasy "amalgamation," as Flores called it. What this suggests is that the most distinctive aspects of magical realism lie at the point where two different realities intersect, perhaps to collide, perhaps to merge. Familiar oppositions—life and death, waking and sleeping, child and adult, civilized and "savage"—are much at home in this genre, though not necessarily with their differences resolved. They may marry or exchange identities; they may agree to disagree. What matters is that the domination of any one way of looking at things is, at least temporarily, placed in jeopardy. Normal notions about time, place, identity, matter and the like are challenged, suspended, lured away from certitude. The results can be exhilarating. Montaigne's famous speculation as to whether, when he thought he was amusing himself with his cat, the truth might in fact be that the cat was amusing itself with him, is almost a magical realist story in miniature. It uses our deep-seated sense of the magic of animals (they seem more fully at home in the world, their poise and beauty give them an air of mysterious completeness) to drive a wedge of doubt into the "realist" assumption that we are superior to animals and can "own" them. Here, in a blacksmith's shop, is Elizabeth Bishop's version of the same insight:

> The horse is the real guest, however. His harness hangs loose like a man's suspenders; they say pleasant things to him; one of his legs is doubled up in an improbably, affectedly polite way, and the bottom of his hoof is laid bare, but he doesn't seem to mind. Manure piles up behind him, suddenly, neatly. He, too, is very much at home. He is enormous. His rump is like a brown, glossy globe of the whole brown world. His ears are secret entrances to the underworld. His nose is supposed to feel like velvet and does, with ink spots under milk all over its pink. Clear, bright-green bits of stiffened froth, like glass, are stuck around his mouth. He wears medals on his chest, too, and one on his forehead, and simpler decorations—red and blue celluloid rings overlapping each other on leather straps. On each temple is a clear glass bulge, like an eyeball, but in them are the heads of two other horses (his dreams?), brightly colored, real and raised, un-touchable, alas, against backgrounds of silver blue. His trophies hang around him, and the cloud of his odor is a chariot in itself.

The observer in this passage is a child, but neither that nor our awareness of the strong metaphorical dimension of the style serves to qualify or interrupt our sense that two kinds of truth, animal magic and everyday existence, are being woven together in a way that delights us, informs us, expands us. Many of our waking moments are spent out of touch with our own imaginations. When something puts us back in touch, without cutting us off from our wakefulness, we feel bigger, wiser, more at home in the world.

Sometimes the intersecting in a magical realist story is large-scale, a colliding of cultures or civilizations, one "primitive" and hence in touch with magic, the other "civilized" and presumably "realistic," i.e., committed to science and wary of illusion and superstition. It is important to recognize this collision in cultural terms because its very scale helps us understand that magical realism is not so much a challenge to the conventions of literary realism, as it is to the basic assumptions of modern positivistic thought, the soil in which literary realism flourished. Magical realism's inquiries drive deep, questioning the political and metaphysical definitions of the real by which most of us live. Perhaps this is one reason why South America has been such a fertile ground for this kind of fiction. Native and colonial cultures have collided there again and again. The primitive and the modern still coexist, cheek by jowl. Peasants, whom we tend to see both as wiser and more credulous than ourselves, still constitute a large segment of society. Political extremes and turmoil have helped nourish a skepticism about the values of the industrial revolution. In writers like Borges, Cortázar, García Márquez and Lispector, "reality" is capable of turning sharp corners and surprising us, a maneuver behind which we sense a biting critique of the vanity of Western civilization and an understanding of cultural relativity. When North American and English writers like Faulkner and Welty, Lawrence and Woolf, bring the same implicit comparison to bear on our own worlds, they remind us that our literary heritage includes writers like Hawthorne and Poe, Dickens and Swift, who questioned the assumptions of reason and science that everything could be accounted for within their terms and by their tools of knowledge.

Our suspicion that there are people among whom genuine magic still survives—American Indians, European peasants, eccentric inventors, clowns, and conjurors—is enough of an opening for that wedge of doubt Montaigne employed. A complementary factor may be found in the way in which modern civilization seems magical to outsiders. After seeing ice through the entranced eyes of the natives of Macondo in García Márquez's *One Hundred Years of Solitude*, we will never take it quite for granted again, and the relativity of "reality" as we know it will have been made clear to us in yet another way. A child's view of a horse, a peasant's view of ice: the real magic of fiction is the way it can bring these to us with a force that enhances our normal consciousness. The relativity just mentioned, which is after all a scientific term used since Einstein, should remind us that science itself has moved from the positivist and materialist views that supported realism to a set of skeptical and pluralistic attitudes matching the new mode of fiction presented here.

While it is exhilarating to watch cultures collide, the juxtaposing of city and country can serve the same purpose, as a number of works in this volume by writers as diverse as Kafka, Calvino, Escarpit and Borges will demonstrate. Magical realism may trace its ancestry to the genres of romance and pastoral, which are in turn derived from ancient classics like *The Odyssey* and *Gilgamesh*, demonstrating how travel broadens and that there are more things in heaven and earth than are dreamed of in our philosophy. Far afield or close to home, they tell us, we may find our settled expectations overturned, our sense of wonder refreshed and renewed. *The Thousand and One Nights* is not magical realism, but it is the right kind of companion for Borges' hero in "The South," Juan Dahlmann, to carry about with him on his journey from city to country, present to past, and from the "real" to the "imagined." In that story, as in so many other of our examples, the intersections are multiple. Indeed, we need to remember that a collision of cultures may be metaphoric, as when the coexistence of childhood and adulthood is suddenly revealed to us (Olesha, Bishop), or when the interpenetration of life and death (Rilke, Lawrence) is exposed. Playing with past and present, near and far, exposes the vulnerability of our norms for time (Carpentier) and space (Nabokov). When we have finished a good magical realist story we cannot say which is the real and which the magical, where fact leaves off and fancy begins. James's Spencer Brydon, in "The Jolly Corner," undertakes a pursuit of what he and we are sure must be mere hypothesis. As its reality dawns on him, and us, we abandon our sense that such firm distinctions are possible. Once outside the story, we may rush to embrace them once more, but they may never again hold quite the same solidity for us. A French critic, Tristan Todorov, has said that in stories of this kind the reader must *hesitate*; if you believe that he who hesitates is lost, this volume is not for you.

The Henry James story will serve to make a further point about magical realism, a way of distinguishing genuine examples (at least as we editors have understood them) and stories that resemble them in some respects. In a magical realist story there must be an irreducible element, something that cannot be explained by logic, familiar knowledge, or received belief. If, after reading "The Jolly Corner," you conclude that Spencer Brydon's experience can be explained as hallucination or neurosis, you will have appealed to that large body of modern orthodoxy (familiar knowledge? received belief?) known as psychology, and the story will not be an example of magical realism for you. To reach that conclusion you will have to ignore the separate fact of Alice Staverton's corroborating dream, the means by which James asserts a reality for the phantom self, an existence outside Brydon's own consciousness. This "difficulty" in the story led one critic, in what is surely an unprecedented example of "irritable reaching after fact" (Keats), to argue that the whole thing was Alice's plot to marry Brydon, and that the apparition was Alice herself in disguise! But even if you manage to "explain" the James story in such terms, you will have difficulty marshalling "evidence" to settle questions arising from other stories in this collection. How is the angel in "A Very Old Man with Enormous Wings" to be accounted for? We learn that he is a phenomenon beyond the ken of the church, as first represented by father Gonzaga and then by the Vatican. Few of us would write him off as the joint hallucination of the whole populace. We must take him as a given, accepted but not explained.

Such accountings, of course, take place on the story's own terms. If we hear of a man with wings, we do not need to verify him immediately by seeing one outside our window. However, we might want some link of prior knowledge we can refer him to. Many stories would give us evidence for a "reasonable" accounting: he was an angel, as such beings are understood and described by religious doctrine; he was somebody's daydream; he was an ordinary man with a pair of false wings fixed to his back. García Márquez refuses that option. He seems to understand that those "reasonable" explanations finally refer to bodies of knowledge and belief outside the story itself, constituting a reassurance that he does not care to provide. Of course we know as we read a story, that on the whole it is fictitious. But we like, most of us, to go into even an illusory labyrinth with a little string to help us get out. In a science fiction story, the string says that science will eventually be able to account for everything the universe may confront us with; we rise to the challenge of verification. In a ghost story, the string says that people have often believed in ghosts and that it will be fun for us to suspend our disbelief accordingly. Some stories, like those of Sholem Aleichem and Isaac Bashevis Singer, are loosely associated with traditional bodies of religious belief; the connection constitutes a kind of mild validation that makes possible a certain detachment on the reader's part; to recall Todorov's criterion, they don't make one *hesitate*.

Most often, magical realism resists our contemporary faith in the idea that things anomalous and unsettling, beyond the grasp of "proof," can generally be accounted for as aberrations of the human mind. Quirks of the individual consciousness don't need to affect our basic sense of what's real, although they may. If the reaction to literary realism (and its earnest laboratory counterpart, naturalism) can be said to have taken one important direction through the *internalization* of the fictional in writers such as Proust, Joyce and Woolf—a turning inward to a more faithful representation of subjectivity, of the shifting but omnipresent screen between ourselves and things beyond us called consciousness—then magical realism can be recognized as a divergent tendency toward a different treatment of the *external*, the world outside consciousness. Even a sensitive reader may feel tempted while reading Kafka to exclaim: "Why, this is a portrayal of insanity!" But that same reader will sense

Kafka's firm resistance to such a conclusion. And so it will be with Rilke, Lawrence, Borges, and all the others here.

The distinction, discussed above, between stories that explain themselves and stories that don't, sounds easier to make than in practice is actually the case. That is because the presence of "explanation" in a story can be a subtle and arguable matter. At one point in our work on this collection, we were trying to choose between two Faulkner stories: "Spotted Horses" and "The Old People." The more we thought about it, the more the latter seemed a clear-cut example of our genre. But why? There was more humor in "Spotted Horses," but we knew from stories like "The Nose," "Gogol's Wife," and "Blacamán the Good, Vendor of Miracles" that magical realism can be wildly funny. It was more a matter of shading and nuance. A magic associated with animals is invoked in both stories, but "Spotted Horses" tends to concentrate on human folly in the form of a bravura treatment of greed and superstition. Magic exists in the story, but we feel detached from it rather than drawn into it. In "The Old People," the reader merges with the magic. One does not *want* to explain the apparition of the deer as superstition or hallucination, but is instead content with the growth of mystery, with full participation in the sense of wonder with which the story closes. Perhaps, it is not only that magic realism makes you hesitate between possibilities; it makes you value that hesitation. Not only does it withhold answers, but it teaches you to enjoy the questions as well.

Is there any such thing as a typical magical realist story? Every reader will find stories that seem central to the concept and others that seem peripheral, but the notion of a prototype or model is too restrictive. If you consider the fundamental patterns these stories may follow, you will discover two options right away. There is the story that offers one fantastic premise and then adheres to logic and natural law. If clouds were manufactured, then what happens in "The Cloud Maker" would lie squarely within the realm of everything we know about human nature. If a severed hand could lead a separate life, then it would probably become a household pet and eventually a nuisance, as in "Major Aranda's Hand." If a woman turned into a porcelain doll, then no doubt her husband would behave much as Tolstoy claims to have done in his letter to his wife's sister. And so it goes. In such stories, the "magical" comes first and the "realism" ensues. A second possibility is a story which begins naturally and with familiar events and details, and then moves toward the extraordinary. It may do so gradually, as in the James, Mann, and Faulkner stories. Or it may change suddenly, as in "The Country Doctor" and "The Aleph."

These possibilities scarcely exhaust the genre. There are stories in this collection which fit neither one of them. The more we have explored magical realism, the more we have been impressed by its range and scope. It accommodates stories of more or less pure fantasy, like the

Michaux and Calvino selections. And it includes stories which are only slightly tinged with strangeness, like "Lyompa" and "The Piano." Some examples are told very simply and straightforwardly, like Babel's "The Sin of Jesus" and Kaleb's "The Guest." In others, style is a strong presence and figurative language colors our sense of the real, as in the selections from Mandelstam, Nabokov, and Bishop. In making our selections, we have tried to do justice to this range of possibilities.

A larger, more comprehensive anthology might give more attention to earlier writers, reaching back to Poe and Hawthorne, even to Ovid and Homer. But we have taken our term to imply a reaction to literary realism, so that most of our examples come either from this century or from the last years of the nineteenth century (Gogol, whose story was written in 1836, is the sole exception). Even within that range, the collecting of examples could go on and on, so we decided, when we had enough superb specimens to make a good-sized book, not to worry too much about the tantalizing possibilities that always exist around the next corner or between the covers of the next book. We do regret the omission of some authors and of second examples by favorite writers due to limitations of space and problems with high permissions costs, but these factors were, of course, beyond our control.

It is important, we think, to take note of the fact that this book began as a collaboration, at Oberlin College, between a teacher and a student. That may help to explain the nature of its appeal and its potential as a textbook. It constitutes a natural meeting ground. Young people have in recent years demonstrated a strong appetite for literature connected with fantasy. They read Tolkien; they read *Watership Down*; they read the Dune trilogy; they read Carlos Castenada. At the same time, their teachers are naturally anxious to introduce them to serious and substantial texts that represent a literary tradition. In the case of fiction, this tradition is a mixture of realistic and nonrealistic writings. It includes authors not represented here, but many of its best practitioners can indeed be found in this book.

One value of this collection, then, may lie in its ability to bridge the differences of appetite and enthusiasm that naturally separate different generations. *Magical Realist Fiction* says, or implies, that good fiction may partake of both fact and fancy, dream and waking, positivism and relativism. It shows students that what they liked in Tolkien and Castenada is present, perhaps in a more comprehensive form, in Kafka, Borges, Faulkner, Woolf, and Nabokov. And it reminds the teacher that recent fiction has gone beyond the realist tradition without altogether abandoning its values. The book wasn't created with this bridging effect in mind, but that is one of its most notable possibilities.

Another virtue of this collection, as we see it, lies in its international character. It is less risky, obviously, to teach materials only in one's own language, sticking with English and American fiction. But the world we live in has seen, and is seeing, some very substantial changes, and it's probably fair to say that these days a literate person ought to be someone for whom names like Borges and Calvino are familiar parts of an expanding literary heritage. There is no anthology currently on the market providing anything like a survey of this new heritage. This one at least provides a beginning.

We are especially indebted to Vinio Rossi and Kathy Spahn; both had a familiarity with magical realism that they were very generous in sharing. Many others—Stuart Friebert, Andrew Hoover, Marjorie Hoover, Mark Strand, Harriet Turner, David Walker, and Franz Wright—provided valuable leads. Other anthologies, particularly Barbara Howes' *The Eye of the Heart*, Randall Jarrell's forgotten classic, *The Anchor Book of Stories*, J.M. Cohen's *Latin American Writing Today*, and Jerome Beaty's *Fiction* (1973) in the Norton Introduction to Literature Series, made our task much easier. While one editor, David Young, has written this introduction, all the ideas in it were evolved jointly; it should be regarded, like the book itself, as the product of an agreeable and instructive collaboration.

Notes

The paper by Angel Flores, "Magical Realism in Spanish American Fiction" was published in *Hispania*, vol. 38, no. 2 (May, 1955). Gregory Rabassa's protest against the term was registered in "Beyond Magical Realism; Thoughts on the Art of Gabriel García Márquez," in *Books Abroad*, vol. 47, no. 3 (Summer, 1973). Tzvetan Todorov's book is entitled *The Fantastic: A Structural Approach to a Literary Genre* (Case Western Reserve, 1973, viz. pp. 25 and 31).

As we completed work on this volume, we discovered an anthology of Canadian short stories, *Magic Realism*, edited by Geoff Hancock (Toronto: Aya Press, 1980) that should certainly be of interest to the readers of this collection.

NIKOLAI GOGOL

NIKOLAI GOGOL (1809–1852), the Russian novelist and dramatist, has variously been seen as a romantic writer, an early realist, and a satirist of unparalleled gifts. His best-known works are the novel Dead Souls (1842) and the play The Inspector General (1836), but short stories like "The Nose" and "The Overcoat" are close behind in popularity. Misguided criticism about his fiction dismayed Gogol, and he turned to religious faith for comfort, spending most of his later years in Rome. Before he died, he destroyed the manuscript of the sequel to Dead Souls, on which he had been working the last ten years of his life.

Gogol is an exception to our general rule for this anthology; that is, to select mainly twentieth-century writers with a few also from the late nineteenth century. The reason for our choice is that Gogol is simply too important to ignore. If Russian fiction, as someone has remarked, came out of Gogol's overcoat, then magical realism might be said to have come out of his nose. The matter-of-fact way in which "The Nose" asks us to accept the departure, adventures, and return of Kovalyov's nose, as well as the teasing by the narrator, who obfuscates, blusters, hedges, and generally tweaks our noses, is not only wonderful in itself, but a remarkable prototype for fiction that was mainly produced in this century by innovators like Kafka and Borges. Gogol deserves his special place in this anthology, and it is a pleasure to introduce readers who may not have encountered such writing previously to a story so remarkable for its time (1836) and so important to the kind of fiction this book features. We are delighted to present this classic in a new translation by Olga Markof-Belaeff, commissioned especially for this anthology.

The Nose

Nikolai Gogol

I

A N UNUSUALLY odd event took place in St. Petersburg on March twenty-fifth. Ivan Yakovlevich, the barber who lives on Voznesensky Avenue (his last name is not known and even his shop sign, which features a gentleman with a lathered cheek and the announcement, "And they let blood too," reveals nothing else), woke up rather early and sensed the aroma of hot bread. Sitting up on his bed, he saw that his spouse, a rather respectable lady who liked to drink coffee very much, was removing freshly baked loaves from the oven.

"I won't have coffee today, Praskovya Osipovna," Ivan Yakovlevich said. "Instead, I'd like to have a bit of warm bread with onions." (In fact, Ivan Yakovlevich would have liked to have had both but he knew that it was absolutely impossible to ask for two things at once because Praskovya Osipovna did not like such fancies at all.) "Let the dolt eat bread, it's even better for me," the wife thought to herself. "There will be coffee left over." And she threw a loaf on the table.

Ivan Yakovlevich put on his tailcoat over his shirt for propriety's sake, sat down at the table and having poured some salt and prepared two onions, took a knife and with a serious face began to slice the bread. He cut the bread in half and looked inside. To his surprise, he saw something white. He carefully poked it with the knife and felt it with his finger. "It's solid," he remarked to himself. "What could it be?"

He reached in and pulled out—a nose! Ivan Yakovlevich's hands dropped. He rubbed his eyes and felt again: a nose, no question about it!

11

And what is more, it seemed to be someone familiar. Horror distorted Ivan Yakovlevich's face. But his horror was nothing compared with the indignation that seized his wife.

"Where did you cut off that nose, you beast?" she yelled in anger. "Cheat! Drunkard! I'll report you to the police myself. You brigand! Three people have told me already that you pull on noses so hard when you shave that they can hardly stay on."

But Ivan Yakovlevich was petrified. He had realized that this nose belonged to none other than Collegiate Assessor Kovalyov, whom he shaved every Wednesday and Sunday.

"Wait, Praskovya Osipovna! I'll wrap it in a rag and put it away in a corner—let it sit there for a bit; then I'll take it out."

"I won't hear of it! You want me to have a cut-off nose lying about my room? You dried-up crust! All you ever do is run your razor up and down the strap; soon you'll be completely incapable of fulfilling your duty. You slut! You scoundrel! You want me to answer to the police on your account? Oh you slob. You stupid blockhead! Out, out! I don't care where you take it, just get it out of my sight!"

Ivan Yakovlevich was stunned. He thought and thought and did not know what to think.

"How the hell did it happen," he said finally, scratching behind his ear. "I couldn't tell you for sure whether I was drunk last night or not. And it must be an impossible event by any reckoning, since bread is baked stuff and a nose is something else completely. I can't figure it out!"

Ivan Yakovlevich fell silent. The thought that the police might find a nose on him and he might be accused drove him into a total stupor. He was already having visions of a crimson collar beautifully embroidered in silver, a sword...and his whole body trembled. Finally, he got out his underwear and boots, pulled on all that junk and, wrapping the nose in a rag, went out into the street to the accompaniment of Praskovya Osipovna's hefty reproaches.

He wanted to get rid of it somehow: either to slip it behind a pillar next to the gate or sort of let it drop nonchalantly and then turn into an alley. Unfortunately, he kept running into acquaintances who immediately launched into questioning: "Where are you going?" or "Whom are you setting out to shave so early?"—so that Ivan Yakovlevich just could not find the right moment. Once he had already dropped the nose when a constable pointed with his halberd from a distance and added: "Pick it up! You dropped something over there!" So Ivan Yakovlevich was forced to pick up the nose and put it in his pocket. Desperation seized him, especially since more and more people appeared on the street as stores and vending stands opened.

He decided to walk toward St. Isaac's Bridge—with luck he might be able to throw it into the Neva. But I must apologize, I still haven't said anything about Ivan Yakovlevich, a man respectable in many ways.

Ivan Yakovlevich, like any decent Russian tradesman, was a hopeless drunk. And even though he shaved other people's chins every day, his own was always unshaven. Ivan Yakovlevich's tailcoat (Ivan Yakovlevich never wore frockcoats) was mottled; that is it was black, but covered with brownish-yellow and grey spots. The collar was oily and bits of thread hung where three buttons used to be. Ivan Yakovlevich was a great cynic and when Collegiate Assessor Kovalyov said to him during shaving, "Your hands always stink, Ivan Yakovlevich!" he would answer with the question, "Why would they smell?" "I don't know why, pal, but they do," the Collegiate Assessor would reply and Ivan Yakovlevich, taking a pinch of snuff, would lather Kovalyov's cheek in response, under his nose, behind the ear, and under his chin—in short, everywhere he felt like.

This worthy citizen was already on St. Isaac's Bridge. First he looked all around, then he leaned over the railing as if to look under the bridge—to see if there were many fish—and quietly tossed the rag with the nose. He felt as if he had shed a hundred pounds. Ivan Yakovlevich even smiled. Instead of going to shave clerks' chins, he set out for an establishment with the sign "Food and Tea" to get a glass of punch when he suddenly saw at the end of the bridge a precinct policeman of dignified appearance with spreading sideburns, a three-cornered hat, and a sword. He froze. Meanwhile the policeman wagged his finger at him, saying:

"Come over here, buddy!"

Ivan Yakovlevich, who knew what was expected, pulled off his cap, and walking up briskly, said:

"Good health to you, your honor!"

"No, no, buddy, not 'your honor'; now tell me what you were doing there as you were standing on the bridge."

"By God, sir, I had been out shaving and only looked to see if the current was swift."

"You are lying! You won't get away with it. Come on, own up!"

"Sir, I'm ready to shave you twice a week, or even three times without any argument," Ivan Yakovlevich replied.

"No, pal, that's nonsense! I have three barbers who give me shaves and consider it a great honor, too. Now, why don't you tell me what you were doing there?"

Ivan Yakovlevich went pale.... But here the events fog up completely and what happened next is absolutely unknown.

II

Collegiate Assessor Kovalyov woke up rather early and went "brrr..." with his mouth, something he always did when he woke up even though he could not explain why. Kovalyov stretched and demanded that a small mirror that was standing on the table be handed to him. He wanted to look at a small pimple that had come out on his nose the day before, but to his enormous surprise he saw that he had a completely smooth spot instead of a nose. Frightened, Kovalyov asked for water and rubbed his eyes with a towel: that's right, no nose! He began to feel with his hand to see if he was asleep; it seemed he wasn't. Collegiate Assessor Kovalyov jumped out of bed, shook himself: no nose! He asked to be dressed immediately and rushed directly to the chief of police.

But in the meantime, it is necessary to say something about Kovalyov so that the reader should know what kind of collegiate assessor he was. Collegiate assessors who acquire the rank with the help of learned diplomas can't be compared at all to those collegiate assessors who are made in the Caucasus. These are two completely different categories. Learned collegiate assessors... But Russia is such a wonderful country that if you say anything about one collegiate assessor, all collegiate assessors from Riga to Kamchatka will inevitably take it personally. The same applies to all professions and ranks. Kovalyov was a Caucasus collegiate assessor. He had held the rank only two years, could not forget it for a minute, and in order to acquire even more dignity and weight he never called himself "Collegiate Assessor," but "Major." "Listen, dearie," he would usually say to a woman who sold shirt fronts upon meeting her on the street, "Come to my house; I live on Sadovaya Street. Just ask: does Major Kovalyov live here? Anyone will show you." If he came across one that was pretty, he would give her an additional secret request, adding: "Ask for Major Kovalyov's apartment, honey." That is why we will call this collegiate assessor "major" from now on.

Major Kovalyov was in the habit of taking a stroll on Nevsky Avenue every day. His shirt collar was always exceedingly clean and starched. His whiskers were of the sort one can still see on provincial and district land surveyors, architects, and regimental doctors, and also on men with different kinds of police duties and in general on those men who have full ruddy cheeks and play whist very well—these whiskers run down the very center of the cheek and straight to the nose. Major Kovalyov wore many heart-shaped fobs and crested signets, some stamped Wednesday, Thursday, Monday, and the like. Major Kovalyov had come to St. Petersburg on business, namely in search of a position, as a vice-governor if possible and if not, as a senior clerk in some prominent department. Major Kovalyov was also not averse to getting married, but only if the bride had a two hundred thousand ruble dowry. And thus the readers may judge for themselves what sort of situation this major found himself in when he saw, instead of a fairly handsome and regular nose, a most stupid, even and smooth spot.

To make things worse, there were no cabs in sight on the street and he was forced to walk, wrapped in his cloak and his face covered with a

handkerchief, as if he had a nosebleed. . . ." But maybe I just imagined it;
a nose couldn't disappear just like that," he thought and stepped inside
a pastry shop with the intention of taking a look in a mirror. Fortunately,
there was no one in the store. Sleepy-eyed boys were sweeping the rooms
and setting up chairs, some were bringing out trays of hot meat pies; the
tables and chairs were strewn with yesterday's coffee-stained newspapers. "Thank God, there is no one here," he muttered, "now I can take a
look." He came up to a mirror timidly and looked. "What the hell, such
rubbish!" he muttered and spat. "If at least there were something instead
of a nose, but—nothing. . . !"

He bit his lip in frustration and left the pastry shop determined,
contrary to his custom, not to look or smile at anyone. Suddenly he
stopped dead in his tracks by the entrance to a house; an indescribable
event had occurred in front of his eyes. A carriage had stopped at the
entrance, its doors opened, a gentleman in uniform jumped out holding
his head low and ran up the steps. What horror and, at the same time
amazement, seized Kovalyov when he realized that it was his very own
nose! Everything seemed to have been turned upside down after this
extraordinary sight. He felt he could barely stand up but decided,
trembling as in a fever, to wait at any cost until his nose returned to the
carriage. Two minutes later, the nose did in fact come out. He was
wearing a gold-embroidered uniform, suede breeches, and a sword.
Judging by his plumed hat, he held the rank of state councilor. Everything indicated that he was going out to pay a visit. He glanced in
both directions, shouted "Let's go!" to the coachman, got in and drove
off.

Poor Kovalyov almost lost his mind. He didn't even know what to
think of such a strange event. How could it really be that a nose which
was on his face yesterday, was now walking and riding, and in uniform!
He ran after the carriage, which luckily drove for a short distance and
stopped outside Kazan Cathedral. He rushed to the church pushing his
way through a crowd of old beggar women with wrapped faces and just
slits for eyes, at whom he used to laugh so much, and went in. There
were only a few people praying, all of them stood near the entrance door.
Kovalyov felt so distraught that he did not have the strength to pray and
searched every corner with his eyes, looking for the gentleman. He finally
saw him standing on the side. The nose had hidden his face entirely
behind his large standing collar and prayed with an expression of utmost
piety. "How am I going to come up to him," Kovalyov thought. "You can
tell by his uniform, his hat, by every thing that he is a state councilor. The
devil knows how one should do it!"

He began to clear his throat nearby but the nose would not abandon
his pious pose for a minute and continued his assiduous devotions.

"My dear sir," Kovalyov said, inwardly forcing himself to be bold,
"dear sir. . . ."

"What do you wish?" the nose answered, turning.

"It seems odd. . . dear sir. . . it seems to me. . .you should know your place. And suddenly I find you, and where? In church. You must admit. . . ."

"I beg your pardon, I can't seem to grasp your meaning. . . . Do explain."

"How can I explain," Kovalyov thought and, mustering courage, began:

"Of course. . .I am, by the way, a major. For me to walk around without a nose, you must agree, is unseemly. A street vendor who sells peeled oranges on Voskresensky Bridge could sit about without a nose; but I have the intention of securing. . .and in addition, I am acquainted with many ladies in houses. Chekhtaryova, a state councilor's wife, and others. . . . You be the judge. . .I don't know, dear sir"—here Major Kovalyov shrugged his shoulders—"forgive me. . .if one were to look upon the matter in accordance with the laws of honor and duty. . .you can understand yourself. . . ."

"I don't understand anything at all," the nose replied. "Be so kind as to speak clearly."

"Dear sir," Kovalyov said with dignity, "I don't know what I am to make of your words. . . . The whole matter seems to be quite obvious. . . . Or if you want. . . . But then, you are my very own nose!"

The nose looked at the major and his brow clouded slightly.

"You are mistaken, dear sir. I am by myself. Besides, there can be no close connection between us. Judging by the buttons on your uniform, you must serve in the Senate or, at least, in the Ministry of Justice. And I am in academics."

Having said this, the nose turned away and resumed praying. Kovalyov was completely confused; he didn't know what to think. The pleasant rustle of ladies' dresses was heard at this moment: an older lady came up, all swathed in lace, and a thin one beside her, in a white dress that was outlined charmingly on her graceful waist, and a cream-colored hat as light as a pastry. Snuffbox in hand, a tall footman with large whiskers and an elaborate cape stopped behind them.

Kovalyov moved closer, pulled out his batiste shirt collar, arranged the fobs that dangled from a gold chain and, smiling in all directions, turned his attention to the airy lady who, leaning slightly like a spring flower, raised her white transparent fingers to her brow. Kovalyov's smile spread even wider when he glimpsed under her brim her round, luminously white chin and part of her cheek, tinged with the color of the first spring rose. But suddenly he leaped back as if burned. He had remembered that he had absolutely nothing instead of a nose; tears appeared in his eyes. He turned in order to tell the gentleman in uniform directly that he only pretended to be a state councilor, that he was a rogue and a scoundrel, and nothing else but his very own nose. . . . But the nose was no longer there, for he had driven away, probably to pay someone another visit.

Kovalyov was plunged into despair. He went back and, stopping under the cathedral's colonnade, looked closely in all directions in the hope of catching sight of the nose. He remembered very well that the nose wore a plumed hat and that his uniform was embroidered with gold but he hadn't noticed his cloak, nor the color of his carriage, nor horses; not even whether he had a footman in the back and in what kind of livery. Besides, there were so many carriages rushing past in every direction and at such speed that it would be impossible to tell them apart. Even if he had spotted one of them, he would have no means to stop it. It was a wonderful and sunny day. There were masses of people on Nevsky Avenue. A flowery cascade of ladies poured all over the sidewalk from the Police to the Anichkin Bridges. There came a court councilor of his acquaintance, a man he addressed as lieutenant colonel, especially in the presence of others. And there was Yarygin, a department head in the Senate, a great friend who always lost after eight rubbers of whist. And there was another major who was made assessor in the Caucasus; he was waving his arm for Kovalyov to come over....

"Oh, hell!" Kovalyov exclaimed. "Cabbie, take me straight to the Chief of Police!"

Kovalyov got in the cab and kept repeating: "Get going!"

"Is the Chief of Police in?" he demanded in the foyer.

"Not at all," the doorman replied, "he has just left."

"Can't be!"

"Yes," the doorman added, "it's not been long, but he is gone. Had you come a little earlier, you might have found him at home."

Kovalyov, always pressing the handkerchief to his face, got in the cab again and shouted desperately:

"Let's go!"

"Where?" asked the driver.

"Go straight!"

"Straight where? There is a turn here: right or left?"

This question made Kovalyov stop and think again. Given his situation, he should first apply at the Office of Public Order, not just because it was connected directly with the police, but because its orders were carried out more quickly. It would be irrational to seek satisfaction through the superiors of that office which the nose had declared as his own, since it was evident from the nose's own replies that this man held nothing sacred and that he could lie in this case just as he had lied when he said that he had never laid eyes on Kovalyov before. Thus, Kovalyov was ready to set out for the Office of Public Order when it occurred to him that this rogue and scoundrel, who had already behaved so shamelessly during their first meeting, could somehow slip out of the city—then all inquiries would be in vain or could become prolonged, God forbid, over a whole month. Finally, it seemed that heaven itself had inspired him. He decided to go directly to a newspaper office and place a timely announcement with a detailed description of all the particulars so that anyone who came across his nose could present him immediately at Kovalyov's house or, at least, report his whereabouts. So, with this decision, he told the cabdriver to go to the newspaper office. On the way there, he kept thumping the driver's back with his fist and repeating: "Faster, you scoundrel! Faster, you crook!" "Oh sir!" the driver complained, shaking his head and whipping his horse, whose coat was as long as a lap dog's. The droshky finally stopped and Kovalyov, out of breath, ran into a small office where a white-haired clerk in an old tailcoat and glasses sat holding a quill pen in his teeth and counted copper coins.

"Who takes advertisements here?" Kovalyov shouted. "Oh, hello!"

"My pleasure," said the old clerk glancing up for a second and looking again at the neat piles of money.

"I would like to publish...."

"Excuse me. Please wait a bit," the clerk muttered as he wrote down a figure with one hand and moved two beads on an abacus with the fingers of his left.

A footman in a braided coat and an appearance that showed he belonged to an aristocratic house was standing by the desk with a note in his hand. The footman thought it proper to reveal his sociability:

"Would you believe, the little mongrel isn't even worth eighty kopecks, that is I wouldn't give eight pennies for it, but the Countess loves it, she really does, so there are a hundred rubles for whoever finds it! Now, to put it plainly, people's tastes are completely incompatible; if you like to hunt—keep a setter, or a poodle: don't scrimp—spend five hundred, or even a thousand, as long as it's a good dog."

The grizzled clerk was listening to all this with an understanding demeanor and at the same time busied himself with his calculations: he was counting the characters in the notice. A great number of old women, shop assistants, and yardkeepers stood all around with scraps of paper in hand. One of the notes stated that a sober-minded coachman was available for service; another offered a barely-used carriage that had been brought from Paris in 1814; a nineteen-year-old serf girl was also available, much practiced in doing laundry but equally good for other kinds of work; a sturdy droshky with one spring missing; a young, fiery dapple-grey horse, seventeen years old; new turnip and radish seeds, imported from London; a summer house with land, two horse stalls and room for a magnificent birch or pine grove; there was also an offer to those desiring to buy old shoe soles inviting them for re-auctioning every day between eight and three. The room in which this group had gathered was very small and the air exceedingly heavy. But Collegiate Assessor Kovalyov could not smell the odors because he had again covered his face with the handkerchief and because his very own nose was God knows in what kinds of places.

"My good sir, allow me to inquire...I have a great need," he said at last, impatiently.

"Right away, right away! Two rubles, forty-three kopecks! One moment! One ruble, sixty-four kopecks!" the gray-mar. 1 gentleman was saying, as he tossed notes at the eyes of the old women and porters. "What is it you'd like?" he stated finally, turning to Kovalyov.

"I request..." said Kovalyov, "a fraud or perhaps a knavery has taken place, I can't seem to find out what just yet. I only ask that it be published that the one who will haul the scoundrel before me will be sufficiently rewarded."

"Allow me to inquire as to your name?"

"No, why the name? I can't tell you my name. I have many acquaintances: Chekhtaryova, the wife of a state councilor, Pelageya Grigoryevna Podtochina, a staff officer's wife... What if they should find out, God forbid! Simply write: the collegiate assessor or, better yet, a gentleman presently ranked major."

"And the runaway was your servant?"

"What do you mean my servant? That wouldn't be such a dirty trick as this! My...my nose ran away...."

"Hm, that's an odd name! And did this Mr. Nosov get away with a lot of your money?"

"It's my nose...you got it all wrong! My nose, my very own nose has taken off to parts unknown. The devil is playing tricks on me!"

"But how could he have taken off? I don't quite get it."

"I can't tell you how, but the important thing is that he is driving around town calling himself a state councilor. That's why I'm asking you to announce that whoever catches him, should bring him to me in the briefest possible time. You be the judge, now really what am I to do without such a visible part of the body. It's not like some little toe that I can shove in a boot and no one's the wiser if it's missing. Thursdays, I visit Chekhtaryova, a state councilor's wife. Pelageya Grigoryevna Podtochina, a staff officer's wife, she has a very pretty daughter too, is also a very good acquaintance; now you be the judge, what am I to do now...I can't go to see them now...."

The clerk was deep in thought as his tightly pressed lips indicated.

"No, I can't publish an announcement like that in the papers," he finally said after a long silence.

"What? How so?"

"Just so. The newspaper might lose its reputation. If everyone starts writing that his nose has run off, then...As it is, people are saying that a lot of incongruities and false rumors are being printed."

"But how is this matter an incongruity? No, there is nothing of the sort here."

"That is what you think. And just last week we had exactly the same case. An official came, just as you have and bought a notice (it came to two rubles and seventy-three kopecks), the advertisement was about a lost black-haired poodle. Who would think there was anything to it. And it turned out to be libel: the poodle was a treasurer. I forget in which department."

"I'm not advertising about a poodle, but about my very own nose, so it's almost as if about my own self."

"No, I can't accept an advertisement like that at all."

"But I really have lost my nose!"

"See a doctor, if you lost it. They say there are people who can implant any sort of nose you wish. Although, I must say that you strike me as a jolly fellow who enjoys a good joke among friends."

"I swear to you, by all that is holy! If it comes to that, I can even show you!"

"Don't trouble yourself," the clerk continued while taking snuff. "On the other hand, if it's not an inconvenience," he added, moved by curiosity, "I would fancy a look."

The Collegiate Assessor removed the handkerchief from his face.

"Really now, it is extremely odd," the clerk said. "The spot is perfectly smooth, like a fresh pancake. Yes, it's unbelievably flat!"

"You won't argue now, will you? You can see for yourself that it must be published. I would be particularly grateful to you and very happy that this occasion has given me the pleasure of making your acquaintance...."

It was evident that the Major had decided to grovel a bit.

"Of course, it is no big matter to have it published," said the clerk, "but I don't see any benefit for you in it. If you really want to, why don't you give it to someone with a flair for writing, let him describe it as a rare work of nature and publish the piece in the *Northern Bee* (here he took a pinch of snuff) for the edification of our youth or, simply, (here he blew his nose) for the benefit of general curiosity."

The Collegiate Assessor lost all hope. He looked down at the paper and noticed at the bottom of the page an advertisement about a performance. He caught the name of a very pretty actress and was already searching his pocket for a five-ruble note (for Kovalyov thought that staff officers should sit in the orchestra) when the thought of his nose ruined everything.

Even the clerk seemed moved by Kovalyov's predicament. He wished to alleviate Kovalyov's grief and thought it proper to express his concern in a few words: "I'm really very sad that such an anecdote befell you. Care for some snuff? It clears headaches and spells of melancholy; it is even beneficial with respect to hemorrhoids."

Saying this, the clerk offered his snuffbox, flipping its lid rather nimbly, which showed some lady in a hat.

This unintentional gesture made Kovalyov lose his patience.

"I do not understand how you find room for jesting," he said testily. "Don't you see that I lack that which I need for smelling? To hell with your tobacco! I can't stand the sight of it any more, and not just your vile Berezinsky, but even if you offered me the purest rappé."

Having said that, he left the newspaper office in deep distress and headed to see the precinct captain, a man who was very fond of sugar. His waiting room, which served also as a dining room, was furnished with numerous sugar loaves—tokens of the local merchants' friendship. At this time, the cook was pulling off his uniform boots; his sword and military raiment hung peacefully in the corners and his three-year-old son was already playing with his awesome three-cornered hat. The captain was ready to savor the pleasures of peace after a life of battle and campaigning.

Kovalyov entered just as he stretched, yawned, and exclaimed: "Time for a couple hours' snooze!" And so one could foresee that the arrival of the Collegiate Assessor was totally untimely; and I don't think he would have been received very warmly, had he even brought several pounds of tea or wool cloth with him.

The precinct captain was a great supporter of all the arts and industries but he preferred legal tender above all. "This is the real thing," he would usually say. "There is nothing better: you don't have to feed it, it doesn't take up much room, it always fits in the pocket, and it won't break if you drop it."

The captain addressed Kovalyov rather dryly and said that the the afternoon was no time to start an investigation since nature had prescribed that one should rest after eating (this revealed to the Collegiate Assessor that the captain was not unfamiliar with the wisdom of the ancients), that a respectable man would never have his nose torn off, and that there are many majors roaming the world who do not have their underwear in proper order and who hang around unseemly places.

Right on target! One must note that Kovalyov was an exceedingly sensitive fellow; while he could forgive almost anything said about his own person, he was completely unforgiving when it came to his rank and title. He even thought that while anything about the lower officer ranks could be allowed on the stage, staff officers should never be attacked. The precinct captain's rude reception baffled Kovalyov to the point that, shaking his head and spreading his hands somewhat, he uttered with dignity: "I confess that I have nothing more to add to your offensive statement," and walked out.

He returned home barely able to walk. It was dusk. His apartment seemed sorry and incredibly repulsive after all these fruitless searches. In the foyer he saw his servant Ivan, who was lying on a dirty leather sofa, spitting at the ceiling and hitting the same spot with considerable success. The servant's indifference enraged him and he struck him on the forehead with his hat, adding: "You swine, you are always up to no good!"

Ivan sprung up and started pulling off Kovalyov's cape.

Entering his room, the Major, tired and sad, threw himself into a chair and, letting out several sighs, at last said: "My God! My God! What did I do to deserve this? Had I lost an arm or a leg, it would be better; even the ears—it would be bad, but still bearable. But without his nose a man is the hell knows what, neither fish nor fowl, not a proper citizen, fit only for the rubbish heap. Had it been lopped off in battle or in a duel, or had I lost it myself; but it disappeared just like that, for no good reason!. . .But no, it can't be," he added after some thought. "It is impossible for a nose to disappear, no way. I must be dreaming or hallucinating. Maybe I drank aftershave instead of water by mistake. That dolt Ivan didn't tidy up and I probably just grabbed it."

To make sure that he wasn't drunk, the Major pinched himself so hard that he let out a scream. The pain assured him completely that he was acting and living in reality. He crept up to a mirror with his eyes closed at first in the hope that perhaps his nose would appear in its proper place. He jumped back that very instant, saying: "What a vile sight!"

'This was, indeed, puzzling. Had a button, a silver spoon or something like that disappeared. . .but this? And in his own apartment! Major Kovalyov, having considered all the circumstances, supposed as closest to the truth the complicity of none other than Podtochina, a staff officer's wife, who wanted him to marry her daughter. He too liked to flirt with her occasionally but avoided a final settlement. When the mother told him directly that she wanted to marry off her daughter to him, he gently cast off with his compliments, saying that he was still too young and should serve another five years to be an even forty-two. And thus Podtochina had decided to ruin him, probably out of revenge, and had hired old witches because it was absolutely impossible to assume that the nose had been cut off: no one had come into his room and Ivan Yakovlevich the barber had shaved him on Wednesday, and during all of Wednesday and Thursday his nose had been intact—this he knew and remembered very well. Besides, he would have felt pain, and undoubtedly the wound could not have healed so quickly and been as smooth as a pancake. He considered a number of plans: whether to subpoena Podtochina to court or to go to her and make a direct accusation. His thoughts were interrupted by light flashing through all the cracks in the door, a fact that indicated that Ivan had already lit a candle in the foyer. Soon Ivan himself appeared carrying the candle in front of him and lighting up the room brightly. Kovalyov's first thought was to grab the handkerchief and cover that spot which, even yesterday, held a nose so that the stupid servant should not be distracted upon noticing his master's strange deficiency.

No sooner had Ivan retired to his lair, when an unfamiliar voice was heard in the foyer:

"Does Collegiate Assessor Kovalyov live here?"

"Come in. Major Kovalyov is in," said Kovalyov, rising hurriedly and opening the door.

A handsome police officer entered. His sideburns were neither too light, nor too dark and his cheeks were rather full. He was the same policeman that stood, at the beginning of our tale, at one end of St. Isaac's Bridge.

"Have you lost your nose?"

"That's right."

"It has been found."

"What do you mean?" Major Kovalyov shouted. He was speechless with joy. He stared at the constable standing before him and on whose plump lips and cheeks the flickering light of the candle danced brightly. "How could it be?"

"A strange coincidence: He was intercepted almost on the highway. He was boarding the stagecoach bound for Riga. And he had a passport made out a long time ago in another official's name. And the odd thing is, I took him for a gentleman also. But, fortunately, I had my glasses and saw immediately that he was a nose. Because I am nearsighted, you see, and were you to stand before me, all I would see is that you have a face, but would not notice your nose, or beard, or anything else. My mother-in-law, that is my wife's mother, also can't see anything."

Kovalyov was beside himself.

"Where is he? Where? I'll run there at once."

"Don't worry. Knowing that you need him, I brought him with me. It's also strange that the main conspirator in this affair is that scoundrel of a barber from Voznesenskaya Street, who is now in jail. I've suspected him for a long time of drunkenness and stealing. Just the other day he pocketed a dozen buttons in a shop. Your nose is just as it used to be."

Saying this, the constable reached into his pocket and pulled out the nose wrapped in a piece of paper.

"So, there he is,' shouted Kovalyov. "It's him, all right. Do have a cup of tea with me."

"I would consider it a great pleasure, but it is impossible—I must stop by the jail. . . Groceries are so expensive now. . . My mother-in-law, that is my wife's mother, lives in my house, and the children also; the eldest is especially promising: a very bright lad, but there are no means for his education."

Kovalyov caught on and snatching a ten-ruble note from the table, stuffed it in the constable's hand. The latter bowed and stepped through the door, and almost instantaneously his voice could be heard on the street outside where he was reproaching a stupid peasant right on the teeth for driving a cart on the boulevard.

After the constable had left, the Collegiate Assessor remained in an indefinable state and only after several minutes regained the ability to see and feel: such was the effect of his unexpected joy. Using both hands, he carefully picked up the newly-found nose and examined it closely.

"It's him, it's him," said Major Kovalyov. "There is the pimple on the left side which popped up yesterday."

The Major almost laughed with happiness.

But there is nothing permanent in this world, and so the second minute of happiness is not as vivid as the first, and the third is even feebler, and finally happiness merges imperceptibly with the usual state of one's soul. Thus, a water ripple caused by the fall of a pebble finally blends with the smooth surface. Kovalyov began thinking and realized that the matter was not over: the nose was found but it still had to be attached, placed on its habitual spot.

"And what if it doesn't stick?" The question, addressed to himself, made the Major grow pale. Seized by inexpressible fear, he dashed to the table and pulled up the mirror in order to avoid placing the nose askew. His hands trembled. He placed the nose cautiously on its former site. Oh, horrors! The nose would not stick!. . . He held it to its mouth, warming it slightly with his breath, and again applied it to the smooth spot located between both cheeks; but the nose would not stay on.

"Go on, you dummy, stay!" Kovalyov said to his nose. But the nose seemed wooden and fell on the table with a strange thud, like a piece of cork. The Major's face twisted. "Won't it grow back on?" he said in fear. But no matter how many times he brought it to its proper place, his efforts met with no success.

He called Ivan and sent him to fetch the doctor who lived in the best apartment on the second floor of the same building. The doctor was a handsome man; he had luxurious jet-black sideburns, a fresh and healthy wife, he ate crisp apples every morning, and kept his mouth impeccably clean, rinsing it in the morning for three-quarters of an hour at a stretch and polishing his teeth with five brushes of assorted kinds. The doctor appeared instantly. Having asked when the mishap had occurred, he raised Major Kovalyov's chin and rapped him with his thumb on the very spot where the nose had been, with the result that the Major jerked his head back so violently that he struck it against the wall. The physician said that it was nothing and, suggesting that the Major move away from the wall, asked him to bend his head to the right. Feeling the spot where the nose had been, the doctor uttered "Hm!" He then commanded that he bend his head to the left and said "Hm!" In conclusion, he rapped him with his thumb again so that Major Kovalyov jerked his head like a horse having its teeth inspected. After this research, the physician shook his head and said: "No, it is impossible. You had better remain this way because one could make it worse. Of course, one could reattach it. I could, perhaps, do that right now; but I assure you, you would be worse off."

"That's great! How can I remain without a nose?" Kovalyov asked. "It can't get worse than now. This is hell knows what! How will I show myself in this vile shape? I have acquaintances. I am due at two house parties today, I know many people: state councilor's wife Chekhtaryova, Podtochina, a staff-officer's wife. . . although after her recent action, I will deal with her only through the police. Be so kind," Kovalyov implored, "isn't there some way? Put it on somehow, even if it's not too well, just so it stays on. I can even prop it with my hand when necessary. I don't even dance, by the way, so I won't hurt it with a careless movement. Please rest assured that my gratitude for your visits, insofar as my finances permit. . . . "

"Would you believe," said the doctor in a voice neither loud, nor soft, but exceptionally persuasive and mesmerizing, "I never heal out of greed. This is contrary to my rules and to my art. True, I charge for my visits, but only so as not to offend with a refusal. Of course, I could reattach your nose; but I assure you with my honor, since you won't take my word, that this would be far worse for you. Let nature take its course. Wash frequently with cold water and I assure you that without your nose you will be as healthy as when you had it. I suggest that you put your nose in a jar of alcohol or, better still, pour into it two tablespoons of spiced vodka and warm vinegar. You could collect a handsome sum for it. Why, even I might take it, if the price is reasonable."

"No, no! I'll never sell it!" Kovalyov cried desperately. "I'd have it spoil first!"

"Excuse me!" said the doctor, bowing. "I only wanted to be useful to you. . . Well then! At least, you saw my efforts."

Having said this, the doctor walked grandly out of the room. Kovalyov, in his deep melancholy, did not even notice the doctor's face but saw only the snow-white shirtcuffs peeking from the sleeves of the man's black tailcoat.

He decided that the next day, before lodging a formal complaint, he would write to the staff officer's wife to see whether she would be inclined to return without a fight that which was his. The letter was as follows:

Dear Madam, Alexandra Grigoryevna,

I am unable to understand your strange action. Rest assured, that by acting in this manner you will gain nothing and will not force me to marry your daughter. Believe me, I am fully familiar with the entire story of my nose and also with the fact that you, and no one else, is the principal participant. Its sudden separation from its place, escape and masquerade, first as an official and then as himself, is nothing but the consequence of spells cast by you or by those who practice such ignoble pursuits. I, for my own part, consider it my duty to warn you: if the abovementioned nose is not back in its place today, I will be forced to seek the protection of the law.

However, I have the honor of remaining

Your obedient servant,
Plato Kovalyov

Dear Sir, Plato Kuzmich,

I was extremely surprised by your letter. To be frank, I never expected . . . especially concerning unjustified accusations on your part. Be notified that the official mentioned by you was never received in my house, neither in disguise, nor under his own appearance. True, I was occasionally visited by Philip Ivanovich Potanchikov. And although he, indeed, sought the hand of my daughter, being himself of sober, good character and great learning, but I never gave him any hopes. You also mention a nose. If you mean by this that I wanted to pull your nose, that is, to refuse you formally, then I am surprised that you yourself mention this, while I, as you know, was of a totally different opinion and if you propose formally to my daughter right now, I am ready to satisfy you immediately, because this always constituted my most earnest wish, in the hope of which I remain always ready to serve you.

Alexandra Podtochina

"No," said Kovalyov, having read the reply. "She is truly innocent. It can't be! A person guilty of a crime could not have written that letter." The Collegiate Assessor was knowledgeable in this because he had been sent on investigations while in the Caucasus. "But how, by what means could this have happened? Only the devil can figure it out!" he said finally, letting his hands drop.

Meanwhile, rumors about this extraordinary event spread throughout the capital and, as usual, not without special embellishments. At that time everyone's minds were attuned to the extraordinary: just a short time before, the public had been amused by experiments in magnetism. Furthermore, the story of the dancing chairs on Konyushennaya Street was still alive; and so it is not surprising that soon it was said that the nose of Collegiate Assessor Kovalyov goes strolling on Nevsky Avenue precisely at three o'clock. A multitude of the curious gathered each day. Someone said that the nose was presently in Junker's store, and lo, such a huge crowd gathered and shoved near Junker's that the police had to get involved. A respectable-looking entrepreneur with sideburns, who sold various cookies next to the theatre entrance, made excellent, sturdy wooden benches and invited the curious to stand on them at the price of eighty kopecks a head. A worthy colonel left his house early on purpose and made his way through the crowd with great difficulty; but to his great indignation, instead of a nose, he saw in the store window a common woolen vest and the lithograph of a young girl rearranging her stocking while a dandy wearing an open vest and a goatee spies on her from behind a tree—a picture which had hung in the same place over ten years. Stepping aside, the colonel announced with chagrin: "How dare they confuse the people with such stupid and improbable rumors."

There was another rumor to the effect that Major Kovalyov's nose did not stroll on Nevsky Avenue, but in the gardens of the Tauride Palace, that he had been there for a long time; that Khosrow–Mirza, when he was living in the Palace, was very impressed by this strange play of nature. Some students from the Academy of Surgeons headed there. An aristocratic, respected lady requested in a special letter to the supervisor of the Palace gardens that he show this rare phenomenon to her children and, if possible, provide an explanation that would be edifying and instructive to the youths.

High society was exceptionally happy with these developments, especially the perennial guests of all sorts of parties who liked to make the ladies laugh and whose supply of anecdotes had been completely exhausted. A small faction of respectable and well-intentioned people were very displeased. One gentleman proclaimed irately that he did not understand how in our enlightened age such incongruous inventions could be spread and that he was surprised that the government paid no attention to it. It seems that this gentleman belonged to that class of people who would like to involve the government in everything, including his own daily quarrels with his wife. After this . . . but here the entire event is again concealed by fog and what happened afterwards is absolutely unknown.

III

Utter nonsense is going on in the world. Sometimes there is no verisimilitude at all: suddenly that selfsame nose that drove around with the rank of a state councilor and caused such a stir throughout the city reappeared as if nothing had happened in its proper place, that is between the two cheeks of Major Kovalyov. This happened around the seventh day of April. Kovalyov woke up and, glancing in the mirror by chance, saw—his nose! He grabbed it with his hand—his nose, all right! "Hey!" Kovalyov shouted and was ready to break into a barefoot jig across the room, when Ivan interrupted him. Kovalyov immediately ordered a wash and, washing, looked again in the mirror—his nose! He looked again while drying with a towel—his nose!

"Take a look, Ivan, I think I have a pimple on my nose," he said while thinking: "What if Ivan says, 'No, sir. You don't have a nose, let alone a pimple.'"

But Ivan replied: "No, sir. There is no pimple, the nose is clear."

"Great, what the hell!" said the Major to himself and snapped his fingers. Ivan Yakovlevich, the barber, looked in through the door at this time. His timid manner reminded one of a cat that had just been thrashed for stealing bacon.

"First things first: Are your hands clean?" shouted Kovalyov from afar.

"They are clean."

"You are lying."

"I swear they are clean, sir."

"They better be."

Kovalyov sat down. Ivan Yakovlevich covered him with the cloth and, with the aid of a brush, instantaneously transformed his chin and parts of his cheeks into the kind of cream that is served at merchants' weddings.

"Now look there," Ivan Yakovlevich said to himself glancing at the nose and, tilting his head to the other side, looked at it at an angle. "There! Now if you go on and think about it," he continued, examining the nose at length. Finally, he raised two fingers as lightly and carefully as can be imagined, in order to grasp it by the tip. Such was Ivan Yakovlevich's system.

"Hey, hey, watch it!" Kovalyov shouted.

Ivan Yakovlevich let his hands drop, stunned and confused as never before. At last, he began to tickle carefully under the chin with his razor. Although it was very awkward and difficult to shave without holding the olfactory portion of the body, nevertheless, by somehow propping his rough thumb against Kovalyov's cheek and lower gum, he overcame all obstacles and completed the shave.

When all was ready, Kovalyov hurried with his dressing, took a cab and drove directly to the pastry shop. "Boy, a cup of chocolate!" he shouted as he entered and ran to the mirror—the nose was there! He turned around merrily and looked satirically, squinting one eye somewhat, at two officers, one of whom sported a nose no larger than a vest button. Having done that, he headed for the offices of the department where he was seeking the position of vice-governor or, at worst, a senior clerkship. On his way through the reception room, he glanced at a mirror—the nose was there! Later, he went to see another collegiate assessor or major, a great mocker to whose pointed barbs Kovalyov often replied: "I know you, you are a real pin-sticker!" On his way there, he thought: "If even the major does not burst out laughing when he sees me, then it's a sure sign that everything is there and in its right place."

But the collegiate assessor said nothing. "Well, well, the devil take it!"

Kovalyov thought. He ran into Podtochina and her daughter on the street, greeted them and was met with joyful exclamations—that meant that everything was fine and he had no defects. He chatted with them for a long while and made a point of taking out his snuffbox and spending a long time stuffing his nose in both entrances, muttering under his breath: "So there, you womenfolk, you hens! I won't marry the daughter, no sir. Just so, paramour, anytime!" And from then on, Major Kovalyov strolled as if nothing had happened along Nevsky Avenue, went to the theatre, and everywhere else. And his nose sat on his face as if nothing had happened, showing no hint that it had wandered off. And afterwards, Major Kovalyov was always seen in good humor, smiling, chasing after absolutely all the the pretty ladies, and was even observed stopping at a shop in the Merchants' Mall in order to buy a decoration ribbon of some kind, for an unknown purpose, since he had not been awarded any decorations.

So this is the strange story that took place in the northern capital of our vast country! Only now, everything considered, we can see that there is much in it that is improbable. Not to speak of the fact that the supernatural separation of the nose and its appearance in various places is indeed strange, but why couldn't Kovalyov have guessed that he couldn't place an advertisement about his nose in the newspapers? And I don't mean here that I think that advertisements are expensive—that's nonsense. I'm not one of those greedy people. But it is unseemly, it is awkward, it is not good! And then again, how did the nose end up inside baked bread and how did Ivan Yakovlevich himself...? No, I don't understand it at all, I absolutely don't. But what is even stranger and even more incomprehensible is the fact that writers pick such topics. I must admit this is completely inconceivable, it's really...no, no, I can't understand it at all. First of all, there is absolutely no benefit to the community, and secondly,...no, secondly there is no benefit also. I simply don't know what it is....

But then, however, in addition, but, of course, one could allow this and that, and the third, maybe even...well, but doesn't one find incongruities everywhere?... And yet, if you think about it, there really is something to it. Say what you may, but such events do happen—rarely, but they do.

Translated by Olga Markof-Belaeff

LEO TOLSTOY

*L*EO TOLSTOY (1826–1910), the author of War and Peace (1865–1869) and
Anna Karenina (1875–1877), might scarcely seem to belong in an anthology of this
kind, but the fact is that the range of Toystoy's writing was considerable and that he could turn
his powerful imagination to almost any account. One might argue that some of his later tales for
peasants, (like "How Much Land Does a Man Need?"), are in the magical realist vein, or even
that later short novels like The Kreutzer Sonata (1899) can be considered in light of this mode
of exposition. The present selection, however, is an earlier piece, and something that Tolstoy
himself did not consider a story at all, but rather a sort of joke perpetrated in a letter to his wife's
sister. The effect of removing it from the letters and treating it as a short piece of magical realist
fiction is done to show how great writers can display creativity outside the boundaries of their
serious work, and how magical realism can make its appearance when the assumptions of realism
are temporarily abandoned.

The Porcelain Doll

Leo Tolstoy

A LETTER written six months after his marriage by Tolstoy to his wife's younger sister, the Natasha of *War and Peace*. The first few lines are in his wife's handwriting, the rest in his own.

21st March 1863

Why, Tanya, have you dried up?... You don't write to me at all and I so love receiving letters from you, and you have not yet replied to Levochka's [Tolstoy's] crazy epistle, of which I did not understand a word.

23rd March

There, she began to write and suddenly stopped, because she could not continue. And do you know why, Tanya dear? A strange thing has befallen her and a still stranger thing has befallen me. As you know, like the rest of us she has always been made of flesh and blood, with all the advantages and disadvantages of that condition: she breathed, was warm and sometimes hot, blew her nose (and how loud!) and so on, and above all she had control of her limbs, which—both arms and legs—could assume different positions: in a word she was corporeal like all of us. Suddenly on March 21st 1863, at ten o'clock in the evening, this extraordinary thing befell her and me. Tanya! I know you always loved her (I do not know what feeling she will arouse in you now); I know you felt a sympathetic interest in me, and I know your reasonableness, your sane view of the important affairs of life, and your love of your parents (please prepare them and inform them of this event), and so I write to tell you just how it happened.

I got up early that day and walked and rode a great deal. We lunched and dined together and had been reading (she was still able to read) and I felt tranquil and happy. At ten o'clock I said goodnight to Auntie (Sonya was still then as usual and said she would follow me) and I went off to bed. Through my sleep I heard her open the door and heard her breathe as she undressed...I heard how she came out from behind the screen and approached the bed. I opened my eyes...and saw—not the Sonya you and I have known—but a porcelain Sonya! Made of that very porcelain about which your parents had a dispute. You know those porcelain dolls with bare cold shoulders, and necks and arms bent forward, but made of the same lump of porcelain as the body. They have black painted hair arranged in large waves, the paint of which gets rubbed off at the top, and protruding porcelain eyes that are too wide and are also painted black at the corners, and the stiff porcelain folds of their skirts are made of the same one piece of porcelain as the rest. And Sonya was like that! I touched her arm—she was smooth, pleasant to feel, and cold porcelain. I thought I was asleep and gave myself a shake, but she remained like that and stood before me immovable. I said: Are you porcelain? And without opening her mouth (which remained as it was, with curved lips painted bright red) she replied: Yes, I am porcelain. A shiver ran down my back. I looked at her legs: they also were porcelain and (you can imagine my horror) fixed on a porcelain stand, made of one piece with herself, representing the ground and painted green to depict grass. By her left leg, a little above and at the back of the knee, there was a porcelain column, colored brown and probably representing the stump of a tree. This too was in one piece with her. I understood that without this stump she could not remain erect, and I became very sad, as you who loved her can imagine. I still did not believe my senses and began to call her. She could not move without that stump and its base, and only rocked a little—together with the base—to fall in my direction. I heard how the porcelain base knocked against the floor. I touched her again, and she was all smooth, pleasant, and cold porcelain. I tried to lift her hand, but could not. I tried to pass a finger, or even a nail, between her elbow and her side—but it was impossible. The obstacle was the same porcelain mass, such as is made at Auerbach's, and of which sauce-boats are made. She was planned for external appearance only. I began to examine her chemise, it was all of one piece with the body, above and below. I looked more closely, and noticed that at the bottom a bit of the fold of her chemise was broken off and it showed brown. At the top of her head it showed white where the paint had come off a little. The paint had also come off a lip in one place, and a bit was chipped off one shoulder. But it was all so well made and so natural that it was still our same Sonya. And the chemise was one I knew, with lace, and there was a knot of black hair behind but of porcelain, and the fine slender hands, and large eyes, and the lips—all were the same, but of porcelain. And the dimple in her chin and the small bones in front of her shoulders were there too, but of porcelain. I was in a terrible state and did not know what to say or do or think. She would have been glad to help me, but what could a porcelain creature do? The half-closed eyes, the eyelashes and eyebrows, were all like her living self when looked at from a distance. She did not look at me, but past me at her bed. She evidently wanted to lie down, and rocked on her pedestal all the time. I quite lost control of myself, seized her, and tried to take her to her bed. My fingers made no impression on her cold porcelain body, and what surprised me yet more was that she had become as light as an empty flask. And suddenly she seemed to shrink, and became quite small, smaller than the palm of my hand, although she still looked just the same. I seized a pillow, put her in a corner of it, pressed down another corner with my fist, and placed her there, then I took her nightcap, folded it in four, and covered her up to the head with it. She lay there still just the same. Then I extinguished the candle and placed her under my beard. Suddenly I heard her voice from the corner of the pillow: "Leva, why have I become porcelain?" I did not know what to reply. She said again: "Does it make any difference that I am porcelain?" I did not want to grieve her, and said that it did not matter. I felt her again in the dark—she was still as before, cold and porcelain. And her stomach was the same as when she was alive, protruding upwards—rather unnatural for a porcelain doll. Then I experienced a strange feeling. I suddenly felt it pleasant that she should be as she was, and ceased to feel surprised—it all seemed natural. I took her out, passed her from one hand to the other, and tucked her under my head. She liked it all. We fell asleep. In the morning I got up and went out without looking at her. All that had happened the day before seemed so terrible. When I returned for lunch she had again become such as she always was. I did not remind her of what had happened the day before, fearing to grieve her and Auntie. I have not yet told anyone but you about it. I thought it had all passed off, but all these days, every time we are alone together, the same thing happens. She suddenly becomes small and porcelain. In the presence of others she is just as she used to be. She is not oppressed by this, nor am I. Strange as it may seem, I frankly confess that I am glad of it, and though she is porcelain we are very happy.

I write to you of all this, dear Tanya, only that you should prepare her parents for the news, and through papa should find out from the doctors what this occurrence means, and whether it will not be bad for our expected child. Now we are alone, and she is sitting under my necktie and I feel how her sharp little nose cuts into my neck. Yesterday she had been left in a room by herself. I went in and saw that Dora (our little dog) had dragged her into a corner, was playing with her, and nearly broke her. I whipped Dora, put Sonya in my waistcoat pocket and took her to my study. Today however I am expecting from Tula a small wooden box I have ordered, covered outside with morocco and lined inside with raspberry-colored velvet, with a place arranged in it for her so that she can be laid in it with her elbows, head, and back all supported evenly so that she cannot break. I shall also cover it completely with chamois leather.

I had written this letter when suddenly a terrible misfortune occurred. She was standing on the table, when Natalya Petrovna pushed against her in passing, and she fell and broke off a leg above the knee with the stump. Alexey says that it can be mended with a cement made of the white of eggs. If such a recipe is known in Moscow please send me it.

Translated by Aylmer Maude

THOMAS MANN

*T*HOMAS MANN (1875–1955), *Germany's great novelist of this century, is justly famous for large-scale masterpieces like* Buddenbrooks (1901), The Magic Mountain (1924), *and* Doctor Faustus (1947). *But he was also one of the finest short-story writers of modern Europe.* "Tonio Kröger," "Death in Venice," "Disorder and Early Sorrow," *and* "Mario and the Magician," *among others, show his masterful ability to comment on the social problems that led to the destruction of German culture and the rise of National Socialism. The short stories tend to depict illness and obsession in melancholy, haunted characters. Mann had to leave Germany when Hitler came to power in 1933, and he settled in the United States, becoming a citizen in 1944.*

The early story we have chosen for this anthology, "The Wardrobe" (1899), *was written while Mann was in his twenties. It preshadows the themes and style of mature work and is, at the same time, a persuasive instance of magical realism. No attempt is made to account for the beautiful young woman in the wardrobe who tells stories to the dying youth, either as h hallucination or as some manifestation of death from traditional folklore. The story cultivates a strangeness that does not include the grotesque elements found in many other magical realist stories, and it is interesting to note that our selection from Milan Kundera's novel (1980) mentions this story with admiration.*

The Wardrobe

Thomas Mann

IT WAS cloudy, cool, and half-dark when the Berlin-Rome express drew in at a middle-size station on its way. Albrecht van der Qualen, solitary traveller in a first-class compartment with lace covers over the plush upholstery, roused himself and sat up. He felt a flat taste in his mouth, and in his body the none-too-agreeable sensations produced when the train comes to a stop after a long journey and we are aware of the cessation of rhythmic motion and conscious of calls and signals from without. It is like coming to oneself out of drunkenness or lethargy. Our nerves, suddenly deprived of the supporting rhythm, feel bewildered and forlorn. And this the more if we have just roused out of the heavy sleep one falls into in a train.

Albrecht van der Qualen stretched a little, moved to the window, and let down the pane. He looked along the train. Men were busy at the mail van, unloading and loading parcels. The engine gave out a series of sounds, it snorted and rumbled a bit, standing still, but only as a horse stands still, lifting its hoof, twitching its ears, and awaiting impatiently the signal to go on. A tall, stout woman in a long raincoat, with a face expressive of nothing but worry, was dragging a hundred-pound suitcase along the train, propelling it before her with pushes from one knee. She was saying nothing, but looking heated and distressed. Her upper lip stuck out, with little beads of sweat upon it—altogether she was a pathetic figure. "You poor dear thing," van der Qualen thought. "If I could help you, soothe you, take you in—only for the sake of that upper lip. But each for himself, so things are arranged in life; and I stand here at this

39

moment perfectly carefree, looking at you as I might at a beetle that has fallen on its back."

It was half-dark in the station shed. Dawn or twilight—he did not know. He had slept, who could say whether for two, five, or twelve hours? He had sometimes slept for twenty-four, or even more, unbrokenly, an extraordinarily profound sleep. He wore a half-length dark-brown winter overcoat with a velvet collar. From his features it was hard to judge his age: one might actually hesitate between twenty-five and the end of the thirties. He had a yellowish skin, but his eyes were black like live coals and had deep shadows round them. These eyes boded nothing good. Several doctors, speaking frankly as man to man, had not given him many more months.—His dark hair was smoothly parted on one side.

In Berlin—although Berlin had not been the beginning of his journey—he had climbed into the train just as it was moving off— incidentally with his red leather handbag. He had gone to sleep and now at waking felt himself so completely absolved from time that a sense of refreshment streamed through him. He rejoiced in the knowledge that at the end of the thin gold chain he wore round his neck there was only a little medallion in his waistcoat pocket. He did not like to be aware of the hour or of the day of the week, and moreover he had no truck with the calendars. Some time ago he had lost the habit of knowing the day of the month or even the month of the year. Everything must be in the air—so he put it in his mind, and the phrase was comprehensive though rather vague. He was seldom or never disturbed in this program, as he took pains to keep all upsetting knowledge at a distance from him. After all, was it not enough for him to know more or less what season it was? "It is more or less autumn," he thought, gazing out into the damp and gloomy train shed. "More I do not know. Do I even know where I am?"

His satisfaction at this thought amounted to a thrill of pleasure. No, he did not know where he was! Was he still in Germany? Beyond a doubt. In North Germany? That remained to be seen. While his eyes were still heavy with sleep the window of his compartment had glided past an illuminated sign; it probably had the name of the station on it, but not the picture of a single letter had been transmitted to his brain. In still dazed condition he had heard the conductor call the name two or three times, but not a syllable had he grasped. But out there in a twilight of which he knew not so much as whether it was morning or evening lay a strange place, an unknown town.—Albrecht van der Qualen took his felt hat out of the rack, seized his red leather handbag, the strap of which secured a red and white silk and wool plaid into which was rolled an umbrella with a silver crook—and although his ticket was labelled Florence, he left the compartment and the train, walked along the shed, deposited his luggage at the cloakroom, lighted a cigar, thrust his hands—he carried neither stick nor umbrella—into his overcoat pockets, and left the station.

Outside in the damp, gloomy, and nearly empty square five or six hackney coachmen were snapping their whips, and a man with braided cap and long cloak in which he huddled shivering inquired politely: "*Hotel zum braven Mann?*" Van der Qualen thanked him politely and held on his way. The people whom he met had their coat-collars turned up; he put his up too, nestled his chin into the velvet, smoked, and went his way, not slowly and not too fast.

He passed along a low wall and an old gate with two massive towers; he crossed a bridge with statues on the railings and saw the water rolling slow and turbid below. A long wooden boat, ancient and crumbling, came by, sculled by a man with a long pole in the stern. Van der Qualen stood for a while leaning over the rail of the bridge. "Here," he said to himself, "is a river; here is *the* river. It is nice to think that I call it that because I do not know its name."—Then he went on.

He walked straight on for a little, on the pavement of a street which was neither very narrow nor very broad; then he turned off to the left. It was evening. The electric arc-lights came on, flickered, glowed, sputtered, and then illuminated the gloom. The shops were closing. "So we may say that it is in every respect autumn," thought van der Qualen, proceeding along the wet black pavement. He wore no galoshes, but his boots were very thicksoled, durable, and firm, and withal not lacking in elegance.

He held to the left. Men moved past him, they hurried on their business or coming from it. "And I move with them," he thought, "and am as alone and as strange as probably no man has ever been before. I have no business and no goal. I have not even a stick to lean upon. More remote, freer, more detached, no one can be, I owe nothing to anybody, nobody owes anything to me. God has never held out His hand over me, He knows me not at all. Honest unhappiness without charity is a good thing; a man can say to himself: I owe God nothing."

He soon came to the edge of the town. Probably he had slanted across it at about the middle. He found himself on a broad suburban street with trees and villas, turned to his right, passed three or four cross-streets almost like village lanes, lighted only be lanterns, and came to a stop in a somewhat wider one before a wooden door next to a commonplace house painted a dingy yellow, which had nevertheless the striking feature of very convex and quite opaque plate-glass windows. But on the door was a sign: "In this house on the third floor there are rooms to let." "Ah!" he remarked; tossed away the end of his cigar, passed through the door along a boarding which formed the dividing line between two properties, and then turned left through the door of the house itself. A shabby grey runner ran across the entry. He covered it in two steps and began to mount the simple wooden stair.

The doors to the several apartments were very modest too; they had white glass panes with woven wire over them and on some of them were name-plates. The landings were lighted by oil lamps. On the third story, the top one, for the attic came next, were entrances right and left, simple brown doors without name-plates. Van der Qualen pulled the brass bell in the middle. It rang, but there was no sign from within. He knocked left. No answer. He knocked right. He heard light steps within, very long, like strides, and the door opened.

A woman stood there, a lady, tall, lean, and old. She wore a cap with a large pale-lilac bow and an old-fashioned, faded black gown. She had a sunken birdlike face and on her brow there was an eruption, a sort of fungus growth. It was rather repulsive.

"Good evening," said van der Qualen. "The rooms?"

The old lady nodded; she nodded and smiled slowly, without a word, understandingly, and with her beautiful long white hand made a slow, languid, and elegant gesture towards the next, the left-hand door. Then she retired and appeared again with a key. "Look," he thought, standing behind her as she unlocked the door; "you are like some kind of banshee, a figure out of Hoffmann, madam." She took the oil lamp from its hook and ushered him in.

It was a small, low-ceilinged room with a brown floor. Its walls were covered with straw-colored matting. There was a window at the back in the right-hand wall, shrouded in long, thin white muslin folds. A white door also on the right led into the next room. This room was pathetically bare, with staring white walls, against which three straw chairs, painted pink, stood out like strawberries from whipped cream. A wardrobe, a washing-stand with a mirror. . . The bed, a mammoth mahogany piece, stood free in the middle of the room.

"Have you any objections?" asked the old woman, and passed her lovely long, white hand lightly over the fungus growth on her forehead.— It was as though she had said that by accident because she could not think for the moment of a more ordinary phrase. For she added at once: "—so to speak?"

"No, I have no objections," said van der Qualen. "The rooms are rather cleverly furnished. I will take them. I'd like to have somebody fetch my luggage from the station, here is the ticket. You will be kind enough to make up the bed and give me some water. I'll take the house key now, and the key to the apartment. . . . I'd like a couple of towels. I'll wash up and go into the city for supper and come back later."

He drew a nickel case out of his pocket, took out some soap, and began to wash his face and hands, looking as he did so through the convex window-panes far down over the muddy, gas-lit suburban streets, over the arc-lights and the villas.—As he dried his hands he went over to the wardrobe. It was a square one, varnished brown, rather shaky, with a simple curved top. It stood in the center of the right-hand wall exactly in the niche of a second white door, which of course led into the rooms to which the main and middle door on the landing gave access. "Here is something in the world that is well arranged," thought van der Qualen.

"This wardrobe fits into the door niche as though it were made for it." He opened the wardrobe door. It was entirely empty, with several rows of hooks in the ceiling; but it proved to have no back, being closed behind by a piece of rough, common grey burlap, fastened by nails or tacks at the four corners.

Van der Qualen closed the wardrobe door, took his hat, turned up the collar of his coat once more, put out the candle, and set forth. As he went through the front room he thought he heard mingled with the sound of his own steps a sort of ringing in the other room: a soft, clear, metallic sound—but perhaps he was mistaken. As though a gold ring were to fall into a silver basin, he thought, as he locked the outer door. He went down the steps and out of the gate and took the way to the town.

In a busy street he entered a lighted restaurant and sat down at one of the front tables, turning his back to all the world. He ate a *soupe aux fines herbes* with croutons, a steak with a poached egg, a compote and wine, a small piece of green gorgonzola and half a pear. While he paid and put on his coat he took a few puffs from a Russian cigarette, then lighted a cigar and went out. He strolled for a while, found his homeward route into the suburb, and went leisurely back.

The house with the plate-glass windows lay quite dark and silent when van der Qualen opened the house door and mounted the dim stair. He lighted himself with matches as he went, and opened the left-hand brown door in the third story. He laid hat and overcoat on the divan, lighted the lamp on the big writing-table, and found there his handbag as well as the plaid and umbrella. He unrolled the plaid and got a bottle of cognac, then a little glass and took a sip now and then as he sat in the arm-chair finishing his cigar. "How fortunate, after all," thought he, "that there is cognac in the world." Then he went into the bedroom, where he lighted the candle on the night-table, put out the light in the other room, and began to undress. Piece by piece he put down his good, unobtrusive grey suit on the red chair beside the bed; but then as he loosened his braces he remembered his hat and overcoat, which still lay on the couch. He fetched them into the bedroom and opened the wardrobe . . . He took a step backwards and reached behind him to clutch one of the large dark red mahogany balls which ornamented the bedposts. The room, with its four white walls, from which the three pink chairs stood out like strawberries from whipped cream, lay in the unstable light of the candle. But the wardrobe over there was open and it was not empty. Somebody was standing in it, a creature so lovely that Albrecht van der Qualen's heart stood still a moment and then in long, deep, quiet throbs resumed its beating. She was quite nude and one of her slender arms reached up to crook a forefinger round one of the hooks in the ceiling of the wardrobe. Long waves of brown hair rested on the childlike shoulders— they breathed that charm to which the only answer is a sob. The candlelight was mirrored in her narrow black eyes. Her mouth was a little large, but it had an expression as sweet as the lips of sleep when after long days of pain they kiss our brow. Her ankles nestled and her slender limbs clung to one another.

Albrecht van der Qualen rubbed one hand over his eyes and stared...and he saw that down in the right corner the sacking was loosened from the back of the wardrobe. "What—" said he..."won't you come in—or how should I put it—out? Have a little glass of cognac? Half a glass?" But he expected no answer to this and he got none. Her narrow, shining eyes, so very black that they seemed bottomless and inexpressive—they were directed upon him, but aimlessly and somewhat blurred, as though they did not see him.

"Shall I tell you a story?" she said suddenly in a low, husky voice.

"Tell me a story," he answered. He had sunk down in a sitting posture on the edge of the bed, his overcoat lay across his knees with his folded hands resting upon it. His mouth stood a little open, his eyes half-closed. But the blood pulsated warm and mildly through his body and there was a gentle singing in his ears. She had let herself down in the cupboard and embraced a drawn-up knee with her slender arms, while the other leg stretched out before her. Her little breasts were pressed together by her upper arm, and the light gleamed on the skin of her flexed knee. She talked...talked in a soft voice, while the candle-flame performed its noiseless dance.

Two walked on the heath and her head lay on his shoulder. There was a perfume from all growing things, but the evening mist already rose from the ground. So it began. And often it was in verse, rhyming in that incomparably sweet and flowing way that comes to us now and again in the half-slumber of fever. But it ended badly; a sad ending: the two holding each other indissolubly embraced, and while their lips rest on each other, one stabbing the other above the waist with a broad knife—and not without good cause. So it ended. And then she stood up with an infinitely sweet and modest gesture, lifted the grey sacking at the right-hand corner—and was no more there.

From now on he found her every evening in his wardrobe and listened to her stories—how many evenings? How many days, weeks, or months did he remain in this house and in this city? It would profit nobody to know. Who would care for a miserable statistic? And we are aware that Albrecht van der Qualen had been told by several physicians that he had but a few months to live. She told him stories. They were sad stories, without relief; but they rested like a sweet burden upon the heart and made it beat longer and more blissfully. Often he forgot himself.—His blood swelled up in him, he stretched out his hands to her, and she did not resist him. But then for several evenings he did not find her in the wardrobe, and when she came back she did not tell him anything for several evenings and then by degrees resumed, until he again forgot himself.

How long it lasted—who knows? Who even knows whether Albrecht van der Qualen actually awoke on that grey afternoon and went into the unknown city; whether he did not remain asleep in his first-class carriage and let the Berlin-Rome express bear him swiftly over the mountains? Would any of us care to take the responsibility of giving a definite answer? It is all uncertain. "Everything must be in the air..."

Translated by H. T. Lowe-Porter

HUGO VON HOFMANNSTHAL

*H*UGO VON HOFMANNSTHAL (1874–1929), *the Austrian writer, was a poet, a dramatist, and a librettist, whose experiments with fiction have not attracted much attention. Through the nineties von Hofmannsthal was primarily occupied with lyric poetry and verse drama; as the century changed he became more fully committed to writing in dramatic form. In 1908, he began his collaboration with the composer Richard Strauss, which was to last some twenty years and result in the librettos of a number of important operas, among them Elektra and Der Rosenkavalier. He died of a heart attack while dressing for the funeral of a favorite son who had committed suicide.*

Von Hofmannsthal's prose has a feverish particularity that reflects both the experimentation of his period and his own considerable gifts of observation and expression. "A Tale of the Cavalry," a haunting story of military skirmishes, in which the hero's confrontation with an image or double of himself is never fully accounted for, shows the sureness of touch and execution he could bring to narrative.

A Tale of
The Cavalry

Hugo von Hofmannsthal

O N JULY 22, 1848, before six o'clock in the morning, the second
squadron of Wallmodern cuirassiers, a troop of cavalry a hundred
and seven strong under Captain Baron Rofrano, left the Casino San
Alessandro and took the road to Milan. The wide, sunny landscape lay in
untroubled peace; from distant mountain peaks, morning clouds rose
like steady plumes of smoke into the radiant sky. Not a breath of air
stirred the corn. Here and there, between clumps of trees fresh-bathed in
the morning air, there was a bright gleam of a house or a church. Hardly
had the troop left the foremost outposts of its own army about a mile
behind them when they caught sight of a glint of weapons in the
corn-fields, and the vanguard reported enemy infantry. The squadron
drew up for the attack by the side of the highroad; over their heads
cannon-balls flew, whizzing with a strangely loud, mewing noise; they
attacked across country, driving before them like quails a troop of men
irregularly armed. They belonged to the Manara Legion, and wore
strange headgear. The prisoners were sent back in charge of a corporal
and eight men. Outside a beautiful villa approached by an avenue of
ancient cypresses, the vanguard reported suspicious figures. Anton
Lerch, the sergeant, dismounted, took twelve men armed with carbines,
whom he posted at the windows, and captured eighteen students of the
Pisan Legion, well-bred, handsome young men with white hands and
long hair. Half-an-hour later the squadron stopped a wayfarer in the

Bergamasque costume whose very guilelessness and insignificance aroused suspicion. Sewn into the lining of his coat he was carrying detailed plans of the greatest importance relating to the formation of irregular corps in the Giudicaria and their liaison with the Piedmontese army. About ten o'clock, a herd of cows fell into the squadron's hands. Immediately afterwards, they encountered a strong enemy detachment which fired on the vanguard from a cemetery wall. The front line, under Lieutenant Count Trautsohn, vaulted over the low wall and laid about them among the graves on the enemy, most of whom escaped in wild confusion into the church and through the vestry door into a dense thicket. The twenty-seven new prisoners reported themselves as Neapolitan irregulars under Papal officers. The squadron had lost one man. Corporal Wotrubek, with two men, Dragoons Holl and Haindl, riding round the thicket, captured a light howitzer drawn by two farm-horses by knocking the guard senseless, taking the horses by the bridles, and turning them round. Corporal Wotrubek was sent back to headquarters, slightly wounded, to report these skirmishes and the other successes of the day, the prisoners were also sent back, while the howitzer was taken on by the squadron which, deducting the escort, now numbered seventy-eight men.

Since the prisoners declared with one voice that the city of Milan had been abandoned by the enemy troops, regular and irregular, and stripped of artillery and ammunition, the captain could not deny himself and his men the pleasure of riding into the great, beautiful, defenseless city. Amid the ringing of noonday bells, under the march trumpeted into the steely, glittering sky by the four buglers, to rattle against a thousand windows and re-echo on seventy-eight cuirasses and seventy-eight upright, naked swords, with streets to right and left swarming like a broken anthill with gaping faces, watching pallid, cursing figures slipping into house-doors, drowsy windows flung wide open by the bare arms of unknown beauty, past Santa Babila, San Fedele, San Carlo, past the famous white marble cathedral, San Satiro, San Giorgio, San Lorenzo, San Eustorgio, their ancient bronze doors all opening wide on silvery saints and brocade-clad women with shining eyes, on candle-light and fumes of incense, on the alert for shots from a thousand attics, dark archways, and low shop-stalls, yet seeing at every turn mere half-grown girls and boys with flashing teeth and black hair, looking down on it all from their trotting horses, their eyes glittering in masks of blood-spattered dust, in at the Porta Venezia, out at the Porta Ticinese—thus the splendid squadron rode through Milan.

Not far from the Porta Ticinese, on a rampart set with fine plane-trees, it seemed to Sergeant Anton Lerch that he saw, at the ground-floor window of a new, bright-yellow house, a woman's face he knew. Curious to know more, he turned in his saddle; a slight stiffness in his horse's gait made him suspect a stone in one of its foreshoes, and as he was riding in the rear of the squadron, and could break file without disturbance, he made up his mind to dismount, even going so far as to back his horse into the entry of the house. Hardly had he raised the second white-socked hoof of his bay to inspect the shoe when a door leading straight into the front of the entry actually opened to show a woman, sensual-looking and still not quite past her youth, in a somewhat dishevelled bedgown, and behind her a sunny room with a few pots of basil and red pelargonium in the windows, while his sharp eyes caught in a pier-glass the reflection of the other side of the room, which was filled with a large white bed and a papered door, through which a stout, clean-shaven, elderly man was just withdrawing.

As there struggled back into the sergeant's mind the woman's name and a great many other things besides—that she was the widow or divorced wife of a Croat paymaster, that, nine or ten years before, he had on occasion spent the evening or half the night in Vienna with her and her accredited lover of the moment—he tried to distinguish, under her present stoutness, the full yet slender figure of those days. But standing there, she gave him a fawning Slav smile which sent the blood pulsing into his thick neck and under his eyes, and he was daunted by a certain archness in the way she spoke to him, by her bedgown and the furniture in the room behind. At the very moment, however, when with heavy eyes he was watching a big fly crawl over the woman's comb, when he had no thought in mind but of his hand on the warm, cool neck, brushing it away, the memory of the skirmishes and other lucky chances of the day came flooding back upon him, and he pressed her head forward with a heavy hand, saying: "Vuic"—he had not pronounced her name for ten years at least, and had completely forgotten her first name—"a week from now we shall occupy the town and these shall be my quarters," and he pointed to the half-open door of the room. Meanwhile he heard door after door slam in the house, felt his horse urging him to be gone, first by a dumb dragging at the bridle, then by loud neighing after the others. He mounted and trotted off after the squadron with no answer from Vuic save an evasive laugh and a toss of the head. But the word, once spoken, made him feel its power within him. Riding beside the main column of the squadron, his bay a little jaded, under the heavy, metallic glow of the sky, half blinded by the cloud of dust that moved with the riders, the sergeant, in his imagination, slowly took possession of the room with the mahogany furniture and the pots of basil, and at the same time entered into a life of peace still irradiated by war, an atmosphere of comfort and pleasant brutality with no officer to give him orders, a slippered life with the hilt of his sabre sticking through the left-hand pocket of his dressing-gown. And the stout, clean-shaven man who had vanished through the papered door, something between a priest and a pensioned footman, played an important part in it all, more important, even, than the fine, broad bed and Vuic's white skin. The clean-shaven man was now a somewhat servile companion who told court gossip and brought presents of tobacco and capons, now he was hard pressed and had to pay blackmail, was involved in many intrigues, was in the confidence of the Piedmontese, was the Pope's cook, procurer, owner of suspect houses with gloomy pavilions for political meetings, and swelled up into a huge, bloated figure from which, if it were tapped in twenty places, gold, not blood would pour.

There were no further surprises for the squadron that afternoon, and there was nothing to check the sergeant's musings. But there had awakened in him a craving for strokes of luck, for prize moneys, for ducats suddenly falling into his pockets. And the thorn which festered in his flesh, round which all wishes and desires clustered, was the anticipation of his first entrance into the room with the mahogany furniture.

When the squadron, its horses fed and half-rested, attempted towards evening to advance by a detour on Lodi and the Adda bridge, where there was every prospect of an encounter with the enemy, a village lying in a dark hollow off the highroad with a half-ruined church spire looked enticing and suspicious enough to attract the sergeant's attention. Beckoning to two dragoons, Holl and Scarmolin, he broke away from the squadron's route with them, and, so inflamed was his imagination that it swelled to the hope of surprising in the village some ill-defended enemy general, or of winning some other great prize. Having arrived at the wretched and seemingly deserted place, he ordered Scarmolin to reconnoitre the houses from the outside to the left, Holl to the right, while he himself, pistol in hand, set off at the gallop through the village. Soon, feeling under his feet hard flagstones which were coated with some slippery kind of grease, he had to put his horse to the walk. Deathly silence reigned in the village—not a child, not a bird, not a breath of air. To right and left there stood foul hovels, the mortar scaling from their walls, with obscene drawings in charcoal here and there on the bare bricks. Between the naked doorposts the sergeant caught sight from time to time of a dirty, half-naked figure lounging on a bed or hobbling through the room as if on broken hips. His horse advanced painfully, pushing its haunches leadenly forward. As he turned and bent to look at its hind shoe, shuffling footsteps issued from a house; he sat upright, and a woman whose face he could not see passed close in front of his mount. She was only half-dressed, her ragged, filthy gown of flowered silk, half torn off her shoulders, trailed in the gutter, there were dirty slippers on her feet. She passed so close in front of his horse that the breath from its nostrils stirred the bunch of greasy curls that hung down her bare neck under an old straw hat, yet she made no move to hurry, nor did she make way for the rider. From a door-step to the left, two rats, bleeding in their death-agony, rolled into the middle of the street, the under one screaming so desperately that the sergeant's horse stopped, staring at the ground, its head averted and its breathing audible. A pressure on its flank sent it forward again, the woman having disappeared in an entry before the sergeant could see her face. A dog ran out busily with upraised head, dropped a bone in the middle of the street and set about burying it between the paving-stones. It was a dirty white bitch with trailing teats; she scraped with fiendish intentness, then took the bone between her teeth and carried it away. As she began to dig again, three dogs ran up, two of them mere puppies with soft bones and loose skin; unable to bark or bite, they pulled at each other's muzzles with blunt teeth. The dog which had come with them was a pale yellow greyhound, its body so bloated that it could only drag itself along on its four skinny legs. The body was taut as a drum, so that its head looked far too small; there was a dreadful look of pain and fear in its restless little eyes. Two other dogs ran up at once, one thin and white, with black furrows running from its reddened eyes, and hideous in its avidity, the other a vile dachshund with long legs. This dog raised its head towards the sergeant and looked at him. It must have been very old. Its eyes were fathomlessly weary and sad. But the bitch ran to and fro in silly haste before the rider, the two puppies snapped soundlessly with their muzzles round the horse's fetlocks, and the greyhound dragged its hideous body close in front of the horse's hoofs. The bay could not advance a step. But when, having drawn his pistol to shoot one of the dogs, it misfired, the sergeant spurred his horse on both flanks and thundered away over the paving-stones. After a few bounds he was brought up short by a cow which a lad was dragging to the shambles at the end of a tight-stretched rope. But the cow, shrinking from the smell of blood and the fresh hide of a calf nailed to the doorpost, planted its hoofs firm on the ground, drew the reddish haze of the sunset in through dilated nostrils and, before the lad could drag her across the road with stick and rope, tore away with piteous eyes a mouthful of the hay which the sergeant had tied on the front of his saddle.

He had now left the last house of the village behind him and, riding between two low and crumbling walls, could see his way ahead on the farther side of an old single-span bridge over an apparently dry ditch. He felt in his horse's step such an unutterable heaviness that every foot of the walls to right and left, and even every single one of the centipedes and wood-lice which housed in them, passed toilsomely before his eyes, and it seemed to him that he had spent eternity riding through the hideous village. But as, at the same time, he heard a great rasping breath from his horse's chest without at once realizing what it was, he looked above and beside him, and then ahead to see whence it came, and in doing so became aware, on the farther side of the bridge and at the same distance from it as himself, of a man of his own regiment, a sergeant riding a bay with white-socked forefeet. But as he knew that there was no other horse of the kind in the whole squadron but the one on which he was at that moment mounted, and as he still could not recognize the face of the other rider, he impatiently spurred his horse into a very lively trot, where-upon the other mended his pace in exactly the same way till there was only a stone's throw between them. And now, as the two horses, each from its own side, placed the same white-socked forefoot on the bridge, the sergeant, recognizing with starting eyes his own wraith, reined in his horse aghast, and stretched his right hand with stiffened fingers towards the being, while the wraith, also reining in its horse and raising its right hand, was suddenly there no longer; Holl and Scarmolin appeared from the dry ditch to left and right quite unperturbed, while loud and near at hand the bugles of the squadron sounded the attack.

Taking a rise in the ground at full speed, the sergeant saw the squadron already galloping towards a thicket from which enemy cavalry, armed with pikes, were pouring, and as he gathered the four loose reins in his left hand and wound the hand-strap round his right, he saw the fourth rank leave the squadron and slacken its pace, was already on the thundering earth, now in the thick smell of dust, now in the midst of the enemy, struck at a blue arm wielding a pike, saw close at hand the captain's face with starting eyes and savagely bared teeth, was suddenly wedged in among enemy faces and foreign colors, dived below whirling blades, lunged at the next man's neck and unseated him, saw Scarmolin beside him, laughing, hew off the fingers of a man's bridle hand and strike deep into the horse's neck, felt the thick of battle slacken, and was suddenly alone on the bank of a brook behind an enemy officer on an iron-grey horse. The officer put his horse to the jump across the brook, the horse refused. The officer pulled it round, turning towards the sergeant a young, very pale face and the mouth of a pistol, then a sabre was driven into his mouth with the full force of a galloping horse in its tiny point. The sergeant snatched back his sabre, and at the very spot where the fingers of the fallen rider had opened, laid hold of the snaffle of the iron-grey, which, light and airy as a fawn, lifted its hoofs across its dying master.

As the sergeant rode back with his splendid prize, the sun, setting in a thick mist, cast a vast crimson haze over the fields. Even on untrodden ground there seemed to lie whole pools of blood. A crimson glow lay on white uniforms and laughing faces, cuirasses and saddle-cloths sparkled and shone, and three little fig trees on which the men had wiped the grooves in their sabres glowed deepest of all. The captain came to a halt by the blood-stained trees, beside the bugler of the squadron, who raised his crimson-dripping bugle to his lips and blew. The sergeant rode from line to line and saw that the squadron had not lost a man, but had taken nine horses. He rode up to the captain to report, the iron-grey still beside him, capering with upraised head and wide nostrils, like the young, vain, beautiful horse it was. The captain hardly listened to the report. He made a sign to Lieutenant Count Trautsohn, who at once dismounted, unharnessed the captured light howitzer, ordered the gun to be dragged away by a detachment of six men and sunk in a swamp formed by the brook, having driven away the now useless draught-horses with a blow from the flat of his sabre, and silently resumed his place at the head of the first rank. During this time, the squadron, drawn up in two ranks, was not really restless, yet there was a strange feeling in the air; the elation of four successful skirmishes in one day found vent in outbursts of suppressed laughter and smothered shouts to each other. Even the horses were restless, especially those flanking the prizes. What with all these windfalls, the parade-ground seemed too small to hold them; in the pride of victory, the men felt they must scatter, swarm in upon a new enemy, fling themselves upon him, and carry off yet more horses.

At that moment Captain Baron Rofrano rode up to the front rank of his squadron and, raising his big eyelids from his rather sleepy blue eyes, gave, audibly but without raising his voice, the command "Release led horses." The squadron stood still as death. Only the iron-grey beside the sergeant stretched its neck, almost touching with its nostrils the forehead of the captain's mount. The captain sheathed his sabre, drew a pistol from its holster and, wiping a little dust from its shining barrel with the back of his bridle-hand, repeated the command, raising his voice slightly and beginning to count, "One...two..." When he had counted "two," he fixed his veiled eyes on the sergeant, who sat motionless in his saddle, staring him full in the face. While Anton Lerch's steady, unflinching gaze, flashing now and then an oppressed, doglike look, seemed to express a kind of servile trust born of many years of service, his mind was almost unaware of the huge tension of the moment, but was flooded with visions of an alien ease, and from depths in him unknown to himself there rose a bestial anger against the man before him who was taking away his horse, a dreadful rage against the face, the voice, the bearing, the whole being of the man, such as can only arise, in some mysterious fashion, through years of close companionship. Whether something of the same sort was going on in the captain's mind too, or whether he felt the silently spreading danger of critical situations coming to a head in this moment of mute insubordination, we cannot know. Raising his arm with a negligent, almost graceful gesture, he counted "three" with a contemptuous curl of his upper lip, the shot cracked, and the sergeant, hit in the forehead, reeled, his body across his horse's neck, then fell between the iron-grey and the bay. He had not reached the ground, however, before all the other noncommissioned officers and men had driven off their captured horses with a twist of the rein or a kick, and the captain quietly putting away his pistol, was able to rally his squadron, still twitching from the lightning stroke, against the enemy, who seemed to be gathering in the distant, shadowy dusk. The enemy, however, did not engage the new attack, and not long after, the squadron arrived unmolested at the southern outposts of its own army.

Translated by Mary Hottinger and
Tania and James Stern

HENRY JAMES

H ENRY JAMES (1843–1916), born into a wealthy American family, became a European whose subsequent residence in France and England indicated no loss of interest in his native country. Most of his fiction reflects a concern with the relationships between a more civilized but less morally-sound Europe, and an earnest and idealistic but far less worldly America. Almost all of his great novels, including The American (1877), The Portrait of a Lady (1881), The Ambassadors (1903), and The Golden Bowl (1904), can be said to share this preoccupation.

James's novels, however, constitute only one part of his achievement. He experimented with drama, with mixed results, and was a master of the short story and the novella. In these shorter forms, he was capable of combining the psychological realism of his novels with other possibilities. Thus, "The Turn of the Screw," a novella, is an admirable variation on gothic fiction, while "The Jolly Corner" (1908), also a sort of ghost story, is a compelling example of early magical realism. Critical interpretations have attempted to resolve the mystery of this story by explaining the apparition as Spencer Brydon's hallucination or even as Alice Staverton's hoax! The ghost's resistance to such clarification, however, indicates the success of the story as an example of the magical realist mode and as one of the more successful and engrossing pieces of shorter fiction Henry James produced.

The Jolly Corner

Henry James

I

"EVERY ONE asks me what I 'think' of everything," said Spencer Brydon; "and I make answer as I can—begging or dodging the question, putting them off with any nonsense. It wouldn't matter to any of them really," he went on, "for, even were it possible to meet in that stand-and-deliver way so silly a demand on so big a subject, my 'thoughts' would still be almost altogether about something that concerns only myself." He was talking to Miss Staverton, with whom for a couple of months now he had availed himself of every possible occasion to talk; this disposition and this resource, this comfort and support, as the situation in fact presented itself, having promptly enough taken the first place in the considerable array of rather unattenuated surprises attending his so strangely belated return to America. Everything was somehow a surprise; and that might be natural when one had so long and so consistently neglected everything, taken pains to give surprises so much margin for play. He had given them more than thirty years— thirty-three, to be exact; and they now seemed to him to have organised their performance quite on the scale of that licence. He had been twenty-three on leaving New York—he was fifty-six today: unless indeed he were to reckon as he had sometimes, since his repatriation, found himself feeling; in which case he would have lived longer than is often allotted to man. It would have taken a century, he repeatedly said to himself, and said also to Alice Staverton, it would have taken a longer absence and a more averted mind than those even of which he had been

59

guilty, to pile up the differences, the newnesses, the queernesses, above all the bignesses, for the better or the worse, that at present assaulted his vision wherever he looked.

The great fact all the while however had been the incalculability; since he *had* supposed himself, from decade to decade, to be allowing, and in the most liberal and intelligent manner, for brilliancy of change. He actually saw that he had allowed for nothing; he missed what he would have been sure of finding, he found what he would never have imagined. Proportions and values were upside-down; the ugly things he had expected, the ugly things of his far-away youth, when he had too promptly waked up to a sense of the ugly—these uncanny phenomena placed him rather, as it happened, under the charm; whereas the "swagger" things, the modern, the monstrous, the famous things, those he had more particularly, like thousands of ingenuous enquirers every year, come over to see, were exactly his sources of dismay. They were as so many set traps for displeasure, above all for reaction, of which his restless tread was constantly pressing the spring. It was interesting, doubtless, the whole show, but it would have been too disconcerting hadn't a certain finer truth saved the situation. He had distinctly not, in this steadier light, come over *all* for the monstrosities; he had come, not only in the last analysis but quite on the face of the act, under an impulse with which they had nothing to do. He had come—putting the thing pompously—to look at his "property," which he had thus for a third of a century not been within four thousand miles of; or, expressing it less sordidly, he had yielded to the humor of seeing again his house on the jolly corner, as he usually, and quite fondly, described it—the one in which he had first seen the light, in which various members of his family had lived and had died, in which the holidays of his overschooled boyhood had been passed and the few social flowers of his chilled adolescence gathered, and which, alienated then for so long a period, had, through the successive deaths of his two brothers and the termination of old arrangements, come wholly into his hands. He was the owner of another, not quite so "good"—the jolly corner having been, from far back, superlatively extended and consecrated; and the value of the pair represented his main capital, with an income consisting, in these later years, of their respective rents which (thanks precisely to their original excellent type) had never been depressingly low. He could live in "Europe," as he had been in the habit of living, on the product of these flourishing New York leases, and all the better since, that of the second structure, the mere number in its long row, having within a twelvemonth fallen in, renovation at a high advance had proved beautifully possible.

These were items of property indeed, but he had found himself since his arrival distinguishing more than ever between them. The house within the street, two bristling blocks westward, was already in course of reconstruction as a tall mass of flats; he had acceded, some time before, to overtures for this conversion—in which, now that it was going forward, it had been not the least of his astonishments to find himself able, on the spot, and though without a previous ounce of such experience, to participate with a certain intelligence, almost with a certain authority. He had lived his life with his back so turned to such concerns and his face addressed to those of so different an order that he scarce knew what to make of this lively stir, in a compartment of his mind never yet penetrated, of a capacity for business and a sense for construction. These virtues, so common all round him now, had been dormant in his own organism—where it might be said of them perhaps that they had slept the sleep of the just. At present, in the splendid autumn weather—the autumn at least was a pure boon in the terrible place—he loafed about his "work" undeterred, secretly agitated; not in the least "minding" that the whole proposition, as they said, was vulgar and sordid, and ready to climb ladders, to walk the plank, to handle materials and look wise about them, to ask questions, in fine, and challenge explanations and really "go into" figures.

It amused, it verily quite charmed him; and, by the same stroke, it amused, and even more, Alice Staverton, though perhaps charming her perceptibly less. She wasn't however going to be better off for it, as *he* was—and so astonishingly much: nothing was now likely, he knew, ever to make her better off than she found herself, in the afternoon of life, as the delicately frugal possessor and tenant of the small house in Irving Place to which she had subtly managed to cling through her almost unbroken New York career. If he knew the way to it now better than to any other address among the dreadful multiplied numberings which seemed to him to reduce the whole place to some vast ledger-page, overgrown, fantastic, of ruled and criss-crossed lines and figures—if he had formed, for his consolation, that habit, it was really not a little because of the charm of his having encountered and recognised, in the vast wilderness of the wholesale, breaking through the mere gross generalisation of wealth and force and success, a small still scene where items and shades, all delicate things, kept the sharpness of the notes of a high voice perfectly trained, and where economy hung about like the scent of a garden. His old friend lived with one maid and herself, dusted her relics and trimmed her lamps and polished her silver; she stood off, in the awful modern crush, when she could, but she sallied forth and did battle when the challenge was really to "spirit," the spirit she after all confessed to, proudly and a little shyly, as to that of the better time, that of *their* common, their quite far-away and antediluvian social period and order. She made use of the street-cars when need be, the terrible things that people scrambled for as the panic-stricken at sea scramble for the boats; she affronted, inscrutably, under stress, all the public concussions and ordeals; and yet, with that slim mystifying grace of her appearance, which defied you to say if she were a fair young woman who looked older through trouble, or a fine smooth older one who looked young through successful indifference; with her precious reference, above all, to memories and histories into which he could enter, she was as exquisite for him as some pale pressed flower (a rarity to begin with), and, failing other sweetnesses, she was a sufficient reward of his effort. They had communities of knowledge, "their" knowledge (this discriminating possessive was always on her lips) of presences of the other age, presences all overlaid, in his case, by the experience of a man and the freedom of a wanderer, overlaid by pleasure, by infidelity, by passages of life that were strange and dim to her, just by "Europe" in short, but still unobscured, still exposed and cherished, under that pious visitation of the spirit from which she had never been diverted.

She had come with him one day to see how his "apartment-house" was rising; he had helped her over gaps and explained to her plans, and while they were there had happened to have, before her, a brief but lively discussion with the man in charge, the representative of the building-firm that had undertaken his work. He had found himself quite "standing-up" to this personage over a failure on the latter's part to observe some detail of one of their noted conditions, and had so lucidly argued his case that, besides ever so prettily flushing, at the time, for sympathy in his triumph, she had afterwards said to him (though to a slightly greater effect of irony) that he had clearly for too many years neglected a real gift. If he had but stayed at home he would have anticipated the inventor of the skyscraper. If he had but stayed at home he would have discovered his genius in time really to start some new variety of awful architectural hare and run it till it burrowed in a goldmine. He was to remember these words, while the weeks elapsed, for the small silver ring they had sounded over the queerest and deepest of his own lately most disguised and most muffled vibrations.

It had begun to be present to him after the first fortnight, it had broken out with the oddest abruptness, this particular wanton wonderment: it met him there—and this was the image under which he himself judged the matter, or at least, not a little, thrilled and flushed with it—very much as he might have been met by some strange figure, some unexpected occupant, at a turn of one of the dim passages of an empty house. The quaint analogy quite hauntingly remained with him, when he didn't indeed rather improve it by a still intenser form: that of his opening a door behind which he would have made sure of finding nothing, a door into a room shuttered and void, and yet so coming, with a great suppressed start, on some quite erect confronting presence, something planted in the middle of the place and facing him through the dusk. After that visit to the house in construction he walked with his companion to see the other and always so much the better one, which in the eastward direction formed one of the corners, the "jolly" one precisely, of the street now so generally dishonoured and disfigured in its westward reaches, and of the comparatively conservative Avenue. The Avenue still had pretensions, as Miss Staverton said, to decency; the old people had mostly gone, the old names were unknown, and here and there an old association seemed to stray, all vaguely, like some very aged person, out too late, whom you might meet and feel the impulse to watch or follow, in kindness, for safe restoration to shelter.

They went in together, our friends; he admitted himself with his key, as he kept no one there, he explained, preferring, for his reasons, to leave the place empty, under a simple arrangement with a good woman living in the neighbourhood and who came for a daily hour to open windows and dust and sweep. Spencer Brydon had his reasons and was growingly aware of them; they seemed to him better each time he was there, though he didn't name them all to his companion, any more than he told her as yet how often, how quite absurdly often, he himself came. He only let her see for the present, while they walked through the great blank rooms, that absolute vacancy reigned and that, from top to bottom, there was nothing but Mrs. Muldoon's broom-stick, in a corner, to tempt the burglar. Mrs. Muldoon was then on the premises, and she loquaciously attended the visitors, preceding them from room to room and pushing back shutters and throwing up sashes—all to show them, as she remarked, how little there was to see. There was little indeed to see in the great gaunt shell where the main dispositions and the general apportion-ment of space, the style of an age of ampler allowances, had nevertheless for its master their honest pleading message, affecting him as some good old servant's, some lifelong retainer's appeal for a character, or even for a retiring-pension; yet it was also a remark of Mrs. Muldoon's that, glad as she was to oblige him by her noonday round, there was a request she greatly hoped he would never make of her. If he should wish her for any reason to come in after dark she would just tell him, if he "plased," that he must ask it of somebody else.

The fact that there was nothing to see didn't militate for the worthy woman against what one *might* see, and she put it frankly to Miss Staverton that no lady could be expected to like, could she? "scraping up to thim top storeys in the ayvil hours." The gas and the electric light were off the house, and she fairly evoked a gruesome vision of her march through the great grey rooms—so many of them as there were too!—with her glimmering taper. Miss Staverton met her honest glare with a smile and the profession that she herself certainly would recoil from such an adventure. Spencer Brydon meanwhile held his peace—for the moment; the question of the "evil" hours in his old home had already become too grave for him. He had begun some time since to "crape," and he knew just why a packet of candles addressed to that pursuit had been stowed by his own hand, three weeks before, at the back of a drawer of the fine old sideboard that occupied, as a "fixture," the deep recess in the dining-room. Just now he laughed at his companions—quickly however changing the subject; for the reason that, in the first place, his laugh struck him even at that moment as starting the odd echo, the conscious human resonance (he scarce knew how to qualify it) that sounds made while he was there alone sent back to his ear or his fancy; and that, in the second, he imagined Alice Staverton for the instant on the point of asking him, with a divination, if he ever so prowled. There were divinations he was unprepared for, and he had at all events averted enquiry by the time Mrs. Muldoon had left them, passing on to other parts.

There was happily enough to say, on so consecrated a spot, that could be said freely and fairly; so that a whole train of declarations was precipitated by his friend's having herself broken out, after a yearning look round: "But I hope you don't mean they want you to pull *this* to pieces!" His answer came, promptly, with his re-awakened wrath: it was of course exactly what they wanted, and what they were "at" him for, daily, with the iteration of people who couldn't for their life understand a man's liability to decent feelings. He had found the place, just as it stood and beyond what he could express, an interest and a joy. There were values other than the beastly rent-values, and in short, in short—! But it was thus Miss Staverton took him up. "In short you're to make so good a thing of your skyscraper that, living in luxury on *those* ill-gotten gains, you can afford for a while to be sentimental here!" Her smile had for him, with the words, the particular mild irony with which he found half her talk suffused; an irony without bitterness and that came, exactly, from her having so much imagination—not, like the cheap sarcasms with which one heard most people, about the world of "society," bid for the reputation of cleverness, from nobody's really having any. It was agreeable to him at this very moment to be sure that when he had answered, after a brief demur, "Well yes: so, precisely, you may put it!" her imagination would still do him justice. He explained that even if never a dollar were to come to him from the other house he would nevertheless cherish this one; and he dwelt, further, while they lingered and wandered, on the fact of the stupefaction he was already exciting, the positive mystification he felt himself create.

He spoke of the value of all he read into it, into the mere sight of the walls, mere shapes of the rooms, mere sound of the floors, mere feel, in his hand, of the old silver-plated knobs of the several mahogany doors, which suggested the pressure of the palms of the dead; the seventy years of the past in fine that these things represented, the annals of nearly three generations, counting his grandfather's, the one that had ended there, and the impalpable ashes of his long-extinct youth, afloat in the very air like microscopic motes. She listened to everything; she was a woman who answered intimately but who utterly didn't chatter. She scattered abroad therefore no cloud of words; she could assent, she could agree, above all she could encourage, without doing that. Only at the last she went a little further than he had done himself. "And then how do you know? You may still, after all, want to live here." It rather indeed pulled him up, for it wasn't what he had been thinking, at least in her sense of the words. "You mean I may decide to stay on for the sake of it?"

"Well, *with* such a home—!" But, quite beautifully, she had too much tact to dot so monstrous an *i*, and it was precisely an illustration of the way she didn't rattle. How could any one—of any wit—insist on any one else's "wanting" to live in New York?

"Oh," he said, "I *might* have lived here (since I had my opportunity early in life); I might have put in here all these years. Then everything would have been different enough—and, I dare say, 'funny' enough. But that's another matter. And then the beauty of it—I mean of my perversity, of my refusal to agree to a 'deal'—is just in the total absence of a reason. Don't you see that if I had a reason about the matter at all it would *have* to be the other way, and would then be inevitably a reason of dollars? There are no reasons here *but* of dollars. Let us therefore have none whatever— not the ghost of one."

They were back in the hall then for departure, but from where they stood the vista was large, through an open door, into the great square main saloon, with its almost antique felicity of brave spaces between windows. Her eyes came back from that reach and met his own a moment. "Are you very sure the 'ghost' of one doesn't, much rather, serve—?"

He had a positive sense of turning pale. But it was as near as they were then to come. For he made answer, he believed, between a glare and a grin: "Oh ghosts—of course the place must swarm with them! I should be ashamed of it if it didn't. Poor Mrs. Muldoon's right, and it's why I haven't asked her to do more than look in."

Miss Staverton's gaze again lost itself, and things she didn't utter, it was clear, came and went in her mind. She might even for the minute, off there in the fine room, have imagined some element dimly gathering. Simplified like the death-mask of a handsome face, it perhaps produced for her just then an effect akin to the stir of an expression in the "set" commemorative plaster. Yet whatever her impression may have been she produced instead a vague platitude. "Well, if it were only furnished and lived in—!"

She appeared to imply that in case of its being still furnished he might have been a little less opposed to the idea of a return. But she passed straight into the vestibule, as if to leave her words behind her, and the next moment he had opened the house-door and was standing with her on the steps. He closed the door and, while he re-pocketed his key, looking up and down, they took in the comparatively harsh actuality of the Avenue, which reminded him of the assault of the outer light of the Desert on the traveller emerging from an Egyptian tomb. But he risked before they stepped into the street his gathered answer to her speech.

"For me it *is* lived in. For me it *is* furnished." At which it was easy for her to sigh "Ah yes—!" all vaguely and discreetly; since his parents and his favourite sister, to say nothing of other kin, in numbers, had run their course and met their end there. That represented, within the walls, ineffaceable life.

It was a few days after this that, during an hour passed with her again, he had expressed his impatience of the too flattering curiosity— among the people he met—about his appreciation of New York. He had arrived at none at all that was socially producible, and as for that matter of his "thinking" (thinking the better or the worse of anything there) he was wholly taken up with one subject of thought. It was mere vain egoism, and it was moreover, if she liked, a morbid obsession. He found all things come back to the question of what he personally might have been, how he might have led his life and "turned out," if he had not so, at the outset, given it up. And confessing for the first time to the intensity within him of this absurd speculation—which but proved also, no doubt, the habit of too selfishly thinking—he affirmed the impotence there of any other source of interest, any other native appeal. "What would it have made of me, what would it have made of me? I keep for ever wondering, all idiotically; as if I could possibly know! I see what it has made of dozens of others, those I meet, and it positively aches within me, to the point of exasperation, that it would have made something of me as well. Only I can't make out *what*, and the worry of it, the small rage of curiosity never to be satisfied, brings back what I remember to have felt, once or twice, after judging best, for reasons, to burn some important letter unopened. I've been sorry, I've hated it—I've never known what was in the letter. You may of course say it's a trifle—!"

"I don't say it's a trifle," Miss Staverton gravely interrupted.

She was seated by her fire, and before her, on his feet and restless, he turned to and fro between this intensity of his idea and a fitful and unseeing inspection, through his single eyeglass, of the dear little old objects on her chimney-piece. Her interruption made him for an instant look at her harder. "I shouldn't care if you did!" he laughed, however; "and it's only a figure, at any rate, for the way I now feel. *Not* to have followed my perverse young course—and almost in the teeth of my father's curse, as I may say; not to have kept it up, so, 'over there', from that day to this, without a doubt or a pang; not, above all, to have liked it, to have loved it, so much, loved it, no doubt, with such an abysmal conceit of my own preference: some variation from *that*, I say, must have produced some different effect for my life and for my 'form.' I should have stuck here—if it had been possible; and I was too young, at twenty-three, to judge, *pour deux sous*, whether it *were* possible. If I had waited I might have seen it was, and then I might have been, by staying here, something nearer to one of these types who have been hammered so hard and made so keen by their conditions. It isn't that I admire them so much—the question of any charm in them, or of any charm, beyond that of the rank money-passion, exerted by their condition *for* them, has nothing to do with the matter: it's only a question of what fantastic, yet perfectly possible, development of my own nature I mayn't have missed. It comes over me that I had then a strange *alter ego* deep down somewhere within me, as the full-blown flower is in the small tight bud, and that I just took the course, I just transferred him to the climate, that blighted him for once and for ever."

"And you wonder about the flower," Miss Staverton said. "So do I, if you want to know; and so I've been wondering these several weeks. I believe in the flower," she continued, "I feel it would have been quite splendid, quite huge and monstrous."

"Monstrous above all!" her visitor echoed; "and I imagine, by the same stroke, quite hideous and offensive."

"You don't believe that," she returned; "if you did you wouldn't wonder. You'd know, and that would be enough for you. What you feel—and what I feel *for* you—is that you'd have had power."

"You'd have liked me that way?" he asked.

She barely hung fire. "How should I not have liked you?"

"I see. You'd have liked me, have preferred me, a billionaire!"

"How should I not have liked you?" she simply again asked.

He stood before her still—her question kept him motionless. He took it in, so much there was of it; and indeed his not otherwise meeting it testified to that. "I know at least what I am," he simply went on; "the other side of the medal's clear enough. I've not been edifying—I believe I'm thought in a hundred quarters to have been barely decent. I've followed strange paths and worshipped strange gods; it must have come to you again and again—in fact you've admitted to me as much—that I was leading, at any time these thirty years, a selfish frivolous scandalous life. And you see what it has made of me."

She just waited, smiling at him. "You see what it has made of *me*."

"Oh you're a person whom nothing can have altered. You were born to be what you are, anywhere, anyway: you've the perfection nothing else could have blighted. And don't you see how, without my exile, I shouldn't have been waiting till now—?" But he pulled up for the strange pang.

"The great thing to see, " she presently said, "seems to me to be that it has spoiled nothing. It hasn't spoiled your being here at last. It hasn't spoiled this. It hasn't spoiled your speaking—" She also however faltered.

He wondered at everything her controlled emotion might mean. "Do you believe then—too dreadfully!—that I *am* as good as I might ever have been?"

"Oh no! Far from it!" With which she got up from her chair and was nearer to him. "But I don't care," she smiled.

"You mean I'm good enough?"

She considered a little. "Will you believe it if I say so? I mean will you let that settle your question for you?" And then as if making out in his face that he drew back from this, that he had some idea which, however absurd, he couldn't yet bargain away: "Oh you don't care either—but very differently: you don't care for anything but yourself."

Spencer Brydon recognised it—it was in fact what he had absolutely professed. Yet he importantly qualified. "*He* isn't myself. He's the just so totally other person. But I do want to see him," he added. "And I can. And I shall."

Their eyes met for a minute while he guessed from something in hers that she divined his strange sense. But neither of them otherwise expressed it, and her apparent understanding, with no protesting shock, no easy derision, touched him more deeply than anything yet, constituting for his stifled perversity, on the spot, an element that was like breathable air. What she said however was unexpected. "Well, *I've* seen him."

"You—?"

"I've seen him in a dream."

"Oh a 'dream'—!" It let him down.

"But twice over," she continued. "I saw him as I see you now."

"You've dreamed the same dream—?"

"Twice over," she repeated. "The very same."

This did somehow a little speak to him, as it also gratified him. "You dream about me at that rate?"

"Ah about *him!*" she smiled.

His eyes again sounded her. "Then you know all about him." And as she said nothing more: "What's the wretch like?"

She hesitated, and it was as if he were pressing her so hard that, resisting for reasons of her own, she had to turn away. "I'll tell you some other time!"

II

It was after this that there was most of a virtue for him, most of a cultivated charm, most of a preposterous secret thrill, in the particular form of surrender to his obsession and of address to what he more and more believed to be his privilege. It was what in these weeks he was living for—since he really felt life to begin but after Mrs. Muldoon had retired from the scene and, visiting the ample house from attic to cellar, making sure he was alone, he knew himself in safe possession and, as he tacitly expressed it, let himself go. He sometimes came twice in the twenty-four hours; the moments he liked best were those of gathering dusk, of the short autumn twilight; this was the time of which, again and again, he found himself hoping most. Then he could, as seemed to him, most intimately wander and wait, linger and listen, feel his fine attention, never in his life before so fine, on the pulse of the great vague place: he preferred the lampless hour and only wished he might have prolonged each day the deep crepuscular spell. Later—rarely much before midnight, but then for a considerable vigil—he watched with his glimmering light; moving slowly, holding it high, playing it far, rejoicing above all, as much as he might, in open vistas, reaches of communication between rooms and by passages; the long straight chance or show, as he would have called it, for the revelation he pretended to invite. It was a practice he found he could perfectly "work" without exciting remark; no one was in the least the wiser for it; even Alice Staverton, who was moreover a well of discretion, didn't quite fully imagine.

He let himself in and let himself out with the assurance of calm proprietorship; and accident so far favoured him that, if a fat Avenue "officer" had happened on occasion to see him entering at eleven-thirty, he had never yet, to the best of his belief, been noticed as emerging at two. He walked there on the crisp November nights, arrived regularly at the evening's end; it was as easy to do this after dining out as to take his way to a club or to his hotel. When he left his club, if he hadn't been dining out, it was ostensibly to go to his hotel; and when he left his hotel, if he had spent a part of the evening there, it was ostensibly to go to his club. Everything was easy in fine; everything conspired and promoted: there was truly even in the strain of his experience something that glossed over, something that salved and simplified, all the rest of consciousness. He circulated, talked, renewed, loosely and pleasantly, old relations—met indeed, so far as he could, new expectations and seemed to make out on the whole that in spite of the career, of such different contacts, which he had spoken of to Miss Staverton as ministering so little, for those who might have watched it, to edification, he was positively rather liked than not. He was a dim secondary social success— and all with people who had truly not an idea of him. It was all mere surface sound, this murmur of their welcome, this popping of their corks—just as his gestures of response were the extravagant shadows, emphatic in proportion as they meant little, of some game of *ombres chinoises*. He projected himself all day, in thought, straight over the bristling line of hard unconscious heads and into the other, the real, the waiting life; the life that, as soon as he had heard behind him the click of his great house-door, began for him, on the jolly corner, as beguilingly as the slow opening bars of some rich music follows the tap of the conductor's wand.

He always caught the first effect of the steel point of his stick on the old marble of the hall pavement, large black-and-white squares that he remembered as the admiration of his childhood and that had then made in him, as he now saw, for the growth of an early conception of style. This effect was the dim reverberating tinkle as of some far-off bell hung who should say where?—in the depths of the house, of the past, of that mystical other world that might have flourished for him had he not, for weal or woe, abandoned it. On this impression he did ever the same thing; he put his stick noiselessly away in a corner—feeling the place once more in the likeness of some great glass bowl, all precious concave crystal, set delicately humming by the play of a moist finger round its edge. The concave crystal held, as it were, this mystical other world, and the indescribably fine murmur of its rim was the sigh there, the scarce audible pathetic wail to his strained ear, of all the old baffled forsworn possibilities. What he did therefore by this appeal of his hushed presence was to wake them into such measure of ghostly life as they might still enjoy. They were shy, all but unappeasably shy, but they weren't really sinister; at least they weren't as he had hitherto felt them—before they had taken the Form he so yearned to make them take, the Form he at moments saw himself in the light of fairly hunting on tiptoe, the points of his evening-shoes, from room to room and from storey to storey.

That was the essence of his vision—which was all rank folly, if one would, while he was out of the house and otherwise occupied, but which took on the last verisimilitude as soon as he was placed and posted. He knew what he meant and what he wanted; it was as clear as the figure on a cheque presented in demand for cash. His *alter ego* "walked"—that was the note of his image of him, while his image of his motive for his own odd pastime was the desire to waylay him and meet him. He roamed, slowly, warily, but all restlessly, he himself did—Mrs. Muldoon had been right, absolutely, with her figure of their "craping"; and the presence he watched for would roam restlessly too. But it would be as cautious and as shifty; the conviction of its probable, in fact its already quite sensible, quite audible evasion of pursuit grew for him from night to night, laying on him finally a rigor to which nothing in his life had been comparable. It has been the theory of many superficially-judging persons, he knew, that he was wasting that life in a surrender to sensations, but he had tasted of no pleasure so fine as his actual tension, had been introduced to no sport that demanded at once the patience and the nerve of this stalking of a creature more subtle, yet at bay perhaps more formidable, than any beast of the forest. The terms, the comparisons, the very practices of the chase positively came again into play; there were even moments when passages of his occasional experience as a sportsman, stirred memories, from his younger time, of moor and mountain and desert, revived for him—and to the increase of his keenness—by the tremendous force of analogy. He found himself at moments—once he had placed his single light on some mantel-shelf or in some recess—stepping back into shelter or shade, effacing himself behind a door or in an embrasure, as he had sought of old the vantage of rock and tree; he found himself holding his breath and living in the joy of the instant, the supreme suspense created by big game alone.

He wasn't afraid (though putting himself the question as he believed gentlemen on Bengal tiger-shoots or in close quarters with the great bear of the Rockies had been known to confess to having put it); and this indeed—since here at least he might be frank!—because of the impression, so intimate and so strange, that he himself produced as yet a dread, produced certainly a strain, beyond the liveliest he was likely to feel. They fell for him into categories, they fairly became familiar, the signs, for his own perception, of the alarm his presence and his vigilance created; though leaving him always to remark, portentously, on his probably having formed a relation, his probably enjoying a consciousness, unique in the experience of man. People enough, first and last, had been in terror of apparitions, but who had ever before so turned the tables and become himself, in the apparitional world, an incalculable terror? He might have found this sublime had he quite dared to think of it; but he didn't too much insist, truly, on that side of his privilege. With habit and repetition he gained to an extraordinary degree the power to penetrate the dusk of distances and the darkness of corners, to resolve back into their innocence the treacheries of uncertain light, the evil-looking forms taken in the gloom by mere shadows, by accidents of the air, by shifting effects of perspective; putting down his dim luminary he could still wander on without it, pass into other rooms and, only knowing it was there behind him a case of need, see his way about, visually project for his purpose a comparative clearness. It made him feel, this acquired faculty, like some monstrous stealthy cat; he wondered if he would have glared at these moments with large shining yellow eyes, and what it mightn't verily be, for the poor hard-pressed *alter ego*, to be confronted with such a type.

He liked however the open shutters; he opened everywhere those Mrs. Muldoon had closed, closing them as carefully afterwards, so that she shouldn't notice: he liked—oh this he did like, and above all in the upper rooms!—the sense of the hard silver of the autumn stars through the window panes, and scarcely less the flare of the streetlamps below, the white electric luster which it would have taken curtains to keep out. This was human actual social; this was of the world he had lived in, and he was more at his ease certainly for the countenance, coldly general and impersonal, that all the while and in spite of his detachment it seemed to give him. He had support of course mostly in the rooms at the wide front and the prolonged side; it failed him considerably in the central shades and the parts at the back. But if he sometimes, on his rounds, was glad of his optical reach, so none the less often the rear of the house affected him as the very jungle of his prey. The place was there more subdivided; a large "extension" in particular, where small rooms for servants had been multiplied, abounded in nooks and corners, in closets and passages, in the ramifications especially of an ample back staircase over which he leaned, many a time, to look far down—not deterred from his gravity even while aware that he might, for a spectator, have figured some solemn simpleton playing at hide-and-seek. Outside in fact he might himself make that ironic *rapprochement*; but within the walls, and in spite of the clear windows, his consistency was proof against the cynical light of New York.

It had belonged to that idea of the exasperated consciousness of his victim to become a real test for him; since he had quite put it to himself from the first that, oh distinctly! he could "cultivate" his whole perception. He had felt it as above all open to cultivation—which indeed was but another name for his manner of spending his time. He was bringing it on, bringing it to perfection, by practice; in consequence of which it had grown so fine that he was now aware of impressions, attestations of his general postulate, that couldn't have broken upon him at once. This was the case more specifically with a phenomenon at last quite frequent for him in the upper rooms, the recognition—absolutely unmistakable, and by a turn dating from a particular hour, his resumption of his campaign after a diplomatic drop, a calculated absence of three nights—of his being definitely followed, tracked at a distance carefully taken and to the express end that he should the less confidently, less arrogantly, appear to himself merely to pursue. It worried, it finally quite broke him up, for it proved, of all the conceivable impressions, the one least suited to his book. He was kept in sight while remaining himself—as regards the essence of his position—sightless, and his only recourse then was in abrupt turns, rapid recoveries of ground. He wheeled about, retracing his steps, as if he might so catch in his face at least the stirred air of some other quick revolution. It was indeed true that his fully dislocalised thought of these manoeuvres recalled to him Pantaloon, at the Christmas farce, buffeted and tricked from behind by ubiquitous Harlequin; but it left intact the influence of the conditions themselves each time he was reexposed to them, so that in fact this association, had he suffered it to become constant, would on a certain side have but ministered to his intenser gravity. He had made, as I have said, to create on the premises the baseless sense of a reprieve, his three absences; and the result of the third was to confirm the after-effect of the second.

On his return, that night—the night succeeding his last intermission—he stood in the hall and looked up the staircase with a certainty more intimate than any he had yet known. "He's *there*, at the top, and waiting—not, as in general, falling back for disappearance. He's holding his ground, and it's the first time—which is a proof, isn't it? that something has happened for him." So Brydon argued with his hand on the banister and his foot on the lowest stair; in which position he felt as never before the air chilled by his logic. He himself turned cold in it, for he seemed of a sudden to know what now was involved. "Harder pressed?—yes, he takes it in, with its thus making clear to him that I've come, as they say, 'to stay.' He finally doesn't like and can't bear it, in the sense, I mean, that his wrath, his menaced interest, now balances with his dread. I've hunted him till he has 'turned': that, up there, is what has happened—he's the fanged or the antlered animal brought at last to bay." There came to him, as I say—but determined by an influence beyond my notation!—the acuteness of this certainty; under which however the next moment he had broken into a sweat that he would as little have consented to attribute to fear as he would have dared immediately to act upon it for enterprise. It marked none the less a prodigious thrill, a thrill that represented sudden dismay, no doubt, but also represented, and with the selfsame throb, the strangest, the most joyous, possibly the next minute almost the proudest, duplication of consciousness.

"He has been dodging, retreating, hiding, but now, worked up to anger, he'll fight!"—this intense impression made a single mouthful as it were, of terror and applause. But what was wondrous was that the applause for the felt fact, was so eager, since, if it was his other self he was running to earth, this ineffable identity was thus in the last resort not unworthy of him. It bristled there—somewhere near at hand, however unseen still—as the hunted thing, even as the trodden worm of the adage *must* at last bristle; and Brydon at this instant tasted probably of a sensation more complex than had ever before found itself consistent with sanity. It was as if it would have shamed him that a character so associated with his own should triumphantly succeed in just skulking, should to the end not risk the open, so that the drop of this danger was, on the spot, a great lift of the whole situation. Yet with another rare shift of the same subtlety he was already trying to measure by how much more he himself might now be in peril of fear; so rejoicing that he could in another form, actively inspire that fear, and simultaneously quaking for the form in which he might passively know it.

The apprehension of knowing it must after a little have grown in him, and the strangest moment of his adventure perhaps, the most memorable or really most interesting, afterwards, of his crisis, was the lapse of certain instants of concentrated conscious *combat*, the sense of a need to hold on to something, even after the manner of a man slipping and slipping on some awful incline; the vivid impulse, above all, to move, to act, to charge, somehow and upon something—to show himself, in a word, that he wasn't afraid. The state of "holding-on" was thus the state to which he was momentarily reduced; if there had been anything, in the great vacancy, to seize, he would presently have been aware of having clutched it as he might under a shock at home have clutched the nearest chair-back. He had been surprised at any rate—of this he *was* aware—into something unprecedented since his original appropriation of the place; he had closed his eyes, held them tight, for a long minute, as with that instinct of dismay and that terror of vision. When he opened them the room, the other contiguous rooms, extraordinarily, seemed lighter—so light, almost, that at first he took the change for day. He stood firm, however that might be, just where he had paused; his resistance had helped him—it was as if there were something he had tided over. He knew after a little what this was—it had been in the imminent danger of flight. He had stiffened his will against going; without this he would have made for the stairs, and it seemed to him that, still with his eyes closed, he would have descended them, would have known how, straight and swiftly to the bottom.

Well, as he had held out, here he was—still at the top, among the more intricate upper rooms and with the gauntlet of the others, of all the rest of the house, still to run when it should be his time to go. He would go at his time—only at his time: didn't he go every night very much at the same hour? He took out his watch—there was light for that: it was scarcely a quarter past one, and he had never withdrawn so soon. He reached his lodgings for the most part at two—with his walk of a quarter of an hour. He would wait for the last quarter—he wouldn't stir till then; and he kept his watch there with his eye on it, reflecting while he held it that this deliberate wait, a wait with an effort, which he recognised, would serve perfectly for the attestation he desired to make. It would prove his courage—unless indeed the latter might most be proved by his budging at last from his place. What he mainly felt now was that, since he hadn't originally scuttled, he had his dignities—which had never in his life seemed so many—all to preserve and to carry aloft. This was before him in truth as a physical image, an image almost worthy of an age of greater romance. That remark indeed glimmered for him only to glow the next instant with a finer light; since what age of romance, after all, could have matched either the state of his mind or, "objectively," as they said, the wonder of his situation? The only difference would have been that, brandishing his dignities over his head as in a parchment scroll, he might then—that is in the heroic time—have proceeded downstairs with a drawn sword in his other grasp.

At present, really, the light he had set down on the mantel of the next room would have to figure his sword; which utensil, in the course of a minute, he had taken the requisite number of steps to possess himself of. The door between the rooms was open, and from the second another door opened to a third. These rooms, as he remembered, gave all three upon a common corridor as well, but there was a fourth, beyond them, without issue save through the preceding. To have moved, to have heard his step again, was appreciably a help; though even in recognizing this he lingered once more a little by the chimney-piece on which his light had rested. When he next moved, just hesitating where to turn, he found himself considering a circumstance that, after his first and comparatively vague apprehension of it, produced in him the start that often attends some pang of recollection, the violent shock of having ceased happily to forget. He had come into sight of the door in which the brief chain of communication ended and which he now surveyed from the nearer threshold the one not directly facing it. Placed at some distance to the left of this point, it would have admitted him to the last room of the four, the room without other approach or egress, had it not, to his intimate conviction, been closed *since* his former visitation, the matter probably of a quarter of an hour before. He stared with all his eyes at the wonder of the fact, arrested again where he stood and again holding his breath while he sounded its sense. Surely it had been *subsequently* closed—that is it had been on his previous passage indubitably open!

He took it full in the face that something had happened between— that he couldn't not have noticed before (by which he meant on his original tour of all the rooms that evening) that such a barrier had exceptionally presented itself. He had indeed since that moment undergone an agitation so extraordinary that it might have muddled for him any earlier view; and he tried to convince himself that he might perhaps then have gone into the room and, inadvertently, automatically, on coming out, have drawn the door after him. The difficulty was that this exactly was what he never did; it was against his whole policy, as he might have said, the essence of which was to keep vistas clear. He had them from the first, as he was well aware, quite on the brain: the strange apparition, at the far end of one of them, of his baffled "prey" (which had become by so sharp an irony so little the term now to apply!) was the form of success his imagination had most cherished, projecting into it always a refinement of beauty. He had known fifty times the start of perception that had afterwards dropped; had fifty times gasped to himself "There!" under some fond brief hallucination. The house, as the case stood, admirably lent itself; he might wonder at the taste, the native architecture of the particular time, which could rejoice so in the multiplication of doors—the opposite extreme to the modern, the actual almost complete proscription of them; but it had fairly contributed to provoke this obsession of the presence encountered telescopically, as he might say, focussed and studied in diminishing perspective and as by a rest for the elbow.

It was with these considerations that his present attention was charged—they perfectly availed to make what he saw portentous. He *couldn't*, by any lapse, have blocked that aperture; and if he hadn't, if it was unthinkable, why what else was clear but that there had been another agent? Another agent?—he had been catching, as he felt, a moment back, the very breath of him; but when had he been so close as in this simple, this logical, this completely personal act? It was so logical, that is, that one might have *taken* it for personal; yet for what did Brydon take it, he asked himself, while, softly panting, he felt his eyes almost leave their sockets. Ah this time at last they *were*, the two, the opposed projections of him, in presence; and this time, as much as one would, the question of danger loomed. With it rose, as not before, the question of courage—for what he knew the blank face of the door to say to him was "Show us how much you have!" It stared, it glared back at him with that challenge; it put to him the two alternatives: should he just push it open or not? Oh to have this consciousness was to *think*—and to think, Brydon knew, as he stood there, was, with the lapsing moments, not to have acted! Not to have acted—that was the misery and the pang—was even still not act; was in fact *all* to feel the thing in another, in a new and terrible way. How long did he pause and how long did he debate? There was presently nothing to measure it; for his vibration had already changed—as just by the effect of its intensity. Shut up there, at bay, defiant, and with the prodigy of the thing palpably proveably *done*, thus giving notice like some stark signboard—under that accession of accent the situation itself had turned; and Brydon at last remarkably made up his mind on what it had turned to.

It had turned altogether to a different admonition; to a supreme hint, for him, of the value of Discretion! This slowly dawned, no doubt—for it could take its time; so perfectly, on his threshold, had he been stayed, so little as yet had he either advanced or retreated. It was the strangest of all things that now when, by his taking ten steps and applying his hand to a latch, or even his shoulder and his knee, if necessary, to a panel, all the hunger of his prime need might have been met, his high curiosity crowned, his unrest assuaged—it was amazing, but it was also exquisite and rare, that insistence should have, at a touch, quite dropped from him. Discretion—he jumped at that; and yet not, verily, at such a pitch, because it saved his nerves or his skin, but because; much more valuably, it saved the situation. When I say he "jumped" at it I feel the consonance of this term with the fact that—at the end indeed of I know not how long—he did move again, he crossed straight to the door. He wouldn't touch it—it seemed now that he might *if* he would: he would only just wait there a little, to show, to prove, that he wouldn't. He had thus another station, close to the thin partition by which revelation was denied him; but with his eyes bent and his hands held off in a mere intensity of stillness. He listened as if there had been something to hear, but this attitude, while it lasted, was his own communication. "If you won't then—good: I spare you and I give up. You affect me as by the appeal positively for pity: you convince me that for reasons rigid and sublime—what do I know?—we both of us should have suffered. I respect them then, and, though moved and privileged as, I believe, it has never been given to man, I retire, I renounce—never, on my honor, to try again. So rest for ever—and let *me!*"

That, for Brydon was the deep sense of this last demonstration—solemn, measured, directed, as he felt it to be. He brought it to a close, he turned away; and now verily he knew how deeply he had been stirred. He retraced his steps, taking up his candle, burnt, he observed, well-nigh to the socket, and marking again, lighten it as he would, the distinctness of his footfall; after which, in a moment, he knew himself at the other side of the house. He did there what he had not yet done at these hours—he opened half a casement, one of those in the front, and let in the air of the night; a thing he would have taken at any time previous for a sharp rupture of his spell. His spell was broken now, and it didn't matter—broken by his concession and his surrender, which made it idle henceforth that he should ever come back. The empty street—its other life so marked even by the great lamplit vacancy—was within call, within touch; he stayed there as to be in it again, high above it though he was still perched; he watched as for some comforting common fact, some vulgar human note, the passage of a scavenger or a thief, some night-bird however base. He would have blessed that sign of life; he would have welcomed positively the slow approach of his friend the policeman, whom he had hitherto only sought to avoid, and was not sure that if the patrol had come into sight he might not have felt the impulse to get into relation with it, to hail it, on some pretext, from his fourth floor.

The pretext that wouldn't have been too silly or too compromising, the explanation that would have saved his dignity and kept his name, in such a case, out of the papers, was not definite to him: he was so occupied with the thought of recording his Discretion—as an effect of the vow he had just uttered to his intimate adversary—that the importance of this loomed large and something had overtaken all ironically his sense of proportion. If there had been a ladder applied to the front of the house, even one of the vertiginous perpendiculars employed by painters and roofers and sometimes left standing overnight, he would have managed somehow, astride of the window-still, to compass by outstretched leg and arm that mode of descent. If there had been some such uncanny thing as he had found in his room at hotels, a workable fire escape in the form of notched cable or a canvas shoot, he would have availed himself of it as a proof—well, of his present delicacy. He nursed that sentiment, as the question stood, a little in vain, and even—at the end of he scarce knew, once more, how long—found it, as by the action on his mind of the failure of response of the outer world, sinking back to vague anguish. It seemed to him he had waited an age for some stir of the great grim hush; the life of the town was itself under a spell—so unnaturally, up and down the whole prospect of known and rather ugly objects, the blankness and the silence lasted. Had they ever, he asked himself, the hardfaced houses, which had begun to look livid in the dim dawn, had they ever spoken so little to any need of his spirit? Great builded voids, great crowded stillnesses put on, often, in the heart of cities, for the small hours, a sort of sinister mask, and it was of this large collective negation that Brydon presently became conscious—all the more that the break of day was, almost incredibly, now at hand, proving to him what a night he had made of it.

He looked again at his watch, saw what had become of his time-values (he had taken hours for minutes—not, as in other tense situations, minutes for hours) and the strange air of the streets was but the weak, the sullen flush of a dawn in which everything was still locked up. His choked appeal from his own open window had been the sole note of life, and he could but break off at last as for a worse despair. Yet while so deeply demoralised he was capable again of an impulse denoting—at least by his present measure—extraordinary resolution; of retracing his steps to the spot where he had turned cold with the extinction of his last pulse of doubt as to there being in the place another presence than his own. This required an effort strong enough to sicken him; but he had his reason, which over-mastered for the moment everything else. There was the whole of the rest of the house to traverse, and how should he screw himself to that if the door he had seen closed were at present open? He could hold to the idea that the closing had practically been for him an act of mercy, a chance offered him to descend, depart, get off the ground and never again profane it. This conception held together, it worked; but what it meant for him depended now clearly on the amount of forbearance his recent action, or rather his recent inaction, had engendered. The image of the "presence," whatever it was, waiting there for him to go—this image had not yet been so concrete for his nerves as when he stopped short of the point at which certainty would have come to him. For, with all his resolution, or more exactly with all his dread, he did stop short—he hung back from really seeing. The risk was too great and his fear too definite: it took at this moment an awful specific form.

He knew—yes, as he had never known anything—that, *should* he see the door open, it would all too abjectly be the end of him. It would mean that the agent of his shame—for his shame was the deep abjection—was once more at large and in general possession; and what glared him thus in the face was the act that this would determine for him. It would send him straight about to the window he had left open, and by that window, be long ladder and dangling rope as absent as they would, he saw himself uncontrollably insanely fatally take his way to the street. The hideous chance of this he at least could avert; but he could only avert it by recoiling in time from assurance. He had the whole house to deal with, this fact was still there; only he now knew that uncertainty alone could start him. He stole back from where he had checked himself—merely to do so was suddenly like safety—and, making blindly for the greater staircase, left gaping rooms and sounding passages behind. Here was the top of the stairs, with a fine large dim descent and three spacious landings to mark off. His instinct was all for mildness, but his feet were harsh on the floors, and, strangely, when he had in a couple of minutes become aware of this, it counted somehow for help. He couldn't have spoken, the tone of his voice would have scared him, and the common conceit or resource of "whistling in the dark" (whether literally or figuratively) have appeared basely vulgar; yet he liked none the less to hear himself go, and when he had reached his first landing—taking it all with no rush, but quite steadily—that stage of success drew from him a gasp of relief.

The house, withal, seemed immense, the scale of space again inordinate; the open rooms, to no one of which his eyes deflected, gloomed in their shuttered state like mouths of caverns; only the high skylight that formed the crown of the deep well created for him a medium in which he could advance, but which might have been, for queerness of color, some watery under-world. He tried to think of something noble, as that his property was really grand, a splendid possession; but this nobleness took the form too of the clear delight with which he was finally to sacrifice it. They might come in now, the builders, the destroyers—they might come as soon as they would. At the end of two flights he had dropped to another zone, and from the middle of the third, with only one more left, he recognised the influence of the lower windows, of half-drawn blinds, of the occasional gleam of street-lamps, of the glazed spaces of the vestibule. This was the bottom of the sea, which showed an illumination of its own and which he even saw paved—when at a given moment he drew up to sink a long look over the banisters— with the marble squares of his childhood. By that time indubitably he felt, as he might have said in a commoner cause, better; it had allowed him to stop and draw breath, and the ease increased with the sight of the old black-and-white slabs. But what he most felt was that now surely, with the element of impunity pulling him as by hard firm hands, the case was settled for what he might have seen above had he dared that last look. The closed door, blessedly remote now, was still closed—and he had only in short to reach that of the house.

He came down further, he crossed the passage forming the access to the last flight; and if here again he stopped an instant it was almost for the sharpness of the thrill of assured escape. It made him shut his eyes—which opened again to the straight slope of the remainder of the stairs. Here was impunity still, but impunity almost excessive; inasmuch as the side-lights and the high fan-tracery of the entrance were glimmering straight into the hall; an appearance produced, he the next instant saw, by the fact that the vestibule gaped wide, that the hinged halves of the inner door had been thrown far back. Out of that again the *question* sprang at him, making his eyes, as he felt, half-start from his head, as they had done, at the top of the house, before the sign of the other door. If he had left that one open, hadn't he left this one closed, and wasn't he now in the *most* immediate presence of some inconceivable occult activity? It was as sharp, the question, as a knife in his side, but the answer hung fire still and seemed to lose itself in the vague darkness to which the thin admitted dawn, glimmering archwise over the whole outer door, made a semicircular margin, a cold silvery nimbus that seemed to play a little as he looked—to shift and expand and contract.

It was as if there had been something within it, protected by indistinctness and corresponding in extent with the opaque surface behind, the painted panels of the last barrier to his escape, of which the key was in his pocket. The indistinctness mocked him even while he stared, affected him as somehow shrouding or challenging certitude, so that after faltering an instant on his step he let himself go with the sense that here *was* at last something to meet, to touch, to take, to know—something all unnatural and dreadful, but to advance upon which was the condition for him either of liberation or of supreme defeat. The penumbra, dense and dark, was the virtual screen of a figure which stood in it as still as some image erect in a niche or as some black-vizored sentinel guarding a treasure. Brydon was to know afterwards, was to recall and make out, the particular thing he had believed during the rest of his descent. He saw, in its great grey glimmering margin, the central vagueness diminish, and he felt it to be taking the very form toward which, for so many days, the passion of his curiosity had yearned. It gloomed, it loomed, it was something, it was somebody, the prodigy of a personal presence.

Rigid and conscious, spectral yet human, a man of his own substance and stature waited there to measure himself with his power to dismay. This only could it be—this only till he recognised, with his advance, that what made the face dim was the pair of raised hands that covered it and in which, so far from being offered in defiance, it was buried as for dark depreciation. So Brydon, before him, took him in; with every fact of him now, in the higher light, hard and acute—his planted stillness, his vivid truth, his grizzled bent head and white masking hands, his queer actuality of evening-dress, of dangling double eye-glass, of gleaming silk lappet and white linen, of pearl button and gold watch-guard and polished shoe. No portrait by a great modern master could have presented him with more intensity, thrust him out of his frame with more art, as if there had been "treatment," of the consummate sort, in his every shade and salience. The revulsion, for our friend, had become, before he knew it, immense—this drop, in the act of apprehension, to the sense of his adversary's inscrutable manoeuvre. That meaning at least, while he gaped, it offered him; for he could but gape at his other self in this other anguish, gape as a proof that *he*, standing there for the achieved, the enjoyed, the triumphant life, couldn't be faced in his triumph. Wasn't the proof in the splendid covering hands, strong and completely spread?—so spread and so intentional that, in spite of a special verity that surpassed every other, the fact that one of these hands had lost two fingers, which were reduced to stumps, as if accidentally shot away, the face was effectually guarded and saved.

"Saved," though, *would* it be?—Brydon breathed his wonder till the very impunity of his attitude and the very insistence of his eyes produced, as he felt, a sudden stir which showed the next instant as a deeper portent, while the head raised itself, the betrayal of a braver purpose. The hands, as he looked, began to move, to open; then, as if deciding in a flash, dropped from the face and left it uncovered and presented. Horror, with the sight, had leaped into Brydon's throat, gasping there in a sound he couldn't utter; for the bared identity was too hideous as *his*, and his glare was the passion of his protest. The face, *that* face, Spencer Brydon's?—he searched it still, but looking away from it in dismay and denial, falling straight from his height of sublimity. It was unknown, inconceivable, awful, disconnected from any possibility—! He had been "sold," he inwardly moaned, stalking such game as this: the presence before him was a presence, the horror within him a horror, but the waste of his nights had been only grotesque and the success of his adventure an irony. Such an identity fitted his at *no* point, made its alternative monstrous. A thousand times yes, as it came upon him nearer now—the face was the face of a stranger. It came upon him nearer now, quite as one of those expanding fantastic images projected by the magic lantern of childhood; for the stranger, whoever he might be, evil, odious, blatant, vulgar, had advanced as for aggression, and he knew himself give ground. Then harder pressed still, sick with the force of his shock, and falling back as under the hot breath and the roused passion of a life larger than his own, a rage of personality before which his own collapsed, he felt the whole vision turn to darkness and his very feet give way. His head went round; he was going; he had gone.

III

What had next brought him back, clearly—though after how long?—was Mrs. Muldoon's voice, coming to him from quite near, from so near that he seemed presently to see her as kneeling on the ground before him while he lay looking up at her; himself not wholly on the ground, but half-raised and upheld conscious, yes, of tenderness of support and, more particularly, of a head pillowed in extraordinary softness and faintly refreshing fragrance. He considered, he wondered, his wit but half at his service; then another face intervened, bending more directly over him, and he finally knew that Alice Staverton had made her lap an ample and perfect cushion to him, and that she had to this end seated herself on the lowest degree of the staircase, the rest of his long person remaining stretched on his old black-and-white slabs. They were cold, these marble squares of his youth; but *he* somehow was not, in his rich return of consciousness—the most wonderful hour, little by little, that he had ever known, leaving him, as it did, so gratefully, so abysmally passive, and yet as with a treasure of intelligence waiting all round him for quiet appropriation; dissolved, he might call it, in the air of the place and producing the golden glow of a late autumn afternoon. He had come back, yes—come back from further away than any man but himself had ever travelled; but it was strange how with this sense what he had come back *to* seemed really the great thing, and as if his prodigious journey had been all for the sake of it. Slowly but surely his consciousness grew, his vision of his state thus completing itself: he had been miraculously *carried* back—lifted and carefully borne as from where he had been picked up, the uttermost end of an interminable grey passage. Even with this he was suffered to rest, and what had now brought him to knowledge was the break in the long mild motion.

It had brought him to knowledge, to knowledge—yes, this was the beauty of his state; which came to resemble more and more that of a man who has gone to sleep on some news of a great inheritance, and then, after dreaming it away, after profaning it with matters strange to it, has waked up again to serenity of certitude and has only to lie and watch it grow. This was the drift of his patience—that he had only to let it shine on him. He must moreover, with intermissions, still have been lifted and borne; since why and how else should he have known himself, later on, with the afternoon glow intenser, no longer at the foot of his stairs—situated as these now seemed at that dark other end of his tunnel—but on a deep window-bench of his high saloon, over which had been spread, couch-fashion, a mantle of soft stuff lined with grey fur that was familiar to his eyes and that one of his hands kept fondly feeling as for its pledge of truth. Mrs. Muldoon's face had gone, but the other, the second he had recognised, hung over him in a way that showed how he was still propped and pillowed. He took it all in, and the more he took it the more it seemed to suffice: he was as much at peace as if he had had food and drink. It was the two women who had found him, on Mrs. Muldoon's having plied, at her usual hour, her latch-key—and on her having above all arrived while Miss Staverton still lingered near the house. She had been turning away, all anxiety, from worrying the vain bell-handle—her calculation having been of the hour of the good woman's visit; but the latter, blessedly, had come up while she was still there, and they had entered together. He had then lain, beyond the vestibule, very much as he was lying now—quite, that is, as he appeared to have fallen, but all so wondrously without bruise or gash; only in a depth of stupor. What he most took in, however, at present, with the steadier clearance, was that Alice Staverton had for a long unspeakable moment not doubted he was dead.

"It must have been that I was." He made it out as she held him. "Yes—I can only have died. You brought me literally to life. Only," he wondered, his eyes rising to her, "only, in the name of all the benedictions, how?"

It took her but an instant to bend her face and kiss him, and something in the manner of it, and in the way her hands clasped and locked his head while he felt the cool charity and virtue of her lips, something in all this beatitude somehow answered everything. "And now I keep you," she said.

"Oh, keep me, keep me!" he pleaded while her face still hung over him: in response to which it dropped again and stayed close, clingingly close. It was the seal of their situation—of which he tasted the impress for a long blissful moment in silence. But he came back. "Yet how did you know—?"

"I was uneasy. You were to have come, you remember—and you had sent no word."

"Yes, I remember—I was to have gone to you at one today." It caught on to their "old" life and relation—which were so near and so far. "I was still out there in my strange darkness—where was it, what was it? I must have stayed there so long." He could but wonder at the depth and the duration of his swoon.

"Since last night?" she asked with a shade of fear for her possible indiscretion.

"Since this morning—it must have been: the cold dim dawn of today. Where have I been," he vaguely wailed, "where have I been?" He felt her hold him close, and it was as if this helped him now to make in all security his mild moan. "What a long dark day!"

All in her tenderness she had waited a moment. "In the cold dim dawn?" she quavered.

But he had already gone on piecing together the parts of the whole prodigy. "As I didn't turn up you came straight—?"

She barely cast about. "I went first to your hotel—where they told me of your absence. You had dined out last evening and hadn't been back since. But they appeared to know you had been at your club."

"So you had the idea of *this*—?"

"Of what?" she asked in a moment.

"Well—of what has happened."

"I believed at least you'd have been here. I've known, all along," she said, "that you've been coming."

" 'Known' it—?"

"Well, I've believed it. I said nothing to you after that talk we had a month ago—but I felt sure. I knew you *would*," she declared.

"That I'd persist, you mean?"

"That you'd see him."

"Ah but I didn't!" cried Brydon with his long wail. "There's some-body—an awful beast; whom I brought, too horribly, to bay. But it's not me."

At this she bent over him again, and her eyes were in his eyes. "No—it's not you." And it was as if, while her face hovered, he might have made out in it, hadn't it been so near, some particular meaning blurred by a smile. "No, thank heaven," she repeated—"it's not you! Of course it wasn't to have been."

"Ah but it *was*," he gently insisted. And he stared before him now as he had been staring for so many weeks. "I was to have known myself."

"You couldn't!" she returned consolingly. And then reverting, and as if to account further for what she had herself done, "But it wasn't only *that*, that you hadn't been at home," she went on, "I waited till the hour at which we had found Mrs. Muldoon that day of my going with you; and she arrived, as I've told you, while, failing to bring any one to the door, I lingered in my despair on the steps. After a little, if she hadn't come, by such a mercy, I should have found means to hunt her up. But it wasn't," said Alice Staverton, as if once more with her fine intention — "it wasn't only that."

His eyes, as he lay turned back to her. "What more then?"

She met it, the wonder she had stirred. "In the cold dim dawn, you say? Well, in the cold dim dawn of this morning I too saw you."

"Saw *me*—?"

"Saw *him*," said Alice Staverton. "It must have been at the same moment."

He lay an instant taking it in—as if he wished to be quite reasonable. "At the same moment?"

"Yes—in my dream again, the same one I've named to you. He came back to me. Then I knew it for a sign. He had come to you."

At this Brydon raised himself; he had to see her better. She helped him when she understood his movement, and he sat up, steadying himself beside her there on the window-bench and with his right hand grasping her left. "*He* didn't come to me."

"You came to yourself," she beautifully smiled.

"Ah I've come to myself now—thanks to you, dearest. But this brute, with his awful face—this brute's a black stranger. He's none of *me*, even as I *might* have been," Brydon sturdily declared.

But she kept the clearness that was like the breath of infallibility. "Isn't the whole point that you'd have been different?"

He almost scowled for it. "As different as *that*—?"

Her look again was more beautiful to him than the things of this world. "Haven't you exactly wanted to know *how* different? So this morning," she said, "you appeared to me."

"Like *him*?"

"A black stranger!"

"Then how did you know it was I?"

"Because, as I told you weeks ago, my mind, my imagination, had worked so over what you might, what you mightn't have been—to show you, you see, how I've thought of you. In the midst of that you came to me—that my wonder might be answered. So I knew," she went on; "and believed that, since the question held you too so fast, as you told me that day, you too would see for yourself. And when this morning I again saw I knew it would be because you had—and also then, from the first moment, because you somehow wanted me. *He* seemed to tell me of that. So why," she strangely smiled, "shouldn't I like him?"

It brought Spencer Brydon to his feet. "You 'like' that horror—?"

"I *could* have liked him. And to me," she said, "he was no horror. I had accepted him."

"'Accepted'—?" Brydon oddly sounded.

"Before, for the interest of his difference—yes. And as *I* didn't disown him, as *I* knew him—which you at last, confronted with him in his difference, so cruelly didn't, my dear—well, he must have been, you see, less dreadful to me. And it may have pleased him that I pitied him."

She was beside him on her feet, but still holding his hand—still with her arm supporting him. But though it all brought for him thus a dim light, "You 'pitied' him?" he grudgingly, resentfully asked.

"He has been unhappy; he has been ravaged," she said.

"And haven't I been unhappy? Am not I—you've only to look at me!—ravaged?"

"Ah I don't say I like him *better*," she granted after a thought. "But he's grim, he's worn—and things have happened to him. He doesn't make shift, for sight, with your charming monocle."

"No"—it struck Brydon: "I couldn't have sported mine 'downtown.' They'd have guyed me there."

"His great convex pince-nez—I saw it, I recognised the kind—is for his poor ruined sight. And his poor right hand—!"

"Ah!" Brydon winced—whether for his proved identity or for his lost fingers. Then, "He has a million a year," he lucidly added. "But he hasn't you."

"And he isn't—no, he isn't—*you!*" she murmured as he drew her to his breast.

RAINER MARIA RILKE

*R*AINER MARIA RILKE (1875–1926) is known primarily as one of the great poets
of the twentieth century, but he experimented with fiction and drama as well, most
notably in his novel of 1910, The Notebooks of Malte Laurids Brigge. The novel's hero is a
Danish poet living in Paris, and the story mixes childhood reminiscence with terrifying adult
experience in a nightmarish urban world. The model may be Goethe's semi-autobiographical
novel, The Sorrows of Young Werther, but the manner and shape of Rilke's book are distinctly
modern. Rilke was trying to face and conquer his worst fears so that he could continue as a poet,
and he spared himself and his readers no scenes or images that might further that goal. The result
is an uneven, disquieting, often quite beautiful book, with passages that, once read, never leave
the memory.

    Our purpose here is to demonstrate the unique effects Rilke achieved by combining
narration with a poet's way of seeing the world, a "magical realist" trademark. The novel is full
of anecdotes of the most extraordinary kind, and both of the sections cited here show Rilke's
remarkable imagination harnessed to the fictional mode. The first, which we have called "The
Death of Chamberlain Brigge," is organized around a central metaphor, the various ways of
objectifying and personifying death. The tale might appear to be reminiscent of Kafka if it did not
flicker nervously through so many points of view, including that of the delicate knickknacks in the
death chamber! The second selection, which we have called "The Hand," enters the child's
world and its inarticulate fears in a similarly extraordinary way. The tale's point of view is dual,
combining the narrator's present understanding with the child's wonder and terror. Critics will
continue to argue about the success of the novel as a whole, but Rilke's narrative mastery in
passages such as these is beyond dispute.

The Death of Chamberlain Brigge

Rainer Maria Rilke

WHEN I think back to my home, where there is nobody left now, I imagine that formerly this must have been otherwise. Formerly one knew (or perhaps one guessed it) that one had one's death within one, as a fruit its kernel. The children had a little death within them and the grown-ups a big one. The women had it in their womb and the men in their breast. One *had* it, and that gave one a singular dignity and a quiet pride.

My grandfather, old Chamberlain Brigge, still looked as if he carried a death within him. And what a death it was: two months long and so loud that it could be heard as far off as the manor farm.

The long, old manor house was too small for this death; it seemed as if wings would have to be added, for the chamberlain's body grew larger and larger, and he wanted continually to be carried out of one room into another, falling into a terrible rage when, though the day had not yet come to an end, there was no room left in which he had not already lain. Then the whole troop of men-servants, maids and dogs, that he always had about him, had to go upstairs with him, under the usherance of the

Excerpt from *The Notebooks of Malte Laurids Brigge.*

major-domo, into the room in which his saintly mother had died, which had been kept exactly as she had left it twenty-three years before and in which no one else had ever been allowed to set foot. Now the whole pack burst in. The curtains were drawn back, and the robust light of a summer afternoon inspected all the shy, frightened objects and turned clumsily around in the suddenly opened-up mirrors. And the people did likewise. There were chamber-maids who, in their curiosity, did not know where their hands were loitering, young men-servants who gaped at everything, and older retainers who went about trying to recollect all that had been told them about this close-locked room in which they now found themselves at last.

But the dogs especially seemed to find their sojourn in a room where everything had a smell uncommonly exciting. The tall, lean Russian wolfhounds ran busily back and forth behind the armchairs, crossed the apartment in long dance-steps with a swinging movement, reared like heraldic animals, and looked, resting their slender paws on the white-and-gold window-sill, with tense pointed faces and backdrawn foreheads, to right and left out into the courtyard. Small glove-yellow dachshunds sat in the large silk-upholstered easy-chair near the window, looking as though everything were quite in order, and a sullen-looking rubican setter rubbed his back along the edge of a giltlegged table, causing the Sèvres cups on its painted tray to tremble.

Yes, for these absent-minded, drowsy things it was a terrible time. From books that some hasty hand had clumsily opened rose-leaves would tumble, to be trampled underfoot; small fragile objects were seized, and, when they were immediately broken, quickly put back again; many hidden things, too, were thrust beneath curtains, or even flung behind the gilt net-work of the fire-screen and from time to time something fell, fell muffled on carpeting, fell clear on the hard parquetry, but here and there it smashed, shattering sharply or cracking apart almost inaudibly, for these things, pampered as they were, could not survive any sort of fall.

And had it occurred to anyone to ask what caused all this, what had called down upon this anxiously guarded room the full measure of destruction,—there would have been but *one* answer: Death.

The death of Chamberlain Christoph Detlev Brigge at Ulsgaard. For he lay, welling large out of his dark blue uniform, in the middle of the floor and never stirred. In his big, stranger's face, no longer familiar to anyone, the eyes had fallen shut: he did not see what was happening. They had tried at first to lay him on the bed, but this he had resisted, for he detested beds since those first nights in which his illness had grown. Besides, the bed up there had proved too small, so nothing else remained but to lay him thus upon the carpet; for downstairs again he had refused to go.

So now he lay there, and one might think that he had died. The dogs, as it slowly began to grow dark, had one after the other squeezed through the crack in the door. Only the rubican setter with the sullen face sat beside his master, and one of his broad, tufted forepaws lay on Christoph Detlev's big, grey hand. Most of the servants, too, were now standing outside in the white corridor, which was brighter than the room; those, however, who still remained within glanced furtively now and then at the great darkening heap in the middle, and they wished that it were nothing more than a large garment over some rotten thing.

But it was soemthing more. It was a voice, that voice which seven weeks before no one had known yet: for it was not the voice of the chamberlain. It was not Christoph Detlev to whom this voice belonged, but Christoph Detlev's death.

Christoph Detlev's death had been living at Ulsgaard for many, many days now and had spoken to everyone and demanded: demanded to be carried, demanded the blue room, demanded the little salon, demanded the large hall. Demanded the dogs, demanded that people should laugh, talk, play and be quiet and all at the same time. Demanded to see friends, women, and people who were dead, and demanded to die itself: demanded. Demanded and shouted.

For when night had fallen and those of the overwearied domestics who were not on watch tried to go to sleep, then Christoph Detlev's death would shout, shout and groan, roar so long and so constantly that the dogs, at first howling along with him, were silent and did not dare lie down, but stood on their long, slender, trembling legs, and were afraid. And when they heard it in the village roaring through the spacious, silvery, Danish summer night, they rose from their beds as if there were a thunderstorm, put on their clothes and remained sitting round the lamp without a word until it was over. And women near their time were laid in the most remote rooms and in the most impenetrable closets; but they heard it, they heard it, as if it were in their own bodies, and they pled to be allowed to get up too, and came, white and wide, and sat among the others with their blurred faces. And the cows that were calving at that time were helpless and bound, and from the body of one they tore the dead fruit with all the entrails, as it would not come at all. And everyone did their daily work badly and forgot to bring in the hay, because they spent the day dreading the night and because they were so fagged out by all their continuous watchings and terrified arisings, that they could not remember anything. And when they went on Sundays to the white, peaceful church, they prayed that there might no longer be a master at Ulsgaard: for this was a dreadful master. And what they all thought and prayed the pastor said aloud from the height of his pulpit; for he also had no nights any more and could not understand God. And the bell said it, having found a terrible rival that boomed the whole night through, and against which, even though it took to sounding with all its metal, it could do nothing. Indeed, they all said it; and there was one among the young men who dreamed that he had gone to the manor-house and killed the master with his pitch-fork; and they were so exasperated, so done, so overwrought, that they all listened as he told his dream, and, quite unconsciously, looked at him to see if he were really equal to such a deed. Thus did they feel and speak throughout the whole district where, only a few weeks before, the chamberlain had been loved and pitied. But though they talked thus, nothing changed. Christoph Detlev's death, which dwelt at Ulsgaard, was not to be hurried. It had come to stay for ten weeks, and for ten weeks it stayed. And during that time it was more master than ever Christoph Detlev Brigge had been; it was like a king who, afterward and forever, is called the Terrible.

That was not the death of just any dropsical person; it was the wicked, princely death which the chamberlain had carried within him and nourished on himself his whole life long. All excess of pride, will and lordly vigor that he himself had not been able to consume in his quiet days, had passed into his death, that death which now sat, dissipating, at Ulsgaard.

How the chamberlain would have looked at anyone who asked of him that he should die any other death than this. He was dying his own hard death.

And when I think of the others whom I have seen or about whom I have heard: it is always the same. They all have had a death of their own. Those men who carried theirs inside their armor, within, like a prisoner; those women who grew very old and small, and then on a huge bed, as on a stage, before the whole family, the household and the dogs, passed away in discreet and seigniorial dignity. Even the children, and the very little ones at that, did not die just any child's death; they pulled themselves together and died that which they already were, and that which they would have become.

And what a melancholy beauty it gave to women when they were pregnant and stood there, and in their big bodies, upon which their slender hands instinctively rested, were *two* fruits: a child and a death. Did not the dense, almost nourishing smile on their quite vacant faces come from their sometimes thinking that both were growing?

Translated by M.D. Herter-Norton

The Hand

Rainer Maria Rilke

O NCE, WHEN it had grown almost dark during this story, I was
on the point of telling Maman about the hand: at that moment I
could have done it. I had taken a long breath in order to begin; but then it
occurred to me how well I had understood the servant's not being able to
approach their faces. And in spite of the waning light I feared what
Maman's face would be like when it should see what I had seen. I quickly
took another breath, to make it appear that that was all I had meant to do.
A few years later, after the remarkable night in the gallery at Urnekloster, I
went about for days with the intention of taking little Erik into my
confidence. But after our nocturnal conversation he had once more
closed himself completely to me, avoided me, I believe that he despised
me. And just for this reason I wanted to tell him about "the hand." I
imagined I would rise in his estimation (and I wanted that keenly for
some reason) if I could make him understand that I had really had that
experience. But Erik was so clever at evasion that I never got to it. And
then we did leave right afterward. So, strangely enough, this is the first
time I am relating (and after all only for myself) an occurrence that now
lies far back in the days of my childhood.

How small I must still have been I see from the fact that I was
kneeling on the armchair in order to reach comfortably up to the table on
which I was drawing. It was an evening, in winter, in our apartment in
town, if I am not mistaken. The table stood in my room, between the
windows, and there was no lamp in the room save that which shone on

Excerpt from The Notebooks of Malte Laurids Brigge.

my papers and on Mademoiselle's book; for Mademoiselle sat next me, her chair pushed back a little, and was reading. She was far away when she read, and I don't know whether she was in her book; she could read for hours, she seldom turned the leaves, and I had the impression that the pages became steadily fuller under her eyes, as though she looked words into them, certain words that she needed and that were not there. So it seemed to me as I went on drawing. I was drawing slowly, without any very decided intention, and when I didn't know what to do next, I would survey the whole with head bent a little to the right; in that position it always came to me soonest what was lacking. They were officers on horseback, who were riding into battle, or they were in the midst of it, and that was far simpler, for in that case, almost all one needed to draw was the smoke that enveloped everything. Maman, it is true, always insists that they were islands I was painting; islands with large trees and a castle and a flight of steps and flowers along the edge that were supposed to be reflected in the water. But I think she is making that up, or it must have been later.

It is certain that on that particular evening I was drawing a knight, a solitary, easily recognizable knight, on a strikingly caparisoned horse. He became so gaily-colored that I had to change crayons frequently, but the red was most in demand, and for it I reached again and again. Now I needed it once more, when it rolled (I can see it yet) right across the lighted sheet to the edge of the table and, before I could stop it, fell past me and disappeared. I needed it really urgently, and it was very annoying to clamber down after it. Awkward as I was, I had to make all sorts of preparations to get down; my legs seemed to me far too long, I could not pull them out from under me; the too-prolonged kneeling posture had numbed my limbs; I could not tell what belonged to me, and what to the chair. At last I did arrive down there, somewhat bewildered, and found myself on a fur rug that stretched from under the table as far as the wall. But here a fresh difficulty arose. My eyes, accustomed to the brightness above and all inspired with the colors on the white paper, were unable to distinguish anything at all beneath the table, where the blackness seemed to me so dense that I was afraid I should knock against it. I therefore relied on my sense of touch, and kneeling, supported on my left hand, I combed around with my other hand in the cool, long-haired rug, which felt quite friendly; only that no pencil was to be found. I imagined I must be losing a lot of time, and was about to call to Mademoiselle and ask her to hold the lamp for me, when I noticed that to my involuntarily strained eyes the darkness was gradually growing more penetrable. I could already distinguish the wall at the back, which ended in a light-colored molding; I oriented myself with regard to the legs of the table; above all I recognized my own outspread hand moving down there all alone, a little like an aquatic animal, examining the ground. I watched it, as I remember still, almost with curiosity; it seemed as if it knew things

I had never taught it, groping down there so independently, with movements I had never noticed in it before. I followed it up as it pressed forward, I was interested in it, ready for all sorts of things. But how should I have been prepared to see suddenly come to meet it out of the wall another hand, a larger, extraordinarily thin hand, such as I had never seen before. It came groping in similar fashion from the other side, and the two outspread hands moved blindly toward one another. My curiosity was not yet used up but suddenly it came to an end, and there was only terror. I felt that one of the hands belonged to me, and that it was committing itself to something irreparable. With all the authority I had over it, I checked it and drew it back flat and slowly, without taking my eyes off the other, which went on groping. I realized that it would not leave off; I cannot tell how I got up again. I sat deep in the armchair, my teeth chattered, and I had so little blood in my face that it seemed to me there could be no more blue in my eyes. Mademoiselle—, I wanted to say and could not, but at that she took fright of her own accord, and, flinging her book away, knelt beside the chair and cried out my name; I believe she shook me. But I was perfectly conscious. I swallowed a couple of times; for now I wanted to tell about it.

But how? I made an indescribable effort to master myself, but it was not to be expressed so that anyone could understand. If there were words for this occurrence, I was too little to find them. And suddenly the fear seized me that nevertheless they might suddenly be there, beyond my years, these words, and it seemed to me more terrible than anything else that I should then have to say them. To live through once again the reality down there, differently, conjugated, from the beginning; to hear myself admitting it—for that I had no strength left.

It is of course imagination on my part to declare now that I already at that time felt that something had entered into my life, directly into mine, with which I alone should have to go about, always and always. I see myself lying in my little crib and not sleeping and somehow vaguely foreseeing that life would be like this: full of many special things that are meant for *one* person alone and that cannot be told. Certain it is that a sad and heavy pride gradually arose in me. I pictured to myself how one would go about, full of what is inside one, and silent. I felt an impetuous sympathy for grown-ups; I admired them, and proposed to tell them that I admired them. I proposed to tell it to Mademoiselle at the next opportunity.

Translated by M.D. Herter-Norton

D. H. LAWRENCE

D. H. LAWRENCE (1885–1930) *wrote fiction, poetry, literary criticism, drama, and also was a painter. He is best-known as a novelist (Sons and Lovers, Women in Love, Lady Chatterley's Lover), a fact that has obscured the sometimes extraordinary achievement of his short stories. In theory, Lawrence felt that a writer should not tip the fictional balance by interjecting opinions and prejudices; in practice, given his many strong views, he found this difficult. Readers of his novels must succumb to a kind of insistence that Lawrence cannot afford in shorter forms, so that his stories combine his often visionary insights and psychological probing with an attractive economy and uncharacteristic understatement. The best stories present their characters and worlds with a minimum of commentary, and the results can be stunning.*

North American and English writers who have ventured into magical realism usually have a touch of the visionary about them, and Lawrence was no exception. He believed that we live in the midst of forces, both internal and external, of which we are largely ignorant, and that these forces—many of them linked to our sexuality—are capable of asserting themselves suddenly and dramatically. Some of his stories contain supernatural manifestations that cannot be explained on the level of ordinary reality and reveal the power of unconscious will. "The Rocking-Horse Winner," an anthology favorite, is about a young boy who learns to predict race results in response to the desperate greed of his family and destroys himself in the process. A late story, "The Woman Who Rode Away," tells of a woman who wills her own death as a sacrifice in an Indian rite. Both of these stories might have been included in this collection, but the ones we have chosen are, we feel, both subtler and better examples of Lawrence's magical realism.

Lawrence grew up in Nottinghamshire, the son of a coalminer father and a schoolteacher mother who had ambitions for her gifted son. "Odour of Chrysanthemums" (1914) draws on Lawrence's deep knowledge of that world. The magical factor in this acute portrait of working-class life is death, which, as in Rilke's short piece, is not only a vehicle for grief and horror, but a means to a transcendent insight into human dignity and worth, a disruption of the ordinary by which the characters can break out of their limitations. Sightlessness functions similarly in the second story, "The Blind Man" (1922), bursting the barriers of convention and repression in the tender but ironic conclusion. Here, as elsewhere in Lawrence, the power of touch is given extraordinary meaning; simple physical contact becomes a metaphor for psychological and spiritual encounter that reminds us of the powerful moments of transformation and recognition that often characterize myth.

Odour of Chrysanthemums

D. H. Lawrence

I

THE SMALL locomotive engine, Number 4, came clanking, stumbling down from Selston with seven full wagons. It appeared round the corner with loud threats of speed, but the colt that it startled from among the gorse, which still flickered indistinctly in the raw afternoon, out-distanced it at a canter. A woman, walking up the railway line to Underwood, drew back into the hedge, held her basket aside, and watched the footplate of the engine advancing. The trucks thumped heavily past, one by one, with slow inevitable movement, as she stood insignificantly trapped between the jolting black wagons and the hedge; then they curved away towards the coppice where the withered oak leaves dropped noiselessly, while the birds, pulling at the scarlet hips beside the track, made off into the dusk that had already crept into the spinney. In the open, the smoke from the engine sank and cleaved to the rough grass. The fields were dreary and forsaken, and in the marshy strip that led to the whimsey, a reedy pit-pond, the fowls had already abandoned their run among the alders, to roost in the tarred fowl-house. The pit-bank loomed up beyond the pond, flames like red sores licking its ashy sides, in the afternoon's stagnant light. Just beyond rose the tapering chimneys and the clumsy black headstocks of Brinsley Colliery. The two wheels were spinning fast up against the sky, and the winding engine rapped out its little spasms. The miners were being turned up.

The engine whistled as it came into the wide bay of railway lines beside the colliery, where rows of trucks stood in harbor.

Miners, single, trailing and in groups, passed like shadows diverging home. At the edge of the ribbed level of sidings squat a low cottage, three steps down from the cinder track. A large bony vine clutched at the house, as if to claw down the tiled roof. Round the bricked yard grew a few wintry primroses. Beyond, the long garden sloped down to a bush-covered brook course. There were some twiggy apple trees, winter-crack trees, and ragged cabbages. Beside the path hung dishevelled pink chrysanthemums, like pink cloths hung on bushes. A woman came stooping out of the felt-covered fowl-house, half-way down the garden. She closed and padlocked the door, then drew herself erect, having brushed some bits from her white apron.

She was a tall woman of imperious mien, handsome, with definite black eyebrows. Her smooth black hair was parted exactly. For a few moments she stood steadily watching the miners as they passed along the railway: then she turned towards the brook course. Her face was calm and set, her mouth was closed with disillusionment. After a moment she called:

"John!" There was no answer. She waited, and then said distinctly: "Where are you?"

"Here!" replied a child's sulky voice from among the bushes. The woman looked piercingly through the dusk.

"Are you at that brook?" she asked sternly.

For answer the child showed himself before the raspberry-canes that rose like whips. He was a small, sturdy boy of five. He stood quite still, defiantly.

"Oh!" said the mother, conciliated. "I thought you were down at that wet brook—and you remember what I told you—"

The boy did not move or answer.

"Come, come on in," she said more gently, "it's getting dark. There's your grandfather's engine coming down the line!"

The lad advanced slowly, with resentful, taciturn movement. He was dressed in trousers and waistcoat of cloth that was too thick and hard for the size of the garments. They were evidently cut down from a man's clothes.

As they went slowly towards the house he tore at the ragged wisps of chrysanthemums and dropped the petals in handfuls along the path.

"Don't do that—it does look nasty," said his mother. He refrained, and she, suddenly pitiful, broke off a twig with three or four wan flowers and held them against her face. When mother and son reached the yard her hand hesitated, and instead of laying the flower aside, she pushed it in her apron-band. The mother and son stood at the foot of the three steps looking across the bay of lines at the passing home of the miners.

The trundle of the small train was imminent. Suddenly the engine loomed past the house and came to a stop opposite the gate.

The engine-driver, a short man with round gray beard, leaned out of the cab high above the woman.

"Have you got a cup of tea?" he said in a cheery, hearty fashion.

It was her father. She went in, saying she would mash. Directly, she returned.

"I didn't come to see you on Sunday," began the little gray-bearded man.

"I didn't expect you," said his daughter.

The engine-driver winced; then, reassuming his cheery, airy manner, he said:

"Oh, have you heard then? Well, and what do you think—?"

"I think it is soon enough," she replied.

At her brief censure the little man made an impatient gesture, and said coaxingly, yet with dangerous coldness:

"Well, what's a man to do? It's no sort of life for a man of my years, to sit at my own hearth like a stranger. And if I'm going to marry again it may as well be soon as late—what does it matter to anybody?"

The woman did not reply, but turned and went into the house. The man in the engine-cab stood assertive, till she returned with a cup of tea and a piece of bread and butter on a plate. She went up the steps and stood near the footplace of the hissing engine.

"You needn't 'a' brought me bread an' butter," said her father. "But a cup of tea"—he sipped appreciatively—"it's very nice." He sipped for a moment or two, then: "I hear as Walter's got another bout on," he said.

"When hasn't he?" said the woman bitterly.

"I heerd tell of him in the 'Lord Nelson' braggin' as he was going to spend that b—afore he went: half a sovereign that was."

"When?" asked the woman.

"A' Sat'day night—I know that's true."

"Very likely," she laughed bitterly. "He gives me twenty-three shillings."

"Aye, it's a nice thing, when a man can do nothing with his money but make a beast of himself!" said the gray-whiskered man. The woman turned her head away. Her father swallowed the last of his tea and handed her the cup.

"Aye," he sighed, wiping his mouth. "It's a settler, it is—"

He put his hand on the lever. The little engine strained and groaned, and the train rumbled towards the crossing. The woman again looked across the metals. Darkness was settling over the spaces of the railway and trucks; the miners, in gray somber group, were still passing home. The winding engine pulsed hurriedly, with brief pauses. Elizabeth Bates looked at the dreary flow of men, then she went indoors. Her husband did not come.

The kitchen was small and full of firelight; red coals piled glowing up the chimney mouth. All the life of the room seemed in the white, warm hearth and the steel fender reflecting the red fire. The cloth was laid for tea; cups glinted in the shadows. At the back, where the lowest stairs protruded into the room, the boy sat struggling with a knife and a piece of white wood. He was almost hidden in the shadow. It was half-past four. They had but to await the father's coming to begin tea. As the mother watched her son's sullen little struggle with the wood, she saw herself in his silence and pertinacity; she saw the father in her child's indifference to all but himself. She seemed to be occupied by her husband. He had probably gone past his home, slunk past his own door, to drink before he came in, while his dinner spoiled and wasted in waiting. She glanced at the clock, then took the potatoes to strain them in the yard. The garden and fields beyond the brook were closed in uncertain darkness. When she rose with the saucepan, leaving the drain steaming into the night behind her, she saw the yellow lamps were lit along the high road that went up the hill away beyond the space of the railway lines and the field.

Then again she watched the men trooping home, fewer now and fewer.

Indoors the fire was sinking and the room was dark red. The woman put her saucepan on the hob, and set a batter-pudding near the mouth of the oven. Then she stood unmoving. Directly, gratefully, came quick young steps to the door. Someone hung on the latch a moment, then a little girl entered and began pulling off her outdoor things, dragging a mass of curls, just ripening from gold to brown, over her eyes with her hat.

Her mother chid her for coming late from school, and said she would have to keep her at home the dark winter days.

"Why, mother, it's hardly a bit dark yet. The lamp's not lighted, and my father's not home."

"No, he isn't. But it's a quarter to five! Did you see anything of him?"

The child became serious. She looked at her mother with large wistful blue eyes.

"No, mother, I've never seen him. Why? Has he come up an' gone past, to Old Brinsley? He hasn't, mother, 'cos I never saw him."

"He'd watch that," said the mother bitterly, "he'd take care as you didn't see him. But you may depend upon it, he's seated in the 'Prince o' Wales.' He wouldn't be this late."

The girl looked at her mother piteously.

"Let's have our teas, mother, should we?" said she.

The mother called John to table. She opened the door once more and looked out across the darkness of the lines. All was deserted: she could not hear the winding engines.

"Perhaps," she said to herself, "he's stopped to get some ripping done."

They sat down to tea. John, at the end of the table near the door, was almost lost in the darkness. Their faces were hidden from each other. The girl crouched against the fender slowly moving a thick piece of bread before the fire. The lad, his face a dusky mark on the shadow, sat watching her who was transfigured in the red glow.

"I do think it's beautiful to look in the fire," said the child.

"Do you?" said her mother. "Why?"

"It's so red, and full of little caves—and it feels so nice, and you can fair smell it."

"It'll want mending directly," replied her mother, "and then if your father comes he'll carry on and say there never is a fire when a man comes home sweating from the pit. A public house is always warm enough."

There was silence till the boy said complainingly: "Make haste, our Annie."

"Well, I am doing! I can't make the fire do it no faster, can I?"

"She keeps wafflin it about so's to make 'er slow," grumbled the boy.

"Don't have such an evil imagination, child," replied the mother.

Soon the room was busy in the darkness with the crisp sound of crunching. The mother ate very little. She drank her tea determinedly, and sat thinking. When she rose her anger was evident in the stern unbending of her head. She looked at the pudding in the fender, and broke out:

"It is a scandalous thing as a man can't even come home to his dinner! If it's crozzled up to a cinder I don't see why I should care. Past his very door he goes to get to a public house, and here I sit with his dinner waiting for him—"

She went out. As she dropped piece after piece of coal on the red fire, the shadows fell on the walls, till the room was almost in total darkness.

"I canna see," grumbled the invisible John. In spite of herself, the mother laughed.

"You know the way to your mouth," she said. She set the dustpan outside the door. When she came again like a shadow on the hearth, the lad repeated, complaining sulkily:

"I canna see."

"Good gracious!" cried the mother irritably, "you're as bad as your father if it's a bit dusk!"

Nevertheless, she took a paper spill from a sheaf on the mantelpiece and proceeded to light the lamp that hung from the ceiling in the middle of the room. As she reached up, her figure displayed itself just rounding with maternity.

"Oh, mother—!" exclaimed the girl.

"What?" said the woman, suspended in the act of putting the lampglass over the flame. The copper reflector shone handsomely on her, as she stood with uplifted arm, turning to face her daughter.

"You've got a flower in your apron!" said the child, in a little rapture at this unusual event.

"Goodness me!" exclaimed the woman, relieved. "One would think the house was afire." She replaced the glass and waited a moment before turning up the wick. A pale shadow was seen floating vaguely on the floor.

"Let me smell!" said the child, still rapturously, coming forward and putting her face to her mother's waist.

"Go along, silly!" said the mother, turning up the lamp. The light revealed their suspense so that the woman felt it almost unbearable. Annie was still bending at her waist. Irritably, the mother took the flowers out from her apron-band.

"Oh, mother—don't take them out!" Annie cried, catching her hand and trying to replace the sprig.

"Such nonsense!" said the mother, turning away. The child put the pale chrysanthemums to her lips, murmuring:

"Don't they smell beautiful!"

Her mother gave a short laugh.

"No," she said, "not to me. It was chrysanthemums when I married him, and chrysanthemums when you were born, and the first time they ever brought him home drunk, he'd got brown chrysanthemums in his buttonhole."

She looked at the children. Their eyes and their parted lips were wondering. The mother sat rocking in silence for some time. Then she looked at the clock.

"Twenty minutes to six!" In a tone of fine bitter carelessness she continued: "Eh, he'll not come now till they bring him. There he'll stick! But he needn't come rolling in here in his pit-dirt, for *I* won't wash him. He can lie on the floor—Eh, what a fool I've been, what a fool! And this is what I came here for, to this dirty hole, rats and all, for him to slink past his very door. Twice last week—he's begun now—"

She silenced herself, and rose to clear the table.

While for an hour or more the children played, subduedly intent, fertile of imagination, united in fear of the mother's wrath, and in dread of their father's homecoming, Mrs. Bates sat in her rocking-chair making a "singlet" of thick cream-colored flannel, which gave a dull wounded sound as she tore off the gray edge. She worked at her sewing with energy, listening to the children, and her anger wearied itself, lay down to rest, opening its eyes from time to time and steadily watching, its ears raised to listen. Sometimes even her anger quailed and shrank, and the mother suspended her sewing, tracing the footsteps that thudded along the sleepers outside; she would lift her head sharply to bid the children "hush," but she recovered herself in time, and the footsteps went past the gate, and the children were not flung out of their play-world.

But at last Annie sighed, and gave in. She glanced at her wagon of slippers, and loathed the game. She turned plaintively to her mother.

"Mother!"—but she was inarticulate.

John crept out like a frog from under the sofa. His mother glanced up.

"Yes," she said, "just look at those shirtsleeves!"

The boy held them out to survey them, saying nothing. Then somebody called in a hoarse voice away down the line, and suspense bristled in the room, till two people had gone by outside, talking.

"It is time for bed," said the mother.

"My father hasn't come," wailed Annie plaintively. But her mother was primed with courage.

"Never mind. They'll bring him when he does come—like a log." She meant there would be no scene. "And he may sleep on the floor till he wakes himself. I know he'll not go to work tomorrow after this!"

The children had their hands and faces wiped with a flannel. They were very quiet. When they had put on their nightdresses, they said their prayers, the boy mumbling. The mother looked down at them, at the brown silken bush of intertwining curls in the nape of the girl's neck, at the little black head of the lad, and her heart burst with anger at their father, who caused all three such distress. The children hid their faces in her skirts for comfort.

When Mrs. Bates came down, the room was strangely empty, with a tension of expectancy. She took up her sewing and stitched for some time without raising her head. Meantime her anger was tinged with fear.

II

The clock struck eight and she rose suddenly, dropping her sewing on her chair. She went to the stair-foot door, opened it, listening. Then she went out, locking the door behind her.

Something scuffled in the yard, and she started, though she knew it was only the rats with which the place was overrun. The night was very dark. In the great bay of railway lines, bulked with trucks, there was no trace of light, only away back she could see a few yellow lamps at the pit-top, and the red smear of the burning pit-bank on the night. She hurried along the edge of the track, then, crossing the converging lines, came to the stile by the white gates, whence she emerged on the road. Then the fear which had led her shrank. People were walking up to New Brinsley; she saw the lights in the houses; twenty yards farther on were the broad windows of the 'Prince of Wales,' very warm and bright, and the loud voices of men could be heard distinctly. What a fool she had been to imagine that anything had happened to him! He was merely drinking over there at the 'Prince of Wales.' She faltered. She had never yet been to fetch him, and she never would go. So she continued her walk toward the long straggling line of houses, standing back on the highway. She entered a passage between the dwellings.

"Mr. Rigley?—Yes! Did you want him? No, he's not in at this minute."

The raw-boned woman leaned forward from her dark scullery and peered at the other, upon whom fell a dim light through the blind of the kitchen window.

"Is it Mrs. Bates?" she asked in a tone tinged with respect.

"Yes. I wondered if your Master was at home. Mine hasn't come yet."

"Asn't 'e! Oh, Jack's been 'ome an' 'ad 'is dinner an' gone out. 'E's just gone for 'alf an hour afore bed-time. Did you call at the 'Prince of Wales'?"

"No—"

"No, you didn't like—! It's not very nice." The other woman was indulgent. There was an awkward pause. "Jack never said nothink about—about your Master," she said.

"No!—I expect he's stuck in there!"

Elizabeth Bates said this bitterly, and with recklessness. She knew that the woman across the yard was standing at her door listening, but she did not care. As she turned:

"Stop a minute! I'll just go an' ask Jack if 'e knows anythink," said Mrs. Rigley.

"Oh no—I wouldn't like to put—!"

"Yes, I will, if you'll just step inside an' see as th' childer doesn't come downstairs and set theirselves afire."

Elizabeth Bates, murmuring a remonstrance, stepped inside. The other woman apologized for the state of the room.

The kitchen needed apology. There were little frocks and trousers and childish undergarments on the squab and on the floor, and a litter of playthings everywhere. On the black American cloth of the table were pieces of bread and cake, crusts, slops, and a teapot with cold tea.

"Eh, ours is just as bad," said Elizabeth Bates, looking at the woman, not at the house. Mrs. Rigley put a shawl over her head and hurried out, saying:

"I shanna be a minute."

The other sat, noting with faint disapproval the general untidiness of the room. Then she fell to counting the shoes of various sizes scattered over the floor. There were twelve. She sighed and said to herself:

"No wonder!"—glancing at the litter. There came the scratching of two pairs of feet on the yard, and the Rigleys entered. Elizabeth Bates rose. Rigley was a big man, with very large bones. His head looked particularly bony. Across his temple was a blue scar, caused by a wound got in the pit, a wound in which the coal-dust remained blue like tattooing.

"Asna 'e come whoam yit?" asked the man, without any form of greeting, but with deference and sympathy. "I couldna say wheer he is—'e's non ower theer!"—he jerked his head to signify the 'Prince of Wales.'

"'E's 'appen gone up to th' 'Yew,'" said Mrs. Rigley.

There was another pause. Rigley had evidently something to get off his mind:

"Ah left 'im finishin' a stint," he began. "Loose-all 'ad bin gone about ten minutes when we com'n away, an' I shouted: 'Are ter comin', Walt?' an' 'e said: 'Go on, Ah shanna be but a'ef a minnit,' so we com'n ter th' bottom, me an' Bowers, thinkin' as 'e wor just behint, an' 'ud come up i' th' next bantle—"

He stood perplexed, as if answering a charge of deserting his mate. Elizabeth Bates, now again certain of disaster, hastened to reassure him:

"I expect 'e's gone up to th' 'Yew Tree,' as you say. It's not the first time. I've fretted myself into a fever before now. He'll come home when they carry him."

"Ay, isn't it too bad!" deplored the other woman.

"I'll just step up to Dick's an' see if 'e *is* theer," offered the man, afraid of appearing alarmed, afraid of taking liberties.

"Oh, I wouldn't think of bothering you that far," said Elizabeth Bates, with emphasis, but he knew she was glad of his offer.

As they stumbled up the entry, Elizabeth Bates heard Rigley's wife run across the yard and open her neighbor's door. At this, suddenly all the blood in her body seemed to switch away from her heart.

"Mind!" warned Rigley. "Ah've said many a time as Ah'd fill up them ruts in this entry, sumb'dy 'll be breakin' their legs yit."

She recovered herself and walked quickly along with the miner.

"I don't like leaving the children in bed, and nobody in the house," she said.

"No, you dunna!" he replied courteously. They were soon at the gate of the cottage.

"Well, I shanna be many minnits. Dunna you be frettin' now, 'e'll be all right," said the butty.

"Thank you very much, Mr. Rigley," she replied.

"You're welcome!" he stammered, moving away. "I shanna be many minnits."

The house was quiet. Elizabeth Bates took off her hat and shawl, and rolled back the rug. When she had finished, she sat down. It was a few minutes past nine. She was startled by the rapid chuff of the winding engine at the pit, and the sharp whirr of the brakes on the rope as it descended. Again she felt the painful sweep of her blood, and she put her hand to her side, saying aloud: "Good gracious!—it's only the nine o'clock deputy going down," rebuking herself.

She sat still, listening. Half an hour of this, and she was wearied out.

"What am I working myself up like this for?" she said pitiably to herself, "I s'll only be doing myself some damage."

She took out her sewing again.

At a quarter to ten there were footsteps. One person! She watched for the door to open. It was an elderly woman, in a black bonnet and a black woollen shawl—his mother. She was about sixty years old, pale, with blue eyes, and her face all wrinkled and lamentable. She shut the door and turned to her daughter-in-law peevishly.

"Eh, Lizzie, whatever shall we do, whatever shall we do!" she cried.

Elizabeth drew back a little, sharply.

"What is it, mother?" she said.

The elder woman seated herself on the sofa.

"I don't know, child, I can't tell you!"—she shook her head slowly. Elizabeth sat watching her, anxious and vexed.

"I don't know," replied the grandmother, sighing very deeply. "There's no end to my troubles, there isn't. The things I've gone through, I'm sure it's enough—!" She wept without wiping her eyes, the tears running.

"But, mother," interrupted Elizabeth, "what do you mean? What is it?"

The grandmother slowly wiped her eyes. The fountains of her tears were stopped by Elizabeth's directness. She wiped her eyes slowly.

"Poor child! Eh, you poor thing!" she moaned. "I don't know what we're going to do, I don't—and you as you are—it's a thing, it is indeed!"

Elizabeth waited.

"Is he dead?" she asked, and at the words her heart swung violently, though she felt a slight flush of shame at the ultimate extravagance of the question. Her words sufficiently frightened the old lady, almost brought her to herself.

"Don't say so, Elizabeth! We'll hope it's not as bad as that; no, may the Lord spare us that, Elizabeth. Jack Rigley came just as I was sittin' down to a glass afore going to bed, an' 'e said: "Appen you'll go down th' line, Mrs. Bates. Walt's had an accident. 'Appen you'll go an' sit wi' 'er till we can get him home.' I hadn't time to ask him a word afore he was gone. An' I put my bonnet on an' come straight down, Lizzie. I thought to myself: 'Eh, that poor blessed child, if anybody should come an' tell her of a sudden, there's no knowin' what'll 'appen to 'er.' You mustn't let it upset you, Lizzie—or you know what to expect. How long is it, six months—or is it five, Lizzie? Ay!"—the old woman shook her head—"time slips on, it slips on! Ay!"

Elizabeth's thoughts were busy elsewhere. If he was killed—would she be able to manage on the little pension and what she could earn?—she counted up rapidly. If he was hurt—they wouldn't take him to the hospital—how tiresome he would be to nurse!—but perhaps she'd be able to get him away from the drink and his hateful ways. She would—while he was ill. The tears offered to come to her eyes at the picture. But what sentimental luxury was this she was beginning? She turned to consider the children. At any rate she was absolutely necessary for them. They were her business.

"Ay!" repeated the old woman, "it seems but a week or two since he brought me his first wages. Ay—he was a good lad, Elizabeth, he was, in his way. I don't know why he got to be such a trouble, I don't. He was a happy lad at home, only full of spirits. But there's no mistake he's been a handful of trouble, he has! I hope the Lord'll spare him to mend his ways. I hope so, I hope so. You've had a sight o' trouble with him, Elizabeth, you have indeed. But he was a jolly enough lad wi' me, he was, I can assure you. I don't know how it is . . ."

The old woman continued to muse aloud, a monotonous irritating sound, while Elizabeth thought concentratedly, startled once, when she heard the winding-engine chuff quickly, and the brakes skirr with a shriek. Then she heard the engine more slowly, and the brakes made no sound. The old woman did not notice. Elizabeth waited in suspense. The mother-in-law talked, with lapses into silence.

"But he wasn't your son, Lizzie, an' it makes a difference. Whatever he was, I remember him when he was little, an' I learned to understand him and to make allowances. You've got to make allowances for them—"

It was half-past ten, and the old woman was saying: "But it's trouble from beginning to end; you're never too old for trouble, never too old for that—" when the gate banged back, and there were heavy feet on the steps.

"I'll go, Lizzie, let me go," cried the old woman, rising. But Elizabeth was at the door. It was a man in pit-clothes.

"They're bringin' 'im, Missis," he said. Elizabeth's heart halted a moment. Then it surged on again, almost suffocating her.

"Is he—is it bad?" she asked.

The man turned away, looking at the darkness:

"The doctor says 'e'd been dead hours. 'E saw 'im i' th' lamp-cabin."

The old woman, who stood just behind Elizabeth, dropped into a chair, and folded her hands, crying: "Oh, my boy, my boy!"

"Hush!" said Elizabeth, with a sharp twitch of a frown. "Be still, mother, don't waken th' children: I wouldn't have them down for anything!"

The old woman moaned softly, rocking herself. The man was drawing away. Elizabeth took a step forward.

"How was it?" she asked.

"Well, I couldn't say for sure," the man replied, very ill at ease. "'E wor finishin' a stint an' th' butties 'ad gone, an' a lot o' stuff come down atop 'n 'im.'

"And crushed him?" cried the widow, with a shudder.

"No," said the man, "it fell at th' back of 'im. 'E wor under th' face, an' it niver touched 'im. It shut 'im in. It seems 'e wor smothered."

Elizabeth shrank back. She heard the old woman behind her cry: "What?—what did 'e say it was?"

The man replied, more loudly: "'E wor smothered!"

Then the old woman wailed aloud, and this relieved Elizabeth.

"Oh, mother," she said, putting her hand on the old woman, "don't waken th' children, don't waken th' children."

She wept a little, unknowing, while the old mother rocked herself and moaned. Elizabeth remembered that they were bringing him home, and she must be ready. "They'll lay·him in the parlor," she said to herself, standing a moment pale and perplexed.

Then she lighted a candle and went into the tiny room. The air was cold and damp, but she could not make a fire, there was no fireplace. She set down the candle and looked round. The candlelight glittered on the luster-glasses on the two vases that held some of the pink chrysanthemums, and on the dark mahogany. There was a cold, deathly smell of chrysanthemums in the room. Elizabeth stood looking at the flowers. She turned away, and calculated whether there would be room to lay him on the floor, between the couch and the chiffonier. She pushed the chairs aside. There would be room to lay him down and to step round him. Then she fetched the old red tablecloth, and another old cloth, spreading them down to save her bit of carpet. She shivered on leaving the parlor; so, from the dresser drawer she took a clean shirt and put it at the fire to air. All the time her mother-in-law was rocking herself in the chair and moaning.

"You'll have to move from there, mother," said Elizabeth. "They'll be bringing him in. Come in the rocker."

The old mother rose mechanically, and seated herself by the fire, continuing to lament. Elizabeth went into the pantry for another candle, and there, in the little pent-house under the naked tiles, she heard them coming. She stood still in the pantry doorway, listening. She heard them pass the end of the house, and come awkwardly down the three steps, a jumble of shuffling footsteps and muttering voices. The old woman was silent. The men were in the yard.

Then Elizabeth heard Matthews, the manager of the pit, say: "You go in first, Jim. Mind!"

The door came open, and the two women saw a collier backing into the room, holding one end of a stretcher, on which they could see the nailed pit-boots of the dead man. The two carriers halted, the man at the head stooping to the lintel of the door.

"Wheer will you have him?" asked the manager, a short, white-bearded man.

Elizabeth roused herself and came from the pantry carrying the unlighted candle.

"In the parlor," she said.

"In there, Jim!" pointed the manager, and the carriers backed round into the tiny room. The coat with which they had covered the body fell off as they awkwardly turned through the two doorways, and the women saw their man, naked to the waist, lying stripped for work. The old woman began to moan in a low voice of horror.

"Lay th' stretcher at th' side," snapped the manager, "an' put 'im on th' cloths. Mind now, mind! Look you now—!"

One of the men had knocked off a vase of chrysanthemums. He stared awkwardly, then they set down the stretcher. Elizabeth did not look at her husband. As soon as she could get in the room, she went and picked up the broken vase and the flowers.

"Wait a minute!" she said.

The three men waited in silence while she mopped up the water with a duster.

"Eh, what a job, what a job, to be sure!" the manager was saying, rubbing his brow with trouble and perplexity. "Never knew such a thing in my life, never! He'd no business to ha' been left. I never knew such a thing in my life! Fell over him clean as a whistle, an' shut him in. Not four foot of space, there wasn't—yet it scarce bruised him."

He looked down at the dead man, lying prone, half naked, all grimed with coal-dust.

"Sphyxiated," the doctor said. It *is* the most terrible job I've ever known. Seems as if it was done o' purpose. Clean over him, an' shut 'im in, like a mouse-trap"—he made a sharp, descending gesture with his hand.

The colliers standing by jerked aside their heads in hopeless comment.

The horror of the thing bristled upon them all.

Then they heard the girl's voice upstairs calling shrilly: "Mother, mother—who is it? Mother, who is it?"

Elizabeth hurried to the foot of the stairs and opened the door:

"Go to sleep!" she commanded sharply. "What are you shouting about? Go to sleep at once—there's nothing—"

Then she began to mount the stairs. They could hear her on the boards, and on the plaster floor of the little bedroom. They could hear her distinctly:

"What's the mater now?—what's the matter with you, silly thing?"— her voice was much agitated, with an unreal gentleness.

"I thought it was some men come," said the plaintive voice of the child. "Has he come?"

"Yes, they've brought him. There's nothing to make a fuss about. Go to sleep now, like a good child."

They could hear her voice in the bedroom, they waited whilst she covered the children under the bedclothes.

"Is he drunk?" asked the girl, timidly, faintly.

"No! No—he's not! He—he's asleep."

"Is he asleep downstairs?"

"Yes—and don't make a noise."

There was silence for a moment, then the men heard the frightened child again:

"What's that noise?"

"It's nothing, I tell you, what are you bothering for?"

The noise was the grandmother moaning. She was oblivious of everything, sitting on her chair rocking and moaning. The manager put his hand on her arm and bade her "Sh—sh!!"

The old woman opened her eyes and looked at him. She was shocked by this interruption, and seemed to wonder.

"What time is it?" the plaintive thin voice of the child, sinking back unhappily into sleep, asked this last question.

"Ten o'clock," answered the mother more softly. Then she must have bent down and kissed the children.

Matthews beckoned to the men to come away. They put on their caps and took up the stretcher. Stepping over the body, they tiptoed out of the house. None of them spoke till they were far from the wakeful children.

When Elizabeth came down she found her mother alone on the parlor floor, leaning over the dead man, the tears dropping on him.

"We must lay him out," the wife said. She put on the kettle, then returning knelt at the feet, and began to unfasten the knotted leather laces. The room was clammy and dim with only one candle, so that she had to bend her face almost to the floor. At last she got off the heavy boots and put them away.

"You must help me now," she whispered to the old woman. Together they stripped the man.

When they arose, saw him lying in the naive dignity of death, the women stood arrested in fear and respect. For a few moments they remained still, looking down, the old mother whimpering. Elizabeth felt countermanded. She saw him, how utterly inviolable' he lay in himself. She had nothing to do with him. She could not accept it. Stooping, she laid her hand on him, in claim. He was still warm, for the mine was hot where he had died. His mother had his face between her hands, and was murmuring incoherently. The old tears fell in succession as drops from wet leaves; the mother was not weeping, merely her tears flowed. Elizabeth embraced the body of her husband, with cheek and lips. She seemed to be listening, inquiring, trying to get some connection. But she could not. She was driven away. He was impregnable.

She rose, went into the kitchen, where she poured warm water into a bowl, brought soap and flannel and a soft towel.

"I must wash him," she said.

Then the old mother rose stiffly, and watched Elizabeth as she carefully washed his face, carefully brushing the big blond moustache from his mouth with the flannel. She was afraid with a bottomless fear, so she ministered to him. The old woman, jealous, said:

"Let me wipe him!"—and she kneeled on the other side drying slowly as Elizabeth washed, her big black bonnet sometimes brushing the dark head of her daughter-in-law. They worked thus in silence for a long time. They never forgot it was death, and the touch of the man's dead body gave them strange emotions, different in each of the women; a great dread possessed them both, the mother felt the lie was given to her womb, she was denied; the wife felt the utter isolation of the human soul, the child within her was a weight apart from her.

At last it was finished. He was a man of handsome body, and his face showed no traces of drink. He was blond, full-fleshed, with fine limbs. But he was dead.

"Bless him," whispered his mother, looking always at his face, and speaking out of sheer terror. "Dear lad—bless him!" She spoke in a faint, sibilant ecstasy of fear and mother love.

Elizabeth sank down again to the floor, and put her face against his neck, and trembled and shuddered. But she had to draw away again. He was dead, and her living flesh had no place against his. A great dread and weariness held her: she was so unavailing. Her life was gone like this.

"White as milk he is, clear as a twelve-month baby, bless him, the darling!" the old mother murmured to herself. "Not a mark on him, clear and clean and white, beautiful as ever a child was made," she murmured with pride. Elizabeth kept her face hidden.

"He went peaceful, Lizzie—peaceful as sleep. Isn't he beautiful, the lamb? Ay—he must ha' made his peace, Lizzie. 'Appen he made it all right, Lizzie, shut in there. He'd have time. He wouldn't look like this if he hadn't made his peace. The lamb, the dear lamb. Eh, but he had a hearty laugh. I loved to hear it. He had the heartiest laugh, Lizzie, as a lad—"

Elizabeth looked up. The man's mouth was fallen back, slightly open under the cover of the moustache. The eyes, half shut, did not show glazed in the obscurity. Life with its smoky burning gone from him, had left him apart and utterly alien to her. And she knew what a stranger he was to her. In her womb was ice of fear, because of this separate stranger with whom she had been living as one flesh. Was this what it all meant—utter, intact separateness, obscured by heat of living? In dread she turned her face away. The fact was too deadly. There had been nothing between them, and yet they had come together, exchanging their nakedness repeatedly. Each time he had taken her, they had been two isolated beings, far apart as now. He was no more responsible than she. The child was like ice in her womb. For as she looked at the dead man, her mind, cold and detached, said clearly: "Who am I? What have I been doing? I have been fighting a husband who did not exist. *He* existed all the time. What wrong have I done? What was that I have been living with?

There lies the reality, this man." And her soul died in her for fear: she knew she had never seen him, he had never seen her, they had met in the dark and had fought in the dark, not knowing whom they met nor whom they fought. And now she saw, and turned silent in seeing. For she had been wrong. She had said he was something he was not; she had felt familiar with him. Whereas he was apart all the while, living as she never lived, feeling as she never felt.

In fear and shame she looked at his naked body, that she had known falsely. And he was the father of her children. Her soul was torn from her body and stood apart. She looked at his naked body and was ashamed, as if she had denied it. After all, it was itself. It seemed awful to her. She looked at his face, and she turned her own face to the wall. For his look was other than hers, his way was not her way. She had denied him what he was—she saw it now. She had refused him as himself. And this had been her life, and his life. She was grateful to death, which restored the truth. And she knew she was not dead.

And all the while her heart was bursting with grief and pity for him. What had he suffered? What stretch of horror for this helpless man! She was rigid with agony. She had not been able to help him. He had been cruelly injured, this naked man, this other being, and sh could make no reparation. There were the children—but the children belonged to life. This dead man had nothing to do with them. He and she were only channels through which life had flowed to issue in the children. She was a mother—but how awful she knew it now to have been a wife. And he, dead now, how awful he must have felt it to be a husband. She felt that in the next world he would be a stranger to her. If they met there, in the beyond, they would only be ashamed of what had been before. The children had come, for some mysterious reason, out of both of them. But the children did not unite them. Now he was dead, she knew how eternally he was apart from her, how eternally he had nothing more to do with her. She saw this episode of her life closed. They had denied each other in life. Now he had withdrawn. An anguish came over her. It was finished then: it had become hopeless between them long before he died. Yet he had been her husband. But how little!

"Have you got his shirt, 'Lizabeth?"

Elizabeth turned without answering, though she strove to weep and behave as her mother-in-law expected. But she could not, she was silenced. She went into the kitchen and returned with the garment.

"It is aired," she said, grasping the cotton shirt here and there to try. She was almost ashamed to handle him; what right had she or anyone to lay hands on him; but her touch was humble on his body. It was hard work to clothe him. He was so heavy and inert. A terrible dread gripped her all the while: that he could be so heavy and utterly inert, unresponsive, apart. The horror of the distance between them was almost too much for her—it was so infinite a gap she must look across.

At last it was finished. They covered him with a sheet and left him lying, with his face bound. And she fastened the door of the little parlour, lest the children should see what was lying there. Then, with peace sunk heavy on her heart, she went about making tidy the kitchen. She knew she submitted to life, which was her immediate master. But from death, her ultimate master, she winced with fear and shame.

The Blind Man

D. H. Lawrence

ISABEL PERVIN was listening for two sounds—for the sound of wheels on the drive outside and for the noise of her husband's footsteps in the hall. Her dearest and oldest friend, a man who seemed almost indispensable to her living, would drive up in the rainy dusk of the closing November day. The trap had gone to fetch him from the station. And her husband, who had been blinded in Flanders, and who had a disfiguring mark on his brow, would be coming in from the out-houses.

He had been home for a year now. He was totally blind. Yet they had been very happy. The Grange was Maurice's own place. The back was a farmstead, and the Wernhams, who occupied the rear premises, acted as farmers. Isabel lived with her husband in the handsome rooms in front. She and he had been almost entirely alone together since he was wounded. They talked and sang and read together in a wonderful and unspeakable intimacy. Then she reviewed books for a Scottish newspaper, carrying on her old interest, and he occupied himself a good deal with the farm. Sightless, he could still discuss everything with Wernham, and he could also do a good deal of work about the place—menial work, it is true, but it gave him satisfaction. He milked the cows, carried in the pails, turned the separator, attended to the pigs and horses. Life was still very full and strangely serene for the blind man, peaceful with the almost incomprehensible peace of immediate contact in darkness. With his wife he had a whole world, rich and real and invisible.

They were newly and remotely happy. He did not even regret the loss of his sight in these times of dark, palpable joy. A certain exultance swelled his soul.

But as time wore on, sometimes the rich glamour would leave them. Sometimes, after months of this intensity, a sense of burden overcame Isabel, a weariness, a terrible ennui, in that silent house approached between a colonnade of tall-shafted pines. Then she felt she would go mad, for she could not bear it. And sometimes he had devastating fits of depression, which seemed to lay waste his whole being. It was worse than depression—a black misery, when his own life was a torture to him, and when his presence was unbearable to his wife. The dread went down to the roots of her soul as these black days recurred. In a kind of panic she tried to wrap herself up still further in her husband. She forced the old spontaneous cheerfulness and joy to continue. But the effort it cost her was almost too much. She knew she could not keep it up. She felt she would scream with the strain, and would give anything, anything, to escape. She longed to possess her husband utterly; it gave her inordinate joy to have him entirely to herself. And yet, when again he was gone in a black and massive misery, she could not bear him, she could not bear herself; she wished she could be snatched away off the earth altogether, anything rather than live at this cost.

Dazed, she schemed for a way out. She invited friends, she tried to give him some further connection with the outer world. But it was no good. After all their joy and suffering, after their dark, great year of blindness and solitude and unspeakable nearness, other people seemed to them both shallow, prattling, rather impertinent. Shallow prattle seemed presumptuous. He became impatient and irritated, she was wearied. And so they lapsed into their solitude again. For they preferred it.

But now, in a few weeks' time, her second baby would be born. The first had died, an infant, when her husband first went out to France. She looked with joy and relief to the coming of the second. It would be her salvation. But also she felt some anxiety. She was thirty years old, her husband was a year younger. They both wanted the child very much. Yet she could not help feeling afraid. She had her husband on her hands, a terrible joy to her, and a terrifying burden. The child would occupy her love and attention. And then, what of Maurice? What would he do? If only she could feel that he, too, would be at peace and happy when the child came! She did so want to luxuriate in a rich, physical satisfaction of maternity. But the man, what would he do? How could she provide for him, how avert those shattering black moods of his, which destroyed them both?

She sighed with fear. But at this time Bertie Reid wrote to Isabel. He was her old friend, a second or third cousin, a Scotsman, as she was a Scotswoman. They had been brought up near to one another, and all her life he had been her friend, like a brother, but better than her own brothers. She loved him—though not in the marrying sense. There was a sort of kinship between them, an affinity. They understood one another instinctively. But Isabel would never have thought of marrying Bertie. It would have seemed like marrying in her own family.

Bertie was a barrister and a man of letters, a Scotsman of the intellectual type, quick, ironical, sentimental, and on his knees before the women he adored but did not want to marry. Maurice Pervin was different. He came of a good old country family—the Grange was not a very great distance from Oxford. He was passionate, sensitive, perhaps over-sensitive, wincing—a big fellow with heavy limbs and a forehead that flushed painfully. For his mind was slow, as if drugged by the strong provincial blood that beat in his veins. He was very sensitive to his own mental slowness, his feelings being quick and acute. So that he was just the opposite to Bertie, whose mind was much quicker than his emotions, which were not so very fine.

From the first the two men did not like each other. Isabel felt that they *ought* to get on together. But they did not. She felt that if only each could have the clue to the other there would be such a rare understanding between them. It did not come off, however. Bertie adopted a slightly ironical attitude, very offensive to Maurice, who returned the Scotch irony with English resentment, a resentment which deepened sometimes into stupid hatred.

This was a little puzzling to Isabel. However, she accepted it in the course of things. Men were made freakish and unreasonable. Therefore, when Maurice was going out to France for the second time, she felt that, for her husband's sake, she must discontinue her friendship with Bertie. She wrote to the barrister to this effect. Bertram Reid simply replied that in this, as in all other matters, he must obey her wishes, if these were indeed her wishes.

For nearly two years nothing had passed between the two friends. Isabel rather gloried in the fact; she had no compunction. She had one great article of faith, which was, that husband and wife should be so important to one another, that the rest of the world simply did not count. She and Maurice were husband and wife. They loved one another. They would have children. Then let everybody and everything else fade into insignificance outside this connubial felicity. She professed herself quite happy and ready to receive Maurice's friends. She was happy and ready: the happy wife, the ready woman in possession. Without knowing why, the friends retired abashed, and came no more. Maurice, of course, took as much satisfaction in this connubial absorption as Isabel did.

He shared in Isabel's literary activities, she cultivated a real interest in agriculture and cattle-raising. For she, being at heart perhaps an emotional enthusiast, always cultivated the practical side of life, and prided herself on her mastery of practical affairs. Thus the husband and wife had spent the five years of their married life. The last had been one of blindness and unspeakable intimacy. And now Isabel felt a great indifference coming over her, a sort of lethargy. She wanted to be allowed to bear her child in peace, to nod by the fire and drift vaguely, physically, from day to day. Maurice was like an ominous thunder-cloud. She had to keep waking up to remember him.

When a little note came from Bertie, asking if he were to put up a tombstone to their dead friendship, and speaking of the real pain he felt on account of her husband's loss of sight, she felt a pang, a fluttering agitation of reawakening. And she read the letter to Maurice.

"Ask him to come down," he said.

"Ask Bertie to come here!" she re-echoed.

"Yes—if he wants to."

Isabel paused for a few moments.

"I know he wants to—he'd only be too glad," she replied. "But what about you, Maurice? How would you like it?"

"I should like it."

"Well—in that case—But I thought you didn't care for him—"

"Oh, I don't know. I might think differently of him now," the blind man replied. It was rather abstruse to Isabel.

"Well, dear," she said, "if you're quite sure—"

"I'm sure enough. Let him come," said Maurice.

So Bertie was coming, coming this evening, in the November rain and darkness. Isabel was agitated, racked with her old restlessness and indecision. She had always suffered from this pain of doubt, just an agonizing sense of uncertainty. It had begun to pass off, in the lethargy of maternity. Now it returned, and she resented it. She struggled as usual to maintain her calm, composed, friendly bearing, a sort of mask she wore over all her body.

A woman had lighted a tall lamp beside the table, and spread the cloth. The long dining-room was dim, with its elegant but rather severe pieces of old furniture. Only the round table glowed softly under the light. It had a rich, beautiful effect. The white cloth glistened and dropped its heavy, pointed lace corners almost to the carpet, the china was old and handsome, creamy-yellow, with a blotched pattern of harsh red and deep blue, the cups large and bell-shaped, the teapot gallant. Isabel looked at it with superficial appreciation.

Her nerves were hurting her. She looked automatically again at the high, uncurtained windows. In the last dusk she could just perceive outside a huge fir tree swaying its boughs: it was as if she thought it rather than saw it. The rain came flying on the window panes. Ah, why had she no peace? These two men, why did they tear at her? Why did they not come—why was there this suspense?

She sat in a lassitude that was really suspense and irritation. Maurice, at least, might come in—there was nothing to keep him out. She rose to her feet. Catching sight of her reflection in a mirror, she glanced at herself with a slight smile of recognition, as if she were an old friend to herself. Her face was oval and calm, her nose a little arched. Her neck made a beautiful line down to her shoulder. With hair knotted loosely behind, she had something of a warm, maternal look. Thinking this of herself, she arched her eyebrows and her rather heavy eyelids, with a little flicker of a smile, and for a moment her gray eyes looked amused and wicked, a little sardonic, out of her transfigured Madonna face.

Then, resuming her air of womanly patience—she was really fatally self-determined—she went with a little jerk toward the door. Her eyes were slightly reddened.

She passed down the wide hall, and through a door at the end. Then she was in the farm premises. The scent of dairy, and of farm-kitchen, and of farmyard and of leather almost overcame her: but particularly the scent of dairy. They had been scalding out the pans. The flagged passage in front of her was dark, puddled and wet. Light came out from the open kitchen door. She went forward and stood in the doorway. The farm-people were at tea, seated at a little distance from her, round a long, narrow table, in the center of which stood a white lamp. Ruddy faces, ruddy hands holding food, red mouths working, heads bent over the tea-cups: men, land-girls, boys: it was tea-time, feeding-time. Some faces caught sight of her. Mrs. Wernham, going round behind the chairs with a large black teapot, halting slightly in her walk, was not aware of her for a moment. Then she turned suddenly.

"Oh, is it Madam!" she exclaimed. "Come in, then, come in! We're at tea." And she dragged forward a chair.

"No, I won't come in," said Isabel. "I'm afraid I interrupt your meal."

"No—no—not likely, Madam, not likely."

"Hasn't Mr. Pervin come in, do you know?"

"I'm sure I couldn't say! Missed him, have you, Madam?"

"No, I only wanted him to come in," laughed Isabel, as if shyly.

"Wanted him, did ye? Get up, boy—get up, now—"

Mrs. Wernham knocked one of the boys on the shoulder. He began to scrape to his feet, chewing largely.

"I believe he's in top stable," said another face from the table.

"Ah! No, don't get up. I'm going myself," said Isabel.

"Don't you go out of a dirty night like this. Let the lad go. Get along wi' ye, boy," said Mrs. Wernham.

"No, no," said Isabel, with a decision that was always obeyed. "Go on with your tea, Tom. I'd like to go across to the stable, Mrs. Wernham."

"Did ever you hear tell!" exclaimed the woman.

"Isn't the trap late?" asked Isabel.

"Why, no," said Mrs. Wernham, peering into the distance at the tall, dim clock. "No, Madam—we can give it another quarter or twenty minutes yet, good—yes, every bit of a quarter."

"Ah! It seems late when darkness falls so early," said Isabel.

"It do, that it do. Bother the days, that they draw in so," answered Mrs. Wernham. "Proper miserable!"

"They are," said Isabel, withdrawing.

She pulled on her overshoes, wrapped a large tartan shawl around her, put on a man's felt hat, and ventured out along the causeways of the first yard. It was very dark. The wind was roaring in the great elms behind the out-houses. When she came to the second yard the darkness seemed deeper. She was unsure of her footing. She wished she had brought a lantern. Rain blew against her. Half she liked it, half she felt unwilling to battle.

She reached at last the just visible door of the stable. There was no sign of a light anywhere. Opening the upper half, she looked in: into a simple well of darkness. The smell of horses, ammonia, and of warmth was startling to her, in that full night. She listened with all her ears, but could hear nothing save the night, and the stirring of a horse.

"Maurice!" she called, softly and musically, though she was afraid. "Maurice—are you there?"

Nothing came from the darkness. She knew the rain and wind blew in upon the horses, the hot animal life. Feeling it wrong, she entered the stable, and drew the lower half of the door shut, holding the upper part close. She did not stir, because she was aware of the presence of the dark hindquarters of the horses, though she could not see them, and she was afraid. Something wild stirred in her heart.

She listened intensely. Then she heard a small noise in the distance—far away, it seemed—the chink of a pan, and a man's voice speaking a brief word. It would be Maurice, in the other part of the stable. She stood motionless, waiting for him to come through the partition door. The horses were so terrifyingly near to her, in the invisible.

The loud jarring of the inner door-latch made her start; the door was opened. She could hear and feel her husband entering and invisibly passing among the horses near to her, in darkness as they were, actively intermingled. The rather low sound of his voice as he spoke to the horses came velvety to her nerves. How near he was, and how invisible! The darkness seemed to be in a strange swirl of violent life, just upon her. She turned giddy.

Her presence of mind made her call, quietly and musically:

"Maurice! Maurice—dea-ar!"

"Yes," he answered. "Isabel?"

She saw nothing, and the sound of his voice seemed to touch her.

"Hello!" she answered cheerfully, straining her eyes to see him. He was still busy, attending to the horses near her, but she saw only darkness. It made her almost desperate.

"Won't you come in, dear?" she said.

"Yes, I'm coming. Just half a minute. *Stand over—now!* Trap's not come, has it?"

"Not yet," said Isabel.

His voice was pleasant and ordinary, but it had a slight suggestion of the stable to her. She wished he would come away. While he was so utterly invisible she was afraid of him.

"How's the time?" he asked.

"Not yet six," she replied. She disliked to answer into the dark. Presently he came very near to her, and she retreated out of doors.

"The weather blows in here," he said, coming steadily forward, feeling for the doors. She shrank away. At last she could dimly see him.

"Bertie won't have much of a drive," he said, as he closed the doors.

"He won't indeed!" said Isabel calmly, watching the dark shape at the door.

"Give me your arm, dear," she said.

She pressed his arm close to her, as she went. But she longed to see him, to look at him. She was nervous. He walked erect, with face rather lifted, but with a curious tentative movement of his powerful, muscular legs. She could feel the clever, careful, strong contact of his feet with the earth, as she balanced against him. For a moment he was a tower of darkness to her, as if he rose out of the earth.

In the house-passage he wavered, and went cautiously, with a curious look of silence about him as he felt for the bench. Then he sat down heavily. He was a man with rather sloping shoulders, but with heavy limbs, powerful legs that seemed to know the earth. His head was small, usually carried high and light. As he bent down to unfasten his gaiters and boots he did not look blind. His hair was brown and crisp, his hands were large, reddish, intelligent, the veins stood out in the wrists; and his thighs and knees seemed massive. When he stood up his face and neck were surcharged with blood, the veins stood out on his temples. She did not look at his blindness.

Isabel was always glad when they had passed through the dividing door into their own regions of repose and beauty. She was a little afraid of him, out there in the animal grossness of the back. His bearing also changed, as he smelled the familiar, indefinable odor that pervaded his wife's surroundings, a delicate, refined scent, very faintly spicy. Perhaps it came from the potpourri bowls.

He stood at the foot of the stairs, arrested, listening. She watched him, and her heart sickened. He seemed to be listening to fate.

"He's not here yet," he said. "I'll go up and change."

"Maurice," she said, "you're not wishing he wouldn't come, are you?"

"I couldn't quite say," he answered. "I feel myself rather on the *qui vive*."

"I can see you are," she answered. And she reached up and kissed his cheek. She saw his mouth relax into a slow smile.

"What are you laughing at?" she said roguishly.

"You consoling me," he answered.

"Nay," she answered. "Why should I console you? You know we love each other—you know *how* married we are! What does anything else matter?"

"Nothing at all, my dear."

He felt for her face, and touched it, smiling.

"*You're* all right, aren't you?" he asked, anxiously.

"I'm wonderfully all right, love," she answered. "It's you I am a little troubled about, at times."

"Why me?" he said, touching her cheeks delicately with the tips of his fingers. The touch had an almost hyponotizing effect on her.

He went away upstairs. She saw him mount into the darkness, unseeing and unchanging. He did not know that the lamps on the upper corridor were unlighted. He went on into the darkness with unchanging step. She heard him in the bathroom.

Pervin moved about almost unconsciously in his familiar surroundings, dark though everything was. He seemed to know the presence of objects before he touched them. It was a pleasure to him to rock thus through a world of things, carried on the floor in a sort of blood-prescience. He did not think much or trouble much. So long as he kept this sheer immediacy of blood-contact with the substantial world he was happy, he wanted no intervention of visual consciousness. In this state there was a certain rich positivity, bordering sometimes on rapture. Life seemed to move in him like a tide lapping, lapping, and advancing, enveloping all things darkly. It was a pleasure to stretch forth the hand and meet the unseen object, clasp it, and possess it in pure contact. He did not try to remember, to visualize. He did not want to. The new way of consciousness substituted itself in him.

The rich suffusion of this state generally kept him happy, reaching its culmination in the consuming passion for his wife. But at times the flow would seem to be checked and thrown back. Then it would beat inside him like a tangled sea, and he was tortured in the shattered chaos of his own blood. He grew to dread this arrest, this throw-back, this chaos inside himself, when he seemed merely at the mercy of his own powerful and conflicting elements. How to get some measure of control or surety, this was the question. And when the question rose maddening in him, he would clench his fists as if he would *compel* the whole universe to submit to him. But it was in vain. He could not even compel himself.

Tonight, however, he was still serene, though little tremors of unreasonable exasperation ran through him. He had to handle the razor very carefully, as he shaved, for it was not at one with him, he was afraid of it. His hearing also was too much sharpened. He heard the woman lighting the lamps on the corridor, and attending to the fire in the visitor's room. And then, as he went to his room he heard the trap arrive. Then came Isabel's voice, lifted and calling, like a bell ringing:

"Is it you, Bertie? Have you come?"

And a man's voice answered out of the wind:

"Hello, Isabel! There you are."

"Have you had a miserable drive? I'm so sorry we couldn't send a closed carriage. I can't see you at all, you know."

"I'm coming. No, I liked the drive—it was like Perthshire. Well, how are you? You're looking fit as ever, as far as I can see."

"Oh, yes," said Isabel. "I'm wonderfully well. How are you? Rather thin, I think—"

"Worked to death—everybody's old cry. But I'm all right, Ciss. How's Pervin?—isn't he here?"

"Oh, yes, he's upstairs changing. Yes, he's awfully well. Take off your wet things; I'll send them to be dried."

"And how are you both, in spirits? He doesn't fret?"

"No—no, not at all. No, on the contrary, really. We've been wonderfully happy, incredibly. It's more than I can understand—so wonderful: the nearness, and the peace—"

"Ah! Well, that's awfully good news—"

They moved away. Pervin heard no more. But a childish sense of desolation had come over him, as he heard their brisk voices. He seemed shut out—like a child that is left out. He was aimless and excluded, he did not know what to do with himself. The helpless desolation came over him. He fumbled nervously as he dressed himself, in a state almost of childishness. He disliked the Scotch accent in Bertie's speech, and the slight response it found on Isabel's tongue. He disliked the slight purr of complacency in the Scottish speech. He disliked intensely the glib way in which Isabel spoke of their happiness and nearness. It made him recoil. He was fretful and beside himself like a child, he had almost a childish nostalgia to be included in the life circle. And at the same time he was a man, dark and powerful and infuriated by his own weakness. By some fatal flaw, he could not be by himself, he had to depend on the support of another. And this very dependence enraged him. He hated Bertie Reid, and at the same time he knew the hatred was nonsense, he knew it was the outcome of his own weakness.

He went downstairs. Isabel was alone in the dining-room. She watched him enter, head erect, his feet tentative. He looked so strong-blooded and healthy, and, at the same time, cancelled. Cancelled—that was the word that flew across her mind. Perhaps it was his scars suggested it.

"You heard Bertie come, Maurice?" she said.

"Yes—isn't he here?"

"He's in his room. He looks very thin and worn."

"I suppose he works himself to death."

A woman came in with a tray—and after a few minutes Bertie came down. He was a little dark man, with a very big forehead, thin, wispy hair, and sad, large eyes. His expression was inordinately sad—almost funny. He had odd, short legs.

Isabel watched him hesitate under the door, and glance nervously at her husband. Pervin heard him and turned.

"Here you are, now," said Isabel. "Come, let us eat."

Bertie went across to Maurice.

"How are you, Pervin?" he said, as he advanced.

The blind man stuck his hand out into space, and Bertie took it.

"Very fit. Glad you've come," said Maurice.

Isabel glanced at them, and glanced away, as if she could not bear to see them.

"Come," she said. "Come to table. Aren't you both awfully hungry? I am, tremendously."

"I'm afraid you waited for me," said Bertie, as they sat down.

Maurice had a curious monolithic way of sitting in a chair, erect and distant. Isabel's heart always beat when she caught sight of him thus.

"No," she replied to Bertie. "We're very little later than usual. We're having a sort of high tea, not dinner. Do you mind? It gives us such a nice long evening uninterrupted."

"I like it," said Bertie.

Maurice was feeling, with curious little movements, almost like a cat kneading her bed, for his place, his knife and fork, his napkin. He was getting the whole geography of his cover into his consciousness. He sat erect and inscrutable, remote-seeming. Bertie watched the static figure of the blind man, the delicate tactile discernment of the large, ruddy hands, and the curious mindless silence of the brow, above the scar. With difficulty he looked away, and without knowing what he did, picked up a little crystal bowl of violets from the table, and held them to his nose.

"They are sweet-scented," he said. "Where do they come from?"

"From the garden—under the windows," said Isabel.

"So late in the year—and so fragrant! Do you remember the violets under Aunt Bell's south wall?"

The two friends looked at each other and exchanged a smile, Isabel's eyes lighting up.

"Don't I?" she replied. "*Wasn't* she queer!"

"A curious old girl," laughed Bertie. "There's a streak of freakishness in the family, Isabel."

"Ah—but not in you and me, Bertie," said Isabel. "Give them to Maurice, will you?" she added, as Bertie was putting down the flowers. "Have you smelled the violets, dear? Do!—they are so scented."

Maurice held out his hand, and Bertie placed the tiny bowl against his large, warm-looking fingers. Maurice's hand closed over the thin white fingers of the barrister. Bertie carefully extricated himself. Then the two watched the blind man smelling the violets. He bent his head and seemed to be thinking. Isabel waited.

"Aren't they sweet, Maurice?" she said at last, anxiously.

"Very," he said. And he held out the bowl. Bertie took it. Both he and Isabel were a little afraid, and deeply disturbed.

The meal continued. Isabel and Bertie chatted spasmodically. The blind man was silent. He touched his food repeatedly, with quick, delicate touches of his knife-point, then cut irregular bits. He could not bear to be helped. Both Isabel and Bertie suffered: Isabel wondered why. She did not suffer when she was alone with Maurice. Bertie made her conscious of a strangeness.

After the meal the three drew their chairs to the fire, and sat down to talk. The decanters were put on a table near at hand. Isabel knocked the logs on the fire, and clouds of brilliant sparks went up the chimney. Bertie noticed a slight weariness in her bearing.

"You will be glad when your child comes now, Isabel?" he said.

She looked up to him with a quick wan smile.

"Yes, I shall be glad," she answered. "It begins to seem long. Yes, I shall be very glad. So will you, Maurice, won't you?" she added.

"Yes, I shall," replied her husband.

"We are both looking forward so much to having it," she said.

"Yes, of course," said Bertie.

He was a bachelor, three or four years older than Isabel. He lived in beautiful rooms overlooking the river, guarded by a faithful Scottish manservant. And he had his friends among the fair sex—not lovers, friends. So long as he could avoid any danger of courtship or marriage, he adored a few good women with constant and unfailing homage, and he was chivalrously fond of quite a number. But if they seemed to encroach on him, he withdrew and detested them.

Isabel knew him very well, knew his beautiful constancy, and kindness, also his incurable weakness, which made him unable ever to enter into close contact of any sort. He was ashamed of himself, because he could not marry, could not approach women physically. He wanted to do so. But he could not. At the center of him he was afraid, helplessly and even brutally afraid. He had given up hope, had ceased to expect any more that he could escape his own weakness. Hence he was a brilliant and successful barrister, also *littérateur* of high repute, a rich man, and a great social success. At the center he felt himself neuter, nothing.

Isabel knew him well. She despised him even while she admired him. She looked at his sad face, his little short legs, and felt contempt of him. She looked at his dark gray eyes, with their uncanny, almost child-like intuition, and she loved him. He understood amazingly—but she had no fear of his understanding. As a man she patronized him.

And she turned to the impassive, silent figure of her husband. He sat leaning back, with folded arms, and face a little uptilted. His knees were straight and massive. She sighed, picked up the poker, and again began to prod the fire, to rouse the clouds of soft, brilliant sparks.

"Isabel tells me," Bertie began suddenly, "that you have not suffered unbearably from the loss of sight."

Maurice straightened himself to attend, but kept his arms folded.

"No," he said, "not unbearably. Now and again one struggles against it, you know. But there are compensations."

"They say it is much worse to be stone deaf," said Isabel.

"I believe it is," said Bertie. "Are there compensations?" he added, to Maurice.

"Yes. You cease to bother about a great many things." Again Maurice stretched his figure, stretched the strong muscles of his back, and leaned backwards, with uplifted face.

"And that is a relief," said Bertie. "But what is there in place of the bothering? What replaces the activity?"

There was a pause. At length the blind man replied, as out of a negligent, unattentive thinking:

"Oh, I don't know. There's a good deal when you're not active."

"Is there?" said Bertie. "What, exactly? It always seems to me that when there is no thought and no action, there is nothing."

Again Maurice was slow in replying.

"There is something," he replied. "I couldn't tell you what it is."

And the talk lapsed once more, Isabel and Bertie chatting gossip and reminiscence, the blind man silent.

At length Maurice rose restlessly, a big, obtrusive figure. He felt tight and hampered. He wanted to go away.

"Do you mind," he said, "if I go and speak to Wernham?"

"No—go along, dear," said Isabel.

And he went out. A silence came over the two friends. At length Bertie said:

"Nevertheless, it is a great deprivation, Cissie."

"It is, Bertie. I know it is."

"Something lacking all the time," said Bertie.

"Yes, I know. And yet—and yet—Maurice is right. There is something else, something *there*, which you never knew was there, and which you can't express."

"What is there?" asked Bertie.

"I don't know—it's awfully hard to define it—but something strong and immediate. There's something strange in Maurice's presence—indefinable—but I couldn't do without it. I agree that it seems to put one's mind to sleep. But when we're alone I miss nothing; it seems awfully rich, almost splendid, you know."

"I'm afraid I don't follow," said Bertie.

They talked desultorily. The wind blew loudly outside, rain chattered on the window-panes, making a sharp drum-sound, because of the closed, mellow-golden shutters inside. The logs burned slowly, with hot, almost invisible small flames. Bertie seemed uneasy, there were dark circles round his eyes. Isabel, rich with her approaching maternity, leaned looking into the fire. Her hair curled in odd, loose strands, very pleasing to the man. But she had a curious feeling of old woe in her heart, old, timeless night-woe.

"I suppose we're all deficient somewhere," said Bertie.

"I suppose so," said Isabel wearily.

"Damned, sooner or later."

"I don't know," she said, rousing herself, "I feel quite all right, you know. The child coming seems to make me indifferent to everything, just placid. I can't feel that there's anything to trouble about, you know."

"A good thing, I should say," he replied slowly.

"Well, there it is. I suppose it's just Nature. If only I felt I needn't trouble about Maurice, I should be perfectly content—"

"But you feel you must trouble about him?"

"Well—I don't know—" She even resented this much effort.

The evening passed slowly. Isabel looked at the clock. "I say," she said. "It's nearly ten o'clock. Where can Maurice be? I'm sure they're all in bed at the back. Excuse me a moment."

She went out, returning almost immediately.

"It's all shut up and in darkness," she said. "I wonder where he is. He must have gone out to the farm—"

Bertie looked at her.

"I suppose he'll come in," he said.

"I suppose so," she said. "But it's unusual for him to be out now."

"Would you like me to go out and see?"

"Well—if you wouldn't mind. I'd go, but—" She did not want to make the physical effort.

Bertie put on an old overcoat and took a lantern. He went out from the side door. He shrank from the wet and roaring night. Such weather had a nervous effect on him: too much moisture everywhere made him feel almost imbecile. Unwilling, he went through it all. A dog barked violently at him. He peered in all the buildings. At last, as he opened the upper door of a sort of intermediate barn, he heard a grinding noise, and looking in, holding up his lantern, saw Maurice, in his shirt-sleeves, standing listening, holding the handle of a turnip-pulper. He had been pulping sweet roots, a pile of which lay dimly heaped in a corner behind him.

"That you, Wernham?" said Maurice, listening.

"No, it's me," said Bertie.

A large, half-wild gray cat was rubbing at Maurice's leg. The blind man stooped to rub its sides. Bertie watched the scene, then unconsciously entered and shut the door behind him. He was in a high sort of barn-place, from which, right and left, ran off the corridors in front of the stalled cattle. He watched the slow, stooping motion of the other man, as he caressed the great cat.

Maurice straightened himself.

"You came to look for me?" he said.

"Isabel was a little uneasy," said Bertie.

"I'll come in. I like messing about doing these jobs."

The cat had reared her sinister, feline length against his leg, clawing at his thigh affectionately. He lifted her claws out of his flesh.

"I hope I'm not in your way at all at the Grange here," said Bertie, rather shy and stiff.

"My way? No, not a bit. I'm glad Isabel has somebody to talk to. I'm afraid it's I who am in the way. I know I'm not very lively company. Isabel's all right, don't you think? She's not unhappy, is she?"

"I don't think so."

"What does she say?"

"She says she's very content—only a little troubled about you."

"Why me?"

"Perhaps afraid that you might brood," said Bertie cautiously.

"She needn't be afraid of that." He continued to caress the flattened gray head of the cat with his fingers. "What I am a bit afraid of," he resumed, "is that she'll find me a dead weight, always alone with me down here."

"I don't think you need think that," said Bertie, though this was what he feared himself.

"I don't know," said Maurice. "Sometimes I feel it isn't fair that she's saddled with me." Then he dropped his voice curiously. "I say," he asked, secretly struggling, "is my face much disfigured? Do you mind telling me?"

"There is the scar," said Bertie, wondering. "Yes, it is a disfigurement. But more pitiable than shocking."

"A pretty bad scar, though," said Maurice.

"Oh, yes."

There was a pause.

"Sometimes I feel I am horrible," said Maurice, in a low voice, talking as if to himself. And Bertie actually felt a quiver of horror.

"That's nonsense," he said.

Maurice again straightened himself, leaving the cat.

"There's no telling," he said. Then again, in an odd tone, he added: "I don't really know you, do I?"

"Probably not," said Bertie.

"Do you mind if I touch you?"

The lawyer shrank away instinctively. And yet, out of very philanthropy, he said, in a small voice: "Not at all."

But he suffered as the blind man stretched out a strong, naked hand to him. Maurice accidentally knocked off Bertie's hat.

"I thought you were taller," he said, starting. Then he laid his hand on Bertie Reid's head, closing the dome of the skull in a soft, firm grasp, gathering it, as it were; then, shifting his grasp and softly closing again, with a fine, close pressure, till he had covered the skull and the face of the smaller man, tracing the brows, and touching the full, closed eyes, touching the small nose and the nostrils, the rough, short moustache, the mouth, the rather strong chin. The hand of the blind man grasped the shoulder, the arm, the hand of the other man. He seemed to take him, in the soft, traveling grasp.

"You seem young," he said quietly, at last.

The lawyer stood almost annihilated, unable to answer.

"Your head seems tender, as if you were young," Maurice repeated. "So do your hands. Touch my eyes, will you?—touch my scar."

Now Bertie quivered with revulsion. Yet he was under the power of the blind man, as if hypnotized. He lifted his hand, and laid the fingers on the scar, on the scarred eyes. Maurice suddenly covered them with his own hand, pressed the fingers of the other man upon his disfigured eye-sockets, trembling in every fiber, and rocking slightly, slowly, from side to side. He remained thus for a minute or more, whilst Bertie stood as if in a swoon, unconscious, imprisoned.

Then suddenly Maurice removed the hand of the other man from his brow, and stood holding it in his own.

"Oh, my God," he said, "we shall know each other now, shan't we? We shall know each other now."

Bertie could not answer. He gazed mute and terror-struck, overcome by his own weakness. He knew he could not answer. He had an unreasonable fear, lest the other man should suddenly destroy him. Whereas Maurice was actually filled with hot, poignant love, the passion of friendship. Perhaps it was this very passion of friendship which Bertie shrank from most.

"We're all right together now, aren't we?" said Maurice. "It's all right now, as long as we live, so far as we're concerned."

"Yes," said Bertie, trying by any means to escape.

Maurice stood with head lifted, as if listening. The new delicate fulfillment of mortal friendship had come as a revelation and surprise to him, something exquisite and unhoped-for. He seemed to be listening to hear if it were real.

Then he turned for his coat.

"Come," he said, "we'll go to Isabel."

Bertie took the lantern and opened the door. The cat disappeared. The two men went in silence along the causeways. Isabel, as they came, thought their footsteps sounded strange. She looked up pathetically and anxiously for their entrance. There seemed a curious elation about Maurice. Bertie was haggard, with sunken eyes.

"What is it?" she asked.

"We've become friends," said Maurice, standing with his feet apart, like a strange colossus.

"Friends!" re-echoed Isabel. And she looked again at Bertie. He met her eyes with a furtive, haggard look; his eyes were as if glazed with misery.

"I'm so glad," she said, in sheer perplexity.

"Yes," said Maurice.

He was indeed so glad. Isabel took his hand with both hers, and held it fast.

"You'll be happier now, dear," she said.

But she was watching Bertie. She knew that he had one desire—to escape from this intimacy, this friendship, which had been thrust upon him. He could not bear it that he had been touched by the blind man, his insane reserve broken in. He was like a mollusc whose shell is broken.

FRANZ KAFKA

*F*RANZ KAFKA *(1883–1924) published only a small portion of his fiction during his lifetime and did not live to see the way his brilliant experiments made him one of the most influential writers of this century. He completed one novel,* The Trial, *and left two others—*The Castle *and* Amerika—*unfinished, but his major achievement lies in the genre of the short story.*

It is widely recognized that Kafka's art grew in part from his desperate relationship with his strong-willed and domineering father, but it is also clear to anyone who follows the curve of his development that what began as direct expression of his neurosis soon developed an independence and universality that were crucial to his growth as an artist. So much is known about Kafka's difficulties with his health, relationships, and inner life that there is a temptation to reduce his stories to expressions of them, but the point is surely not where the problems began but what they ended as. Lots of people have problems with their parents; few could resolve and transform these difficulties in such creative ways. Moreover, it is clear in retrospect that Kafka also drew on his social alienation—he was a German-speaking Jew born and raised in Prague, a man of two cultures living in a third—for the terror and comedy that pervade his fiction.

Kafka's fictional technique, often imitated but never matched, combines fantastic and dreamlike events with a deadpan manner. Grotesque characters and preposterous transformations are presented matter of factly, in a fictional style that is both accessible in its simplicity and frightening in its apparent serenity. The resulting atmosphere recalls dreams and folktales, but it also cultivates understatement, provoking us to supply emotions that the narrators withhold, and pursuing a comic effect that is, of course, deadly earnest.

The two examples chosen for this collection show Kafka's talent for very short pieces, "The Bucket Rider" *(1921), and for more sustained narrative,* "A Country Doctor" *(1919). In both cases, the world of the story is established quickly, with a few bold strokes, and the narrative seems to flow effortlessly toward an inevitable conclusion.* "The Bucket Rider," *Max Brod tells us, was partly inspired by the Prague coal famine of the winter of 1916–1917; Kafka has transformed that particular reality into a parable of human suffering and indifference.* "A Country Doctor," *being longer and more complex, is less obviously a parable, but readers quickly sense the ways in which it can be interpreted as a metaphor for dilemmas of several kinds: psychological, social, and metaphysical. It invites rich speculation but resists definitive interpretation. Kafka's suggestiveness is what we finally learn to prize most: his way with questions rather than answers.*

A Country Doctor

Franz Kafka

I WAS in great perplexity; I had to start on an urgent journey; a seriously ill patient was waiting for me in a village ten miles off; a thick blizzard of snow filled all the wide spaces between him and me; I had a gig, a light gig with big wheels, exactly right for our country roads; muffled in furs, my bag of instruments in my hand, I was in the courtyard all ready for the journey; but there was no horse to be had, no horse. My own horse had died in the night, worn out by the fatigues of this icy winter; my servant girl was now running round the village trying to borrow a horse; but it was hopeless, I knew it, and I stood there forlornly, with the snow gathering more and more thickly upon me, more and more unable to move. In the gateway the girl appeared, alone, and waved the lantern; of course, who would lend a horse at this time for such a journey? I strode through the courtyard once more; I could see no way out; in my confused distress I kicked at the dilapidated door of the year-long uninhabited pigsty. It flew open and flapped to and fro on its hinges. A steam and smell as of horses came out from it. A dim stable lantern was swinging inside from a rope. A man, crouching on his hams in that low space, showed an open blue-eyed face. "Shall I yoke up?" he asked, crawling out on all fours. I did not know what to say and merely stooped down to see what else was in the sty. The servant girl was standing beside me. "You never know what you're going to find in your own house," she said, and we both laughed. "Hey there, Brother, hey there, Sister!" called the groom, and two horses, enormous creatures with powerful flanks, one after the other, their legs tucked close to their bodies, each well-shaped head lowered like a camel's, by sheer strength of buttocking squeezed out through the door hole which they filled entirely. But at once they were standing up, their legs long and their bodies steaming thickly. "Give him a hand," I said, and the willing girl hurried to help the groom with the harnessing. Yet hardly was she beside him when the groom chipped hold of her and pushed his face against hers. She screamed and fled back to me; on her cheek stood out in red the marks of two rows of teeth. "You brute," I yelled in fury, "do you want a whipping?" but in the same moment reflected that the man was a stranger; that I did not know where he came from, and that of his own free will he was helping me out when everyone else had failed me. As if he knew my thoughts he took no offense at my threat but, still busied with the horses, only turned round once towards me. "Get in," he said then, and indeed everything was ready. A magnificent pair of horses, I observed, such as I had never sat behind, and I climbed in happily. "But I'll drive, you don't know the way," I said. "Of course," said he, "I'm not coming with you anyway, I'm staying with Rose." "No," shrieked Rose, fleeing into the house with a justified presentiment that her fate was inescapable; I heard the door chain rattle as she put it up; I heard the key turn in the lock; I could see, moreover, how she put out the lights in the entrance hall and in further flight all through the rooms to keep herself from being discovered. "You're coming with me," I said to the groom, "or I won't go, urgent as my journey is. I'm not thinking of paying for it by handing the girl over to you." "Gee up!" he said; clapped his hands; the gig whirled off like a log in a freshet; I could just hear the door of my house splitting and bursting as the groom charged at it and then I was deafened and blinded by a storming rush that steadily buffeted all my senses. But this only for a moment, since, as if my patient's farmyard had opened out just before my courtyard gate, I was already there; the horses had come quietly to a standstill; the blizzard had stopped; moonlight all around; my patient's parents hurried out of the house, his sister behind them; I was almost lifted out of the gig; from their confused ejaculations I gathered not a word; in the sickroom the air was almost unbreathable; the neglected stove was smoking; I wanted to push open a window; but first I had to look at my patient. Gaunt, without any fever, not cold, not warm, with vacant eyes, without a shirt, the youngster heaved himself up from under the feather bedding, threw his arms round my neck, and whispered in my ear: "Doctor, let me die." I glanced round the room; no one had heard it; the parents were leaning forward in silence waiting for my verdict; the sister had set a chair for my handbag; I opened the bag and hunted among my instruments; the boy kept clutching at me from his bed to remind me of his entreaty; I picked up a pair of tweezers, examined them in the candlelight and laid them down again. "Yes," I thought blasphemously, "in cases like this the gods are helpful, send the missing horse, add to it a second because of the urgency, and to crown everything bestow even a groom—" And only now did I remember Rose again; what was I to do, how could I rescue her, how could I pull her away from under that groom at ten miles' distance, with a team of horses I couldn't control. These horses, now, they had somehow slipped the reins loose, pushed the windows open from outside, I did not know how; each of them had stuck a head in at a window and, quite unmoved by the startled cries of the family, stood eyeing the patient. "Better go back at once," I thought, as if the horses were summoning me to the return journey, yet I permitted the patient's sister, who fancied that I was dazed by the heat, to take my fur coat from me. A glass of rum was poured out for me, the old man clapped me on the shoulder, a familiarity justified by this offer of his treasure. I shook my head; in the narrow confines of the old man's thoughts I felt ill; that was my only reason for refusing the drink. The mother stood by the bedside and cajoled me towards it; I yielded, and, while one of the horses whinnied loudly to the ceiling, laid my head to the boy's breast, which shivered under my wet beard. I confirmed what I already knew; the boy was quite sound, something a little wrong with his circulation, saturated with coffee by his solicitous mother, but sound and best turned out of bed with one shove. I am no world reformer and so I let him lie. I was the district doctor and did my duty to the uttermost, to the point where it became almost too much. I was badly paid and yet generous and helpful to the poor. I had still to see that Rose was all right, and then the boy might have his way and I wanted to die too. What was I doing there in that endless winter! My horse was dead, and not a single person in the village would lend me another. I had to get my team out of the pigsty; if they hadn't chanced to be horses I should have had to travel with swine. That was how it was. And I nodded to the family. They knew nothing about it, and, had they known, would not have believed it. To write prescriptions is easy, but to come to an understanding with people is hard. Well, this should be the end of my visit, I had once more been called out needlessly, I was used to that, the whole district made my life a torment with my night bell, but that I should have to sacrifice Rose this time as well, the pretty girl who had lived in my house for years almost without my noticing her—that sacrifice was too much to ask, and I had somehow to get it reasoned out in my head with the help of what craft I could muster, in order not to let fly at this family, which with the best will in the world could not restore Rose to me. But as I shut my bag and put an arm out for my fur coat, the family meanwhile standing together, the father sniffing at the glass of rum in his hand, the mother, apparently disappointed in me—why, what do people expect?—biting her lips with tears in her eyes, the sister fluttering a blood-soaked towel, I was somehow ready to admit conditionally that the boy might be ill after all. I went towards him, he welcomed me smiling as if I were bringing him the most nourishing invalid broth—ah, now both horses were whinnying together; the noise, I suppose, was ordained by heaven to assist my examination of the patient—and this time I discovered that the boy was indeed ill. In his right side, near the hip, was an open wound as big as the palm of my hand. Rose-red, in many variations of shade, dark in the hollows, lighter at the edges, softly granulated, with irregular clots of blood, open as a surface mine to the daylight. That was how it looked from a distance. But on a closer inspection there was another complication. I could not help a low whistle of surprise. Worms, as thick and as long as my little finger, themselves rose-red and blood-spotted as well, were wriggling from their fastness in the interior of the wound towards the light, with small white heads and many little legs. Poor boy, you were past helping. I had discovered your great wound; this blossom in your side was destroying you. The family was pleased; they saw me busying myself; the sister told the mother, the mother the father, the father told several guests who were coming in, through the moonlight at the open door, walking on tiptoe, keeping their balance with outstretched arms. "Will you save me?" whispered the boy with a sob, quite blinded by the life within his wound. That is what people are like in my district. Always expecting the impossible from the doctor. They have lost their ancient beliefs; the parson sits at home and unravels his vestments, one after another; but the doctor is supposed to be omnipotent with his merciful surgeon's hand. Well, as it pleases them; I have not thrust my services on them; if they misuse me for sacred ends, I let that happen to me too; what better do I want, old country doctor that I am, bereft of my servant girl! And so they came, the family and the village elders, and stripped my clothes off me; a school choir with the teacher at the head of it stood before the house and sang these words to an utterly simple tune:

> Strip his clothes off, then he'll heal us,
> If he doesn't, kill him dead!
> Only a doctor, only a doctor.

Then my clothes were off and I looked at the people quietly, my fingers in my beard and my head cocked to one side. I was altogether composed and equal to the situation and remained so, although it was no help to me, since they now took me by the head and feet and carried me to the bed. They laid me down in it next to the wall, on the side of the wound. Then they all left the room; the door was shut; the singing stopped; clouds covered the moon; the bedding was warm around me; the horses' heads in the open windows wavered like shadows. "Do you know," said a voice in my ear, "I have very little confidence in you. Why, you were only blown in here, you didn't come on your own feet. Instead of helping me, you're cramping me on my deathbed. What I'd like best is to scratch your eyes out." "Right," I said, "it is a shame. And yet I am a doctor. What am I to do? Believe me, it is not too easy for me either." "Am I supposed to be content with this apology? Oh, I must be, I can't help it. I always have to put up with things. A fine wound is all I brought into the world; that was my sole endowment." "My young friend," said I, "your mistake is: you have not a wide enough view. I have been in all the sickrooms, far and wide, and I tell you: your wound is not so bad. Done in a tight corner with two strokes of the ax. Many a one proffers his side and can hardly hear the ax in the forest, far less that it is coming nearer to him." "Is that really so, or are you deluding me in my fever?" "It is really so, take the word of honor of an official doctor." And he took it and lay still. But now it was time for me to think of escaping. The horses were still standing faithfully in their places. My clothes, my fur coat, my bag were quickly collected; I didn't want to waste time dressing; if the horses raced home as they had come, I should only be springing, as it were, out of this bed into my own. Obediently a horse backed away from the window; I threw my bundle into the gig; the fur coat missed its mark and was caught on a hook only by the sleeve. Good enough. I swung myself onto the horse. With the reins loosely trailing, one horse barely fastened to the other, the gig swaying behind, my fur coat last of all in the snow. "Gee up!" I said, but there was no galloping; slowly, like old men, we crawled through the snowy wastes; a long time echoed behind us the new but faulty song of the children:

> O be joyful, all you patients,
> The doctor's laid in bed beside you!

Never shall I reach home at this rate; my flourishing practice is done for; my successor is robbing me, but in vain, for he cannot take my place; in my house the disgusting groom is raging; Rose is his victim; I do not want to think about it any more. Naked, exposed to the frost of this most unhappy of ages, with an earthly vehicle, unearthly horses, old man that I am, I wander astray. My fur coat is hanging from the back of the gig, but I cannot reach it, and none of my limber pack of patients lifts a finger. Betrayed! Betrayed! A false alarm on the night bell once answered—it cannot be made good, not ever.

Translated by Willa and Edwin Muir

The Bucket Rider

Franz Kafka

COAL ALL spent; the bucket empty; the shovel useless; the stove breathing out cold; the room freezing; the trees outside the window rigid, covered with rime; the sky a silver shield against anyone who looks for help from it. I must have coal; I cannot freeze to death; behind me is the pitiless stove, before me the pitiless sky, so I must ride out between them and on my journey seek aid from the coaldealer. But he has already grown deaf to ordinary appeals; I must prove irrefutably to him that I have not a single grain of coal left, and that he means to me the very sun in the firmament. I must approach like a beggar, who, with the death rattle already in his throat, insists on dying on the doorstep, and to whom the cook accordingly decides to give the dregs of the coffeepot; just so must the coaldealer, filled with rage, but acknowledging the command "Thou shalt not kill," fling a shovelful of coal into my bucket.

My mode of arrival must decide the matter; so I ride off on the bucket. Seated on the bucket, my hands on the handle, the simplest kind of bridle, I propel myself with difficulty down the stairs; but once downstairs my bucket ascends, superbly, superbly; camels humbly squatting on the ground do not rise with more dignity, shaking themselves under the sticks of their drivers. Through the hard-frozen streets we go at a regular canter; often I am upraised as high as the first story of a house; never do I sink as low as the house doors. And at last I float at an extraordinary height above the vaulted cellar of the dealer, whom I see far below crouching over his table, where he is writing; he has opened the door to let out the excessive heat.

"Coaldealer!" I cry in a voice burned hollow by the frost and muffled in the cloud made by my breath, "please, coaldealer, give me a little coal. My bucket is so light that I can ride on it. Be kind. When I can I'll pay you."

The dealer puts his hand to his ear. "Do I hear right?" he throws the question over his shoulder to his wife. "Do I hear right? A customer."

"I hear nothing," says his wife, breathing in and out peacefully while she knits on, her back pleasantly warmed by the heat.

"Oh yes, you must hear," I cry. "It's me; an old customer; faithful and true; only without means at the moment."

"Wife," says the dealer, "it's someone, it must be; my ears can't have deceived me so much as that; it must be an old, a very old customer, that can move me so deeply."

"What ails you, man?" says his wife, ceasing from her work for a moment and pressing her knitting to her bosom. "It's nobody, the street is empty, all our customers are provided for; we could close down the shop for several days and take a rest."

"But I'm sitting up here on the bucket," I cry, and numb, frozen tears dim my eyes, "please look up here, just once; you'll see me directly; I beg you, just a shovelful; and if you give me more it'll make me so happy that I won't know what to do. All the other customers are provided for. Oh, if I could only hear the coal clattering into the bucket!"

"I'm coming," says the coaldealer, and on his short legs he makes to climb the steps of the cellar, but his wife is already beside him, holds him back by the arm and says: "You stay here; seeing you persist in your fancies I'll go myself. Think of the bad fit of coughing you had during the night. But for a piece of business, even if it's one you've only fancied in your head, you're prepared to forget your wife and child and sacrifice your lungs. I'll go."

"Then be sure to tell him all the kinds of coal we have in stock! I'll shout out the prices after you."

"Right," says his wife, climbing up to the street. Naturally she sees me at once. "Frau Coaldealer," I cry, "my humblest greetings; just one shovelful of coal; here in my bucket; I'll carry it home myself. One shovelful of the worst you have. I'll pay you in full for it, of course, but not just now, not just now." What a knell-like sound the words "not just now" have, and how bewilderingly they mingle with the evening chimes that fall from the church steeple nearby!

"Well, what does he want?" shouts the dealer. "Nothing," his wife shouts back, "there's nothing here; I see nothing, I hear nothing; only six striking, and now we must shut up the shop. The cold is terrible; tomorrow we'll likely have lots to do again."

She sees nothing and hears nothing; but all the same she loosens her apron strings and waves her apron to waft me away. She succeeds, unluckily. My bucket has all the virtues of a good steed except powers of resistance, which it has not; it is too light; a woman's apron can make it fly through the air.

"You bad woman!" I shout back, while she, turning into the shop, half-contemptuous, half-reassured, flourishes her fist in the air. "You bad woman! I begged you for a shovelful of the worst coal and you would not give it me." And with that I ascend into the regions of the ice mountains and am lost forever.

Translated by Willa and Edwin Muir

ISAAC BABEL

*I*SAAC BABEL (1894–ca. 1940) was born in Odessa, the one Russian city where a large Jewish population was permitted and where Jewish culture and intellectual life flourished. His literary aspirations led him to St. Petersburg, where he lived illegally, and into the Russian army. His famous collection of stories, Red Cavalry (1923), stemmed directly from his experience as supply officer for a Cossack regiment in Poland. As Stalinist repression set in, Babel fell from favor and was arrested in 1937. He died, sometime around 1940, in a Russian concentration camp.

While his canon is small, the range of Babel's fiction is quite impressive, from realistic sketches of army life to vivid tales of the Jewish ghetto in Odessa, highly flavored with folklore and local color. At all times he writes an arresting, rhythmic prose, which is said to be difficult to reproduce in English. We have chosen to represent him with a story which may at first glance appear to belong to folklore and traditional storytelling methods, but which, on closer inspection, breaks with those conventions and has a meaning and emphasis that are quite unusual.

The Sin of Jesus

Isaac Babel

ARINA WAS a servant at the hotel. She lived next to the main staircase, while Seryoga, the janitor's helper, lived over the back stairs. Between them there was shame. On Palm Sunday Arina gave Seryoga a present—twins. Water flows, stars shine, a man lusts, and soon Arina was big again, her sixth month was rolling by—they're slippery, a woman's months. And now, Seryoga must go into the army. There's a mess for you!

So Arina goes and says: "No sense, Seryoga. There's no sense in my waiting for you. For four years we'll be parted, and in four years, whichever way you look at it, I'll be sure to bring two or three more into this world. It's like walking around with your skirt turned up, working at the hotel. Whoever stops here, he's your master, let him be a Jew, let him be anybody at all. By the time you come home, my insides will be no good any more. I'll be a used-up woman, no match for you."

"That's so," Seryoga nodded.

"There's many that want me. Trofimych the contractor—but he's no gentleman. And Isai Abramych, the warden of Nikolo-Svyatsky Church, a feeble old man, but anyway I'm sick to the stomach of your murderous strength. I tell you this now, and I say it like I would at confession, I've got the wind plain knocked out of me. I'll spill my load in three months, then I'll take the baby to the orphanage and marry the old man."

When Seryoga heard this, he took off his belt and beat her like a hero, right on the belly.

"Look out there," Arina says to him, "go soft on the belly. It's your stuffing, no one else's."

There was no end to the beating, no end to the man's tears and the woman's blood, but that is neither here nor there.

Then the woman came to Jesus Christ.

"So on and so forth," she says, "Lord Jesus, I am the woman from the Hotel Madrid and Louvre, the one on Tverskaya Street. Working at the hotel, it's just like going around with your skirt up. Just let a man stop there, and he's your lord and master, let him be a Jew, let him be anyone at all. There is another slave of yours walking the earth, the janitor's helper, Seryoga. Last year on Palm Sunday I bore him twins."

And so she described it all to the Lord.

"And what if Seryoga were not to go into the army after all?" the Saviour suggested.

"Try and get away with it—not with the policeman around. He'll drag him off as sure as daylight."

"Oh yes, the policeman," the Lord bowed His head, "I never thought of him. Then perhaps you ought to live in purity for a while? "

"For four years?" the woman cried. "To hear you talk, all people should deny their animal nature. That's just your old ways all over again. And where will the increase come from? No, you'd better give me some sensible advice."

The Lord's cheeks turned scarlet, the woman's words had touched a tender spot. But He said nothing. You cannot kiss your own ear—even God knows that.

"I'll tell you what, God's servant, glorious sinner, maiden Arina," the Lord proclaimed in all His glory, "I have a little angel here in heaven, hanging around uselessly. His name is Alfred. Lately he's gotten out of hand altogether, keeps crying and nagging all the time: "What have you done to me, Lord? Why do you turn me into an angel in my twentieth year, and me a hale young fellow?' So I'll give you Alfred the angel as a husband for four years. He'll be your prayer, he'll be your protection, and he'll be your solace. And as for offspring, you've nothing to worry about—you can't bear a duckling from him, let alone a baby, for there's a lot of fun in him, but no seriousness."

"That's just what I need," the maid Arina wept gratefully. "Their seriousness takes me to the doorstep of the grave three times every two years."

"You'll have a sweet respite, God's child Arina. May your prayer be light as a song. Amen."

And so it was decided. Alfred was brought in—a frail young fellow, delicate, two wings fluttering behind his pale-blue shoulders, rippling with rosy light like two doves playing in heaven. Arina threw her hefty arms about him, weeping out of tenderness, our of her woman's soft heart.

"Alfred, my soul, my consolation, my bridegroom . . ."

In parting, the Lord gave her strict instructions to take off the angel's wings every night before he went to bed. His wings were attached to hinges, like a door, and every night she was to take them off and wrap them in a clean sheet, because they were brittle, his wings, and could snap as he tossed in bed—for what were they made of but the sighs of babes, no more than that.

For the last time the Lord blessed the union, while the choir of bishops, called in for the occasion, rendered thunderous praises. No food was served, not a crumb—that wasn't the style in heaven—and then Arina and Alfred, their arms about each other, ran down a silken ladder, straight back to earth. They came to Petrovka, the street where nothing but the best is sold. The woman would do right by her Alfred for he, if one might say so, not only lacked socks, but was altogether as natural as when his mother bore him. And she bought him patent-leather half-boots, checked jersey trousers, a fine hunting jacket, and an electric-blue vest.

"The rest," she says, "we'll find at home."

That day Arina begged off from work. Seryoga came and raised a fuss, but she did not even come out to him, only said from behind her locked door:

"Sergey Nifantyich, I am at present a-washing my feet and beg you to retire without further noise."

He went away without a word—the angel's power was already beginning to manifest itself!

In the evening Arina set out a supper fit for a merchant—the woman had devilish vanity! A half-pint of vodka, wine on the side, a Danube herring with potatoes, a samovar of tea. When Alfred had partaken of all these earthly blessings, he keeled over in a dead sleep. Quick as a wink, Arina lifted off his wings from the hinges, packed them away, and carried him to bed in her arms.

There it lies, the snowy wonder on the eiderdown pillows of her tattered, sinful bed, sending forth a heavenly radiance: moon-silver shafts of light pass and repass, alternate with red ones, float across the floor, sway over his shining feet. Arina weeps and rejoices, sings and prays. Arina, thou hast been granted a happiness unheard of on this battered earth. Blessed art thou among women!

They had drunk the vodka to the last drop, and now it took effect. As soon as they fell asleep, she went and rolled over on top of Alfred with her hot, six-months-big belly. Not enough for her to sleep with an angel, not enough that nobody beside her spat at the wall, snored and snorted—that wasn't enough for the clumsy, ravening slut. No, she had to warm her belly too, her burning belly big with Seryoga's lust. And so she smothered him in her fuddled sleep, smothered him like a week-old babe in the midst of her rejoicing, crushed him under her bloated weight, and he gave up the ghost, and his wings, wrapped in her sheet, wept pale tears.

Dawn came—and all the trees bowed low to the ground. In distant northern forests each fir tree turned into a priest, each fir tree bent its knees in silent worship.

Once more the woman stands before the Lord's throne. She is broad in the shoulders, mighty, the young corpse drooping in her huge red arms.

"Behold, Lord ..."

But here the gentle heart of Jesus could endure no more, and He cursed the woman in His anger:

"As it is on earth, so shall it be with you, Arina, from this day on."

"How is it then, Lord?" the woman replied in a scarcely audible voice. "Was it I who made my body heavy, was it I that brewed vodka on earth, was it I that created a woman's soul, stupid and lonely?"

"I don't wish to be bothered with you," exclaimed the Lord Jesus. "You've smothered my angel, you filthy scum."

And Arina was thrown back to earth on a putrid wind, straight down to Tverskaya Street, to the Hotel Madrid and Louvre, where she was doomed to spend her days. And once there, the sky was the limit. Seryoga was carousing, drinking away his last days, seeing as he was a recruit. The contractor Trofimych, just come from Kolomna, took one look at Arina, hefty and red-cheeked: "Oh, you cute little belly," he said, and so on and so forth.

Isai Abramych, the old codger, heard about this cute little belly, and he was right there too, wheezing toothlessly:

"I cannot wed you lawfully," he said, "after all that happened. However, I can lie with you the same as anyone."

The old man ought to be lying in cold mother earth instead of thinking of such things, but no, he too must take his turn at spitting into her soul. It was as though they had all slipped the chain—kitchen-boys, merchants, foreigners. A fellow in trade—he likes to have his fun.

And that is the end of my tale.

Before she was laid up, for three months had rolled by in the meantime, Arina went out into the back yard, behind the janitor's rooms, raised her monstrous belly to the silken sky, and said stupidly:

"See, Lord, what a belly! They hammer at it like peas falling in a colander. And what sense there's in it I just can't see. But I've had enough."

With His tears Jesus laved Arina when He heard these words. The Saviour fell on His knees before her.

"Forgive me, little Arina. Forgive your sinful God for all He has done to you ..."

But Arina shook her head and would not listen.

"There's no forgiveness for you, Jesus Christ," she said. "No forgiveness, and never will be."

Translated by Mirra Ginsburg

YURI OLESHA

YURI OLESHA (1899–1960), like many Russian writers of his generation, began as a supporter of the Revolution and soon grew disillusioned with it. Some of his writing satirizes the soviet bureaucracy, most notably the short novel Envy (1928), which he also turned into a play. Other pieces look beyond the exasperations of social injustice to large matters of life and death, as in the story included here, "Lyompa," an extraordinary blend of realism and wonder. It shows us an animistic world that we soon come to realize is the child's sense of reality, and at the same time it takes us beyond the child's understanding, to the terrible fact of death. For the most part it accomplishes this quite simply, through careful selection of detail and striking metaphor. "Lyompa" may be the one story by Olesha that fully deserves to be thought of as magic realist, but it is as deserving of that designation as a story could possibly be.

Olesha found it impossible to pursue a career as a writer of serious fiction. The predominant aesthetic of socialist realism fit neither his satirical nor his magical-realist tendencies. Therefore, he turned to journalism. Olesha was imprisoned in the Stalinist purges of 1938 and again after World War II, yet he managed to survive and was freed during Khrushchev's "thaw." He died in 1960. Readers of "Lyompa" will share our sense of loss that such a gifted writer did not develop the potential which lies behind this splendidly realized study in magical realism.

Lyompa

Yuri Olesha

YOUNG ALEXANDER was planing wood in the kitchen. The cuts on his fingers were covered with golden, appetizing scabs.

The kitchen gave onto the courtyard. It was spring and the doors were always open. There was grass growing near the entrance. Water poured from a pail glistened on the stone slabs. A rat appeared in the garbage can. Finely sliced potatoes were frying in the kitchen. The primus stoves were burning; their life began in a burst of splendor when the orange flame shot ceiling-high. It ended in a quiet blue flame. Eggs jumped around in boiling water. One of the tenants was cooking crabs. With two fingers, he picked up a live crab by the waist. The crabs were greenish, the color of the waterpipes. Two or three drops suddenly shot out of the tap. The tap was discreetly blowing its nose. Then, upstairs somewhere, pipes began talking in a variety of voices. The dusk was becoming perceptible. One glass continued to glisten on the window sill, as it received the last rays of the setting sun. The taps chattered. All sorts of moving and knocking started up around the stove.

The dusk was magnificent. People were eating peanuts. There was singing. The yellow light from the rooms fell on the dark sidewalk. The grocery store was brightly lit.

In the room next to the kitchen lay Ponomarev, critically ill. He lay in his room alone. There was a candle burning; a medicine bottle with a prescription attached to it stood on a table at his head.

When people came to see Ponomarev, he said to them:

"You can congratulate me: I'm dying."

In the evening he became delirious. The bottle was staring at him.

153

The prescription was like the train of a wedding dress, the bottle a princess on her wedding day. The bottle had a long name. He wanted to write a treatise. He was talking to his blanket.

"You ought to be ashamed of yourself. . ."

The blanket sat next to him, lay next to him, told him the latest news.

There were only a few things around the sick man: the medicine, the spoon, the light, the wallpaper. The other things had left. When he found he was critically ill and about to die, he realized how huge and varied was the world of things and how few were the things that remained to him. Every day fewer of these things were left. A familiar object like a railroad ticket was already irretrievably remote. First, the number of things on the periphery, far away from him, decreased; then this depletion drew closer to the center, reaching deeper and deeper, toward the courtyard, the house, the corridor, the room, his heart.

At first, the disappearance of things did not particularly sadden the sick man.

The countries had gone: America; then the possibilities: being handsome, rich, having a family (he was single). . . Actually, his sickness was unrelated to their disappearance. They had slipped away as he had grown older. But he was really hurt to realize that even the things moving parallel with his course were growing more remote. In a single day he was abandoned by the street, his job, the mail, horses. Then the disappearances began to occur at a mad rate, right there, alongside him: already the corridor had slipped out of reach and, in his very room, his coat, the door key, his shoes had lost all significance. Death was destroying things on its way to him. Death had left him only a few things, from an infinite number; things he would never have permitted in his house by choice. He had things forced on him. He had the frightening visits and looks of people he knew. He saw he had no chance of defending himself from the intrusion of these unsolicited and, to him, useless things. But now they were compulsory, the only ones. He had lost the right to choose.

Young Alexander was making a model plane.

The boy was much more serious and complex than people imagined. He kept cutting his fingers, bleeding, littering the floor with his shavings, leaving dirty marks with his glue, scrounging bits of silk, crying, being pushed around. The grownups considered themselves absolutely right, although the boy acted in a perfectly adult way, as only a very small number of adults are capable of acting. He acted scientifically. He was following a blueprint in constructing his model, making calculations, respecting the laws of nature. To adult attacks he could have opposed an explanation of the laws, a demonstration of his experiments. He remained silent, however, feeling it was not right for him to look more serious than adults.

The boy was surrounded by rubber bands, coils of wire, sheets of plywood, silk, and the smell of glue. Above him the sky glistened. Under his feet, insects crawled over the stones, and a stone had a little petrified shell embedded in it.

From time to time, while the boy was deep in his work, another boy, quite tiny, would approach him. He was naked except for a tiny pair of blue trunks. He touched things and got in the way. Alexander would chase him away. The naked boy, who looked as if he were made of rubber, wandered all over the house. In the corridor was a bicycle leaning with its pedal against the wall. The pedal had scratched the paint, and the bike gripped the wall by the scratch.

The little boy dropped in on Ponomarev. The child's head bounced around like a ball near the edge of the bed. The sick man's temples were pale, like those of a blind man. The boy came close to Ponomarev's head and examined it. He thought it had always been this way in the world: a bearded man lying in a bed in a room. The little boy had just learned to recognize things; he did not yet know how to distinguish time in their existence.

He turned away and walked around the room. He saw the floorboards, the dust between them, the cracks in the plaster. Around him lines joined and moved and bodies formed. Sometimes a wonderful pattern of light appeared. The child started rushing toward it, but before he had even taken a full step, the change of distance killed the illusion. The child looked up, back, behind the fireplace, searching for it and moving his hands in bewilderment. Each second gave him a new thing. There was an amazing spider over there. The spider vanished at the boy's mere desire to touch it with his hand.

The vanishing things left the dying man nothing but their names.

There was an apple in the world. It glistened amidst the leaves; it seized little bits of the day and gently twirled them round: the green of the garden, the outline of the window. The law of gravity awaited it under the tree, on the black earth, on the knoll. Beady ants scampered among the knolls. Newton sat in the garden. There were many causes hidden inside the apple, causes that could determine a multitude of effects. But none of these causes had anything to do with Ponomarev. The apple had become an abstraction. The fact that the flesh of a thing had disappeared while the abstraction remained was painful to him.

"I thought there was no outside world," he mused. "I thought my eye and my ear ruled things. I thought the world would cease to exist when I ceased to exist. But I still exist! So why don't the things? I thought they got their shape, their weight, their color from my brain. But they have left me, leaving behind only useless names, names that pester my brain."

Ponomarev looked at the child nostalgically. The child walked around. Things rushed to meet him. He smiled at them, not knowing any of them by name. He left the room and the magnificent procession of things trailed after him.

"Listen," the sick man called out to the child, "do you know that when I die, nothing will remain? They will all be gone—the courtyard, the tree, Daddy, Mummy. I'll take everything along with me."

A rat got into the kitchen.

Ponomarev listened: the rat was making itself at home, rattling the plates, opening the tap, making scraping sounds in the bucket.

"Why, someone must be washing dishes in there," Ponomarev decided.

Immediately he became worried: perhaps the rat had a proper name people did not know. He wondered what this name could be. He was delirious. As he thought, fear seized him more and more powerfully. He knew that at any cost he must stop thinking about the rat's name. But he kept searching for it, knowing that as soon as he found that meaningless, horrifying name, he would die.

"Lyompa!" he suddenly shouted in a terrifying voice.

The house was asleep. It was very early in the morning, just after five. Young Alexander was awake. The kitchen door giving onto the courtyard was open. The sun was still down somewhere.

The dying man was wandering about in the kitchen. He was bent forward, arms extended, wrists hanging limp. He was collecting things to take away with him.

Alexander dashed across the courtyard. The model plane flew ahead of him. It was the last thing Ponomarev saw.

He did not collect it. It flew away.

Later that day, a blue coffin with yellow ornaments made its appearance in the kitchen. The little rubber boy stared at it from the corridor, his little hands holding one another behind his back. The coffin had to be turned every which way to get it through the door. It banged against a shelf. Pans fell to the floor. There was a brief shower of plaster. Alexander climbed on the stove and helped to pull the box through. When the coffin finally got into the corridor, it immediately became black and the rubber boy ran along the passage, his feet slapping the floor:

"Grandpa! Grandpa! They've brought you a coffin."

Translated by Andrew R. MacAndrew

OSIP
EMILIEVICH
MANDELSTAM

*O*SIP EMILIEVICH MANDELSTAM (1891–1938), *one of the great poets of this century, was born in Warsaw, grew up in St. Petersburg, and died as one of Stalin's countless victims in a camp for political prisoners near Vladivostock. He had first been arrested in 1934 for writing a satirical poem about Stalin; from then on it was not a matter of whether his defiance would cost him his life, but only when. By writing the poem and reading it aloud to a group of friends, one of whom promptly reported it to the secret police, Mandelstam can be said to have provoked his own death; for a poet of his integrity and authority, life in Russia had become intolerable.*

Mandelstam's prose consists mostly of autobiographical pieces, literary criticism, and travel writing. His one experimental novel, The Egyptian Stamp (1928), shows what this remarkable poet could do when he turned to fiction. As in the cases of Rilke and Elizabeth Bishop, a poet's sensibility, when trained on the conventions and procedures of ordinary fiction, can produce the extraordinary blend called magical realism.

The first chapter of The Egyptian Stamp, translated admirably by Clarence Brown (who has also collaborated with W. S. Merwin on the best translations of Mandelstam's poems) is presented here. This small sample will demonstrate the remarkable, and initially disorienting, texture of Mandelstam's prose. Different realities are mingled in an extravagant blend of possibilities, shifting ground and point of view without warning. Brilliant metaphors enhance the strangeness and wonder of the story. The narrator, who owes more than a little to Gogol's narrator in "The Nose," means to tell the story of a man named Parnok, whose coat is taken by his tailor while he is sleeping, and who goes to reclaim it the next day. The narrator, however, is easily distracted by the wonderful objects that make up the world—a grand piano, for example, is

157

"like a lacquered black meteor fallen from the sky"—and has trouble carrying the narrative forward. In the same way, Parnok is easily distracted from his mission by a map of the hemispheres and a partition on which a number of pictures have been pasted. The tension between narrative and a contrary impulse to extract things from the stream of time and the normal relationships of cause and effect, is what creates the delightful, if somewhat bewildering, world of The Egyptian Stamp. Readers intrigued by it will want to seek out the whole work, partly to see what becomes of Parnok and partly for the brilliant textures and arresting metaphors that Mandelstam brings to his storytelling.

The Egyptian Stamp

Osip Emilievich Mandelstam

I do not like rolled-up manuscripts. Some of them are heavy and smeared with time, like the trumpet of the archangel.

THE POLISH serving girl had gone into the church of Guarenghi to gossip and to pray to the Holy Virgin.

That night there had been a dream of a Chinaman, bedecked in ladies' handbags, like a necklace of partridges, and of an American duel in which the opponents fired their pistols at cabinets of chinaware, at inkpots, and at family portraits.

I propose to you, my family, a coat of arms: a glass of boiled water. In the rubbery aftertaste of Petersburg's boiled water I drink my unsuccessful domestic immortality. The centrifugal force of time has scattered our Viennese chairs and Dutch plates with little blue flowers. Nothing is left. Thirty years have passed like a slow fire. For thirty years a cold white flame has licked at the backs of mirrors, where the bailiff's tags are attached.

But how can I tear myself away from you, dear Egypt of objects? The clear eternity of dining room, bedroom, study. With what excuse cover my guilt? You wish Walhalla? The warehouses of Kokorev! Go there for salvation! Already the porters, dancing in horror, are lifting the grand

Excerpt from *The Egyptian Stamp.*

piano (a Mignon) like a lacquered black meteor fallen from the sky. Bast mats are spread like the chasubles of priests. The cheval-glass floats sideways down the staircase, maneuvering its palm-tree length about the landings.

That evening Parnok had hung his morning coat on the back of a Viennese chair so that during the night it might rest its shoulders and arm holes and have out its sleep in the solid slumber of a cheviot. Who knows? Perhaps on its Viennese chair the morning coat turns somersaults, becomes young again—in short, frolics about? This invertebrate companion of young men pines for the triptych of mirrors at the fashionable tailor's. At the fitting it had been a simple sack—something like a knight's armor or a dubious camisole—which the artistic tailor had covered with designs in his Pythagorean chalk and inspired with life and fluent ease:

—Go, my beauty, and live! Strut at concerts, give talks, love, and make your mistakes!

—Oh, Mervis, Mervis, what have you done? Why have you deprived Parnok of his earthly shell, why parted him from his beloved sister?

—Is he asleep?

—He's sleep! The scamp—it's a pity to waste electric light on him!

The last coffee beans disappeared down the crater of the coffee-grinder, shaped like a barrel-organ.

The abduction was accomplished.

Mervis carried her off like a Sabine woman.

We count by years, but in reality, in any apartment on Kamenoostrovskij, time is cleft into dynasties and centuries.

The management of a house is always rather grand. One cannot embrace the termini of a life: from the moment when one has comprehended the gothic German alphabet all the way to the golden fat of the university's *piroshki.*

The proud and touchy odor of gasoline and the greasy smell of the dear old kerosene protect the apartment, vulnerable as it is to attack from the kitchen, where porters break through with their catapults of firewood. Dusty rags and brushes warm up its white blood.

In the beginning there had been a workbench here—and Il'in's map of the hemispheres.

From this Parnok drew solace. He was consoled by the linen paper, which could not be torn. Poking with his penholder at oceans and continents, he plotted the itineraries of grandiose voyages, comparing the airy outlines of Aryan Europe with the blunt boot of Africa, with inexpressive Australia. In South America, beginning with Patagonia, he also found a certain keenness.

His respect for Il'in's map had remained in Parnok's blood since those fabulous years when he imagined that the aquamarine and ochre hemispheres, like two enormous balls held in the net of latitudes, had been empowered for their visual mission by the white-hot chancellery in the very bowels of the earth and that, like nutritional pills, they contained within themselves condensed space and distance.

Is it not with the same feeling that a singer of the Italian school, preparing to take off on her tour of a still young America, covers the geographical chart with her voice, measures the ocean with its metallic timbre, and checks the inexperienced pulse of the steamship engines with roulades and tremolos...

Upside down on the retina of her eye are those same two Americas, like two green gamebags containing Washington and the Amazon. By her maiden voyage on the salt sea she inaugurates the map as she reads her fortune in dollars and Russian hundred-rouble notes with their wintry crunch.

The fifties deceived her. No *bel canto* could have brightened them up. Everywhere the same low sky like a draped ceiling, the same smoky reading rooms, the same lances of the *Times* and the *Gazettes* plunged into the heart's core of the century. And, finally, Russia ...

Her little ears will begin to tickle: *kreshchatik, shchastie* and *shchavel'*. And her mouth will be stretched to her ears by the unheard of, the impossible sound bI.

And then the Cavalier Guards will flock to the church of Guarenghi for the singing of the requiem. The golden vultures will rend to pieces the Roman Catholic songstress.

How high they placed her! Could that really be death? Death would not dare to open its mouth in the presence of the diplomatic corps.

—We shall overwhelm her with plumes, with gendarmes, with Mozart!

At this moment the delirious images of the novels of Balzac and Stendhal flitted through his mind: young men in the act of conquering Paris and flicking at their shoes with handkerchiefs as they stand at the entrances of private residences—and off he went to recapture his morning coat.

The tailor Mervis lived on Monetnaja, right next to the lycée, but it was difficult to say whether he worked for the students; that was rather taken for granted, as it is taken for granted that a fisherman on the Rhine catches trout and not some sort of filth. Everything indicated that the mind of Mervis was occupied by something more important than his job as tailor. It was not for nothing that his relatives came running to him from distant places just as his client backed away in stupefaction and repentance.

—Who will give my children their roll and butter? said Mervis, gesturing with his hand as though he were scooping up some butter, and in the birdy air of the tailor's apartment Parnok had a vision not only of butter molded in the shape of a star and crimped with dewy petals but even of a bunch of radishes. Then Mervis cleverly turned the conversation first to the lawyer Grusenberg, who had ordered a senator's uniform from him in January, and then for some reason to his son Aron, a student at the Conservatory, became confused, began to fluster, and plunged behind a partition.

—Well, thought Parnok, perhaps it had to turn out this way. Perhaps the morning coat is no longer here, perhaps he actually did sell it, as he says, to pay for the cheviot.

Furthermore, if one thinks about it, Mervis has no real feeling for the cutting of a morning coat. With him it always turns out to be a frock coat—something obviously more familiar to him.

Lucien de Rubempré wore rough linen underwear and an awkward suit sewn by the village tailor; he ate chestnuts in the street and was terrified of concierges. Once, on a fortunate day for himself, he was shaving when the future came to life in his lather.

Parnok stood alone, forgotten by the tailor Mervis and his family. His gaze fell on the partition, behind which hummed a woman's contralto like viscous Jewish honey. This partition, pasted over with pictures, resembled a rather bizarre iconostasis.

There, dressed in a fur coat and with a distorted face, was Pushkin, whom some gentry resembling torchbearers were carrying out of a carriage, narrow as a sentry box, and, disregarding the astonished coachman in his archbishop's cap, were about to fling into the doorway. Alongside this the old-fashioned pilot of the nineteenth century, Santos-Dumont, in his double-breasted jacket behung with pendants, having been thrown by the play of elements from the basket of his balloon, was depicted hanging by a rope and peering at a soaring condor. There was next a representation of some Dutchmen on stilts, who were running all about their little country like cranes.

Translated by Clarence Brown

VIRGINIA WOOLF

*V*IRGINIA WOOLF (1882–1941) *was one of the major experimental novelists of this century. Despite severe episodes of mental illness—she was manic-depressive and eventually committed suicide because she feared further attacks—she managed an impressive canon not only of fiction but of first-rate literary journalism and feminist writing. In addition, she was the center of the Bloomsbury Group, an informal network of intellectuals and artists who profoundly influenced modern art and thought. With her husband Leonard Woolf, she founded the Hogarth Press, which helped introduce the work of new writers like T. S. Eliot.*

In her novels, which were in strong reaction to the naturalistic mode in fiction, Virginia Woolf showed great interest in the exploration of consciousness. Her initial influence in that area was Henry James, and her experiments led her into the technique called "stream of consciousness" that was also being explored by James Joyce. The emphasis on the inner world of her characters and the relativity of experience imposed by individual consciousness took her in a different direction from magical realism (see Introduction), but that her fiction often shared common ground with the tradition we have associated with Kafka and Borges is shown not only by the present selection but by moments in some of her novels such as Mrs. Dalloway (1925), To the Lighthouse (1927), or The Waves (1931), where ordinary reality drops away and is replaced by a greatly expanded sense of time and space. Our selection is from Orlando (1928), one of her most unusual novels, a bravura fantasy about a character who lives three-and-a-half centuries and changes from a man to a woman. It can be said to continue a tradition composed of works like Gargantuas, Gulliver's Travels, and Alice in Wonderland, and to anticipate the exploration of the origins of fiction in romances and tales by writers like Borges and Calvino. In that respect, as well as in its strong interest in the relation between creativity and the breakdown of gender differences, Orlando can be said to have been ahead of its time.

It is customary to point out that Virginia Woolf is a great stylist, meaning that her use of language is original, distinctive, and unusually expressive. This observation is sometimes a covert gesture of dismissal, as if implying that a novelist should have better things to do than produce "purple passages" and special effects through language. But style, as Proust tells us, is for the writer not merely a matter of technique, but of vision, a truth that could be illustrated by countless passages from Virginia Woolf's great body of fiction and is certainly exemplified, though perhaps not very typically, in the selection presented here.

The Great Frost

Virginia Woolf

THE GREAT Frost was, historians tell us, the most severe that has ever visited these islands. Birds froze in mid-air and fell like stones to the ground. At Norwich a young countrywoman started to cross the road in her usual robust health and was seen by the onlookers to turn visibly to powder and be blown in a puff of dust over the roofs as the icy blast struck her at the street corner. The mortality among sheep and cattle was enormous. Corpses froze and could not be drawn from the sheets. It was no uncommon sight to come upon a whole herd of swine frozen immovable upon the road. The fields were full of shepherds, ploughmen, teams of horses, and little bird-scaring boys all struck stark in the act of the moment, one with his hand to his nose, another with the bottle to his lips, a third with a stone raised to throw at the raven who sat, as if stuffed, upon the hedge within a yard of him. The severity of the frost was so extraordinary that a kind of petrifaction sometimes ensued; and it was commonly supposed that the great increase of rocks in some parts of Derbyshire was due to no eruption, for there was none, but to the solidification of unfortunate wayfarers who had been turned literally to stone where they stood. The Church could give little help in the matter, and though some landowners had these relics blessed, the most part preferred to use them either as landmarks, scratching-posts for sheep, or, when the form of the stone allowed, drinking troughs for cattle, which purposes they serve, admirably for the most part, to this day.

But while the country people suffered the extremity of want, and the

Excerpt from the novel *Orlando*.

trade of the country was at a standstill, London enjoyed a carnival of the utmost brilliancy. The Court was at Greenwich, and the new King seized the opportunity that his coronation gave him to curry favour with the citizens. He directed that the river, which was frozen to a depth of twenty feet and more for six or seven miles on either side, should be swept, decorated, and given all the semblance of a park or pleasure ground, with arbours, mazes, alleys, drinking booths, etc., at his expense. For himself and the courtiers, he reserved a certain space immediately opposite the Palace gates; which, railed off from the public only by a silken rope, became at once the centre of the most brilliant society in England. Great statesmen, in their beards and ruffs, dispatched affairs of state under the crimson awning of the Royal Pagoda. Soldiers planned the conquest of the Moor and the downfall of the Turk in striped arbours surmounted by plumes of ostrich feathers. Admirals strode up and down the narrow pathways, glass in hand, sweeping the horizon and telling stories of the north-west passage and the Spanish Armada. Lovers dallied upon divans spread with sables. Frozen roses fell in showers when the Queen and her ladies walked abroad. Coloured balloons hovered motionless in the air. Here and there burnt vast bonfires of cedar and oak wood, lavishly salted, so that the flames were of green, orange, and purple fire. But however fiercely they burnt, the heat was not enough to melt the ice which, though of singular transparency, was yet of the hardness of steel. So clear indeed was it that there could be seen, congealed at a depth of several feet, here a porpoise, there a flounder. Shoals of eels lay motionless in a trance, but whether their state was one of death or merely of suspended animation which the warmth would revive puzzled the philosophers. Near London Bridge where the river had frozen to a depth of some twenty fathoms, a wrecked wherry boat was plainly visible, lying on the bed of the river where it had sunk last autumn, overladen with apples. The old bumboat woman, who was carrying her fruit to market on the Surrey side, sat there in her plaids and farthingales with her lap full of apples, for all the world as if she were about to serve a customer, though a certain blueness about the lips hinted the truth. 'Twas a sight King James specially liked to look upon, and he would bring a troupe of courtiers to gaze with him. In short, nothing could exceed the brilliancy and gaiety of the scene by day. But it was at night that the carnival was at its merriest. For the frost continued unbroken; the nights were of perfect stillness; the moon and stars blazed with the hard fixity of diamonds, and to the fine music of flute and trumpet the courtiers danced.

Orlando, it is true, was none of those who tread lightly the coranto and lavolta; he was clumsy and a little absent-minded. He much preferred the plain dances of his own country, which he had danced as a child, to these fantastic foreign measures. He had indeed just brought his feet together about six in the evening of the seventh of January at the finish of some such quadrille or minuet when he beheld, coming from the pavilion of the Muscovite Embassy, a figure, which, whether boy's or woman's, for the loose tunic and trousers of the Russian fashion served to disguise the sex, filled him with the highest curiosity. The person, whatever the name or sex, was about middle height, very slenderly fashioned, and dressed entirely in oyster-coloured velvet, trimmed with some unfamiliar greenish-coloured fur. But these details were obscured by the extraordinary seductiveness which issued from the whole person. Images, metaphors of the most extreme and extravagant, twined and twisted in his mind. He called her a melon, a pineapple, an olive tree, an emerald, and a fox in the snow all in the space of three seconds; he did not know whether he had heard her, tasted her, seen her, or all three together. (For though we must pause not a moment in the narrative we may here hastily note that all his images at this time were simple in the extreme to match his senses and were mostly taken from things he had liked the taste of as a boy. But if his senses were simple they were at the same time extremely strong. To pause therefore and seek the reason of things is out of the question.) . . . A melon, an emerald, a fox in the snow—so he raved, so he called her. When the boy, for alas, a boy it must be—no woman could skate with such speed and vigour—swept almost on tiptoe past him, Orlando was ready to tear his hair with vexation that the person was of his own sex, and thus all embraces were out of the question. But the skater came closer. Legs, hands, carriage, were a boy's, but no boy ever had a mouth like that; no boy had those breasts; no boy had those eyes which looked as if they had been fished from the bottom of the sea. Finally, coming to a stop and sweeping a curtsey with the utmost grace to the King, who was shuffling past on the arm of some Lord-in-waiting, the unknown skater came to a standstill. She was not a handsbreadth off. She was a woman. Orlando stared; trembled; turned hot; turned cold; longed to hurl himself through the summer air; to crush acorns beneath his feet; to toss his arms with the beech trees and the oaks. As it was, he drew his lips up over his small white teeth; opened them perhaps half an inch as if to bite; shut them as if he had bitten. The Lady Euphrosyne hung upon his arm.

The stranger's name, he found, was the Princess Marousha Stanilovska Dagmar Natasha Iliana Romanovitch, and she had come in the train of the Muscovite Ambassador, who was her uncle perhaps, or perhaps her father, to attend the coronation. Very little was known of the Muscovites. In their great beards and furred hats they sat almost silent; drinking some black liquid which they spat out now and then upon the ice. None spoke English, and French with which some at least were familiar was then little spoken at the English Court.

It was through this accident that Orlando and the Princess became acquainted. They were seated opposite each other at the great table spread under a huge awning for the entertainment of the notables. The Princess was placed between two young Lords, one Lord Francis Vere and the other the young Earl of Moray. It was laughable to see the predicament she soon had them in, for though both were fine lads in their way, the babe unborn had as much knowledge of the French tongue as they had. When at the beginning of dinner the Princess turned to the Earl and said, with a grace which ravished his heart, "*Je crois avoir fait la connaissance d'un gentilhomme qui vous était apparenté en Pologne l'été dernier,*" or "*La beauté des dames de la cour d'Angleterre me met dans le ravissement. On ne peut voir une dame plus gracieuse que votre reine, ni une coiffure plus belle que la sienne,*" both Lord Francis and the Earl showed the highest embarrassment. The one helped her largely to horse-radish sauce, the other whistled to his dog and made him beg for a marrow bone. At this the Princess could no longer contain her laughter, and Orlando, catching her eyes across the boars' heads and stuffed peacocks, laughed too. He laughed, but the laugh on his lips froze in wonder. Whom had he loved, what had he loved, he asked himself in a tumult of emotion, until now? An old woman, he answered, all skin and bone. Red-cheeked trulls too many to mention. A puling nun. A hard-bitten, cruel-mouthed adventuress. A nodding mass of lace and ceremony. Love had meant to him nothing but sawdust and cinders. The joys he had had of it tasted insipid in the extreme. He marvelled how he could have gone through with it without yawning. For as he looked the thickness of his blood melted; the ice turned to wine in his veins; he heard the waters flowing and the birds singing; spring broke over the hard wintry landscape; his manhood woke; he grasped a sword in his hand; he charged a more daring foe than Pole or Moor; he dived in deep water; he saw the flower of danger growing in a crevice; he stretched his hand—in fact he was rattling off one of his most impassioned sonnets when the Princess addressed him, "Would you have the goodness to pass the salt?"

He blushed deeply.

"With all the pleasure in the world, Madame," he replied, speaking French with a perfect accent. For, heaven be praised, he spoke the tongue as his own; his mother's maid had taught him. Yet perhaps it would have been better for him had he never learnt that tongue; never answered that voice; never followed the light of those eyes. . . .

BRUNO SCHULZ

*B*RUNO SCHULZ (1892–1942), *one of the most talented Eastern European writers of this century, led a secluded life in Drogobych in southeastern Poland, where he taught art in a secondary school. He was hesitant about publishing his work, and it was not until 1934 that his first collection of stories appeared,* Cinnamon Shops, *which has been translated in English under the title* The Street of Crocodiles. *This entire book is a wonderful excursion into the private and fantastic world of childhood memories, imbued with lush, poetic visions, and superficially resembling an autobiographical novel. A further collection of stories,* Sanatorium under the Sign of the Hourglass, *was published in 1937, and his only other known work consisted of a translation of Kafka's* The Trial, *and an unfinished novel,* The Messiah. *Another one of the tragic victims of the Holocaust, Schulz, who was Jewish, perished under the Nazi regime in 1942.*

Schulz was a solitary individual, living apart in his complex, inner dreamworld, and although certainly influenced to some extent by Mann, Freud, Rilke, and Kafka, he struck out to explore his own fertile, imaginative territory. All of Schulz's writing is richly textured in layer upon layer of deft description, and yet, as in all good examples of magical realism, most of the stories are grounded in reality, in this case the often drab reality of ordinary life.

Like Kafka, Schulz found his Jewish ancestry problematical, and even though he spoke German fluently, he was more comfortable writing in Polish. Again like Kafka, he suffered from periods of depression and encountered failed relationships, so he confronted the mystery of existence by creating his own fantastic cosmos. But central to Schulz's mythology is a remarkably eccentric father figure, based loosely on Schulz's own merchant father. This character is otherworldly and wizard-like, usually pathetically obsessed, but Schulz regards him with much affection and awe, as contrasted with the domineering and threatening father in Kafka's fiction. The title story of The Street of Crocodiles *presented here is inspired in part by the father figure. An imprecise and undecided reality unfolds so cleverly before the reader's eyes that one relishes each sleight of hand in the tricky narration and, as is typical of magical realist fiction, the question of what is "reality" becomes the main focal point.*

The Street of
Crocodiles

Bruno Schulz

M Y FATHER kept in the lower drawer of his large desk an old and
beautiful map of our city. It was a whole folio sheaf of
parchment pages which, originally fastened with strips of linen, formed
an enormous wall map, a bird's-eye panorama.

Hung on the wall, the map covered it almost entirely and opened a
wide view on the valley of the River Tysmienica, which wound itself like a
wavy ribbon of pale gold, on the maze of widely spreading ponds and
marshes, on the high ground rising toward the south, gently at first, then
in ever tighter ranges, in a chessboard of rounded hills, smaller and paler
as they receded toward the misty yellow fog of the horizon. From that
faded distance of the periphery, the city rose and grew toward the center
of the map, an undifferentiated mass at first, a dense complex of blocks
and houses, cut by deep canyons of streets, to become on the first plan a
group of single houses, etched with the sharp clarity of a landscape seen
through binoculars. In that section of the map, the engraver concentrated on the complicated and manifold profusion of streets and alley-
ways, the sharp lines of cornices, architraves, archivolts, and pilasters, lit
by the dark gold of a late and cloudy afternoon which steeped all corners
and recesses in the deep sepia of shade. The solids and prisms of that
shade darkly honeycombed the ravines of streets, drowning in a warm
color here half a street, there a gap between houses. They dramatized
and orchestrated in a bleak romantic chiaroscuro the complex
architectural polyphony.

On that map, made in the style of baroque panoramas, the area of the Street of Crocodiles shone with the empty whiteness that usually marks polar regions or unexplored countries of which almost nothing is known. The lines of only a few streets were marked in black and their names given in simple, unadorned lettering, different from the noble script of the other captions. The cartographer must have been loath to include that district in the city and his reservations found expression in the typographical treatment.

In order to understand these reservations, we must draw attention to the equivocal and doubtful character of that peculiar area, so unlike the rest of the city.

It was an industrial and commercial district, its soberly utilitarian character glaringly underlined. The spirit of the times, the mechanism of economics, had not spared our city and had taken root in a sector of its periphery which then developed into a parasitical quarter.

While in the old city a nightly semiclandestine trade prevailed, marked by ceremonious solemnity, in the new district modern, sober forms of commercial endeavor had flourished at once. The pseudo-Americanism, grafted on the old, crumbling core of the city, shot up here in a rich but empty and colorless vegetation of pretentious vulgarity. One could see there cheap jerry-built houses with grotesque façades, covered with a monstrous stucco of cracked plaster. The old, shaky suburban houses had large hastily constructed portals grafted on to them which only on close inspection revealed themselves as miserable imitations of metropolitan splendor. Dull, dirty, and faulty glass panes in which dark pictures of the street were wavily reflected, the badly planed wood of the doors, the gray atmosphere of those sterile interiors where the high shelves were cracked and the crumbling walls were covered with cobwebs and thick dust, gave these shops the stigma of some wild Klondike. In row upon row there spread tailors' shops, general outfitters, china stores, drugstores, and barbers' saloons. Their large gray display windows bore slanting semicircular inscriptions in thick gilt letters: CONFISERIE, MANUCURE, KING OF ENGLAND.

The old established inhabitants of the city kept away from that area where the scum, the lowest orders had settled—creatures without character, without background, moral dregs, that inferior species of human being which is born in such ephemeral communities. But on days of defeat, in hours of moral weakness, it would happen that one or another of the city dwellers would venture half by chance into that dubious district. The best among them were not entirely free from the temptation of voluntary degradation, of breaking down the barriers of hierarchy, of immersion in that shallow mud of companionship, of easy intimacy, of dirty intermingling. The district was an El Dorado for such moral deserters. Everything seemed suspect and equivocal there, everything promised with secret winks, cynically stressed gestures, raised eyebrows, the fulfillment of impure hopes, everything helped to release the lowest instincts from their shackles.

Only a few people noticed the peculiar characteristics of that district: the fatal lack of color, as if that shoddy, quickly-growing area could not afford the luxury of it. Everything was gray there, as in black-and-white photographs or in cheap illustrated catalogues. This similarity was real rather than metaphorical because at times, when wandering in those parts, one in fact gained the impression that one was turning the pages of a prospectus, looking at columns of boring commercial advertisements, among which suspect announcements nestled like parasites, together with dubious notices and illustrations with a double meaning. And one's wandering proved as sterile and pointless as the excitement produced by a close study of pornographic albums.

If one entered for example a tailor's shop to order a suit—a suit of cheap elegance characteristic of the district—one found that the premises were large and empty, the rooms high and colorless. Enormous shelves rose in tiers into the undefined height of the room and drew one's eyes toward the ceiling which might be the sky—the shoddy, faded sky of that quarter. On the other hand, the storerooms, which could be seen through the open door, were stacked high with boxes and crates— an enormous filing cabinet rising to the attic to disintegrate into the geometry of emptiness, into the timbers of a void. The large gray windows, ruled like the pages of a ledger, did not admit daylight yet the shop was filled with a watery anonymous gray light which did not throw shadows and did not stress anything. Soon, a slender young man appeared, astonishingly servile, agile, and compliant, to satisfy one's requirements and to drown one in the smooth flow of his cheap sales talk. But when, talking all the time, he unrolled an enormous piece of cloth, fitting, folding, and draping the steam of material, forming it into imaginary jackets and trousers, that whole manipulation seemed suddenly unreal, a sham comedy, a screen ironically placed to hide the true meaning of things.

The tall dark salesgirls, each with a flaw in her beauty (appropriately for that district of remaindered goods), came and went, stood in the doorways watching to see whether the business entrusted to the experienced care of the salesman had reached a suitable point. The salesman simpered and pranced around like a transvestite. One wanted to lift up his receding chin or pinch his pale powdered cheek as with a stealthy meaningful look he discreetly pointed to the trademark on the material, a trademark of transparent symbolism.

Slowly the selection of the suit gave place to the second stage of the plan. The effeminate and corrupted youth, receptive to the client's most intimate stirrings, now put before him a selection of the most peculiar trademarks, a whole library of labels, a cabinet displaying the collection of a sophisticated connoisseur. It then appeared that the outfitter's shop was only a façade behind which there was an antique shop with a collection of highly questionable books and private editions. The servile salesman opened further storerooms, filled to the ceiling with books, drawings, and photographs. These engravings and etchings were beyond our boldest expectations: not even in our dreams had we anticipated such depths of corruption, such varieties of licentiousness.

The salesgirls now walked up and down between the rows of books, their faces, like gray parchment, marked with the dark greasy pigment spots of brunettes, their shiny dark eyes shooting out sudden zigzag cockroachy looks. But even their dark blushes, the piquant beauty spots, the traces of down on their upper lips betrayed their thick, black blood. Their overintense coloring, like that of an aromatic coffee, seemed to stain the books which they took into their olive hands, their touch seemed to run on the pages and leave in the air a dark trail of freckles, a smudge of tobacco, as does a truffle with its exciting, animal smell.

In the meantime, lasciviousness had become general. The salesman, exhausted by his eager importuning, slowly withdrew into feminine passivity. He now lay on one of the many sofas which stood between the bookshelves, wearing a pair of deeply cut silk pajamas. Some of the girls demonstrated to one another the poses and postures of the drawings on the book jackets, while others settled down to sleep on makeshift beds. The pressure on the client had eased. He was now released from the circle of eager interest and left more or less alone. The salesgirls, busy talking, ceased to pay any attention to him. Turning their backs on him they adopted arrogant poses, shifting their weight from foot to foot, making play with their frivolous footwear, abandoning their slim bodies to the serpentine movements of their limbs and thus laid siege to the excited onlooker whom they pretended to ignore behind a show of assumed indifference. This retreat was calculated to involve the guest more deeply, while appearing to leave him a free hand for his own initiative.

But let us take advantage of that moment of inattention to escape from these unexpected consequences of an innocent call at the tailor's, and slip back into the street.

No one stops us. Through the corridors of books, from between the long shelves filled with magazines and prints, we make our way out of the shop and find ourselves in that part of the Street of Crocodiles where from the higher level one can see almost its whole length down to the distant, as yet unfinished buildings of the railway station. It is, as usual in that district, a gray day, and the whole scene seems at times like a photograph in an illustrated magazine, so gray, so one-dimensional are the houses, the people and the vehicles. Reality is as thin as paper and betrays with all its cracks its imitative character. At times one has the impression that it is only the small section immediately before us that falls into the expected pointillistic picture of a city thoroughfare, while on either side, the improvised masquerade is already disintegrating and, unable to endure, crumbles behind us into plaster and sawdust, into the storeroom of an enormous, empty theater. The tenseness of an artificial pose, the assumed earnestness of a mask, an ironical pathos tremble on this façade.

But far be it from us to wish to expose this sham. Despite our better judgment we are attracted by the tawdry charm of the district. Besides, that pretense of a city has some of the feature of self-parody. Rows of small, one-story suburban houses alternate with many storied buildings which, looking as if made of cardboard, are a mixture of blind office windows, of gray-glassed display windows, of fascia, of advertisements and numbers. Among the houses the crowds stream by. The street is as broad as a city boulevard, but the roadway is made, like village squares, of beaten clay, full of puddles and overgrown with grass. The street traffic of that area is a byword in the city; all its inhabitants speak about it with pride and a knowing look. That gray, impersonal crowd is rather self-conscious of its role, eager to live up to its metropolitan aspirations. All the same, despite the bustle and sense of purpose, one has the impression of a monotonous, aimless wandering, of a sleepy procession of puppets. An atmosphere of strange insignificance pervades the scene. The crowd flows lazily by, and, strange to say, one can see it only indistinctly; the figures pass in gentle disarray, never reaching complete sharpness of outline. Only at times do we catch among the turmoil of many heads a dark vivacious look, a black bowler hat worn at an angle, half a face split by a smile formed by lips which had just finished speaking, a foot thrust forward to take a step and fixed forever in that position.

A peculiarity of that district are the cabs, without coachmen, driving along unattended. It is not as if there were no cabbies, but mingling with the crowd and busy with a thousand affairs of their own, they do not bother about their carriages. In that area of sham and empty gestures no one pays much attention to the precise purpose of a cab ride and the passengers entrust themselves to these erratic conveyances with the thoughtlessness which characterizes everything here. From time to time one can see them at dangerous corners, leaning far out from under the broken roof of a cab as, with the reins in their hands, they perform with some difficulty the tricky maneuver of overtaking.

There are also trams here. In them the ambition of the city councilors has achieved its greatest triumph. The appearance of these trams, though, is pitiful, for they are made of papier-mâché with warped sides dented from the misuse of many years. They often have no fronts, so that in passing one can see the passengers, sitting stiffly and behaving with great decorum. These trams are pushed by the town porters. The strangest thing of all is, however, the railway system in the Street of Crocodiles.

Occasionally, at different times of day toward the end of the week, one can see groups of people waiting at a crossroads for a train. One is never sure whether the train will come at all or where it will stop if it does. It often happens, therefore, that people wait in two different places, unable to agree where the stop is. They wait for a long time standing in a black, silent bunch alongside the barely visible lines of the track, their faces in profile: a row of pale cut-out paper figures, fixed in an expression of anxious peering.

At last the train suddenly appears: one can see it coming from the expected side street, low like a snake, a miniature train with a squat, puffing locomotive. It enters the black corridor, and the street darkens from the coal dust scattered by the line of carriages. The heavy breathing of the engine and the wave of a strange sad seriousness, the suppressed hurry and excitement transform the street for a moment into the hall of a railway station in the quickly falling winter dusk.

A black market in railway tickets and bribery in general are the special plagues of our city.

At the last moment, when the train is already in the station, negotiations are conducted in nervous haste with corrupt railway officials. Before these are completed, the train starts, followed slowly by a crowd of disappointed passengers who accompany it a long way down the line before finally dispersing.

The street, reduced for a moment to form an improvised station filled with gloom and the breath of distant travel, widens out again, becomes lighter and again allows the carefree crowd of chattering passers-by to stroll past the shop windows—those dirty gray squares filled with shoddy goods, tall wax dummies, and barbers' dolls.

Showily dressed in long lace-trimmed gowns, prostitutes have begun to circulate. They might even be the wives of hairdressers or restaurant bandleaders. They advance with a brisk rapacious step, each with some small flaw in her evil corrupted face; their eyes have a black, crooked squint, or they have harelips, or the tips of their noses are missing.

The inhabitants of the city are quite proud of the odor of corruption emanating from the Street of Crocodiles. "There is no need for us to go short of anything," they say proudly to themselves, "we even have truly metropolitan vices." They maintain that every woman in that district is a tart. In fact, it is enough to stare at any of them, and at once you meet an insistent clinging look which freezes you with the certainty of fulfillment. Even the schoolgirls wear their hair ribbons in a characteristic way and walk on their slim legs with a peculiar step, an impure expression in their eyes that foreshadows their future corruption.

And yet, and yet—are we to betray the last secret of that district, the carefully concealed secret of the Street of Crocodiles?

Several times during our account we have given warning signals, we have intimated delicately our reservations. An attentive reader will therefore not be unprepared for what is to follow. We spoke of the imitative, illusory character of that area, but these words have too precise and definite a meaning to describe its half-baked and undecided reality.

Our language has no definitions which would weigh, so to speak, the grade of reality, or define its suppleness. Let us say it bluntly: the misfortune of that area is that nothing ever succeeds there, nothing can ever reach a definite conclusion. Gestures hang in the air, movements are prematurely exhausted and cannot overcome a certain point of inertia. We have already noticed the great bravura and prodigality in intentions, projects, and anticipations which are one of the characteristics of the district. It is in fact no more than a fermentation of desires, prematurely aroused and therefore impotent and empty. In an atmosphere of excessive facility, every whim flies high, a passing excitement swells into an empty parasitic growth; a light gray vegetation of fluffy weeds, of colorless poppies sprouts forth, made from a weightless fabric of nightmares and hashish. Over the whole area there floats the lazy licentious smell of sin, and the houses, the shops, the people seem sometimes no more than a shiver on its feverish body, the gooseflesh of its febrile dreams. Nowhere as much as there do we feel threatened by possibilities, shaken by the nearness of fulfillment, pale and faint with the delightful rigidity of realization. And that is as far as it goes.

Having exceeded a certain point of tension, the tide stops and begins to ebb, the atmosphere becomes unclear and troubled, possibilities fade and decline into a void, the crazy gray poppies of excitement scatter into ashes.

We shall always regret that, at a given moment, we had left the slightly dubious tailor's shop. We shall never be able to find it again. We shall wander from shop sign to shop sign and make a thousand mistakes. We shall enter scores of shops, see many which are similar. We shall wander along shelves upon shelves of books, look through magazines and prints, confer intimately and at length with young women of imperfect beauty, with an excessive pigmentation who yet would not be able to understand our requirements.

We shall get involved in misunderstandings until all our fever and excitement have spent themselves in unnecessary effort, in futile pursuit.

Our hopes were a fallacy, the suspicious appearance of the premises and of the staff were a sham, the clothes were real clothes, and the salesman had no ulterior motives. The women of the Street of Crocodiles are depraved to only a modest extent, stifled by thick layers of moral prejudice and ordinary banality. In that city of cheap human material, no instincts can flourish, no dark and unusual passions can be aroused.

The Street of Crocodiles was a concession of our city to modernity and metropolitan corruption. Obviously, we were unable to afford anything better than a paper imitation, a montage of illustrations cut out from last year's moldering newspapers.

Translated by Celina Wieniewska

VLADIMIR NABOKOV

VLADIMIR NABOKOV (1899–1977) has the rare distinction of being a great writer in two languages, Russian and English. In one sense, his life was a series of deprivations. He lost his aristocratic inheritance and native country to the Bolsheviks, his father (a distinguished liberal statesman) to an assassin's bullet, his second home country to Hitler and fascism, and finally the rest of Europe to World War II. He emigrated to America, began again, unknown as a writer and taking on a new language. He supported himself by lecturing on Russian and modern literature, most notably at Cornell. His breakthrough came with Lolita (1955), which was turned down by a series of American publishers but eventually became both a bestseller and a classic, enabling its author to retire from teaching and move to Switzerland, where he spent his final years.

Nabokov's response to the series of deprivations that drove him into exile more than once and cut him off from his cultural heritage was to pour his energies and loyalties into the service of art, which he believed could make existence bearable. Art was not an escape for Nabokov—his novels fiercely reflected the insane century in which they were written—but it was that part of life in which he could encounter beauty and accept pain. It allows him and us to be at our best: most humane, most imaginative, most liberated from the prison of time and historical circumstance. This is not "art for art's sake" but "art for life's sake," a desperate remedy against hopelessness. Nabokov's public mask was sardonic, arrogant, even unfeeling; it never deceives those who have read him carefully. Nabokov's novels could only have been written by a man of unusual compassion, a tender scientist of human loss.

It is as easy to represent Nabokov's excellence by means of his short fiction as by excerpts from his novels. Like Lawrence and Faulkner, he kept his allegiance to the short story alive throughout his career. "A Visit to the Museum" (1939) is a tour de force on the idea of museums (compare the "composite archetypes," such as libraries, cities, and labyrinths, in other magical realists, most notably Borges and Calvino), as well as the painful comedy of exile. One could say of this story that the museum becomes an emblem of human attempts to arrest and defeat time and change by labeling, displaying, and modeling them, and that exile becomes a metaphor for the human condition; but one should not lose sight of the steadily building comedy it produces. The mixture of laughter and suffering is typically "Nabokovian."

The Visit to the Museum

Vladimir Nabokov

SEVERAL YEARS ago a friend of mine in Paris—a person with oddities, to put it mildly—learning that I was going to spend two or three days at Montisert, asked me to drop in at the local museum where there hung, he was told, a portrait of his grandfather by Leroy. Smiling and spreading out his hands, he related a rather vague story to which I confess I paid little attention, partly because I do not like other people's obtrusive affairs, but chiefly because I had always had doubts about my friend's capacity to remain this side of fantasy. It went more or less as follows: after the grandfather died in their St. Petersburg house back at the time of the Russo-Japanese War, the contents of his apartment in Paris were sold at auction. The portrait, after some obscure peregrinations, was acquired by the museum of Leroy's native town. My friend wished to know if the portrait was really there; if there, if it could be ransomed; and if it could, for what price. When I asked why he did not get in touch with the museum, he replied he had written several times, but had never received an answer.

I made an inward resolution not to carry out the request—I could always tell him I had fallen ill or changed my itinerary. The very notion of seeing sights, whether they be museums or ancient buildings, is loathsome to me; besides, the good freak's commission seemed absolute nonsense. It so happened, however, that, while wandering about Montisert's empty streets in search of a stationery store, and cursing the spire of a long-necked cathedral, always the same one, that kept popping up at the end of every street, I was caught in a violent downpour which immediately went about accelerating the fall of the maple leaves, for the fair weather of a southern October was holding on by a mere thread. I dashed for cover and found myself on the steps of the museum.

It was a building of modest proportions, constructed of many-colored stones, with columns, a gilt inscription over the frescoes of the pediment, and a lion-legged stone bench on either side of the bronze door. One of its leaves stood open, and the interior seemed dark against the shimmer of the shower. I stood for a while on the steps, but, despite the overhanging roof, they were gradually growing speckled. I saw that the rain had set in for good, and so, having nothing better to do, I decided to go inside. No sooner had I trod on the smooth, resonant flagstones of the vestibule than the clatter of a moved stool came from a distant corner, and the custodian—a banal pensioner with an empty sleeve—rose to meet me, laying aside his newspaper and peering at me over his spectacles. I paid my franc and, trying not to look at some statues at the entrance (which were as traditional and as insignificant as the first number in a circus program), I entered the main hall.

Everything was as it should be: gray tints, the sleep of substance, matter dematerialized. There was the usual case of old, worn coins resting in the inclined velvet of their compartments. There was, on top of the case, a pair of owls, Eagle Owl and Long-eared, with their French names reading "Grand Duke" and "Middle Duke" if translated. Venerable minerals lay in their open graves of dusty papier-mâché; a photograph of an astonished gentleman with a pointed beard dominated an assortment of strange black lumps of various sizes. They bore a great resemblance to frozen frass, and I paused involuntarily over them, for I was quite at a loss to guess their nature, composition and function. The custodian had been following me with felted steps, always keeping a respectful distance; now, however, he came up, with one hand behind his back and the ghost of the other in his pocket, and gulping, if one judged by his Adam's apple.

"What are they?" I asked.

"Science has not yet determined," he replied, undoubtedly having learned the phrase by rote. "They were found," he continued in the same phony tone, "in 1895, by Louis Pradier, Municipal Councillor and Knight of the Legion of Honor," and his trembling finger indicated the photograph.

"Well and good," I said, "but who decided, and why, that they merited a place in the museum?"

"And now I call your attention to this skull!" the old man cried energetically, obviously changing the subject.

"Still, I would be interested to know what they are made of," I interrupted.

"Science..." he began anew, but stopped short and looked crossly at his fingers, which were soiled with dust from the glass.

I proceeded to examine a Chinese vase, probably brought back by a naval officer; a group of porous fossils; a pale worm in clouded alcohol; a

red-and-green map of Montisert in the seventeenth century; and a trio of
rusted tools bound by a funereal ribbon—a spade, a mattock and a pick.
"To dig in the past," I thought absent-mindedly, but this time did not
seek clarification from the custodian, who was following me noiselessly
and meekly, weaving in and out among the display cases. Beyond the first
hall there was another, apparently the last, and in its center a large
sarcophagus stood like a dirty bathtub, while the walls were hung with
paintings.

At once my eye was caught by the portrait of a man between two
abominable landscapes (with cattle and "atmosphere"). I moved closer
and, to my considerable amazement, found the very object whose
existence had hitherto seemed to me but the figment of an unstable
mind. The man, depicted in wretched oils, wore a frock coat, whiskers
and a large pince-nez on a cord; he bore a likeness to Offenbach, but, in
spite of the work's vile conventionality, I had the feeling one could make
out in his features the horizon of a resemblance, as it were, to my friend.
In one corner, meticulously traced in carmine against a black background, was the signature *Leroy* in a hand as commonplace as the work
itself.

I felt a vinegarish breath near my shoulder, and turned to meet the
custodian's kindly gaze. "Tell me," I asked, "supposing someone wished
to buy one of these paintings, whom should he see?"

"The treasures of the museum are the pride of the city," replied the
old man, "and pride is not for sale."

Fearing his eloquence, I hastily concurred, but nevertheless asked for
the name of the museum's director. He tried to distract me with the story
of the sarcophagus, but I insisted. Finally he gave me the name of one M.
Godard and explained where I could find him.

Frankly, I enjoyed the thought that the portrait existed. It is fun to be
present at the coming true of a dream, even if it is not one's own. I
decided to settle the matter without delay. When I get in the spirit, no
one can hold me back. I left the museum with a brisk, resonant step, and
found that the rain had stopped, blueness had spread across the sky, a
woman in besplattered stockings was spinning along on a silver-shining
bicycle, and only over the surrounding hills did clouds still hang. Once
again the cathedral began playing hide-and-seek with me, but I outwitted
it. Barely escaping the onrushing tires of a furious red bus packed with
singing youths, I crossed the asphalt thoroughfare and a minute later
was ringing at the garden gate of M. Godard. He turned out to be a thin,
middle-aged gentleman in high collar and dickey, with a pearl in the knot
of his tie, and a face very much resembling a Russian wolfhound; as if
that were not enough, he was licking his chops in a most doglike manner,
while sticking a stamp on an envelope, when I entered his small but
lavishly furnished room with its malachite inkstand on the desk and a
strangely familiar Chinese vase on the mantel. A pair of fencing foils hung

crossed over the mirror, which reflected the narrow gray back of his head. Here and there photographs of a warship pleasantly broke up the blue flora of the wallpaper.

"What can I do for you?" he asked, throwing the letter he had just sealed into the wastebasket. This act seemed unusual to me; however, I did not see fit to interfere. I explained in brief my reason for coming, even naming the substantial sum with which my friend was willing to part, though he had asked me not to mention it, but wait instead for the museum's terms.

"All this is delightful," said M. Godard. "The only thing is, you are mistaken—there is no such picture in our museum."

"What do you mean there is no such picture? I have just seen it! Portrait of a Russian nobleman, by Gustave Leroy."

"We do have one Leroy," said M. Godard when he had leafed through an oilcloth notebook and his black fingernail had stopped at the entry in question. "However, it is not a portrait but a rural landscape: The Return of the Herd."

I repeated that I had seen the picture with my own eyes five minutes before and that no power on earth could make me doubt its existence.

"Agreed," said M. Godard, "but I am not crazy either. I have been curator of our museum for almost twenty years now and know this catalog as well as I know the Lord's Prayer. It says here Return of the Herd and that means the herd is returning, and, unless perhaps your friend's grandfather is depicted as a shepherd, I cannot conceive of his portrait's existence in our museum."

"He is wearing a frock coat," I cried. "I swear he is wearing a frock coat!"

"And how did you like our museum in general?" M. Godard asked suspiciously. "Did you appreciate the sarcophagus?"

"Listen," I said (and I think there was already a tremor in my voice), "do me a favor—let's go there this minute, and let's make an agreement that if the portrait is there, you will sell it."

"And if not?" inquired M. Godard.

"I shall pay you the sum anyway."

"All right," he said. "Here, take this red-and-blue pencil and using the red—the red, please—put it in writing for me."

In my excitement I carried out his demand. Upon glancing at my signature, he deplored the difficult pronunciation of Russian names. Then he appended his own signature and, quickly folding the sheet, thrust it into his waistcoat pocket.

"Let's go," he said, freeing a cuff.

On the way he stepped into a shop and bought a bag of sticky-looking caramels which he began offering me insistently: when I flatly refused, he tried to shake out a couple of them into my hand. I pulled my hand away. Several caramels fell on the sidewalk; he stopped to pick them up and then overtook me at a trot. When we drew near the museum we saw the red tourist bus (now empty) parked outside.

"Aha," said M. Godard, pleased. "I see we have many visitors today."

He doffed his hat and, holding it in front of him, walked decorously up the steps.

All was not well at the museum. From within issued rowdy cries, lewd laughter, and even what seemed like the sound of a scuffle. We entered the first hall; there the elderly custodian was restraining two sacrilegists who wore some kind of festive emblems in their lapels and were altogether very purple-faced and full of pep as they tried to extract the municipal councillor's merds from beneath the glass. The rest of the youths, members of some rural athletic organization, were making noisy fun, some of the worm in alcohol, others of the skull. One joker was in rapture over the pipes of the steam radiator, which he pretended was an exhibit; another was taking aim at an owl with his fist and forefinger. There were about thirty of them in all, and their motion and voices created a condition of crush and thick noise.

M. Godard clapped his hands and pointed at a sign reading "Visitors to the Museum must be decently attired." Then be pushed his way, with me following, into the second hall. The whole company immediately swarmed after us. I steered Godard to the portrait; he froze before it, chest inflated, and then stepped back a bit, as if admiring it, and his feminine heel trod on somebody's foot.

"Splendid picture," he exclaimed with genuine sincerity. "Well, let's not be petty about this. You were right, and there must be an error in the catalog."

As he spoke, his fingers, moving as it were on their own, tore up our agreement into little bits which fell like snowflakes into a massive spittoon.

"Who's the old ape?" asked an individual in a striped jersey, and, as my friend's grandfather was depicted holding a glowing cigar, another funster took out a cigarette and prepared to borrow a light from the portrait.

"All right, let us settle on the price," I said, "and, in any case, let's get out of here."

"Make way, please!" shouted M. Godard, pushing aside the curious.

There was an exit, which I had not noticed previously, at the end of the hall and we thrust our way through to it.

"I can make no decision," M. Godard was shouting above the din. "Decisiveness is a good thing only when supported by law. I must first discuss the matter with the mayor, who has just died and has not yet been elected. I doubt that you will be able to purchase the portrait but nonetheless I would like to show you still other treasures of ours."

We found ourselves in a hall of considerable dimensions. Brown books, with a half-baked look and coarse, foxed pages, lay open under glass on a long table. Along the walls stood dummy soldiers in jack boots with flared tops.

"Come, let's talk it over," I cried out in desperation, trying to direct M. Godard's evolutions to a plush-covered sofa in a corner. But in this I was prevented by the custodian. Flailing his one arm, he came running after us, pursued by a merry crowd of youths, one of whom had put on his head a copper helmet with a Rembrandtesque gleam.

"Take it off, take it off!" shouted M. Godard, and someone's shove made the helmet fly off the hooligan's head with a clatter.

"Let us move on," said M. Godard, tugging at my sleeve, and we passed into the section of Ancient Sculpture.

I lost my way for a moment among some enormous marble legs, and twice ran around a giant knee before I again caught sight of M. Godard, who was looking for me behind the white ankle of a neighboring giantess. Here a person in a bowler, who must have clambered up her, suddenly fell from a great height to the stone floor. One of his companions began helping him up, but they were both drunk, and, dismissing them with a wave of the hand, M. Godard rushed on to the next room, radiant with Oriental fabrics; there hounds raced across azure carpets, and a bow and quiver lay on a tiger skin.

Strangely, though, the expanse and motley only gave me a feeling of oppressiveness and imprecision, and, perhaps because new visitors kept dashing by or perhaps because I was impatient to leave the unnecessarily spreading museum and amid calm and freedom conclude my business negotiations with M. Godard, I began to experience a vague sense of alarm. Meanwhile we had transported ourselves into yet another hall, which must have been really enormous, judging by the fact that it housed the entire skeleton of a whale, resembling a frigate's frame; beyond were visible still other halls, with the oblique sheen of large paintings, full of storm clouds, among which floated the delicate idols of religious art in blue and pink vestments; and all this resolved itself in an abrupt turbulence of misty draperies, and chandeliers came aglitter and fish with translucent frills meandered through illuminated aquariums. Racing up a staircase, we saw, from the gallery above, a crowd of gray-haired people with umbrellas examining a gigantic mock-up of the universe.

At last, in a somber but magnificent room dedicated to the history of steam machines, I managed to halt my carefree guide for an instant.

"Enough!" I shouted. "I'm leaving. We'll talk tomorrow."

He had already vanished. I turned and saw, scarcely an inch from me, the lofty wheels of a sweaty locomotive. For a long time I tried to find the way back among models of railroad stations. How strangely glowed the violet signals in the gloom beyond the fan of wet tracks, and what spasms shook my poor heart! Suddenly everything changed again: in front of me stretched an infinitely long passage, containing numerous office cabinets and elusive, scurrying people. Taking a sharp turn, I found myself amid a thousand musical instruments; the walls, all mirror, reflected an enfilade of grand pianos, while in the center there was a pool with a bronze Orpheus atop a green rock. The aquatic theme did not end here as, racing back, I ended up in the Section of Fountains and Brooks, and it was difficult to walk along the winding, slimy edges of those waters.

Now and then, on one side or the other, stone stairs, with puddles on the steps, which gave me a strange sensation of fear, would descend into misty abysses, whence issued whistles, the rattle of dishes, the clatter of typewriters, the ring of hammers and many other sounds, as if, down there, were exposition halls of some kind or other, already closing or not yet completed. Then I found myself in darkness and kept bumping into unknown furniture until I finally saw a red light and walked out onto a platform that clanged under me—and suddenly, beyond it, there was a bright parlor, tastefully furnished in Empire style, but not a living soul, not a living soul. . . . By now I was indescribably terrified, but every time I turned and tried to retrace my steps along the passages, I found myself in hitherto unseen places—a greenhouse with hydrangeas and broken windowpanes with the darkness of artificial night showing through beyond; or a deserted laboratory with dusty alembics on its tables. Finally I ran into a room of some sort with coatracks monstrously loaded down with black coats and astrakhan furs; from beyond a door came a burst of applause, but when I flung the door open, there was no theater, but only a soft opacity and splendidly counterfeited fog with the perfectly convincing blotches of indistinct streetlights. More than convincing! I advanced, and immediately a joyous and unmistakable sensation of reality at last replaced all the unreal trash amid which I had just been dashing to and fro. The stone beneath my feet was real sidewalk, powdered with wonderfully fragrant, newly fallen snow in which the infrequent pedestrians had already left fresh black tracks. At first the quiet and the snowy coolness of the night, somehow strikingly familiar, gave me a pleasant feeling after my feverish wanderings. Trustfully, I started to conjecture just where I had come out, and why the snow, and what were those lights exaggeratedly but indistinctly beaming here and there in the brown darkness. I examined and, stooping, even touched a round spur stone on the curb, then glanced at the palm of my hand, full of wet granular cold, as if hoping to read an explanation there. I felt how lightly, how naïvely I was clothed, but the distinct realization that I had escaped from the museum's maze was still so strong that, for the first two or three minutes, I experienced neither surprise nor fear. Continuing my leisurely examination, I looked up at the house beside which I was standing and was immediately struck by the sight of iron steps and railings that descended into the snow on their way to the cellar. There was a twinge in my heart, and it was with a new, alarmed curiosity that I glanced at the pavement, at its white cover along which stretched black lines, at the brown sky across which there kept sweeping a mysterious light, and at the massive parapet some distance away. I sensed that there was a drop beyond it; something was creaking and gurgling down there. Further on, beyond the murky cavity, stretched a chain of fuzzy lights. Scuffling along the snow in my soaked shoes, I walked a few paces, all the time glancing at the dark house on my right; only in a single window did a lamp glow softly under its green-glass shade. Here, a locked wooden gate.... There, what must be the shutters of a sleeping shop.... And by the light of a streetlamp whose shape had long been shouting to me its impossible message, I made out the ending of a sign—"...*inka Sapog'* ("...*oe Repair"*)—but no, it was not the snow that had obliterated the "hard sign" at the end. "No, no, in a minute I shall wake up," I said aloud, and, trembling, my heart pounding, I turned, walked on, stopped again. From somewhere came the receding sound of hooves, the snow sat like a skullcap on a slightly leaning spur stone, and indistinctly showed white on the woodpile on the other side of the fence, and already I knew, irrevocably, where I was. Alas, it was not the Russia I remembered, but the factual Russia of today, forbidden to me, hopelessly slavish, and hopelessly my own native land. A semiphantom in a light foreign suit, I stood on the impassive snow of an October night, somewhere on the Moyka or the Fontanka Canal, or perhaps on the Obvodny, and I had to do something, go somewhere, run, desperately protect my fragile, illegal life. Oh, how many times in my sleep I had experienced a similar sensation! Now, though, it was reality. Everything was real—the air that seemed to mingle with scattered snowflakes, the still unfrozen canal, the floating fish house, and that peculiar squareness of the darkened and the yellow windows. A man in a fur cap, with a briefcase under his arm, came toward me out of the fog, gave me a startled glance, and turned to look again when he had passed me. I waited for him to disappear and then, with a tremendous haste, began pulling out everything I had in my pockets, ripping up papers, throwing them into the snow and stamping them down. There were some documents, a letter from my sister in Paris, five hundred francs, a handkerchief, cigarettes; however, in order to shed all the integument of exile, I would have to tear off and destroy my clothes, my linen, my shoes, everything, and remain ideally naked; and, even though I was already shivering from my anguish and from the cold, I did what I could.

But enough. I shall not recount how I was arrested, nor tell of my subsequent ordeals. Suffice it to say that it cost me incredible patience and effort to get back abroad, and that, ever since, I have forsworn carrying out commissions entrusted one by the insanity of others.

Translated by Dmitri Nabokov and the author

MARÍA LUISA BOMBAL

M ARÍA LUISA BOMBAL (1910–1980), the Chilean novelist and short-story writer, has long been recognized as an important and influential author in Latin America. She was hailed immediately for her first two novels, The Final Mist (1935) and The Shrouded Woman (1938). Bombal has only recently come to the attention of English-speaking audiences, mostly through selections in anthologies; it was not until 1980 that New Islands, a full-length collection of her poignant stories written during the 1930s, appeared in English. She lived in the United States from 1940 until 1970, at which time she returned to Chile. In 1977 she received the Chilean Academy of Arts and Letters prize for her novella The Story of María Griselda.

Bombal, trained in literature and philosophy at the Sorbonne, displays a consummate sense of craft, blending a rich, descriptive sensibility with a precision of language. Her stories are usually intricately patterned, often with several plot lines. In many of her stories, Bombal addresses modern feminist concerns, depicting women ensnared in difficult situations. These haunting characters, locked into traditional roles, struggle to break out with only moderate success.

The evocative nature of Bombal's writing is perfectly illustrated in her masterpiece, New Islands, where she utilizes her extraordinary stylistic techniques to their fullest. This story is set in a lake district on the Argentine pampas that exudes a hallucinatory ambience, a place where new islands may appear magically and where exotic images blossom under Bombal's touch. Through lucid, but feverish prose, she expertly captures the confusion of the disconcerting love relationship. Her final grotesque revelation may very well have served as inspiration for such writers as Cortázar and García Márquez.

New Islands

María Luisa Bombal

ALL NIGHT long a howling wind had raged across the pampa. Now and then it would slip inside the house through cracks in the doors and window frames, sending ripples through the mosquito netting. Each time this happened, Yolanda would turn on the light, which flickered, held for a moment, and then faded out again. At dawn, when her brother Federico came into the room, she lay on her left shoulder, breathing with difficulty, moaning in her sleep.

"Yolanda! Yolanda!"

She sat up like a shot. In order to see Federico, she parted her long black hair and tossed it over her shoulders.

"Were you dreaming?" he asked.

"Oh, yes—horrible dreams."

"Why must you always sleep in that position? It's bad for your heart."

"I know, I know. What time is it? And where are you off to so early in all this wind?"

"The lakes. It seems another island has emerged. That makes four so far. Some people from La Figura hacienda have come to see them. So we'll be having guests later. I wanted to let you know before I left."

Without shifting her position, Yolanda regarded her brother: a thin, white-haired man whose tight-fitting riding boots lent him an air of youth. Men—how absurd they were! Always in motion, forever willing to take an interest in everything. Upon retiring for the night, they demand to be awakened at daybreak. If they go to a fireplace, they remain standing, ready to run to the other end of the room—ready always to escape, to flee

191

toward the futile. And they cough and smoke, speak loud as if they feared silence—indeed, as if tranquility were a mortal enemy.

"It's all right, Federico."

"So long, then."

The door slams; Federico's spurs jingle on the tile floor in the corridor. Yolanda closes her eyes once more and, delicately, using elaborate care, sinks back onto the pillows on her left shoulder, curling herself as usual into that position which Federico claims is so damaging to one's heart. Breathing heavily, she sighs, falling suddenly into one of her disturbing dreams—dreams from which, morning after morning, she wakes pale and exhausted, as if she had been battling insomnia throughout the entire night.

The visitors from La Figúra hacienda, meanwhile, had reached the grassy bank where the lakes began. Daylight was spreading across the water, unfurling over the landscape like a fire. Out there against the horizon, barely visible under the cloudy sky, were the new islands: still smoking from the fiery effort that had lifted them from who knows what stratified depths.

"Four, four new islands!" the people shouted.

The wind did not subside until nightfall, by which time the men were returning from hunting.

Do, re, mi, fa, sol, la, ti, do...Do, re, mi, fa, sol, la, ti, do...

The notes rise and fall, rise and fall like round, limpid crystal bubbles carried on the wind from the house, now flattened in the distance, to burst over the hunters like solemn, regulated raindrops.

Do, re, mi, fa, sol, la, ti, do...

It's Yolanda practicing, Sylvester says to himself. He pauses a moment to shift the carbine slung on his left shoulder, his heavy body trembling slightly.

Among the bushes bordering the lawn there are white flowers that appear touched by frost. Juan Manuel bends over to examine one.

"Don't touch them," Sylvester warns. "They turn yellow. They're Yolanda's camellias," he adds with a smile.

That humble smile which does not suit him, thinks Juan Manuel. As soon as he relaxes his proud countenance, you see how old he is.

The house is in total darkness, but the notes continue to flow regularly: Do, re, mi, fa, sol, la, ti, do...Do, re, mi, fa, sol, la, ti, do...

"Have you met my sister Yolanda, Juan Manuel?"

On Federico's question, the woman sitting in shadow at the piano gives the stranger her hand, withdrawing it immediately. She then rises, so slowly that she seems to grow upright, uncoiling like a beautiful snake. Very tall, she is extremely slender. Juan Manuel follows her with his eyes as she quickly and quietly turns on the lamps.

She is exactly like her name, thinks Juan Manuel. Pale, angular, and a bit savage. And there is something odd about her that I cannot place. But of course, he realizes as she glides through the door and disappears—her feet are too small. How strange that she can support such a long body on such tiny feet.

How dull this dinner among men, Juan Manuel decides. Among ten hunters thwarted by the wind who gulp down their food without a single manly deed to boast about. And Yolanda, he reflects, why doesn't she preside over the table now that Federico's wife is in Buenos Aires? What an extraordinary figure she makes! Ugly? Pretty? Fragile, that's it, very fragile. And that dark and brilliant gaze of hers—aggressive yet hunted...Whom does she look like? What does she resemble?

Juan Manuel lifts his glass, staring at the wine. Across from him sits Sylvester, who is drinking heavily and talking and laughing in a loud voice. He seems desperate.

The hunters stir the coals with a scoop and tongs, scattering ashes over the multiple fiery eyes which refuse to close—this the final act in a long and boring evening.

And now suddenly the grass and the trees in the garden begin to shiver in the cold night breeze. Large insects beat their wings against the lantern illuminating the long open corridor. Leaning on Juan Manuel, Sylvester staggers toward his room, his feet slipping on the tiles that shine with vapor as if they had just been washed. His footsteps send frogs scurrying off to hide timidly in dark corners.

The iron grilles slamming shut across the doors seem in the silence of the night to echo the useless volley of shots fired by the hunters. Sylvester throws his heavy body on the bed and buries his emaciated face in his hands. His sighs irritate Juan Manuel—he who always detested sharing a room with anyone, let alone with a drunkard who moans.

"Oh, Juan Manuel, Juan Manuel..."

"What's the matter, Don Sylvester? You don't feel well?"

"Oh, my boy—who could know, who could know!..."

"Know what, Don Sylvester?"

"This," said the old man, taking his wallet from his jacket and handing it to Juan Manuel. "Look for the letter. Read it. Yes, a letter. That one, yes. Read it and tell me if you understand it."

An elongated, wavering handwriting flows like smoke across the yellowed, wrinkled pages: *Sylvester, I cannot marry you. Believe me, I have thought it over at great length. It isn't possible, it just isn't. Nevertheless, I love you, Sylvester, I love you and I suffer. But I cannot. Forget me. In vain I ask myself what might save me. A son, perhaps, a child whose sweet weight I could feel inside me forever. Forever! Not to see him grow, separated from me! Myself attached forever to that tiny heart, possessed always by that presence! I weep, Sylvester, I weep; and I cannot explain myself.—Yolanda.*

"I don't understand," Juan Manuel whispers uneasily.

"I have been trying for thirty years to understand," said Sylvester. "I loved her. You cannot know how much I loved her. No one loves like that any more, Juan Manuel...One night, two weeks before we were to be married, she sent me this letter. Afterwards she refused to offer any explanation, and I was never permitted to see her alone. I waited, telling myself that time would solve everything. I am still waiting."

Juan Manuel seemed confused. "Was it the mother, Don Sylvester? Was she also named Yolanda?"

"What? I am speaking of the one and only Yolanda, who tonight has again rejected me. This evening when I saw her, I said to myself: Maybe now that so many years have passed, Yolanda will at long last give me an explanation. But, as usual, she left the room. Sometimes, you know, Federico tries to talk to her about all this. But she starts trembling and runs away, as always..."

The far-off chugging of a train can now be heard. The steady insistent clacking seems to increase Juan Manuel's uneasiness.

"Yolanda was your fiancée, Don Sylvester?"

"Yes, my fiancée...my fiancée..."

Juan Manuel stares coldly at Sylvester's disoriented gestures, his swollen, sixty-year-old body so disastrously preserved. Don Sylvester, his father's old friend, and Yolanda's fiancé.

"Then she is not a young girl, Don Sylvester?"

Sylvester laughs stupidly.

"How old is she?" Juan Manuel inquires.

Sylvester rubs his forehead, eyes closed, trying to count. "Let's see, at that time I was twenty...no, twenty-three..."

But Juan Manuel hardly listens, momentarily relieved by a consoling reflection: What does age matter when one is so prodigiously young!

"Therefore she must be..."

Sylvester's words dissolve in a hacking cough. And again Juan Manuel feels a resurgence of the anxiety that holds him attentive to the secret Sylvester is drunkenly unraveling. And that train in the distance, coming closer now, its regular rhythm as laden with suspense as a drum roll—like a threat not yet become reality. The muffled, monotonous pounding unnerves him, growing louder and louder until, like one seeking escape, he goes to the window, pushes it open, and bends into the night. The headlights of the express glare across the immense plain like malevolent eyes.

"Damned train!" he grumbles. "When will it pass?"

Sylvester comes over to lean beside him, breathing deep as he gestures toward the two shimmering lights.

"It just left Lobos," he explains. "It generally takes half an hour to go by here."

She is fragile and her feet are too small for her height.

"How old is she, Don Sylvester?"

"I don't remember. I'll tell you tomorrow."

But why? Juan Manuel asks himself. Why this preoccupation with a woman I have seen only once in my life? Do I desire her? The train. Oh, that monotonous hissing monster advancing slowly, inexorably across the pampa! What's wrong with me? It must be that I am tired, he thinks, closing the window.

Meanwhile, she is at one end of the garden, leaning against the fence overlooking the hill as if she were bending over the rail of a ship anchored on the prairie. In the sky, a single motionless star: a large red star that seems about to shake loose from its orbit and spin off into infinite space. Juan Manuel stands beside her at the fence, gazing, too, at the pampa now submerged in the dark saturnine twilight. He speaks. What does he say? He whispers words of destiny in her ear. And now he takes her in his arms. And now the arms around her waist tremble, slide lower, caressing her gently. And she tosses, struggles, gripping the wooden rail to better resist. And then she wakes to find herself clutching the sheets, sobbing deep in her throat.

For a long time she weeps without moving, listening to the house quaver. The mirror moves slightly. A withered camellia blossom falls from a vase, dropping on the carpet with the soft thick sound of ripe fruit.

She waits for the train to go by and then, listening to its receding sonic boom, she drifts back to sleep, lying on her left shoulder.

In the morning the wind has resumed its fierce race across the pampa. But this day the hunters are in no mood to waste their ammunition in a gale. Instead, they launch two boats, bound for those new islands afloat on the horizon, rising from a cloud of foam and wheeling birds.

They land proudly, boisterously, carbines on their shoulders as they leap to shore, only to discover an oppressive, foul-smelling atmosphere that stops them in their tracks. After a brief pause they advance, stepping in amazement on slimy weeds that seem to be oozing from the hot and shifting soil. They stagger on amid spirals of sea gulls that swoop around them, flashing by their faces and screeching as they dip and rise. At one point, Juan Manuel lurches as the edge of a wing flails his chest.

And still they advance, crushing under their boots frenzied silver fish stranded by the tide. Farther on, they find more strange vegetation: low bushes of pink coral, which they struggle for some time to uproot, pulling and pulling until their hands bleed.

The sea gulls cluster round them in ever-tightening spirals. Low, running clouds skim by overhead, weaving a vertiginous pattern of shadows. The fumes rising from the earth grow more dense by the moment. Everything boils, shakes violently, trembles. The hunters cannot see; can hardly breathe. Disheartened and afraid, they flee to their boats, return in silence to the mainland.

All afternoon they sat around a bonfire, chatting with the peons who periodically fed the flames with eucalyptus branches, waiting for the wind to abate. But again, as if to exasperate them, the wind did not die down until dusk.

Do, re, mi, fa, sol, la, ti, do. . .Once again, that methodical scale drifts toward them from the house. Juan Manuel pricks up his ears.

Do, re, mi, fa, sol, la, ti, do. . .Do, re, mi, fa, sol, la, ti, do. . .Do, re, mi, fa. . .Do, re, mi, fa. . .—the piano insists. And those notes repeated over and over beat against Juan Manuel's heart, striking where the sea gull's wing had wounded him that morning. Without knowing why, he gets to his feet and starts walking toward that music chiming endlessly through the trees like a summons.

As he reaches the camellia bushes, the piano suddenly falls silent. He enters the darkened drawing room almost at a run, sees logs burning in the fireplace, the piano open. . .But where is Yolanda?

At the far end of the garden she leans against the fence, as if resting on the rail of a ship anchored on the pampa. And now she trembles, hearing the rustle of the lowermost pine-tree branches being brushed aside by someone coming up cautiously behind her. If only it were Juan Manuel!

She slowly turns her head. It is him, in the flesh this time. Oh, his dark, golden complexion in the gray twilight! Golden as though he were enveloped by a sunray. Joining her at the fence, he, too, stares out across the pampa. Frogs begin to sing in the irrigation ditches; and it is as if night were being ushered in by thousands of crystal bells.

Now he looks at her and smiles. Oh, his fine white teeth! They must be cold and hard like tiny chips of ice. And that warm virile odor he gives off, piercing her with pleasure. How sad to resist such pleasure, to shun that circle formed by this strong, beautiful man and his shadow!

"Yolanda," he murmurs.

She feels upon hearing her name that a sudden intimacy exists between them. How marvelous that he called her by name! It would seem that now they are linked by a long and passionate past. Not sharing a past—that was what held them apart and inhibited them.

"All night long I dreamed of you, Juan Manuel, all night long. . ."

He embraces her; she does not reject him. But she obliges his arm to remain chastely around her waist.

"Someone is calling me," she says abruptly, moving out of his embrace and running off. The pine branches she hastily brushes aside rebound with a snap in Juan Manuel's face, scratching his cheek. Disconcerted by a woman for the first time in his life, he runs after her.

She is dressed in white. Only now, as she goes over to her brother to light his pipe—gravely and meticulously, as if performing a trifling daily ritual—only now does he notice that she is wearing a long gown. She has put it on to dine with them. Then Juan Manuel remembers the mud on his boots and rushes to his room to clean them.

On his return to the drawing room, he finds Yolanda seated on a sofa in front of the fireplace. The dancing flames alternately lighten and darken her black eyes. With her arms crossed behind her neck, she is long and slender like a sword, or like...like what? In vain Juan Manuel searches for the proper simile.

"Dinner is served," the maid announces.

As Yolanda rises, her flame-lightened pupils are suddenly extinguished. And going past Juan Manuel, she casts those opaque black eyes on him, the sheer tulle sleeve of her dress grazing his chest like a wing. And in that instant the simile comes to him.

"Now I know what you look like," he whispers. "A sea gull."

Uttering a strange, hoarse cry, Yolanda collapses on the carpet. Momentarily stunned, the others now rush to her side, pick her up, carry her unconscious form to the sofa. Federico sends the maid scurrying for water. Turning angrily to Juan Manuel, he asks: "What did you say to her? What did you *say?*"

"I told her..." Juan Manuel begins; then lapses into silence, feeling a sudden stab of guilt—fearing, without knowing why, to reveal a secret which is not his.

Yolanda, meanwhile, comes to. Sighing, she presses her heart with both hands, as if recovering from a fright. She half sits up, then stretches out on her left shoulder.

"No," Federico protests, "not on your heart. It's bad for you."

She gives him a weak smile, whispers as she waves him away: "I know, I know. Now please leave me alone."

And there is such sad vehemence, such weariness in her gesture, that everyone moves off into the next room without objecting—everyone except Juan Manuel, who remains standing beside the fireplace.

Pale and motionless, Yolanda sleeps, or pretends to sleep, while Juan Manuel, a silent sentinel, waits anxiously for a sign—be it to stay or go.

At daybreak on this third morning the hunters gather once more at the edge of the lakes, which today at last are calm. Mute, they contemplate the smooth surface of the water, shocked into silence by the vista on that distant gray horizon.

For the new islands have vanished.

Again they launch boats, Juan Manuel setting off alone in a dinghy. He rows determinedly, skirting the old islands, which teem with wildlife, refusing to be tempted like his companions by the lashing sound of wings, of cooing and small sharp cries—the old islands, where things rattle and crack like rattan splitting, where the banks are covered with oozy moving flowers spread out like a bed of slime. Soon Juan Manuel is lost in the distance, a receding silhouette rowing a zigzagging course in search of the exact spot where only yesterday they had landed to explore the four new islands. Where was the first one? Here. No, there. No, rather, here. He leans over the water to look for it, though he knows that his eyes could never see the muddy bottom, where, after its vertiginous plunge, the island sank into silt and algae.

Within the circle of a nearby whirlpool something soft and transparent floats: a small jellyfish. Plucking it from the water in his handkerchief, Juan Manuel ties the four corners of the cloth over it like a pouch.

The day is drawing to a close when Yolanda brings her horse to a halt at the base of the hill and opens the gate for the returning hunters. Setting off again, she rides on ahead to the house, the skirt of her tweed riding habit brushing the bushes. And Juan Manuel notes that, though she is mounted in the old-fashioned way, sitting genteelly sidesaddle, with her hair streaming around her face she looks like an Amazon huntress. The light is fading fast, giving way to a dusky bluish spectrum. A chorus of long-tailed magpies croaks by overhead before fluttering down on the naked branches of the now ashen forest.

Juan Manuel suddenly recalls a painting that still hangs in the corridor of his old hacienda in Adrogué: a tall, pensive Amazon equestrienne who, having surrendered to her horse's will, seems to wander lost and disheartened among dry leaves at dusk. The picture is entitled "Autumn," or "Sadness"—he does not remember which.

On the night table in his room he finds a letter from his mother. *Since you are not here, I will take the orchid for Elsa tomorrow*, she writes. Tomorrow. That is today, he realizes. Today, then, is the fifth anniversary of his wife's death. Five years already. Her name was Elsa. He had never grown accustomed to the fact that she had such a lovely name. "And your name is *Elsa*," he would say as he embraced her, as if that alone were a miracle more breathtaking even than her fair beauty and placid smile. Elsa! The perfection of her features! Her translucent complexion, under which ran veins that seemed the fine blue strokes of a master watercolorist. So many years of love! And then that deadly disease. Like a piercing knife comes the memory of that night when, covering her face with her hands to ward off his kiss, she had cried: "I don't want you to see me like this, so ugly...not even after death. You must cover my face with orchids. You have to promise me..."

But Juan Manuel does not want to begin thinking of all that. Desolate, he tosses the letter on the night table without reading further.

The same serene twilight suffusing the pampa washes over Buenos Aires, inundating in steel blue the stones and the air and the mist-covered trees in Recoleta Square.

Juan Manuel's mother walks confidently through a labyrinth of narrow streets. Never has she lost her way in this intricate city, for as a child her parents taught her how to find her bearings in any quarter. And here is their dwelling—the small cold crypt where parents, grandparents, and so many ancestors rest. So many in such a narrow chamber! If only it were true that each of them sleeps alone with his past and his present, isolated yet side by side! But no, that isn't possible. She lays her spray of orchids on the ground, rummaging through her purse for the key. Then, before the altar, she makes the sign of the cross and checks that the candelabra are well polished, that the white altar cloth is well starched. She sighs and descends into the crypt, holding nervously on to the bronze railing. An oil lamp hangs from the low ceiling, its flame mirrored in the black marble floor and shining on the bronze rings of the various compartments arranged sequentially by date. Here all is order and solemn indifference.

Outside, the drizzle starts up again. The raindrops rebound audibly on the concrete streets. But here everything seems remote: the rain, the city, the obligations that await her at home. And now she sighs again, going over to the smallest and newest compartment, and places the orchids at the head of the casket—where Elsa's face reposes. Poor Juan Manuel, she thinks.

She tries unsuccessfully to feel sadness for her daughter-in-law's fate. But that rancor she admits only to the priest persists in her heart, despite the dozens of rosaries and the multiple short prayers her confessor orders her to recite as penance.

She stares hard at the casket, wishing her eyes could pierce the metal liner, wanting to see, to know, to verify. . . Dead for five years! She was so fragile. Perhaps the plain gold ring has already slipped off her frivolous crumbling fingers, fallen into that dusty hole that was once her bosom. Maybe so. But is she dead? No. She has won in spite of everything. One never dies entirely, that is the truth. That strong dark little boy who continues their line, the grandson who has become her only reason for living, has the blue and candid eyes of Elsa.

At three o'clock in the morning Juan Manuel finally resolves to abandon the armchair beside the fireplace where, nearly stupefied by the heat of the flames, he has been smoking and drinking listlessly for hours. He hops over the dogs asleep in the doorway and starts down the long, open corridor. He feels lazy and tired, very tired. Last night Sylvester, he thinks, and tonight me. I am completely drunk.

Sylvester is asleep. He must have dropped off unexpectedly, because the lamp on the night table is still lit.

His mother's letter lies where he left it, still half open. A long postscript scribbled by his son brings a brief smile to his lips. He tries to decipher the winding infantile handwriting through blurred eyes: *Papá.*

Grandma says I can write to you here. I have learned three more words from the new geography book you gave me. And I am going to write the words and the definitions from memory.

Aerolite: Name given to pieces of minerals that fall from outer space to the earth's surface. Aerolites are planetary fragments that float in space and...

"Aiee!" Juan Manuel moans to himself, staggering as he shakes his head to blot out the definition, those evocative, dazzling words that blind him as though a thousand tiny suns were bursting in front of his eyes.

Hurricane: Violent swirling wind made up of various opposing air masses that form whirlwinds...

"That boy!" Juan Manuel groans. And he feels chilled to the bone, while a tremendous roaring pounds his brain like icy waves pounding a beach.

Halo: Luminous circle that sometimes surrounds the moon.

A light mist seeping through the open window obscures his vision, a blue mist that enfolds him softly. "Halo," he murmurs. An immense tenderness comes over him. Yolanda! If only he could see her, talk to her!

If only he could stand at her bedroom door and listen to her breathing.

Everyone, everything is asleep. How many doors he had to open, some by force, as he crept across the east wing of that old hacienda, hooding the lamp flame with his cupped hand! How many empty, dusty rooms where furniture lay piled in the corners, and how many others in which, as he passed by, unrecognizable people sighed and turned under the sheets!

He had chosen the way of ghosts and murderers.

And now that he has his ear against Yolanda's door, all he can hear is the beating of his own heart.

A piece of furniture must, no doubt, block the door from the inside; a very light piece of furniture, since he shoves it aside with little effort. Who is moaning? Juan Manuel turns up the lamp; the room at first seems to spin, then becomes quiet and orderly as his eyes adjust.

He see a narrow bed veiled by mosquito netting where Yolanda sleeps on her left side, her dark curly hair covering her face like a latticework of luxuriant vines. She moans, caught in some nightmare. Juan Manuel sets the lamp on the floor, parts the mosquito netting, and takes her hand. She clutches his fingers as he helps her to rise from the pillows, to escape from the dream and the weight of that monstrous hair which must have pinned her down in those dark regions of sleep.

She opens her eyes at last, sighs with relief, and whispers: "Thank you."

"Thank you," she repeats, fixing him with her somnambulant eyes. "Oh, it was awful!" she explains. "I was in a horrible place. In a park I often visit in my sleep. A park. Giant plants. Ferns tall as trees. And silence...I don't know how to describe it...Silence as green as chloroform...and suddenly, beneath the silence, a low buzzing sound, growing louder, coming nearer...Death, it is death. And then I tried to escape, to wake up. Because if I did not wake up, if death ever found me in that park, I would be doomed to stay forever, don't you think?"

Juan Manuel makes no reply, fearing to shatter this intimacy with the sound of his voice.

Taking a deep breath, Yolanda continues. "They say that in sleep we return to those places where we lived in a prior existence. I, too, sometimes return to a certain Creole house. A room, a patio, a room, another patio with a fountain in the center. I go there and..."

She falls silent and looks at him.

The moment he feared so much has come. The moment when, lucid at last and free from terror, she asks herself how and why this man is sitting on the edge of her bed. He waits, resigned for the imperious "Out of here!" and that solemn gesture with which women are reported to show one the door in instances like this.

But no. Yolanda puts her head on his chest, pressing against his heart.

Astonished, Juan Manuel does not move. Oh, that delicate temple and the smell of flowering honeysuckle coming from those locks of hair pressed against his lips! He remains motionless for a long time. Motionless, tender, full of wonder—as if an unexpected and priceless treasure had fallen into his arms by accident.

Yolanda! His embrace tightens, pressing her to him. But she cries out—a brief, husky, strange cry—and grabs his arms. They struggle, Juan Manuel entangling himself in her thick, sweet-scented hair. He grapples until he is able to seize her by the neck, and then he brutally throws her down on her back.

Gasping, she tosses her head from side to side, weeping as Juan Manuel kisses her mouth and caresses one of her breasts, small and hard like the camellias she cultivates. So many tears. Running silently down her cheeks, so many tears. Falling on the pillow like hot watery pearls, dropping into the hollow of his hand still gripping her neck.

Ashamed, his passion ebbing, Juan Manuel relaxes his embrace.

"Do you hate me, Yolanda?"

She is silent, inert.

"Shall I stay?"

Closing her eyes, she whispers: "No, please go."

The wooden floorboards creak as he crosses to the lamp and goes to the door, leaving Yolanda submerged in shadow.

On the fourth day, a fine mist shrouds the pampa in a white cottony silence that muffles and shortens the sound of the hunters' guns out on the islands and blinds the frightened storks planing in to seek sanctuary on the lake.

And Yolanda—what is she doing? Juan Manuel wonders. What is she doing while he drags his mud-heavy boots through the reeds, killing birds without reason or passion? Maybe she is in the orchard looking for the last strawberries, or pulling up the first radishes: *One must grasp the leaves tight and take them with a single pull, tearing them out of the dark earth like tiny red hearts.* Or it may be that she is in the house, standing on a stool by an open cupboard, the maid handing her a stack of freshly ironed sheets which she will carefully arrange in even piles. And if she were waiting at the window for his return? Anything is possible with a woman like Yolanda, such a strange woman, one who resembles a... But he checks himself, afraid of hurting her in his thoughts.

Twilight again. The hunter gazes across the shadowy pampa, trying to locate the hill and the house. A distant light blinks on amid the fog, pointing the way like a miniature lighthouse.

He drags his boat up the bank and starts across the grassland toward the light. On the way he puts to flight a few head of grazing cattle, their hair twisted into curls by the damp breath of the fog. He leaps barbed-wire fences, the fog clinging to the points like fleece. He sidesteps the thick clumps of thistle that glisten silvery and phosphorescent in the darkness.

Reaching the gate, he crosses the park and goes past the camellias in the garden to a certain window, where he wipes the pane free of fog and then stands transfixed as before his eyes a fairy tale unfolds.

Yolanda is standing naked in the bathroom, absorbed in the contemplation of her right shoulder.

Her right shoulder—on which something light and flexible looms, drooping down to cover a small portion of her back. A wing, or rather, the beginning of a wing. Or more exactly, the stump of a wing. A small atrophied member which she now strokes carefully, as if dreading the touch.

The rest of her body is exactly as he had imagined: slender, proud, and white.

A hallucination, Juan Manuel thinks to himself as he drives crazily, his hands shaking on the steering wheel, along the highway. The long walk, the fog, the weariness, and this state of anxiety I've been living in for the last few days have all combined to make me see what does not exist. Should I go back? But how would I explain my abrupt departure? Don't think about it until you get to Buenos Aires. That's the best thing to do.

By the time he reaches the suburbs of the city, a fine powdery mist coats the windshield. The windshield wipers click like nickel swords, tic-tac, tic-tac, back and forth with a regularity as implacable as his anguish.

He crosses Buenos Aires, dark and deserted in the light shower which bursts into heavy rain as he opens the gate and starts up the walk to his house.

"What's the matter?" his mother asks. "Why have you come back at this hour?"

"My son?"

"Sleeping. It's eleven o'clock, Juan Manuel."

"I want to see him. Good night, Mother."

The old woman shrugs her shoulders and pads off to her room wrapped in a long robe. No, she will never grow accustomed to her son's whims. He is very bright, a fine lawyer; but she would have preferred him less talented and more conventional, like everyone else's sons.

Juan Manuel goes into his son's bedroom and turns on the light. Curled up next to the wall, his head covered by the sheets, the boy resembles a ball of white twine. Uncovering him, Juan Manuel thinks: He sleeps like an untamed little animal. In spite of the fact that he is nine years old, and notwithstanding his meticulous grandmother.

"Billy, wake up."

The boy sits up in bed, blinks his eyes, and grants his father a sleepy smile.

"I brought you a gift, Billy."

The boy stretches out his hand. Searching through his pockets, Juan Manuel takes out the handkerchief tied into a pouch and hands it to his son. Billy unties the knots and spreads the handkerchief open. Finding nothing, he looks up at his father with a trusting expression, waiting for an explanation.

"It was a kind of flower, Billy—a magnificent jellyfish, I swear. I fished it from the lake for you...and it has disappeared..."

The boy thinks for a moment and then cries triumphantly: "No, Papa, it didn't disappear; it *melted*. Because jellyfish are made out of water, just water. I learned it in the geography book you gave me."

Outside, the rain lashes the great leaves of the palm tree in the corner of their garden, its shiny-as-patent-leather branches thrashing against the walls.

"You're right, Billy. It melted."

"But...jellyfish live in the sea, Papa. How did they get to the lakes?"

"I don't know, son," says Juan Manuel, suddenly tired of the conversation, his mind whirling.

Maybe I should telephone Yolanda, he thinks. Everything might seem less vague, less dreadful if I could hear her voice—which, like all other voices under similar circumstances, would simply sound distant, a bit surprised by an unexpected call.

He covers Billy and arranges the pillows. Then he goes back down the solemn staircase in that huge house, so cold and ugly in the rain and lightning. The telephone hangs in the hall—another of his mother's inspirations. As he unhooks the small tube-like receiver, a flash of lightning illuminates the front windows from top to bottom. He asks the operator for a number, and while he waits, the deafening thunderclap rolls over the sleeping city like a train roaring through his living room.

And my call, he thinks, now races through the wires under the rain. Now it is passing through Rivadavia with its line of darkened streetlights, and now it is zooming by the suburbs with their muddy flooding pathways, taking now to the freeway and flying along that straight and lonely road until, by now surely, it reaches the vast pampa with its occasional small villages, going like a bullet now across provincial cities where the asphalt glistens like water under the moonlight, and now perhaps shooting out into open country alone in the rain again, hurtling past a closed railway station, and then dashing across the pasture to the hill, along the poplar-lined drive to dive into the house. And now it rings insistently, echoing and reechoing in the large deserted drawing room, where the wooden floors creak and the roof leaks in one corner.

The ringing resounds for a long time, vibrating hoarsely in Juan Manuel's ear, echoing sharply in the empty drawing room while he waits anxiously. Then someone suddenly lifts the receiver at the other end. But before the voice can say a word, Juan Manuel slams the receiver onto its hook.

Thinking: If I had said, "I can't go through with it, Yolanda. I've thought it out, believe me. It just isn't possible." If I had at least confirmed my doubts about that horror. But i'm afraid to know the truth.

He climbs the staircase slowly

There was something more cruel, more punishing than death, after all. And he had believed that death was the final mystery, the ultimate suffering!

Death—that blind alley!

While he grew older, Elsa would remain eternally young, preserved forever at age thirty-three as on the day she departed from this life. And the day would come when Billy would be older than his mother, when he would know more of the world than she.

Think of it: Elsa's hands become dust, yet her very gestures perpetuated in her letters, in the sweater she knitted for him; and those luminous irises of her now empty eyes still shining with life in her photographs...Elsa erased, fixed in the earth but yet living in their memory and still part of their everyday life as though her spirit kept growing and could react even to things she once ignored.

Nevertheless, Juan Manuel now knows that there is a condition far more cruel and incomprehensible than any of death's little corollaries, for he has perceived a new mystery: a suffering consisting of amazement and fear.

The light from Billy's bedroom throws a shaft into the dark corridor, inviting him to enter once more in hope of finding his son still awake. But

Billy is asleep, and so Juan Manuel looks around the room for something to distract himself and thereby ease his anguish. He goes to Billy's desk and turns the pages of the new geography book. *History of the Earth...The Sidereal Phase of the Earth...Life in the Paleozoic Era...*

And then he reads: *How beautiful must this silent landscape have been in which giant lycopodiums and equisetums raised themselves to such a height, and where mammoth ferns swayed like trees in the humid air...*

What landscape is this? he wonders. I cannot have seen it before, surely. Why, then, does it seem so familiar? He turns the page, reading at random:...*In any case, it is during the Carboniferous Period when swarms of flying insects appear over the now arborescent regions. During the Late Carboniferous there were insects which possessed three pairs of wings. The most remarkable insects of this Period were very large, similar in shape to our present-day dragonflies but much bigger, having a wingspan of sixty-five centimeters...*

Yolanda's dreams, he realizes. The sweet and terrible secret of her shoulder. Perhaps this was where the explanation of the mystery lay.

But Juan Manuel feels incapable of soaring into the intricate galleries of Nature in order to arrive at the mystery's origin. He fears losing his way in that wild world with its disorderly and poorly mapped pathways, strewn with an unsystematic confusion of clues; fears falling into some dark abyss that no amount of logic will lead him out of. And abandoning Yolanda once more, he closes the book, turns off the light, and leaves the room.

Translated by Richard and Lucia Cunningham

HENRI MICHAUX

*H*ENRI MICHAUX *(born 1899), the eminent French poet, essayist, and painter, is indisputably one of the most original and prolific of all contemporary artists, unmatched for the imaginative breadth of his oeuvre and for the power of his daring inventiveness. Born in Belgium, Michaux rejected his middle-class upbringing at an early age and moved to Paris in 1922. He soon plunged into extensive travels throughout Asia and South America, and some of these experiences have been recorded in two provocative volumes, Ecuador (1929) and A Barbarian in Asia (1933). Michaux might claim Swift, Rabelais, and Lautréamont as his literary ancestors, but he has always shunned involvement with popular trends. He treasures his privacy above all else and lives as a near recluse, preferring to go it alone as he persistently tackles the challenges of inward voyages in his explorations of emotional turbulence. In his work, he has created a dense, personal world, bubbling over with sardonic humor, where he invents new words and new beings. In this fusion of the real and the unreal, he attacks the blind futility of convention, conjuring up a realm where the bizarre, the humorous, and the terrifying all mingle.*

From 1954 to 1964, he participated in carefully monitored studies of hallucinogenic drugs. His fascinating insights on his reactions to these powerful stimulants appear in Miserable Miracle *(1956) and* The Major Ordeals of the Mind *(1966). He has over thirty major poetry volumes and perhaps forty shorter texts to his credit. One of his finest collections,* Selected Writings: The Space Within *(1944), includes selections from eight books of prose poems and free verse that were published between 1927 and 1941. As a kind of philosophical outcast from literary society, he rejected the Grand Prix des Lettres, offered for the entirety of his work, in 1965. His paintings, first exhibited in 1937, are displayed in many museums throughout the world. In 1978, the Guggenheim Museum in New York City mounted a major retrospective of Michaux's work.*

In the passages from In the Land of Magic *(1941) that follow, the reader will discover a country where the impossible is realizable, where volition reigns supreme. It is hard not to be charmed by the mysterious activities that one encounters there. Some episodes describe the difficult apprenticeship of the Mages; others show their mischievous tricks as they play havoc with the laws of nature. As André Gide so aptly put it, "Michaux excels in making us feel intuitively both the strangeness of natural things and the naturalness of strange things."*

In the Land
of Magic

Henri Michaux

YOU SEE the cage, you hear fluttering. You note the indisputable noise of the beak sharpening itself against the bars. But no birds at all.

In one of these empty cages I heard the most intense screeching of parrakeets in my life. But honestly, not one could be seen.

Yet what a noise! As if three, four dozen were in the cage:

"Are they not crowded together in this little cage?" I asked mechanically, but adding to my question, in the course of hearing myself ask it, a mocking tone.

"Yes, indeed...," its Master firmly replied, "that is why they make such a racket. They would like more room."

Walking on the two banks of a stream is a laborious exercise.

Rather frequently you see a man (a student in magic) going upstream that way, walking on the one bank and the other at the same time: being very preoccupied, he does not see you. For what he is performing is delicate and tolerates no inattention. He would very soon find himself back on one bank, and how disgraceful that would be!

In the evening you often see fires in the country. These fires are not

Excerpt from *In the Land of Magic*.

fires. They burn nothing whatever. A strand of a cobweb that passed through the very center of one of them would hardly (and only if it was terribly intense) be consumed.

These fires, in short, are without heat.

But they have a brightness which nothing in nature approaches (though less than that of the electric arc).

These conflagrations charm and terrify, without any danger too, and the fire stops as suddenly as it appeared.

I have seen water which keeps from flowing. If the water is in the habit, if it is your water, it doesn't spread, even if the bottle breaks into four pieces.

It just waits for you to put it into another. It doesn't try to spread outside.

Is it the Mage's power at work?

Yes and no, apparently no, the Mage possibly being unaware of the breaking of the bottle and of the pains the water is taking to hold in place.

But he should not make the water wait too long, for this position is uncomfortable and difficult for it to hold and, without exactly letting go, it might stretch pretty far out.

Of course it must be your water and not water of five minutes ago, water that you have just drawn. That would flow out at once. What would prevent it?

Somebody is talking. Suddenly he is seized by an irrepressible, explosive sneezing, that nothing led him to anticipate. The Listeners understand: "Somebody has pinched his cord," they think, and they go off laughing. These internal reminders, inflicted by the Mages, go as far as spasms, contractions, or angina pectoris.

They call it *"pinching the cord."* They also say, without further explanation: "Somebody has pinched it hard."

People have been observed in agony who had nothing wrong with them except that somebody was carefully pinching their *"it."*

The Mages love darkness. The novices have an absolute need for it. They try their hand, if I may put it that way, in chests, wardrobes, linen closets, boxes, cellars, garrets, staircases.

There wasn't a day at my house that something out of the ordinary didn't come from the cupboard, perhaps a toad, perhaps a rat, aware of its own awkwardness and vanishing on the spot without being able to scamper off.

You could find anything including hanged men, mock ones of course, who didn't even have real ropes.

Who would maintain that he could get used to this in the long run?

But an apprehension always held me back for a second, my hand undecidedly on the door handle.

One day a bloody head rolled over my new jacket without even making a stain.

After a moment—horrible—may I never have one like it again—I closed the door.

This must have been a Novice, this Mage, to have been incapable of making a stain on such a clean jacket.

But the head, its weight, its general appearance, had been well imitated. With a sickening fright I felt it falling upon me, when it disappeared.

The child, the chief's child, the patient's child, the plowman's child, the fool's child, the Mage's child, the child is born with twenty-two folds. It's a matter of unfolding himself. The life of the man is then complete. Under that form he dies. There are no more folds for him to undo.

Rarely does a man die without having a few more folds to undo. This has occurred, however. Parallel to this operation the man forms a nucleus. The inferior races, such as *the white race*, see the nucleus rather than the unfolded fold. But the Mage sees the unfolded fold.

Only the unfolded fold is important. The rest is mere epiphenomenon.

The hunchback? A poor wretch, unconsciously obsessed by paternity (rather hot for sex, to be sure, but paternity is what itches him most, they claim).

To comfort him they draw out of his hump another hunchback, a very little one.

What a strange tête-à-tête, when they look at each other for the first time, the old one comforted, the other already bitter and loaded with the extreme dejection of the infirm.

The hunchbacks whom one draws out for them are not true hunchbacks, needless to say, nor really offspring, nor really alive. They disappear after several days without leaving any traces.

But the hunchback has got a grip on himself, and that is not the least of miracles.

Of course shock is indispensable. Shock is what chiefly counts; the galvanization of the individual, who at first is all a-tremble from it.

On the other hand, if the hunchback looks with indifference at the little creature drawn from his hump, the effort is wasted.

You can draw two dozen out of him without any effect, without the slightest improvement in him.

What to make of it? You have there a true, perfect hunchback.

Suddenly you feel a touch. But nothing is really visible beside you, especially if the day is no longer perfectly clear, at the end of the afternoon (the time when *they* come out).

You feel uneasy. You shut the doors and windows. It seems then as if a creature truly in air (as the Medusa is at once in water and made of water), a transparent, massive, elastic one, is trying to pass through the window which resists your pull. A Medusa of air has come in!

You naturally try to explain the thing away to yourself. But the unbearable impression magnifies frightfully, you go out screaming "Myah!" and throw yourself into the street on the run.

Although they know perfectly well that the stars are something besides huge lights on the surface of the sky, they cannot prevent themselves from making star-likenesses to delight their children, to delight themselves, somewhat for practice, out of magical spontaneity.

One who has only a small courtyard builds a ceiling swarming with stars which is the most beautiful thing I have seen. The wretched little yard, surrounded by walls so tired as to seem almost plaintive, under this private sky which sparkles and rumbles with stars—what a show! I've often considered and tried to calculate how high up these stars might be; without succeeding, for if several neighbors take advantage of them, their number is not very large and they seem rather fluffy. On the other hand, they never pass *under* a cloud.

At any rate I've noticed that great care is used to keep them away from the vicinity of the moon, no doubt for fear of absent-mindedly making them pass in front of it.

It seems that this, more than any other manifestation of magical force, arouses envy and desire. The neighbors fight, fight nastily, try to filch the stars from next door. And endless retaliations follow.

Among the people who work at small trades, among the torch-placers, goiter-charmers, noise-effacers, the Water Shepherd is conspicuous for his personal charm and that of his occupation.

The Water Shepherd whistles at a spring and presto! it disengages itself from its bed and goes forward following him. It follows him, growing larger as it passes other bodies of water.

Sometimes he prefers to keep the streamlet as it is, small size, collecting here and there only what is needed to keep it from dwindling away, taking special care when it passes through sandy ground.

I've seen one of these shepherds—out of fascination I stuck with him—who, with a little stream of nothing at all, with a piece of water as big as a boot, gave himself the satisfaction of crossing a great dark river. The waters did not mix, he recovered his little stream intact on the other bank.

A neat trick which the newcomer to stream-leading will not succeed in duplicating. In a second the waters would mix and he might just as well go look for a new spring.

In any case, a tail of the stream necessarily disappears, but enough remains to water an orchard or fill an empty ditch.

He had better not delay, for being very weak it is ready to play itself out. This water is out-of-date.

They say that if one could free the water of all needle-fish, bathing would be something so unspeakably delicious that it is just as well not to dream about it, for it will never, never be.

They try none the less. They use a fishing pole for the purpose.

The fishing pole for fishing for needle-fish has to be fine, fine, fine. The line has to be absolutely invisible and to drop slowly, imperceptibly into the water.

Unfortunately the needle-fish himself is practically invisible.

One of their ways of testing: the bundle of snakes. It confers the right to the second-degree beret. The candidate for the obtainment of the second magical beret has to go seek out the snake. Every snake is considered suitable. None should be rejected. There are some venomous ones, there are some which cannot endure being together. There are little ones and big ones. Need I mention that they are slippery, that they tend to coil up on themselves (against the rules!) and with each other (against the rules!).

What he has to bring back is a good-sized, well-compacted bundle, tied by three pieces of string or willow twigs.

Such are the difficulties for the obtention of the second-degree beret. Without a grip on the snakes, no magic for him. If the candidate is accepted, they send him the exact double of his head, formed by magic. Otherwise it's a melon.

The malefactors there, when taken red-handed, have their faces torn out on the spot. The mage-executioner arrives at once.

Incredible will power is necessary to pull out a face, accustomed as it is to its man.

Little by little, the face works loose, starts to come off.

The executioner redoubles his efforts, braces himself, breathes mightily.

Finally he tears it out.

If the operation is well done, the whole thing detaches itself, forehead, eyes, cheeks, the whole front of the face as if cleaned off by some sort of corrosive sponge.

A thick and dark blood gushes from pores that are everywhere generously open.

The next day an enormous, round, scabby clot has been formed which can inspire nothing but fear.

He who has seen one always remembers it. He has his nightmares to remind him.

If the operation is not well done, because of the malefactor's being particularly robust, only his nose and eyes get torn off. This is at least some result, for the tearing-off is purely magical, and the executioner's fingers are really unable to touch or even to graze the face to be pulled out.

Placed in the center of perfectly empty arenas, the accused man is questioned. In an occult way. The question resounds in a profound silence, but still forcefully for him.

Reflected by the steps, it rebounds, comes back, falls down, and drops on his head like a city tumbling in ruins.

Under squeezing waves, comparable only to successive catastrophes, he loses all resistance and confesses his crime. He cannot not confess.

Deafened, turned to a rag, with aching and echoing head, with the feeling of having had to do with ten thousand accusers, he leaves the arena, where the most absolute silence has not ceased to reign....

Translated by Richard Ellmann

WILLIAM
FAULKNER

W ILLIAM FAULKNER (1897–1962) lived most of his life in northern Mississippi (Oxford), which he recreated in fictional—one might even say mythical—terms as Yoknapatawpha County, in a series of novels and short stories whose power, scope, and complexity give support to his position as the major North American novelist of this century. In the size and imaginative coherence of his accomplishment, he bears comparison to Proust and Joyce, and if his work is uneven and often overwritten, that may serve to remind us of problems and ambitions he shares with predecessors like Melville and Whitman.

Faulkner's subject is the American South, more particularly its historical tragedies—slavery and the Civil War—and the context they provide for individual destinies. Some of his characters are self-made American dreamers (e.g., Thomas Sutpen, a kind of grotesque Great Gatsby), others are driven by obsessive visions of such varying ideals as wealth, honor, love, and social justice. Nearly all of them fail, some comically, some tragically. All of them exist in an engrossing tension between social and historical change on the one hand and individual destiny on the other.

There are hints and glances at magical realism throughout Faulkner's fiction, but it is in his hunting stories, stories of the remaining wilderness, that he delves deepest into this genre. "The Old People," which is part of Faulkner's Go Down, Moses (1942), a work made up of short stories linked to each other in a way that forms a novel, exemplifies this side of his work movingly and beautifully. It is a story of initiation that seems to look back to the beginning of time, as suggested by its opening sentence: "At first there was nothing." Magical realism, as we have noted in the introduction to this anthology, often takes place at the intersection of two cultures, and the wisdom that is handed down to "the boy" by the archetypally named Indian, Sam Fathers, includes not only the knowledge of the hunter but the religious attitudes toward nature and animals that characterized the neolithic civilizations of North America. This story provides us with an engrossing narrative; it also takes in a timescape that is unusual in fiction, especially fiction of the realistic sort.

In his 1982 Nobel Prize acceptance speech, Gabriel García Márquez recalled Faulkner's acceptance of the same prize in 1950 and acknowledged the older writer as his master. Certainly the relations between Faulkner's Yoknapatawpha and García Márquez's Macondo are fascinating to contemplate, as are the two writers' experiments with convoluted time and extended syntax. The note of acknowledgment also serves to remind us that the ties between North American and South American literature will always have special meaning. It shows that North American writers need to be conscious that their own tradition is not only continental but hemispheric as well.

The Old People

William Faulkner

I

AT FIRST there was nothing. There was the faint, cold, steady rain, the gray and constant light of the late November dawn, with the voices of the hounds converging somewhere in it and toward them. Then Sam Fathers, standing just behind the boy as he had been standing when the boy shot his first running rabbit with his first gun and almost with the first load it ever carried, touched his shoulder and he began to shake, not with any cold. Then the buck was there. He did not come into sight; he was just there, looking not like a ghost but as if all of light were condensed in him and he were the source of it, not only moving in it but disseminating it, already running, seen first as you always see the deer, in that split second after he has already seen you, already slanting away in that first soaring bound, the antlers even in that dim light looking like a small rocking-chair balanced on his head.

"Now," Sam Fathers said, "shoot quick, and slow."

The boy did not remember that shot at all. He would live to be eighty, as his father and his father's twin brother and their father in his turn had lived to be, but he would never hear that shot nor remember even the shock of the gun-butt. He didn't even remember what he did with the gun afterward. He was running. Then he was standing over the buck where it lay on the wet earth still in the attitude of speed and not looking at all dead, standing over it shaking and jerking, with Sam Fathers beside him again, extending the knife. "Don't walk up to him in front," Sam said. "If he ain't dead, he will cut you all to pieces with his feet. Walk up to him

217

from behind and take him by the horn first, so you can hold his head down until you can jump away. Then slip your other hand down and hook your fingers in his nostrils."

The boy did that—drew the head back and the throat taut and drew Sam Fathers' knife across the throat and Sam stooped and dipped his hands in the hot smoking blood and wiped them back and forth across the boy's face. Then Sam's horn rang in the wet gray woods and again and again; there was a boiling wave of dogs about them, with Tennie's Jim and Boon Hogganbeck whipping them back after each had had a taste of the blood, then the men, the true hunters—Walter Ewell whose rifle never missed, and Major de Spain and old General Compson and the boy's cousin, McCaslin Edmonds, grandson of his father's sister, sixteen years his senior and, since both he and McCaslin were only children and the boy's father had been nearing seventy when he was born, more his brother than his cousin and more his father than either—sitting their horses and looking down at them: at the old man of seventy who had been a Negro for two generations now but whose face and bearings were still those of the Chickasaw chief who had been his father; and the white boy of twelve with the prints of the bloody hands on his face, who had nothing to do now but stand straight and not let the trembling show.

"Did he do all right, Sam?" his cousin McCaslin said.

"He done all right," Sam Fathers said.

They were the white boy, marked forever, and the old dark man sired on both sides by savage kings, who had marked him, whose bloody hands had merely formally consecrated him to that which, under the man's tutelage, he had already accepted, humbly and joyfully, with abnegation and with pride too; the hands, the touch, the first worthy blood which he had been found at last worthy to draw, joining him and the man forever, so that the man would continue to live past the boy's seventy years and then eighty years, long after the man himself had entered the earth as chiefs and kings entered it;—the child, not yet a man, whose grandfather had lived in the same country and in almost the same manner as the boy himself would grow up to live, leaving his descendants in the land in his turn as his grandfather had done, and the old man past seventy whose grandfathers had owned the land long before the white men ever saw it and who had vanished from it now with all their kind, what of blood they left behind them running now in another race and for a while even in bondage and now drawing toward the end of its alien and irrevocable course, barren, since Sam Fathers had no children.

His father was Ikkemotubbe himself, who had named himself Doom. Sam told the boy about that—how Ikkemotubbe, old Issetibbeha's sister's son, had run away to New Orleans in his youth and returned seven years later with a French companion calling himself the Chevalier Soeur-Blonde de Vitry, who must have been the Ikkemotubbe of his family too and who was already addressing Ikkemotubbe as *Du Homme*;—returned, came home again, with his foreign Aramis and the quadroon slave woman who was to be Sam's mother, and a gold-laced hat and coat and a wicker wine-hamper containing a litter of month-old puppies and a gold snuff-box filled with a white powder resembling fine sugar. And how he was met at the River landing by three or four companions of his bachelor youth, and while the light of a smoking torch gleamed on the glittering braid of the hat and coat Doom squatted in the mud of the land and took one of the puppies from the hamper and put a pinch of the white powder on its tongue and the puppy died before the one who was holding it could cast it away. And how they returned to the Plantation where Issetibbeha, dead now, had been succeeded by his son, Doom's fat cousin Moketubbe, and the next day Moketubbe's eight-year-old son died suddenly and that afternoon, in the presence of Moketubbe and most of the others (the People, Sam Fathers called them) Doom produced another puppy from the wine-hamper and put a pinch of the white powder on its tongue and Moketubbe abdicated and Doom became in fact The Man which his French friend already called him. And how on the day after that, during the ceremony of accession, Doom pronounced a marriage between the pregnant quadroon and one of the slave men which he had just inherited (that was how Sam Fathers got his name, which in Chickasaw had been Had-Two-Fathers) and two years later sold the man and woman and the child who was his own son to his white neighbor, Carothers McCaslin.

That was seventy years ago. The Sam Fathers whom the boy knew was already sixty—a man not tall, squat rather, almost sedentary, flabby-looking though he actually was not, with hair like a horse's mane which even at seventy showed no trace of white and a face which showed no age until he smiled, whose only visible trace of Negro blood was a slight dullness of the hair and the fingernails, and something else which you did notice about the eyes, which you noticed because it was not always there, only in repose and not always then—something not in their shape nor pigment but in their expression, and the boy's cousin McCaslin told him what that was: not the heritage of Ham, not the mark of servitude but of bondage; the knowledge that for a while that part of his blood had been the blood of slaves. "Like an old lion or a bear in a cage," McCaslin said. "He was born in the cage and has been in it all his life; he knows nothing else. Then he smells something. It might be anything, any breeze blowing past anything and then into his nostrils. But there for a second was the hot sand or the cane-brake that he never even saw himself, might not even know if he did see it and probably does know he couldn't hold his own with it if he got back to it. But that's not what he smells then. It was the cage he smelled. He hadn't smelled the cage until that minute. Then the hot sand or the brake blew into his nostrils and blew away, and all he could smell was the cage. That's what makes his eyes look like that."

"Then let him go!" the boy cried. "Let him go!"

His cousin laughed shortly. Then he stopped laughing, making the sound that is. It had never been laughing. "His cage ain't McCaslins," he said. "He was a wild man. When he was born, all his blood on both sides, except the little white part, knew things that had been tamed out of our blood so long ago that we have not only forgotten them, we have to live together in herds to protect ourselves from our own sources. He was the direct son not only of a warrior but of a chief. Then he grew up and began to learn things, and all of a sudden one day he found out that he had been betrayed, the blood of the warriors and chiefs had been betrayed. Not by his father," he added quickly. "He probably never held it against old Doom for selling him and his mother into slavery, because he probably believed the damage was already done before then and it was the same warriors' and chiefs' blood in him and Doom both that was betrayed through the black blood which his mother gave him. Not betrayed by the black blood and not wilfully betrayed by his mother, but betrayed by her all the same, who had bequeathed him not only the blood of slaves but even a little of the very blood which had enslaved it; himself his own battleground, the scene of his own vanquishment and the mausoleum of his defeat. His cage aint us," McCaslin said. "Did you ever know anybody yet, even your father and Uncle Buddy, that ever told him to do or not do anything that he ever paid any attention to?"

That was true. The boy first remembered him as sitting in the door of the plantation blacksmith-shop, where he sharpened plow-points and mended tools and even did rough carpenter-work when he was not in the woods. And sometimes, even when the woods had not drawn him, even with the shop cluttered with work which the farm waited on, Sam would sit there, doing nothing at all for half a day or a whole one, and no man, neither the boy's father and twin uncle in their day nor his cousin McCaslin after he became practical though not yet titular master, ever to say to him, "I want this finished by sundown" or "why wasn't this done yesterday?" And once each year, in the late fall, in November, the boy would watch the wagon, the hooped canvas top erected now, being loaded—the food, hams and sausage from the smokehouse, coffee and flour and molasses from the commissary, a whole beef killed just last night for the dogs until there would be meat in camp, the crate containing the dogs themselves, then the bedding, the guns, the horns and lanterns and axes, and his cousin McCaslin and Sam Fathers in their hunting clothes would mount to the seat and with Tennie's Jim sitting on the dog-crate they would drive away to Jefferson, to join Major de Spain and General Compson and Boon Hogganbeck and Walter Ewell and go on into the big bottom of the Tallahatchie where the deer and bear were, to be gone two weeks. But before the wagon was even loaded the boy would find that he could watch no longer. He would go away, running almost, to stand behind the corner where he could not see the wagon and nobody could see him, not crying, holding himself rigid except for trembling, whispering to himself: "Soon now. Soon now. Just three more years" (or two or one more) "and I will be ten. Then Cass said I can go."

White man's work, when Sam did work. Because he did nothing else: farmed no allotted acres of his own, as the other ex-slaves of old Carothers McCaslin did, performed no field-work for daily wages as the younger and newer Negroes did—and the boy never knew just how that had been settled between Sam and old Carothers, or perhaps with old Carothers' twin sons after him. For, although Sam lived among the Negroes, in a cabin among the other cabins in the quarters, and consorted with Negroes (what of consorting with anyone Sam did after the boy got big enough to walk alone from the house to the blacksmith-shop and then to carry a gun) and dressed like them and talked like them and even went with them to the Negro church now and then, he was still the son of that Chickasaw chief and the Negroes knew it. And, it seemed to the boy, not only Negroes. Boon Hogganbeck's grandmother had been a Chickasaw woman too, and although the blood had run white since and Boon was a white man, it was not chief's blood. To the boy at least, the difference was apparent immediately you saw Boon and Sam together, and even Boon seemed to know it was there—even Boon, to whom in his tradition it had never occurred that anyone might be better born than himself. A man might be smarter, he admitted that, or richer (luckier, he called it) but not better born. Boon was a mastiff, absolutely faithful, dividing his fidelity equally between Major de Spain and the boy's cousin McCaslin, absolutely dependent for his very bread and dividing that impartially too between Major de Spain and McCaslin, hardy, generous, courageous enough, a slave to all the appetites and almost unratiocina-tive. In the boy's eyes at least it was Sam Fathers, the Negro, who bore himself not only toward his cousin McCaslin and Major de Spain but toward all white men, with gravity and dignity and without servility or recourse to that impenetrable wall of ready and easy mirth which Negroes sustain between themselves and white men, bearing himself toward his cousin McCaslin not only as one man to another but as an older man to a younger.

He taught the boy the woods, to hunt, when to shoot and when not to shoot, when to kill and when not to kill, and better, what to do with it afterward. Then he would talk to the boy, the two of them sitting beneath the close fierce stars on a summer hilltop while they waited for the hounds to bring the fox back within hearing, or beside a fire in the November or December woods while the dogs worked out a coon's trail along the creek, or fireless in the pitch dark and heavy dew of April mornings while they squatted beneath a turkey-roost. The boy would never question him; Sam did not react to questions. The boy would just wait and then listen and Sam would begin, talking about the old days and the People whom he had not had time ever to know and so could not remember (he did not remember ever having seen his father's face), and in place of whom the other race into which his blood had run supplied him with no substitute.

And as he talked about those old times and those dead and vanished men of another race from either that the boy knew, gradually to the boy those old times would cease to be old times and would become a part of the boy's present, not only as if they had happened yesterday but as if they were still happening, the men who walked through them actually walking in breath and air and casting an actual shadow on the earth they had not quitted. And more: as if some of them had not happened yet but would occur tomorrow, until at last it would seem to the boy that he himself had not come into existence yet, that none of his race nor the other subject race which his people had brought with them into the land had come here yet; that although it had been his grandfather's and then his father's and uncle's and was now his cousin's and someday would be his own land which he and Sam hunted over, their hold upon it actually was as trivial and without reality as the now faded and archaic script in the chancery book in Jefferson which allocated it to them and that it was he, the boy, who was the guest here and Sam Fathers' voice the mouthpiece of the host.

Until three years ago there had been two of them, the other a full-blood Chickasaw, in a sense even more incredibly lost than Sam Fathers. He called himself Jobaker, as if it were one word. Nobody knew his history at all. He was a hermit, living in a foul little shack at the forks of the creek five miles from the plantation and about that far from any other habitation. He was a market hunter and fisherman and he consorted with nobody, black or white; no Negro would even cross his path and no man dared approach his hut except Sam. And perhaps once a month the boy would find them in Sam's shop—two old men squatting on their heels on the dirt floor, talking in a mixture of Negroid English and flat hill dialect and now and then a phrase of that old tongue which as time went on and the boy squatted there too listening, he began to learn. Then Jobaker died. That is, nobody had seen him in some time. Then one morning Sam was missing, nobody, not even the boy, knew when nor where, until that night when some Negroes hunting in the creek bottom saw the sudden burst of flame and approached. It was Jobaker's hut, but before they got anywhere near it, someone shot at them from the shadows beyond it. It was Sam who fired, but nobody ever found Jobaker's grave.

The next morning, sitting at breakfast with his cousin, the boy saw Sam pass the dining-room window and he remembered then that never in his life before had he seen Sam nearer the house than the blacksmith-shop. He stopped eating even; he sat there and he and his cousin both heard the voices from beyond the pantry door, then the door opened and Sam entered, carrying his hat in his hand but without knocking as anyone else on the place except a house servant would have done, entered just far enough for the door to close behind him and stood looking at neither of them—the Indian face above the nigger clothes, looking at something over their heads or at something not even in the room.

"I want to go," he said. "I want to go to the Big Bottom to live."

"To live?" the boy's cousin said.

"At Major de Spain's and your camp, where you go to hunt," Sam said. "I could take care of it for you all while you aint there. I will build me a little house in the woods, if you rather I didn't stay in the big one."

"What about Isaac here?" his cousin said. "How will you get away from him? Are you going to take him with you?" But still Sam looked at neither of them, standing just inside the room with that face which showed nothing, which showed that he was an old man only when it smiled.

"I want to go," he said. "Let me go."

"Yes," the cousin said quietly. "Of course. I'll fix it with Major de Spain. You want to go soon?"

"I'm going now," Sam said. He went out. And that was all. The boy was nine then; it seemed perfectly natural that nobody, not even his cousin McCaslin, should argue with Sam. Also, since he was nine now, he could understand that Sam could leave him and their days and nights in the woods together without any wrench. He believed that he and Sam both knew that this was not only temporary but that the exigencies of his maturing, of that for which Sam had been training him all his life some day to dedicate himself, required it. They had settled that one night last summer while they listened to the hounds bringing a fox back up the creek valley; now the boy discerned in that very talk under the high, fierce August stars a presage, a warning, of this moment today. "I done taught you all there is of this settled country," Sam said. "You can hunt it good as I can now. You are ready for the Big Bottom now, for bear and deer. Hunter's meat," he said. "Next year you will be ten. You will write your age in two numbers and you will be ready to become a man. Your pa" (Sam always referred to the boy's cousin as his father, establishing even before the boy's orphanhood did that relation between them not of the ward to his guardian and kinsman and chief and head of his blood, but of the child to the man who sired his flesh and his thinking too.) "promised you can go with us then." So the boy could understand Sam's going. But he couldn't understand why now, in March, six months before the moon for hunting.

"If Jobaker's dead like they say," he said, "and Sam hasn't got anybody but us at all kin to him, why does he want to go to the Big Bottom now, when it will be six months before we get there?"

"Maybe that's what he wants," McCaslin said. "Maybe he wants to get away from you a little while."

But that was all right. McCaslin and other grown people often said things like that and he paid no attention to them, just as he paid no attention to Sam saying he wanted to go to the Big Bottom to live. After all, he would have to live there for six months, because there would be no use in going at all if he was going to turn right around and come back. And, as Sam himself had told him, he already knew all about hunting in this settled country that Sam or anybody else could teach him. So it would be all right. Summer, then the bright days after the first frost, then the cold and himself on the wagon with McCaslin this time and the moment would come and he would draw the blood, the big blood which would make him a man, a hunter, and Sam would come back home with them and he too would have outgrown the child's pursuit of rabbits and 'possums. Then he too would make one before the winter fire, talking of the old hunts and the hunts to come as hunters talked.

So Sam departed. He owned so little that he could carry it. He walked. He would neither let McCaslin send him in the wagon, nor take a mule to ride. No one saw him go even. He was just gone one morning, the cabin which had never had very much in it, vacant and empty, the shop in which there never had been very much done, standing idle. Then November came at last, and now the boy made one—himself and his cousin McCaslin and Tennie's Jim, and Major de Spain and General Compson and Walter Ewell and Boon and old Uncle Ash to do the cooking, waiting for them in Jefferson with the other wagon, and the surrey in which he and McCaslin and General Compson and Major de Spain would ride.

Sam was waiting at the camp to meet them. If he was glad to see them, he did not show it. And if, when they broke camp two weeks later to return home, he was sorry to see them go, he did not show that either. Because he did not come back with them. It was only the boy who returned, returning solitary and alone to the settled familiar land, to follow for eleven months the childish business of rabbits and such while he waited to go back, having brought with him, even from his brief first sojourn, an unforgettable sense of the big woods—not a quality dangerous or particularly inimical, but profound, sentient, gigantic and brooding, amid which he had been permitted to go to and fro at will, unscathed, why he knew not, but dwarfed and, until he had drawn honorably blood worthy of being drawn, alien.

Then November, and they would come back. Each morning Sam would take the boy out to the stand allotted him. It would be one of the poorer stands of course, since he was only ten and eleven and twelve and he had never even seen a deer running yet. But they would stand there, Sam a little behind him and without a gun himself, as he had been standing when the boy shot the running rabbit when he was eight years old. They would stand there in the November dawns, and after a while they would hear the dogs. Sometimes the chase would sweep up and past quite close, belling and invisible; once they heard the two heavy reports of Boon Hogganbeck's old gun with which he had never killed anything larger than a squirrel and that sitting, and twice they heard the flat unreverberant clap of Walter Ewell's rifle, following which you did not even wait to hear his horn.

"I'll never get a shot," the boy said. "I'll never kill one."

"Yes, you will," Sam said. "You wait. You'll be a hunter. You'll be a man."

But Sam wouldn't come out. They would leave him there. He would come as far as the road where the surrey waited, to take the riding horses back, and that was all. The men would ride the horses and Uncle Ash and Tennie's Jim and the boy would follow in the wagon with Sam, with the camp equipment and the trophies, the meat, the heads, the antlers, the good ones, the wagon winding on among the tremendous gums and cypresses and oaks where no axe save that of the hunter had ever sounded between the impenetrable walls of cane and brier—the two changing yet constant walls just beyond which the wilderness whose mark he had brought away forever on his spirit even from that first two weeks seemed to lean, stooping a little, watching them and listening, not quite inimical because they were too small, even those such as Walter and Major de Spain and old General Compson who had killed many deer and bear, their sojourn too brief and too harmless to excite to that, but just brooding, secret, tremendous, almost inattentive.

Then they would emerge, they would be out of it, the line as sharp as the demarcation of a doored wall. Suddenly skeleton cotton- and corn-fields would flow away on either hand, gaunt and motionless beneath the gray rain; there would be a house, barns, fences, where the hand of man had clawed for an instant, holding, the wall of the wilderness behind them now, tremendous and still and seemingly impenetrable in the gray and fading light, the very tiny orifice through which they had emerged apparently swallowed up. The surrey would be waiting, his cousin McCaslin and Major de Spain and General Compson and Walter and Boon dismounted beside it. Then Sam would get down from the wagon and mount one of the horses and, with the others on a rope behind him, he would turn back. The boy would watch him for a while against that tall and secret wall, growing smaller and smaller against it, never looking back. Then he would enter it, returning to what the boy believed, and thought that his cousin McCaslin believed, was his loneliness and solitude.

II

So the instant came. He pulled trigger and Sam Fathers marked his face with the hot blood which he had spilled and he ceased to be a child and became a hunter and a man. It was the last day. They broke camp that afternoon and went out, his cousin and Major de Spain and General

Compson and Boon on the horses. Walter Ewell and the Negroes in the wagon with him and Sam and his hide and antlers. There could have been (and were) other trophies in the wagon. But for him they did not exist, just as for all practical purposes he and Sam Fathers were still alone together as they had been that morning. The wagon wound and jolted between the slow and shifting yet constant walls from beyond and above which the wilderness watched them pass, less than inimical now and never to be inimical again since the buck still and forever leaped, the shaking gun-barrels coming constantly and forever steady at last, crashing, and still out of his instant of immortality the buck sprang, forever immortal;—the wagon jolting and bouncing on, the moment of the buck, the shot, Sam Fathers and himself and the blood with which Sam had marked him forever one with the wilderness which had accepted him since Sam said that he had done all right, when suddenly Sam reined back and stopped the wagon and they all heard the unmistakable and unforgettable sound of a deer breaking cover.

Then Boon shouted from beyond the bend of the trail and while they sat motionless in the halted wagon. Walter and the boy already reaching for their guns, Boon came galloping back, flogging his mule with his hat, his face wild and amazed as he shouted down at them. Then the other riders came around the bend, also spurring.

"Get the dogs!" Boon cried. "Get the dogs! If he had a nub on his head, he had fourteen points! Laying right there by the road in that pawpaw thicket! If I'd a knowed he was there, I could have cut his throat with my pocket knife!"

"Maybe that's why he run," Walter said. "He saw you never had your gun." He was already out of the wagon with his rifle. Then the boy was out too with his gun, and the other riders came up and Boon got off his mule somehow and was scrabbling and clawing among the duffel in the wagon, still shouting, "Get the dogs! Get the dogs!" And it seemed to the boy too that it would take them forever to decide what to do—the old men in whom the blood ran cold and slow, in whom during the intervening years between them and himself the blood had become a different and colder substance from that which ran in him and even in Boon and Walter.

"What about it, Sam?" Major de Spain said. "Could the dogs bring him back?"

"We wont need the dogs," Sam said. "If he dont hear the dogs behind him, he will circle back in here about sundown to bed."

"All right," Major de Spain said. "You boys take the horses. We'll go on out to the road in the wagon and wait there." He and General Compson and McCaslin got into the wagon and Boon and Walter and Sam and the boy mounted the horses and turned back and out of the trail. Sam led them for an hour through the gray and unmarked afternoon whose light was little different from what it had been at dawn and which would become darkness without any graduation between. Then Sam stopped them.

"This is far enough," he said. "He'll be coming upwind, and he dont want to smell the mules." They tied the mounts in a thicket. Sam led them on foot now, unpathed through the markless afternoon, the boy pressing close behind him, the two others, or so it seemed to the boy, on his heels. But they were not. Twice Sam turned his head slightly and spoke back to him across his shoulder, still walking: "You got time. We'll get there fore he does."

So he tried to go slower. He tried deliberately to decelerate the dizzy rushing of time in which the buck which he had not even seen was moving, which it seemed to him must be carrying the buck farther and farther and more and more irretrievably away from them even though there were no dogs behind him now to make him run, even though, according to Sam, he must have completed his circle now and was heading back toward them. They went on; it could have been another hour or twice that or less than half, the boy could not have said. Then they were on a ridge. He had never been in here before and he could not see that it was a ridge. He just knew that the earth had risen slightly because the underbrush had thinned a little, the ground sloping invisibly away toward a dense wall of cane. Sam stopped. "This is it," he said. He spoke to Walter and Boon: "Follow this ridge and you will come to two crossings. You will see the tracks. If he crosses, it will be at one of these three."

Walter looked about for a moment. "I know it," he said. "I've even seen your deer. I was in here last Monday. He aint nothing but a yearling."

"A yearling?" Boon said. He was panting from the walking. His face still looked a little wild. "If the one I saw was any yearling, I'm still in kindergarden."

"Then I must have seen a rabbit," Walter said. "I always heard you quit school altogether two years before the first grade."

Boon glared at Walter. "If you dont want to shoot him, get out of the way," he said. "Set down somewhere. By God, I—"

"Aint nobody going to shoot him standing here," Sam said quietly.

"Sam's right," Walter said. He moved, slanting the worn, silver-colored barrel of his rifle downward to walk with it again. "A little more moving and a little more quiet too. Five miles is still Hogganbeck range, even if he wasn't downwind." They went on. The boy could still hear Boon talking, though presently that ceased too. Then once more he and Sam stood motionless together against a tremendous pin oak in a little thicket, and again there was nothing. There was only the soaring and somber solitude in the dim light, there was the thin murmur of the faint cold rain which had not ceased all day. Then, as if it had waited for them to find their positions and become still, the wilderness breathed again. It seemed to lean inward above them, above himself and Sam and Walter and Boon in their separate lurking-places, tremendous, attentive, impartial and omniscient, the buck moving in it somewhere, not running yet since he had not been pursued, not frightened yet and never fearsome but just alert also as they were alert, perhaps already circling back, perhaps quite near, perhaps conscious also of the eye of the ancient immortal Umpire. Because he was just twelve then, and that morning something had happened to him: in less than a second he had ceased forever to be the child he was yesterday. Or perhaps that made no difference, perhaps even a city-bred man, let alone a child, could not have understood it; perhaps only a country-bred one could comprehend loving the life he spills. He began to shake again.

"I'm glad it's started now," he whispered. He did not move to speak; only his lips shaped the expiring words: "Then it will be gone when I raise the gun—"

Nor did Sam. "Hush," he said.

"Is he that near?" the boy whispered. "Do you think—"

"Hush," Sam said. So he hushed. But he could not stop the shaking. He did not try, because he knew it would go away when he needed the steadiness—had not Sam Fathers already consecrated and absolved him from weakness and regret too?—not from love and pity for all which lived and ran and then ceased to live in a second in the very midst of splendor and speed, but from weakness and regret. So they stood motionless, breathing deep and quiet and steady. If there had been any sun, it would be near to setting now; there was a condensing, a densifying, of what he had thought was the gray and unchanging light until he realized suddenly that it was his own breathing, his heart, his blood—something, all things, and that Sam Fathers had marked him indeed, not as a mere hunter, but with something Sam had had in his turn of his vanished and forgotten people. He stopped breathing then; there was only his heart, his blood, and in the following silence the wilderness ceased to breathe also, leaning, stooping overhead with its breath held, tremendous and impartial and waiting. Then the shaking stopped too, as he had known it would, and he drew back the two heavy hammers of the gun.

Then it had passed. It was over. The solitude did not breathe again yet; it had merely stopped watching him and was looking somewhere else, even turning its back on him, looking on away up the ridge at another point, and the boy knew as well as if he had seen him that the buck had come to the edge of the cane and had either seen or scented them and faded back into it. But the solitude did not breathe again. It should have suspired again then but it did not. It was still facing, watching, what it had been watching and it was not here, not where he and Sam stood; rigid, not breathing himself, he thought, cried *No! No!* knowing already that it was too late, thinking with the old despair of two and three years ago: *I'll never get a shot*. Then he heard it—the flat single clap of Walter Ewell's rifle which never missed. Then the mellow sound of the horn came down the ridge and something went out of him and he knew then he had never expected to get the shot at all.

"I reckon that's it," he said. "Walter got him." He had raised the gun slightly without knowing it. He lowered it again and had lowered one of the hammers and was already moving out of the thicket when Sam spoke.

"Wait."

"Wait?" the boy cried. And he would remember that—how he turned upon Sam in the truculence of a boy's grief over the missed opportunity, the missed luck. "What for? Dont you hear that horn?"

And he would remember how Sam was standing. Sam had not moved. He was not tall, squat rather and broad, and the boy had been growing fast for the past year or so and there was not much difference between them in height, yet Sam was looking over the boy's head and up the ridge toward the sound of the horn and the boy knew that Sam did not even see him; that Sam knew he was still there beside him but he did not see the boy. Then the boy saw the buck. It was coming down the ridge, as if it were walking out of the very sound of the horn which related its death. It was not running, it was walking, tremendous, unhurried, slanting and tilting its head to pass the antlers through the undergrowth, and the boy standing with Sam beside him now instead of behind him as Sam always stood, and the gun still partly aimed and one of the hammers still cocked.

Then it saw them. And still it did not begin to run. It just stopped for an instant, taller than any man, looking at them; then its muscles suppled, gathered. It did not even alter its course, not fleeing, not even running, just moving with that winged and effortless ease with which deer move, passing within twenty feet of them, its head high and the eye not proud and not haughty but just full and wild and unafraid, and Sam standing beside the boy now, his right arm raised at full length, palm-outward, speaking in that tongue which the boy had learned from listening to him and Jobaker in the blacksmith shop, while up the ridge Walter Ewell's horn was still blowing them in to a dead buck.

"Oleh, Chief," Sam said. "Grandfather."

When they reached Walter, he was standing with his back toward them, quite still, bemused almost, looking down at his feet. He didn't look up at all.

"Come here, Sam," he said quietly. When they reached him he still did not look up, standing above a little spike buck which had still been a fawn last spring. "He was so little I pretty near let him go," Walter said. "But just look at the track he was making. It's pretty near big as a cow's. If there were any more tracks here beside the ones he is laying in, I would swear there was another buck here that I never even saw."

III

It was dark when they reached the road where the surrey waited. It was turning cold, the rain had stopped, and the sky was beginning to blow clear. His cousin and Major de Spain and General Compson had a fire going. "Did you get him?" Major de Spain said.

"Got a good-sized swamp-rabbit with spike horns," Walter said. He slid the little buck down from his mule. The boy's cousin McCaslin looked at it.

"Nobody saw the big one?" he said.

"I dont even believe Boon saw it," Walter said. "He probably jumped somebody's stray cow in that thicket." Boon started cursing, swearing at Walter and at Sam for not getting the dogs in the first place and at the buck and all.

"Never mind," Major de Spain said. "He'll be here for us next fall. Let's get started home."

It was after midnight when they let Walter out at his gate two miles from Jefferson and later still when they took General Compson to his house and then returned to Major de Spain's, where he and McCaslin would spend the rest of the night, since it was still seventeen miles home. It was cold, the sky was clear now; there would be a heavy frost by sunup and the ground was already frozen beneath the horses' feet and the wheels and beneath their own feet as they crossed Major de Spain's yard and entered the house, the warm dark house, feeling their way up the dark stairs until Major de Spain found a candle and lit it, and into the strange room and the big deep bed, the still cold sheets until they began to warm to their bodies and at last the shaking stopped and suddenly he was telling McCaslin about it while McCaslin listened, quietly until he had finished. "You don't believe it," the boy said. "I know you don't—"

"Why not?" McCaslin said. "Think of all that has happened here, on this earth. All the blood hot and strong for living, pleasuring, that has soaked back into it. For grieving and suffering too, of course, but still getting something out of it for all that, getting a lot out of it, because after all you don't have to continue to bear what you believe is suffering; you can always choose to stop that, put an end to that. And even suffering and grieving is better than nothing; there is only one thing worse than not being alive, and that's shame. But you can't be alive forever, and you always wear out life long before you have exhausted the possibilities of living. And all that must be somewhere; all that could not have been invented and created just to be thrown away. And the earth is shallow; there is not a great deal of it before you come to the rock. And the earth dont want to just keep things, hoard them; it wants to use them again. Look at the seed, the acorns, at what happens even to carrion when you try to bury it: it refuses too, seethes and struggles too until it reaches light and air again, hunting the sun still. And they—" the boy saw his hand in silhouette for a moment against the window beyond which, accustomed to the darkness now, he could see sky where the scoured and icy stars glittered "—·they don't want it, need it. Besides, what would it want, itself, knocking around out there, when it never had enough time about the earth as it was, when there is plenty of room about the earth, plenty of places still unchanged from what they were when the blood used and pleasured in them while it was still blood?"

"But we want them," the boy said. "We want them too. There is plenty of room for us and them too."

"That's right," McCaslin said. "Suppose they dont have substance, cant cast a shadow—"

"But I saw it!" the boy cried. "I saw him!"

"Steady," McCaslin said. For an instant his hand touched the boy's flank beneath the covers. "Steady. I know you did. So did I. Sam took me in there once after I killed my first deer."

EUDORA WELTY

*E*UDORA WELTY (born 1909), one of America's finest and funniest writers, has lived all her life in Jackson, Mississippi, drawing on that town and the surrounding region for her rich and varied fiction. While she has written several novels (the best being The Optimist's Daughter, published in 1969), she is most celebrated for her stories. The publication of her Collected Stories in 1980 was a triumphant event.

If one compares Welty to other Southern writers such as Faulkner and Flannery O'Connor, one discovers that the grotesque and the gothic play a smaller role in her fiction. The critic who saw her characters as "cruel parodies of 'normality' " and declared that she lacked sympathy for them could not have been more mistaken. While her characters suffer from various limitations—they are provincial, uneducated, usually poor, and full of such typical failings as greed, prejudice, and egotism—they are always seen sympathetically, even lovingly, and they rise above their foolishness to a curious kind of dignity. In fact, like the characters of García Márquez, Olesha, and Kaleb, they are peasants, and the observation in the Introduction that we tend to see peasants both as wiser and more credulous than ourselves is useful in trying to assess the complex attitudes that lie behind Welty's fiction.

The long and beautiful story "Moon Lake," from The Golden Apples (1949), is centered on the events of a potential drowning. Set in a girls' camp that is unmistakably real, it is nevertheless stocked with myth and magic at every turn, from its figures of speech—a cat jumps down from a post "like something poured out of a bottle," a funnel of bees passes by "like something from another planet"—to its very names: Moon Lake, Easter, and the wonderfully titled book that is bouncing around the camp: The Re-Creation of Brian Kent. If magical realism is in somewhat short supply in North American fiction, an example as stunning as this one certainly helps to offset the shortage!

Moon Lake

Eudora Welty

FROM THE beginning his martyred presence seriously affected them. They had a disquieting familiarity with it, hearing the spit of his despising that went into his bugle. At times they could hardly recognize what he thought he was playing. Loch Morrison, Boy Scout and Life Saver, was under the ordeal of a week's camp on Moon Lake with girls.

Half the girls were county orphans, wished on them by Mr. Nesbitt and the Men's Bible Class after Billy Sunday's visit to town; but all girls, orphans and Morgana girls alike, were the same thing to Loch; maybe he threw in the two counselors too. He was hating every day of the seven. He hardly spoke; he never spoke first. Sometimes he swung in the trees; Nina Carmichael in particular would hear him crashing in the foliage somewhere when she was lying rigid in siesta.

While they were in the lake, for the dip or the five-o'clock swimming period in the afternoon, he stood against a tree with his arms folded, jacked up one-legged, sitting on his heel, as absolutely tolerant as an old fellow waiting for the store to open, being held up by the wall. Waiting for the girls to get out, he gazed upon some undisturbed part of the water. He despised their predicaments, most of all their not being able to swim. Sometimes he would take aim and from his right cheek shoot an imaginary gun at something far out, where they never were. Then he resumed his pose. He had been roped into this by his mother.

At the hours too hot for girls he used Moon Lake. He dived high off the crosspiece nailed up in the big oak, where the American Legion dived. He went through the air rocking and jerking like an engine, splashed in, climbed out, spat, climbed up again, dived off. He wore a long bathing suit which stretched longer from Monday to Tuesday and from Tuesday to Wednesday and so on, yawning at the armholes toward infinity, and it looked black and formal as a minstrel suit as he stood skinny against the clouds as on a stage.

He came and got his food and turned his back and ate it all alone like a dog and lived in a tent by himself, apart like a nigger, and dived alone when the lake was clear of girls. That way, he seemed able to bear it; that would be his life. In early evening, in moonlight sings, the Boy Scout and Life Saver kept far away. They would sing "When all the little ships come sailing home," and he would be roaming off; they could tell about where he was. He played taps for them, invisibly then, and so beautifully they wept together, whole tentfuls some nights. Off with the whip-poor-wills and the coons and the owls and the little bobwhites—down where it all sloped away, he had pitched his tent, and slept there. Then at reveille, how he would spit into that cornet.

Reveille was his. He harangued the woods when the little minnows were trembling and running wizardlike in the water's edge. And how lovely and altered the trees were then, weighted with dew, leaning on one another's shoulders and smelling like big wet flowers. He blew his horn into their presence—trees' and girls'—and then watched the Dip.

"Good morning, Mr. Dip, Dip, Dip, with your water just as cold as ice!" sang Mrs. Gruenwald hoarsely. She took them for the dip, for Miss Moody said she couldn't, simply couldn't.

The orphans usually hung to the rear, and every other moment stood swayback with knees locked, the shoulders of their wash dresses ironed flat and stuck in peaks, and stared. For swimming they owned no bathing suits and went in in their underbodies. Even in the water they would stand swayback, each with a fist in front of her over the rope, locking over the flat surface as over the top of a tall mountain none of them could ever get over. Even at this hour of the day, they seemed to be expecting little tasks, something more immediate—little tasks that were never given out.

Mrs. Gruenwald was from the North and said "dup." "Good morning, Mr. Dup, Dup, Dup, with your water just as cold as ice!" sang Mrs. Gruenwald, fatly capering and leading them all in a singing, petering-out string down to the lake. She did a sort of little rocking dance in her exhortation, broad in her bathrobe. From the tail end of the line she looked like a Shredded Wheat Biscuit box rocking on its corners.

Nina Carmichael thought, There is nobody and nothing named Mr. Dip, it is not a good morning until you have had coffee, and the water is the temperature of a just-cooling biscuit, thank Goodness. I hate this little parade of us girls, Nina thought, trotting fiercely in the center of it. It ruins the woods, all right. "Gee, we think you're mighty nice," they sang to Mr. Dip, while the Boy Scout, waiting at the lake, watched them go in.

"Watch out for mosquitoes," they called to one another, lyrically because warning wasn't any use anyway, as they walked out of their kimonos and dropped them like the petals of one big scattered flower on the bank behind them, and exposing themselves felt in a hundred places at once the little pangs. The orphans ripped their dresses off over their heads and stood in their underbodies. Busily they hung and piled their dresses on a cedar branch, obeying one of their own number, like a whole flock of ferocious little birds with pale topknots building themselves a nest. The orphan named Easter appeared in charge. She handed her dress wrong-side-out to a friend, who turned it and hung it up for her, and waited standing very still, her little fingers locked.

"Let's let the orphans go in the water first and get the snakes stirred up, Mrs. Gruenwald," Jinny Love Stark suggested first off, in the cheerful voice she adopted toward grown people. "Then they'll be chased away by the time *we* go in."

That made the orphans scatter in their pantie-waists, outwards from Easter; the little gauzes of gnats they ran through made them beat their hands at the air. They ran back together again, to Easter, and stood excitedly, almost hopping.

"I think we'll all go in in one big bunch," Mrs. Gruenwald said. Jinny Love lamented and beat against Mrs. Gruenwald, Mrs. Gruenwald's solid, rope-draped stomach all but returning her blows. "All take hands— march! Into the water! *Don't* let the stobs and cypress roots break your legs! *Do* your best! Kick!, Stay on top if you can and hold the rope if necessary!"

Mrs. Gruenwald abruptly walked away from Jinny Love, out of the bathrobe, and entered the lake with a vast displacing. She left them on the bank with her Yankee advice.

The Morgana girls might never have gone in if the orphans hadn't balked. Easter came to a dead stop at Moon Lake and looked at it squinting as though it floated really on the Moon. And mightn't it be on the Moon?—it was a strange place, Nina thought, unlikely—and three miles from Morgana, Mississippi, all the time. The Morgana girls pulled the orphans' hands and dragged them in, or pushed suddenly from behind, and finally the orphans took hold of one another and waded forward in a body, singing "Good Morning" with their stiff, chip-like lips. None of them could or would swim, ever, and they just stood waist-deep and waited for the dip to be over. A few of them reached out and caught the struggling Morgana girls by the legs as they splashed from one barky post to another, to see how hard it really was to stay up.

"Mrs. Gruenwald, look, they want to drown us."

But Mrs. Gruenwald all this time was rising and sinking like a whale, she was in a sea of her own waves and perhaps of self-generated cold, out in the middle of the lake. She cared little that Morgana girls who learned to swim were getting a dollar from home. She had deserted them, no, she had never really been with them. Not only orphans had she deserted. In the water she kept so much to the profile that her single pushing-out eyeball looked like a little bottle of something. It was said she believed in evolution.

While the Boy Scout in the rosy light under the green trees twirled his horn so that it glittered and ran a puzzle in the sun, and emptied the spit out of it, he yawned, snappingly—as if he would bite the day, as quickly as Easter had bitten Deacon Nesbitt's hand on Opening Day.

"Gee, we think you're mighty nice," they sang to Mr. Dip, gasping, pounding their legs in him. If they let their feet go down, the invisible bottom of the lake felt like soft, knee-deep fur. The sharp hard knobs came up where least expected. The Morgana girls of course wore bathing slippers, and the mud loved to suck them off. The alligators had been beaten out of this lake, but it was said that water snakes—pilots—were swimming here and there; they would bite you but not kill you; and one cottonmouth moccasin was still getting away from the niggers—if the niggers were still going after him; he would kill you. These were the chances of getting sucked under, of being bitten, and of dying three miles away from home.

The brown water cutting her off at the chest, Easter looked directly before her, wide awake, unsmiling. Before she could hold a stare like that, she would have had to swallow something big—so Nina felt. It would have been something so big that it didn't matter to her what the inside of a snake's mouth was lined with. At the other end of her gaze the life saver grew almost insignificant. Her gaze moved like a little switch or wand, and the life saver scratched himself with his bugle, raked himself, as if that eased him. Yet the flick of a blue-bottle fly made Easter jump.

They swam and held to the rope, hungry and waiting. But they had to keep waiting till Loch Morrison blew his horn before they could come out of Moon Lake. Mrs. Gruenwald, who capered before breakfast, believed in evolution, and put her face in the water, was quarter of a mile out. If she said anything, they couldn't hear her for the frogs.

II

Nina and Jinny Love, with the soles of their feet shocked from the walk, found Easter ahead of them down at the spring.

For the orphans, from the first, sniffed out the way to the spring by themselves, and they could get there without stops to hold up their feet and pull out thorns and stickers, and could run through the sandy bottoms and never look down where they were going, and could grab hold with their toes on the sharp rutted path up the pine ridge and down. They clearly could never get enough of skimming over the silk-slick needles and setting prints of their feet in the bed of the spring to see them dissolve away under their eyes. What was it to them if the spring was muddied by the time Jinny Love Stark got there?

The one named Easter could fall flat as a boy, elbows cocked, and drink from the cup of her hand with her face in the spring. Jinny Love prodded Nina, and while they looked on Easter's drawers, Nina was opening the drinking cup she had brought with her, then collapsing it, feeling like a lady with a fan. That way, she was going over a thought, a fact: Half the people out here with me are orphans. Orphans. Orphans. She yearned for her heart to twist. But it didn't, not in time. Easter was through drinking—wiping her mouth and flinging her hand as if to break the bones, to get rid of the drops, and it was Nina's turn with her drinking cup.

Nina stood and bent over from the waist. Calmly, she held her cup in the spring and watched it fill. They could all see how it spangled like a cold star in the curling water. The water tasted the silver cool of the rim it went over running to her lips, and at moments the cup gave her teeth a pang. Nina heard her own throat swallowing. She paused and threw a smile about her. After she had drunk she wiped the cup on her tie and collapsed it, and put the little top on, and its ring over her finger. With that, Easter, one arm tilted, charged against the green bank and mounted it. Nina felt her surveying the spring and all from above. Jinny Love was down drinking like a chicken, kissing the water only.

Easter was dominant among the orphans. It was not that she was so bad. The one called Geneva stole, for example, but Easter was dominant for what she was in herself—for the way she held still, sometimes. All orphans were at once wondering and stoic—at one moment loving everything too much, the next folding back from it, tightly as hard green buds growing in the wrong direction, closing as they go. But it was as if Easter signaled them. Now she just stood up there, watching the spring, with the name Easter—tacky name, as Jinny Love Stark was the first to say. She was medium size, but her hair seemed to fly up at the temples, being cropped and wiry, and this crest made her nearly as tall as Jinny Love Stark. The rest of the orphans had hair paler than their tanned foreheads—straight and tow, the greenish yellow of cornsilk that dimmed black at the roots and shadows, with burnt-out-looking bangs like young boys' and old men's hair; that was from picking in the fields. Easter's hair was a withstanding gold. Around the back of her neck beneath the hair was a dark band on her skin like the mark a gold bracelet leaves on the arm. It came to the Morgana girls with a feeling of elation: the ring was pure dirt. They liked to look at it, or to remember, too late, what it was—as now, when Easter had already lain down for a drink and left the spring. They liked to walk behind her and see her back, which seemed spectacular from crested gold head to hard, tough heel. Mr. Nesbitt, from the Bible Class, took Easter by the wrist and turned her around to him and looked just as hard at her front. She had started her breasts. What Easter did was to bite his right hand, his collection hand. It was wonderful to have with them someone dangerous but not, so far, or provenly, bad. When Nina's little lead-mold umbrella, the size of a clover, a Crackerjack prize, was stolen the first night of camp, that was Geneva, Easter's friend.

Jinny Love, after wiping her face with a hand-made handkerchief, pulled out a deck of cards she had secretly brought in her middy pocket. She dropped them down, bright blue, on a sandy place by the spring. "Let's play cassino. Do they call you *Easter?*"

Down Easter jumped, from the height of the bank. She came back to them. "Cassino, what's that?"

"All right, what do *you* want to play?"

"All right, I'll play you mumblety-peg."

"I don't know how you play that!" cried Nina.

"Who would ever want to know?" asked Jinny Love, closing the circle.

Easter flipped out a jack-knife and with her sawed fingernail shot out three blades.

"Do you carry that in the orphan asylum?" Jinny Love asked with some respect.

Easter dropped to her scarred and coral-colored knees. They saw the dirt. "Get down if you want to play me mumblety-peg," was all she said, "and watch out for your hands and faces."

They huddled down on the piney sand. The vivid, hurrying ants were everywhere. To the squinted eye they looked like angry, orange ponies as they rode the pine needles. There was Geneva, skirting behind a tree, but she never came close or tried to get in the game. She pretended to be catching doodlebugs. The knife leaped and quivered in the sandy arena smoothed by Easter's hand.

"I may not know how to play, but I bet I win," Jinny Love said.

Easter's eyes, lifting up, were neither brown nor green nor cat; they had something of metal, flat ancient metal, so that you could not see into them. Nina's grandfather had possessed a box of coins from Greece and Rome. Easter's eyes could have come from Greece or Rome that day. Jinny Love stopped short of apprehending this, and only took care to watch herself when Easter pitched the knife. The color in Easter's eyes could have been found somewhere, away—away, under lost leaves— strange as the painted color of the ants. Instead of round black holes in the center of her eyes, there might have been women's heads, ancient.

Easter, who had played so often, won. She nodded and accepted Jinny Love's barrette and from Nina a blue jay feather which she transferred to her own ear.

"I wouldn't be surprised if you cheated, and don't know what you had to lose if you lost," said Jinny Love thoughtfully but with an admiration almost fantastic in her.

Victory with a remark attached did not crush Easter at all, or she

scarcely listened. Her indifference made Nina fall back and listen to the
spring running with an endless sound and see how the July light like
purple and yellow birds kept flickering under the trees when the wind
blew. Easter turned her head and the new feather on her head shone
changeably. A black funnel of bees passed through the air, throwing a
funneled shadow, like a visitor from nowhere, another planet.

"We have to play again to see whose the drinking cup will be," Easter
said, swaying forward on her knees.

Nina jumped to her feet and did a cartwheel. Against the spinning
green and blue her heart pounded as heavily as she touched lightly.

"You ruined the game," Jinny Love informed Easter. "You don't know
Nina." She gathered up her cards. "You'd think it was made of fourteen-
carat gold, and didn't come out of the pocket of an old suitcase, that
cup."

"I'm sorry," said Nina sincerely.

As the three were winding around the lake, a bird flying above the
opposite shore kept uttering a cry and then diving deep, plunging into
the trees there, and soaring to cry again.

"Hear him?" one of the niggers said, fishing on the bank; it was
Elberta's sister Twosie, who spoke as if a long, long conversation had
been going on, into which she would intrude only the mildest words.
"Know why? Know why, in de sky, he say 'Spirit? Spirit?' And den he
dive *boom* and say 'GHOST'?"

"Why does he?" said Jinny Love, in a voice of objection.

"Yawl knows. *I* don't know," said Twosie, in her little high, helpless
voice, and she shut her eyes. They couldn't seem to get on by her. On fine
days there is danger of some sad meeting, the positive danger of it. "*I*
don't know what he say dat for." Twosie spoke pitifully, as though
accused. She sighed. "Yawl sho ain't got yo' eyes opem good, yawl. Yawl
don't know what's out here in woods wid you."

"Well, what?"

"Yawl walk right by mans wid great big gun, could jump out at yawl.
Yawl don't eem smellim."

"You mean Mr. Holifield? That's a flashlight he's got." Nina looked at
Jinny Love for confirmation. Mr. Holifield was their handy man, or rather
simply "the man to be sure and have around the camp." He could be
found by beating for a long time on the porch of the American Legion
boat house—he slept heavily. "He hasn't got a gun to jump out with."

"I know who you mean. I hear those boys. Just some big boys, like the
MacLain twins or somebody, and who cares about them?" Jinny Love
with her switch indented the thick mat of hair on Twosie's head and
prodded and stirred it gently. She pretended to fish in Twosie's woolly
head. "Why ain't *you* scared, then?"

"I is."

Twosie's eyelids fluttered. Already she seemed to be fishing in her night's sleep. While they gazed at her crouched, devoted figure, from which the long pole hung, so steady and beggarlike and ordained an appendage, all their passions flew home again and went huddled and soft to roost.

Back at the camp, Jinny Love told Miss Moody about the great big jack-knife. Easter gave it up.

"I didn't mean you couldn't *drink* out of my cup," Nina said, waiting for her. "Only you have to hold it carefully, it leaks. It's engraved."

Easter wouldn't even try it, though Nina dangled it on its ring right under her eyes. She didn't say anything, not even "It's pretty." Was she even thinking of it? Or if not, what did she think about?

"Sometimes orphans act like deaf-and-dumbs," said Jinny Love.

III

"Nina!" Jinny Love whispered across the tent, during siesta. "What do you think you're reading?"

Nina closed *The Re-Creation of Brian Kent.* Jinny Love was already coming directly across the almost-touching cots to Nina's, walking on her knees and bearing down over Gertrude, Etoile, and now Geneva.

With Jinny Love upon her, Geneva sighed. Her sleeping face looked as if she didn't want to. She slept as she swam, in her pantie-waist, she was in running position and her ribs went up and down frantically—a little box in her chest that expanded and shut without a second's rest between. Her cheek was pearly with afternoon moisture and her kitten-like teeth pearlier still. As Jinny Love hid her and went over, Nina seemed to see her still; even her vaccination mark looked too big for her.

Nobody woke up from being walked over, but after Jinny Love had fallen in bed with Nina, Easter gave a belated, dreaming sound. She had not even been in the line of march; she slept on the cot by the door, curved shell-like, both arms forward over her head. It was an inward sound she gave—now it came again—of such wholehearted and fateful concurrence with the thing dreamed, that Nina and Jinny Love took hands and made wry faces at each other.

Beyond Easter's cot the corona of afternoon flared and lifted in an intensity that came through the eyelids. There was nothing but light out there. True, the black Negroes inhabited it. Elberta moved slowly through it, as if she rocked a baby with her hips, carrying a bucket of scraps to throw in the lake—to get hail Columbia for it later. Her straw hat spiraled rings of orange and violet, like a top. Far, far down a vista of intolerable light, a tiny daub of black cotton, Twosie had stationed herself at the edge of things, and slept and fished.

Eventually there was Exum wandering with his fish pole—he could dance on a dime, Elberta said, he used to work for a blind man. Exum was smart for twelve years old; too smart. He found that hat he wore—not a sign of the owner. He had a hat like new, filled out a little with peanut shells inside the band to correct the size, and he like a little black peanut in it. It stood up and away from his head all around, and seemed only following him—on runners, perhaps, like those cartridges for change in Spights' store.

Easter's sighs and her prolonged or half-uttered words now filled the tent, just as the heat filled it. Her words fell in threes, Nina observed, like the mourning-dove's call in the woods.

Nina and Jinny Love lay speechless, doubling for themselves the already strong odor of Sweet Dreams Mosquito Oil, in a trance of endurance through the hour's siesta. Entwined, they stared—orphan-like themselves—past Easter's cot and through the tent opening as down a long telescope turned on an incandescent star, and saw the spiral of Elberta's hat return, and saw Exum jump over a stick and on the other side do a little dance in a puff of dust. They could hear the intermittent crash, splash of Loch Morrison using their lake, and Easter's voice calling again in her sleep, her unintelligible words.

But however Nina and Jinny Love made faces at they knew not what, Easter concurred; she thoroughly agreed.

The bugle blew for swimming. Geneva jumped so hard she fell off her cot. Nina and Jinny Love were indented with each other, like pressed leaves, and jumped free. When Easter, who had to be shaken, sat up drugged and stupid on her cot, Nina ran over to her.

"Listen. Wake up. Look, you can go in in my bathing shoes today."

She felt her eyes glaze with this plan of kindness as she stretched out her limp red shoes that hung down like bananas under Easter's gaze. But Easter dropped back on the cot and stretched her legs.

"Never mind your shoes. I don't have to go in the lake if I don't want to."

"You do. I never heard of that. Who picked you out? You do," they said, all gathering.

"You make me."

Easter yawned. She fluttered her eyes and rolled them back—she loved doing that. Miss Moody passed by and beamed in at them hovered around Easter's passive and mutinous form. All along she'd been afraid of some challenge to her counselorship, from the way she hurried by now, almost too daintily.

"Well, *I* know," Jinny Love said, sidling up. "I know as much as you know, Easter." She made a chant, which drove her hopping around the tent pole in an Indian step. "You don't have to go, if you don't want to go. And if it ain't so, you still don't have to go, if you don't want to go." She kissed her hand to them.

Easter was silent—but if she groaned when she waked, she'd only be imitating herself.

Jinny Love pulled on her bathing cap, which gave way and came down over her eyes. Even in blindness, she cried, "So you needn't think you're the only one, Easter, not always. What do you say to that?"

"I should worry, I should cry," said Easter, lying still, spread-eagled.

"Let's us run away from basket weaving," Jinny Love said in Nina's ear, a little later in the week.

"Just as soon."

"Grand. They'll think we're drowned."

They went out the back end of the tent, barefooted; their feet were as tough as anybody's by this time. Down in the hammock, Miss Moody was reading *The Re-Creation of Brian Kent* now. (Nobody knew whose book that was, it had been found here, the covers curled up like side combs. Perhaps anybody at Moon Lake who tried to read it felt cheated by the title, as applying to camp life, as Nina did, and laid it down for the next person.) Cat, the niggers' cat, was sunning on a post and when they approached jumped to the ground like something poured out of a bottle, and went with them, in front.

They trudged down the slope past Loch Morrison's tent and took the track into the swamp. There they moved single file between two walls; by lifting their arms they could have touched one or the other pressing side of the swamp. Their toes exploded the dust that felt like the powder clerks pump into new kid gloves, as Jinny Love said twice. They were eye to eye with the finger-shaped leaves of the castor bean plants, put out like those gypsy hands that part the curtains at the back of rolling wagons, and wrinkled and coated over like the fortune-teller's face.

Mosquitoes struck at them; Sweet Dreams didn't last. The whining lifted like a voice, saying "I don't want..." At the girls' shoulders Queen Anne's lace and elderberry and blackberry thickets, loaded heavily with flower and fruit and smelling with the melony smell of snake, overhung the ditch to touch them. The ditches had dried green or blue bottoms, cracked and glazed—like a dropped vase. "I hope we don't meet any nigger men," Jinny Love said cheerfully.

Sweet bay and cypress and sweetgum and live oak and swamp maple closing tight made the wall dense, and yet there was somewhere still for the other wall of vine; it gathered itself on the ground and stacked and tilted itself in the trees; and like a table in the tree the mistletoe hung up there black in the zenith. Buzzards floated from one side of the swamp to the other, as if choice existed for them—raggedly crossing the sky and shadowing the track, and shouldering one another on the solitary limb of a moon-white sycamore. Closer to the ear than lips could begin words came the swamp sounds—closer to the ear and nearer to the dreaming mind. They were a song of hilarity of Jinny Love, who began to skip. Periods of silence seemed hoarse, or the suffering from hoarseness, otherwise inexplicable, as though the world could stop. Cat was stalking

something at the black edge of the ditch. The briars didn't trouble Cat at
all, it was they that seemed to give way beneath that long, boatlike belly.

The track serpentined again, and walking ahead was Easter. Geneva
and Etoile were playing at her side, edging each other out of her shadow,
but when they saw who was coming up behind them, they turned and
ran tearing back towards camp, running at angles, like pullets, leaving a
cloud of dust as they passed by.

"Wouldn't you know!" said Jinny Love.

Easter was going unconcernedly on, her dress stained green behind;
she ate something out of her hand as she went.

"We'll soon catch up—don't hurry."

The reason orphans were the way they were lay first in nobody's
watching them, Nina thought, for she felt obscurely like a trespasser.
They, they were not answerable. Even on being watched, Easter remained not answerable to a soul on earth. Nobody cared! And so, in this
beatific state, something came out of *her*.

"Where are you going?"

"Can we go with you, Easter?"

Easter, her lips stained with blackberries, replied, "It ain't my road."

They walked along, one on each side of her. Though they automatically stuck their tongues out at her, they ran their arms around her waist.
She tolerated the closeness for a little while; she smelled of orphan-
starch, but she had a strange pure smell of sweat, like a sleeping baby,
and in her temple, so close then to their eyes, the skin was transparent
enough for a little vein to be seen pounding under it. She seemed very
tender and very small in the waist to be trudging along so doggedly,
when they had her like that.

Vines, a magnificent and steamy green, covered more and more of
the trees, played over them like fountains. There were stretches of water
below them, blue-black, netted over with half-closed waterlilies. The hori-
zontal limbs of cypresses grew a short, pale green scruff like bird feathers.

They came to a tiny farm down here, the last one possible before the
muck sucked it in—a patch of cotton in flower, a house whitewashed in
front, a clean-swept yard with a little iron pump standing in the middle
of it like a black rooster. These were white people—an old woman in a
sunbonnet came out of the house with a galvanized bucket, and pumped
it full in the dooryard. That was an excuse to see people go by.

Easter, easing out of the others' clasp, lifted her arm halfway and
turning for an instant, gave two waves of the hand. But the old woman
was prouder than she.

Jinny Love said, "How would you all like to live there?"

Cat edged the woods onward, and at moments vanished into a
tunnel in the briars. Emerging from other tunnels, he—or she—glanced
up at them with a face more mask-like than ever.

"There's a short-cut to the lake." Easter, breaking and darting ahead, suddenly went down on her knees and slid under a certain place in the barbed wire fence. Rising, she took a step inward, sinking down as she went. Nina untwined her arm from Jinny Love's and went after her.

"I might have known you'd want us to go through a barbed wire fence." Jinny Love sat down where she was, on the side of the ditch, just as she would take her seat on a needlepoint stool. She jumped up once, and sat back. "Fools, fools!" she called. "Now I think you've made me turn my ankle. Even if I wanted to track through the mud, I couldn't!"

Nina and Easter, dipping under a second, unexpected fence, went on, swaying and feeling their feet pulled down, reached to the trees. Jinny Love was left behind in the heartless way people and incidents alike are thrown off in the course of a dream, like the gratuitous flowers scattered from a float—rather in celebration. The swamp was now all-enveloping, dark and at the same time vivid, alarming—it was like being inside the chest of something that breathed and might turn over.

Then there was Moon Lake, a different aspect altogether. Easter climbed the slight rise ahead and reached the pink, grassy rim and the innocent open. Here it was quiet, until, fatefully, there was one soft splash.

"You see the snake drop off in the water?" asked Easter.

"Snake?"

"Out of that tree."

"You can have him."

"There he is: coming up!" Easter pointed.

"That's probably a different one," Nina objected in the voice of Jinny Love.

Easter looked both ways, chose, and walked on the pink sandy rim with its purpled lip, her blue shadow lolling over it. She went around a bend, and straight to an old gray boat. Did she know it would be there? It was in some reeds, looking mysterious to come upon and yet in place, as an old boat will. Easter stepped into it and hopped to the far seat that was over the water, and dropping to it lay back with her toes hooked up. She looked falling over backwards. One arm lifted, curved over her head, and hung till her finger touched the water.

The shadows of the willow leaves moved gently on the sand, deep blue and narrow, long crescents. The water was quiet, the color of pewter, marked with purple stobs, although where the sun shone right on it the lake seemed to be in violent agitation, almost boiling. Surely a little chip would turn around and around in it. Nina dropped down on the flecked sandbar. She fluttered her eyelids, half closed them, and the world looked struck by moonlight.

"Here I come," came Jinny Love's voice. It hadn't been long. She came twitching over their tracks along the sandbar, her long soft hair blowing up like a skirt in a play of the breeze in the open. "But I don't choose to sit myself in a leaky boat," she was calling ahead. "I choose the land."

She took her seat on the very place where Nina was writing her name. Nina moved her finger away, drawing a long arrow to a new place. The sand was coarse like beads and full of minute shells, some shaped exactly like bugles.

"Want to hear about my ankle?" Jinny Love asked. "It wasn't as bad as I thought. I must say you picked a queer place, I saw an *owl*. It smells like the school basement to me—peepee and old erasers." Then she stopped with her mouth a little open, and was quiet, as though something had been turned off inside her. Her eyes were soft, her gaze stretched to Easter, to the boat, the lake—her long oval face went vacant.

Easter was lying rocked in the gentle motion of the boat, her head turned on its cheek. She had not said hello to Jinny Love anew. Did she see the drop of water clinging to her lifted finger? Did it make a rainbow? Not to Easter: her eyes were rolled back, Nina felt. Her own hand was writing in the sand. Nina, Nina, Nina. Writing, she could dream that her self might get away from her—that here in this faraway place she could tell her self, by name, to go or to stay. Jinny Love had begun building a sand castle over her foot. In the sky clouds moved no more perceptibly than grazing animals. Yet with a passing breeze, the boat gave a knock, lifted and fell. Easter sat up.

"Why aren't we out in the boat?" Nina, taking a strange and heady initiative, rose to her feet. "Out there!" A picture in her mind, as if already furnished from an eventual and appreciative distance, showed the boat floating where she pointed, far out in Moon Lake with three girls sitting in the three spaces. "We're coming, Easter!"

"Just as I make a castle. *I'm* not coming," said Jinny Love. "Anyway, there's stobs in the lake. We'd be upset, ha ha."

"What do I care, I can swim!" Nina cried at the water's edge.

"You can just swim from the first post to the second post. And that's in front of camp, not here."

Firming her feet in the sucking, minnowy mud, Nina put her weight against the boat. Soon her legs were half hidden, the mud like some awful kiss pulled at her toes, and all over she tautened and felt the sweat start out of her body. Roots laced her feet, knotty and streaming. Under water, the boat was caught too, but Nina was determined to free it. She saw that there was muddy water in the boat too, which Easter's legs, now bright pink, were straddling. Suddenly all seemed easy.

"It's coming loose!"

At the last minute, Jinny Love, who had extracted her foot from the castle with success, hurried over and climbed to the middle seat of the boat, screaming. Easter sat up swaying with the dip of the boat; the energy seemed all to have gone out of her. Her lolling head looked pale and featureless as a pear beyond the laughing face of Jinny Love. She had not said whether she wanted to go or not—yet surely she did, she had been in the boat all along, she had discovered the boat.

For a moment, with her powerful hands, Nina held the boat back. Again she thought of a pear—not the everyday gritty kind that hung on the tree in the backyard, but the fine kind sold on trains and at high prices, each pear with a paper cone wrapping it alone—beautiful, symmetrical, clean pears with thin skins, with snow-white flesh so juicy and tender that to eat one baptized the whole face, and so delicate that while you urgently ate the first half, the second half was already beginning to turn brown. To all fruits, and especially to those fine pears, something happened—the process was so swift, you were never in time for them. It's not the flowers that are fleeting, Nina thought, it's the fruits—it's the time when things are ready that they don't stay. She even went through the rhyme, "Pear tree by the garden gate, How much longer must I wait?"—thinking it was the pears that asked it, not the picker.

Then she climbed in herself, and they were rocking out sideways on the water.

"Now what?" said Jinny Love.

"This is all right for me," said Nina.

"Without oars?—Ha ha."

"Why didn't you tell me, then!—But I don't care now."

"You never are as smart as you think."

"Wait till you find out where we get to."

"I guess you know Easter can't swim. She won't even touch water with her foot."

"What do you think a *boat's* for?"

But a soft tug had already stopped their drifting. Nina with a dark frown turned and looked down.

"A chain! An old mean chain!"

"That's how smart you are."

Nina pulled the boat in again—of course nobody helped her!—burning her hands on the chain, and kneeling outward tried to free the other end. She could see now through the reeds that it was wound around and around an old stump, which had almost grown over it in places. The boat had been chained to the bank since maybe last summer.

"No use hitting it," said Jinny Love.

A dragonfly flew about their heads. Easter only waited in her end of the boat, not seeming to care about the disappointment either. If this was their ship, she was their figurehead, turned on its back, sky-facing. She wouldn't be their passenger.

"You thought we'd all be out in the middle of Moon Lake by now, didn't you?" Jinny Love said, from her lady's seat. "Well, look where we are."

"Oh, Easter! Easter! I wish you still had your knife!"

"—But let's don't go back yet," Jinny Love said on shore. "I don't think they've missed us." She started a sand castle over her other foot.

"You make me sick," said Easter suddenly.

"Nina, let's pretend Easter's not with us."

"But that's what *she* was pretending."

Nina dug into the sand with a little stick, printing "Nina" and then "Easter."

Jinny Love seemed stunned, she let sand run out of both fists. "But how could you ever know what Easter was pretending?"

Easter's hand came down and wiped her name clean; she also wiped out "Nina." She took the stick out of Nina's hand and with a formal gesture, as if she would otherwise seem to reveal too much, wrote for herself. In clear, high-waisted letters the word "Esther" cut into the sand. Then she jumped up.

"Who's that?" Nina asked.

Easter laid her thumb between her breasts, and walked about.

"Why, I call that 'Esther.'"

"Call it 'Esther' if you want to, I call it 'Easter.'"

"Well, sit down...."

"And I named myself."

"How could you? Who let you?"

"I let myself name myself."

"Easter, I believe you," said Nina. "But I just want you to spell it right. Look—E-A-S—"

"I should worry, I should cry."

Jinny Love leaned her chin on the roof of her castle to say, "I was named for my maternal grandmother, so my name's Jinny Love. It couldn't be anything else. Or anything better. You see? Easter's just not a real name. It doesn't matter how she spells it, Nina, nobody ever had it. Not around here." She rested on her chin.

"I have it."

"Just see how it looks spelled right." Nina lifted the stick from Easter's fingers and began to print, but had to throw herself bodily over the name to keep Easter from it. "Spell it right and it's real!" she cried.

"But right or wrong, it's tacky," said Jinny Love. "You can't get me mad over it. All I can concentrate on out here is missing the figs at home."

"'Easter' is real beautiful!" Nina said distractedly. She suddenly threw the stick into the lake, before Easter could grab it, and it trotted up and down in a crucible of sun-filled water. "I thought it was the day you were found on a doorstep," she said sullenly—even distrustfully.

Easter sat down at last and with slow, careful movements of her palms rubbed down the old bites on her legs. Her crest of hair dipped downward and she rocked a little, up and down, side to side, in a rhythm. Easter never did intend to explain anything unless she had to—or to force your explanations. She just had hopes. She hoped never to be sorry. Or did she?

"I haven't got no father. I never had, he ran away. I've got a mother. When I could walk, then my mother took me by the hand and turned me in, and I remember it. I'm going to be a singer."

It was Jinny Love, starting to clear her throat, who released Nina. It was Jinny Love, escaping, burrowing her finger into her castle, who was now kind, pretending Easter had never spoken. Nina banged Jinny Love on the head with her fist. How good and hot her hair was! Like hot glass. She broke the castle from her tender foot. She wondered if Jinny Love's head would break. Not at all. You couldn't learn anything through the head.

"Ha, ha, ha!" yelled Jinny Love, hitting back.

They were fighting and hitting for a moment. Then they lay quiet, tilted together against the crumbled hill of sand, stretched out and looking at the sky where now a white tower of cloud was climbing.

Someone moved; Easter lifted to her lips a piece of cross-vine cut back in the days of her good knife. She brought up a kitchen match from her pocket, lighted up, and smoked.

They sat up and gazed at her.

"If you count much on being a singer, that's not a very good way to start," said Jinny Love. "Even boys, it stunts their growth."

Easter once more looked the same as asleep in the dancing shadows, except for what came out of her mouth, more mysterious, almost, than words.

"Have some?" she asked, and they accepted. But theirs went out.

Jinny Love's gaze was fastened on Easter, and she dreamed and dreamed of telling on her for smoking, while the sun, even through leaves, was burning her pale skin pink, and she looked the most beautiful of all: she felt temptation. But what she said was, "Even after all this is over, Easter, I'll always remember you."

Off in the thick of the woods came a fairy sound, followed by a tremulous silence, a holding apart of the air.

"What's that?" cried Easter sharply. Her throat quivered, the little vein in her temple jumped.

"That's Mister Loch Morrison. Didn't you know he had a horn?"

There was another fairy sound, and the pried-apart gentle silence. The woods seemed to be moving after it, running—the world pellmell. Nina could see the boy in the distance, too, and the golden horn tilted up. A few minutes back her gaze had fled the present and this scene; now she put the horn blower into his visionary place.

"Don't blow that!" Jinny Love cried out this time, jumping to her feet and stopping up her ears, stamping on the shore of Moon Lake. "You shut up! We can hear!—Come on," she added prosaically to the other two. "It's time to go. I reckon they've worried enough." She smiled. "Here comes Cat."

Cat always caught something; something was in his—or her—mouth, a couple of little feet or claws bouncing under the lifted whiskers. Cat didn't look especially triumphant; just through with it.

They marched on away from their little boat.

IV

One clear night the campers built a fire up above the spring, cooked supper on sticks around it, and after stunts, a recitation of "How They Brought the Good News from Ghent to Aix" by Gertrude Bowles, and the ghost story about the bone, they stood up on the ridge and poured a last song into the woods—"Little Sir Echo."

The fire was put out and there was no bright point to look into, no circle. The presence of night was beside them—a beast in gossamer, with no shine of outline, only of ornament—rings, earrings....

"March!" cried Mrs. Gruenwald, and stamped down the trail for them to follow. They went single file on the still-warm pine needles, soundlessly now. Not far away there were crackings of twigs, small, regretted crashes; Loch Morrison, supperless for all they knew, was wandering around by himself, sulking, alone.

Nobody needed light. The night sky was pale as a green grape, transparent like grape flesh over each tree. Every girl saw moths—the beautiful ones like ladies, with long legs that were wings—and the little ones, mere bits of bark. And once against the night, just before Little Sister Spights' eyes, making her cry out, hung suspended a spider—a body no less mysterious than the grape of the air, different only a little.

All around swam the fireflies. Clouds of them, trees of them, islands of them floating, a lower order of brightness—one could even get into a tent by mistake. The stars barely showed their places in the pale sky—small and far from this bright world. And the world would be bright as long as these girls held awake, and could keep their eyes from closing. And the moon itself shone—taken for granted.

Moon Lake came in like a flood below the ridge; they trailed downward. Out there Miss Moody would sometimes go in a boat; sometimes she had a late date from town, "Rudy" Spights or "Rudy" Loomis, and then they could be seen drifting there after the moon was up, far out on the smooth bright surface. ("And she lets him hug her out there," Jinny Love had instructed them "Like this." She had seized, of all people, Etoile, whose name rhymed with tinfoil. "Hands off," said Etoile.) Twice Nina had herself seen the silhouette of the canoe on the bright water, with the figures at each end, like a dark butterfly with wings spread open and still. Not tonight!

Tonight, it was only the niggers, fishing. But their boat must be full of silver fish! Nina wondered if it was the slowness and near-fixity of boats out on the water that made them so magical. Their little boat in the reeds that day had not been far from this one's wonder, after all. The turning of water and sky, of the moon, or the sun, always proceeded, and there was this magical hesitation in their midst, of a boat. And in the boat, it was not so much that they drifted, as that in the presence of a boat the world drifted, forgot. The dreamed-about changed places with the dreamer.

Home from the wild moonlit woods, the file of little girls wormed into the tents, which were hot as cloth pockets. The candles were lighted by Miss Moody, dateless tonight, on whose shelf in the flare of nightly revelation stood her toothbrush in the glass, her hand-painted celluloid powder box, her Honey and Almond cream, her rouge and eyebrow tweezers, and at the end of the line the bottle of Compound, containing true and false unicorn and the life root plant.

Miss Moody, with a fervent frown which precluded interruption, sang in soft tremolo as she rubbed the lined-up children with "Sweet Dreams."

> "Forgive me
> O please forgive me
> I didn't mean to make
> You cry!
> I love you and I need you—"

They crooked and bent themselves and lifted nightgowns to her silently while she sang. Then when she faced them to her they could look into the deep tangled rats of her puffed hair and at her eyebrows which seemed fixed for ever in that elevated line of adult pleading.

> "Do anything but don't say good-bye!"

And automatically they almost said, "Good-bye!" Her hands rubbed and cuffed them while she sang, pulling to her girls all just alike, as if girlhood itself were an infinity, but a commodity. ("I'm ticklish," Jinny Love informed her every night.) Her look of pleading seemed infinitely perilous to them. Her voice had the sway of an aerialist crossing the high wire, even while she sang out of the nightgown coming down over her head.

There were kisses, prayers. Easter, as though she could be cold tonight, got into bed with Geneva. Geneva like a little June bug hooked onto her back. The candles were blown. Miss Moody ostentatiously went right to sleep. Jinny Love cried into her pillow for her mother, or perhaps for the figs. Just outside their tent, Citronella burned in a saucer in the weeds—Citronella, like a girl's name.

Luminous of course but hidden from them, Moon Lake streamed out in the night. By moonlight sometimes it seemed to run like a river. Beyond the cry of the frogs there were the sounds of a boat moored somewhere, of its vague, clumsy reaching at the shore, those sounds that are recognized as being made by something sightless. When did boats have eyes—once? Nothing watched that their little part of the lake stayed roped off and protected; was it there now, the rope stretched frail-like between posts that swayed in mud? That rope was to mark how far the girls could swim. Beyond lay the deep part, some bottomless parts, said Moody. Here and there was the quicksand that stirred your footprint and kissed your heel. All snakes, harmless and harmful, were freely playing now; they put a trailing, moony division between weed and weed—bright, turning, bright and turning.

Nina still lay dreamily, or she had waked in the night. She heard Gertrude Bowles gasp in a dream, beginning to get her stomach ache, and Etoile begin, slowly, her snore. She thought: Now I can think, in between them. She could not even feel Miss Moody fretting.

The orphan! she thought exultantly. The other way to live. There were secret ways. She thought, Time's really short, I've been only thinking like the others. It's only interesting, only worthy, to try for the fiercest secrets. To slip into them all—to change. To change for a moment into Gertrude, into Mrs. Gruenwald, into Twosie—into a boy. To *have been* an orphan.

Nina sat up on the cot and stared passionately before her at the night—the pale dark roaring night with its secret step, the Indian night. She felt the forehead, the beaded stars, look in thoughtfully at her.

The pondering night stood rude at the tent door, the opening fold would let it stoop in—it, him—he had risen up inside. Long-armed, or long-winged, he stood in the center there where the pole went up. Nina lay back, drawn quietly from him. But the night knew about Easter. All about her. Geneva had pushed her to the very edge of the cot. Easter's hand hung down, opened outward. Come here, night, Easter might say, tender to a giant, to such a dark thing. And the night, obedient and graceful, would kneel to her. Easter's calloused hand hung open there to the night that had got wholly into the tent.

Nina let her own arm stretch forward opposite Easter's. Her hand too opened, of itself. She lay there a long time motionless, under the night's gaze, its black cheek, looking immovably at her hand, the only part of her now which was not asleep. Its gesture was like Easter's, but Easter's hand slept and her own hand knew—shrank and knew, yet offered still.

"Instead . . . me instead. . . ."

In the cup of her hand, in her filling skin, in the fingers' bursting weight and stillness, Nina felt it: compassion and a kind of competing that were all one, a single ecstasy, a single longing. For the night was not impartial. No, the night loved some more than others, served some more than others. Nina's hand lay open there for a long time, as if its fingers would be its eyes. Then it too slept. She dreamed her hand was helpless to the tearing teeth of wild beasts. At reveille she woke up lying on it. She could not move it. She hit it and bit it until like a cluster of bees it stung back and came to life.

V

They had seen, without any idea of what he would do—and yet it was just like him—little old Exum toiling up the rough barky ladder and dreaming it up, clinging there monkeylike among the leaves, all eyes and wrinkled forehead.

Exum was apart too, boy and nigger to boot; he constantly moved along an even further fringe of the landscape than Loch, wearing the man's stiff straw hat brilliant as a snowflake. They would see Exum in the hat bobbing along the rim of the swamp like a fisherman's cork, elevated just a bit by the miasma and illusion of the landscape he moved in. It was Exum persistent as a little bug, inching along the foot of the swamp wall, carrying around a fishing cane and minnow can, fishing around the bend from their side of the lake, catching all kinds of things. Things, things. He claimed all he caught, gloating—dangled it and loved it, clasped it with suspicious glee—wouldn't a soul dispute him that? The Boy Scout asked him if he could catch an electric eel and Exum promised it readily—a gift; the challenge was a siesta-long back-and-forth across the water.

Now all rolling eyes, he hung on the ladder, too little to count as looking—too everything-he-was to count as anything.

Beyond him on the diving-board, Easter was standing—high above the others at their swimming lesson. She was motionless, barefooted, and tall with her outgrown, printed dress on her and the sky under her. She had not answered when they called things up to her. They splashed noisily under her calloused, coral-colored foot that hung over.

"How are you going to get down, Easter!" shouted Gertrude Bowles.

Miss Moody smiled understandingly up at Easter. How far, in the water, could Miss Parnell Moody be transformed from a schoolteacher? They had wondered. She wore a canary yellow bathing cap lumpy over her hair, with a rubber butterfly on the front. She wore a brassiere and bloomers under her bathing suit because, said Jinny Love, that was exactly how good she was. She scarcely looked for trouble, immediate trouble—though this was the last day at Moon Lake.

Exum's little wilted black fingers struck at his lips as if playing a tune on them. He put out a foolishly long arm. He held a green willow switch. Later they every one said they saw him—but too late. He gave Easter's heel the tenderest, obscurest little brush, with something of nigger persuasion about it.

She dropped like one hit in the head by a stone from a sling. In their retrospect, her body, never turning, seemed to languish upright for a moment, then descend. It went to meet and was received by blue air. It dropped as if handed down all the way and was let into the brown water almost on Miss Moody's crown, and went out of sight at once. There was something so positive about its disappearance that only the instinct of caution made them give it a moment to come up again; it didn't come up.

Then Exum let loose a girlish howl and clung to the ladder as though a fire had been lighted under it.

Nobody called for Loch Morrison. On shore, he studiously hung his bugle on the tree. He was enormously barefooted. He took a frog dive and when he went through the air they noticed that the powdered-on dirt gave him lavender soles. Now he swam destructively into the water, cut through the girls, and began to hunt Easter where all the fingers began to point.

They cried while he hunted, their chins dropping into the brown buggy stuff and their mouths sometimes swallowing it. He didn't give a glance their way. He stayed under as though the lake came down a lid on him, at each dive. Sometimes, open-mouthed, he appeared with something awful in his hands, showing not them, but the world, or himself—long ribbons of green and terrible stuff, shapeless black matter, nobody's shoe. Then he would up-end and go down, hunting her again. Each dive was a call on Exum to scream again.

"Shut up! Get out of the way! You stir up the lake!" Loch Morrison yelled once—blaming them. They looked at one another and after one loud cry all stopped crying. Standing in the brown that cut them off where they waited, ankle-deep, waist-deep, knee-deep, chin-deep, they made a little V., with Miss Moody in front and partly obscuring their vision with her jerky butterfly cap. They felt his insult. They stood so still as to be almost carried away, in the pictureless warm body of lake around them, until they felt the weight of the currentless water pulling anyhow. Their shadows only, like the curled back edges of a split drum, showed where they each protruded out of Moon Lake.

Up above, Exum howled, and further up, some fulsome, vague clouds with uneasy hearts blew peony-like. Exum howled up, down, and all around. He brought Elberta, mad, from the cook tent, and surely Mrs. Gruenwald was dead to the world—asleep or reading—or she would be coming too, by now, capering down her favorite trail. It was Jinny Love, they realized, who had capered down, and now stood strangely signaling from shore. The painstaking work of Miss Moody, white bandages covered her arms and legs; poison ivy had appeared that morning. Like Easter, Jinny Love had no intention of going in the lake.

"Ahhhhh!" everybody said, long and drawn out, just as he found her.

Of course he found her, there was her arm sliding through his hand. They saw him snatch the hair of Easter's head, the way a boy will snatch anything he wants, as if he won't have invisible opponents snatching first. Under the water he joined himself to her. He spouted, and with engine-like jerks brought her in.

There came Mrs. Gruenwald. With something like a skip, she came to a stop on the bank and waved her hands. Her middy blouse flew up, showing her loosened corset. It was red. They treasured that up. But her voice was pre-emptory.

"This minute! Out of the lake! Out of the lake, out-out! Parnell! Discipline! March them out."

"One's drowned!" shrieked poor Miss Moody.

Loch stood over Easter. He sat her up, folding, on the shore, wheeled her arm over, and by that dragged her clear of the water before he dropped her, a wrapped bundle in the glare. He shook himself in the sun like a dog, blew his nose, spat, and shook his ears, all in a kind of leisurely trance that kept Mrs. Gruenwald off—as though he had no notion that he was interrupting things at all. Exum could now be heard shrieking for Miss Marybelle Steptoe, the lady who had had the camp last year and was now married and living in the Delta.

Miss Moody and all her girls now came out of the lake. Tardy, drooping, their hair heavy-wet and their rubber shoes making wincing sounds, they edged the shore.

Loch returned to Easter, spread her out, and then they could all get at her, but they watched the water lake in her lap. The sun like a weight fell on them. Miss Moody wildly ran and caught up Easter's ankle and pushed on her, like a lady with a wheelbarrow. The Boy Scout looped Easter's arms like sashes on top of her and took up his end, the shoulders. They carried her, looking for shade. One arm fell, touching ground. Jinny Love, in the dazzling bandages, ran up and scooped Easter's arm in both of hers. They proceeded, zigzag, Jinny Love turning her head toward the rest of them, running low, bearing the arm.

They put her down in the only shade on earth, after all, the table under the tree. It was where they ate. The table was itself still mostly tree, as the ladder and diving board were half tree too; a camp table had to be round and barky on the underside, and odorous of having been chopped down. They knew that splintery surface, and the ants that crawled on it. Mrs. Gruenwald, with her strong cheeks, blew on the table, but she might have put a cloth down. She stood between table and girls; her tennis shoes, like lesser corsets, tied her feet solid there; and they did not go any closer, but only to where they could see.

"I got her, please ma'am."

In the water, the life saver's face had held his whole impatience; now it was washed pure, blank. He pulled Easter his way, away from Miss Moody—who, however, had got Easter's sash ends wrung out—and then, with a turn, hid her from Mrs. Gruenwald. Holding her folded up to him, he got her clear, and the next moment, with a spread of his hand, had her lying there before him on the table top.

They were silent. Easter lay in a mold of wetness from Moon Lake, on her side; sharp as a flatiron her hipbone pointed up. She was arm and leg to leg in a long fold, wrong-colored and pressed together as unopen leaves are. Her breasts, too, faced together. Out of the water Easter's hair was darkened, and lay over her face in long fern shapes. Miss Moody laid it back.

"You can tell she's not breathing," said Jinny Love.

Easter's nostrils were pinched-looking like an old country woman's. Her side fell slack as a dead rabbit's in the woods, with the flowers of her orphan dress all running together in some antic of their own, some belated mix-up of the event. The Boy Scout had only let her go to leap onto the table with her. He stood over her, put his hands on her, and rolled her over; they heard the distant-like knock of her forehead on the solid table, and the knocking of her hip and knee.

Exum was heard being whipped in the willow clump; then they remembered Elberta was his mother. "You little black son-a-bitch!" they heard her yelling, and he howled through the woods.

Astride Easter the Boy Scout lifted her up between his legs and dropped her. He did it again, and she fell on one arm. He nodded—not to them.

There was a sigh, a Morgana sigh, not an orphans'. The orphans did not press forward, or claim to own or protect Easter any more. They did nothing except mill a little, and yet their group was delicately changed. In Nina's head, where the world was still partly leisurely, came a recollected scene: birds on a roof under a cherry tree; they were drunk.

The Boy Scout, nodding, took Easter's hair and turned her head. He left her face looking at them. Her eyes were neither open nor altogether shut but as if her ears heard a great noise, back from the time she fell; the whites showed under the lids pale and slick as watermelon seeds. Her lips were parted to the same degree; her teeth could be seen smeared with black mud.

The Boy Scout reached in and gouged out her mouth with his hand, an unbelievable act. She did not alter. He lifted up, screwed his toes, and with a groan of his own fell upon her and drove up and down upon her, into her, gouging the heels of his hands into her ribs again and again. She did not alter except that she let a thin stream of water out of her mouth, a dark stain down the fixed cheek. The children drew together. Life-saving was much worse than they had dreamed. Worse still was the careless-ness of Easter's body.

Jinny Love volunteered once more. She would wave a towel over things to drive the mosquitoes, at least, away. She chose a white towel. Her unspotted arms lifted and criss-crossed. She faced them now; her expression quietened and became ceremonious.

Easter's body lay up on the table to receive anything that was done to it. If *he* was brutal, her self, her body, the withheld life, was brutal too. While the Boy Scout as if he rode a runaway horse clung momently to her and arched himself off her back, dug his knees and fists into her and was flung back careening by his own tactics, she lay there.

Let him try and try!

The next thing Nina knew was a scent of home, an adult's thumb in her shoulder, and a cry, "Now what?" Miss Lizzie Stark pushed in front of her, where her hips and black purse swung to a full stop, blotting out everything. She was Jinny Love's mother and had arrived on her daily visit to see how the camp was running.

They never heard the electric car coming, but usually they saw it, watched for it in the landscape, as out of place as a piano rocking over the holes and taking the bumps, making a high wall of dust.

Nobody dared tell Miss Lizzie; only Loch Morrison's grunts could be heard.

"Some orphan get too much of it?" Then she said more loudly, "But what's *he* doing to her? Stop that."

The Morgana girls all ran to her and clung to her skirt.

"Get off me," she said. "Now look here, everybody. I've got a weak heart. You all know that.—Is that *Jinny Love?*"

"Leave me alone, Mama," said Jinny Love, waving the towel.

Miss Lizzie, whose hands were on Nina's shoulders, shook Nina. "Jinny Love Stark, come here to me, Loch Morrison, get off that table and shame on you."

Miss Moody was the one brought to tears. She walked up to Miss Lizzie holding a towel in front of her breast and weeping. "He's our life saver, Miss Lizzie. Remember? Our Boy Scout. Oh, mercy, I'm thankful you've come, he's been doing that a long time. Stand in the shade, Miss Lizzie."

"Boy Scout? Why, he ought to be—he ought to be—I can't stand it, Parnell Moody."

"Can't any of us help it, Miss Lizzie. Can't any of us. It's what he came for." She wept.

"That's Easter," Geneva said. "That is."

"He ought to be put out of business," Miss Lizzie Stark said. She stood in the center of them all, squeezing Nina uncomfortably for Jinny Love, who flouted her up in front, and Nina could look up at her. The white rice powder which she used on the very front of her face twinkled on her faint mustache. She smelled of red pepper and lemon juice—she had been making them some mayonnaise. She was valiantly trying to make up for all the Boy Scout was doing by what she was thinking of him: that he was odious. Miss Lizzie's carelessly flung word to him on sight—the first day—had been, "You little rascal, I bet you run down and pollute the spring, don't you?" "Nome," the Boy Scout had said, showing the first evidence of his gloom.

"Tears won't help, Parnell," Miss Lizzie said. "Though some don't know what tears are." She glanced at Mrs. Gruenwald, who glanced back from another level; she had brought herself out a chair. "And our last afternoon. I'd thought we'd have a treat."

They looked around as here came Marvin, Miss Lizzie's yard boy, holding two watermelons like a mother with twins. He came toward the table and just stood there.

"Marvin. You can put those melons down, don't you see the table's got somebody on it?" Miss Lizzie said. "Put 'em down and wait."

Her presence made this whole happening seem more in the nature of things. They were glad Miss Lizzie had come! It was somehow for this that they had given those yells of Miss Lizzie as Camp Mother. Under her gaze the Boy Scout's actions seemed to lose a good deal of significance. He was reduced almost to a nuisance—a mosquito, with a mosquito's proboscis. "Get him off her," Miss Lizzie repeated, in her rich and yet careless, almost humorous voice, knowing it was no good. "Ah, get him off her." She stood hugging the other little girls, several of them, warmly. Her gaze only hardened on Jinny Love; they hugged her all the more.

She loved them. It seemed the harder it was to get out here and the harder a time she found them having, the better she appreciated them. They remembered now—while the Boy Scout still drove up and down on Easter's muddy back—how they were always getting ready for Miss Lizzie; the tents even now were straight and the ground picked up and raked for her, and the tea for supper was already made and sitting in a tub in the lake; and sure enough, the niggers' dog had barked at the car just as always, and now here she was. She could have stopped everything; and she hadn't stopped it. Even her opening protests seemed now like part of things—what she was supposed to say. Several of the little girls looked up at Miss Lizzie instead of at what was on the table. Her powdered lips flickered, her eyelids hooded her gaze, but she was there.

On the table, the Boy Scout spat, and took a fresh appraisal of Easter. He reached for a hold on her hair and pulled her head back. No longer were her lips faintly parted—her mouth was open. It gaped. So did his. He dropped her, the head with its suddenness bowed again on its cheek, and he started again.

"Easter's dead! Easter's d—" cried Gertrude Bowles in a rowdy voice, and she was slapped rowdily across the mouth to cut off the word, by Miss Lizzie's hand.

Jinny Love, with a persistence they had not dreamed of, deployed the towel. Could it be owing to Jinny Love's always being on the right side that Easter mustn't dare die and bring all this to a stop? Nina thought, It's I that's thinking. Easter's not thinking at all. And while not thinking, she is not dead, but unconscious, which is even harder to be. Easter had come among them and had held herself untouchable and intact. Of course, for one little touch could smirch her, make her fall so far, so deep.—Except that by that time they were all saying the nigger deliberately poked her off in the water, meant her to drown.

"Don't touch her," they said tenderly to one another.

"Give up! Give up! Give up!" screamed Miss Moody—she who had rubbed them all the same, as if she rubbed chickens for the frying pan. Miss Lizzie without hesitation slapped her too.

"Don't touch her."

For they were crowding closer to the table all the time.

"If Easter's dead, I get her coat for winter, all right," said Geneva.

"Hush, orphan."

"Is she then?"

"You shut up." The Boy Scout looked around and panted at Geneva. "You can ast *me* when I ast you to ast me."

The niggers' dog was barking again, had been barking.

"Now who?"

"A big boy. It's old Ran MacLain and he's coming."

"He would."

He came right up, wearing a cap.

"Get away from me, Ran MacLain," Miss Lizzie called toward him. "You and dogs and guns, keep away. We've already got all we can put up with out here."

She put her foot down on his asking any questions, getting up on the table, or leaving, now that he'd come. Under his cap bill, Ran MacLain set his gaze—he was twenty-three, his seasoned gaze—on Loch and Easter on the table. He could not be prevented from considering them all. He moved under the tree. He held his gun under his arm. He let two dogs run loose, and almost imperceptibly, he chewed gum. Only Miss Moody did not move away from him.

And pressing closer to the table, Nina almost walked into Easter's arm flung out over the edge. The arm was turned at the elbow so that the hand opened upward. It held there the same as it had held when the night came in and stood in the tent, when it had come to Easter and not to Nina. It was the one hand, and it seemed the one moment.

"Don't touch her."

Nina fainted. She woke up to the cut-onion odor of Elberta's under-arm. She was up on the table with Easter, foot to head. There was so much she loved at home, but there was only time to remember the front yard. The silver, sweet-smelling paths strewed themselves behind the lawn mower, the four-o'clocks blazed. Then Elberta raised her up, she got down from the table, and was back with the others.

"Keep away. Keep away, I told you you better keep away. Leave me alone," Loch Morrison was saying with short breaths. "I dove for her, didn't I?"

They hated him, Nina most of all. Almost, they hated Easter.

They looked at Easter's mouth and at the eyes where they were contemplating without sense the back side of the light. Though she had bullied and repulsed them earlier, they began to speculate in another kind of allurement: was there danger that Easter, turned in on herself, might call out to them after all, from the other, worse, side of it? Her secret voice, if soundless then possibly visible, might work out of her terrible mouth like a vine, preening and sprung with flowers. Or a snake would come out.

The Boy Scout crushed in her body and blood came out of her mouth. For them all, it was like being spoken to.

"Nina, you! Come stand right here in my skirt," Miss Lizzie called. Nina went and stood under the big bosom that started down, at the neck of her dress, like a big cloven white hide.

Jinny Love was catching her mother's eye. Of course she had stolen brief rests, but now her white arms lifted the white towel and whipped it bravely. She looked at them until she caught their eye—as if in the end the party was for *her*.

Marvin had gone back to the car and brought two more melons, which he stood holding.

"Marvin. We aren't ready for our watermelon. I told you."

"Oh, Ran. How could you? Oh, Ran."

That was Miss Moody in still a third manifestation.

By now the Boy Scout seemed for ever part of Easter and she part of him, he in motion on the up-and-down and she stretched across. He was dripping, while her skirt dried on the table; so in a manner they had changed places too. Was time moving? Endlessly, Ran MacLain's dogs frisked and played, with the niggers' dog between.

Time was moving because in the beginning Easter's face—the curve of her brow, the soft upper lip and the milky eyes—partook of the swoon of her fall—the almost forgotten fall that bathed her so purely in blue for that long moment. The face was set now, and ugly with that rainy color of seedling petunias, the kind nobody wants. Her mouth surely by now had been open long enough, as long as any gape, bite, cry, hunger, satisfaction lasts, any one person's grief, or even protest.

Not all the children watched, and their heads all were beginning to hang, to nod. Everybody had forgotten about crying. Nina had spotted three little shells in the sand she wanted to pick up when she could. And suddenly this seemed to her one of those moments out of the future, just as she had found one small brief one out of the past; this was far, far ahead of her—picking up the shells, one, another, another, without time moving any more, and Easter abandoned on a little edifice, beyond dying and beyond being remembered about.

"I'm so tired!" Gertrude Bowles said. "And hot. Ain't you tired of Easter, laying up there on that table?"

"My arms are about to break, you all," and Jinny Love stood and hugged them to her.

"I'm so tired of Easter," Gertrude said.

"Wish she'd go ahead and die and get it over with," said Little Sister Spights, who had been thumb-sucking all afternoon without a reprimand.

"I give up," said Jinny Love.

Miss Lizzie beckoned, and she came. "I and Nina and Easter all went out in the woods, and I was the only one that came back with poison ivy," she said, kissing her mother.

Miss Lizzie sank her fingers critically into the arms of the girls at her skirt. They all rose on tiptoe. Was Easter dead then?

Looking out for an instant from precarious holds, they took in sharply for memory's sake that berated figure, the mask formed and set on the face, one hand displayed, one jealously clawed under the waist, as if á secret handful had been groveled for, the spread and spotted legs. It was a betrayed figure, the betrayal was over, it was a memory. And then as the blows, automatic now, swung down again, the figure itself gasped.

"Get back. Get back." Loch Morrison spoke between cruel, gritted teeth to them, and crouched over.

And when they got back, her toes webbed outward. Her belly arched and drew up from the board under her. She fell, but she kicked the Boy Scout.

Ridiculously, he tumbled backwards off the table. He fell almost into Miss Lizzie's skirt; she halved herself on the instant, and sat on the ground with her lap spread out before her like some magnificent hat that has just got crushed. Ran MacLain hurried politely over to pick her up, but she fought him off.

"Why don't you go home—now!" she said.

Before their eyes, Easter got to her knees, sat up, and drew her legs up to her. She rested her head on her knees and looked out at them, while she slowly pulled her ruined dress downward.

The sun was setting. They felt it directly behind them, the warmth flat as a hand. Easter leaned slightly over the table's edge, as if to gaze down at what might move, and blew her nose; she accomplished that with the aid of her finger, like people from away in the country. Then she sat looking out again; in another moment her legs dropped and hung down. The girls looked back at her, through the yellow and violet streams of dust—just now reaching them from Ran MacLain's flivver—the air coarse as sacking let down from the tree branches. Easter lifted one arm and shaded her eyes, but the arm fell in her lap like a clod.

There was a sighing sound from them. For the first time they noticed there was an old basket on the table. It held their knives, forks, tin cups and plates.

"Carry me." Easter's words had no inflection. Again, "Carry me." She held out her arms to them, stupidly.

Then Ran MacLain whistled to his dogs.

The girls ran forward all together. Mrs. Gruenwald's fists rose in the air as if she lifted—no, rather had lowered—a curtain and she began with a bleating sound, "Pa-a-ack—"

"—up your troubles in your old kit bag
And smile, smile, smile!"

The Negroes were making a glorious commotion, all of them came up
now, and then Exum escaped them all and ran waving away to the
woods, dainty as a loosened rabbit.

"Who was he, that big boy?" Etoile was asking Jinny Love.

"Ran MacLain, slow-poke."

"What did he want?"

"He's just waiting on the camp. *They're* coming out tomorrow,
hunting. I heard all he said to Miss Moody."

"Did Miss Moody *know* him?"

"Anybody knows him, and his twin brother too."

Nina, running up in the front line with the others, sighed—the sigh
she gave when she turned in her examination papers at school. Then
with each step she felt a defiance of her own. She screamed, "Easter!"

In that passionate instant, when they reached Easter and took her
up, many feelings returned to Nina, some joining and some conflicting.
At least what had happened to Easter was out in the world, like the table
itself. There it remained—mystery, if only for being hard and cruel and,
by something Nina felt inside her body, murderous.

Now they had Easter and carried her up to the tent, Mrs. Gruenwald
still capering backwards and leading on,

"—in your old kit bag!
Smile, girls-instead-of-boys, that's the style!"

Miss Lizzie towered along darkly, groaning. She grabbed hold of Little
Sister Spights, and said, "Can *you* brush me off!" She would be taking
charge soon, but for now she asked for a place to sit down and a glass of
cold water. She did not speak to Marvin yet; he was shoving the
watermelons up onto the table.

Their minds could hardly capture it again, the way Easter was
standing free in space, then handled and turned over by the blue air
itself. Some of them looked back and saw the lake, rimmed around with
its wall-within-walls of woods, into which the dark had already come.
There were the water wings of Little Sister Spights, floating yet, white as a
bird. "I know another Moon Lake," one girl had said yesterday. "Oh, my
child, Moon Lakes are all over the world," Mrs. Gruenwald had interrupted. "I know of one in Austria. . ." And into each fell a girl, they dared,
now, to think.

The lake grew darker, then gleamed, like the water of a rimmed well.
Easter was put to bed, they sat quietly on the ground outside the tent,
and Miss Lizzie sipped water from Nina's cup. The sky's rising clouds

lighted all over, like one spread-out blooming mimosa tree that could be seen from where the trunk itself should rise.

VI

Nina and Jinny Love, wandering down the lower path with arms entwined, saw the Boy Scout's tent. It was after the watermelon feast, and Miss Lizzie's departure. Miss Moody, in voile and tennis shoes, had a date with old "Rudy" Loomis, and Mrs. Gruenwald was trying to hold the girls with a sing before bedtime. Easter slept; Twosie watched her.

Nina and Jinny Love could hear the floating songs, farewell-like, the cheers and yells between. An owl hooted in a tree, closer by. The wind stirred.

On the other side of the tent wall the slats of the Boy Scout's legs shuttered open and shut like a fan when he moved back and forth. He had a lantern in there, or perhaps only a candle. He finished off his own shadow by opening the flap of his tent. Jinny Love and Nina halted on the path, quiet as old campers.

The Boy Scout, little old Loch Morrison, was undressing in his tent for the whole world to see. He took his time wrenching off each garment; then he threw it to the floor as hard as he would throw a ball; yet that seemed, in him, meditative.

His candle—for that was all it was—jumping a little now, he stood there studying and touching his case of sunburn in a Kress mirror like theirs. He was naked and there was his little tickling thing hung on him like the last drop on the pitcher's lip. He ceased or exhausted study and came to the tent opening again and stood leaning on one raised arm, with his weight on one foot—just looking out into the night, which was clamorous.

It seemed to them he had little to do!

Hadn't he surely, just before they caught him, been pounding his chest with his fists? Bragging on himself? It seemed to them they could still hear in the beating air of night the wild tattoo of pride he must have struck off. His silly, brief, overriding little show they could well imagine there in his tent of separation in the middle of the woods, in the night. Minnowy thing that matched his candle flame, naked as he was with that, he thought he shone forth too. Didn't he?

Nevertheless, standing there with the tent slanting over him and his arm knobby as it reached up and his head bent a little, he looked rather at loose ends.

"We can call like an owl," Nina suggested. But Jinny Love thought in terms of the future. "I'll tell on him, in Morgana tomorrow. He's the most conceited Boy Scout in the whole troop; and's bowlegged.

"You and I will always be old maids," she added.

Then they went up and joined the singing.

ANÍBAL
MONTEIRO
MACHADO

ANÍBAL MONTEIRO MACHADO (1895–1964), a Brazilian author, was trained for the legal profession. However, ill-suited by temperament for this kind of work, he eventually turned his full attention to his real love—writing. For a short period, he taught literature in secondary schools, but fortunately he was rescued from this job through the efforts of his friends, when they secured a position for him as a public official. For the last twenty-five years of his life, his house in Ipanema served as a literary meeting place for his peers.

Machado became known for his periodical publications long before the appearance of his first book, Vila Feliz (1944), from which "The Piano" has been selected. This carefully executed piece is a perfect illustration of an inanimate object, here in the form of a piano, suddenly coming to life as the center of attention, causing widespread repercussions with devastating aftereffects, both socially and spiritually, for its owners. The seemingly simple task of disposing of this cumbersome instrument results in countless absurdities.

Machado also composed essays, prose poems, a novel, and two plays, one of which was based on "The Piano." Because he wrote with so much care, he has left behind a small, but exceptionally brilliant body of work.

The Piano

Aníbal Monteiro Machado

"ROSÁLIA!" SHOUTED João de Oliveira to his wife, who was upstairs. "I told the guy to get out. What a nerve! He laughed at it. He said it wasn't worth even five hundred cruzeiros."

"It's an old trick," she replied. "He wants to get it for nothing and then sell it to somebody else. That's how these fellows get rich."

But Rosália and Sara looked somewhat alarmed as they came downstairs. The family approached the old piano respectfully, as if to console it after the insult.

"We'll get a good price for it, you'll see," asserted Oliveira, gazing at the piano with a mixture of affection and apprehension. "They don't make them like this any more."

"Put an ad in the paper," said Rosália, "and they'll come flocking. The house will be like this with people." She joined the tips of the fingers of her right hand in customary token of an immense crowd. "It's a pity to have to give it up."

"Ah, it's a love of a piano!" said João. "Just looking at it you think you hear music." He caressed its oaken case.

"Well, come on, João. Let's put the ad in."

It had to be sold so that the little parlor could be made into a bedroom for Sara and her intended, a lieutenant in the artillery. Besides, the price would pay for her trousseau.

Three mornings later, the piano was adorned with flowers for the sacrifice, and the house was ready to receive prospective buyers.

The first to arrive were a lady and her daughter. The girl opened the piano and played a few chords.

"It's no good at all, Mama."

The lady stood up, looked at it, and noticed that the ivory was missing from some of the keys. She took her daughter by the hand and walked out, muttering as she went: "Think of coming all this distance to look at a piece of junk."

The Oliveira family had no time to feel resentment, for three new candidates appeared, all at the same time: an elderly lady who smelled like a rich widow, a young girl wearing glasses and carrying a music portfolio, and a redheaded man in a worn, wrinkled suit.

"I was here ahead of you," said the young girl to the old lady. "It doesn't really matter. I only came because my mother wanted me to. There must be plenty of others for sale. But I'd just like to say that I was ringing the doorbell while you were still getting off the bus. We came in together but I got here first."

This rivalry for priority pleased the Oliveiras. They thought it wise, however, to break up the argument, so they smiled at everyone and offered them all coffee. The young girl went over to the piano, while the redheaded man stood at a distance and evaluated it with a cool eye. At this moment a lady entered holding a schoolgirl by the hand. They sat down distrustfully.

Suddenly the young girl began to play, and the whole room hung on the notes that she extracted from the keyboard. Off-pitch, metallic, horrible notes. The Oliveiras anxiously studied the faces of their visitors. The redheaded man remained utterly impassive. The others glanced at one another as if seeking a common understanding. The newly arrived lady made a wry face. The perfumed old lady seemed more tolerant and looked indulgently at the old piano case.

It was a jury trial and the piano was the accused. The young girl continued to play, as if she were wringing a confession from it. The timbre suggested that of a decrepit, cracked-voiced soprano with stomach trouble. Some of the notes did not play at all. Doli joined in with her barking, a bitch's well-considered verdict. A smile passed around the room. No one was laughing, however. The girl seemed to be playing now out of pure malice, hammering at the dead keys and emphasizing the cacophony. It was a dreadful situation.

"There's something you ought to know about this piano," explained João de Oliveira. "It's very sensitive to the weather, it changes a great deal with variations in temperature."

The young girl stopped abruptly. She rose, put on some lipstick, and picked up her music portfolio.

"I don't know how you had the nerve to advertise this horror," she said, speaking to João but looking disdainfully as Rosália as if she had been the horror.

And she left.

João said nothing for a moment. After all, the insult had been directed at the old piano, not at him. Nevertheless, he felt constrained to declare that it was a genuine antique.

"They don't make them like this any more," he said emphatically. "They just don't make them."

There was a long silence. The status of the piano had reached its nadir. Finally the redheaded man spoke: "What are you asking for it?"

In view of what had happened, João de Oliveira lowered substantially the price he had had in mind.

"Five contos," he said timidly.

He looked at everyone to see the effect. There was a silent response. Oliveira felt cold. Was the price monstrously high? Only the old lady showed any delicacy at all: she said she would think it over. But, through her veil of mercy, João perceived her decision.

As they all were leaving, a man about to enter stepped out of their way.

"Did you come about the piano?" asked one of them. "Well, you'll..."

But Oliveira interrupted.

"Come in," he said cheerfully. "It's right here. Lots of people have been looking at it."

The man was middle-aged, with a shock of grayish hair. He lifted the lid of the piano and examined the instrument at length. "Probably a music teacher," thought João.

The man did not ask the price. "Thank you," he said and left.

The house was empty again. Sara returned to her room. Rosália and João looked at each other in disappointment.

"Nobody understands its value," commented João sadly. "If I can't get a decent price for it, I'd rather not sell it at all."

"But how about Sara's trousseau?" said Rosália.

"I'll borrow the money."

"You'd never be able to pay it back out of your salary."

"We'll postpone the marriage."

"They love each other, João. They'll want to get married no matter what, trousseau or no trousseau...."

At this moment, Sara could be heard shouting from her room that she could not possibly get married without two new slips and so forth.

"The thing is," Rosália went on, "this house is about the size of a matchbox. Where can we put the newlyweds? We'll have to give up the piano to make room for them. Nobody nowadays has enough room."

Sara's voice was heard again: "No, don't sell the piano. It's so pretty..."

"It's also so silent," interrupted her mother. "You never play it any more. All you ever play is the victrola."

She went to her daughter's room to speak further with her. Strange that Sara should talk like that. Rosália put the dilemma flatly: "A husband or a piano. Choose."

"Oh, a husband!" replied Sara with voluptuous conviction. "Of course."

She hugged her pillow.

"So...?"

"You're always against it, Rosália," shouted João de Oliveira.

"Against what?"

"Our piano."

"Oh, João, how can you say such a thing!"

The next day, as soon as he got back from work, João de Oliveira asked about the piano.

"Did any people answer the ad, Rosália?"

Yes, there had been several telephone calls for information about the piano, and an old man had come and looked at it. Also, the redheaded man had come again.

"Did any of them say anything about buying it?" asked João.

"No. But the two men who came to the house looked at it a long time."

"They did? Did they look at it with interest? With admiration?"

"It's hard to say."

"Yes, they admired it," said Sara. "Especially the old man. He almost ate it with his eyes."

João de Oliveira was touched. It was no longer a matter of price. He just wanted his piano to be treated with consideration and respect, that's all. Maybe it wasn't worth a lot of money but it certainly deserved some courteous attention. He was sorry he hadn't been there, but what his daughter told him of the old man's respectful attitude consoled him for the contumely of the day before. That man must understand the soul of antique furniture.

"Did he leave his address, Sara? No? Oh, well...he'll probably be back."

He rose from his chair and walked around the old instrument. He smiled at it lovingly.

"My piano," he said softly. He ran his hand over the varnished wood as if he were caressing an animal.

No candidate the next day. Only a voice with a foreign accent asking if it was new. Rosália replied that it wasn't but that they had taken such good care of it that it almost looked like new.

"Tomorrow is Saturday," thought Oliveira. "There's bound to be a lot of people."

There were two, a man and a little girl, and they came in a limousine. The man looked at the modest house of the Oliveira family and considered it useless to go in. Nevertheless, he went to the door and asked the make and age of the piano.

"Thank you. There's no need for me to see it," he replied to João's insistence that he look at it. "I thought it would be a fairly new piano. Good luck..."

And he went away.

João was grief-stricken. Ever since he had inherited the piano he had prized it dearly. He had never thought he would have to part with it. Worst of all, no one appreciated it, no one understood its value.

No one, except possibly the fellow who came the next Wednesday. He praised the piano in the most enthusiastic terms, said it was marvelous, and refused to buy. He said that if he paid so low a price for it he would feel he was stealing it, and that João and Rosália were virtually committing a crime in letting this precious thing get out of their hands. Oliveira did not exactly understand.

"Does he mean what he says?" he asked Rosália.

"I think he's just trying to be funny," she replied.

"I don't know. Maybe not."

Rosália was the first to lose hope. Her main concern now, when her husband came home from work, was to alleviate his suffering.

"How many today?"

"Nobody. Two telephone calls. They didn't give their names but they said they'd probably come and look at it."

Her voice was calm, soothing.

"How about the redheaded fellow?"

"I'm sure he'll be back."

For several days no one came or telephoned. João de Oliveira's feelings may be compared to those of a man who sees his friend miss a train: he is sad for his friend's sake and he is happy because he will continue for a time to have the pleasure of his company. João sat down near the piano and enjoyed these last moments with it. He admired its dignity. He confided his thoughts to it. Three generations had played it. How many people it had induced to dream or to dance! All this had passed away, but the piano remained. It was the only piece of furniture that bespoke the presence of his forebears. It was sort of eternal. It and the old oratory upstairs.

"Sara, come and play that little piece by Chopin. See if you remember it."

"I couldn't Papa. The piano sounds terrible."

"Don't say that," Rosália whispered. "Can't you see how your father feels?"

Whenever Sara's eyes lit on the piano, they transformed it into a nuptial bed in which she and the lieutenant were kissing and hugging.

For days and days no prospective buyer appeared. Nothing but an occasional telephone call from the redheaded man, as if he had been a doctor verifying the progress of a terminal case. The advertisement was withdrawn.

"Well, João, what are we going to do about it?"

"What are we going to do about what, Rosália?"

"The piano!"

"I'm not going to sell it," João shouted. "These leeches don't give a damn about the piano; they just want a bargain. I'd rather give it away to someone who'll take good care of it, who knows what it represents."

He was walking back and forth agitatedly. Suddenly the expression of his face changed.

"Listen, Rosália. Let's phone our relatives in Tijuca."

Rosália understood his purpose and was pleased.

"Hello! Is Messias there? He went out? Oh, is this Cousin Miquita? Look...I want to give you our piano as a present.... Yes, as a present.... No, it's not a joke.... Really.... Right.... Exactly.... So it won't go out of the family.... Fine. Have it picked up here sometime soon.... You're welcome. I'm glad to do it...."

After he had hung up he turned to his wife.

"You know what? She didn't believe me at first. She thought it was All Fools' Day."

Rosália was delighted. João walked over to the old piano as if to confer with it about what he had just done.

"My conscience is clear," he thought. "You will not be rejected. You will stay in the family, with people of the same blood. My children's children will know and respect you; you will play for them. I'm sure you understand and won't be angry with us."

"When will they come for it?" interrupted Rosália, eager to get the room ready for the bridal couple.

The next day Messias telephoned his relatives in Ipanema. Did they really mean to give him a piano? It was too much. He was grateful but they really shouldn't. When his wife told him, he could hardly believe it.

"No, it's true, Messias. You know, our house is about as big as a nutshell. We can't keep the piano here, and João doesn't want it to fall into the hands of strangers. If you people have it, it's almost the same as if it were still with us. Are you going to send for it soon?"

Several days went by. No moving van came. Mr. and Mrs. Oliveira thought the silence of their relatives in Tijuca extremely odd.

"Something's wrong. Telephone them, Rosália."

Cousin Miquita answered. She was embarrassed. The moving men asked a fortune for the job.

"I guess it's the gasoline shortage.... Wait a few more days. Messias will arrange something. We're delighted about getting the piano. We think of nothing else, Rosália."

This last sentence struck a false note, thought Rosália. After a week, João de Oliveira telephoned again.

"Do you want it or don't you, Messias?"

"João, you can't imagine how terrible we feel about this," came the stammered reply. "You give us a fine present and we can't accept it. They're asking an arm and a leg to move it here. And, anyway, we really have no room for it. We haven't even got enough room for the stuff we have now. We should have thought of this before. Miquita feels awful about it."

"In short, you don't want the piano."

"We want it.... But we don't...we can't..."

João de Oliveira hung up. He was beginning to understand.

"You see, Rosália. We can't even give the piano away. We can't even give it away."

"What can you do, João! Everything ends up with nobody wanting it."

After a few minutes of silent despondence, they were aroused by Sara, who interspersed her sobs with words of bitter desperation. Her mother comforted her.

"Don't worry, child. It'll be all right. We'll sell it for whatever we can get."

"I want it out right away, Mama. In a few days I'm to be married and my room isn't even ready yet. None of our things are in here. Only that terrible piano ruining my life, that piano that nobody wants."

"Speak softly, dear. Your father can hear you."

"I want him to hear me," she cried, with another sob. She wiped her eyes.

João de Oliveira slept little that night. He was meditating about life. His thoughts were confused and generally melancholy. They induced in him a fierce rage against both life and the piano. He left the house early and went to a nearby bar, where he talked with several men.

"What is my husband doing in a place like that?" Rosália asked herself. João was never a drinker.

Oliveira came back accompanied by a shabbily dressed Negro and two husky Portuguese in work clothes. He showed them the piano. They hefted it and said they doubted if they could handle it, just the three of them.

Rosália and Sara looked on in amazement.

"Have you found a buyer?" asked Rosália.

"No, wife. Nobody will buy this piano."

"You're giving it away?"

"No, wife. Nobody wants it even for free."

"Then what are you doing, João? What in the world are you doing?"

João's eyes watered but his face hardened.

"I'm going to throw it in the ocean."

"Oh, no, Papa!" exclaimed Sara. "That's crazy!"

The Oliveiras could not see the ocean from their windows, but they could smell it and hear it, for they were only three blocks from the avenue that ran along the beach.

The men were waiting, talking among themselves.

"What a courageous thing to do, João!" said his wife. "But shouldn't we talk it over first? Is there no other way out? People will think it funny, throwing a piano into the water."

"What else can we do, Rosália? Lots of ships go to the bottom of the ocean. Some of them have pianos on board."

This irrefutable logic silenced his wife. João seemed to take heart.

"Okeh, you fellows," he cried. "Up with it! Let's go!"

One of the Portuguese came forward and said humbly, on behalf of his colleagues and himself, that they couldn't do it. They hoped he would excuse them, but it would hurt their conscience to throw something like that in the sea. It almost seemed like a crime.

"Boss, why don't you put an ad in the paper? The piano is in such good condition."

"Yes, I know," replied Oliveira ironically. "You may go."

The men left. For a moment the Negro entertained the idea that he might take the piano for himself. He stared at it. He was fascinated by the idea of owning something, and a fine, luxurious thing at that. It was a dream that could become an immediate reality. But where would he take it? He had no house.

Rosália rested her head on her husband's shoulder and fought back the tears.

"Ah, João, what a decision you have made!"

"But if nobody wants it, and if it can't stay here..."

"I know, João. But I can't help feeling sad. It's always been with us. Doesn't it seem cruel, after all these years, to throw it in the ocean? Look at it, standing there, knowing nothing about what's going to happen to it. It's been there almost twenty years, in that corner, never doing any harm..."

"We must try to avoid sentimentality, Rosália."

"She looked at him with admiration.

"All right, João. Do what you must."

Groups of Negro boys, ragged but happy, start out from the huts at Pinto and Latolandia where they live, and stroll through the wealthy neighborhoods. One can always find them begging nickels for ice cream, gazing in rapture at the posters outside the movie houses, or rolling on the sand in Leblon.

That morning a southwester was whipping the Atlantic into a fury. The piano, needless to say, remained as tranquil as ever. And imposing in the severity of its lines.

Preparations for the departure were under way. João de Oliveira asked his wife and daughter to remove the parts that might possibly be useful. Accordingly, the bronze candlesticks were taken off, then the pedals and metal ornaments, and finally the oak top.

"Ugh!" exclaimed Sara. "It looks so different."

Without mentioning it to his family, João de Oliveira had recruited a bunch of Negro boys. They were waiting impatiently outside the door. Oliveira now told them to come in, the strongest ones first.

It was twenty after four in the afternoon when the funeral cortege started out. A small crowd on the sidewalk made way for it. The piano moved slowly and irregularly. Some people came up to observe it more closely. Rosália and her daughter contemplated it sadly from the porch, their arms around each other's shoulders. They could not bring themselves to accompany it. The cook was wiping her eyes on her apron.

"Which way?" asked the Negro boys when the procession reached the corner. They were all trying to hold the piano at the same time, with the result that it almost fell.

"Which way?" they repeated.

"To the sea!" cried João de Oliveira. And with the grand gesture of a naval commander he pointed toward the Atlantic.

"To the sea! To the sea!" echoed the boys in chorus.

They began to understand that the piano was going to be destroyed, and this knowledge excited them. They laughed and talked animatedly among themselves. The hubbub inspired the little bitch Doli to leap in the air and bark furiously.

The balconies of the houses were crowded, chiefly with young girls.

"Mother of heaven!" they exclaimed. "What is it?" And, incredulously, "A piano!"

"It came from ninety-nine," cried a Negro urchin, running from house to house to inform the families.

"Why, that's where Sara lives."

"It's João de Oliveira's house."

An acquaintance ran out to learn the facts from Oliveira himself.

"What's wrong, João?"

"Nothing's wrong. I know what I'm doing. Just everybody keep out of the way."

"But why don't you sell it?"

"I'll sell it, all right. I'll sell it to the Atlantic Ocean. See it there? The ocean..."

With the air of a somewhat flustered executioner, he resumed his command.

"More to the left, fellows.... Careful, don't let it drop.... Just the big boys now, everybody else let go."

From time to time one of the boys would put his arm inside the piano and run his hand along the strings. The sound was a sort of death rattle.

A lady on a balcony shouted at João, "Would you sell it?"

"No, madam, it's not for sale. I'll give it away. You want it?"

The lady reddened, felt offended, and went into her house. João made his offer more general.

"Anyone around here want a piano?"

At number forty-three a family of Polish refugees accepted. They were astounded, but they accepted.

"Then it's yours," shouted João de Oliveira.

The Polish family came down and stood around the piano.

"We'll take it, all right. . . . But. . . our house is very small. Give us a couple of days to get ready for it."

"Now or never!" replied Oliveira. "Here it is, right outside your house. You don't want it? Okeh, fellows, let's go."

The piano moved closer and closer to the sea. It swayed like a dead cockroach carried by ants.

João de Oliveira distinguished only a few of the exclamations coming from the doors, windows, and balconies of the houses.

"This is the craziest thing I ever heard of," someone shouted from a balcony.

"Crazy?" replied João de Oliveira, looking up at the speaker. "Okeh then you take it. Take it. . . . "

Farther on, the scene was repeated. Everyone thought it was a crazy thing to do and everyone wanted the piano; but as soon as the owner offered immediate possession, there was just embarrassed silence. After all, who is prepared to receive a piano at a moment's notice?

João de Oliveira proceeded resolutely, accompanied by a buzz of comments and lamentations. He decided to make no more replies.

A group of motorcycle policemen stopped the procession and surrounded the old piano. João de Oliveira gave a detailed explanation. They asked to see his documents. He went back to the house and got them. He thought the requirement natural enough, for the nation was at war. But he resented having had to give an explanation, for he was acting pursuant to a personal decision for which he was accountable to no one outside the family. He certainly had a right to throw away his own property. This thought reawakened his affection for the instrument. Placing his hand on the piano as if on the forehead of a deceased friend, he felt deeply moved and began to discourse on its life.

"It's an antique, one of the oldest pianos in Brazil."

It had belonged to his grandparents, who had been in the service of the Empire.

"It was a fine piano, you may believe me. Famous musicians played on it. They say that Chopin preferred it over all others. But what does this matter? No one appreciates it any more. Times have changed. . . . Sara, my daughter, is getting married. She'll live with us. The house is small. What can I do? No one wants it. This is the only way out."

And he nodded toward the sea.

The Negro boys were growing impatient with the interruptions. They were eager to see the piano sink beneath the waves. Almost as impatient as these improvised movers, were the people who had joined the procession, including delivery men, messenger boys, a few women, and a great many children.

The police examined the interior of the piano but found nothing suspicious. They returned Oliveira's papers and suggested that he hurry so that traffic would not be impeded.

A photographer asked some of the people to form a group and snapped their picture. João de Oliveira was on the left side in a pose expressing sadness. Then he became annoyed with all these interruptions that prolonged the agony of his piano.

Night fell rapidly. A policeman observed that after six o'clock they would not be permitted to go on. They would have to wait till the next day.

The Negro boys dispersed. They were to be paid later, at Oliveira's house. People were amazed that evening at the number of young Negroes strolling around with small, ivory-plated pieces of wood in their hands.

The piano remained there on the street where they had left it, keeled over against the curb. A ridiculous position. Young men and women on their evening promenade soon surrounded it and made comments.

When he got home, João de Oliveira found some of Sara's girl friends there, eagerly questioning her about the piano.

It was still dark when João and his wife awoke to the loud sound of rain. Wind, rain, and the roar of the surf. They lit the light and looked at each other.

"I was thinking about the piano, Rosália."

"So was I, João. Poor thing! Out in the rain there...and it's so cold!"

The water must be getting into the works and ruining everything...the felt, the strings. It's terrible, isn't it, Rosália?"

"We did an ungrateful thing, João."

"I don't even like to think about it, Rosália."

João de Oliveira looked out the window. Flashes of lightning illuminated the trees, revealing branches swaying wildly in the wind. João went back to bed and slept fitfully. He awoke again and told his wife that he had been listening to the piano.

"I heard everything that was ever played on it. Many different hands. My grandmother's hands, my mother's, yours, my aunt's, Sara's. More than twenty hands, more than a hundred white fingers were pressing the keys. I never heard such pretty music. It was sublime, Rosália. The dead hands sometimes played better than the live ones. Lots of young girls from earlier generations were standing around the piano, listening. Couples who later got married were sitting nearby, holding hands. I don't know why, but after a while they all looked at me—with contempt. Suddenly the hands left the piano, but it kept on playing. The Funeral March. Then the piano shut by itself.... There was a torrent of water. The piano let itself get swept along...toward the ocean. I shouted to it but it wouldn't listen to me. It seemed to be offended, Rosália, and it just kept on going.... I stood there in the street, all alone. I began to cry..."

João de Oliveira was breathing hard. The mysterious concert had left him in a state of emotion. He felt remorseful.

The rain stopped. As soon as it was light, João went out to round up the Negro boys. All he wanted now was to get the thing over with as quickly as possible.

The wind was still strong, and the ocean growled as if it were digesting the storm of the night before. The boys came, but in smaller numbers than before. Several grown men were among them. João de Oliveira, in a hoarse voice, assumed command again.

On the beach the piano moved more slowly. Finally the long tongues of the waves began to lick it.

Some families stood on the sidewalk, watching the spectacle. Oliveira's crew carried and pushed the piano far enough for the surf to take charge and drag it out to sea. Two enormous waves broke over it without effect. The third made it tremble. The fourth carried it away forever.

João de Oliveira stood there, knee deep in water, with his mouth open. The sea seemed enormously silent. No one could tell that he was crying, for the tears on his cheeks were indistinguishable from the drops of spray.

Far off, he saw Sara with her head resting on the lieutenant's shoulder. Doli was with her, her snout expressing inquiry and incipient dismay; she had always slept next to the piano. João was glad that Rosália had not come.

Many people appeared later on the beach, asking one another what had happened. It seemed at first that an entire Polish family had drowned. Subsequently, it was learned that only one person had drowned. Some said it was a child. Others insisted that it was a lady who had had an unhappy love affair. Only later was it generally known that the person who had drowned was a piano.

People posted themselves at their windows to watch João de Oliveira come back from the beach.

"That's the man!" someone announced.

Oliveira walked slowly, staring at the ground. Everyone felt respect for him.

"It's gone, Rosália," he said as he entered the house. "It has passed the point of no return."

"Before we talk about it, João, go change your clothes."

"Our piano will never come back, Rosália."

"Of course it won't come back. That's why you threw it in the sea."

"Who knows," said Sara. "Maybe it'll be washed up on a beach somewhere."

"Let's not think about it any more. It's over. It's finished. Sara, it's time you did your room."

There was a pause, after which João resumed his lamentation.

"I saw the waves swallow it."

"Enough, my husband. Enough!"

"It came back to the surface twice."

"It's all over! Let's not think about it any more."

"I didn't mention it to anybody so they wouldn't think I went crazy. . . though they're beginning to think I'm crazy anyway. . . . The fact is, I'm probably the most rational man in the whole neighborhood. . . . But a little while ago I clearly heard the piano play the Funeral March."

"That was in your dream last night," Rosália reminded him.

"No, it was there by the sea, in broad daylight. Didn't you hear it, Sara? Right afterward, it was covered all with foam, and the music stopped."

He nodded his head, expressing hopelessness before the inevitable. He was talking as if to himself.

"It must be far away by now. Under the water, moving along past strange sights. The wrecks of ships. Submarines. Fishes. Until yesterday it had never left this room. . . Years from now it will be washed up on some island in an ocean on the other side of the world. And when Sara, Rosália, and I are dead, it will still remember the music it made in this house."

He left the room. Sara, alone, looked at the place where the piano had been. Again, she pictured the conjugal bed there, but this time she felt a little guilty.

Her thoughts were interrupted by a knock at the door. A fellow came in with an official notice. Some unidentified person had told the police that a secret radio was hidden in the piano and that her father had wanted to get rid of it. He was to appear at the district police station and answer questions. Well, it was the sort of thing you had to expect in wartime. Nothing anyone could do about it.

Oliveira spent the rest of the day at the police station. He came home late.

"What a life, Rosália!" he said as he fell dejected into the armchair. "What a life! We can't even throw away things that belong to us."

João felt oppressed, stifled. He meditated awhile and then spoke again.

"Have you ever noticed, Rosália, how people hate to get rid of old things? How they cling to them?"

"Not only old things," replied Rosália. "Old ideas too."

Doli was sniffing the area where the piano had been. She wailed a little and fell asleep.

The doorbell rang. A man entered and drew some papers from a briefcase. He said he came from the Port Captain's office.

"Are you João de Oliveira?"

"Yes, I am João de Oliveira."

"What did you cast in the sea this morning?"

Oliveira was stupefied.

"Out here we're not in that port, my dear sir. It's ocean."

"Are you going to give me a vocabulary lesson, Mr. Oliveira?"

The man repeated his previous question and explained that regulations now forbade the placing of objects in or on the sea without a license.

"Have you a license?"

Oliveira humbly asked whether what he had done was in any way offensive or bad.

"That's not the question. Don't you know that we're at war? That our coasts must be protected? That the Nazis are always watching for an opportunity?"

"But it was just a piano, sir."

"It's still a violation. Anyway, was it really a piano? Are you absolutely sure?"

"I think I am," João blurted, looking at his daughter and his wife. "Wasn't it a piano, Rosália? Wasn't it, Sara?"

"Where's your head, João?" exclaimed Rosália. "You know it was a piano."

Her husband's doubt surprised everyone. He seemed to be musing.

"I thought a person could throw anything in the ocean that he wanted to."

"No, indeed! That's all we need...."

João arose. He looked delirious.

"Suppose I want to throw myself in the sea. Can I?"

"It all depends," replied the man from the Port Captain's office.

"Depends on whom? On me and nobody else! I'm a free man. My life belongs to me."

"Much less than you think," said the man.

Sara broke into the smile with which she always greeted the lieutenant, who had just come in. She ran to kiss him.

"See our room, darling. It looks good now, doesn't it?"

"Yes, real good. Where are you going to put the new one?"

"The new one?"

"Yes. Aren't you going to get another?"

Sara and her mother exchanged glances of amazement.

"I'm crazy for a piano," said Sara's fiancé. "You have no idea how it relaxes me. All day long I have to hear guns shooting. A little soft music in the evening ..."

Sara had a fit of coughing. João de Oliveira went out the door. He felt suffocated; he needed to breathe.

Who else would come out of the night and make new demands of him? How could he have known that a piano hidden from the world, living in quiet anonymity, was really an object of public concern? Why hadn't he just left it where it was?

It was miles away now, traveling.... Far away, riding the southern seas.... And free. More so than he or Sara or Rosália. It was he, João de Oliveira, who now felt abandoned. For himself and for his family. It wasn't their piano any more. It was a creature loose in the world. Full of life and pride, moving boldly through the seven seas. Sounding forth. Embraced by all the waters of the world. Free to go where it wished, to do what it wished.

Beneath the trees in front of the house, the Negro boys were waiting for their second day's pay. They had worked hard. It was so dark that he could scarcely distinguish their shaved heads. In the midst of them he saw a vaguely familiar form. The person opened the garden gate and asked permission to enter.

With some difficulty João recognized the redheaded man, but he was wholly unprepared for what the man was about to say:

"I've come back about the piano. I think I can make you a reasonable offer."

Translated by William L. Grossman

JORGE LUIS BORGES

*J*ORGE LUIS BORGES (born 1899), Argentine fiction writer, poet, essayist, and critic, while not widely known until the 1960s, is a magical realist who ranks with Kafka as a father of the genre in this century. He has served as an invaluable model for younger Latin American writers like Fuentes, Cortázar, and García Márquez, but his influence, also reflected in writers like Italo Calvino, is truly international. If he has not been awarded the Nobel Prize, it is probably because he has written no novels. Yet the whole point of his fiction is to challenge realism and, along with it, the idea that novels are any more inevitable than dinosaurs. The questions he poses about writing and reading, and the nature of literary texts, are so radical and searching that many readers are not quite ready to face them. Writers, on the other hand, appreciate both the force and the originality of Borges' fiction, and it would be hard to find a good writer who does not admire him. García Márquez, for example, has said that Borges has done more for the Spanish language than any writer since Cervantes.

The extraordinary range of Borges' work is difficult to represent with two selections. So effective is his compression, his stories often seem to contain whole novels, as well as philosophical problems and existential paradoxes. His command of ideas and narrative possibilities is such that at times he begins to seem omniscient. The two stories presented here are among a dozen we would like to have used. "The Aleph" (1945) is rich in irony at the expense of its superior narrator, who is too firmly convinced that he understands the mysterious relationship of life and art. It may be said to exist for the sake of the list it arrives at, one of the most extraordinary catalogues in literature, and surely one of the most endearing attempts to represent "reality" since Homer's description of the Shield of Achilles in The Iliad. "The South" (1952) must finally be read on several levels, with the reader entertaining a number of conjectures about the reality on which it is based. At some point, we come to suspect that we may have collaborated with the author, and perhaps with the main character, in a death that may not have occurred. The story of Juan Dahlmann helps us discover that we are all romantics to some degree.

Readers who enjoy these stories will want to seek out others. Our own favorites include "Funes, the Memorious," "The Garden of Forking Paths," "The Babylon Lottery," and the remarkable "Tlön, Uqbar, Orbis Tertius." Borges is an engrossing and captivating author; readers may find themselves drawn toward the conclusion that collections like Ficciones, ostensibly separate stories, are in fact the most extraordinary novels that our century has produced.

The Aleph

Jorge Luis Borges

O God! I could be bounded in a nutshell, and count myself a King of infinite space....

HAMLET, II, 2

But they will teach us that Eternity is the Standing still of the Present Time, a Nunc-stans *(as the Schools call it); which neither they, nor any else understand, no more than they would a* Hic-stans *for an Infinite greatness of Place.*

LEVIATHAN, IV, 46

O N THE burning February morning Beatriz Viterbo died, after braving an agony that never for a single moment gave way to self-pity or fear, I noticed that the sidewalk billboards around Constitution Plaza were advertising some new brand or other of American cigarettes. The fact pained me, for I realized that the wide and ceaseless universe was already slipping away from her and that this slight change was the first of an endless series. The universe may change but not me, I thought with a certain sad vanity. I knew that at times my fruitless devotion had annoyed her; now that she was dead, I could devote myself to her memory, without hope but also without humiliation. I recalled that the thirtieth of April was her birthday; on that day to visit her house on Garay Street and pay my respects to her father and to Carlos

Dedicated to Estela Canto by the author.

Argentino Daneri, her first cousin, would be an irreproachable and perhaps unavoidable act of politeness. Once again I would wait in the twilight of the small, cluttered drawing room, once again I would study the details of her many photographs: Beatriz Viterbo in profile and in full color; Beatriz wearing a mask, during the Carnival of 1921; Beatriz at her First Communion; Beatriz on the day of her wedding to Roberto Alessandri; Beatriz soon after her divorce, at a luncheon at the Turf Club; Beatriz at a seaside resort in Quilmes with Delia San Marco Porcel and Carlos Argentino; Beatriz with the Pekinese lapdog given her by Villegas Haedo; Beatriz, front and three-quarter views, smiling, hand on her chin. . . . I would not be forced, as in the past, to justify my presence with modest offerings of books—books whose pages I finally learned to cut beforehand, so as not to find out, months later, that they lay around unopened.

Beatriz Viterbo died in 1929. From that time on, I never let a thirtieth of April go by without a visit to her house. I used to make my appearance at seven-fifteen sharp and stay on for some twenty-five minutes. Each year, I arrived a little later and stayed a little longer. In 1933, a torrential downpour coming to my aid, they were obliged to ask me to dinner. Naturally, I took advantage of that lucky precedent. In 1934, I arrived, just after eight, with one of those large Santa Fe sugared cakes, and quite matter-of-factly I stayed to dinner. It was in this way, on these melancholy and vainly erotic anniversaries, that I came into the gradual confidences of Carlos Argentino Daneri.

Beatriz had been tall, frail, slightly stooped; in her walk there was (if the oxymoron may be allowed) a kind of uncertain grace, a hint of expectancy. Carlos Argentino was pink-faced, overweight, gray-haired, fine-featured. He held a minor position in an unreadable library out on the edge of the Southside of Buenos Aires. He was authoritarian but also unimpressive. Until only recently, he took advantage of his nights and holidays to stay at home. At a remove of two generations, the Italian "S" and demonstrative Italian gestures still survived in him. His mental activity was continuous, deeply felt, far-reaching, and—all in all—meaningless. He dealt in pointless analogies and in trivial scruples. He had (as did Beatriz) large, beautiful, finely shaped hands. For several months he seemed to be obsessed with Paul Fort—less with his ballads than with the idea of a towering reputation. "He is the Prince of poets," Daneri would repeat fatuously. "You will belittle him in vain—but no, not even the most venomous of your shafts will graze him."

On the thirtieth of April, 1941, along with the sugared cake I allowed myself to add a bottle of Argentine cognac. Carlos Argentino tasted it, pronounced it "interesting," and, after a few drinks, launched into a glorification of modern man.

"I view him," he said with a certain unaccountable excitement, "in his inner sanctum, as though in his castle tower, supplied with telephones, telegraphs, phonographs, wireless sets, motion-picture screens, slide projectors, glossaries, timetables, handbooks, bulletins ..."

He remarked that for a man so equipped, actual travel was superfluous. Our twentieth century had inverted the story of Mohammed and the mountain; nowadays, the mountain came to the modern Mohammed.

So foolish did his ideas seem to me, so pompous and so drawn out his exposition, that I linked them at once to literature and asked him why he didn't write them down. As might be foreseen, he answered that he had already done so—that these ideas, and others no less striking, had found their place in the Proem, or Augural Canto, or, more simply, the Prologue Canto of the poem on which he had been working for many years now, alone, without publicity, without fanfare, supported only by those twin staffs universally known as work and solitude. First, he said, he opened the floodgates of his fancy; then, taking up hand tools, he resorted to the file. The poem was entitled *The Earth*; it consisted of a description of the planet, and, of course, lacked no amount of picturesque digressions and bold apostrophes.

I asked him to read me a passage, if only a short one. He opened a drawer of his writing table, drew out a thick stack of papers—sheets of a large pad imprinted with the letter-head of the Juan Crisóstomo Lafinur Library—and, with ringing satisfaction, declaimed:

> Mine eyes, as did the Greek's, have known men's towns and fame,
> The works, the days in light that fades to amber;
> I do not change a fact or falsify a name—
> The *voyage* I set down is...*autour de ma chambre*

"From any angle, a greatly interesting stanza," he said, giving his verdict. "The opening line wins the applause of the professor, the academician, and the Hellenist—to say nothing of the would-be scholar, a considerable sector of the public. The second flows from Homer to Hesiod (generous homage, at the very outset, to the father of didactic poetry), not without rejuvenating a process whose roots go back to Scripture—enumeration, congeries, conglomeration. The third—baroque? decadent? example of the cult of pure form?—consists of two equal hemistichs. The fourth, frankly bilingual, assures me the unstinted backing of all minds sensitive to the pleasures of sheer fun. I should, in all fairness, speak of the novel rhyme in lines two and four, and of the erudition that allows me—without a hint of pedantry!—to cram into four lines three learned allusions covering thirty centuries packed with literature—first to the *Odyssey*, second to *Works and Days*, and third to the immortal bagatelle bequeathed us by the frolicking pen of the Savoyard, Xavier de Maistre. Once more I've come to realize that modern art demands the balm of laughter, the scherzo. Decidedly, Goldoni holds the stage!"

He read me many other stanzas, each of which also won his own approval and elicited his lengthy explications. There was nothing remarkable about them. I did not even find them any worse than the first one. Application, resignation, and chance had gone into the writing; I saw, however, that Daneri's real work lay not in the poetry but in his invention of reasons why the poetry should be admired. Of course, this second phase of his effort modified the writing in his eyes, though not in the eyes of others. Daneri's style of delivery was extravagant, but the deadly drone of his metric regularity tended to tone down and to dull that extravagance.*

Only once in my life have I had occasion to look into the fifteen thousand alexandrines of the *Polyolbion*, that topographical epic in which Michael Drayton recorded the flora, fauna, hydrography, orography, military and monastic history of England. I am sure, however, that this limited but bulky production is less boring than Carlos Argentino's similar vast undertaking. Daneri had in mind to set to verse the entire face of the planet, and, by 1941, had already displaced a number of acres of the State of Queensland, nearly a mile of the course run by the River Ob, a gasworks to the north of Veracruz, the leading shops in the Buenos Aires parish of Concepción, the villa of Mariana Cambaceres de Alvear in the Belgrano section of the Argentine capital, and a Turkish baths establishment not far from the well-known Brighton Aquarium. He read me certain long-winded passages from his Australian section, and at one point praised a word of his own coining, the color "celestewhite," which he felt "actually *suggests* the sky, an element of utmost importance in the landscape of the continent Down Under." But these sprawling, lifeless hexameters lacked even the relative excitement of the so-called Augural Canto. Along about midnight, I left.

Two Sundays later, Daneri rang me up—perhaps for the first time in his life. He suggested we get together at four o'clock "for cocktails in the salon-bar next door, which the forward-looking Zunino and Zungri—my landlords, as you doubtless recall— are throwing open to the public. It's a place you'll really want to get to know."

More in resignation than in pleasure, I accepted. Once there, it was hard to find a table. The "salon-bar," ruthlessly modern, was only barely less ugly than what I had expected; at the nearby tables, the excited customers spoke breathlessly of the sums Zunino and Zungri had

---

*Among my memories are also some lines of a satire in which he lashed out unsparingly at bad poets. After accusing them of dressing their poems in the warlike armor of erudition, and of flapping in vain their unavailing wings, he concluded with this verse:

But they forget, alas, one foremost fact—BEAUTY!

Only the fear of creating an army of implacable and powerful enemies dissuaded him (he told me) from fearlessly publishing this poem.

invested in furnishings without a second thought to cost. Carlos Argentino pretended to be astonished by some feature or other of the lighting arrangement (with which, I felt, he was already familiar), and he said to me with a certain severity, "Grudgingly, you'll have to admit to the fact that these premises hold their own with many others far more in the public eye."

He then reread me four or five different fragments of the poem. He had revised them following his pet principle of verbal ostentation: where at first "blue" had been good enough, he now wallowed in "azures," "ceruleans," and "ultramarines." The word "milky" was too easy for him; in the course of an impassioned description of a shed where wool was washed, he chose such words as "lacteal," "lactescent," and even made one up-"lactinacious." After that, straight out, he condemned our modern mania for having books prefaced, "a practice already held up to scorn by the Prince of Wits in his own graceful preface to the *Quixote*." He admitted, however, that for the opening of his new work an attention-getting foreword might prove valuable—"an accolade signed by a literary hand of renown." He next went on to say that he considered publishing the initial cantos of his poem. I then began to understand the unexpected telephone call; Daneri was going to ask me to contribute a foreword to his pedantic hodgepodge. My fear turned out unfounded; Carlos Argentino remarked, with admiration and envy, that surely he could not be far wrong in qualifying with the epithet "solid" the prestige enjoyed in every circle by Álvaro Melián Lafinur, a man of letters, who would, if I insisted on it, be only too glad to dash off some charming opening words to the poem. In order to avoid ignominy and failure, he suggested I make myself spokesman for two of the book's undeniable virtues—formal perfection and scientific rigor—"inasmuch as this wide garden of metaphors, of figures of speech, of elegances, is inhospitable to the least detail not strictly upholding of truth." He added that Beatriz had always been taken with Álvaro.

I agreed—agreed profusely—and explained for the sake of credibility that I would not speak to Álvaro the next day, Monday, but would wait until Thursday, when we got together for the informal dinner that follows every meeting of the Writers' Club. (No such dinners are ever held, but it is an established fact that the meetings do take place on Thursdays, a point which Carlos Argentino Daneri could verify in the daily papers, and which lent a certain reality to my promise.) Half in prophecy, half in cunning, I said that before taking up the question of a preface I would outline the unusual plan of the work. We then said good-bye.

Turning the corner of Bernardo de Irigoyen, I reviewed as impartially as possible the alternatives before me. They were: a) to speak to Álvaro, telling him this first cousin of Beatriz' (the explanatory euphemism would allow me to mention her name) had concocted a poem that seemed to draw out into infinity the possibilities of cacophony and chaos: *b*) not to say a word to Álvaro. I clearly foresaw that my indolence would opt for *b*.

But first thing Friday morning, I began worrying about the telephone. It offended me that that device, which had once produced the irrecoverable voice of Beatriz, could now sink so low as to become a mere receptacle for the futile and perhaps angry remonstrances of that deluded Carlos Argentino Daneri. Luckily, nothing happened—except the inevitable spite touched off in me by this man, who had asked me to fulfill a delicate mission for him and then had let me drop.

Gradually, the phone came to lose its terrors, but one day toward the end of October it rang, and Carlos Argentino was on the line. He was deeply disturbed, so much so that at the outset I did not recognize his voice. Sadly but angrily he stammered that the now unrestrainable Zunino and Zungri, under the pretext of enlarging their already outsized "salon-bar," were about to take over and tear down his house.

"My home, my ancestral home, my old and inveterate Garay Street home!" he kept repeating, seeming to forget his woe in the music of his words.

It was not hard for me to share his distress. After the age of fifty, all change becomes a hateful symbol of the passing of time. Besides, the scheme concerned a house that for me would always stand for Beatriz. I tried explaining this delicate scruple of regret, but Daneri seemed not to hear me. He said that if Zunino and Zungri persisted in this outrage, Doctor Zunni, his lawyer, would sue *ipso facto* and make them pay some fifty thousand dollars in damages.

Zunni's name impressed me; his firm, although at the unlikely address of Caseros and Tacuari, was nonetheless known as an old and reliable one. I asked him whether Zunni had already been hired for the case. Daneri said he would phone him that very afternoon. He hesitated, then with that level, impersonal voice we reserve for confiding something intimate, he said that to finish the poem he could not get along without the house because down in the cellar there was an Aleph. He explained that an Aleph is one of the points in space that contains all other points.

"It's in the cellar under the dining room," he went on, so overcome by his worries now that he forgot to be pompous. "It's mine—mine. I discovered it when I was a child, all by myself. The cellar stairway is so steep that my aunt and uncle forbade my using it, but I'd heard someone say there was a world down there. I found out later they meant an old-fashioned globe of the world, but at the time I thought they were referring to the world itself. One day when no one was home I started down in secret, but I stumbled and fell. When I opened my eyes, I saw the Aleph."

"The Aleph?" I repeated.

"Yes, the only place on earth where all places are—seen from every angle, each standing clear, without any confusion or blending. I kept the discovery to myself and went back every chance I got. As a child, I did not foresee that this privilege was granted me so that later I could write the poem. Zunino and Zungri will not strip me of what's mine—no, and a thousand times no! Legal code in hand, Doctor Zunni will prove that my Aleph is inalienable."

I tried to reason with him. "But isn't the cellar very dark?" I said.

"Truth cannot penetrate a closed mind. If all places in the universe are in the Aleph, then all stars, all lamps, all sources of light are in it, too."

"You wait there. I'll be right over to see it."

I hung up before he could say no. The full knowledge of a fact sometimes enables you to see all at once many supporting but previously unsuspected things. It amazed me not to have suspected until that moment that Carlos Argentino was a madman. As were all the Viterbos, when you came down to it. Beatriz (I myself often say it) was a woman, a child, with almost uncanny powers of clairvoyance, but forgetfulness, distractions, contempt, and a streak of cruelty were also in her, and perhaps these called for a pathological explanation. Carlos Argentino's madness filled me with spiteful elation. Deep down, we had always detested each other.

On Garay Street, the maid asked me kindly to wait. The master was, as usual, in the cellar developing pictures. On the unplayed piano, beside a large vase that held no flowers, smiled (more timeless than belonging to the past) the large photograph of Beatriz, in gaudy colors. Nobody could see us; in a seizure of tenderness, I drew close to the portrait and said to it, "Beatriz, Beatriz Elena, Beatriz Elena Viterbo, darling Beatriz, Beatriz now gone forever, it's me, it's Borges."

Moments later, Carlos came in. He spoke drily. I could see he was thinking of nothing else but the loss of the Aleph.

"First a glass of pseudo-cognac," he ordered, "and then down you dive into the cellar. Let me warn you, you'll have to lie flat on your back. Total darkness, total immobility, and a certain ocular adjustment will also be necessary. From the floor, you must focus your eyes on the nineteenth step. Once I leave you, I'll lower the trapdoor and you'll be quite alone. You needn't fear the rodents very much—though I know you will. In a minute or two, you'll see the Aleph—the microcosm of the alchemists and Kabbalists, our true proverbial friend, the *multum in parvo!*"

Once we were in the dining room, he added, "Of course, if you don't see it, your incapacity will not invalidate what I have experienced. Now, down you go. In a short while you can babble with *all* of Beatriz' images."

Tired of his inane words, I quickly made my way. The cellar, barely wider than the stairway itself, was something of a pit. My eyes searched the dark, looking in vain for the globe Carlos Argentino had spoken of. Some cases of empty bottles and some canvas sacks cluttered one corner. Carlos picked up a sack, folded it in two, and at a fixed spot spread it out.

"As a pillow," he said, "this is quite threadbare, but if it's padded even a half-inch higher, you won't see a thing, and there you'll lie, feeling ashamed and ridiculous. All right now, sprawl that hulk of yours there on the floor and count off nineteen steps."

I went through with his absurd requirements, and at last he went away. The trapdoor was carefully shut. The blackness, in spite of a chink that I later made out, seemed to me absolute. For the first time, I realized the danger I was in: I'd let myself be locked in a cellar by a lunatic, after gulping down a glassful of poison! I knew that back of Carlos' transparent boasting lay a deep fear that I might not see the promised wonder. To keep his madness undetected, to keep from admitting that he was mad, *Carlos had to kill me*. I felt a shock of panic, which I tried to pin to my uncomfortable position and not to the effect of a drug. I shut my eyes—I opened them. Then I saw the Aleph.

I arrive now at the ineffable core of my story. And here begins my despair as a writer. All language is a set of symbols whose use among its speakers assumes a shared past. How, then, can I translate into words the limitless Aleph, which my floundering mind can scarcely encompass? Mystics, faced with the same problem, fall back on symbols: to signify the godhead, one Persian speaks of a bird that somehow is all birds; Alanus de Insulis, of a sphere whose center is everywhere and circumference is nowhere; Ezekiel, of a four-faced angel who at one and the same time moves east and west, north and south. (Not in vain do I recall these inconceivable analogies; they bear some relation to the Aleph.) Perhaps the gods might grant me a similar metaphor, but then this account would become contaminated by literature, by fiction. Really, what I want to do is impossible, for any listing of an endless series is doomed to be infinitesimal. In that single gigantic instant I saw millions of acts both delightful and awful; not one of them amazed me more than the fact that all of them occupied the same point in space, without overlapping or transparency. What my eyes beheld was simultaneous, but what I shall now write down will be successive, because language is successive. Nonetheless, I'll try to recollect what I can.

On the back part of the step, toward the right, I saw a small iridescent sphere of almost unbearable brilliance. At first I thought it was revolving; then I realized that this movement was an illusion created by the dizzying world it bounded. The Aleph's diameter was probably little more than an inch, but all space was there, actual and undiminished. Each thing (a mirror's face, let us say) was infinite things, since I distinctly saw it from every angle of the universe. I saw the teeming sea; I saw daybreak and nightfall; I saw the multitudes of America; I saw a silvery cobweb in the center of a black pyramid; I saw a splintered labyrinth (it was London); I saw, close up, unending eyes watching themselves in me as in a mirror; I saw all the mirrors on earth and none of them reflected me; I saw in a backyard of Soler Street the same tiles that thirty years before I'd seen in the entrance of a house in Fray Bentos; I saw bunches of grapes, snow, tobacco, lodes of metal, steam; I saw convex equatorial deserts and each one of their grains of sand; I saw a woman in Inverness whom I shall never forget; I saw her tangled hair, her tall figure, I saw the cancer in her breast; I saw a ring of baked mud in a sidewalk, where before there had been a tree; I saw a summer house in Adrogué and a copy of the first English translation of Pliny—Philemon Holland's—and all at the same time saw each letter on each page (as a boy, I used to marvel that the letters in a closed book did not get scrambled and lost overnight); I saw a sunset in Querétaro that seemed to reflect the color of a rose in Bengal; I saw my empty bedroom; I saw in a closet in Alkmaar a terrestrial globe between two mirrors that multiplied it endlessly; I saw horses with flowing manes on a shore of the Caspian Sea at dawn; I saw the delicate bone structure of a hand; I saw the survivors of a battle sending out picture postcards; I saw in a showcase in Mirzapur a pack of Spanish playing cards; I saw the slanting shadows of ferns on a greenhouse floor; I saw tigers, pistons, bison, tides, and armies; I saw all the ants on the planet; I saw a Persian astrolabe; I saw in the drawer of a writing table (and the handwriting made me tremble) unbelievable, obscene, detailed letters, which Beatriz had written to Carlos Argentino; I saw a monument I worshiped in the Chacarita cemetery; I saw the rotted dust and bones that had once deliciously been Beatriz Viterbo; I saw the circulation of my own dark blood; I saw the coupling of love and the modification of death; I saw the Aleph from every point and angle, and in the Aleph I saw the earth and in the earth the Aleph and in the Aleph the earth; I saw my own face and my own bowels; I saw your face; and I felt dizzy and wept, for my eyes had seen that secret and conjectured object whose name is common to all men but which no man has looked upon—the unimaginable universe.

I felt infinite wonder, infinite pity.

"Feeling pretty cockeyed, are you, after so much spying into places where you have no business?" said a hated and jovial voice. "Even if you were to rack your brains, you couldn't pay me back in a hundred years for this revelation. One hell of an observatory, eh, Borges?"

Carlos Argentino's feet were planted on the topmost step. In the sudden dim light, I managed to pick myself up and utter, "One hell of a—yes, one hell of a."

The matter-of-factness of my voice surprised me. Anxiously, Carlos Argentino went on.

"Did you see everything—really clear, in colors?"

At that very moment I found my revenge. Kindly, openly pitying him, distraught, evasive, I thanked Carlos Argentino Daneri for the hospitality of his cellar and urged him to make the most of the demolition to get away from the pernicious metropolis, which spares no one—believe me, I told him, no one! Quietly and forcefully, I refused to discuss the Aleph.

On saying goodbye, I embraced him and repeated that the country, that fresh air and quiet were the great physicians.

Out on the street, going down the stairways inside Constitution Station, riding the subway, every one of the faces seemed familiar to me. I was afraid that not a single thing on earth would ever again surprise me; I was afraid I would never again be free of all I had seen. Happily, after a few sleepless nights, I was visited once more by oblivion.

Postscript of March first, 1943—Some six months after the pulling down of a certain building on Garay Street, Procrustes & Co., the publishers, not put off by the considerable length of Daneri's poem, brought out a selection of its "Argentine sections." It is redundant now to repeat what happened. Carlos Argentino Daneri won the Second National Prize for Literature.* First Prize went to Dr Aita; Third Prize, to Dr. Mario Bonfanti. Unbelievably, my own book *The Sharper's Cards* did not get a single vote. Once again dullness and envy had their triumph! It's been some time now that I've been trying to see Daneri; the gossip is that a second selection of the poem is about to be published. His felicitous pen (no longer cluttered by the Aleph) has now set itself the task of writing an epic on our national hero, General San Martín.

I want to add two final observations: one, on the nature of the Aleph; the other, on its name. As is well known, the Aleph is the first letter of the Hebrew alphabet. Its use for the strange sphere in my story may not be accidental. For the Kabbalah, that letter stands for the *En Soph*, the pure and boundless godhead; it is also said that it takes the shape of a man pointing to both heaven and earth, in order to show that the lower world is the map and mirror of the higher; for Cantor's *Mengenlehre*, it is the symbol of transfinite numbers, of which any part is as great as the whole. I would like to know whether Carlos Argentino chose that name or whether he read it—applied to another point where all points converge—in one of the numberless texts that the Aleph in his cellar revealed to him. Incredible as it may seem, I believe that the Aleph of Garay Street was a false Aleph. ˑ

Here are my reasons. Around 1867, Captain Burton held the post of British Consul in Brazil. In July, 1942, Pedro Henríquez Ureña came across a manuscript of Burton's, in a library at Santos, dealing with the mirror which the Oriental world attributes to Iskander Zu al-Karnayn, or Alexander Bicornis of Macedonia. In its crystal the whole world was reflected. Burton mentions other similar devices—the sevenfold cup of Kai Kosru; the mirror that Tariq ibn-Ziyad found in a tower (*Thousand and One Nights*, 272); the mirror that Lucian of Samosata examined on the

---

* "I received your pained congratulations," he wrote me. "You rage, my poor friend, with envy, but you must confess—even if it chokes you!—that this time I have crowned my cap with the reddest of feathers; my turban with the most *caliph* of rubies."

moon (*True History*, I, 26); the mirrorlike spear that the first book of Capella's *Satyricon* attributes to Jupiter; Merlin's universal mirror, which was "round and hollow ... and seem'd a world of glas" (*The Faerie Queene*, III, 2, 19)—and adds this curious statement: "But the aforesaid objects (besides the disadvantage of not existing) are mere optical instruments. The Faithful who gather at the mosque of Amr, in Cairo, are acquainted with the fact that the entire universe lies inside one of the stone pillars that ring its central court... No one, of course, can actually see it, but those who lay an ear against the surface tell that after some short while they perceive its busy hum... The mosque dates from the seventh century; the pillars come from other temples of pre-Islamic religions, since, as ibn-Khaldun has written; 'In nations founded by nomads, the aid of foreigners is essential in all concerning masonry.'"

Does this Aleph exist in the heart of a stone? Did I see it there in the cellar when I saw all things, and have I now forgotten it? Our minds are porous and forgetfulness seeps in; I myself am distorting and losing, under the wearing away of the years, the face of Beatriz.

Translated by Norman Thomas di Giovanni

The South

Jorge Luis Borges

THE MAN who landed in Buenos Aires in 1871 bore the name of Johannes Dahlmann and he was a minister in the Evangelical Church. In 1939, one of his grandchildren, Juan Dahlmann, was secretary of a municipal library on Calle Córdoba, and he considered himself profoundly Argentinian. His maternal grandfather had been that Francisco Flores, of the Second Line-Infantry Division, who had died on the frontier of Buenos Aires, run through with a lance by Indians from Catriel; in the discord inherent between his two lines of descent, Juan Dahlmann (perhaps driven to it by his Germanic blood) chose the line represented by his romantic ancestor, his ancestor of the romantic death. An old sword, a leather frame containing the daguerreotype of a blank-faced man with a beard, the dash and grace of certain music, the familiar strophes of *Martin Fierro*, the passing years, boredom and solitude, all went to foster this voluntary, but never ostentatious nationalism. At the cost of numerous small privations, Dahlmann had managed to save the empty shell of a ranch in the South which had belonged to the Flores family; he continually recalled the image of the balsamic eucalyptus trees and the great rose-colored house which had once been crimson. His duties, perhaps even indolence, kept him in the city. Summer after summer he contented himself with the abstract idea of possession and with the certitude that his ranch was waiting for him on a precise site in the middle of the plain. Late in February, 1939, something happened to him.

Blind to all fault, destiny can be ruthless at one's slightest distraction. Dahlmann had succeeded in acquiring, on that very afternoon, an imperfect copy of Weil's edition of *The Thousand and One Nights*. Avid to examine this find, he did not wait for the elevator but hurried up the stairs. In the obscurity, something brushed by his forehead: a bat, a bird? On the face of the woman who opened the door to him he saw horror engraved, and the hand he wiped across his face came away red with blood. The edge of a recently painted door which someone had forgotten to close had caused this wound. Dahlmann was able to fall asleep, but from the moment he awoke at dawn the savor of all things was atrociously poignant. Fever wasted him and the pictures in *The Thousand and One Nights* served to illustrate nightmares. Friends and relatives paid him visits and, with exaggerated smiles, assured him that they thought he looked fine. Dahlmann listened to them with a kind of feeble stupor and he marveled at their not knowing that he was in hell. A week, eight days passed, and they were like eight centuries. One afternoon, the usual doctor appeared, accompanied by a new doctor, and they carried him off to a sanitarium on the Calle Ecuador, for it was necessary to X-ray him. Dahlmann, in the hackney coach which bore them away, thought that he would, at last, be able to sleep in a room different from his own. He felt happy and communicative. When he arrived at his destination, they undressed him, shaved his head, bound him with metal fastenings to a stretcher; they shone bright lights on him until he was blind and dizzy, auscultated him, and a masked man stuck a needle into his arm. He awoke with a feeling of nausea, covered with a bandage, in a cell with something of a well about it; in the days and nights which followed the operation he came to realize that he had merely been, up until then, in a suburb of hell. Ice in his mouth did not leave the least trace of freshness. During these days Dahlmann hated himself in minute detail: he hated his identity, his bodily necessities, his humiliation, the beard which bristled upon his face. He stoically endured the curative measures, which were painful, but when the surgeon told him he had been on the point of death from septicemia, Dahlmann dissolved in tears of self-pity for his fate. Physical wretchedness and the incessant anticipation of horrible nights had not allowed him time to think of anything so abstract as death. On another day, the surgeon told him he was healing and that, very soon, he would be able to go to his ranch for convalescence. Incredibly enough, the promised day arrived.

Reality favors symmetries and slight anachronisms: Dahlmann had arrived at the sanitarium in a hackney coach and now a hackney coach was to take him to the Constitución station. The first fresh tang of autumn, after the summer's oppressiveness, seemed like a symbol in nature of his rescue and release from fever and death. The city, at seven in the morning, had not lost that air of an old house lent it by the night; the streets seemed like long vestibules, the plazas were like patios. Dahlmann recognized the city with joy on the edge of vertigo: a second before his eyes registered the phenomena themselves, he recalled the corners, the billboards, the modest variety of Buenos Aires. In the yellow light of the new day, all things returned to him.

Every Argentine knows that the South begins at the other side of Rivadavia. Dahlmann was in the habit of saying that this was no mere convention, that whoever crosses this street enters a more ancient and sterner world. From inside the carriage he sought out, among the new buildings, the iron grill window, the brass knocker, the arched door, the entrance way, the intimate patio.

At the railroad station he noted that he still had thirty minutes. He quickly recalled that in a café on the Calle Brazil (a few dozen feet from Yrigoyen's house) there was an enormous cat which allowed itself to be caressed as if it were a disdainful divinity. He entered the café. There was the cat, asleep. He ordered a cup of coffee, slowly stirred the sugar, sipped it (this pleasure had been denied him in the clinic), and thought, as he smoothed the cat's black coat, that this contact was an illusion and that the two beings, man and cat, were as good as separated by a glass, for man lives in time, in succession, while the magical animal lives in the present, in the eternity of the instant.

Along the next to the last platform the train lay waiting. Dahlmann walked through the coaches until he found one almost empty. He arranged his baggage in the network rack. When the train started off, he took down his valise and extracted, after some hesitation, the first volume of *The Thousand and One Nights*. To travel with this book, which was so much a part of the history of his ill-fortune, was a kind of affirmation that his ill-fortune had been annulled; it was a joyous and secret defiance of the frustrated forces of evil.

Along both sides of the train the city dissipated into suburbs; this sight, and then a view of the gardens and villas, delayed the beginning of his reading. The truth was that Dahlmann read very little. The magnetized mountain and the genie who swore to kill his benefactor are—who would deny it?—marvelous, but not so much more than the morning itself and the mere fact of being. The joy of life distracted him from paying attention to Scheherezade and her superfluous miracles. Dahlmann closed his book and allowed himself to live.

Lunch—the bouillon served in shining metal bowls, as in the remote summers of childhood—was one more peaceful and rewarding delight.

Tomorrow I'll wake up at the ranch, he thought, and it was as if he was two men at a time: the man who traveled through the autumn day and across the geography of the fatherland, and the other one, locked up in a sanitarium and subject to methodical servitude. He saw unplastered brick houses, long and angled, timelessly watching the trains go by; he saw horsemen along the dirt roads; he saw gullies and lagoons and ranches; he saw great luminous clouds that resembled marble; and all these things were accidental, casual, like dreams of the plain. He also thought he recognized trees and crop fields; but he would not have been able to name them, for his actual knowledge of the countryside was quite inferior to his nostalgic and literary knowledge.

From time to time he slept, and his dreams were animated by the impetus of the train. The intolerable white sun of high noon had already become the yellow sun which precedes nightfall, and it would not be long before it would turn red. The railroad car was now also different; it was not the same as the one which had quit the station siding at Constitución; the plain and the hours had transfigured it. Outside, the moving shadow of the railroad car stretched toward the horizon. The elemental earth was not perturbed either by settlements or other signs of humanity. The country was vast but at the same time intimate and, in some measure, secret. The limitless country sometimes contained only a solitary bull. The solitude was perfect, perhaps hostile, and it might have occurred to Dahlmann that he was traveling into the past and not merely south. He was distracted from these considerations by the railroad inspector who, on reading his ticket, advised him that the train would not let him off at the regular station but at another: an earlier stop, one scarcely known to Dahlmann. (The man added an explanation which Dahlmann did not attempt to understand, and which he hardly heard, for the mechanism of events did not concern him.)

The train laboriously ground to a halt, practically in the middle of the plain. The station lay on the other side of the tracks; it was not much more than a siding and a shed. There was no means of conveyance to be seen, but the station chief supposed that the traveler might secure a vehicle from a general store and inn to be found some ten or twelve blocks away.

Dahlmann accepted the walk as a small adventure. The sun had already disappeared from view, but a final splendor exalted the vivid and silent plain, before the night erased its color. Less to avoid fatigue than to draw out his enjoyment of these sights, Dahlmann walked slowly, breathing in the odor of clover with sumptuous joy.

The general store at one time had been painted a deep scarlet, but the years had tempered this violent color for its own good. Something in its poor architecture recalled a steel engraving, perhaps one from an old edition of *Paul et Virginie*. A number of horses were hitched up to the paling. Once inside, Dahlmann thought he recognized the shopkeeper. Then he realized that he had been deceived by the man's resemblance to one of the male nurses in the sanitarium. When the shopkeeper heard Dahlmann's request, he said he would have the shay made up. In order to add one more event to that day and to kill time, Dahlmann decided to eat at the general store.

Some country louts, to whom Dahlmann did not at first pay any attention, were eating and drinking at one of the tables. On the floor, and hanging on to the bar, squatted an old man, immobile as an object. His years had reduced and polished him as water does a stone or the generations of men do a sentence. He was dark, dried up, diminutive, and seemed outside time, situated in eternity. Dahlmann noted with satisfaction the kerchief, the thick poncho, the long *chiripá*, and the colt boots, and told himself, as he recalled futile discussions with people from the Northern counties or from the province of Entre Rios, that gauchos like this no longer existed outside the South.

Dahlmann sat down next to the window. The darkness began overcoming the plain, but the odor and sound of the earth penetrated the iron bars of the window. The shop owner brought him sardines, followed by some roast meat. Dahlmann washed the meal down with several glasses of red wine. Idling, he relished the tart savor of the wine, and let his gaze, now grown somewhat drowsy, wander over the shop. A kerosene lamp hung from a beam. There were three customers at the other table: two of them appeared to be farm workers; the third man, whose features hinted at Chinese blood, was drinking with his hat on. Of a sudden, Dahlmann felt something brush lightly against his face. Next to the heavy glass of turbid wine, upon one of the stripes in the table cloth, lay a spit ball of breadcrumb. That was all: but someone had thrown it there.

The men at the other table seemed totally cut off from him. Perplexed, Dahlmann decided that nothing had happened, and he opened the volume of *The Thousand and One Nights*, by way of suppressing reality. After a few moments another little ball landed on his table, and now the *peones* laughed outright. Dahlmann said to himself that he was not frightened, but he reasoned that it would be a major blunder if he, a convalescent, were to allow himself to be dragged by strangers into some chaotic quarrel. He determined to leave, and had already gotten to his feet when the owner came up and exhorted him in an alarmed voice:

"*Señor* Dahlmann, don't pay any attention to those lads; they're half high."

Dahlmann was not surprised to learn that the other man, now, knew his name. But he felt that these conciliatory words served only to aggravate the situation. Previous to this moment, the *peones'* provocation was directed against an unknown face, against no one in particular, almost against no one at all. Now it was an attack against him, against his name, and his neighbors knew it. Dahlmann pushed the owner aside, confronted the *peones*, and demanded to know what they wanted of him.

The tough with a Chinese look staggered heavily to his feet. Almost in Juan Dahlmann's face he shouted insults, as if he had been a long way off. His game was to exaggerate his drunkness, and this extravagance constituted a ferocious mockery. Between curses and obscenities, he threw a long knife into the air, followed it with his eyes, caught and juggled it, and challenged Dahlmann to a knife fight. The owner objected in a tremulous voice, pointing out that Dahlmann was unarmed. At this point, something unforeseeable occurred.

From a corner of the room, the old ecstatic gaucho—in whom Dahlmann saw a summary and cipher of the South (his South)—threw him a naked dagger, which landed at his feet. It was as if the South had resolved that Dahlmann should accept the duel. Dahlmann bent over to pick up the dagger, and felt two things. The first, that this almost instinctive act bound him to fight. The second, that the weapon, in his torpid hand, was no defense at all, but would merely serve to justify his murder. He had once played with a poniard, like all men, but his idea of fencing and knifeplay did not go further than the notion that all strokes should be directed upwards, with the cutting edge held inwards. *They would not have allowed such things to happen to me in the sanitarium*, he thought.

"Let's get on our way," said the other man.

They went out and if Dahlmann was without hope, he was also without fear. As he crossed the threshold, he felt that to die in a knife fight, under the open sky, and going forward to the attack, would have been a liberation, a joy, and a festive occasion, on the first night in the sanitarium, when they stuck him with the needle. He felt that if he had been able to choose, then, or to dream his death, this would have been the death he would have chosen or dreamt.

Firmly clutching his knife, which he perhaps would not know how to wield, Dahlmann went out into the plain.

Translated by Anthony Kerrigan

OCTAVIO PAZ

*O*CTAVIO PAZ (born 1914) is Mexico's foremost living poet. He is also widely
know as an essayist, critic, editor, and diplomat. Born in Mexico City, he rapidly
assimilated, as a young writer, the influences of such modern poets as T. S. Eliot, St. John
Perse, and André Breton. Attracted to Marxism, like so many South American intellectuals, he
fought on the Republican side in the Spanish Civil War. His diplomatic career brought him to
Paris in the years following World War II, and he was later his country's ambassador to India,
resigning in protest in 1968 over Mexico's brutal suppression of student rioters. He has moved
from Marxism to a form of mysticism, influenced by Hinduism and by his interest in the history
of his country and of Latin America in general. Paz believes that the self is an illusion, and his
important study of Mexican character and culture, The Labyrinth of Solitude (1950), was no
doubt influential in formulating a Latin American existentialism, later realized in novels like
García Márquez's One Hundred Years of Solitude.

Always a theoretician of literature as well as a practitioner, Paz has been steadily attracted
to experimentation. While the results are mainly evidenced in his poetry, they can also be
glimpsed in the delightful story "My Life with the Wave" (1949), a tale that bears traces of
influence from surrealism (Michaux makes an interesting comparison) and at the same time
reflects the deft way of narrative that characterizes so much Latin American fiction.

My Life with the Wave

Octavio Paz

WHEN I left that city, a wave moved ahead of the others. She was tall and light. In spite of the shouts of the others who grabbed her by her floating skirts, she clutched my arm and went leaping off with me. I didn't want to say anything to her, because it hurt me to shame her in front of her friends. Besides, the furious stares of the larger waves paralyzed me. When we got to town, I explained to her that it was impossible, that life in the city was not what she had been able to imagine with all the ingenuousness of a wave that had never left the sea. She watched me gravely: *No, her decision was made. She couldn't go back.* I tried sweetness, harshness, irony. She cried, screamed, hugged, threatened. I had to apologize.

The next day my troubles began. How could we get on the train without being seen by the conductor, the passengers, the police? It's true the rules say nothing in respect to the transport of waves on the railroad, but this very reserve was an indication of the severity with which our act would be judged. After much thought I arrived at the station an hour before departure, took my seat, and, when no one was looking, emptied the tank of the drinking fountain; then, carefully, I poured in my friend.

The first incident arose when the children of a couple nearby loudly declared their thirst. I blocked their way and promised them refreshments and lemonade. They were at the point of accepting when another thirsty passenger approached. I was about to invite her too, but the stare

305

of her companion stopped me short. The lady took a paper cup, approached the tank, and turned the faucet. Her cup was barely half full when I leaped between the woman and my friend. She looked at me in astonishment. While I apoligized, one of the children turned the faucet again. I closed it violently. The lady brought the cup to her lips:

"Agh, this water is salty."

The boy echoed her. Various passengers rose. The husband called the conductor:

"This man put salt in the water."

The conductor called the Inspector:

"So you've placed put substances in the water?"

The Inspector called the police:

"So, you've poisoned the water?"

The police in turn called the Captain:

"So, you're the poisoner?"

The Captain called three agents. The agents took me to an empty car, amidst the stares and whispers of the passengers. At the next station they took me off and pushed and dragged me to the jail. For days no one spoke to me, except during the long interrogations. No one believed me when I explained my story, not even the jailer, who shook his head, saying: "The case is grave, truly grave. You weren't trying to poison the children?"

One day they brought me before the Magistrate. "Your case is difficult," he repeated. "I will assign you to the Penal Judge."

A year passed. Finally they tried me. As there were no victims, my sentence was light. After a short time, my day of freedom arrived.

The Warden called me in:

"Well, now you're free. You were lucky. Lucky there were no victims. But don't let it happen again, because the next time you'll really pay for it. . . ."

And he stared at me with the same solemn stare with which everyone watched me.

The same afternoon I took the train, and after hours of uncomfortable traveling, arrived in Mexico City. I took a cab home. At the door of my apartment I heard laughter and singing. I felt a pain in my chest, like the smack of a wave of surprise when surprise smacks us in the chest: my friend was there, singing and laughing as always.

"How did you get back?"

"Easy: on the train. Someone, after making sure that I was only salt water, poured me into the engine. It was a rough trip: soon I was a white plume of vapor, then I fell in a fine rain on the machine. I thinned out a lot. I lost many drops."

Her presence changed my life. The house of dark corridors and dusty furniture was filled with air, with sun, with green and blue reflections, a numerous and happy populace of reverberations and echoes. How many waves is one wave, and how it can create a beach or a rock or jetty out of a wall, a chest, a forehead that it crowns with foam! Even the abandoned corners, the abject corners of dust and debris were touched by her light hands. Everything began to laugh and everywhere white teeth shone. The sun entered the old rooms with pleasure and stayed for hours when it should have left the other houses, the district, the city, the country. And some nights, very late, the scandalized stars would watch it sneak out of my house.

Love was a game, a perpetual creation. Everything was beach, sand, a bed of sheets that were always fresh. If I embraced her, she would swell with pride, incredibly tall like the liquid stalk of a poplar, and soon that thinness would flower into a fountain of white feathers, into a plume of laughs that fell over my head and back and covered me with whiteness. Or she would stretch out in front of me, infinite as the horizon, until I too became horizon and silence. Full and sinuous, she would envelop me like music or some giant lips. Her presence was a going and coming of caresses, of murmurs, of kisses. Plunging into her waters, I would be drenched to the socks and then, in a wink of an eye, I find myself high above, at a dizzying height, mysteriously suspended, to fall like a stone, and feel myself gently deposited on dry land, like a feather. Nothing is comparable to sleeping rocked in those waters, unless it is waking pounded by a thousand happy light lashes, by a thousand assaults that withdraw laughing.

But I never reached the center of her being. I never touched the nakedness of pain and death. Perhaps it does not exist in waves, that secret place that renders a woman vunerable and moral, that electric button where everything interlocks, twitches, and straightens out, and then swoons. Her sensibility, like that of women, spread in ripples, only they weren't concentric ripples, but rather excentric ones that spread further each time, until they touched other galaxies. To love her was to extend to remote contacts, to vibrate with far-off stars we never suspect. But her center...no, she had no center, just an emptiness like a whirlwind that sucked me in and smothered me.

Stretched out side by side, we exchanged confidences, whispers, smiles. Curled up, she fell on my chest and unfolded there like a vegetation of murmurs. She sang in my ear, a little sea shell. She became humble and transparent, clutching my feet like a small animal, calm water. She was so clear I could read all of her thoughts. On certain nights her skin was covered with phosphorescence and to embrace her was to embrace a piece of night tattooed with fire. But she also became black and bitter. At unexpected hours she roared, moaned, twisted. Her groans woke the neighbors. Upon hearing her, the sea wind would scratch at the door of the house or rave in a loud voice on the roof. Cloudy days irritated her; she broke furniture, said foul words, covered me with insults and gray and greenish foam. She spat, cried, swore, prophesied.

Subject to the moon, the stars, the influence of the light of other worlds, she changed her moods and appearance in a way that I thought fantastic, but it was as fatal as the tide.

She began to complain of solitude. I filled the house with shells and conches, with small sailboats that in her days of fury she shipwrecked (along with the others, laden with images, that each night left my forehead and sunk in her ferocious or gentle whirlwinds). How many little treasures were lost in that time! But my boats and the silent song of the shells were not enough. I had to install a colony of fish in the house. It was not without jealousy that I watched them swimming in my friend, caressing her breasts, sleeping between her legs, adorning her hair with little flashes of color.

Among those fish there were a few particularly repulsive and ferocious ones, little tigers from the aquarium with large fixed eyes and jagged and bloodthirsty mouths. I don't know by what aberration my friend delighted in playing with them, shamelessly showing them a preference whose significance I prefer to ignore. She passed long hours confined with those horrible creatures. One day I couldn't stand it any more; I flung open the door and threw myself on them. Agile and ghostly, they slipped between my hands while she laughed and pounded me until I fell. I thought I was drowning, and when I was purple and at the point of death, she deposited me on the bank and began to kiss me, saying I don't know what things. I felt very weak, fatigued and humiliated. And at the same time her voluptuousness made me close my eyes because her voice was sweet and she spoke to me of the delicious death of the drowned. When I came to my senses, I began to fear and hate her.

I had neglected my affairs. Now I began to visit friends and renew old and dear relations. I met an old girlfriend. Making her swear to keep my secret, I told her of my life with the wave. Nothing moves women so much as the possibility of saving a man. My redeemer employed all of her arts, but what could a woman, master of a limited number of souls and bodies, do faced with my friend who was always changing—and always identical to herself in her incessant metamorphoses.

Winter came. The sky turned gray. Fog fell on the city. A frozen drizzle rained. My friend screamed every night. During the day she isolated herself, quiet and sinister, stuttering a single syllable, like an old woman who mutters in a corner. She became cold; to sleep with her was to shiver all night and to feel, little by little, the blood, bones, and thoughts freeze. She turned deep, impenetrable, restless. I left frequently, and my absences were more prolonged each time. She, in her corner, endlessly howled. With teeth like steel and a corrosive tongue she gnawed the walls, crumbled them. She passed the nights in mourning, reproaching me. She had nightmares, deliriums of the sun, of burning beaches. She dreamt of the pole and of changing into a great block of ice, sailing beneath black skies in nights as long as months. She insulted me.

She cursed and laughed, filled the house with guffaws and phantoms. She summoned blind, quick, and blunt monsters from the deep. Charged with electricity, she carbonized everything she touched. Full of acid, she dissolved whatever she brushed against. Her sweet arms became knotty cords that strangled me. And her body, greenish and elastic, was an implacable whip that lashed and lashed. I fled. The horrible fish laughed with their ferocious grins.

There in the mountains, among the tall pines and the precipices, I breathed the cold thin air like a thought of liberty. I returned at the end of a month. I had decided. It had been so cold over the marble of the chimney, next to the extinct fire, I found a statue of ice. I was unmoved by her wearisome beauty. I put her in a big canvas sack and went out into the streets with the sleeper on my shoulders. In a restaurant in the outskirts I sold her to a waiter friend, who immediately began to chop her into little pieces, which he carefully deposited in the buckets where bottles are chilled.

Translated by Eliot Weinberger

JOHN CHEEVER

JOHN CHEEVER (1912–1982) was a master of lyrical fiction that described the lives of affluent, middle-class Americans. A penetrating observer, he wrote in a style noted for its cool precision and its meticulously rendered detail. Cheever is known for his touches of fantasy, but he is no sentimentalist when it comes to showing the pain, loneliness, or uglier sides of contemporary living.

Cheever's own early experiences in a New England town were perhaps the impetus that encouraged his thematic concerns. He often relishes human eccentricities; many of his protagonists face the dilemma of needing the security of an orderly family life and yet are tempted by the conflicting desire for seeking more adventurous outlets. His work sympathetically exposes weaknesses of human nature, often comically depicting our complicated relationships.

An accomplished novelist, Cheever was famous for such books as The Wapshot Chronicle (1957), winner of the National Book Award, and Falconer (1977), but his stories are unquestionably his true masterpieces. His 1978 collection, The Stories of John Cheever, won both the Pulitzer Prize and an American Book Award.

Our selection here is the title story from his early volume, The Enormous Radio (1953), which clearly shows Cheever's ironic handling of a middle-class family. The aggressive intruder that upsets the delicate domestic balance is simply a radio that somehow manages to pick up voices from neighboring tenants. A sense of magic often enters his stories, which Cheever himself claimed were set "in the long-lost world when the city of New York was still filled with a river light." He qualified this further by stating, "The constants that I look for . . . are a love of light and a determination to trace some moral chain of being."

The Enormous Radio

John Cheever

JIM AND IRENE Westcott were the kind of people who seem to
strike that satisfactory average of income, endeavor, and respecta-
bility that is reached by the statistical reports in college alumni bulletins.
They were the parents of two young children, they had been married
nine years, they lived on the twelfth floor of an apartment house near
Sutton Place, they went to the theatre on an average of 10.3 times a year,
and they hoped someday to live in Westchester. Irene Westcott was a
pleasant, rather plain girl with soft brown hair and a wide, fine forehead
upon which nothing at all had been written, and in the cold weather she
wore a coat of fitch skins dyed to resemble mink. You could not say that
Jim Westcott looked younger than he was, but you could at least say of
him that he seemed to feel younger. He wore his graying hair cut very
short, he dressed in the kind of clothes his class had worn at Andover,
and his manner was earnest, vehement, and intentionally naïve. The
Westcotts differed from their friends, their classmates, and their neighbors only in an interest they shared in serious music. They went to a
great many concerts—although they seldom mentioned this to anyone—
and they spent a good deal of time listening to music on the radio.

Their radio was an old instrument, sensitive, unpredictable, and
beyond repair. Neither of them understood the mechanics of radio—or of
any of the other appliances that surrounded them—and when the
instrument faltered, Jim would strike the side of the cabinet with his

hand. This sometimes helped. One Sunday afternoon, in the middle of a Schubert quartet, the music faded away altogether. Jim struck the cabinet repeatedly, but there was no response; the Schubert was lost to them forever. He promised to buy Irene a new radio, and on Monday when he came home from work he told her that he had got one. He refused to describe it, and said it would be a surprise for her when it came.

The radio was delivered at the kitchen door the following afternoon, and with the assistance of her maid and the handyman Irene uncrated it and brought it into the living room. She was struck at once with the physical ugliness of the large gumwood cabinet. Irene was proud of her living room, she had chosen its furnishings and colors as carefully as she chose her clothes, and now it seemed to her that the new radio stood among her intimate possessions like an aggressive intruder. She was confounded by the number of dials and switches on the instrument panel, and she studied them thoroughly before she put the plug into a wall socket and turned the radio on. The dials flooded with a malevolent green light, and in the distance she heard the music of a piano quintet. The quintet was in the distance for only an instant; it bore down upon her with a speed greater than light and filled the apartment with the noise of music amplified so mightily that it knocked a china ornament from a table to the floor. She rushed to the instrument and reduced the volume. The violent forces that were snared in the ugly gumwood cabinet made her uneasy. Her children came home from school then, and she took them to the Park. It was not until later in the afternoon that she was able to return to the radio.

The maid had given the children their suppers and was supervising their baths when Irene turned on the radio, reduced the volume, and sat down to listen to a Mozart quintet that she knew and enjoyed. The music came through clearly. The new instrument had a much purer tone, she thought, than the old one. She decided that tone was most important and that she could conceal the cabinet behind a sofa. But as soon as she had made her peace with the radio, the interference began. A crackling sound like the noise of a burning powder fuse began to accompany the singing of the strings. Beyond the music, there was a rustling that reminded Irene unpleasantly of the sea, and as the quintet progressed, these noises were joined by many others. She tried all the dials and switches but nothing dimmed the interference, and she sat down, disappointed and bewildered, and tried to trace the flight of the melody. The elevator shaft in her building ran beside the living-room wall, and it was the noise of the elevator that gave her a clue to the character of the static. The rattling of the elevator cables and the opening and closing of the elevator doors were reproduced in her loudspeaker, and, realizing that the radio was sensitive to electrical currents of all sorts, she began to discern through the Mozart the ringing of telephone bells, the dialing of phones, and the lamentation of a vacuum cleaner. By listening more carefully, she was able to distinguish doorbells, elevator bells, electric razors, and Waring mixers, whose sounds had been picked up from the apartments that surrounded hers and transmitted through her loudspeaker. The powerful and ugly instrument, with its mistaken sensitivity to discord, was more than she could hope to master, so she turned the thing off and went into the nursery to see her children.

When Jim Westcott came home that night, he went to the radio confidently and worked the controls. He had the same sort of experience Irene had had. A man was speaking on the station Jim had chosen, and his voice swung instantly from the distance into a force so powerful that it shook the apartment. Jim turned the volume control and reduced the voice. Then, a minute or two later, the interference began. The ringing of telephones and doorbells set in, joined by the rasp of the elevator doors and the whir of cooking appliances. The character of the noise had changed since Irene had tried the radio earlier; the last of the electric razors was being unplugged, the vacuum cleaners had all been returned to their closets, and the static reflected that change in pace that overtakes the city after the sun goes down. He fiddled with the knobs but couldn't get rid of the noises, so he turned the radio off and told Irene that in the morning he'd call the people who had sold it to him and give them hell.

The following afternoon, when Irene returned to the apartment from a luncheon date, the maid told her that a man had come and fixed the radio. Irene went into the living room before she took off her hat or her furs and tried the instrument. From the loudspeaker came a recording of the "Missouri Waltz." It reminded her of the thin, scratchy music from an old-fashioned phonograph that she sometimes heard across the lake where she spent her summers. She waited until the waltz had finished, expecting an explanation of the recording, but there was none. The music was followed by silence, and then the plaintive and scratchy record was repeated. She turned the dial and got a satisfactory burst of Caucasian music—the thump of bare feet in the dust and the rattle of coin jewelry—but in the background she could hear the ringing of bells and a confusion of voices. Her children came home from school then, and she turned off the radio and went to the nursery.

When Jim came home that night, he was tired, and he took a bath and changed his clothes. Then he joined Irene in the living room. He had just turned on the radio when the maid announced dinner, so he left it on, and he and Irene went to the table.

Jim was too tired to make even a pretense of sociability, and there was nothing about the dinner to hold Irene's interest, so her attention wandered from the food to the deposits of silver polish on the candlesticks and from there to the music in the other room. She listened for a few minutes to a Chopin prelude and then was surprised to hear a man's voice break in. "For Christ's sake, Kathy," he said, "do you always have to play the piano when I get home?" The music stopped abruptly. "It's the only chance I have," a woman said. "I'm at the office all day." "So am I," the man said. He added something obscene about an upright piano, and slammed a door. The passionate and melancholy music began again.

"Did you hear that?" Irene asked.

"What?" Jim was eating his dessert.

"The radio. A man said something while the music was still going on—something dirty."

"It's probably a play."

"I don't think it *is* a play," Irene said,

They left the table and took their coffee into the living room. Irene asked Jim to try another station. He turned the knob. "Have you seen my garters?" a man asked. "Button me up," a woman said. "Have you seen my garters?" the man said again. "Just button me up and I'll find your garters," the woman said. Jim shifted to another station. "I wish you wouldn't leave apple cores in the ashtrays," a man said. "I hate the smell."

"This is strange," Jim said.

"Isn't it?" Irene said.

Jim turned the knob again. "'On the coast of Coromandel where the early pumpkins blow,'" a woman with a pronounced English accent said, "'in the middle of the woods lived the Yonghy-Bonghy-Bò. Two old chairs, and half a candle, one old jug without a handle...'"

"My God!" Irene cried. "That's the Sweeneys' nurse."

"'These were all his worldly goods,'" the British voice continued.

"Turn that thing off," Irene said. "Maybe they can hear *us*." Jim switched the radio off. "That was Miss Armstrong, the Sweeneys' nurse," Irene said. "She must be reading to the little girl. They live in 17-B. I've talked with Miss Armstrong in the Park. I know her voice very well. We must be getting other people's apartments."

"That's impossible," Jim said.

"Well, that was the Sweeneys' nurse," Irene said hotly. "I know her voice. I know it very well. I'm wondering if they can hear us."

Jim turned the switch. First from a distance and then nearer, nearer, as if borne on the wind, came the pure accents of the Sweeneys' nurse again: "'*Lady Jingly! Lady Jingly!*'" she said, "'*sitting where the pumpkins blow, will you come and be my wife? said the Yonghy-Bonghy-Bò...*'"

Jim went over to the radio and said "Hello" loudly into the speaker.

"'*I am tired of living singly,*'" the nurse went on, "'*on this coast so wild and shingly, I'm a-weary of my life; if you'll come and be my wife, quite serene would be my life...*'"

"I guess she can't hear us," Irene said. "Try something else."

Jim turned to another station, and the living room was filled with the uproar of a cocktail party that had overshot its mark. Someone was playing the piano and singing the "Whiffenpoof Song," and the voices that surrounded the piano were vehement and happy. "Eat some more sandwiches," a woman shrieked. There were screams of laughter and a dish of some sort crashed to the floor.

"Those must be the Fullers, in 11-E," Irene said. "I knew they were giving a party this afternoon. I saw her in the liquor store. Isn't this too divine? Try something else. See if you can get those people in 18-C."

The Westcotts overheard that evening a monologue on salmon fishing in Canada, a bridge game, running comments on home movies of what had apparently been a fortnight at Sea Island, and a bitter family quarrel about an overdraft at the bank. They turned off their radio at midnight and went to bed, weak with laughter. Sometime in the night, their son began to call for a glass of water and Irene got one and took it to his room. It was very early. All the lights in the neighborhood were extinguished, and from the boy's window she could see the empty street. She went into the living room and tried the radio. There was some faint coughing, a moan, and then a man spoke. "Are you all right, darling?" he asked. "Yes," a woman said wearily. "Yes, I'm all right, I guess," and then she added with great feeling, "But, you know, Charlie, I don't feel like myself any more. Sometimes there are about fifteen or twenty minutes in the week when I feel like myself. I don't like to go to another doctor, because the doctor's bills are so awful already, but I just don't feel like myself, Charlie. I just never feel like myself." They were not young, Irene thought. She guessed from the timbre of their voices that they were middle-aged. The restrained melancholy of the dialogue and the draft from the bedroom window made her shiver, and she went back to bed.

The following morning, Irene cooked breakfast for the family—the maid didn't come up from her room in the basement until ten—braided her daughter's hair, and waited at the door until her children and her husband had been carried away in the elevator. Then she went into the living room and tried the radio. "I don't want to go to school," a child screamed. "I hate school. I won't go to school. I hate school." "You will go to school," an enraged woman said. "We paid eight hundred dollars to get you into that school and you'll go if it kills you." The next number on the dial produced the worn record of the "Missouri Waltz." Irene shifted the control and invaded the privacy of several breakfast tables. She overheard demonstrations of indigestion, carnal love, abysmal vanity, faith, and despair. Irene's life was nearly as simple and sheltered as it appeared to be, and the forthright and sometimes brutal language that came from the loudspeaker that morning astonished and troubled her. She continued to listen until her maid came in. Then she turned off the radio quickly, since this insight, she realized, was a furtive one.

Irene had a luncheon date with a friend that day, and she left her apartment at a little after twelve. There were a number of women in the elevator when it stopped at her floor. She stared at their handsome and impassive faces, their furs, and the cloth flowers in their hats. Which one of them had been to Sea Island? she wondered. Which one had overdrawn her bank account? The elevator stopped at the tenth floor and a woman with a pair of Skye terriers joined them. Her hair was rigged high on her head and she wore a mink cape. She was humming the "Missouri Waltz."

Irene had two Martinis at lunch, and she looked searchingly at her friend and wondered what her secrets were. They had intended to go shopping after lunch, but Irene excused herself and went home. She told the maid that she was not to be disturbed; then she went into the living room, closed the doors, and switched on the radio. She heard, in the course of the afternoon, the halting conversation of a woman entertaining her aunt, the hysterical conclusion of a luncheon party, and a hostess briefing her maid about some cocktail guests. "Don't give the best Scotch to anyone who hasn't white hair," the hostess said. "See if you can get rid of that liver paste before you pass those hot things, and could you lend me five dollars? I want to tip the elevator man."

As the afternoon waned, the conversations increased in intensity. From where Irene sat, she could see the open sky above the East River. There were hundreds of clouds in the sky, as though the south wind had broken the winter into pieces and were blowing it north, and on her radio she could hear the arrival of cocktail guests and the return of children and businessmen from their schools and offices. "I found a good-sized diamond on the bathroom floor this morning," a woman said. "It must have fallen out of that bracelet Mrs. Dunston was wearing last night." "We'll sell it," a man said. "Take it down to the jeweler on Madison Avenue and sell it. Mrs. Dunston won't know the difference, and we could use a couple of hundred bucks..." "'Oranges and lemons, say the bells of St. Clement's,'" the Sweeneys' nurse sang. "'Halfpence and farthings, say the bells of St. Martin's. When will you pay me? say the bells at old Bailey...'" "It's not a hat," a woman cried, and at her back roared a cocktail party. "It's not a hat, it's a love affair. That's what Walter Florell said. He said it's not a hat, it's a love affair," and then, in a lower voice, the same woman added, "Talk to somebody, for Christ's sake, honey, talk to somebody. If she catches you standing here not talking to anybody, she'll take us off her invitation list, and I love these parties."

The Westcotts were going out for dinner that night, and when Jim came home, Irene was dressing. She seemed sad and vague, and he brought her a drink. They were dining with friends in the neighborhood, and they walked to where they were going. The sky was broad and filled with light. It was one of those splendid spring evenings that excite memory and desire, and the air that touched their hands and faces felt very soft. A Salvation Army band was on the corner playing "Jesus Is Sweeter." Irene drew on her husband's arm and held him there for a minute, to hear the music. "They're really such nice people, aren't they?"

she said. "They have such nice faces. Actually, they're so much nicer than a lot of the people we know." She took a bill from her purse and walked over and dropped it into the tambourine. There was in her face, when she returned to her husband, a look of radiant melancholy that he was not familiar with. And her conduct at the dinner party that night seemed strange to him, too. She interrupted her hostess rudely and stared at the people across the table from her with an intensity for which she would have punished her children.

It was still mild when they walked home from the party, and Irene looked up at the spring stars. "'How far that little candle throws its beams,'" she exclaimed. "'So shines a good deed in a naughty world.'" She waited that night until Jim had fallen asleep, and then went into the living room and turned on the radio.

Jim came home at about six the next night. Emma, the maid, let him in, and he had taken off his hat and was taking off his coat when Irene ran into the hall. Her face was shining with tears and her hair was disordered. "Go up to 16-C, Jim!" she screamed. "Don't take off your coat. Go up to 16-C. Mr. Osborn's beating his wife. They've been quarreling since four o'clock, and now he's hitting her. Go up there and stop him."

From the radio in the living room, Jim heard screams, obscenities, and thuds. "You know you don't have to listen to this sort of thing," he said. He strode into the living room and turned the switch. "It's indecent," he said. "It's like looking in windows. You know you don't have to listen to this sort of thing. You can turn it off."

"Oh, it's so horrible, it's so dreadful," Irene was sobbing. "I've been listening all day, and it's so depressing."

"Well, if it's so depressing, why do you listen to it? I bought this damned radio to give you some pleasure," he said. "I paid a great deal of money for it. I thought it might make you happy. I wanted to make you happy."

"Don't, don't, don't, don't quarrel with me," she moaned, and laid her head on his shoulder. "All the others have been quarreling all day. Everybody's been quarreling. They're all worried about money. Mrs. Hutchinson's mother is dying of cancer in Florida and they don't have enough money to send her to the Mayo Clinic. At least, Mr. Hutchinson says they don't have enough money. And some woman in this building is having an affair with the handyman—with that hideous handyman. It's too disgusting. And Mrs. Melville has heart trouble and Mr. Hendricks is going to lose his job in April and Mrs. Hendricks is horrid about the whole thing and that girl who plays the 'Missouri Waltz' is a whore, a common whore, and the elevator man has tuberculosis and Mr. Osborn has been beating Mrs. Osborn." She wailed, she trembled with grief and checked the stream of tears down her face with the heel of her palm.

"Well, why do you have to listen?" Jim asked again. "Why do you have to listen to this stuff if it makes you so miserable?"

"Oh, don't, don't, don't," she cried. "Life is too terrible, too sordid and awful. But we've never been like that, have we, darling? Have we? I mean, we've always been good and decent and loving to one another, haven't we? And we have two children, two beautiful children. Our lives aren't sordid, are they, darling? Are they?" She flung her arms around his neck and drew his face down to hers. "We're happy, aren't we, darling? We are happy, aren't we?"

"Of course we're happy," he said tiredly. He began to surrender his resentment. "Of course we're happy. I'll have that damned radio fixed or taken away tomorrow." He stroked her soft hair. "My poor girl," he said.

"You love me, don't you?" she asked. "And we're not hypercritical or worried about money or dishonest, are we?"

"No, darling," he said.

A man came in the morning and fixed the radio. Irene turned it on cautiously and was happy to hear a California-wine commercial and a recording of Beethoven's Ninth Symphony, including Schiller's "Ode to Joy." She kept the radio on all day and nothing untoward came from the speaker.

A Spanish suite was being played when Jim came home. "Is everything all right?" he asked. His face was pale, she thought. They had some cocktails and went in to dinner to the "Anvil Chorus" from *Il Trovatore*. This was followed by Debussy's "La Mer."

"I paid the bill for the radio today," Jim said. "It cost four hundred dollars. I hope you'll get some enjoyment out of it."

"Oh, I'm sure I will," Irene said.

"Four hundred dollars is a good deal more than I can afford," he went on. "I wanted to get something that you'd enjoy. It's the last extravagance we'll be able to indulge in this year. I see that you haven't paid your clothing bills yet. I saw them on your dressing table." He looked directly at her. "Why did you tell me you'd paid them? Why did you lie to me?"

"I just didn't want you to worry, Jim," she said. She drank some water. "I'll be able to pay my bills out of this month's allowance. There were the slipcovers last month, and that party."

"You've got to learn to handle the money I give you a little more intelligently, Irene," he said. "You've got to understand that we won't have as much money this year as we had last. I had a very sobering talk with Mitchell today. No one is buying anything. We're spending all our time promoting new issues, and you know how long that takes. I'm not getting any younger, you know. I'm thirty-seven. My hair will be gray next year. I haven't done as well as I'd hoped to do. And I don't suppose things will get any better."

"Yes, dear," she said.

"We've got to start cutting down," Jim said. "We've got to think of the children. To be perfectly frank with you, I worry about money a great deal. I'm not at all sure of the future. No one is. If anything should happen to me, there's the insurance, but that wouldn't go very far today. I've worked awfully hard to give you and the children a comfortable life," he said bitterly. "I don't like to see all of my energies, all of my youth, wasted in fur coats and radios and slipcovers and—"

"Please, Jim," she said. "Please. They'll hear us."

"*Who'll hear us?* Emma can't hear us."

"The radio."

"Oh, I'm sick!" he shouted. "I'm sick to death of your apprehensiveness. The radio can't hear us. Nobody can hear us. And what if they can hear us? Who cares?"

Irene got up from the table and went into the living room. Jim went to the door and shouted at her from there. "Why are you so Christly all of a sudden? What's turned you overnight into a convent girl? You stole your mother's jewelry before they probated her will. You never gave your sister a cent of that money that was intended for her—not even when she needed it. You made Grace Howland's life miserable, and where was all your piety and your virtue when you went to that abortionist? I'll never forget how cool you were. You packed your bag and went off to have that child murdered as if you were going to Nassau. If you'd had any reasons, if you'd had any good reasons—"

Irene stood for a minute before the hideous cabinet, disgraced and sickened, but she held her hand on the switch·before she extinguished the music and the voices, hoping that the instrument might speak to her kindly, that she might hear the Sweeneys' nurse. Jim continued to shout at her from the door. The voice on the radio was suave and noncommittal. "An early-morning railroad disaster in Tokyo," the loudspeaker said, "killed twenty-nine people. A fire in a Catholic hospital near Buffalo for the care of blind children was extinguished early this morning by nuns. The temperature is forty-seven. The humidity is eighty-nine."

VJEKOSLAV KALEB

VJEKOSLAV KALEB (born 1905), a Yugoslav novelist and short-story writer, began publishing his stories during the 1940s. He fought on the side of the partisans during World War II and afterwards worked for a film company before becoming a full-time, professional writer in 1957. His work ranges from rustic descriptions of the desolate landscapes of his homeland in the Dalmatian hinterland to wartime and modern urban settings. Kaleb's fiction often skillfully exposes villagers' suspicious attitudes with their characteristic displays of xenophobia. His prose can sometimes be slightly undisciplined, but at its best, it is notable for its sensitivity of observation and for its clear-cut authenticity. Kaleb does not usually concentrate on the dramatic events of a situation, but generally prefers to focus on the complicated, psychological reactions of his characters.

Kaleb has completed one novel, Glorious Dust, which was translated into English in 1960. He has numerous short-story collections in print. In his shorter pieces, he often achieves remarkable effects by carefully juxtaposing bizarre incidents from everyday life with vivid details that yield dramatic discoveries; occasionally it is difficult for the reader to determine the exact results of the described action. This quality of strange uncertainty emanating from Kaleb's best work is very evident in "The Guest," in which a dog, by simply entering a farmer's house, activates an unexpected chain of events, reminiscent of Machado's "The Piano."

The Guest

Vjekoslav Kaleb

THREE OF THEM sat in the dark house under the ceiling of sooty beams: Frane on the log near the fire, Mara at the low table, mixing thick hominy for supper, their half-witted daughter squatting on the chest near the wall, preying like a wild cat.

The day had not been interesting; the boredom of a holiday had worn them out and made them quiet, so they rolled into the evening as if into lukewarm water; nesting in the evening, feeling about its palace with their antennae, seeking pleasure like crabs on a rock.

"Praised be Thy Name...," Mara murmured, glancing through the door at the glow sinking in the west behind the hill and through the leaves of almond and vine, sending only a little of its light into the house; the woman seemed to be afraid of the approaching night, of the uncertain journey through sleep, of vanishing till the morrow.

"With God's help...," she sighed.

The anxiety thawed from Frane's face...he obeyed: the bell from the church flung thin peals of sound which, like night swallows, prodded the darkness in ecstasy and sweetly vanished in the distance. A stretched-out hand made the sign of the cross, a prayer was murmured, the whole soul, sleepy, carried on the waves of the tolling, was lost in the solemn calm of the evening as if in a more beautiful tomorrow.

When the last sound and vibration of the bells had died away slowly, the air was empty again, the pattern of silence fell on all things and pressed them to the earth like a dead body; everything—the whitewashed wall, the earth floor, the old furniture, the bed, the low table

325

in the middle, the chest next to the wall, the hearth, the cask—was frightened into silence. The neighborhood must also have vanished—not a voice came from it.

At last Mara crossed herself again, and seeing that the weak fire was gaining over the light from outside, she lit the little oil-lamp hanging from a beam in the middle of the house.

"There is a little more fuel left in it, let it burn," she said.

Under her dishevelled hair the daughter's eyes flickered with the reflections of the light, kindling a cobweb of reddish-yellow sparks; she stared without a thought through the door into the yard.

"Hem!" She spoke up suddenly, her voice tart, her look focused on the entrance.

Mara looked at her, then at the door.

She started and frowned.

From the door two gentle, intelligent eyes were watching, calm and lonely as two candles at the altar.

It was a big spaniel standing at the door, with long grey hair, his thin brown ears hanging, plastered to his cheeks like two pieces of velvet. He was strangely quiet, solemn, and in color matching the darkness; only his eyes stood out. He looked at the people intensely but acceptingly, expecting a sign of goodwill. Their looks were also fixed for a time upon his intelligent eyes, estimating, trying to find out what he was up to.

They thought he was going to speak.

So they looked at each other for a while like three people and a dog, in expectation, and then the guest realized that nobody was saying a word, and so he stepped over the threshold and entered the house.

"Jesus Christ!" said the young woman quietly, her eyes wide with suspicion.

The beautiful, distinguished-looking beast stopped at the table and looked at the woman again.

His look seemed to her inquisitive, somehow full of wisdom and furtive knowledge. She looked aside.

She turned to her husband.

"H'm, it seems he has got something to tell us!"

"H'm?" His face was more serious now; there was suspicion in it, a shade of fear and respect.

"Yes, yes...that one...."

Dawning hope was perhaps awakening in him like an old memory: a strange, trifling occurrence sometimes brings the desired change to a home. When the light hid like this behind the hill, disappearing, and the darkness covered everything like an old witch, like a clucking hen hatching under her feathers a new tomorrow, then hopes and fears swarmed in silence, by the fire, in the light of the oil-lamp, strangely shaped hopes and fears, like the castles in clouds created by the embers and the bluish flames playing on them. This is a different entertainment every day.

Frane wiped the strange thought from his brow and said, sobered against his will:

"Let's have our supper."

The woman moved towards the table.

She put a yellow lump of hard hominy into a small wooden bowl and passed it to her daughter on the chest, and she and her husband began to eat together from the big bowl.

The dog came to Frane and looked eagerly at the spoonfuls of food, following them with his eyes from bowl to mouth.

The two old people glanced at him with caution, evading his look; their nostrils sniffed the refined scents emanating from the dog, as if a doctor had entered the house.

"Where is His Grace from?" Mara asked vaguely of her husband or the dog, expecting the answer rather from the dog.

And Frane looked inquisitively at the guest.

And he, instead of saying something, just raised his front leg and his front paw dropped on Frane's knee.

Frane was worried. He cut a piece of hominy with his spoon and threw it on the floor.

The dog just looked at the yellow lump on the black floor without budging.

"He must have it on a plate," said the woman. She reached for the wooden plate cautiously, put several lumps of food on it, and took it to a corner of the house.

"Here it is. . .this. . .if you please. . . ."

The dog understood. He took his paw down from Frane's knee, approached the plate, and slowly, beginning with the smaller lumps, ate the hominy.

After this he was not interested in their supper any more, but he sat as before on his hind legs in the middle of the house and began to watch his hosts again, first one, then the other.

It became quite dark, an early autumn evening. The fire in the hearth was dying, the house lit only with the flame of the oil-lamp. Mara, respectful of the guest, raised the wick and improved the flame. A merry grin appeared on the daughter's face, her eyes flickering with curiosity. Frane looked from below his reddish eyebrows, new thoughts cropping up. Suddenly his eyes began to blink, as if he were thinking hard, and then he got up, straightened his back, and stood very solemnly in the middle of the house.

"Pour a little wine," he said significantly.

There were steps in the yard.

Neighbor Špirkan came in.

"Good evening. . . ." He stopped. "And whose dog is this?"

"I don't know," answered Frane.

The neighbor's little son Jerko peeped from the door, with a look of surprise, questioning the dog and the inmates.

"A distinguished-looking animal. Looks like a human being."

"He has said: 'Good evening,'" the daughter remarked.

"H'm?" Špirkan looked at each of them in turn; then at the dog, his eyebrows raised.

The women started, as if stung.

"Has he?. . .I haven't heard!"

Špirkan examined the dog again, more carefully, then he questioned them with his eyes, suspiciously: why were they hiding the truth from him?

But he did not say a word.

Little Jerko ran away from the door.

Frane, as if wanting more light in the room, went to the hearth and put some wood on the fire. He moved with solemnity, taking no notice of Špirkan.

They sat round the fire on the old logs, as if retiring to take counsel. The flashes from the flames began to dance on their faces, and the shadows danced on the wall.

The dog also stepped towards the hearth, but stopped humbly a little away from it. His head and eyes, lit by the fire, stood out against the dark background.

They could see him well. But they shut themselves in this square of the hearth, in its light and warmth, as if protected by a real fence. Somewhere far away they felt the strange animal, with its illuminated face peeping through the wall of darkness into their corner. Who could tell whether these eyes were bringing good or evil?

They worded carefully the thoughts which occurred to them.

"You see, winter's coming. . . ."

"It's a hard lot, brother, hard. . .life's bad for a farmer."

"And Heaven knows if. . . ."

Then some inquisitive people began to drop in from the village:

"Frane's got a strange dog!"

The old bell-ringer Markutina turned up, too, hoarse and asthmatic, with bushy moustache, one eye rolled out, its lids inside out, red like a living wound.

"Oho-ho—who is this guest?" He was a little pleased, as he was always pleased with every change and any news, even if it was not good.

He noticed the calm, intelligent eyes, almost like a human's watching from below.

"You see. . .he looks like a parson. . . ."

"He has said: 'Good evening,'" said the daughter.

"Has he?" Markutina looked round, asking everybody in turn.

"Shut up, you fool!" The mother lost her temper, then glanced cautiously at the dog.

Markutina and Špirkan rolled their eyes doubtfully:

"H'm—who knows where he's come from!" whispered Špirkan.

"A strange dog!" said Kazo.

"Eeeee...."

"Who knows what he is...." said Špirkan and added more loudly, looking at him askance: "Perhaps he understands...."

Šaka, a young, hot-tempered farmer, tall and red in the face, interrupted them harshly:

"Whose is he?"

"God knows," sighed the woman, but the trembling of her upper lip betrayed her pride—she and her husband were obviously most important here. "We were just sitting here, here, when he appeared at the door...."

"And says he: 'Good evening'...ha, ha, ha...." The daughter gave a short peal of laughter and her face contracted as if shivering with cold.

They all fixed their eyes first upon the daughter and then upon the guest sitting quietly in the middle of the house and blinking as if he had nothing to do with what was going on. They meant to enrich time with their expectations, but the dog suddenly got up, approached the bed, sniffed it carefully, and jumped on to it. From the bed, above them, he looked at all the audience, as if asking permission, sniffed the middle of the bed, kneaded it with his paws, turned three times; in an ordinary dog-like way, curled up—and lay down with his snout under his tail.

At once he began to breathe wearily and murmur, closing his eyes.

The audience moved little by little towards the bed, and went on with their business in a circle.

"Look how beautifully he has lain down...like a real gentleman," a woman warbled kindly.

"He has taken his place, as they say...," said Nikac.

"Intruded into another man's house.... And who's to pay for the expenses?" said Frane's sister loudly, so that the guest should hear.

"Ah, you can't help it, the animal is tired.... Who knows how far he's come?" Nikac resumed his flattery.

"Or if the devil himself is in him...." Markutina stopped in fear.

"Of course...what else?..." added Kazo with a breath of malice, eager to spoil Frane's hopes. He turned and moved away a little, as if the guest might jump up in self-defense.

"Whoever he is," Frane flared up like straw on fire, "he's come to my house. There's no need for your quibbling! I shall...." The words were extinguished in doubt.

"This is what I'm going to do." Saka grasped the handle of the axe in the corner.

"No, no...don't!" Mara was afraid.

The dog looked at her, gentle and sleepy, and blinked innocently. It was obvious that he was not trying to follow the conversation.

"Leave him alone, leave him alone...." Frane frowned, pretending boredom.

"Brothers," Špirkan spoke up solemnly, "our village, for instance... Ah, who wants to come to our desert.... What was I going to say?... This must have been an act of grace.... Our village which has been abandoned by God and men...that is to say...." He looked at the dog and stopped, then looked at the others as if asking: Is this how one should put it?—and inviting them to help him.

"What village? Damn the village. I protest...this has nothing to do with the village, this is my house, and I want to have this clearly established...," Frane shouted resolutely and glanced at the dog.

Everybody was silent.

"Eh, my God," Nikac began wisely. "Eh, my God, who knows if we live by what God gives us.... Who knows what brings luck, what brings misfortune...."

Frane looked around the audience expecting approval. They all stood thinking, eager with curiosity, full of their own zest, silent, refusing to deserve the merit for the good or take responsibility for the evil; looking at the fine, distinguished animal with its silky hair and intelligent eyes.

"Let's say the rosary to the glory of Holy Mary," said Špirkan's sister, old spinster Kata.

"H'm?" Everybody stared at her, but the interest was soon exhausted.

Kata's round eyes and her pedantically sharpened mouth showed that she expected her suggestion to become significant.

"I tell you he hasn't come to the house just like that..." Nikac agreed with what he had said before.

Then Špirkan began in a flattering voice, glancing kindly at the dog, unwilling to give offense, even going so far as to praise it:

"Dogs can be very, very intelligent animals...very intelligent.... A major had a dog, and the dog always bought his newspapers for him...."

Markutina understood the policy behind the argument at once, and in order to make a correction, not letting other people overtake him, he said:

"The dog is man's friend.... They say that a dog—and I've heard it with my own ears—has died on his master's grave... The dog's heart broke with grief...like a human being's would, my God, there you are."

"And I've heard," Kazo imposed himself again, speaking softly, covering his mouth so that the dog would not see it, and trying to make Mara hear him, "that once a master's soul entered the body of his dog, and the dog wandered about the world while the master was lying in bed as though dead, until the dog met a man who was willing to carry him over the nine mountains to the fasting waters...."

"What 'fasting waters'?" Šaka asked contemptuously.

"Fasting, fasting, yes...." It was Kazo's turn to show contempt for the question now because he did not know how to answer it. "Over the nine mountains he had to carry the dog."

"For Christ's sake!" exclaimed Mara softly and looked at the dog with fear.

The women's eyes were sparkling.

"Then," Kazo went on, "and then...."

"Ouuuuuuummmmuumm...," murmured the dog in its sleep and Kazo stopped agape.

The silence was intense and watchful.

The hosts were very worried.

Markutina, who was the bell-ringer and the beadle, approached Frane, his face conscious of his professional qualifications, and whispered:

"I would send for the parson," and he looked carefully at the dog.

"Yes," said Frane, "we could, to hear what he would have to say."

"Well, Šaka could go."

Frane took Šaka aside.

"Come, let Luka lend you his horse, and go and bring the parson.... You will be back by nine."

Šaka scratched his head.

"H'm?" And he looked at the dog, sleeping quietly now, very solemn.

Frane managed with difficulty to persuade Šaka to go to the village with another man and bring the parson.

When Šaka was gone, Špirkan spoke up very seriously:

"I wouldn't have sent for the parson...nnno... You see that the beast... I mean this one...is lying quietly like a lamb.... Who knows what a parson's wisdom may bring on us...."

Frane was worried again.

Mara waved her arms.

"Brothers, what's this?... Why has he come to our house?"

"I would kill him, and have done with it!" someone said behind another's back.

"Wait, wait...." Kazo pushed the others aside. "I'll be nice to him and just ask him what he wants...."

"Ah, you, why should you ask him, why should you?... What right do you have to claim wisdom?" Markutina pushed him angrily, afraid that this might come to an end without the parson.

"Well, I, I, I..." Kazo brought his finger close to Markutina's eyes.

"Mmmmm." Markutina turned to him sideways and challenged him with his elbow.

"Nothing, it's nothing..." Frane raised his arms solemnly. "Nothing..." It seemed that he was going to say something very significant.

At this moment the dog got up. He looked absent-mindedly at the audience: he was not surprised that they were so many. He stretched himself very .competently, yawned, and shook in a dog-like way from head to tail. Then he suddenly became matter-of-fact: he jumped to the floor and walked in his most ordinary way to the door, without looking at anybody, not even at Frane, who was standing nearest to him with his arms folded on his breast as if he were in front of his own shop.

Everybody retreated quickly and made way for the dog.

They turned their heads after him, they stretched their necks a little, but their feet remained in the same place.

The dog could be seen in the moonlight outside, stopping at the gate of the yard, raising his leg, like a quite ordinary dog, wetting the threshold, and disappearing into the night.

Translated by Svetozar Koljević

TOMMASO
LANDOLFI

TOMMASO LANDOLFI (born 1908), the Italian writer, is best known for his
ingenious short stories, although he has also published poetry, dramatic works, and
translations. Much admired in Europe, he is represented in English in two major collections,
Gogol's Wife and Other Stories (1963) and Cancerqueen (1971). Landolfi attended the
University of Florence, where he took a degree in Russian literature. It was probably this
background that sparked his obsession with the weighty metaphysical concerns that so intrigued
the great Russian writers. Most of his stories probe an essentially spiritual problem, calling into
question the very underpinnings of reality. His urbane style easily draws us into his clever plots,
but his work demands an attentive and creative effort on the part of the reader. Although he can
be amusing and entertaining, he is not always an easy author to come to grips with.

Landolfi often uses first person narrators who are usually rather obtrusive observers, as in
the bewitching "Gogol's Wife," which is couched as a chapter from a biography of Gogol,
apparently written by a close companion. The narrator is soon exposing the darkest secrets,
gossiping in the name of scholarship and claiming to shed light on Gogol's genius. We have
already seen Gogol's fantastic literary world in his story "The Nose" and now Landolfi does him
one better, caricaturing the petty vices and human folly that Gogol so mocked in his own work.
There is a devastating correlation between the final disclosure in this comical study and Gogol's
real-life frenzied destruction of his last manuscript at the end of his life when he was haunted by
moral and religious difficulties, further aggravated by adverse reactions from the critics about his
work.

Gogol's Wife

Tommaso Landolfi

AT THIS point, confronted with the whole complicated affair of Nikolai Vassilevitch's wife, I am overcome by hesitation. Have I any right to disclose something which is unknown to the whole world, which my unforgettable friend himself kept hidden from the world (and he had his reasons), and which I am sure will give rise to all sorts of malicious and stupid misunderstandings? Something, moreover, which will very probably offend the sensibilities of all sorts of base, hypocritical people, and possibly of some honest people too, if there are any left? And finally, have I any right to disclose something before which my own spirit recoils, and even tends toward a more or less open disapproval?

But the fact remains that, as a biographer, I have certain firm obligations. Believing as I do that every bit of information about so lofty a genius will turn out to be of value to us and to future generations, I cannot conceal something which in any case has no hope of being judged fairly and wisely until the end of time. Moreover, what right have we to condemn? Is it given to us to know, not only what intimate needs, but even what higher and wider ends may have been served by those very deeds of a lofty genius which perchance may appear to us vile? No indeed, for we understand so little of these privileged natures. "It is true," a great man once said, "that I also have to pee, but for quite different reasons."

But without more ado I will come to what I know beyond doubt, and can prove beyond question, about this controversial matter, which will now—I dare to hope—no longer be so. I will not trouble to recapitulate what is already known of it, since I do not think this should be necessary at the present stage of development of Gogol studies.

Let me say it at once: Nikolai Vassilevitch's wife was not a woman. Nor was she any sort of human being, nor any sort of living creature at all, whether animal or vegetable (although something of the sort has some-times been hinted). She was quite simply a balloon. Yes, a balloon; and this will explain the perplexity, or even indignation, of certain biog-raphers who were also the personal friends of the Master, and who complained that, although they often went to his house, they never saw her and "never even heard her voice." From this they deduced all sorts of dark and disgraceful complications—yes, and criminal ones too. No, gentlemen, everything is always simpler than it appears. You did not hear her voice simply because she could not speak, or to be more exact, she could only speak in certain conditions, as we shall see. And it was always, except once, in tête-à-tête with Nikolai Vassilevitch. So let us not waste time with any cheap or empty refutations but come at once to as exact and complete a description as possible of the being or object in question.

Gogol's so-called wife was an ordinary dummy made of thick rubber, naked at all seasons, buff in tint, or as is more commonly said, flesh-colored. But since women's skins are not all of the same color, I should specify that hers was a light-colored, polished skin, like that of certain brunettes. It, or she, was, it is hardly necessary to add, of feminine sex. Perhaps I should say at once that she was capable of very wide alterations of her attributes without, of course, being able to alter her sex itself. She could sometimes appear to be thin, with hardly any breasts and with narrow hips more like a young lad than a woman, and at other times to be excessively well-endowed or—let us not mince matters—fat. And she often changed the color of her hair, both on her head and elsewhere on her body, though not necessarily at the same time. She could also seem to change in all sorts of other tiny particulars, such as the position of moles, the vitality of the mucous membranes and so forth. She could even to a certain extent change the very color of her skin. One is faced with the necessity of asking oneself who she really was, or whether it would be proper to speak of a single "person"—and in fact we shall see that it would be imprudent to press this point.

The cause of these changes, as my readers will already have understood, was nothing else but the will of Nikolai Vassilevitch himself. He would inflate her to a greater or lesser degree, would change her wig and her other tufts of hair, would grease her with ointments and touch her up in various ways so as to obtain more or less the type of woman which suited him at that moment. Following the natural inclinations of his fancy, he even amused himself sometimes by producing grotesque or monstrous forms; as will be readily understood, she became deformed when inflated beyond a certain point or if she remained below a certain pressure.

But Gogol soon tired of these experiments, which he held to be "after all, not very respectful" to his wife, whom he loved in his own way—

however inscrutable it may remain to us. He loved her, but which of these incarnations, we may ask ourselves, did he love? Alas, I have already indicated that the end of the present account will furnish some sort of an answer. And how can I have stated above that it was Nikolai Vassilevitch's will which ruled that woman? In a certain sense, yes, it is true; but it is equally certain that she soon became no longer his slave but his tyrant. And here yawns the abyss, or if you prefer it, the Jaws of Tartarus. But let us not anticipate.

I have said that Gogol obtained with his manipulations *more or less* the type of woman which he needed from time to time. I should add that when, in rare cases, the form he obtained perfectly incarnated his desire, Nikolai Vassilevitch fell in love with it "exclusively," as he said in his own words, and that this was enough to render "her" stable for a certain time—until he fell out of love with "her." I counted no more than three or four of these violent passions—or, as I suppose they would be called today, infatuations—in the life (dare I say in the conjugal life?) of the great writer. It will be convenient to add here that a few years after what one may call his marriage, Gogol had even given a name to his wife. It was Caracas, which is, unless I am mistaken, the capital of Venezuela. I have never been able to discover the reason for this choice: great minds are so capricious!

Speaking only of her normal appearance, Caracas was what is called a fine woman—well built and proportioned in every part. She had every smallest attribute of her sex properly disposed in the proper location. Particularly worthy of attention were her genital organs (if the adjective is permissible in such a context). They were formed by means of ingenious folds in the rubber. Nothing was forgotten, and their operation was rendered easy by various devices, as well as by the internal pressure of the air.

Caracas also had a skeleton, even though a rudimentary one. Perhaps it was made of whalebone. Special care had been devoted to the construction of the thoracic cage, of the pelvic basin and of the cranium. The first two systems were more or less visible in accordance with the thickness of the fatty layer, if I may so describe it, which covered them. It is a great pity that Gogol never let me know the name of the creator of such a fine piece of work. There was an obstinacy in his refusal which was never quite clear to me.

Nikolai Vassilevitch blew his wife up through the anal sphincter with a pump of his own invention, rather like those which you hold down with your two feet and which are used today in all sorts of mechanical workshops. Situated in the anus was a little one-way valve, or whatever the correct technical description would be, like the mitral valve of the heart, which, once the body was inflated, allowed more air to come in but none to go out. To deflate, one unscrewed a stopper in the mouth, at the back of the throat.

And that, I think, exhausts the description of the most noteworthy peculiarities of this being. Unless perhaps I should mention the splendid rows of white teeth which adorned her mouth and the dark eyes which, in spite of their immobility, perfectly simulated life. Did I say simulate? Good heavens, simulate is not the word! Nothing seems to be the word, when one is speaking of Caracas! Even these eyes could undergo a change of color, by means of a special process to which, since it was long and tiresome, Gogol seldom had recourse. Finally, I should speak of her voice, which it was only once given to me to hear. But I cannot do that without going more fully into the relationship between husband and wife, and in this I shall no longer be able to answer to the truth of everything with absolute certitude. On my conscience I could not—so confused, both in itself and in my memory, is that which I now have to tell.

Here, then, as they occur to me, are some of my memories.

The first and, as I said, the last time I ever heard Caracas speak to Nikolai Vassilevitch was one evening when we were absolutely alone. We were in the room where the woman, if I may be allowed the expression, lived. Entrance to this room was strictly forbidden to everybody. It was furnished more or less in the Oriental manner, had no windows and was situated in the most inaccessible part of the house. I did know that she could talk, but Gogol had never explained to me the circumstances under which this happened. There were only the two of us, or three, in there. Nikolai Vassilevitch and I were drinking vodka and discussing Butkov's novel. I remember that we left this topic, and he was maintaining the necessity for radical reforms in the laws of inheritance. We had almost forgotten her. It was then that, with a husky and submissive voice, like Venus on the nuptial couch, she said point-blank: "I want to go poo poo."

I jumped, thinking I had misheard, and looked across at her. She was sitting on a pile of cushions against the wall; that evening she was a soft, blonde beauty, rather well-covered. Her expression seemed commingled of shrewdness and slyness, childishness and irresponsibility. As for Gogol, he blushed violently and, leaping on her, stuck two fingers down her throat. She immediately began to shrink and to turn pale; she took on once again that lost and astonished air which was especially hers, and was in the end reduced to no more than a flabby skin on a perfunctory bony armature. Since, for practical reasons which will readily be divined, she had an extraordinarily flexible backbone, she folded up almost in two, and for the rest of the evening she looked up at us from where she had slithered to the floor, in utter abjection.

All Gogol said was: "She only does it for a joke, or to annoy me, because as a matter of fact she does not have such needs." In the presence of other people, that is to say of me, he generally made a point of treating her with a certain disdain.

We went on drinking and talking, but Nikolai Vassilevitch seemed very much disturbed and absent in spirit. Once he suddenly interrupted what he was saying, seized my hand in his and burst into tears. "What can I do now?" he exclaimed. "You understand, Foma Paskalovitch, that I loved her?"

It is necessary to point out that it was impossible, except by a miracle, ever to repeat any of Caracas' forms. She was a fresh creation every time, and it would have been wasted effort to seek to find again the exact proportions, the exact pressure, and so forth, of a former Caracas. Therefore the plumpish blonde of that evening was lost to Gogol from that time forth forever; this was in fact the tragic end of one of those few loves of Nikolai Vassilevitch, which I described above. He gave me no explanation; he sadly rejected my proffered comfort, and that evening we parted early. But his heart had been laid bare to me in that outburst. He was no longer so reticent with me, and soon had hardly any secrets left. And this, I may say in parenthesis, caused me very great pride.

It seems that things had gone well for the "couple" at the beginning of their life together. Nikolai Vassilevitch had been content with Caracas and slept regularly with her in the same bed. He continued to observe this custom till the end, saying with a timid smile that no companion could be quieter or less importunate than she. But I soon began to doubt this, especially judging by the state he was sometimes in when he woke up. Then, after several years, their relationship began strangely to deteriorate.

All this, let it be said once and for all, is no more than a schematic attempt at an explanation. About that time the woman actually began to show signs of independence or, as one might say, of autonomy. Nikolai Vassilevitch had the extraordinary impression that she was acquiring a personality of her own, indecipherable perhaps, but still distinct from his, and one which slipped through his fingers. It is certain that some sort of continuity was established between each of her appearances— between all those brunettes, those blondes, those redheads and auburn-headed girls, between those plump, those slim, those dusky or snowy or golden beauties, there was a certain something in common. At the beginning of this chapter I cast some doubt on the propriety of considering Caracas as a unitary personality; nevertheless I myself could not quite, whenever I saw her, free myself of the impression that, however unheard of it may seem, this was fundamentally the same woman. And it may be that this was why Gogol felt he had to give her a name.

An attempt to establish in what precisely subsisted the common attributes of the different forms would be quite another thing. Perhaps it was no more and no less than the creative afflatus of Nikolai Vassilevitch himself. But no, it would have been too singular and strange if he had been so much divided off from himself, so much averse to himself. Because whoever she was, Caracas was a disturbing presence and even—it is better to be quite clear—a hostile one. Yet neither Gogol nor I ever succeeded in formulating a remotely tenable hypothesis as to her true nature; when I say formulate, I mean in terms which would be at once rational and accessible to all. But I cannot pass over an extraordinary event which took place at this time.

Caracas fell ill of a shameful disease—or rather Gogol did—though he was not then having, nor had he ever had, any contact with other women. I will not even try to describe how this happened, or where the filthy complaint came from; all I know is that it happened. And that my great, unhappy friend would say to me: "So, Foma Paskalovitch, you see what lay at the heart of Caracas; it was the spirit of syphilis."

Sometimes he would even blame himself in a quite absurd manner; he was always prone to self-accusation. This incident was a real catastrophe as far as the already obscure relationship between husband and wife, and the hostile feelings of Nikolai Vassilevitch himself, were concerned. He was compelled to undergo long-drawn-out and painful treatment—the treatment of those days—and the situation was aggravated by the fact that the disease in the woman did not seem to be easily curable. Gogol deluded himself for some time that, by blowing his wife up and down and furnishing her with the most widely divergent aspects, he could obtain a woman immune from the contagion, but he was forced to desist when no results were forthcoming.

I shall be brief, seeking not to tire my readers, and also because what I remember seems to become more and more confused. I shall therefore hasten to the tragic conclusion. As to this last, however, let there be no mistake. I must once again make it clear that I am very sure of my ground. I was an eyewitness. Would that I had not been!

The years went by. Nikolai Vassilevitch's distaste for his wife became stronger, though his love for her did not show any signs of diminishing. Toward the end, aversion and attachment struggled so fiercely with each other in his heart that he became quite stricken, almost broken up. His restless eyes, which habitually assumed so many different expressions and sometimes spoke so sweetly to the heart of his interlocutor, now almost always shone with a fevered light, as if he were under the effect of a drug. The strangest impulses arose in him, accompanied by the most senseless fears. He spoke to me of Caracas more and more often, accusing her of unthinkable and amazing things. In these regions I could not follow him, since I had but a sketchy acquaintance with his wife, and hardly any intimacy—and above all since my sensibility was so limited compared with his. I shall accordingly restrict myself to reporting some of his accusations, without reference to my personal impressions.

"Believe it or not, Foma Paskalovitch," he would, for example, often say to me: "Believe it or not, *she's aging!*" Then, unspeakably moved, he would, as was his way, take my hands in his. He also accused Caracas of giving herself up to solitary pleasures, which he had expressly forbidden. He even went so far as to charge her with betraying him, but the things he said became so extremely obscure that I must excuse myself from any further account of them.

One thing that appears certain is that toward the end Caracas, whether aged or not, had turned into a bitter creature, querulous, hypocritical and subject to religious excess. I do not exclude the possibility that she may have had an influence on Gogol's moral position during the last period of his life, a position which is sufficiently well known. The tragic climax came one night quite unexpectedly when Nikolai Vassilevitch and I were celebrating his silver wedding—one of the last evenings we were to spend together. I neither can nor should attempt to set down what it was that led to his decision, at a time when to all appearances he was resigned to tolerating his consort. I know not what new events had taken place that day. I shall confine myself to the facts; my readers must make what they can of them.

That evening Nikolai Vassilevitch was unusually agitated. His distaste for Caracas seemed to have reached an unprecedented intensity. The famous "pyre of vanities"—the burning of his manuscripts—had already taken place; I should not like to say whether or not at the instigation of his wife. His state of mind had been further inflamed by other causes. As to his physical condition, this was ever more pitiful, and strengthened my impression that he took drugs. All the same, he began to talk in a more or less normal way about Belinsky, who was giving him some trouble with his attacks on the *Selected Correspondence*. Then suddenly, tears rising to his eyes, he interrupted himself and cried out: "No. No. It's too much, too much. I can't go on any longer," as well as other obscure and disconnected phrases which he would not clarify. He seemed to be talking to himself. He wrung his hands, shook his head, got up and sat down again after having taken four or five anxious steps round the room. When Caracas appeared, or rather when we went in to her later in the evening in her Oriental chamber, he controlled himself no longer and began to behave like an old man, if I may so express myself, in his second childhood, quite giving way to his absurd impulses. For instance, he kept nudging me and winking and senselessly repeating: "There she is, Foma Paskalovitch; there she is!" Meanwhile she seemed to look up at us with disdainful attention. But behind these "mannerisms" one could feel in him a real repugnance, a repugnance which had, I suppose, now reached the limits of the endurable. Indeed . . .

After a certain time Nikolai Vassilevitch seemed to pluck up courage. He burst into tears, but somehow they were more manly tears. He wrung his hands again, seized mine in his, and walked up and down, muttering: "That's enough! We can't have any more of this. This is an unheard of thing. How can such a thing be happening to me? How can a man be expected to put up with *this*?"

He then leapt furiously upon the pump, the existence of which he seemed just to have remembered, and, with it in his hand, dashed like a whirlwind to Caracas. He inserted the tube in her anus and began to inflate her. . . . Weeping the while, he shouted like one possessed: "Oh, how I love her, how I love her, my poor, poor darling!. . . But she's going to burst! Unhappy Caracas, most pitiable of God's creatures! But die she must!"

Caracas was swelling up. Nikolai Vassilevitch sweated, wept and pumped. I wished to stop him but, I know not why, I had not the courage. She began to become deformed and shortly assumed the most monstrous aspect; and yet she had not given any signs of alarm—she was used to these jokes. But when she began to feel unbearably full, or perhaps when Nikolai Vassilevitch's intentions became plain to her, she took on an expression of bestial amazement, even a little beseeching, but still without losing that disdainful look. She was afraid, she was even committing herself to his mercy, but still she could not believe in the immediate approach of her fate; she could not believe in the frightful audacity of her husband. He could not see her face because he was behind her. But I looked at her with fascination, and did not move a finger.

At last the internal pressure came through the fragile bones at the base of her skull, and printed on her face an indescribable rictus. Her belly, her thighs, her lips, her breasts and what I could see of her buttocks had swollen to incredible proportions. All of a sudden she belched, and gave a long hissing groan; both these phenomena one could explain by the increase in pressure, which had suddenly forced a way out through the valve in her throat. Then her eyes bulged frantically, threatening to jump out of their sockets. Her ribs flared wide apart and were no longer attached to the sternum, and she resembled a python digesting a donkey. A donkey, did I say? An ox! An elephant! At this point I believed her already dead, but Nikolai Vassilevitch, sweating, weeping and repeating: "My dearest! My beloved! My best!" continued to pump.

She went off unexpectedly and, as it were, all of a piece. It was not one part of her skin which gave way and the rest which followed, but her whole surface at the same instant. She scattered in the air. The pieces fell more or less slowly, according to their size, which was in no case above a very restricted one. I distinctly remember a piece of her cheek, with some lip attached, hanging on the corner of the mantelpiece. Nikolai Vassilevitch stared at me like a madman. Then he pulled himself together and, once more with furious determination, he began carefully to collect those poor rags which once had been the shining skin of Caracas, and all of her.

"Good-by, Caracas," I thought I heard him murmur, "Good-by! You were too pitiable!" And then suddenly and quite audibly: "The fire! The fire! She too must end up in the fire." He crossed himself—with his left hand, of course. Then, when he had picked up all those shriveled rags, even climbing on the furniture so as not to miss any, he threw them straight on the fire in the hearth, where they began to burn slowly and with an excessively unpleasant smell. Nikolai Vassilevitch, like all Russians, had a passion for throwing important things in the fire.

Red in the face, with an inexpressible look of despair, and yet of sinister triumph too, he gazed on the pyre of those miserable remains. He had seized my arm and was squeezing it convulsively. But those traces of what had once been a being were hardly well alight when he seemed yet again to pull himself together, as if he were suddenly remembering something or taking a painful decision. In one bound he was out of the room.

A few seconds later I heard him speaking to me through the door in a broken, plaintive voice: "Foma Paskalovitch, I want you to promise not to look. *Golubchik*, promise not to look at me when I come in."

I don't know what I answered, or whether I tried to reassure him in any way. But he insisted, and I had to promise him, as if he were a child, to hide my face against the wall and only turn round when he said I might. The door then opened violently and Nikolai Vassilevitch burst into the room and ran to the fireplace.

And here I must confess my weakness, though I consider it justified by the extraordinary circumstances. I looked round before Nikolai Vassilevitch told me I could; it was stronger than me. I was just in time to see him carrying something in his arms, something which he threw on the fire with all the rest, so that it suddenly flared up. At that, since the desire to *see* had entirely mastered every other thought in me, I dashed to the fireplace. But Nikolai Vassilevitch placed himself between me and it and pushed me back with a strength of which I had not believed him capable. Meanwhile the object was burning and giving off clouds of smoke. And before he showed any sign of calming down there was nothing left but a heap of silent ashes.

The true reason why I wished to see was because I had already glimpsed. But it was only a glimpse, and perhaps I should not allow myself to introduce even the slightest element of uncertainty into this true story. And yet, an eyewitness account is not complete without a mention of that which the witness knows with less than complete certainty. To cut a long story short, that something was a baby. Not a flesh and blood baby, of course, but more something in the line of a rubber doll or a model. Something, which, to judge by its appearance, could have been called *Caracas' son*.

Was I mad too? That I do not know, but I do know that this was what I saw, not clearly, but with my own eyes. And I wonder why it was that when I was writing this just now I didn't mention that when Nikolai Vassilevitch came back into the room he was muttering between his clenched teeth: "Him too! Him too!"

And that is the sum of my knowledge of Nikolai Vassilevitch's wife. In the next chapter I shall tell what happened to him afterwards, and that will be the last chapter of his life. But to give an interpretation of his feelings for his wife, or indeed for anything, is quite another and more difficult matter, though I have attempted it elsewhere in this volume, and refer the reader to that modest effort. I hope I have thrown sufficient light on a most controversial question and that I have unveiled the mystery, if not of Gogol, then at least of his wife. In the course of this I have implicitly given the lie to the insensate accusation that he ill-treated or even beat his wife, as well as other like absurdities. And what else can be the goal of a humble biographer such as the present writer but to serve the memory of that lofty genius who is the object of his study?

Translated by Wayland Young

ALFONSO
REYES

*A*LFONSO REYES (1889–1959), *Mexican man of letters and diplomat, was born in Monterey, where his father, a distinguished soldier, was governor of the province. His first diplomatic posting, in Paris, was destroyed by World War I, and he found himself in Madrid, living in poverty, with a wife and child to support. He turned his hand to translating and secretarial work and at the same time began to develop rapidly as an author. By 1920, he had returned to diplomatic service, and the remainder of his career saw him serve as Mexico's ambassador to France, Argentina, and Brazil.*

Reyes is more celebrated as a poet, critic, and essayist, than as a writer of fiction. His poetry is of a rather casual and eclectic sort. His essays are praised as models of their kind. And his scholarship includes a much-admired translation of The Iliad, as well as work on the great Renaissance stylist Gongora. "Major Aranda's Hand" (1955) shows what this nimble mind and cultivated imagination could do when turned to fiction. It has that Latin American sense that reality is invented, intriguing, ineffable. Especially in comparison to something like the Rilke selection we have titled "The Hand," Reyes' selection shows how good-humored and relaxed the Latin temperament could be in the presence of an instability that seems to have made Europeans of the same generation unsettled and nervous.

Major Aranda's Hand

Alfonso Reyes

MAJOR ARANDA suffered the loss of a hand in battle, and, unfortunately for him, it was his right hand. Other people make collections of hands of bronze, of ivory, of glass and of wood; at times they come from religious statues or images; at times they are antique door knockers. And surgeons keep worse things in jars of alcohol. Why not preserve this severed hand, testimony to a glorious deed? Are we sure that the hand is of less value than the brain or the heart?

Let us meditate about it. Aranda did not meditate, but was impelled by a secret instinct. Theological man has been shaped in clay, like a doll, by the hand of God. Biological man evolves thanks to the service of his hand, and his hand has endowed the world with a new natural kingdom, the kingdom of the industries and the arts. If the strong walls of Thebes rose to the music of Amphion's lyre, it was his brother Zethus, the mason, who raised the stones with his hand. Manual laborers appear therefore in archaic mythologies, enveloped in magic vapor: they are the wonder-workers. They are "The Hands Delivering the Fire" that Orozco has painted. In Diego Rivera's mural the hand grasps the cosmic globe that contains the powers of creation and destruction; and in Chapingo the proletarian hands are ready to reclaim the patrimony of the earth.

The other senses remain passive, but the manual sense experiments and adds and, from the spoils of the earth, constructs a human order, the

347

son of man. It models both the jar and the planet; it moves the potter's wheel and opens the Suez Canal.

A delicate and powerful instrument, it possesses the most fortunate physical resources: hinges, pincers, tongs, hooks, bony little chains, nerves, ligaments, canals, cushions, valleys and hillocks. It is soft and hard, aggressive and loving.

A marvelous flower with five petals that open and close like the sensitive plant, at the slightest provocation! Is five an essential number in the universal harmonies? Does the hand belong to the order of the dog rose, the forget-me-not, the scarlet pimpernel? Palmists perhaps are right in substance although not in their interpretations. And if the physiognomists of long ago had gone on from the face to the hand, completing their vague observations, undoubtedly they would have figured out correctly that the face mirrors and expresses but that the hand acts.

There is no doubt about it, the hand deserves unusual respect, and it could indeed occupy the favorite position among the household gods of Major Aranda.

The hand was carefully deposited in a quilted jewel case. The folds of white satin seemed a diminutive Alpine landscape. From time to time intimate friends were granted the privilege of looking at it for a few minutes. It was a pleasing, robust, intelligent hand, still in a rather tense position from grasping the hilt of the sword. It was perfectly preserved.

Gradually this mysterious object, this hidden talisman, became familiar. And then it emigrated from the treasure chest to the showcase in the living room and a place was made for it among the campaign and high military decorations.

Its nails began to grow, revealing a slow, silent, surreptitious life. At one moment this growth seemed something brought on by inertia, at another it was evident that it was a natural virtue. With some repugnance at first, the manicurist of the family consented to take care of those nails each week. The hand was always polished and well cared for.

Without the family knowing how it happened—that's how man is, he converts the statue of the god into a small art object—the hand descended in rank; it suffered a *manus diminutio*; it ceased to be a relic and entered into domestic circulation. After six months it acted as a paperweight or served to hold the leaves of the manuscripts—the major was writing his memoirs now with his left hand; for the severed hand was flexible and plastic and the docile fingers maintained the position imposed upon them.

In spite of its repulsive coldness, the children of the house ended up by losing respect for it. At the end of a year, they were already scratching themselves with it or amused themselves by folding its fingers in the form of various obscene gestures of international folklore.

The hand thus recalled many things that it had completely forgotten. Its personality was becoming noticeable. It acquired its own consciousness and character. It began to put out feelers. Then it moved like a tarantula. Everything seemed an occasion for play. And one day, when it was evident that it had put on a glove all by itself and had adjusted a bracelet on the severed wrist, it did not attract the attention of anyone.

It went freely from one place to another, a monstrous little lap dog, rather crablike. Later it learned to run, with a hop very similar to that of hares, and, sitting back on the fingers, it began to jump in a prodigious manner. One day it was seen spread out on a current of air: it had acquired the ability to fly.

But in doing all these things, how did it orient itself, how did it see? Ah! Certain sages say that there is a faint light, imperceptible to the retina, perhaps perceptible to other organs, particularly if they are trained by education and exercise. Should not the hand see also? Of course it complements its vision with its sense of touch; it almost has eyes in its fingers, and the palm is able to find its bearings through the gust of air like the membranes of a bat. Nanook, the Eskimo, on his cloudy polar steppes, raises and waves the weather vanes to orient himself in an apparently uniform environment. The hand captures a thousand fleeting things and penetrates the translucent currents that escape the eye and the muscles, those currents that are not visible and that barely offer any resistance.

The fact is that the hand, as soon as it got around by itself, became ungovernable, became temperamental. We can say that it was then that it really "got out of hand." It came and went as it pleased. It disappeared when it felt like it; returned when it took a fancy to do so. It constructed castles of improbable balance out of bottles and wineglasses. It is said that it even became intoxicated; in any case, it stayed up all night.

It did not obey anyone. It was prankish and mischievous. It pinched the noses of callers, it slapped collectors at the door. It remained motionless, playing dead, allowing itself to be contemplated by those who were not acquainted with it, and then suddenly it would make an obscene gesture. It took singular pleasure in chucking its former owner under the chin, and it got into the habit of scaring the flies away from him. He would regard it with tenderness, his eyes brimming with tears, as he would regard a son who had proved to be a black sheep.

It upset everything. Sometimes it took a notion to sweep and tidy the house; other times it would mix up the shoes of the family with a true arithmetical genius for permutations, combinations and changes; it would break the window panes by throwing rocks, or it would hide the balls of the boys who were playing in the street.

The major observed it and suffered in silence. His wife hated it, and of course was its preferred victim. The hand, while it was going on to other exercises, humiliated her by giving her lessons in needlework or cooking.

The truth is that the family became demoralized. The one-handed man was depressed and melancholy, in great contrast to his former happiness. His wife became distrustful and easily frightened, almost paranoid. The children became negligent, abandoned their studies, and forgot their good manners. Everything was sudden frights, useless drudgery, voices, doors slamming, as if an evil spirit had entered the house. The meals were served late, sometimes in the parlor, sometimes in a bedroom because, to the consternation of the major, to the frantic protest of his wife, and to the furtive delight of the children, the hand had taken possession of the dining room for its gymnastic exercises, locking itself inside, and receiving those who tried to expel it by throwing plates at their heads. One just had to yield, to surrender with weapons and baggage, as Aranda said.

The old servants, even the nurse who had reared the lady of the house, were put to flight. The new servants could not endure the bewitched house for a single day. Friends and relatives deserted the family. The police began to be disturbed by the constant complaints of the neighbors. The last silver grate that remained in the National Palace disappeared as if by magic. An epidemic of robberies took place, for which the mysterious hand was blamed, though it was often innocent.

The most cruel aspect of the case was that people did not blame the hand, did not believe that there was such a hand animated by its own life, but attributed everything to the wicked devices of the poor one-handed man, whose severed member was now threatening to cost us what Santa Aña's leg cost us. Undoubtedly Aranda was a wizard who had made a pact with Satan. People made the sign of the cross.

In the meantime the hand, indifferent to the harm done to others, acquired an athletic musculature, became robust, steadily got into better shape, and learned how to do more and more things. Did it not try to continue the major's memoirs for him? The night when it decided to get some fresh air in the automobile, the Aranda family, incapable of restraining it, believed that the world was collapsing; but there was not a single accident, nor fines nor bribes to pay the police. The major said that at least the car, which had been getting rusty after the flight of the chauffeur, would be kept in good condition that way.

Left to its own nature, the hand gradually came to embody the Platonic idea that gave it being, the idea of seizing, the eagerness to acquire control. When it was seen how hens perished with their necks twisted or how art objects belonging to other people arrived at the house—which Aranda went to all kinds of trouble to return to their owners, with stammerings and incomprehensible excuses—it was evident that the hand was an animal of prey and a thief.

People now began to doubt Aranda's sanity. They spoke of hallucinations, of "raps" or noises of spirits, and of other things of a like nature. The twenty or thirty persons who really had seen the hand did not appear trustworthy when they were of the servant class, easily swayed by superstitions; and when they were people of moderate culture, they remained silent and answered with evasive remarks for fear of compromising themselves or being subject to ridicule. A round table of the Faculty of Philosophy and Literature devoted itself to discussing a certain anthropological thesis concerning the origin of myths.

There is, however, something tender and terrible in this story. Aranda awoke one night at midnight with shrieks of terror; in strange nuptials the severed hand, the right one, had come to link itself with the left hand, its companion of other days, as if longing to be close to it. It was impossible to detach it. It passed the remainder of the night there, and there it resolved to spend the nights from then on. Custom makes monsters familiar. The major ended by paying no attention to the hand. It even seemed to him that the strange contact made the mutilation more bearable and in some manner comforted his only hand.

The poor left hand, the female, needed the kiss and company of the right hand, the male. Let us not belittle it; in its slowness it tenaciously preserves as a precious ballast the prehistoric virtues: slowness, the inertia of centuries in which our species has developed. It corrects the crazy audacities, the ambitions of the right hand. It has been said that it is fortunate that we do not have two right hands, for in that case we would become lost among the pure subtleties and complexities of virtuosity; we would not be real men; no, we would be sleight-of-hand performers. Gauguin knows well what he is doing when, to restrain his refined sensitivity, he teaches the right hand to paint again with the candor of the left hand.

One night, however, the hand pushed open the library door and became deeply absorbed in reading. It came upon a story by de Maupassant about a severed hand that ends by strangling its enemy. It came upon a beautiful fantasy by Nerval in which an enchanted hand travels the world, creating beauty and casting evil spells. It came upon some notes by the philosopher Gaos about the phenomenology of the hand.... Good heavens! What will be the result of this fearful incursion into the alphabet?

The result is sad and serene. The haughty independent hand that believed it was a person, an autonomous entity, an inventor of its own conduct, became convinced that it was only a literary theme, a matter of fantasy already very much worked over by the pen of writers. With sorrow and difficulty—and, I might almost say, shedding abundant tears—it made its way to the showcase in the living room, settled down in its jewel case, which it first placed carefully among the campaign and high military decorations; and, disillusioned and sorrowful, it committed suicide in its fashion: it let itself die.

The sun was rising when the major, who had spent a sleepless night tossing about, upset by the prolonged absence of his hand, discovered it inert in the jewel case, somewhat darkened, with signs of asphyxiation.

He could not believe his eyes. When he understood the situation, he nervously crumpled the paper on which he was about to submit his resignation from active service. He straightened up to his full height, reassumed his military haughtiness, and, startling his household, shouted at the top of his voice: "Attention! Fall in! All to their posts! Bugler, sound the bugle call of victory!"

Translated by Mildred Johnson

JULIO
CORTÁZAR

*J*ULIO CORTÁZAR (born 1914), *the celebrated Argentine novelist, short-story writer, essayist, and amateur jazz musician, has lived in Paris since the early 1950s where he works as a translator for UNESCO. Cortázar is committed to exploding the old literary forms and experimenting with new structures as he continues his search for the disquieting forces that lurk just beneath the surface of daily existence. All of his work reflects his belief that reality is elusive and best exemplified through fantastic, nearly inexplicable occurrences—the miraculous in the midst of the everyday. His first collection of short stories,* Bestiary (1951), *quickly established him as an unusually talented writer. Readers of his work soon recognize that an atmosphere of hallucination, a poetry of disorientation, pervades all of Cortázar's fiction. His subject is essentially the study of conflicting realities, compulsive imaginings, and complex, swirling perceptions.*

Cortázar is also politically committed and many of his novels, including Hopscotch *(1963), a massive, labyrinthine work that has influenced many writers, and* A Manual for Manuel *(1973), evoke political and social quandaries that shape the lives of his characters.*

He has published many excellent short-fiction collections, such as Cronopios and Famas *(1962),* A Change of Light *(1974, 1978), and perhaps his most famous,* End of the Game and Other Stories *(1967), a special English translation which combines work from* Bestiary *(1951),* Secret Weapons *(1958), and* End of the Game *(1956) . Most of the stories in* End of the Game *dwell on exposing the darker side of man, often with strange and metaphysical implications.*

Both of the following examples from End of the Game *explore the act of experiencing someone else's life, where identities are somehow exchanged through the intensity of imagination. A vivid sense of reality runs through these stories, but we are soon forced into reconsidering it, as Cortázar's multiple possibilities produce a memorable tension. The first piece,* "Axolotl," *quickly bewilders us, leading us into contradictions that make us marvel—the meaning is* especially elusive in the conclusion because we cannot possibly ascertain who or what is recording these thoughts. "The Night Face Up," based on a motorcycle accident Cortázar had in 1952, beautifully melds the worlds of a 20th-century man and a pre-Columbian Indian, as the hallucinations, apparently induced by anaesthesia, take over the mind of the protagonist. At the end, we rejoice in our uncertainty, accepting the magic of Cortázar and taking his creations on their own terms.

Axolotl

Julio Cortázar

THERE WAS a time when I thought a great deal about the axolotls.
I went to see them in the aquarium at the Jardin des Plantes and
stayed for hours watching them, observing their immobility, their faint
movements. Now I am an axolotl.

I got to them by chance one spring morning when Paris was
spreading its peacock tail after a wintry Lent. I was heading down the
boulevard Port-Royal, then I took Saint-Marcel and L'Hôpital and saw
green among all that grey and remembered the lions. I was friend of the
lions and panthers, but had never gone into the dark, humid building
that was the aquarium. I left my bike against the gratings and went to
look at the tulips. The lions were sad and ugly and my panther was
asleep. I decided on the aquarium, looked obliquely at banal fish until,
unexpectedly, I hit it off with the axolotls. I stayed watching them for an
hour and left, unable to think of anything else.

In the library at Sainte-Geneviève, I consulted a dictionary and
learned that axolotls are the larval stage (provided with gills) of a species
of salamander of the genus Ambystoma. That they were Mexican I knew
already by looking at them and their little pink Aztec faces and the
placard at the top of the tank. I read that specimens of them had been
found in Africa capable of living on dry land during the periods of
drought, and continuing their life under water when the rainy season
came. I found their Spanish name, *ajolote*, and the mention that they
were edible, and that their oil was used (no longer used, it said) like
cod-liver oil.

I didn't care to look up any of the specialized works, but the next day

I went back to the Jardin des Plantes. I began to go every morning, morning and afternoon some days. The aquarium guard smiled perplexedly taking my ticket. I would lean up against the iron bar in front of the tanks and set to watching them. There's nothing strange in this, because after the first minute I knew that we were linked, that something infinitely lost and distant kept pulling us together. It had been enough to detain me that first morning in front of the sheet of glass where some bubbles rose through the water. The axolotls huddled on the wretched narrow (only I can know how narrow and wretched) floor of moss and stone in the tank. There were nine specimens, and the majority pressed their heads against the glass, looking with their eyes of gold at whoever came near them. Disconcerted, almost ashamed, I felt it a lewdness to be peering at these silent and immobile figures heaped at the bottom of the tank. Mentally I isolated one, situated on the right and somewhat apart from the others, to study it better. I saw a rosy little body, translucent (I thought of those Chinese figurines of milky glass), looking like a small lizard about six inches long, ending in a fish's tail of extraordinary delicacy, the most sensitive part of our body. Along the back ran a transparent fin which joined with the tail, but what obsessed me was the feet, of the slenderest nicety, ending in tiny fingers with minutely human nails. And then I discovered its eyes, its face. Inexpressive features, with no other trait save the eyes, two orifices, like brooches, wholly of transparent gold, lacking any life but looking, letting themselves be penetrated by my look, which seemed to travel past the golden level and lose itself in a diaphanous interior mystery. A very slender black halo ringed the eye and etched it onto the pink flesh, onto the rosy stone of the head, vaguely triangular, but with curved and irregular sides which gave it a total likeness to a statuette corroded by time. The mouth was masked by the triangular plane of the face, its considerable size would be guessed only in profile; in front a delicate crevice barely slit the lifeless stone. On both sides of the head where the ears should have been, there grew three tiny sprigs red as coral, a vegetal outgrowth, the gills, I suppose. And they were the only thing quick about it; every ten or fifteen seconds the sprig pricked up stiffly and again subsided. Once in a while a foot would barely move, I saw the diminutive toes poise mildly on the moss. It's that we don't enjoy moving a lot, and the tank is so cramped—we barely move in any direction and we're hitting one of the others with our tail or our head—difficulties arise, fights, tiredness. The time feels like it's less if we stay quietly.

It was their quietness that made me lean toward them fascinated the first time I saw the axolotls. Obscurely I seemed to understand their secret will, to abolish space and time with an indifferent immobility. I knew better later; the gill contraction, the tentative reckoning of the delicate feet on the stones, the abrupt swimming (some of them swim with a simple undulation of the body) proved to me that they were capable of escaping that mineral lethargy in which they spent whole hours. Above all else, their eyes obsessed me. In the standing tanks on either side of them, different fishes showed me the simple stupidity of their handsome eyes so similar to our own. The eyes of the axolotls spoke to me of the presence of a different life, of another way of seeing. Glueing my face to the glass (the guard would cough fussily once in a while), I tried to see better those diminutive golden points, that entrance to the infinitely slow and remote world of these rosy creatures. It was useless to tap with one finger on the glass directly in front of their faces; they never gave the least reaction. The golden eyes continued burning with their soft, terrible light; they continued looking at me from an unfathomable depth which made me dizzy.

And nevertheless they were close. I knew it before this, before being an axolotl. I learned it the day I came near them for the first time. The anthropomorphic features of a monkey reveal the reverse of what most people believe, the distance that is traveled from them to us. The absolute lack of similarity between axolotls and human beings proved to me that my recognition was valid, that I was not propping myself up with easy analogies. Only the little hands... But an eft, the common newt, had such hands also, and we are not at all alike. I think it was the axolotls' heads, that triangular pink shape with the tiny eyes of gold. That looked and knew. That laid the claim. They were not *animals*.

It would seem easy, almost obvious, to fall into mythology. I began seeing in the axolotls a metamorphosis which did not succeed in revoking a mysterious humanity. I imagined them aware, slaves of their bodies, condemned infinitely to the silence of the abyss, to a hopeless meditation. Their blind gaze, the diminutive gold disc without expression and nonetheless terribly shining, went through me like a message: "Save us, save us." I caught myself mumbling words of advice, conveying childish hopes. They continued to look at me, immobile; from time to time the rosy branches of the gills stiffened. In that instant I felt a muted pain; perhaps they were seeing me, attracting my strength to penetrate into the impenetrable thing of their lives. They were not human beings, but I had found in no animal such a profound relation with myself. The axolotls were like witnesses of something, and at times like horrible judges. I felt ignoble in front of them; there was such a terrifying purity in those transparent eyes. They were larvas, but larva means disguise and also phantom. Behind those Aztec faces, without expression but of an implacable cruelty, what semblance was awaiting its hour?

I was afraid of them. I think that had it not been for feeling the proximity of other visitors and the guard, I would not have been bold enough to remain alone with them. "You eat them alive with your eyes, hey," the guard said, laughing; he likely thought I was a little cracked. What he didn't notice was that it was they devouring me slowly with their eyes, in a cannabalism of gold. At any distance from the aquarium, I had only to think of them, it was as though I were being affected from a distance. It got to the point that I was going every day, and at night I thought of them immobile in the darkness, slowly putting a hand out which immediately encountered another. Perhaps their eyes could see in the dead of night, and for them the day continued indefinitely. The eyes of axolotls have no lids.

I know now that there was nothing strange, that that had to occur. Leaning over in front of the tank each morning, the recognition was greater. They were suffering, every fiber of my body reached toward that stifled pain, that stiff torment at the bottom of the tank. They were lying in wait for something, a remote dominion destroyed, an age of liberty when the world had been that of the axolotls. Not possible that such a terrible expression which was attaining the overthrow of that forced blankness on their stone faces should carry any message other than one of pain, proof of that eternal sentence, of that liquid hell they were undergoing. Hopelessly, I wanted to prove to myself that my own sensibility was projecting a non-existent consciouness upon the axolotls. They and I knew. So there was nothing strange in what happened. My face was pressed against the glass of the aquarium, my eyes were attempting once more to penetrate the mystery of those eyes of gold without iris, without pupil. I saw from very close up the face of an axolotl immobile next to the glass. No transition and no surprise, I saw my face against the glass, I saw it on the outside of the tank, I saw it on the other side of the glass. Then my face drew back and I understood.

Only one thing was strange: to go on thinking as usual, to know. To realize that was, for the first moment, like the horror of a man buried alive awaking to his fate. Outside, my face came close to the glass again, I saw my mouth, the lips compressed with the effort of understanding the axolotls. I was an axolotl and now I knew instantly that no understanding was possible. He was outside the aquarium, his thinking was a thinking outside the tank. Recognizing him, being him himself, I was an axolotl and in my·world. The horror began—I learned in the same moment—of believing myself prisoner in the body of an axolotl, metamorphosed into him with my human mind intact, buried alive in an axolotl, condemned to move lucidly among unconscious creatures. But that stopped when a foot just grazed my face, when I moved just a little to one side and saw an axolotl next to me who was looking at me, and understood that he knew also, no communication possible, but very clearly. Or I was also in him, or all of us were thinking humanlike, incapable of expression, limited to the golden splendor of our eyes looking at the face of the man pressed against the aquarium.

He returned many times, but he comes less often now. Weeks pass without his showing up. I saw him yesterday, he looked at me for a long time and left briskly. It seemed to me that he was not so much interested in us any more, that he was coming out of habit. Since the only thing I do is think, I could think about him a lot. It occurs to me that at the beginning we continued to communicate, that he felt more than ever one with the mystery which was claiming him. But the bridges were broken between him and me, because what was his obsession is now an axolotl, alien to his human life. I think that at the beginning I was capable of returning to him in a certain way—ah, only in a certain way—and of keeping awake his desire to know us better. I am an axolotl for good now, and if I think like a man it's only because every axolotl thinks like a man inside his rosy stone resemblance. I believe that all this succeeded in communicating something to him in those first days, when I was still he. And in this final solitude to which he no longer comes, I console myself by thinking that perhaps he is going to write a story about us, that, believing he's making up a story, he's going to write all this about axolotls.

Translated by Paul Blackburn

The Night
Face Up

Julio Cortázar

*And at certain periods they went
out to hunt enemies; they called it
the war of the blossom.*

HALFWAY DOWN the long hotel vestibule, he thought that probably he was going to be late, and hurried on into the street to
get out his motorcycle from the corner where the next-door superinten-
dent let him keep it. On the jewelry store at the corner he read that it was
ten to nine; he had time to spare. The sun filtered through the tall
downtown buildings, and he—because for himself, for just going along
thinking, he did not have a name—he swung onto the machine, savoring
the idea of the ride. The motor whirred between his legs, and a cool wind
whipped his pantslegs.

He let the ministries zip past (the pink, the white), and a series of
stores on the main street, their windows flashing. Now he was beginning
the most pleasant part of the run, the real ride: a long street bordered
with trees, very little traffic, with spacious villas whose gardens rambled
all the way down to the sidewalks, which were barely indicated by low
hedges. A bit inattentive perhaps, but tooling along on the right side of
the street, he allowed himself to be carried away by the freshness, by the
weightless contraction of this hardly begun day. This involuntary relaxa-
tion, possibly, kept him from preventing the accident. When he saw that
the woman standing on the corner had rushed into the crosswalk while

he still had the green light, it was already somewhat too late for a simple solution. He braked hard with foot and hand, wrenching himself to the left; he heard the woman scream, and at the collision his vision went. It was like falling asleep all at once.

He came to abruptly. Four or five young men were getting him out from under the cycle. He felt the taste of salt and blood, one knee hurt, and when they hoisted him up he yelped, he couldn't bear the pressure on his right arm. Voices which did not seem to belong to the faces hanging above him encouraged him cheerfully with jokes and assurances. His single solace was to hear someone else confirm that the lights indeed had been in his favor. He asked about the woman, trying to keep down the nausea which was edging up into his throat. While they carried him face up to a nearby pharmacy, he learned that the cause of the accident had gotten only a few scrapes on the legs. "Nah, you barely got her at all, but when ya hit, the impact made the machine jump and flop on its side..." Opinions, recollections of other smashups, take it easy, work him in shoulders first, there, that's fine, and someone in a dustcoat giving him a swallow of something soothing in the shadowy interior of the small local pharmacy.

Within five minutes the police ambulance arrived, and they lifted him onto a cushioned stretcher. It was a relief for him to be able to lie out flat. Completely lucid, but realizing that he was suffering the effects of a terrible shock, he gave his information to the officer riding in the ambulance with him. The arm almost didn't hurt; blood dripped down from a cut over the eyebrow all over his face. He licked his lips once or twice to drink it. He felt pretty good, it had been an accident, tough luck; stay quiet a few weeks, nothing worse. The guard said that the motorcycle didn't seem badly racked up. "Why should it," he replied. "It all landed on top of me." They both laughed, and when they got to the hospital, the guard shook his hand and wished him luck. Now the nausea was coming back little by little; meanwhile they were pushing him on a wheeled stretcher toward a pavilion further back, rolling along under trees full of birds, he shut his eyes and wished he were asleep or chloroformed. But they kept him for a good while in a room with that hospital smell, filling out a form, getting his clothes off, and dressing him in a stiff, greyish smock. They moved his arm carefully, it didn't hurt him. The nurses were constantly making wisecracks, and if it hadn't been for the stomach contractions he would have felt fine, almost happy.

They got him over to X-ray, and twenty minutes later, with the still-damp negative lying on his chest like a black tombstone, they pushed him into surgery. Someone tall and thin in white came over and began to look at the X-rays. A woman's hands were arranging his head, he felt that they were moving him from one stretcher to another. The man in white came over to him again, smiling, something gleamed in his right hand. He patted his cheek and made a sign to someone stationed behind.

It was unusual as a dream because it was full of smells, and he never dreamt smells. First a marshy smell, there to the left of the trail the swamps began already, the quaking bogs from which no one ever returned. But the reek lifted, and instead there came a dark, fresh composite fragrance, like the night under which he moved, in flight from the Aztecs. And it was all so natural, he had to run from the Aztecs who had set out on their manhunt, and his sole chance was to find a place to hide in the deepest part of the forest, taking care not to lose the narrow trail which only they, the Motecas, knew.

What tormented him the most was the odor, as though, notwithstanding the absolute acceptance of the dream, there was something which resisted that which was not habitual, which until that point had not participated in the game. "It smells of war," he thought, his hand going instinctively to the stone knife which was tucked at an angle into his girdle of woven wool. An unexpected sound made him crouch suddenly stock-still and shaking. To be afraid was nothing strange, there was plenty of fear in his dreams. He waited, covered by the branches of a shrub and the starless night. Far off, probably on the other side of the big lake, they'd be lighting the bivouac fires; that part of the sky had a reddish glare. The sound was not repeated. It had been like a broken limb. Maybe an animal that, like himself, was escaping from the smell of war. He stood erect slowly, sniffing the air. Not a sound could be heard, but the fear was still following, as was the smell, that cloying incense of the war of the blossom. He had to press forward, to stay out of the bogs and get to the heart of the forest. Groping uncertainly through the dark, stooping every other moment to touch the packed earth of the trail, he took a few steps. He would have liked to have broken into a run, but the gurgling fens lapped on either side of him. On the path and in darkness, he took his bearings. Then he caught a horrible blast of that foul smell he was most afraid of, and leaped forward desperately.

"You're going to fall off the bed," said the patient next to him. "Stop bouncing around, old buddy."

He opened his eyes and it was afternoon, the sun already low in the oversized windows of the long ward. While trying to smile at his neighbor, he detached himself almost physically from the final scene of the nightmare. His arm, in a plaster cast, hung suspended from an apparatus with weights and pulleys. He felt thirsty, as though he'd been running for miles, but they didn't want to give him much water, barely enough to moisten his lips and make a mouthful. The fever was winning slowly and he would have been able to sleep again, but he was enjoying the pleasure of keeping awake, eyes half-closed, listening to the other patients' conversation, answering a question from time to time. He saw a little white pushcart come up beside the bed, a blond nurse rubbed the front of his thigh with alcohol and stuck him with a fat needle connected to a tube which ran up to a bottle filled with a milky, opalescent liquid. A young intern arrived with some metal and leather apparatus which he adjusted to fit onto the good arm to check something or other. Night fell, and the fever went along dragging him down softly to a state in which things seemed embossed as through opera glasses, they were real and soft and, at the same time, vaguely distasteful; like sitting in a boring movie and thinking that, well, still, it'd be worse out in the street, and staying.

A cup of a marvelous golden broth came, smelling of leeks, celery and parsley. A small hunk of bread, more precious than a whole banquet, found itself crumbling little by little. His arm hardly hurt him at all, and only in the eyebrow where they'd taken stitches a quick, hot pain sizzled occasionally. When the big windows across the way turned to smudges of dark blue, he thought it would not be difficult for him to sleep. Still on his back so a little uncomfortable, running his tongue out over his hot, too-dry lips, he tasted the broth still, and with a sigh of bliss, he let himself drift off.

First there was a confusion, as of one drawing all his sensations, for that moment blunted or muddled, into himself. He realized that he was running in pitch darkness, although, above, the sky criss-crossed with treetops was less black than the rest. "The trail," he thought. "I've gotten off the trail." His feet sank into a bed of leaves and mud, and then he couldn't take a step that the branches of shrubs did not whiplash against his ribs and legs. Out of breath, knowing despite the darkness and silence that he was surrounded, he crouched down to listen. Maybe the trail was very near, with the first daylight he would be able to see it again. Nothing now could help him to find it. The hand that had unconsciously gripped the haft of the dagger climbed like a fen scorpion up to his neck where the protecting amulet hung. Barely moving his lips, he mumbled the supplication of the corn which brings about the beneficent moons, and the prayer to Her Very Highness, to the distributor of all Motecan possessions. At the same time he felt his ankles sinking deeper into the mud, and the waiting in the darkness of the obscure grove of live oak grew intolerable to him. The war of the blossom had started at the beginning of the moon and had been going on for three days and three nights now. If he managed to hide in the depths of the forest, getting off the trail further up past the marsh country, perhaps the warriors wouldn't follow his track. He thought of the many prisoners they'd already taken. But the number didn't count, only the consecrated period. The hunt would continue until the priests gave the sign to return. Everything had its number and its limit, and it was within the sacred period, and he on the other side from the hunters.

He heard the cries and leaped up, knife in hand. As if the sky were aflame on the horizon, he saw torches moving among the branches, very near him. The smell of war was unbearable, and when the first enemy jumped him, leaped at his throat, he felt an almost-pleasure in sinking the stone blade flat to the haft into his chest. The lights were already around him, the happy cries. He managed to cut the air once or twice, then a rope snared him from behind.

"It's the fever," the man in the next bed said. "The same thing happened to me when they operated on my duodenum. Take some water, you'll see, you'll sleep all right."

Laid next to the night from which he came back, the tepid shadow of the ward seemed delicious to him. A violet lamp kept watch high on the far wall like a guardian eye. You could hear coughing, deep breathing, once in a while a conversation in whispers. Everything was pleasant and secure, without the chase, no... But he didn't want to go on thinking about the nightmare. There were lots of things to amuse himself with. He began to look at the cast on his arm, and the pulleys that held it so comfortably in the air. They'd left a bottle of mineral water on the night table beside him. He put the neck of the bottle to his mouth and drank it like a precious liqueur. He could now make out the different shapes in the ward, the thirty beds, the closets with glass doors. He guessed that his fever was down, his face felt cool. The cut over the eyebrow barely hurt at all, like a recollection. He saw himself leaving the hotel again, wheeling out the cycle. Who'd have thought that it would end like this? He tried to fix the moment of the accident exactly, and it got him very angry to notice that there was a void there, an emptiness he could not manage to fill. Between the impact and the moment that they picked him up off the pavement, the passing out or what went on, there was nothing he could see. And at the same time he had the feeling that this void, this nothingness, had lasted an eternity. No, not even time, more as if, in this void, he had passed across something, or had run back immense distances. The shock, the brutal dashing against the pavement. Anyway, he had felt an immense relief in coming out of the black pit while the people were lifting him off the ground. With pain in the broken arm, blood from the split eyebrow, contusion on the knee; with all that, a relief in returning to daylight, to the day, and to feel sustained and attended. That was weird. Someday he'd ask the doctor at the office about that. Now sleep began to take over again, to pull him slowly down. The pillow was so soft, and the coolness of the mineral water in his fevered throat. The violet light of the lamp up there was beginning to get dimmer and dimmer.

As he was sleeping on his back, the position in which he came to did not surprise him, but on the other hand the damp smell, the smell of oozing rock, blocked his throat and forced him to understand. Open the eyes and look in all directions, hopeless. He was surrounded by an absolute darkness. Tried to get up and felt ropes pinning his wrists and ankles. He was staked to the ground on a floor of dank, icy stone slabs. The cold bit into his naked back, his legs. Dully, he tried to touch the amulet with his chin and found they had stripped him of it. Now he was lost, no prayer could save him from the final... From afar off, as though filtering through the rock of the dungeon, he heard the great kettledrums of the feast. They had carried him to the temple, he was in the underground cells of Teocalli itself, awaiting his turn.

He heard a yell, a hoarse yell that rocked off the walls. Another yell, ending in a moan. It was he who was screaming in the darkness, he was screaming because he was alive, his whole body with that cry fended off what was coming, the inevitable end. He thought of his friends filling up the other dungeons, and of those already walking up the stairs of the sacrifice. He uttered another choked cry, he could barely open his mouth, his jaws were twisted back as if with a rope and a stick, and once in a while they would open slowly with an endless exertion, as if they were made of rubber. The creaking of the wooden latches jolted him like a whip. Rent, writhing, he fought to rid himself of the cords sinking into his flesh. His right arm, the strongest, strained until the pain became unbearable and he had to give up. He watched the double door open, and the smell of the torches reached him before the light did. Barely girdled by the ceremonial loincloths, the priests' acolytes moved in his direction, looking at him with contempt. Lights reflected off the sweaty torsos and off the black hair dressed with feathers. The cords went slack, and in their place the grappling of hot hands, hard as bronze; he felt himself lifted, still face up, and jerked along by the four acolytes who carried him down the passageway. The torchbearers went ahead, indistinctly lighting up the corridor with its dripping walls and a ceiling so low that the acolytes had to duck their heads. Now they were taking him out, taking him out, it was the end. Face up, under a mile of living rock which, for a succession of moments, was lit up by a glimmer of torchlight. When the stars came out up there instead of the roof and the great terraced steps rose before him, on fire with cries and dances, it would be the end. The passage was never going to end, but now it was beginning to end, he would see suddenly the open sky full of stars, but not yet, they trundled him along endlessly in the reddish shadow, hauling him roughly along and he did not want that, but how to stop it if they had torn off the amulet, his real heart, the life-center.

In a single jump he came out into the hospital night, to the high, gentle, bare ceiling, to the soft shadow wrapping him round. He thought he must have cried out, but his neighbors were peacefully snoring. The water in the bottle on the night table was somewhat bubbly, a translucent shape against the dark azure shadow of the windows. He panted, looking for some relief for his lungs, oblivion for those images still glued to his eyelids. Each time he shut his eyes he saw them take shape instantly, and he sat up, completely wrung out, but savoring at the same time the surety that now he was awake, that the night nurse would answer if he rang, that soon it would be daybreak, with the good, deep sleep he usually had at that hour, no images, no nothing... It was difficult to keep his eyes open, the drowsiness was more powerful than he. He made one last effort, he sketched a gesture toward the bottle of water with his good hand and did not manage to reach it, his fingers closed again on a black emptiness, and the passageway went on endlessly, rock after rock, with momentary ruddy flares, and face up he choked out a dull moan because the roof was about to end, it rose, was opening like a mouth of shadow, and the acolytes straightened up, and from on high a waning moon fell on a face whose eyes wanted not to see it, were closing and opening desperately, trying to pass to the other side, to find again the bare, protecting ceiling of the ward. And every time they opened, it was night and the moon, while they climbed the great terraced steps, his head hanging down backward now, and up at the top were the bonfires, red columns of perfumed smoke, and suddenly he saw the red stone, shiny with the blood dripping off it, and the spinning arcs cut by the feet of the victim whom they pulled off to throw him rolling down the north steps. With a last hope he shut his lids tightly, moaning to wake up. For a second he thought he had gotten there, because once more he was immobile in the bed, except that his head was hanging down off it, swinging. But he smelled death, and when he opened his eyes he saw the blood-soaked figure of the executioner-priest coming toward him with the stone knife in his hand. He managed to close his eyelids again, although he knew now he was not going to wake up, that he was awake, that the marvelous dream had been the other, absurd as all dreams are—a dream in which he was going through the strange avenues of an astonishing city, with green and red lights that burned without fire or smoke, on an enormous metal insect that whirred away between his legs. In the infinite lie of the dream, they had also picked him up off the ground, someone had approached him also with a knife in his hand, approached him who was lying face up, face up with his eyes closed between the bonfires on the steps.

Translated by Paul Blackburn

ALEJO
CARPENTIER

*A*LEJO CARPENTER (1904–1980) was born in Havana, Cuba. His father was
a French architect, his mother a Russian who had studied medicine in Switzerland.
From this cosmopolitan beginning, Carpentier went on to the wide range of travel and professional activities that have characterized so many Latin American writers. He studied music
and architecture, and worked variously as a teacher, a journalist, the director of a radio station,
and a publisher. Exile from Cuba was a factor in a substantial portion of his life. At one point he
lived for 14 years in Venezuela, but in 1959 he returned to join the government of Fidel Castro.
He died in Paris in 1980.

Carpentier is best-known for three novels: The Lost Steps (1953), about a group of
sophisticates who make an expedition into a primitive wilderness; The Kingdom of This World
(1957); and Explosion in a Cathedral (1962). However, his short fiction, as the present
selection shows, is experimental, imaginative, and deeply interesting. "Journey to the Seed" is
taken from The War of Time (1958), a collection of shorter pieces on the theme of time. It
shows that Carpentier, like other writers of his generation (Paz, Cortázar), had studied and
absorbed the ideas of the French Surrealists, bringing them home to a native story-telling tradition
that was firmly grounded in everyday reality and in the life of the senses. A theoretical telling of
"Journey to the Seed" would be interesting in and of itself, but what makes the story
unforgettable is its mastery of detail. It is magical realism at its finest.

Journey to
the Seed

Alejo Carpentier

I

"WHAT DO you want, old 'un?"

The question fell several times from the top of the scaffolding. But the old man did not reply. He went from one spot to another, poking about, a long monologue of incomprehensible phrases issuing from his throat. They had already brought down the roof-tiles which covered the faded pavings with their earthenware mosaic. Up above, the picks were loosening the masonry, sending the stones rolling down wooden channels in a great cloud of lime and chalk. And through each one of the embrasures which had been cut into the battlements appeared (their secret uncovered) smooth oval or square ceilings, cornices, garlands, denticles, moldings and wall-paper which hung down from the friezes like old, cast-off snake skins. Watching the demolition, a Ceres with a broken nose, a discolored robe and with a blackened crown of maize upon her head stood in her back court upon her fountain of faded masks. Visited by the sun in the dusky hours, the grey fish in her basin yawned in mossy, warm water, their round eyes watching those black workmen in the gap in the sky-line who were gradually reducing the age-old height of the house. The old man had seated himself at the foot of the statue with his stick pointing at his chin. He watched the raising and lowering of buckets in which valuable remains were carried away. There was the

371

sound of muffled street noises and, up above, the pulleys harmonized their disagreeable and grating bird-songs in a rhythm of iron upon stone.

Five o'clock struck. The cornices and entablatures emptied of people. There only remained the hand-ladders ready for the next day's assault. The breeze turned fresher, now that it was relieved of its load of sweat, curses, rope-creakings, axles shrieking for the oil-can, and the slapping of greasy bodies. Twilight arrived earlier for the denuded house. It was clothed in shadows at an hour when the now-fallen upper parapets had been wont to regale the façade with a sparkle of sunlight. Ceres tightened her lips. For the first time, the rooms slept without window-blinds, open on to a landscape of ruins.

Contrary to their wishes, several capitals lay in the grass. Their acanthus leaves revealed their vegetable condition. A climbing plant, attracted by the family resemblance, ventured to stretch its tendrils towards the ionic scrolls. When night fell, the house was nearer the ground. A door-frame still stood on high with planks of shade hanging from its bewildered hinges.

II

Then the dark old man who had not moved from that place, gestured strangely and waved his stick over a cemetery of tiles.

The black and white marble squares flew back and covered the floors again. With sure leaps, stones closed the gaps in the battlements. The walnut panels, garnished with nails, fitted themselves into their frames whilst, with rapid rotations, the screws of the hinges buried themselves in their holes. Raised up by an effort from the flowers, the tiles on the faded pavings put together their broken fragments and in a noisy whirlwind of clay fell like rain upon the roof-tree. The house grew, returned again to its usual proportions, clothed and modest. Ceres was less grey. There were more fish in the fountain. And the murmur of water invoked forgotten begonias.

The old man put a key into the lock of the main door and began to open windows. His heels sounded hollow. When he lit the brass lamps, a yellow tremor ran along the oil of the family portraits and black-robed people murmured in all the galleries to the rhythm of spoons stirred in chocolate bowls.

Don Marcial, Marquis of Capellanías lay on his deathbed, his breast clad in medals, and with an escort of four candles with long beards of melted wax.

III

The candles grew slowly and lost their beads of sweat. When they regained their full height, a nun put them out and drew away her taper.

The wicks became white and threw off their snuff. The house emptied of visitors and the carriages departed into the night. Don Marcial played on an invisible keyboard and opened his eyes.

The blurred and jumbled roof-beams fell gradually back into place. The flasks of medicine, the damask tassels, the scapulary over the head of the bed, the daguerreotypes and the palms of the balcony grille emerged from the mists. Whilst the doctor shook his head with professional condolence, the sick man felt better. He slept for a few hours and awoke with the black beetle-browed regard of Father Anastasio upon him. The confession changed from being frank, detailed and full of sins to being reticent, halting and full of concealments. And after all, what right had that Carmelite friar to interfere in his life? Suddenly Don Marcial felt himself drawn into the middle of the room. The weight on his forehead lifted and he got up with surprising speed. The naked woman who was lounging upon the brocade of the bed searched for her petticoats and bodices and took away with her, soon afterwards, the sound of crushed silk and perfume. Below, in the closed carriage, covering the seat studs, there was an envelope containing gold coins.

Don Marcial did not feel well. As he arranged his tie in front of the pier-glass he found that he looked bloated. He went down to the office where legal men, solicitors and notaries were waiting for him to settle the auctioning of the house. It had all been useless. His belongings would go bit by bit to the highest bidder to the rhythm of hammer-blows upon the table. He greeted them and they left him alone. He thought of the mysteries of the written word, of those black threads which, ravelling and unravelling over wide, filigrained balance sheets, had ravelled and unravelled agreements, oaths, covenants, testimonies, declarations, surnames, titles, dates, lands, trees and stones—a web of threads extracted from the ink-well, threads in which a man's legs became fouled and which formed barriers across the paths, access to which was denied by law; they formed a noose pressing at his throat and muffling his voice as he perceived the dreadful sound of words which floated free. His signature had betrayed him, getting involved in knots and tangles of parchments. Bound by it, the man of flesh became a man of paper.

It was dawn. The dining-room clock had just struck six in the afternoon.

IV

Months of mourning passed, overshadowed by a growing feeling of remorse. At first the idea of bringing another woman into that bedroom seemed almost reasonable to him. But, little by little, the need for a new body was replaced by increasing scruples which reached the point of flagellation. One night, Don Marcial drew blood from his flesh with a strap and immediately felt a more intense desire, though of short duration. It was then that the Marchioness returned, one afternoon, from her ride along the banks of the Almendares. The horses of the calash had no moisture on their manes other than that of their own sweat. But all the rest of the day, they kicked at the panels of the stable as if irritated by the stillness of the low clouds.

At twilight, a basin full of water fell in the Marchioness' bath and broke. Then the May rains made the tank overflow. And the dark old woman who had a touch of the tar-brush and who kept doves under her bed walked through the yard muttering: 'Beware of rivers, child, beware of the running green.' There wasn't a day on which water did not betray its presence. But this presence was finally nothing more than a bowlful spilled upon a Paris gown when they came back from the anniversary ball given by the Captain General of the colony.

Many relatives reappeared. Many friends returned. The chandeliers of the great drawing-room now sparkled very brightly. The cracks in the façades gradually closed. The piano again became a clavichord. The palm trees lost some rings. The climbing plants let go of the first cornice. The rings under Ceres' eyes grew whiter and the capitals seemed newly-carved. Marcial grew livelier and would spend whole afternoons embracing the Marchioness. Crowsfeet, frowns and double chins were erased and the flesh regained its firmness. One day the smell of fresh paint filled the house.

V

The blushes were genuine. Every night the leaves of screens opened wider, skirts fell in the darker corners and there were new barriers of lace. Finally the Marchioness blew out the lamps. Only he spoke in the darkness.

They left for the sugar-mill in a great train of calashes—a shining of sorrel croups, of silver bits and of varnish in the sun. But in the shade of the poinsettias which made the inner portico of the house glow red, they realized that they hardly knew one another. Marcial gave permission for Negro tribal dances and drums in order to divert them a little on those days which were odorous with Cologne perfume, baths of benzoin, with loosened hair and sheets taken from the cupboards which, when opened, spilled out bunches of vetiver herb on to the tiles. A whiff of cane liquor whirled in the breeze with the prayer-bell. The low breezes wafted tidings of reluctant rains whose first, big, noisy drops were sucked in by roofs so dry that they gave out the sound of copper. After a dawn lengthened by an awkward embrace, their disagreements made up, the wound healed, they both went back to the city. The Marchioness changed her travelling dress for a bridal gown and as usual, the couple went to church to recover their liberty. They gave the presents back to relatives and friends and in a flurry of bronze bells, a parade of harnesses, each one took the road back to his own home. Marcial went on visiting María de las Mercedes for some time until the day when the rings were taken to the gold-smith's to be disengraved. There began a new life for Marcial. In the house with the high balconies, Ceres was replaced by an Italian Venus and the masks of the fountain almost imperceptibly pushed out their reliefs on seeing the flames of the oil-lamps still alight when dawn already dappled the sky.

VI

One night when he had been doing a lot of drinking and felt dizzied by the smell of stale tobacco left by his friends, Marcial had the strange sensation that all the clocks in the house were striking five, then half-past four, then half-past three. It was like a distant recognition of other possibilities. Just as one imagines oneself during the lassitude of a sleepless night able to walk on the smooth ceiling among furniture placed amidst the roof-beams and with the floor as a smooth ceiling above. It was a fleeting impression that left not the slightest trace in his mind which was now little inclined to meditation.

And there was a big party in the music-room on the day when he reached his minority. He was happy when he thought that his signature no longer had any legal value and that the moth-eaten registers and the notaries were erased from his world. He was reaching the stage where law courts were no longer to be feared by those whose persons were not held in any regard by the law codes. After getting tipsy on full-bodied wines, the young men took down from the wall a guitar encrusted with mother-of-pearl, a psaltery and a trombone. Someone wound up the clock which played the Tyrolean Cow Song and the Ballad of the Scottish Lakes. Another blew on the hunting horn that had lain coiled in its copper case upon the scarlet felt of a show-case alongside the transverse flute brought from Aránjuez. Marcial who was boldly courting the Campoflorido girl joined in the din and picked out the tune of Trípili-Trápala on the bass notes of the keyboard. Then they all went up into the attic, suddenly remembering that there, under the beams which were once again covered with plaster, were hoarded the dresses and liveries of the House of Capellanías. Along shelves frosted with camphor lay court-gowns, an Ambassador's sword, several braided military jackets, the cloak of a Prince of the Church and long dress-coats with damask buttons and with damp marks in the folds. The shadows were tinted with amaranth ribbons, yellow crinolines, faded tunics and velvet flowers. A tinker's costume with a tasselled hair-net made for a Carnival masquerade won applause. The Campoflorido rounded her shoulders underneath a shawl which was the color of creole flesh and which had been used by a certain grandmother on a night of momentous family decision, in order to receive the waning fires of a rich treasurer of the Order of St Clare.

The young people returned to the music-room in fancy dress. Wearing an alderman's tricorne hat on his head, Marcial struck the floor three times with his stick, and started off the waltz which the mothers found terribly improper for young ladies with that clasping around the waist and the man's hand touching the whalebone supports of their corsets which they had all made from the latest pattern in the "Garden of Fashion." The doors were obscured by maidservants, stable-boys, servants who came from their far-off outbuildings and from stifling basements to marvel at such a riotous party. Later, they played blind man's buff and hide-and-seek. Marcial hid with the Campoflorido girl behind the Chinese screen and imprinted a kiss on her neck and in return received a perfumed handkerchief whose Brussels lace still held the soft warmth from her décolleté. And when, in the twilight, the girls went off to the watchtowers and fortresses which were silhouetted grey-black against the sea, the young men left for the Dance Hall where mulatto girls with huge bracelets swayed so gracefully without ever losing their little high-heeled shoes however agitated the dance. And from behind a neighboring wall in a yard full of pomegranate trees the men of the Cabildo Arará Tres Ojos band beat out a drum roll just as if it were carnival time. Standing on tables and stools, Marcial and his friends applauded the grace of a Negress with greyish kinky hair who was beautiful, almost desirable again when she looked over her shoulder and danced with a proud gesture of defiance.

VII

The visits of Don Abundio, the family notary and executor, grew more frequent. He sat down gravely at the head of Marcial's bed, letting his stick of acana wood fall to the floor in order to wake him up before time. When he opened his eyes, they met an alpaca coat covered with dandruff, a coat whose shining sleeves gathered up titles and rents. There was finally only a small allowance left, one designed to put a check on any folly. It was then that Marcial resolved to enter the Royal Seminary of San Carlos.

After passing his examinations indifferently, he began to frequent the cloisters where he understood less and less of the teachers' explanations. The world of ideas was slowly becoming empty. What had first been a universal assembly of togas, doublets, ruffs and wigs, debaters and sophists took on the immobility of a waxworks museum. Marcial was now content with the scholastic exposition of system and accepted as true what was said in the text book. Over the copper engravings of Natural History were inscribed Lion, Ostrich, Whale, Jaguar. In the same way, Aristotle, Saint Thomas, Bacon and Descartes headed the black pages on which boring catalogues of interpretations of the universe appeared in the margins of the lengthy chapters. Little by little, Marcial left off studying them and found that a great weight was lifted from him. His mind became light and happy when he accepted only an instinctive knowledge of things. Why think of the prism when the clear winter light gave added detail to the fortress of the door? An apple falling from the tree was only an incitement to the teeth. A foot in a bathtub was only a foot in a bathtub. The day on which he left the Seminary, he forgot his books. The gnomon recovered its fairy character; the spectrum became synonymous with the word spectre; the octander was an armour-plated insect with spines on its back.

Several times, he had walked quickly with an anxious heart to visit women who whispered behind blue doors at the foot of the battlements. The memory of one of them who wore embroidered shoes and basil leaves over her ear pursued him like a toothache on hot afternoons. But one day, the anger and threats of his confessor made him weep with fear. He fell for the last time between the sheets of hell and renounced forever his wanderings along quiet streets, and his last-minute cowardice which made him return home angrily after turning his back on a certain cracked pavement (the sign, when he was walking with his eyes lowered, of the half-turn he must make in order to enter the perfumed threshold).

Now he was living his religious crisis, full of amulets, paschal lambs and china doves, Virgins in sky-blue cloaks, angels with swan's wings, the Ass, the Ox and a terrible Saint Dionysius who appeared to him in dreams with a big hollow between his shoulders and the hesitant walk of one who seeks for something he has lost. He stumbled against the bed and Marcial awoke in fear, grasping the rosary of muffled beads. The wicks in their oil vessels gave a sad light to the images which were recovering their pristine colors.

VIII

The furniture grew. It became more and more difficult to keep his arms on the edge of the dining-room table. The cupboards with carved ornices became wider at the front. Stretching their bodies, the Moors on he staircase brought their torches up to the balustrades of the landing. The armchairs were deeper and the rocking-chairs tended to go over backwards. He no longer needed to bend his legs when he lay down at the bottom of the bathtub which had marble rings.

One morning, whilst reading a licentious book, Marcial suddenly felt like playing with the lead soldiers which lay in their wooden boxes. He hid the book again under the wash-basin and opened a drawer covered with spiders' webs. The study table was too small to fit so many persons. For this reason, Marcial sat on the floor. He placed the grenadiers in lines of eight, then the officers on horseback, clustered round the standard-bearer and behind, the artillery with their cannons, gunwads and matchstaffs. Bringing up the rear came fifes and kettledrums and an escort of drummers. The mortars were provided with a spring which enabled them to shoot glass marbles from a yard away.

Bang! Bang! Bang!

Horses fell, standard-bearers fell, drums fell. He had to be called three times by the Negro Eligio before he made up his mind to wash his hands and go down to the dining-room.

From then on, Marcial retained the habit of sitting on the tile floor. When he realized the advantages, he was surprised at not having thought of it before. Grown-ups with their addiction to velvet cushions sweat too much. Some smell of notary—like Don Abundio—because they know nothing of the coolness of marble (whatever the temperature) when one is lying full-length on the floor. It is only from the floor that all the angles and perspectives of a room can be appreciated. There are beauties of wood, mysterious insect paths, shadowy corners which are unknown from a man's height. When it rained, Marcial hid under the clavichord. Each roll of thunder made the box tremble and all the notes sang. From the sky fell thunderbolts which created a cavern full of improvisations—the sounds of an organ, of a pine grove in the wind, of a cricket's mandolin.

IX

That morning, they shut him in his room. He heard murmurs all over the house and the lunch they served him was too succulent for a weekday. There were six cakes from the confectioner's shop on the Alameda when only two could be eaten on Sundays after mass. He amused himself by looking at the travel engravings until the rising buzz which came from under the doors caused him to peep out between the Venetian blinds. Men dressed in black were arriving, carrying a box with bronze handles. He felt like crying but at that moment, Melchor the coachman appeared, displaying a toothy smile over his squeaky boots. They began to play chess. Melchor was knight. He was King. With the floor-tiles as the board, he could advance one at a time whilst Melchor had to jump one to the front and two sideways or vice versa. The game went on until nightfall when the Chamber of Commerce's Fire Brigade went past.

When he got up, he went to kiss the hand of his father who lay on his sick-bed. The Marquis was feeling better and spoke to his son with his normal looks and phrases. His 'Yes, father' and 'No, father' were fitted in between each bead in the rosary of questions like the responses of the acolyte in mass. Marcial respected the Marquis but for reasons which nobody would have guessed. He respected him because of his great height and because he appeared on ball nights with decorations sparkling across his breast; because he envied his sabre and his militia officer's epaulets, because at Christmas he had eaten a whole turkey stuffed with almonds and raisins to win a bet; because, on one occasion, perhaps because he wanted to beat her, he seized one of the mulatto girls who was sweeping in the rotunda and carried her in his arms to his room. Hidden behind a curtain, Marcial saw her emerge a short time later weeping and with her dress unbuttoned, and he was glad she had been punished because she was the one who always emptied the jam-pots that were returned to the larder.

His father was a terrible, magnanimous being whom he ought to love first after God. Marcial felt that he was more God than God because his gifts were daily and tangible. But he preferred the God of heaven because he interfered with him less.

X

When the furniture grew taller and Marcial knew better than anyone else what there was underneath beds, cupboards and escritoires, he had a big secret; life held no charm away from Melchor, the coachman. Neither God nor his father, nor the gilded bishop in the Corpus processions were as important as Melchor.

Melchor came from far away. He was the grandson of conquered princes. In his kingdom, there were elephants, hippopotamus, tigers and giraffes. There men did not work in dark rooms full of parchments like Don Abundio. They lived by being cleverer than the animals. One of them had caught a great crocodile in a blue lake by piercing it with a hook concealed in the tightly-packed bodies of twelve roast geese. Melchor knew songs that were easy to learn because the words had no meaning and were repeated a great deal. He stole sweets from the kitchen, got out at night through the stable door and on one occasion had thrown stones at the police and then had disappeared into the shadows of Amargura street.

On rainy days, his boots were put to dry in front of the kitchen fire. Marcial would have liked to have had feet to fill such boots. The right-hand one was called Calambín. The left-hand one was called Calambán. The man who tamed unbroken horses just by putting his fingers on their lips, this lord of velvet and spurs who wore such tall top hats also knew how cool the marble floor was in summer and hid under the furniture a fruit or cake snatched from the trays which were destined for the big drawing-room. Marcial and Melchor had a secret store full of fruit and almonds which they held in common and called Urí, urí, urá, with understanding laughs. Both of them had explored the house from top to bottom and were the only ones who knew of the existence of a small basement full of Dutch flasks underneath the stables and of twelve dusty butterflies which had just lost their wings in a broken glass box in a disused attic over the maids' rooms.

XI

When Marcial acquired the habit of breaking things, he forgot about Melchor and drew closer to the dogs. There were several of them in the house. There was a big, striped one, a hound with dragging teats, a greyhound who was too old to play with, a woolly dog which the rest chased at certain periods and which the housemaids had to lock up.

Marcial liked Canelo best because he took shoes from out of the bedrooms and dug up the rose-bushes in the garden. He was always black from charcoal or covered with red earth and he used to devour the other dogs' meals, whine without reason and hide stolen bones by the fountain. Occasionally he would finish off a newly-laid egg after sending the hen flying into the air with a swift levering movement of the muzzle. Everyone would kick Canelo. But Marcial fell ill when they took him away. And the dog returned in triumph, wagging its tail after having been abandoned at the other side of the Charity Hospital and recovered a position in the house which the other dogs with their skill at hunting or their alertness as watchdogs never occupied.

Canelo and Marcial used to pee together. Sometimes, they chose the Persian carpet in the drawing-room and upon the wool pile, they outlined the shapes of clouds which would grow slowly bigger. For this they were given the strap. But the beating did not hurt as much as the grown-ups thought. On the contrary, it was an excellent excuse for setting up a concert of howls and of arousing the sympathy of the neighbors. When the cross-eyed woman in the attic called his father a "savage," Marcial looked at Canelo and laughed with his eyes. They cried a bit more to get a biscuit and all was forgotten. Both of them used to eat earth, roll in the sun, drink from the fish-pond and look for shade and perfume under the sweet basil. In hours of the greatest heat, the damp paving-stones were crowded. There was a grey goose with a bag hanging between its bow-legs; there was the old hen with a bare behind and the lizard that croaked and shot out a tongue like a pink tie issuing from its throat; there was the juba snake born in a city without females and the mouse which walled up its hole with the seed of the carey bush. One day they showed Marcial a dog.

'Bow, wow,' he said.

He spoke his own language. He had attained the supreme freedom. He already wanted to reach with his hands things which were out of reach of his hands.

XII

Hunger, thirst, heat, pain, cold. When Marcial had reduced his perception to these essential realities, he renounced light which was now incidental to him. He did not know his name. The baptism with its unpleasant salt was taken away from him and he did not now need smell, hearing or sight. His hands brushed against pleasing forms. He was a totally sentient and tactile being. The universe entered him through all his pores. Then he closed his eyes which only perceived nebulous giants and penetrated into a warm, damp body full of shadows in which he died. The body, on feeling him wrapped in its own substance, slipped towards life.

But now time sped more rapidly and lessened its last hours. The minutes sounded like the slipping of cards under a gambler's thumb.

The birds returned to the egg in a rush of feathers. The fish coagulated into spawn leaving a snowstorm of scales at the bottom of the tank. The palms folded their fronds and disappeared into the earth like closed fans. Stalks sucked in the leaves and the ground drew in all that belonged to it. Thunder resounded in the corridors. Hair grew on the suède of gloves. Woollen shawls lost their dye and plumped out the fleece of distant sheep. Cupboards, escritoires, beds, crucifixes, tables, blinds flew into the night seeking their ancient roots in the jungles. Everything which had nails in it crumbled. A brig (anchored heaven knows where) hurriedly took the marble of the floor-tiles and the fountain back to Italy. The collection of arms, ironwork, the keys, copper-pans, horse-bits from the stables melted, swelling the river of metal which was channelled along roofless galleries into the earth. All was metamorphosed and went back to its primitive condition. The clay became clay again, leaving a desert in place of a house.

XIII

When the workmen came at daybreak to continue the demolition, they found their work finished. Someone had taken away the statue of Ceres which had been sold the day before to an antique-dealer. After lodging a complaint with the Union, the men went and sat on the benches of the city park. Then one of them recalled the very vague story of a Marchioness of Capellanías who had been drowned one May afternoon among the lilies of the Almendares. But nobody paid any attention to the tale, because the sun was traveling from East to West and the hours which grow on the right-hand of clocks must become longer out of laziness since they are those which lead most surely to death.

Translated by Jean Franco

CLARICE LISPECTOR

C LARICE LISPECTOR (1924–1977) is recognized as one of Brazil's greatest writers, both for her novels and her short stories. Born in the Ukraine, she arrived in Brazil as an infant with her immigrant parents. After graduating from law school, she lived for some time in Europe and the United States with her diplomat husband, before settling in Rio de Janeiro in 1959.

Her first novel, Beside the Savage Heart (1944), was favorably received and her fourth novel, The Apple in the Dark (1961), is probably her best-known long work, but it is a rather bleak, hermetic account of alienated characters desperately searching for some meaning in life. Ontologically, Lispector seems to espouse existentialism—her characters are often on the verge of exploding with psychological tension, but they usually resign themselves to the hopelessness of their arbitrary condition. Lispector portrays profound, almost mystical views of the human dilemma in a straightforward but vivid style.

With the appearance of Family Ties (1960), a collection of short stories, Lispector disclosed a more poetic world. Although these stories embody a fairly pessimistic view of life, they are for the most part sensitive studies of the psychological difficulties that must be faced in modern times. Despair, solitude, and the lack of communication are the predominant themes, but Lispector manages to create beautifully crafted pieces that cast their own wondrous glow, even during periods of crisis.

Superbly translated by Elizabeth Bishop, "The Smallest Woman in the World" is an ironic study of racism and sexism. The story takes place in an archetypal, magical-realist setting where two civilizations collide, the modern clashing with the primitive, touching off reactions that test all the characters' accepted beliefs in reality. The pronounced physical and environmental differences, the unresolved emotional uncertainties between the French explorer and Little Flower, and the varied responses to the newspaper account leave the reader, on many levels, immersed in the same uneasy and strange sentiments that the characters are experiencing—an intricate blend of divergent perceptions.

The Smallest
Woman in
the World

Clarice Lispector

IN THE depths of Equatorial Africa the French explorer, Marcel
Pretre, hunter and man of the world, came across a tribe of
surprisingly small pygmies. Therefore he was even more surprised when
he was informed that a still smaller people existed, beyond forests and
distances. So he plunged farther on.

In the Eastern Congo, near Lake Kivu, he really did discover the
smallest pygmies in the world. And—like a box within a box within a
box—obedient, perhaps, to the necessity nature sometimes feels of
outdoing herself—among the smallest pygmies in the world there was
the smallest of the smallest pygmies in the world.

Among mosquitoes and lukewarm trees, among leaves of the most
rich and lazy green, Marcel Pretre found himself facing a woman
seventeen and three-quarter inches high, full-grown, black, silent—
"Black as a monkey," he informed the press—who lived in a treetop with
her little spouse. In the tepid miasma of the jungle, that swells the fruits
so early and gives them an almost intolerable sweetness, she was
pregnant.

So there she stood, the smallest woman in the world. For an instant,
in the buzzing heat, it seemed as if the Frenchman had unexpectedly

reached his final destination. Probably only because he was not insane, his soul neither wavered nor broke its bounds. Feeling an immediate necessity for order and for giving names to what exists, he called her Little Flower. And in order to be able to classify her among the recognizable realities, he immediately began to collect facts about her.

Her race will soon be exterminated. Few examples are left of this species, which, if it were not for the sly dangers of Africa, might have multiplied. Besides disease, the deadly effluvium of the water, insufficient food, and ranging beasts, the great threat to the Likoualas are the savage Bahundes, a threat that surrounds them in the silent air, like the dawn of battle. The Bahundes hunt them with nets, like monkeys. And eat them. Like that: they catch them in nets and eat them. The tiny race, retreating, always retreating, has finished hiding away in the heart of Africa, where the lucky explorer discovered it. For strategic defense, they live in the highest trees. The women descend to grind and cook corn and to gather greens; the men, to hunt. When a child is born, it is left free almost immediately. It is true that, what with the beasts, the child frequently cannot enjoy this freedom for very long. But then it is true that it cannot be lamented that for such a short life there had been any long, hard work. And even the language that the child learns is short and simple, merely the essentials. The Likoualas use few names; they name things by gestures and animal noises. As for things of the spirit, they have a drum. While they dance to the sound of the drum, a little male stands guard against the Bahundes, who come from no one knows where.

That was the way, then, that the explorer discovered, standing at his very feet, the smallest existing human thing. His heart beat, because no emerald in the world is so rare. The teachings of the wise men of India are not so rare. The richest man in the world has never set eyes on such strange grace. Right there was a woman that the greed of the most exquisite dream could never have imagined. It was then that the explorer said timidly, and with a delicacy of feeling of which his wife would never have thought him capable: "You are Little Flower."

At that moment, Little Flower scratched herself where no one scratches. The explorer—as if he were receiving the highest prize for chastity to which an idealistic man dares aspire—the explorer, experienced as he was, looked the other way.

A photograph of Little Flower was published in the colored supplement of the Sunday Papers, life-size. She was wrapped in a cloth, her belly already very big. The flat nose, the black face, the splay feet. She looked like a dog.

On that Sunday, in an apartment, a woman seeing the picture of Little Flower in the paper didn't want to look a second time because "It gives me the creeps."

In another apartment, a lady felt such perverse tenderness for the smallest of the African women that—an ounce of prevention being worth a pound of cure—Little Flower could never be left alone to the tenderness of that lady. Who knows to what murkiness of love tenderness can lead? The woman was upset all day, almost as if she were missing something. Besides, it was spring and there was a dangerous leniency in the air.

In another house, a little girl of five, seeing the picture and hearing the comments, was extremely surprised. In a houseful of adults, this little girl had been the smallest human being up until now. And, if this was the source of all caresses, it was also the source of the first fear of the tyranny of love. The existence of Little Flower made the little girl feel—with a deep uneasiness that only years and years later, and for very different reasons, would turn into thought—made her feel, in her first wisdom, that "sorrow is endless."

In another house, in the consecration of spring, a girl about to be married felt an ecstasy of pity: "Mama, look at her little picture, poor little thing! Just look how sad she is!"

"But," said the mother, hard and defeated and proud, "it's the sadness of an animal. It isn't human sadness."

"Oh, Mama!" said the girl, discouraged.

In another house, a clever little boy had a clever idea: "Mummy, if I could put this little woman from Africa in little Paul's bed when he's asleep? When he woke up wouldn't he be frightened? Wouldn't he howl? When he saw her sitting on his bed? And then we'd play with her! She would be our toy!"

His mother was setting her hair in front of the bathroom mirror at the moment, and she remembered what a cook had told her about life in an orphanage. The orphans had no dolls, and, with terrible maternity already throbbing in their hearts, the little girls had hidden the death of one of the children from the nun. They kept the body in a cupboard and when the nun went out they played with the dead child, giving her baths and things to eat, punishing her only to be able to kiss and console her. In the bathroom, the mother remembered this, and let fall her thoughtful hands, full of curlers. She considered the cruel necessity of loving. And she considered the malignity of our desire for happiness. She considered how ferociously we need to play. How many times we will kill for love. Then she looked at her clever child as if she were looking at a dangerous stranger. And she had a horror of her own soul that, more than her body, had engendered that being, adept at life and happiness. She looked at him attentively and with uncomfortable pride, that child who had already lost two front teeth, evolution evolving itself, teeth falling out to give place to those that could bite better. "I'm going to buy him a new suit," she decided, looking at him, absorbed. Obstinately, she adorned her gap-toothed son with fine clothes; obstinately, she wanted him very clean, as if his cleanliness could emphasize a soothing superficiality, obstinately perfecting the polite side of beauty. Obstinately drawing away from, and drawing him away from, something that ought to be "black as a monkey." Then, looking in the bathroom mirror, the mother gave a deliberately refined and social smile, placing a distance of insuperable millenniums between the abstract lines of her features and the crude face of Little Flower. But, with years of practice, she knew that this was going to be a Sunday on which she would have to hide from herself anxiety, dreams, and lost millenniums.

In another house, they gave themselves up to the enthralling task of measuring the seventeen and three-quarter inches of Little Flower against the wall. And, really, it was a delightful surprise: she was even smaller than the sharpest imagination could have pictured. In the heart of each member of the family was born, nostalgic, the desire to have that tiny and indomitable thing for itself, that thing spared having been eaten, that permanent source of charity. The avid family soul wanted to devote itself. To tell the truth, who hasn't wanted to own a human being just for himself? Which, it is true, wouldn't always be convenient; there are times when one doesn't want to have feelings.

"I bet if she lived here it would end in a fight," said the father, sitting in the armchair and definitely turning the page of the newspaper. "In this house everything ends in a fight."

"Oh, you, José—always a pessimist," said the mother.

"But, Mama, have you thought of the size her baby's going to be?" said the oldest little girl, aged thirteen, eagerly.

The father stirred uneasily behind his paper.

"It should be the smallest black baby in the world," the mother answered, melting with pleasure. "Imagine her serving our table, with her big little belly!"

"That's enough!" growled father.

"But you have to admit," said the mother, unexpectedly offended, "that it is something very rare. You're the insensitive one."

And the rare thing itself?

In the meanwhile, in Africa, the rare thing herself, in her heart—and who knows if the heart wasn't black, too, since once nature has erred she can no longer be trusted—the rare thing herself had something even rarer in her heart, like the secret of her own secret: a minimal child. Methodically, the explorer studied that little belly of the smallest mature human being. It was at this moment that the explorer, for the first time since he had known her, instead of feeling curiosity, or exaltation, or victory, or the scientific spirit, felt sick.

The smallest woman in the world was laughing.

She was laughing, warm, warm—Little Flower was enjoying life. The rare thing herself was experiencing the ineffable sensation of not having been eaten yet. Not having been eaten yet was something that at any other time would have given her the agile impulse to jump from branch to branch. But, in this moment of tranquility, amid the thick leaves of the Eastern Congo, she was not putting this impulse into action—it was entirely concentrated in the smallness of the rare thing itself. So she was laughing. It was a laugh such as only one who does not speak laughs. It was a laugh that the explorer, constrained, couldn't classify. And she kept on enjoying her own soft laugh, she who wasn't being devoured. Not to be devoured is the most perfect feeling. Not to be devoured is the secret goal of a whole life. While she was not being eaten, her bestial laughter was as delicate as joy is delicate. The explorer was baffled.

In the second place, if the rare thing herself was laughing, it was because, within her smallness, a great darkness had begun to move.

The rare thing herself felt in her breast a warmth that might be called love. She loved that sallow explorer. If she could have talked and had told him that she loved him, he would have been puffed up with vanity. Vanity that would have collapsed when she added that she also loved the explorer's ring very much, and the explorer's boots. And when that collapse had taken place, Little Flower would not have understood why. Because her love for the explorer—one might even say "profound love," since, having no other resources, she was reduced to profundity—her profound love for the explorer would not have been at all diminished by the fact that she also loved his boots. There is an old misunderstanding about the word love, and, if many children are born from this misunderstanding, many others have lost the unique chance of being born, only because of the susceptibility that demands that it be me! me! that is loved, and not my money. But in the humidity of the forest these cruel refinements do not exist, and love is not to be eaten, love is to find a boot pretty, love is to like the strange color of a man who isn't black, is to laugh for love of a shiny ring. Little Flower blinked with love, and laughed warmly, small, gravid, warm.

The explorer tried to smile back, without knowing exactly to what abyss his smile responded, and then he was embarrassed as only a very big man can be embarrassed. He pretended to adjust his explorer's hat better; he colored, prudishly. He turned a lovely color, a greenish-pink, like a lime at sunrise. He was undoubtedly sour.

Perhaps adjusting the symbolic helmet helped the explorer to get control of himself, severely recapture the discipline of his work, and go on with his note-taking. He had learned how to understand some of the tribe's few articulate words, and to interpret their signs. By now, he could ask questions.

Little Flower answered "Yes." That it was very nice to have a tree of her own to live in. Because—she didn't say this but her eyes became so dark that they said it—because it is good to own, good to own, good to own. The explorer winked several times.

Marcel Pretre had some difficult moments with himself. But at least he kept busy taking notes. Those who didn't take notes had to manage as best they could:

"Well," suddenly declared one old lady, folding up the newspaper decisively, "well, as I always say: God knows what He's doing."

Translated by Elizabeth Bishop

CARLOS
FUENTES

CARLOS FUENTES (born 1928), the well-known Mexican novelist, was raised far
from his homeland as the son of a diplomat. Fuentes was educated in the United
States, Argentina, Chile, and Switzerland. He eventually returned to Mexico City where he
completed a law degree, but he already realized his true career would be as a man of letters. He
went on to hold various diplomatic posts, culminating in his position as Mexico's ambassador to
France from 1975–1977. Since retiring from active diplomatic service, he has moved to
Princeton, New Jersey, to concentrate on his fiction and to teach at the University of
Pennsylvania and Columbia University.

Like many Latin American writers, Fuentes is concerned with social and political justice,
and he addresses these questions through his fictionalized accounts of the mythical and historical
realities of Mexico. Because he grew up outside of Mexico, his native country became a kind of
imaginary place for him. He took advantage of his unique position as a politically astute, outside
commentator to create his first novel, Where the Air Is Clearer (1958), a lucid indictment of
the shortcomings of Mexican life after the revolution of 1910–1920. His next novel, The
Death of Artemio Cruz (1962), which gained international recognition for its author, describes
the final thoughts of a corrupted revolutionary hero through its dynamic narrative of three
fragmented voices. Subsequent books include Terra Nostra (1976), an ambitious investigation
of the Mediterranean roots of Hispanic culture, The Hydra Head (1978), and most recently,
Distant Relations (1982).

In much of his fiction, Fuentes has experimented with points of view and concepts of
time, and our selection, Aura (1962), is a masterful example. Recounted in second-person
narrative, Aura is an eerie novella that touches on the themes of love, mortality, reincarnation,
and the passage of time (bearing fruitful comparison to Carpentier's "Journey to the Seed"). In a
haunting allegorical style reminiscent of Poe, Hawthorne, and James, Fuentes leaves his
protagonist, Felix Montero, trapped in a somnambulistic world of perpetual twilight. To get the

effect of a dark, enchanted fairy tale, Fuentes creates a wonderful variation on the old witch-figure with magic powers who lures the lover to the beautiful young woman. Montero realizes all too late that he has become a prisoner of occult forces. From the outset, an ominous feeling of unreality abounds—from the intoxicating fragrances of exotic flowers on the dark patio of the rat-infested house lit by flickering votive candles to the writhing jumble of cats on the roof that resemble a smoking ball of flames. As Fuentes has cleverly put it, "Aura is about the life of death," suspenseful to the end and ultimately inexplicable.

Aura

Carlos Fuentes

Man hunts and struggles. Woman intrigues and dreams; she is the mother of fantasy, the mother of the gods. She has second sight, the wings that enable her to fly to the infinite of desire and the imagination... The gods are like men: they are born and they die on a woman's breast....

JULES MICHELET

I

YOU'RE READING the advertisement: an offer like this isn't made every day. You read it and reread it. It seems to be addressed to you and nobody else. You don't even notice when the ash from your cigarette falls into the cup of tea you ordered in this cheap, dirty café. You read it again. "Wanted, young historian, conscientious, neat. Perfect knowledge of colloquial French. Youth...knowledge of French, preferably after living in France for a while... Four thousand pesos a month, all meals, comfortable bedroom-study." All that's missing is your name. The advertisement should have two more words, in bigger, blacker type: Felipe Montero. Wanted, Felipe Montero, formerly on scholarship at the Sorbonne, historian full of useless facts, accustomed to digging among yellowed documents, part-time teacher in private schools, nine hundred pesos a month. But if you read that, you'd be suspicious, and take it as a joke. "Address, Donceles 815." No telephone; come in person.

You leave a tip, reach for your briefcase, get up. You wonder if another young historian, in the same situation you are, has seen this same advertisement, has got ahead of you and taken the job already. You walk down to the corner, trying to forget this idea. As you wait for the bus, you run over the dates you must have on the tip of your tongue so that your sleepy pupils will respect you. The bus is coming now, and you're staring at the tips of your black shoes. You've got to be prepared. You put your hand in your pocket, search among the coins, and finally take out thirty centavos. You've got to be prepared. You grab the hand-rail—the bus slows down but doesn't stop—and jump aboard. Then you shove your way forward, pay the driver the thirty centavos, squeeze yourself in among the passengers already standing in the aisle, hang on to the overhead rail, press your briefcase tighter under your left arm, and automatically put your left hand over the back pocket where you keep your billfold.

This day is just like any other day, and you don't remember the advertisement until the next morning, when you sit down in the same café and order breakfast and open your newspaper. You come to the advertising section and there it is again: *young historian*. The job is still open. You reread the advertisement, lingering over the final words: four thousand pesos.

It's surprising to know that anyone lives on Donceles Street. You always thought that nobody lived in the old centre of the city. You walk slowly, trying to pick out the number 815 in that conglomeration of old colonial mansions, all of them converted into repair shops, jewellery shops, shoe stores, drugstores. The numbers have been changed, painted over, confused. A 13 next to a 200. An old plaque reading 47 over a scrawl in blurred charcoal: *Now* 924. You look up at the second stories. Up there, everything is the same as it was. The jukeboxes don't disturb them. The mercury streetlights don't shine in. The cheap merchandise on sale along the street doesn't have any effect on that upper level; on the baroque harmony of the carved stones; on the battered stone saints with pigeons clustering on their shoulders; on the latticed balconies, the copper gutters, the sandstone gargoyles; on the greenish curtains that darken the long windows; on that window from which someone draws back when you look at it. You gaze at the fanciful vines carved over the doorway, then lower your eyes to the peeling wall and discover 815, *formerly* 69.

You rap vainly with the knocker, that copper head of a dog, so worn and smooth that it resembles the head of a canine foetus in a museum of natural science. It seems as if the dog is grinning at you and you let go of the cold metal. The door opens at the first light push of your fingers, but before going in you give a last look over your shoulder, frowning at the long line of stalled cars that growl, honk, and belch out the unhealthy fumes of their impatience. You try to retain some single image of that indifferent outside world.

You close the door behind you and peer into the darkness of a roofed alleyway. It must be a patio of some sort, because you can smell the mold, the dampness of the plants, the rotting roots, the thick drowsy aroma. There isn't any light to guide you, and you're searching in your coat pocket for the box of matches when a sharp, thin voice tells you, from a distance: "No, it isn't necessary. Please. Walk thirteen steps forward and you'll come to a stairway at your right. Come up, please. There are twenty-two steps. Count them."

Thirteen. To the right. Twenty-two.

The dank smell of the plants is all around you as you count out your steps, first on the paving-stones, then on the creaking wood, spongy from the dampness. You count to twenty-two in a low voice and then stop, with the matchbox in your hand, the briefcase under your arm. You knock on a door that smells of old pine. There isn't any knocker. Finally you push it open. Now you can feel a carpet under your feet, a thin carpet, badly laid. It makes you trip and almost fall. Then you notice the greyish, filtered light that reveals some of the humps.

"Señora," you say, because you seem to remember a woman's voice. "Señora . . ."

"Now turn to the left. The first door. Please be so kind."

You push the door open: you don't expect any of them to be latched, you know they all open at a push. The scattered lights are braided in your eyelashes, as if you were seeing them through a silken net. All you can make out are the dozens of flickering lights. At last you can see that they're votive-lights, all set on brackets or hung between unevenly-spaced panels. They cast a faint glow on the silver objects, the crystal flasks, the gilt-framed mirrors. Then you see the bed in the shadows beyond, and the feeble movement of a hand that seems to be beckoning to you.

But you can't see her face until you turn your back on that galaxy of religious lights. You stumble to the foot of the bed, and have to go around it in order to get to the head of it. A tiny figure is almost lost in its immensity. When you reach out your hand, you don't touch another hand, you touch the ears and thick fur of a creature that's chewing silently and steadily, looking up at you with its glowing red eyes. You smile and stroke the rabbit that's crouched beside her hand. Finally you shake hands, and her cold fingers remain for a long while in your sweating palm.

"I'm Felipe Montero. I read your advertisement."

"Yes, I know. I'm sorry, there aren't any chairs."

"That's all right. Don't worry about it."

"Good. Please let me see your profile. No, I can't see it well enough. Turn towards the light. That's right. Excellent."

"I read your advertisement . . ."

"Yes, of course. Do you think you're qualified? *Avez-vous fait des études?*"

"*À Paris, Madame.*"

"*Ah, oui, ça me fait plaisir, toujours, toujours, d'entendre... oui...vous savez...on était tellement habitué...et après...*"

You move aside so that the light from the candles and the reflections from the silver and crystal show you the silk coif that must cover a head of very white hair, and that frames a face so old it's almost childlike. Her whole body is covered by the sheets and the feather-pillows and the high, tightly-buttoned white collar, all except for her arms, which are wrapped in a shawl, and her pallid hands resting on her stomach. You can only stare at her face until a movement of the rabbit lets you glance furtively at the crusts and bits of bread scattered on the worn-out red silk of the pillows.

"I'll come directly to the point. I don't have many years ahead of me, Señor Montero, and therefore I decided to break a lifelong rule and place an advertisement in the newspaper..."

"Yes, that's why I'm here."

"Of course. So you accept."

"Well, I'd like to know a little more..."

"Yes. You're wondering."

She sees you glance at the night-table, the different-colored bottles, the glasses, the aluminium spoons, the row of pillboxes, the other glasses—all stained with whitish liquids—on the floor within reach of her hand. Then you notice that the bed is hardly raised above the level of the floor. Suddenly the rabbit jumps down and disappears in the shadows.

"I can offer you four thousand pesos."

"Yes, that's what the advertisement said today."

"Ah, then it came out."

"Yes, it came out."

"It has to do with the memoirs of my husband, General Llorente. They must be put in order before I die. I want them to be published. I decided that a short time ago."

"But the General himself? Wouldn't he be able to..."

"He died sixty years ago, Señor. They're his unfinished memoirs. They have to be completed before I die."

"But..."

"I can tell you everything. You'll learn to write in my husband's own style. You'll only have to arrange and read his manuscripts to become fascinated by his style...his clarity...his..."

"Yes, I understand."

"Saga, Saga. Where are you? Ici, Saga..."

"Who?"

"My companion."

"The rabbit?"

"Yes. She'll come back."

When you raise your eyes, which you've been keeping lowered, her lips are closed but you can hear her words again—"She'll come back"— as if the old lady were pronouncing them at that instant. Her lips remain still. You look in back of you and you're almost blinded by the gleam from the religious objects. When you look at her again you see that her eyes have opened very wide, and that they're clear, liquid, enormous, almost the same color as the yellowish whites around them, so that only the black dots of the pupils mar that clarity. It's lost a moment later in the heavy folds of her lowered eyelids, as if she wanted to protect that glance which is now hiding at the back of its dry cave.

"Then you'll stay here. Your room is upstairs. It's sunny there."

"It might be better if I didn't trouble you, Señora. I can go on living where I am and work on the manuscripts there."

"My conditions are that you have to live here. There isn't much time left."

"I don't know if . . ."

"Aura . . ."

The old woman moves for the first time since you entered her room. As she reaches out her hand again you sense that agitated breathing beside you, and another hand reaches out to touch the Señora's fingers. You look around and a girl is standing there, a girl whose whole body you can't see because she's standing so close to you and her arrival was so unexpected, without the slightest sound—not even those sounds that can't be heard but are real anyway because they're remembered immediately afterwards, because in spite of everything they're louder than the silence that accompanies them.

"I told you she'd come back."

"Who?"

"Aura. My companion. My niece."

"Good afternoon."

The girl nods and at the same instant the old lady imitates her gesture.

"This is Señor Montero. He's going to live with us."

You move a few steps so that the light from the candles won't blind you. The girl keeps her eyes closed, her hands folded at her side. She doesn't look at you at first, then little by little she opens her eyes as if she were afraid of the light. Finally you can see that those eyes are sea-green and that they surge, break to foam, grow calm again, then surge again like a wave. You look into them and tell yourself it isn't true, because they're beautiful green eyes just like all the beautiful green eyes you've ever known. But you can't deceive yourself: those eyes do surge, do change, as if offering you a landscape that only you can see and desire.

"Yes. I'm going to live with you."

II

The old woman laughs sharply and tells you that she is grateful for
your kindness and that the girl will show you to your room. You're
thinking about the salary of four thousand pesos, and how the work
should be pleasant because you like these jobs of careful research that
don't include physical effort or going from one place to another or
meeting people you don't want to meet. You're thinking about this as you
follow her out of the room, and you discover that you've got to follow her
with your ears instead of your eyes: you follow the rustle of her skirt, the
rustle of taffeta, and you're anxious now to look into her eyes again. You
climb the stairs behind that sound in the darkness, and you're still
unused to the obscurity. You remember it must be about six in the
afternoon, and the flood of light surprises you when Aura opens the door
to your bedroom—another door without a latch—and steps aside to tell
you: "This is your room. We'll expect you for supper in an hour."

She moves away with that same faint rustle of taffeta, and you weren't
able to see her face again.

You close the door and look up at the skylight that serves as a roof.
You smile when you find that the evening light is blinding compared with
the darkness in the rest of the house, and smile again when you try out
the mattress on the gilded metal bed. Then you glance around the room:
a red wool rug, olive and gold wallpaper, an easy-chair covered in red
velvet, an old walnut desk with a green leather top, an old Argand lamp
with its soft glow for your nights of research, and a bookshelf over the
desk in reach of your hand. You walk over to the other door, and on
pushing it open you discover an outmoded bathroom: a four-legged
bathtub with little flowers painted on the porcelain, a blue hand-basin,
an old-fashioned toilet. You look at yourself in the large oval mirror on
the door of the wardrobe—it's also walnut—in the bathroom hallway.
You move your heavy eyebrows and wide thick lips, and your breath fogs
the mirror. You close your black eyes, and when you open them again the
mirror has cleared. You stop holding your breath and run your hand
through your dark, limp hair; you touch your fine profile, your lean
cheeks; and when your breath hides your face again you're repeating her
name: "Aura."

After smoking two cigarettes while lying on the bed, you get up, put
on your jacket, and comb your hair. You push the door open and try to
remember the route you followed coming up. You'd like to leave the door
open so that the lamplight could guide you, but that's impossible
because the springs close it behind you. You could enjoy playing with
that door, swinging it back and forth. You don't do it. You could take the
lamp down with you. You don't do it. This house will always be in
darkness, and you've got to learn it and relearn it by touch. You grope
your way like a blind man, with your arms stretched out wide, feeling

your way along the wall, and by accident you turn on the light-switch. You stop and blink in the bright middle of that long, empty hall. At the end of it you can see the banister and the spiral staircase.

You count the stairs as you go down: another custom you've got to learn in Señora Llorente's house. You take a step backward when you see the reddish eyes of the rabbit, which turns its back on you and goes hopping away.

You don't have time to stop in the lower hallway because Aura is waiting for you at a half-open stained-glass door, with a candelabra in her hand. You walk towards her, smiling, but you stop when you hear the painful yowling of a number of cats—yes, you stop to listen, next to Aura, to be sure that they're cats—and then follow her to the parlor.

"It's the cats," Aura tells you. "There's lots of rats in this part of the city."

You go through the parlor: furniture upholstered in faded silk; glass-fronted cabinets containing porcelain figurines, musical clocks, medals, glass balls; carpets with Persian designs; pictures of rustic scenes; green velvet curtains. Aura is dressed in green.

"Is your room comfortable?"

"Yes. But I have to get my things from the place where . . ."

"It won't be necessary. The servant has already gone for them."

"You shouldn't have bothered."

You follow her into the dining-room. She places the candelabra in the middle of the table. The room feels damp and cold. The four walls are panelled in dark wood, carved in Gothic style, with fretwork arches and large rosettes. The cats have stopped yowling. When you sit down, you notice that four places have been set. There are two large, covered plates and an old, grimy bottle.

Aura lifts the cover from one of the plates. You breathe in the pungent odor of the liver and onions she serves you, then you pick up the old bottle and fill the cut-glass goblets with that thick red liquid. Out of curiosity you try to read the label on the winebottle, but the grime has obscured it. Aura serves you some whole broiled tomatoes from the other plate.

"Excuse me," you say, looking at the two extra places, the two empty chairs," but are you expecting someone else?"

Aura goes on serving the tomatoes. "No. Señora Consuelo feels a little ill tonight. She won't be joining us."

"Señora Consuelo? Your aunt?"

"Yes. She'd like you to go in and see her after supper."

You eat in silence. You drink that thick wine, occasionally shifting your glance so that Aura won't catch you in the hypnotized stare that you can't control. You'd like to fix the girl's features in your mind. Every time you glance away you forget them again, and an irresistible urge forces you to look at her once more. As usual, she has her eyes lowered. While you're searching for the pack of cigarettes in your coat pocket, you run across that big key, and remember, and say to Aura: "Ah! I forgot that one of the drawers in my desk is locked. I've got my papers in it."

And she murmurs: "Then you want to go out?" She says it as a reproach.

You feel confused, and reach out your hand to her with the key dangling from one finger.

"It isn't important. The servants can go for them tomorrow."

But she avoids touching your hand, keeping her own hands on her lap. Finally she looks up, and once again you question your senses, blaming the wine for your bewilderment, for the dizziness brought on by those shining, clear green eyes, and you stand up after Aura does, running your hand over the wooden back of the Gothic chair, without daring to touch her bare shoulder or her motionless head.

You make an effort to control yourself, diverting your attention away from her by listening to the imperceptible movement of a door behind you—it must lead to the kitchen—or by separating the two different elements that make up the room: the compact circle of light around the candelabra, illuminating the table and one carved wall, and the larger circle of darkness surrounding it. Finally you have the courage to go up to her, take her hand, open it, and place your key-ring in her smooth palm as a token.

She closes her hand, looks up at you, and murmurs, "Thank you." Then she rises and walks quickly out of the room.

You sit down in Aura's chair, stretch your legs, and light a cigarette, feeling a pleasure you've never felt before, one that you knew was part of you but that only now you're experiencing fully, setting it free, bringing it out because this time you know it'll be answered and won't be lost... And Señora Consuelo is waiting for you, as Aura said. She's waiting for you after supper...

You leave the dining-room, and with the candelabra in your hand you walk through the parlor and the hallway. The first door you come to is the old lady's. You rap on it with your knuckles, but there isn't any answer. You knock again. Then you push the door open because she's waiting for you. You enter cautiously, murmuring: "Señora... Señora..."

She doesn't hear you, for she's kneeling in front of that wall of religious objects, with her head resting on her clenched fists. You see her from a distance: she's kneeling there in her coarse woollen nightgown, with her head sunk into her narrow shoulders; she's thin, even emaciated, like a medieval sculpture; her legs are like two sticks, and they're inflamed with erysipelas. While you're thinking of the continual rubbing of that rough wool against her skin, she suddenly raises her fists and strikes feebly at the air, as if she were doing battle against the images you can make out as you tiptoe closer: Christ, the Virgin, St Sebastian, St

Lucia, the Archangel Michael, and the grinning demons in an old print, the only happy figures in that iconography of sorrow and wrath, happy because they're jabbing their pitchforks into the flesh of the damned, pouring cauldrons of boiling water on them, violating the women, getting drunk, enjoying all the liberties forbidden to the saints. You approach that central image, which is surrounded by the tears of Our Lady of Sorrows, the blood of Our Crucified Lord, the delight of Lucifer, the anger of the Archangel, the viscera preserved in bottles of alcohol, the silver heart: Señora Consuelo, kneeling, threatens them with her fists, stammering the words you can hear as you move even closer: "Come, City of God! Gabriel, sound your trumpet! Ah, how long the world takes to die!"

She beats her breast until she collapses in front of the images and candles in a spasm of coughing. You raise her by the elbow, and as you gently help her to the bed you're surprised at her smallness: she's almost a little girl, bent over almost double. You realize that without your assistance she'd have had to get back to bed on her hands and knees. You help her into that wide bed with its bread-crumbs and old feather-pillows, and cover her up, and wait till her breathing is back to normal, while the involuntary tears run down her parchment cheeks.

"Excuse me...excuse me, Señor Montero... Old ladies have nothing left but...the pleasures of devotion... Give me my handkerchief, please."

"Señorita Aura told me..."

"Yes, of course. I don't want to lose any time. We should...we should begin working as soon as possible... Thank you..."

"You should try to rest."

"Thank you... Here..."

The old lady raises her hand to her collar, unbuttons it, and lowers her head to remove the frayed purple ribbon that she hands to you. It's heavy because there's a copper key hanging from it.

"Over in that corner... Open that trunk and bring me the papers at the right, on top of the others... They're tied with a yellow ribbon..."

"I can't see very well..."

"Ah, yes...it's just that I'm so accustomed to the darkness. To my right...keep going till you come to the trunk... They've walled us in, Señor Montero. They've built up all around us and blocked off the light. They've tried to force me to sell, but I'll die first. This house is full of memories for us. They won't take us out of here till I'm dead... Yes, that's it. Thank you. You can begin reading this part. I'll give you the others later. Goodnight, Señor Montero. Thank you. Look, the candelabra has gone out. Light it outside the door, please. No, no, you can keep the key. I trust you."

"Señora, there's a rat's nest in that corner..."

"Rats? I never go over there..."

"You should bring the cats in here."
"The cats? What cats? Goodnight. I'm going to sleep. I'm very tired."
"Goodnight."

III

That same evening you read those yellow papers written in mustard-colored ink, some of them with holes where a careless ash had fallen, others heavily fly-specked. General Llorente's French doesn't have the merits his wife attributed to it. You tell yourself you can make considerable improvements in the style, can tighten up his rambling account of past events: his childhood on an hacienda in Oaxaca, his military studies in France, his friendship with the Duke of Morny and the intimates of Napoleon III, his return to Mexico on the staff of Maximilian, the imperial ceremonies and gatherings, the battles, the defeat in 1867, his exile in France. Nothing that hasn't been described before. As you undress you think of the old lady's distorted notions, the value she attributes to these memories. You smile as you get into bed, thinking of the four thousand pesos.

You sleep soundly until a flood of light wakes you up at six in the morning; that glass roof doesn't have any curtain. You bury your head under the pillow and try to go back to sleep. Ten minutes later you give it up and walk into the bathroom, where you find all your things neatly arranged on a table and your few clothes hanging in the wardrobe. Just as you finish shaving the early morning silence is broken by that painful, desperate yowling.

You try to find out where it's coming from: you open the door to the hallway, but you can't hear anything from there: those cries are coming from up above, from the skylight. You jump up on the chair, from the chair on to the desk, and by supporting yourself on the bookshelf you can reach the skylight. You open one of the windows and pull yourself up to look out at that side garden, that square of yew-trees and brambles where five, six, seven cats—you can't count them, can't hold yourself up there for more than a second—are all twined together, all writhing in flames and giving off a dense smoke that reeks of burnt fur. As you get down again you wonder if you really saw it: perhaps you only imagined it from those dreadful cries that continue, grow less, and finally stop.

You put on your shirt, brush off your shoes with a piece of paper, and listen to the sound of a bell that seems to run through the passageways of the house until it arrives at your door. You look out into the hallway: Aura is walking along it with a bell in her hand. She turns her head to look at you and tells you that breakfast is ready. You try to detain her but she goes down the spiral staircase, still ringing that black-painted bell as if she were trying to wake up a whole asylum, a whole boarding-school.

You follow her in your shirt-sleeves, but when you reach the downstairs hallway you can't find her. The door of the old lady's bedroom opens behind you and you see a hand that reaches out from behind the partly-opened door, set a chamberpot in the hallway and disappears again, closing the door.

In the dining-room your breakfast is already on the table, but this time only one place has been set. You eat quickly, return to the hallway, and knock at Señora Consuelo's door. Her sharp, weak voice tells you to come in. Nothing has changed: the perpetual shadows, the glow of the votive lights and the silver objects.

"Good morning, Señor Montero. Did you sleep well?"

"Yes. I read till quite late."

The old lady waves her hand as if in a gesture of dismissal. "No, no, no. Don't give me your opinion. Work on those pages and when you've finished I'll give you the others."

"Very well. Señora, would I be able to go into the garden?"

"What garden, Señor Montero?"

"The one that's outside my room."

"This house doesn't have any garden. We lost our garden when they built up all around us."

"I think I could work better outdoors."

"This house has only got that dark patio where you came in. My niece is growing some shade-plants there. But that's all."

"It's all right, Señora."

"I'd like to rest during the day. But come to see me tonight."

"Very well, Señora."

You spend all morning working on the papers, copying out the passages you intend to keep, rewriting the ones you think are especially bad, smoking one cigarette after another and reflecting that you ought to space your work so that the job lasts as long as possible. If you can manage to save at least twelve thousand pesos, you can spend a year on nothing but your own work, which you've postponed and almost forgotten. Your great, inclusive work on the Spanish discoveries and conquests in the New World. A work that sums up all the scattered chronicles, makes them intelligible, and discovers the resemblances among all the undertakings and adventures of Spain's Golden Age and all the human prototypes and major accomplishments of the Renaissance. You end up by putting aside the General's tedious pages and starting to compile the dates and summaries of your own work. Time passes and you don't look at your watch until you hear the bell again. Then you put on your coat and go down to the dining-room.

Aura is already seated. This time Señora Llorente is at the head of the table, wrapped in her shawl and nightgown and coif, hunching over her plate. But the fourth place has also been set. You note it in passing: it doesn't bother you any more. If the price of your future creative liberty is to put up with all the manias of this old woman, you can pay it easily. As you watch her eating her soup you try to figure out her age. There's a time after which it's impossible to detect the passing of the years, and Señora Consuelo crossed that frontier a long time ago. The General hasn't mentioned her in what you've already read of the memoirs. But if the General was 42 at the time of the French invasion, and died in 1901, forty years later, he must have died at the age of 82. He must have married the Señora after the defeat at Querétaro and his exile. But she would only have been a girl at that time...

The dates escape you because now the Señora is talking in that thin, sharp voice of hers, that bird-like chirping. She's talking to Aura and you listen to her as you eat, hearing her long list of complaints, pains, suspected illnesses, more complaints about the cost of medicines, the dampness of the house and so forth. You'd like to break in on this domestic conversation to ask about the servant who went for your things yesterday, the servant you've never even glimpsed and who never waits on table. You're about to ask about him but you're suddenly surprised to realize that up to this moment Aura hasn't said a word and is eating with a sort of mechanical fatality, as if she were waiting for some outside impulse before picking up her knife and fork, cutting a piece of liver—yes, it's liver again, apparently the favorite dish in this house—and carrying it to her mouth. You glance quickly from the aunt to the niece, but at that moment the Señora becomes motionless and at the same moment Aura puts her knife on her plate and also becomes motionless, and you remember that the Señora had put down her knife only a fraction of a second earlier.

There are several minutes of silence: you finish eating while they sit there rigid as statues, watching you. At last the Señora says, "I'm very tired. I ought not to eat at the table. Come, Aura, help me to my room."

The Señora tries to hold your attention: she looks directly at you so that you'll keep looking at her, although what she's saying is aimed at Aura. You have to make an effort in order to evade that look, which once again is wide, clear, and yellowish, free of the veils and wrinkles that usually obscure it. Then you glance at Aura, who is staring fixedly at nothing and silently moving her lips. She gets up with a motion like those you associate with dreaming, takes the arm of the bent old lady, and slowly helps her from the dining-room.

Alone now, you help yourself to the coffee that has been there since the beginning of the meal, the cold coffee you sip as you wrinkle your brow and ask yourself if the Señora doesn't have some secret power over her niece: if the girl, your beautiful Aura in her green dress, isn't kept in this dark old house against her will. But it would be so easy for her to escape while the Señora was asleep in her shadowy room. You tell yourself that her hold over the girl must be terrible. And you consider the way out that occurs to your imagination: perhaps Aura is waiting for you to release her from the chains in which the perverse, insane old lady, for some unknown reason, has bound her. You remember Aura as she was a few moments ago, spiritless, hypnotized by her terror, incapable of speaking in front of the tyrant, moving her lips in silence as if she were silently begging you to set her free; so enslaved that she imitated every gesture of the Señora, as if she were permitted to do only what the Señora did.

You rebel against this tyranny: you walk towards the other door, the one at the foot of the staircase, the one next to the old lady's room: that's where Aura must live, because there's no other room in the house. You push the door open and go in. This room is dark also, with whitewashed walls, and the only decoration is an enormous black Christ. At the left there's a door that must lead into the widow's bedroom. You go up to it on tiptoes, put your hands against it, then decide not to open it: you should talk with Aura alone.

And if Aura wants your help she'll come to your room. You go up there for a while, forgetting the yellowed manuscripts and your own notebooks, thinking only about the beauty of your Aura. And the more you think about her, the more you make her yours, not only because of her beauty and your desire, but also because you want to set her free: you've found a moral basis for your desire, and you feel innocent and self-satisfied. When you hear the bell again you don't go down to supper because you can't bear another scene like the one at the middle of the day. Perhaps Aura will realize it and come up to look for you after supper.

You force yourself to go on working on the papers. When you're bored with them you undress slowly, get into bed, and fall asleep at once, and for the first time in years you dream, dream of only one thing, of a fleshless hand that comes towards you with a bell, screaming that you should go away, everyone should go away; and when that face with its empty eye-sockets comes close to yours, you wake up with a muffled cry, sweating, and feel those gentle hands caressing your face, those lips murmuring in a low voice, consoling you and asking you for affection. You reach out your hands to find that other body, that naked body with a key dangling from its neck, and when you recognize the key you recognize the woman who is lying over you, kissing you, kissing your whole body. You can't see her in the black of the starless night, but you can smell the fragrance of the patio plants in her hair, can feel her smooth, eager body in your arms: you kiss her again and don't ask her to speak.

When you free yourself, exhausted, from her embrace, you hear her first whisper: "You're my husband." You agree. She tells you it's daybreak, then leaves you, saying that she'll wait for you that night in her room. You agree again and then fall asleep, relieved, unburdened, emptied of desire, still feeling the touch of Aura's body, her trembling, her surrender.

It's hard for you to wake up. There are several knocks on the door, and at last you get out of bed, groaning and still half-asleep. Aura, on the other side of the door, tells you not to open it: she says that Señora Consuelo wants to talk with you, is waiting for you in her room.

Ten minutes later you enter the widow's sanctuary. She's propped up against the pillows, motionless, her eyes hidden by those drooping, wrinkled, dead-white lids; you notice the puffy wrinkles under her eyes, the utter weariness of her skin.

Without opening her eyes she asks you, "Did you bring the key to the trunk?"

"Yes, I think so... Yes, here it is."

"You can read the second part. It's in the same place. It's tied with a blue ribbon."

You go over to the trunk, this time with a certain disgust: the rats are swarming around it, peering at you with their glittering eyes from the cracks in the rotted floorboards, galloping towards the holes in the rotted walls. You open the trunk and take out the second batch of papers, then return to the foot of the bed. Señora Consuelo is petting her white rabbit. A sort of croaking laugh emerges from her buttoned-up throat, and she asks you, "Do you like animals?"

"No, not especially. Perhaps because I've never had any."

"They're good friends. Good companions. Above all when you're old and lonely."

"Yes, they must be."

"They're always themselves, Señor Montero. They don't have any pretensions."

"What did you say his name is?"

"The rabbit? She's Saga. She's very intelligent. She follows her instincts. She's natural and free."

"I thought it was a male rabbit."

"Oh? Then you still can't tell the difference."

"Well, the important thing is that you don't feel all alone."

"They want us to be alone, Señor Montero, because they tell us that solitude is the only way to achieve saintliness. They forget that in solitude the temptation is even greater."

"I don't understand, Señora."

"Ah, it's better that you don't. Get back to work now, please."

You turn your back on her, walk to the door, leave her room. In the hallway you clench your teeth. Why don't you have courage enough to tell her that you love the girl? Why don't you go back and tell her, once and for all, that you're planning to take Aura away with you when you finish the job? You approach the door again and start pushing it open, still uncertain, and through the crack you see Señora Consuelo standing up, erect, transformed, with a military tunic in her arms: a blue tunic with gold buttons, red epaulettes, bright medals with crowned eagles—a tunic the old lady bites ferociously, kisses tenderly, drapes over her shoulders as she performs a few teetering dance-steps. You close the door.

Yes: "She was fifteen years old when I met her," you read in the second part of the memoirs. *"Elle avait quinze ans lorsque je l'ai connue et, si j'ose le dire, ce sont ses yeux verts qui ont fait ma perdition."* Consuelo's green eyes, Consuelo who was only fifteen in 1867, when General Llorente married her and took her with him into exile in Paris. *"Ma jeune poupée,"* he wrote in a moment of inspiration, *"ma jeune poupée aux yeux verts; je t'ai comblée d'amour."* He described the house they lived in, the outings, the dances, the carriages, the world of the Second Empire, but all in a dull enough way. *"J'ai même supporté ta haine des chats, moi qui aimais tellement les jolies bêtes ..."* One day he found her torturing a cat: she had it clasped between her legs, with her crinoline skirt pulled up, and he didn't know how to attract her attention because it seemed to him that *"tu faisais ça d'une façon si innocente, par pur enfantillage,"* and in fact it excited him so much that if you can believe what he wrote, he made love to her that night with extraordinary passion, *"parce que tu m'avais dit que torturer les chats était ta manière à toi de rendre notre amour favorable, par un sacrifice symbolique ..."* You've figured it up: Señora Consuelo must be 109. Her husband died fifty-nine years ago. *"Tu sais si bien t'habiller, ma douce Consuelo, toujours drappée dans de velours verts, verts comme tes yeux. Je pense que tu seras toujours belle, même dans cent ans ..."* Always dressed in green. Always beautiful, even after a hundred years. *"Tu es si fière de ta beauté; que ne ferais tu pas pour rester toujours jeune?"*

IV

Now you know why Aura is living in this house: to perpetuate the illusion of youth and beauty in that poor, crazed old lady. Aura, kept here like a mirror, like one more icon on that votive wall with its clustered offerings, preserved hearts, imagined saints and demons.

You put the manuscript aside and go downstairs, suspecting there's only one place Aura could be in the morning: the place that greedy old woman has assigned to her.

Yes, you find her in the kitchen, at the moment she's beheading a kid: the vapor that rises from the open throat, the smell of spilt blood, the animal's glazed eyes, all give you nausea. Aura is wearing a ragged, bloodstained dress and her hair is dishevelled; she looks at you without recognition and goes on with her butchering.

You leave the kitchen: this time you'll really speak to the old lady, really throw her greed and tyranny in her face. When you push open the door she's standing behind the veil of lights, performing a ritual with the empty air: one hand stretched out and clenched, as if holding something up, and the other clasped around an invisible object, striking again and again at the same place. Then she wipes her hands against her breast, sighs, and starts cutting the air again, as if—yes, you can see it clearly—as if she were skinning an animal...

You run through the hallway, the parlor, the dining-room, to where Aura is slowly skinning the kid, absorbed in her work, heedless of your entrance or your words, looking at you as if you were made of air.

You climb up to your room, go in, and brace yourself against the door as if you were afraid someone would follow you: panting, sweating, victim of your horror, of your certainty, If something or someone should try to enter, you wouldn't be able to resist, you'd move away from the door, you'd let it happen. Frantically you drag the armchair over to that latchless door, push the bed up against it, then fall on to the bed, exhausted, drained of your will-power, with your eyes closed and your arms wrapped around your pillow...the pillow that isn't yours... nothing is yours.

You fall into a stupor, into the depths of a dream that's your only escape, your only means of saying No to insanity. "She's crazy, she's crazy," you repeat again and again to make yourself sleepy, and you can see her again as she skins the imaginary kid with an imaginary knife. "She's crazy, she's crazy ..."

in the depths of the dark abyss, in your silent dream with its mouths opening in silence, you see her coming towards you from the blackness of the abyss, you see her crawling towards you,

in silence,

moving her fleshless hand, coming towards you until her face touches yours and you see the old lady's bloody gums, her toothless gums, and you scream and she goes away again, moving her hand, sowing the abyss with the yellow teeth she carries in her bloodstained apron:

your scream is an echo of Aura's, she is standing in front of you in your dream, and she's screaming because someone's hands have ripped her green taffeta skirt in two, and then

she turns her head towards you

with the torn folds of the skirt in her hands, turns towards you and laughs silently, with the old lady's teeth superimposed on her own, while her legs, her naked legs, shatter into bits and fly towards the abyss...

There's a knock at the door, then the sound of the bell, the supper bell. Your head aches so much that you can't make out the hands on the clock, but you know it must be late: above your head you can see the night clouds beyond the skylight. You get up painfully, dazed and hungry. You hold the glass pitcher under the faucet, wait for the water to run, fill the pitcher, then pour it into the basin. You wash your face, brush your teeth with your worn toothbrush that's clogged with greenish paste, dampen hair—you don't notice you're doing all this in the wrong order—and comb it meticulously in front of the oval mirror on the walnut wardrobe. Then you tie your tie, put on your jacket and go down to the empty dining-room, where only one place has been set: yours.

Beside your plate, under your napkin, there's an object you start caressing with your fingers: a clumsy little rag doll, filled with a powder that trickles from its badly-sewn shoulder; its face is drawn with India ink, and its body is naked, sketched with a few brushstrokes. You eat the cold supper—liver, tomatoes, wine—with your right hand while holding the doll in your left.

You eat mechanically, without noticing at first your own hypnotized attitude, but later you glimpse a reason for your oppressive sleep, your nightmare, and finally identify your sleep-walking movements with those of Aura and the old lady. You're suddenly disgusted by that horrible little doll, in which you begin to suspect a secret illness, a contagion. You let it fall to the floor. You wipe your lips with the napkin, look at your watch, and remember that Aura is waiting for you in her room.

You go cautiously up to Señora Consuelo's door, but there isn't a sound from within. You look at your watch again: it's barely nine o'clock. You decide to feel your way down to that dark, roofed patio you haven't been in since you came through it, without seeing anything, on the day you arrived here.

You touch the damp, mossy walls, breathe the perfumed air, and try to isolate the different elements you're breathing, to recognize the heavy, sumptuous aromas that surround you. The flicker of your match lights up the narrow, empty patio, where various plants are growing on each side in the loose, reddish earth. You can make out the tall, leafy forms that cast their shadows on the walls in the light of the match; but it burns down, singeing your fingers, and you have to light another one to finish seeing the flowers, fruits and plants you remember reading about in old chronicles, the forgotten herbs that are growing here so fragrantly and drowsily: the long, broad, downy leaves of the henbane; the twining stems with flowers that are yellow outside, red inside; the pointed, heart-shaped leaves of the nightshade; the ash-colored down of the grape-mullein with its clustered flowers; the bushy gatheridge with its white blossoms; the belladonna. They come to life in the flare of your match, swaying gently with their shadows, while you recall the uses of these herbs that dilate the pupils, alleviate pain, reduce the pangs of childbirth, bring consolation, weaken the will, induce a voluptuous calm.

You're all alone with the perfumes when the third match burns out. You go up to the hallway slowly, listen again at Señora Consuelo's door, then tiptoe on to Aura's. You push it open without knocking and go into that bare room, where a circle of light reveals the bed, the huge Mexican crucifix, and the woman who comes towards you when the door is closed. Aura is dressed in green, in a green taffeta robe from which, as she approaches, her moon-pale thighs reveal themselves. The woman, you repeat as she comes close, the woman, not the girl of yesterday: the girl of yesterday—you touch Aura's fingers, her waist—couldn't have been more than 20; the woman of today—you caress her loose black hair, her pallid cheeks—seems to be 40. Between yesterday and today, something about her green eyes has turned hard; the red of her lips has strayed beyond their former outlines, as if she wanted to fix them in a happy grimace, a troubled smile: as if, like that plant in the patio, her smile combined the taste of honey and the taste of gall. You don't have time to think of anything more.

"Sit down on the bed, Felipe."

"Yes."

"We're going to play. You don't have to do anything. Let me do everything myself."

Sitting on the bed, you try to make out the source of that diffuse, opaline light that hardly lets you distinguish the objects in the room, and the presence of Aura, from the golden atmosphere that surrounds them. She sees you looking up, trying to find where it comes from. You can tell from her voice that she's kneeling down in front of you.

"The sky is neither high nor low. It's over us and under us at the same time."

She takes off your shoes and socks and caresses your bare feet.

You feel the warm water that bathes the soles of your feet, while she washes them with a heavy cloth, now and then casting furtive glances at that Christ carved from black wood. Then she dries your feet, takes you by the hand, fastens a few violets in her loose hair, and begins to hum a melody, a waltz, to which you dance with her, held by the murmur of her voice, gliding around to the slow, solemn rhythm she's setting, very different from the light movements of her hands, which unbutton your shirt, caress your chest, reach around to your back and grasp it. You also murmur that wordless song, that melody rising naturally from your throat: you glide around together, each time closer to the bed, until you muffle the song with your hungry kisses on Aura's mouth, until you stop the dance with your crushing kisses on her shoulders and breasts.

You're holding the empty robe in your hands. Aura, squatting on the bed, places an object against her closed thighs, caressing it, summoning you with her hand. She caresses that thin wafer, breaks it against her thighs, oblivious of the crumbs that roll down her hips: she offers you half of the wafer and you take it, place it in your mouth at the same time she does, and swallow it with difficulty. Then you fall on Aura's naked body, you fall on her naked arms, which are stretched out from one side of the bed to the other like the arms of the crucifix hanging on the wall, the black Christ with that scarlet silk wrapped around his thighs, his spread knees, his wounded side, his crown of thorns set on a tangled black wig with silver spangles. Aura opens up like an altar.

You murmur her name in her ear. You feel the woman's full arms against your back. You hear her warm voice in your ear: "Will you love me for ever?"

"For ever, Aura. I'll love you for ever."

"For ever? Do you swear it?"

"I swear it."

"Even though I grow old? Even though I lose my beauty? Even though my hair turns white?"

"For ever, my love, for ever."

"Even if I die, Felipe? Will you love me for ever, even if I die?"

"For ever, for ever. I swear it. Nothing can separate us."

"Come, Felipe, come ..."

When you wake up, you reach out to touch Aura's shoulder, but you only touch the still-warm pillow and the white sheet that covers you.

You murmur her name.

You open your eyes and see her standing at the foot of the bed, smiling but not looking at you. She walks slowly towards the corner of the room, sits down on the floor, places her arms on the knees that emerge from the darkness you can't peer into, and strokes the wrinkled hand that comes forward from the lessening darkness: she's sitting at the feet of the old lady, of Señora Consuelo, who is seated in an armchair you hadn't noticed earlier: Señora Consuelo smiles at you, nodding her head, smiling at you along with Aura, who moves her head in rhythm with the old lady's; they both smile at you, thanking you. You lie back, without any will, thinking that the old lady has been in the room all the time;

you remember her movements, her voice, her dance, though you keep telling yourself she wasn't there.

The two of them get up at the same moment, Consuelo from the chair, Aura from the floor. Turning their backs on you, they walk slowly towards the door that leads to the widow's bedroom, enter that room where the lights are for ever trembling in front of the images, close the door behind them, and leave you to sleep in Aura's bed.

V

Your sleep is heavy and unsatisfying. In your dreams you had already felt the same vague melancholy, the weight on your diaphragm, the sadness that won't stop oppressing your imagination. Although you're sleeping in Aura's room, you're sleeping all alone, far from the body you believe you've possessed.

When you wake up, you look for another presence in the room, and realize it's not Aura who disturbs you but rather the double presence of something that was engendered during the night. You put your hands on your forehead, trying to calm your disordered senses: that dull melancholy is hinting to you in a low voice, the voice of memory and premonition, that you're seeking your other half, that the sterile conception last night engendered your own double.

And you stop thinking, because there are things even stronger than the imagination: the habits that force you to get up, look for a bathroom off this room without finding one, go out into the hallway rubbing your eyelids, climb the stairs tasting the thick bitterness of your tongue, enter your own room feeling the rough bristles on your chin, turn on the bathroom faucets and then slide into the warm water, letting yourself relax into forgetfulness.

But while you're drying yourself, you remember the old lady and the girl as they smiled at you before leaving the room arm in arm; you recall that whenever they're together they always do the same things: they embrace, smile, eat, speak, enter, leave, at the same time, as if one were imitating the other, as if the will of one depended on the existence of the other... You cut yourself lightly on one cheek as you think of these things while you shave; you make an effort to get control of yourself. When you finish shaving you count the objects in your travelling-case, the bottles and tubes which the servant you've never seen brought over from your boarding-house: you murmur the names of these objects, touch them, read the contents and instructions, pronounce the names of the manufacturers, keeping to those objects in order to forget that other one, the one without a name, without a label, without any rational consistency. What is Aura expecting of you? you ask yourself, closing the travelling-case. What does she want, what does she want?

In answer you hear the dull rhythm of her bell in the corridor telling you breakfast is ready. You walk to the door without your shirt on. When you open it you find Aura there: it must be Aura because you see the green taffeta she always wears, though her face is covered with a green veil. You take her by the wrist, that slender wrist which trembles at your touch...

"Breakfast is ready," she says, in the faintest voice you've ever heard.

"Aura. Let's stop pretending."

"Pretending?"

"Tell me if Señora Consuelo keeps you from leaving, from living your own life. Why did she have to be there when you and I... Please tell me you'll go with me when..."

"Go away? Where?"

"Out of this house. Out into the world, to live together. You shouldn't feel bound to your aunt for ever... Why all this devotion? Do you love her that much?"

"Love her?"

"Yes. Why do you have to sacrifice yourself this way?"

"Love her? She loves me. She sacrifices herself for me."

"But she's an old woman, almost a corpse. You can't..."

"She has more life than I do. Yes, she's old and repulsive... Felipe, I don't want to become...to be like her...another..."

"She's trying to bury you alive. You've got to be reborn, Aura."

"You have to die before you can be reborn... No, you don't understand. Forget about it, Felipe. Just have faith in me."

"If you'd only explain."

"Just have faith in me. She's going to be out today for the whole day..."

"She?"

"Yes, the other."

"She's going out? But she never..."

"Yes, sometimes she does. She makes a great effort and goes out. She's going out today. For all day...You and I could..."

"Go away?"

"If you want to."

"Well...perhaps not yet. I'm under contract. But as soon as I can finish the work, then..."

"Ah, yes. But she's going to be out all day. We could do something..."

"What?"

"I'll wait for you this evening in my aunt's bedroom. I'll wait for you as always."

She turns away, ringing her bell like the lepers who use a bell to announce their approach, telling the unwary: "Out of the way, out of the way." You put on your shirt and coat and follow the sound of the bell calling you to the dining-room. In the parlor the widow Llorente comes towards you, bent over, leaning on a knobby cane; she's dressed in an old white gown with a stained and tattered gauze veil. She goes by without looking at you, blowing her nose into a handkerchief, blowing her nose and spitting. She murmurs, "I won't be at home today, Señor Montero. I have complete confidence in your work. Please keep at it. My husband's memoirs must be published."

She goes away, stepping across the carpets with her tiny feet, which are like those of an antique doll, and supporting herself with her cane, and spitting and sneezing as if she wanted to clear something from her congested lungs. It's only by an effort of the will that you keep yourself from following her with your eyes, despite the curiosity you feel at seeing the yellowed bridal gown she's taken from the bottom of that old trunk in her bedroom...

You scarcely touch the cold coffee that's waiting for you in the dining-room. You sit for an hour in the tall arch-back chair, smoking, waiting for the sounds you never hear, until finally you're sure the old lady has left the house and can't catch you at what you're going to do. For the last hour you've had the key to the trunk clutched in your hand, and now you get up and silently walk through the parlor into the hallway, where you wait for another fifteen minutes—your watch tells you how long—with your ear against Señora Consuelo's door. Then you slowly push it open until you can make out, beyond the spider's web of candles, the empty bed on which her rabbit is gnawing at a carrot: the bed that's always littered with scraps of bread, and that you touch gingerly as if you thought the old lady might be hidden among the rumples of the sheets. You walk over to the corner where the trunk is, stepping on the tail of one of those rats; it squeals, escapes from your feet, and scampers off to warn the others. You fit the copper key into the rusted padlock, remove the padlock, and then raise the lid, hearing the creak of the old, stiff hinges. You take out the third portion of the memoirs—it's tied with a red ribbon—and under it you discover those photographs, those old, brittle, dogeared photographs. You pick them up without looking at them, clutch the whole treasure to your breast, and hurry out of the room without closing the trunk, forgetting the hunger of the rats. You close the door, lean against the wall in the hallway until you catch your breath, then climb the stairs to your room.

Up there you read the new pages, the continuation, the events of an agonized century. In his florid language General Llorente describes the personality of Eugenia de Montijo, pays his respects to Napoleon the Small, summons up his most martial rhetoric to declare the Franco-Prussian War, fills whole pages with his sorrow at the defeat, harangues all men of honor about the Republican monster, sees a ray of hope in General Boulanger, sighs for Mexico, believes that in the Dreyfus affair the honor—always that word 'honor'—of the army has asserted itself again...

The brittle pages crumble at your touch: you don't respect them now, you're only looking for a reappearance of the woman with green eyes. "I know why you weep at times, Consuelo. I have not been able to give you children, although you are so radiant with life..." And later: "Consuelo, you should not tempt God. We must reconcile ourselves. Is not my affection enough? I know that you love me; I feel it. I am not asking you for resignation, because that would offend you. I am only asking you to see, in the great love which you say you have for me, something sufficient, something that can fill both of us, without the need of turning to sick imaginings..." On another page: "I told Consuelo that those medicines were utterly useless. She insists on growing her own herbs in the garden. She says she is not deceiving herself. The herbs are not to strengthen the body, but rather the soul..." Later: "I found her in a delirium, embracing the pillow. She cried, 'Yes, yes, yes, I've done it, I've recreated her! I can invoke her, I can give her life with my own life!' It was necessary to call the doctor. He told me he could not quiet her, because the truth was that she was under the effects of narcotics, not of stimulants..." And finally:

"Early this morning I found her walking barefooted through the hallways. I wanted to stop her. She went by without looking at me, but her words were directed to me. 'Don't stop me, she said. 'I'm going towards my youth, and my youth is coming towards me. It's coming in, it's in the garden, it's come back. . .' Consuelo, my poor Consuelo, even the devil was an angel at one time. . ."

There isn't any more. The memoirs of General Llorente end with that sentence: "*Consuelo, le démon aussi était un ange, avant* . . ."

And after the last page, the portraits. The portrait of an elderly gentleman in a military uniform, an old photograph with these words in one corner: "*Moulin, Photographe, 35 Boulevard Haussmann*" and the date "1894." Then the photograph of Aura, of Aura with her green eyes, her black hair gathered in ringlets, leaning against a Doric column with a painted landscape in the background: the landscape of a Lorelei in the Rhine. Her dress is buttoned up to the collar, there's a handkerchief in her hand, she's wearing a bustle: Aura, and the date "1876" in white ink, and on the back of the daguerrotype, in spidery handwriting: "*Fait pour notre dixième anniversaire de mariage*," and a signature in the same hand, "Consuelo Llorente." In the third photograph you see both Aura and the old gentleman, but this time they're dressed in outing-clothes, sitting on a bench in a garden. The photograph has become a little blurred: Aura doesn't look as young as she did in the other picture, but it's she, it's he, it's. . .it's you. You stare and stare at the photographs, then hold them up to the skylight. You cover General Llorente's beard with your finger, and imagine him with black hair, and you only discover yourself: blurred, lost, forgotten, but you, you, you.

Your head is spinning, overcome by the rhythm of that distant waltz, by the odor of damp, fragrant plants; you fall exhausted on the bed, touching your cheeks, your eyes, your nose, as if you were afraid that some invisible hand had ripped off the mask you've been wearing for twenty-seven years, the cardboard features that hid your true face, your real appearance, the appearance you once had but then forgot. You bury your face in the pillow, trying to keep the wind of the past from tearing away your own features, because you don't want to lose them. You lie there with your face in the pillow, waiting for what has to come, for what you can't prevent. You don't look at your watch again, that useless object tediously measuring time in accordance with human vanity, those little hands marking out the long hours that were invented to disguise the real passage of time, which races with a mortal and insolent swiftness no clock could ever measure. A life, a century, fifty years: you can't imagine these lying measurements any longer, you can't hold that bodiless dust within your hands.

When you look up from the pillow, you find you're in darkness. Night has fallen.

Night has fallen. Beyond the skylight the swift black clouds are hiding the moon, which tries to free itself, to reveal its pale, round, smiling face. It escapes for only a moment, then the clouds hide it again. You haven't got any hope left. You don't even look at your watch. You hurry down the stairs, out of that prison cell with its old papers and faded daguerrotypes, and stop at the door of Señora Consuelo's room, and listen to your own voice, muted and transformed after all those hours of silence: "Aura..."

Again: "Aura..."

You enter the room. The votive-lights have gone out. You remember that the old lady has been away all day, without her faithful attention the candles have all burned up. You grope forward in the darkness to the bed.

And again: "Aura."

You hear a faint rustle of taffeta, and the breathing that keeps time with your own. You reach out your hand to touch Aura's green robe.

"No...Don't touch me...Lie down at my side."

You find the edge of the bed, swing up your legs, and remain there stretched out and motionless. You can't help feeling a shiver of fear: "She might come back any minute."

"She won't come back."

"Never?"

"I'm exhausted. She's already exhausted. I've never been able to keep her with me for more than three days."

"Aura..."

You want to put your hand on Aura's breasts. She turns her back: you can tell by the difference in her voice.

"No...Don't touch me..."

"Aura...I love you."

"Yes. You love me. You told me yesterday that you'd always love me."

"I'll always love you, always. I need your kisses, your body..."

"Kiss my face. Only my face."

You bring your lips close to the head that's lying next to yours. You stroke Aura's long black hair. You grasp that fragile woman by the shoulders, ignoring her sharp complaint. You tear off her taffeta robe, embrace her, feel her small and lost and naked in your arms, despite her moaning resistance, her feeble protests, kissing her face without thinking, without distinguishing, and you're touching her withered breasts when a ray of moonlight shines in and surprises you, shines in through a chink in the wall that the rats have chewed open, an eye that lets in a beam of silvery moonlight. It falls on Aura's eroded face, as brittle and yellowed as the memoirs, as creased with wrinkles as the photographs. You stop kissing those fleshless lips, those toothless gums: the ray of moonlight shows you the naked body of the old lady, of Señora Consuelo, limp, spent, tiny, ancient, trembling because you touch her, you love her, you too have come back...

You plunge your face, your open eyes, into Consuelo's silver-white hair, and you'll embrace her again when the clouds cover the moon, when you're both hidden again, when the memory of youth, of youth re-embodied, rules the darkness.

"She'll come back, Felipe. We'll bring her back together. Let me recover my strength and I'll bring her back..."

Translated by Lysander Kemp

ELIZABETH BISHOP

*E*LIZABETH BISHOP (1911–1979) *was one of America's most distinguished poets, known for her inspired, lucid observations of natural surroundings, combined with her ecstatic explorations of subjective feelings. Occasionally her poems verge on the fantastic through the lush use of imagery. Her important volumes include* Poems: North and South—A Cold Spring *(1955), which won the Pulitzer Prize,* Complete Poems *(1969), winner of a* National Book Award, *and* Geography III *(1979). She served as a consultant in poetry at the Library of Congress (1949–50), and then from the early 1950s until 1967, she lived in Brazil. She returned to the United States to teach at Harvard University during the 1970s.*

The story "In the Village," from her book Questions of Travel *(1965), is unusual because Bishop published little prose. This piece seems to have been inspired by her childhood experiences with her grandparents in Nova Scotia. As noted in the* Introduction, *Bishop commands a rich metaphorical style that, without the least suggestion of sentimentality, accurately captures the overwhelmed feelings of a child witnessing adult suffering. The narration unfolds through the little girl's memory, with episodes authentically evolving in fragmented sequences. The whole texture of the story shines with magic, as the child perceives all of the activities around her. Her vision is resonant yet curiously detached, covering an astounding range from the mother's terrifying shriek echoing in the pure blue skies to the beautiful, reassuring clang of the blacksmith's anvil.*

In the Village

Elizabeth Bishop

A SCREAM, the echo of a scream, hangs over that Nova Scotian village. No one hears it; it hangs there forever, a slight stain in those pure blue skies, skies that travellers compare to those of Switzerland, too dark, too blue, so that they seem to keep on darkening a little more around the horizon—or is it around the rims of the eyes?—the color of the cloud of bloom on the elm trees, the violet on the fields of oats; something darkening over the woods and waters as well as the sky. The scream hangs like that, unheard, in memory—in the past, in the present, and those years between. It was not even loud to begin with, perhaps. It just came there to live, forever—not loud, just alive forever. Its pitch would be the pitch of my village. Flick the lightning rod on top of the church steeple with your fingernail and you will hear it.

She stood in the large front bedroom with sloping walls on either side, papered in wide white and dim-gold stripes. Later, it was she who gave the scream.

The village dressmaker was fitting a new dress. It was her first in almost two years and she had decided to come out of black, so the dress was purple. She was very thin. She wasn't at all sure whether she was going to like the dress or not and she kept lifting the folds of the skirt, still unpinned and dragging on the floor around her, in her thin white hands, and looking down at the cloth.

"Is it a good shade for me? Is it too bright? I don't know. I haven't worn colors for so long now... How long? Should it be black? Do you think I should keep on wearing black?"

Drummers sometimes came around selling gilded red or green

421

books, unlovely books, filled with bright new illustrations of the Bible stories. The people in the pictures wore clothes like the purple dress, or like the way it looked then.

It was a hot summer afternoon. Her mother and her two sisters were there. The older sister had brought her home, from Boston, not long before, and was staying on, to help. Because in Boston she had not got any better, in months and months—or had it been a year? In spite of the doctors, in spite of the frightening expenses, she had not got any better.

First, she had come home, with her child. Then she had gone away again, alone, and left the child. Then she had come home. Then she had gone away again, with her sister; and now she was home again.

Unaccustomed to having her back, the child stood now in the doorway, watching. The dressmaker was crawling around and around on her knees eating pins as Nebuchadnezzar had crawled eating grass. The wallpaper glinted and the elm trees outside hung heavy and green, and the straw matting smelled like the ghost of hay.

Clang.

Clang.

Oh, beautiful sounds, from the blacksmith's shop at the end of the garden! Its gray roof, with patches of moss, could be seen above the lilac bushes. Nate was there—Nate, wearing a long black leather apron over his trousers and bare chest, sweating hard, a black leather cap on top of dry, thick, black-and-gray curls, a black sooty face; iron filings, whiskers, and gold teeth, all together, and a smell of red-hot metal and horses' hoofs.

Clang.

The pure note: pure and angelic.

The dress was all wrong. She screamed.

The child vanishes.

Later they sit, the mother and the three sisters, in the shade on the back porch, sipping sour, diluted ruby: raspberry vinegar. The dressmaker refuses to join them and leaves, holding the dress to her heart. The child is visiting the blacksmith.

In the blacksmith's shop things hang up in the shadows and shadows hang up in the things, and there are black and glistening piles of dust in each corner. A tub of night-black water stands by the forge. The horseshoes sail through the dark like bloody little moons and follow each other like bloody little moons to drown in the black water, hissing, protesting.

Outside, along the matted eaves, painstakingly, sweetly, wasps go over and over a honeysuckle vine.

Inside, the bellows creak. Nate does wonders with both hands; with one hand. The attendant horse stamps his foot and nods his head as if agreeing to a peace treaty.

Nod.

And nod.

A Newfoundland dog looks up at him and they almost touch noses, but not quite, because at the last moment the horse decides against it and turns away.

Outside in the grass lie scattered big, pale granite discs, like mill-stones, for making wheel rims on. This afternoon they are too hot to touch.

Now it is settling down, the scream.

Now the dressmaker is at home, basting, but in tears. It is the most beautiful material she has worked on in years. It has been sent to the woman from Boston, a present from her mother-in-law, and heaven knows how much it cost.

Before my older aunt had brought her back, I had watched my grandmother and younger aunt unpacking her clothes, her "things." In trunks and barrels and boxes they had finally come, from Boston, where she and I had once lived. So many things in the village came from Boston, and even I had once come from there. But I remembered only being here, with my grandmother.

The clothes were black, or white, or black-and-white.

"Here's a mourning hat," says my grandmother, holding up something large, sheer, and black, with large black roses on it; at least I guess they are roses, even if black.

"There's that mourning coat she got the first winter," says my aunt.

But always I think they are saying "morning." Why, in the morning, did one put on black? How early in the morning did one begin? Before the sun came up?

"Oh, here are some house dresses!"

They are nicer. Clean and starched, stiffly folded. One with black polka dots. One of fine black-and-white strips with black grosgrain bows. A third with a black velvet bow and on the bow a pin of pearls in a little wreath.

"Look. She forgot to take it off."

A white hat. A white embroidered parasol. Black shoes with buckles glistening like the dust in the blacksmith's shop. A silver mesh bag. A silver calling-card case on a little chain. Another bag of silver mesh, gathered to a tight, round neck of strips of silver that will open out, like the hatrack in the front hall. A silver-framed photograph, quickly turned over. Handkerchiefs with narrow black hems—"morning handkerchiefs." In bright sunlight, over breakfast tables, they flutter.

A bottle of perfume has leaked and made awful brown stains.

Oh, marvelous scent, from somewhere else! It doesn't smell like that here; but there, somewhere, it does, still.

A big bundle of postcards. The curdled elastic around them breaks. I gather them together on the floor.

Some people wrote with pale-blue ink, and some with brown, and some with black, but mostly blue. The stamps have been torn off many of them. Some are plain, or photographs, but some have lines of metallic crystals on them—how beautiful!—silver, gold, red, and green, or all four mixed together, crumbling off, sticking in the lines on my palms. All the cards like this I spread on the floor to study. The crystals outline the buildings on the cards in a way buildings never are outlined but should be—if there were a way of making the crystals stick. But probably not; they would fall to the ground, never to be seen again. Some cards, instead of lines around the buildings, have words written in their skies with the same stuff, crumbling, dazzling and crumbling, raining down a little on little people who sometimes stand about below: pictures of Pentecost? What are the messages? I cannot tell, but they are falling on those specks of hands, on the hats, on the toes of their shoes, in their paths—wherever it is they are.

Postcards come from another world, the world of the grandparents who send things, the world of sad brown perfume, and morning. (The gray postcards of the village for sale in the village store are so unilluminating that they scarcely count. After all, one steps outside and immediately sees the same thing: the village, where we live, full size, and in color.)

Two barrels of china. White with a gold band. Broken bits. A thick white teacup with a small red-and-blue butterfly on it, painfully desirable. A teacup with little pale-blue windows in it.

"See the grains of rice?" says my grandmother, showing me the cup against the light.

Could you poke the grains out? No, it seems they aren't really there any more. They were put there just for a while and then they left something or other behind. What odd things people do with grains of rice, so innocent and small! My aunt says that she has heard they write the Lord's Prayer on them. And make them make those little pale-blue lights.

More broken china. My grandmother says it breaks her heart. "Why couldn't they have got it packed better? Heaven knows what it cost."

"Where'll we put it all? The china closet isn't nearly big enough."

"It'll just have to stay in the barrels."

"Mother, you might as well use it."

"No," says my grandmother.

"Where's the silver, Mother?"

"In the vault in Boston."

Vault. Awful word. I run the tip of my finger over the rough, jewelled lines on the postcards, over and over. They hold things up to each other and exclaim, and talk, and exclaim, over and over.

"There's that cake basket."

"Mrs. Miles . . ."

"Mrs. Miles' spongecake . . ."

"She was very fond of her."

Another photograph—"Oh, that *Negro* girl! That friend."

"She went to be a medical missionary. She had a letter from her, last winter, From Africa."

"They were great friends."

They show me the picture. She, too, is black-and-white, with glasses on a chain. A morning friend.

And the smell, the wonderful smell of the dark-brown stains. Is it roses?

A tablecloth.

"She did beautiful work," says my grandmother.

"But look—it isn't finished."

Two pale, smooth wooden hoops are pressed together in the linen. There is a case of little ivory embroidery tools.

I abscond with a little ivory stick with a sharp point. To keep it forever I bury it under the bleeding heart by the crab-apple tree, but it is never found again.

Nate sings and pumps the bellows with one hand. I try to help, but he really does it all, from behind me, and laughs when the coals blow red and wild.

"Make me a ring! Make me a ring, Nate!"

Instantly it is made; it is mine.

It is too big and still hot, and blue and shiny. The horseshoe nail has a flat oblong head, pressing hot against my knuckle.

Two men stand watching, chewing or spitting tobacco, matches, horseshoe nails—anything, apparently, but with such presence; they are perfectly at home. The horse is the real guest, however. His harness hangs loose like a man's suspenders; they say pleasant things to him; one of his legs is doubled up in an improbable, affectedly polite way, and the bottom of his hoof is laid bare, but he doesn't seem to mind. Manure piles up behind him, suddenly, neatly. He, too, is very much at home. He is enormous. His rump is like a brown, glossy globe of the whole brown world. His ears are secret entrances to the underworld. His nose is supposed to feel like velvet and does, with ink spots under milk all over its pink. Clear bright-green bits of stiffened froth, like glass, are stuck around his mouth. He wears medals on his chest, too, and one on his forehead, and simpler decorations—red and blue celluloid rings overlapping each other on leather straps. On each temple is a clear glass bulge, like an eyeball, but in them are the heads of two other little horses (his dreams?), brightly colored, real and raised, untouchable, alas, against backgrounds of silver blue. His trophies hang around him, and the cloud of his odor is a chariot in itself.

At the end, all four feet are brushed with tar, and shine, and he expresses his satisfaction, rolling it from his nostrils like noisy smoke, as he backs into the shafts of his wagon.

The purple dress is to be fitted again this afternoon but I take a note to Miss Gurley to say the fitting will have to be postponed. Miss Gurley seems upset.

"Oh dear. And how is—" And she breaks off.

Her house is littered with scraps of cloth and tissue-paper patterns, yellow, pinked, with holes in the shapes of A, B, C, and D in them, and numbers; and threads everywhere like a fine vegetation. She has a bosom full of needles with threads ready to pull out and make nests with. She sleeps in her thimble. A gray kitten once lay on the treadle of her sewing machine, where she rocked it as she sewed, like a baby in a cradle, but it got hanged on the belt. Or did she make that up? But another gray-and-white one lies now by the arm of the machine, in imminent danger of being sewn into a turban. There is a table covered with laces and braids, embroidery silks, and cards of buttons of all colors—big ones for winter coats, small pearls, little glass ones delicious to suck.

She has made the very dress I have on, "for twenty-five cents." My grandmother said my other grandmother would certainly be surprised at that.

The purple stuff lies on a table; long white threads hang all about it. Oh, look away before it moves by itself, or makes a sound; before it echoes, echoes, what it has heard!

Mysteriously enough, poor Miss Gurley—I know she is poor—gives me a five-cent piece. She leans over and drops it in the pocket of the red-and-white dress that she has made herself. It is very tiny, very shiny. King George's beard is like a little silver flame. Because they look like herring- or maybe salmon-scales, five-cent pieces are called "fish-scales." One heard of people's rings being found inside fish, or their long-lost jackknives. What if one could scrape a salmon and find a little picture of King George on every scale?

I put my five-cent piece in my mouth for greater safety on the way home, and swallow it. Months later, as far as I know, it is still in me, transmuting all its precious metal into my growing teeth and hair.

Back home, I am not allowed to go upstairs. I heard my aunts running back and forth and something like a tin washbasin falls bump in the carpeted upstairs hall.

My grandmother is sitting in the kitchen stirring potato mash for tomorrow's bread and crying into it. She gives me a spoonful and it tastes wonderful but wrong. In it I think I taste my grandmother's tears; then I kiss her and taste them on her cheek.

She says it is time for her to get fixed up, and I say I want to help her brush her hair. So I do, standing swaying on the lower rung of the back of her rocking chair.

The rocking chair has been painted and repainted so many times that it is as smooth as cream—blue, white, and gray all showing through.

My grandmother's hair is silver and in it she keeps a great many celluloid combs, at the back and sides, streaked gray and silver to match. The one at the back has longer teeth than the others and a row of sunken silver dots across the top, beneath a row of little balls. I pretend to play a tune on it; then I pretend to play a tune on each of the others before we stick them in, so my grandmother's hair is full of music. She laughs. I am so pleased with myself that I do not feel obliged to mention the five-cent piece. I drink a rusty, icy drink out of the biggest dipper; still, nothing much happens.

We are waiting for a scream. But it is not screamed again, and the red sun sets in silence.

Every morning I take the cow to the pasture we rent from Mr. Chisolm. She, Nelly, could probably go by herself just as well, but I like marching through the village with a big stick, directing her.

This morning it is brilliant and cool. My grandmother and I are alone again in the kitchen. We are talking. She says it is cool enough to keep the oven going, to bake the bread, to roast a leg of lamb.

"Will you remember to go down to the brook? Take Nelly around by the brook and pick me a big bunch of mint. I thought I'd make some mint sauce."

"For the leg of lamb?"

"You finish your porridge."

"I think I've had enough now..."

"Hurry up and finish that porridge."

There is talking on the stairs.

"No, now wait," my grandmother says to me. "Wait a minute."

My two aunts come into the kitchen. She is with them, wearing the white cotton dress with black polka dots and the flat black velvet bow at the neck. She comes and feeds me the rest of the porridge herself, smiling at me.

"Stand up now and let's see how tall you are," she tells me.

"Almost to your elbow," they say. "See how much she's grown."

"Almost."

"It's her hair."

Hands are on my head, pushing me down; I slide out from under them. Nelly is waiting for me in the yard, holding her nose just under in the watering trough. My stick waits against the door frame, clad in bark.

Nelly looks up at me, drooling glass strings. She starts off around the corner of the house without a flicker of expression.

Switch. Switch. How annoying she is!

But she is a Jersey and we think she is very pretty. "From in front," my aunts sometimes add.

She stops to snatch at the long, untrimmed grass around the gatepost.

"Nelly!"

Whack! I hit her hipbone.

On she goes without even looking around. Flop, flop, down over the dirt sidewalk into the road, across the village green in front of the Presbyterian church. The grass is gray with dew; the church is dazzling. It is high-shouldered and secretive; it leans backwards a little.

Ahead, the road is lined with dark, thin old elms; grass grows long and blue in the ditches. Behind the elms the meadows run along, peacefully, greenly.

We pass Mrs. Peppard's house. We pass Mrs. McNeil's house. We pass Mrs. Geddes's house. We pass Hills' store.

The store is high, and a faded gray-blue, with tall windows, built on a long, high stoop of gray-blue cement with an iron hitching rail along it. Today, in one window there are big cardboard easels, shaped like houses—complete houses and houses with the roofs lifted off to show glimpses of the rooms inside, all in different colors—with cans of paint in pyramids in the middle. But they are an old story. In the other window is something new: shoes, single shoes, summer shoes, each sitting on top of its own box with its mate beneath it, inside, in the dark. Surprisingly, some of them appear to be exactly the colors and texture of pink and blue blackboard chalks, but I can't stop to examine them now. In one door, great overalls hang high in the air on hangers. Miss Ruth Hill looks out the other door and waves. We pass Mrs. Captain Mahon's house.

Nelly tenses and starts walking faster, making over to the right. Every morning and evening we go through this. We are approaching Miss Spencer's house. Miss Spencer is the milliner the way Miss Gurley is the dressmaker. She has a very small white house with the doorstep right on the sidewalk. One front window has lace curtains with a pale-yellow window shade pulled all the way down, inside them; the other one has a shelf across it on which are displayed four summer hats. Out of the corner of my eye I can see that there is a yellow chip straw with little wads of flamingo-colored feathers around the crown, but again there is no time to examine anything.

On each side of Miss Spencer's door is a large old lilac bush. Every time we go by Nelly determines to brush off all her flies on these bushes—brush them off forever, in one fell swoop. Then Miss Spencer is apt to come to the door and stand there, shaking with anger, between the two bushes still shaking from Nelly's careening passage, and yell at me, sometimes waving a hat in my direction as well.

Nelly leaning to the right, breaks into a cow trot. I run up with my stick.

Whack!

"Nelly!"

Whack!

Just this once she gives in and we rush safely by.

Then begins a long, pleasant stretch beneath the elms. The Presbyterian manse has a black iron fence with openwork foursided pillars, like tall, thin bird cages, bird cages for storks. Dr. Gillespie, the minister, appears just as we come along, and rides slowly toward us on his bicycle.

"Good day." He even tips his hat.

"Good day."

He wears the most interesting hat in the village: a man's regular stiff straw sailor, only it is black. Is there a possibility that he paints it at home, with something like stove polish? Because once I had seen one of my aunts painting a straw-colored hat navy blue.

Nelly, oblivious, makes cow flops. Smack. Smack. Smack. Smack.

It is fascinating. I cannot take my eyes off her. Then I step around them: fine dark-green and lacy and watery at the edges.

We pass the McLeans', whom I know very well. Mr. McLean is just coming out of his new barn with the tin hip roof and with him is Jock, their old shepherd dog, long-haired, black and white and yellow. He runs up barking deep, cracked, soft barks in the quiet morning. I hesitate.

Mr. McLean bellows, "Jock! You! Come back here! Are you trying to frighten her?"

To me he says, "He's twice as old as you are."

Finally I pat the big round warm head.

We talk a little. I ask the exact number of Jock's years but Mr. McLean has forgotten.

"He hasn't hardly a tooth in his head and he's got rheumatism. I hope we'll get him through next winter. He still wants to go to the woods with me and it's hard for him in the snow. We'll be lost without him."

Mr. McLean speaks to me behind one hand, not to hurt Jock's feelings: "*Deaf as a post.*"

Like anybody deaf, Jock puts his head to one side.

"He used to be the best dog at finding cows for miles around. People used to come from away down the shore to borrow him to find their cows for them. And he'd always find them. The first year we had to leave him behind when we went up to the mountain to get the cows I thought it would kill him. Well, when his teeth started going he couldn't do much with the cows any more. Effie used to say, 'I don't know how we'd run the farm without him.' "

Loaded down with too much black and yellow and white fur, Jock smiles, showing how few teeth he has. He has yellow caterpillars for eyebrows.

Nelly has gone on ahead. She is almost up the hill to Chisolms' when I catch up with her. We turn in to their steep, long drive, through a steep, bare yard crowded with unhappy apple trees. From the top, though, from the Chisolms' back yard, one always stops to look at the view.

There are the tops of all the elm trees in the village and there, beyond them, the long green marshes, so fresh, so salt. Then the Minas Basin, with the tide halfway in or out, the wet red mud glazed with sky blue until it meets the creeping lavender-red water In the middle of the view, like one hand of a clock pointing straight up, is the steeple of the Presbyterian church. We are in the "Maritimes" but all that means is that we live by the sea.

Mrs. Chisolm's pale frantic face is watching me out the kitchen window as she washes the breakfast dishes. We wave, but I hurry by because she may come out and ask questions. But her questions are not as bad perhaps as those of her husband, Mr. Chisolm, who wears a beard. One evening he had met me in the pasture and asked me how my soul was. Then he held me firmly by both hands while he said a prayer, with his head bowed, Nelly right beside us chewing her cud all the time. I had felt a soul, heavy in my chest, all the way home.

I let Nelly through the set of bars to the pasture where the brook is, to get the mint. We both take drinks and I pick a big bunch of mint, eating a little, scratchy and powerful. Nelly looks over her shoulder and comes back to try it, thinking, as cows do, it might be something especially for her. Her face is close to mine and I hold her by one horn to admire her eyes again. Her nose is blue and as shiny as something in the rain. At such close quarters my feelings for her are mixed. She gives my bare arm a lick, scratchy and powerful, too, almost upsetting me into the brook; then she goes off to join a black-and-white friend she has here, mooing to her to wait until she catches up.

For a while I entertain the idea of not going home today at all, of staying safely here in the pasture all day, playing in the brook and climbing on the squishy, moss-covered hummocks in the swampy part. But an immense, sibilant, glistening loneliness suddenly faces me, and the cows are moving off to the shade of the fir trees, their bells chiming softly, individually.

On the way home there are the four hats in Miss Spencer's window to study, and the summer shoes in Hills'. There is the same shoe in white, in black patent leather, and in the chalky, sugary, unearthly pinks and blues. It has straps that button around the ankle and above, four of them, about an inch wide and an inch apart, reaching away up.

In those unlovely gilded red and green books, filled with illustrations of the Bible stories, the Roman centurions wear them, too, or something very like them.

Surely they are my size. Surely, this summer, pink or blue, my grandmother will buy me a pair!

Miss Ruth Hill gives me a Moirs' chocolate out of the glass case. She talks to me: "How is she? We've always been friends. We played together from the time we were babies. We sat together in school. Right from primer class on. After she went away, she always wrote to me—even after she got sick the first time."

Then she tells a funny story about when they were little.

That afternoon, Miss Gurley comes and we go upstairs to watch the purple dress being fitted again. My grandmother holds me against her knees. My younger aunt is helping Miss Gurley, handing her the scissors when she asks. Miss Gurley is cheerful and talkative today.

The dress is smaller now; there are narrow, even folds down the skirt; the sleeves fit tightly, with little wrinkles over the thin white hands. Everyone is very pleased with it; everyone talks and laughs.

"There. You see? It's so becoming."

"I've never seen you in anything more becoming."

"And it's so nice to see you in color for a change."

And the purple is real, like a flower against the gold-and-white wallpaper.

On the bureau is a present that has just come, from an uncle in Boston whom I do not remember. It is a gleaming little bundle of flat, triangular satin pillows—sachets, tied together with a white satin ribbon, with an imitation rosebud on top of the bow. Each is a different faint color; if you take them apart, each has a different faint scent. But tied together the way they came, they make one confused, powdery one.

The mirror has been lifted off the bureau and put on the floor against the wall.

She walks slowly up and down and looks at the skirt in it.

"I think that's about right," says Miss Gurley, down on her knees and looking into the mirror, too, but as if the skirt were miles and miles away.

But, twitching the purple skirt with her thin white hands, she says desperately, "I don't know what they're wearing any more. I have no *idea*!" It turns to a sort of wail.

"Now, now," soothes Miss Gurley. "I do think that's about right. Don't you?" She appeals to my grandmother and me.

Light, musical, constant sounds are coming from Nate's shop. It sounds as though he were making a wheel rim.

She sees me in the mirror and turns on me: "Stop sucking your thumb!"

Then in a moment she turns to me again and demands, "Do you know what I want?"

"No."

"I want some humbugs. I'm dying for some humbugs. I don't think I've had any humbugs for years and years and years. If I give you some pennies, will you go to Mealy's and buy me a bag?"

To be sent on an errand! Everything is all right.

Humbugs are a kind of candy, although not a kind I am particularly fond of. They are brown, like brook water, but hard, and shaped like little twisted pillows. They last a long time, but lack the spit-producing brilliance of cherry or strawberry.

Mealy runs a little shop where she sells candy and bananas and oranges and all kinds of things she crochets. At Christmas, she sells toys, but only at Christmas. Her real name is Amelia. She also takes care of the telephone switchboard for the village, in her dining room.

Somebody finds a black pocketbook in the bureau. She counts out five big pennies into my hand, in a column, then one more.

"That one's for you. So you won't eat up all my humbugs on the way home."

Further instructions:

"Don't run all the way."

"Don't stop on the bridge."

I do run, by Nate's shop, glimpsing him inside, pumping away with one hand. We wave. The beautiful, big Newfoundland dog is there again and comes out, bounding along with me a ways.

I do not stop on the bridge but slow down long enough to find out the years on the pennies. King George is much bigger than on a five-cent piece, brown as an Indian in copper, but he wears the same clothes; on a penny, one can make out the little ermine trimmings on his coat.

Mealy has a bell that rings when you go in so that she'll hear you if she's at the switchboard. The shop is a step down, dark, with a counter along one side. The ceiling is low and the floor has settled well over to the counter side. Mealy is broad and fat and it looks as though she and the counter and the showcase, stuffed dimly with things every which way, were settling down together out of sight.

Five pennies buys a great many humbugs. I must not take too long to decide what I want for myself. I must get back quickly, quickly, while Miss Gurley is there and everyone is upstairs and the dress is still on. Without taking time to think, quickly I point at the brightest thing. It is a ball, glistening solidly with crystals of pink and yellow sugar, hung, impractically, on an elastic, like a real elastic ball. I know I don't even care for the inside of it, which is soft, but I wind most of the elastic around my arm, to keep the ball off the ground, at least, and start hopefully back.

But one night, in the middle of the night, there is a fire. The church bell wakes me up. It is in the room with me; red flames are burning the wallpaper beside the bed. I suppose I shriek.

The door opens. My younger aunt comes in. There is a lamp lit in the hall and everyone is talking at once.

"Don't cry!" my aunt almost shouts at me. "It's just a fire. Way up the road. It isn't going to hurt you. Don't *cry!*"

"Will! Will!" My grandmother is calling my grandfather. "Do you have to go?"

"No, don't go, Dad!"

"It looks like McLean's place." My grandfather sounds muffled.

"Oh, not their new barn!" My grandmother.

"You can't tell from here." He must have his head out the window.

"*She's* calling for you. Mother." My older aunt. "I'll go."

"No. *I'll* go." My younger aunt.

"Light that other lamp, girl."

My older aunt comes to my door. "It's way off. It's nowhere near us. The men will take care of it. Now you go to sleep." But she leaves my door open.

"Leave her door open," calls my grandmother just then. "Oh, why do they have to ring the bell like that? It's enough to terrify anybody. Will, be *careful*."

Sitting up in bed, I see my grandfather starting down the stairs, tucking his nightshirt into his trousers as he goes.

"Don't make so much noise!" My older aunt and my grandmother seem to be quarreling.

"Noise! I can't hear myself think, with that bell!"

"I bet Spurgeon's ringing it!" They both laugh.

"It must have been heat lightning," says my grandmother, now apparently in her bedroom, as if it were all over.

"*She's* all right. Mother." My younger aunt comes back. "I don't think she's scared. You can't see the glare so much on that side of the house."

Then my younger aunt comes into my room and gets in bed with me. She says to go to sleep, it's way up the road. The men have to go; my grandfather has gone. It's probably somebody's barn full of hay, from heat lightning. It's been such a hot summer there's been a lot of it. The church bell stops and her voice is suddenly loud in my ear over my shoulder. The last echo of the bell lasts for a long time.

Wagons rattle by.

"Now they're going down to the river to fill the barrels," my aunt is murmuring against my back.

The red flame dies down on the wall, then flares again.

Wagons rattle by in the dark. Men are swearing at the horses.

"Now they're coming back with the water. Go to sleep."

More wagons; men's voices. I suppose I go to sleep.

I wake up and it is the same night, the night of the fire. My aunt is getting out of bed, hurrying away. It is still dark and silent now, after the fire. No, not silent; my grandmother is crying somewhere, not in her room. It is getting gray. I hear one wagon, rumbling far off, perhaps crossing the bridge.

But now I am caught in a skein of voices, my aunts' and my grandmother's, saying the same things over and over, sometimes loudly, sometimes in whispers:

"Hurry. For heaven's sake, *Shut the door!*"

"Sh!"

"Oh, we can't go on like this, we. . ."

"It's too dangerous. Remember that. . ."

"Sh! Don't let her. . ."

A door slams.

A door opens. The voices begin again.

I am struggling to free myself.

Wait. Wait. No one is going to scream.

Slowly, slowly it gets daylight. A different red reddens the wallpaper. Now the house is silent. I get up and dress by myself and go downstairs. My grandfather is in the kitchen alone, drinking his tea. He has made the oatmeal himself, too. He gives me some and tells me about the fire very cheerfully.

It had not been the McLeans' new barn after all, but someone else's barn, off the road. All the hay was lost but they had managed somehow to save part of the barn.

But neither of us is really listening to what he is saying; we are listening for sounds from upstairs. But everything is quiet.

On the way home from taking Nelly to the pasture I go to see where the barn was. There are people still standing around, some of them the men who got up in the night to go to the river. Everyone seems quite cheerful there, too, but the smell of burned hay is awful, sickening.

Now the front bedroom is empty. My older aunt has gone back to Boston and my other aunt is making plans to go there after a while, too.

There has been a new pig. He was very cute to begin with, and skidded across the kitchen linoleum while everyone laughed. He grew and grew. Perhaps it is all the same summer, because it is unusually hot and something unusual for a pig happens to him; he gets sunburned. He really gets sunburned, bright pink, but the strangest thing of all, the curled-up end of his tail gets so sunburned it is brown and scorched. My grandmother trims it with the scissors and it doesn't hurt him.

Sometime later this pig is butchered. My grandmother, my aunt, and I shut ourselves in the parlor. My aunt plays a piece on the piano called "Out in the Fields." She plays it and plays it; then she switches to Mendelssohn's "War March of the Priests."

The front room is empty. Nobody sleeps there. Clothes are hung there.

Every week my grandmother sends off a package. In it she puts cake and fruit, a jar of preserves, Moirs' chocolates.

Monday afternoon every week.

Fruit, cake, Jordan almonds, a handkerchief with a tatted edge.

Fruit. Cake. Wild-strawberry jam. A New Testament.

A little bottle of scent from Hills' store, with a purple silk tassel fastened to the stopper.

Fruit. Cake. "Selections from Tennyson."

A calendar, with a quotation from Longfellow for every day.

Fruit. Cake. Moirs' chocolates.

I watch her pack them in the pantry. Sometimes she sends me to the store to get things at the last minute.

The address of the sanitarium is in my grandmother's handwriting, in purple indelible pencil, on smoothed-out wrapping paper. It will never come off.

I take the package to the post office. Going by Nate's, I walk far out in the road and hold the package on the side away from him.

He calls to me. "Come here! I want to show you something."

But I pretend I don't hear him. But at any other time I still go there just the same.

The post office is very small. It sits on the side of the road like a package once delivered by the post office. The government has painted its clapboards tan, with a red trim. The earth in front of it is worn hard. Its face is scarred and scribbled on, carved with initials. In the evening, when the Canadian Pacific mail is due, a row of big boys leans against it, but in the daytime there is nothing to be afraid of. There is no one in front, and inside it is empty. There is no one except the postmaster, Mr. Johnson, to look at my grandmother's purple handwriting.

The post office tilts a little, like Mealy's shop, and inside it looks as chewed as a horse's manger. Mr. Johnson looks out through the little window in the middle of the bank of glass-fronted boxes, like an animal looking out over its manger. But he is dignified by the thick, bevelled-edged glass boxes with their solemn, upright gold-and-black-shaded numbers.

Ours is 21. Although there is nothing in it, Mr. Johnson automatically cocks his eye at it from behind when he sees me.

21.

"Well, well. Here we are again. Good day, good day," he says.

"Good day, Mr. Johnson."

I have to go outside again to hand him the package through the ordinary window, into his part of the post office, because it is too big for the little official one. He is very old, and nice. He has two fingers missing on his right hand where they were caught in a threshing machine. He wears a navy-blue cap with a black leather visor, like a ship's officer, and a shirt with feathery brown stripes, and a big gold collar button.

"Let me see. Let me see. Let me see. Hm," he says to himself, weighing the package on the scales, jiggling the bar with the two remaining fingers and thumb.

"Yes. Yes. Your grandmother is very faithful."

Every Monday afternoon I go past the blacksmith's shop with the package under my arm, hiding the address of the sanitarium with my arm and my other hand.

Going over the bridge, I stop and stare down into the river. All the little trout that have been too smart to get caught—for how long now?—are there, rushing in flank movements, foolish assaults and retreats, against and away from the old sunken fender of Malcolm McNeil's Ford. It has lain there for ages and is supposed to be a disgrace to us all. So are the tin cans that glint there, brown and gold.

From above, the trout look as transparent as the water, but if one did catch one, it would be opaque enough, with a little slick moonwhite belly with a pair of tiny, pleated, rose-pink fins on it. The leaning willows soak their narrow yellowed leaves.

Clang.

Clang.

Nate is shaping a horseshoe.

Oh, beautiful pure sound!

It turns everything else to silence.

But still, once in a while, the river gives an unexpected gurgle. "*Slp,*" it says, out of glassy-ridged brown knots sliding along the surface.

Clang.

And everything except the river holds its breath.

Now there is no scream. Once there was one and it settled slowly down to earth one hot summer afternoon; or did it float up, into that dark, too dark, blue sky? But surely it has gone away, forever.

Clang.

It sounds like a bell buoy out at sea.

It is the elements speaking: earth, air, fire, water.

All those other things—clothes, crumbling postcards, broken china; things damaged and lost, sickened or destroyed; even the frail almost-lost scream—are they too frail for us to hear their voices long, too mortal?

Nate!

Oh, beautiful sound, strike again!

ITALO CALVINO

ITALO CALVINO (born 1923), the Italian author, is among the most versatile and gifted fiction writers in the world. With each new book, he engages readers in formal and stylistic experiments that reaffirm his position as a recognized master of fantasy. He has focused his work on the world of imagination and has moved easily from the neorealism in The Path to the Nest of Spiders *(1947), a novel based on his experiences in the Resistance during the war, to progressively more visionary and magical tales. Among these are* The Baron in the Trees *(1957),* The Nonexistent Knight *(1959),* Cosmicomics *(1965), winner of a National Book Award for the remarkable translations of William Weaver,* Invisible Cities *(1974), and* If on a Winter's Night a Traveler *(1979). Calvino also collected and retold 200 traditional Italian tales in his outstanding compilation,* Italian Folktales *(1956).*

Calvino grew up in a scientific atmosphere—his parents were agronomists and his father taught science at the University of Turin—but his most vivid childhood memories are of adventure books and romances. His first story presented here, "The Distance of the Moon," has been selected from Cosmicomics, *which combines scientific knowledge with Calvino's talent for conjuring up an enchanted tale. Often Calvino will deliberately set himself a seemingly impossible task as he attempts to find new ways of exploring realities left untouched or ignored by other writers. In* Cosmicomics, *he tries to melt together the vivid images of fiction with the abstractions of science. He bases each story on a dry, scientific premise related to the evolution of the cosmos, which becomes the starting point for a personal account by the ubiquitous narrator, Qfwfq, of exactly how these mind-boggling events took place. In the context of a moving and chatty style, desiccated scientific notions suddenly bubble to life, enacted by lovable characters.*

Calvino will often work on several projects at once, accumulating material as inspiration strikes him and then filing it away under related subject matter until he feels that a folder might contain enough material for a full-length book. Apparently, the selections from Invisible Cities *were created in this manner and perhaps they resemble prose poems more than anything else, having been influenced by Rimbaud's* Illuminations. *In this book, the Venetian traveler Marco Polo describes to Kublai Khan the utterly fantastic places and cities he has visited in the empire,* most nearly beyond comprehension. We have chosen a few samples of these magical places that often exist only through the realization of some grand obsession. After a small taste, most readers yearn to explore this captivating book further—as Calvino describes it, each section is "like a love poem to a city when it is immensely difficult to live there."

The Distance
of the Moon

Italo Calvino

At one time, according to Sir George H. Darwin, the Moon was very close to the Earth. Then the tides gradually pushed her far away: the tides that the Moon herself causes in the Earth's waters, where the Earth slowly loses energy.

HOW WELL I know!—*old Ofwfq cried,*—the rest of you can't remember, but I can. We had her on top of us all the time, that enormous Moon: when she was full—nights as bright as day, but with a butter-colored light—it looked as if she were going to crush us; when she was new, she rolled around the sky like a black umbrella blown by the wind; and when she was waxing, she came forward with her horns so low she seemed about to stick into the peak of a promontory and get caught there. But the whole business of the Moon's phases worked in a different way then: because the distances from the Sun were different, and the orbits, and the angle of something or other, I forget what; as for eclipses, with Earth and Moon stuck together the way they were, why, we had eclipses every minute: naturally, those two big monsters managed to put each other in the shade constantly, first one, then the other.

Orbit? Oh, elliptical, of course: for a while it would huddle against us and then it would take flight for a while. The tides, when the Moon swung closer, rose so high nobody could hold them back. There were nights when the Moon was full and very, very low, and the tide was so high that the Moon missed a ducking in the sea by a hair's-breadth; well, let's say a few yards anyway. Climb up on the Moon? Of course we did. All you had to do was row out to it in a boat and, when you were underneath, prop a ladder against her and scramble up.

The spot where the Moon was lowest, as she went by, was off the Zinc Cliffs. We used to go out with those little rowboats they had in those days, round and flat, made of cork. They held quite a few of us: me, Captain Vhd Vhd, his wife, my deaf cousin, and sometimes little Xlthlx—she was twelve or so at that time. On those nights the water was very calm, so silvery it looked like mercury, and the fish in it, violet-colored, unable to resist the Moon's attraction, rose to the surface, all of them, and so did the octopuses and the saffron medusas. There was always a flight of tiny creatures—little crabs, squid, and even some weeds, light and filmy, and coral plants—that broke from the sea and ended up on the Moon, hanging down from that lime-white ceiling, or else they stayed in midair, a phosporescent swarm we had to drive off, waving banana leaves at them.

This is how we did the job: in the boat we had a ladder: one of us held it, another climbed to the top, and a third, at the oars, rowed until we were right under the Moon; that's why there had to be so many of us (I only mentioned the main ones). The man at the top of the ladder, as the boat approached the Moon, would become scared and start shouting: "Stop! Stop! I'm going to bang my head!" That was the impression you had, seeing her on top of you, immense, and all rough with sharp spikes and jagged, saw-tooth edges. It may be different now, but then the Moon, or rather the bottom, the underbelly of the Moon, the part that passed closest to the Earth and almost scraped it, was covered with a crust of sharp scales. It had come to resemble the belly of a fish, and the smell too, as I recall, if not downright fishy, was faintly similar, like smoked salmon.

In reality, from the top of the ladder, standing erect on the last rung, you could just touch the Moon if you held your arms up. We had taken the measurements carefully (we didn't yet suspect that she was moving away from us); the only thing you had to be very careful about was where you put your hands. I always chose a scale that seemed fast (we climbed up in groups of five or six at a time), then I would cling first with one hand, then with both, and immediately I would feel ladder and boat drifting away from below me, and the motion of the Moon would tear me from the Earth's attraction. Yes, the Moon was so strong that she pulled you up; you realized this the moment you passed from one to the other: you had to swing up abruptly, with a kind of somersault, grabbing the scales, throwing your legs over your head, until your feet were on the Moon's surface. Seen from the Earth, you looked as if you were hanging there with your head down, but for you, it was the normal position, and the only odd thing was that when you raised your eyes you saw the sea above you, glistening, with the boat and the others upside down, hanging like a bunch of grapes from the vine.

My cousin, the Deaf One, showed a special talent for making those leaps. His clumsy hands, as soon as they touched the lunar surface (he was always the first to jump up from the ladder), suddenly became deft and sensitive. They found immediately the spot where he could hoist himself up; in fact just the pressure of his palms seemed enough to make him stick to the satellite's crust. Once I even thought I saw the Moon come toward him, as he held out his hands.

He was just as dextrous in coming back down to Earth, an operation still more difficult. For us, it consisted in jumping, as high as we could, our arms upraised (seen from the Moon, that is, because seen from the Earth it looked more like a dive, or like swimming downwards, arms at our sides), like jumping up from the Earth in other words, only now we were without the ladder, because there was nothing to prop it against on the Moon. But instead of jumping with his arms out, my cousin bent toward the Moon's surface, his head down as if for a somersault, then made a leap, pushing with his hands. From the boat we watched him, erect in the air as if he were supporting the Moon's enormous ball and were tossing it, striking it with his palms; then, when his legs came within reach, we managed to grab his ankles and pull him down on board.

Now, you will ask me what in the world we went up on the Moon for; I'll explain it to you. We went to collect the milk, with a big spoon and a bucket. Moon-milk was very thick, like a kind of cream cheese. It formed in the crevices between one scale and the next, through the fermentation of various bodies and substances of terrestrial origin which had flown up from the prairies and forests and lakes, as the Moon sailed over them. It was composed chiefly of vegetal juices, tadpoles, bitumen, lentils, honey, starch crystals, sturgeon eggs, molds, pollens, gelatinous matter, worms, resins, pepper, mineral salts, combustion residue. You had only to dip the spoon under the scales that covered the Moon's scabby terrain, and you brought it out filled with that precious muck. Not in the pure state, obviously; there was a lot of refuse. In the fermentation (which took place as the Moon passed over the expanses of hot air above the deserts) not all the bodies melted; some remained stuck in it: fingernails and cartilage, bolts, sea horses, nuts and peduncles, shards of crockery, fishhooks, at times even a comb. So this paste, after it was collected, had to be refined, filtered. But that wasn't the difficulty: the hard part was transporting it down to the Earth. This is how we did it: we hurled each spoonful into the air with both hands, using the spoon as a catapult. The cheese flew, and if we had thrown it hard enough, it stuck to the ceiling, I mean the surface of the sea. Once there, it floated, and it was easy enough to pull it into the boat. In this operation, too, my deaf cousin displayed a special gift; he had strength and a good aim; with a single, sharp throw, he could send the cheese straight into a bucket we held up to him from the boat. As for me, I occasionally misfired; the contents of the spoon would fail to overcome the Moon's attraction and they would fall back into my eye.

I still haven't told you everything, about the things my cousin was good at. That job of extracting lunar milk from the Moon's scales was child's play to him: instead of the spoon, at times he had only to thrust his bare hand under the scales, or even one finger. He didn't proceed in any orderly way, but went to isolated places, jumping from one to the other, as if he were playing tricks on the Moon, surprising her, or perhaps tickling her. And wherever he put his hand, the milk spurted out as if from a nanny goat's teats. So the rest of us had only to follow him and collect with our spoons the substance that he was pressing out, first here, then there, but always as if by chance, since the Deaf One's movements seemed to have no clear, practical sense. There were places, for example, that he touched merely for the fun of touching them: gaps between two scales, naked and tender folds of lunar flesh. At times my cousin pressed not only his fingers but—in a carefully gauged leap—his big toe (he climbed onto the Moon barefoot) and this seemed to be the height of amusement for him, if we could judge by the chirping sounds that came from his throat as he went on leaping.

The soil of the Moon was not uniformly scaly, but revealed irregular bare patches of pale, slippery clay. These soft areas inspired the Deaf One to turn somersaults or to fly almost like a bird, as if he wanted to impress his whole body into the Moon's pulp. As he ventured farther in this way, we lost sight of him at one point. On the Moon there were vast areas we had never had any reason or curiosity to explore, and that was where my cousin vanished; I had suspected that all those somersaults and nudges he indulged in before our eyes were only a preparation, a prelude to something secret meant to take place in the hidden zones.

We fell into a special mood on those nights off the Zinc Cliffs: gay, but with a touch of suspense, as if inside our skulls, instead of the brain, we felt a fish, floating, attracted by the Moon. And so we navigated, playing and singing. The Captain's wife played the harp; she had very long arms, silvery as eels on those nights, and armpits as dark and mysterious as sea urchins; and the sound of the harp was sweet and piercing, so sweet and piercing it was almost unbearable, and we were forced to let out long cries, not so much to accompany the music as to protect our hearing from it.

Transparent medusas rose to the sea's surface, throbbed there a moment, then flew off, swaying toward the Moon. Little Xlthlx amused herself by catching them in midair, though it wasn't easy. Once, as she stretched her little arms out to catch one, she jumped up slightly and was also set free. Thin as she was, she was an ounce or two short of the weight necessary for the Earth's gravity to overcome the Moon's attraction and bring her back: so she flew up among the medusas, suspended over the sea. She took fright, cried, then laughed and started playing, catching shellfish and minnows as they flew, sticking some into her mouth and chewing them. We rowed hard, to keep up with the child: the Moon ran off in her ellipse, dragging that swarm of marine fauna through the sky, and a train of long, entwined seaweeds, and Xlthlx hanging there in the midst. Her two wispy braids seemed to be flying on their own, outstretched toward the Moon; but all the while she kept wriggling and kicking at the air, as if she wanted to fight that influence, and her socks—she had lost her shoes in the flight—slipped off her feet and swayed, attracted by the Earth's force. On the ladder, we tried to grab them.

The idea of eating the little animals in the air had been a good one; the more weight Xlthlx gained, the more she sank toward the Earth; in fact, since among those hovering bodies hers was the largest, mollusks and seaweeds and plankton began to gravitate about her, and soon the child was covered with siliceous little shells, chitinous carapaces, and fibers of sea plants. And the farther she vanished into that tangle, the more she was freed of the Moon's influence, until she grazed the surface of the water and sank into the sea.

We rowed quickly, to pull her out and save her: her body had remained magnetized, and we had to work hard to scrape off all the things encrusted on her. Tender corals were wound about her head, and every time we ran the comb through her hair there was a shower of crayfish and sardines; her eyes were sealed shut by limpets clinging to the lids with their suckers; squids' tentacles were coiled around her arms and her neck; and her little dress now seemed woven only of weeds and sponges. We got the worst of it off her, but for weeks afterwards she went on pulling out fins and shells, and her skin, dotted with little diatoms, remained affected forever, looking—to someone who didn't observe her carefully—as if it were faintly dusted with freckles.

This should give you an idea of how the influences of Earth and Moon, practically equal, fought over the space between them. I'll tell you something else: a body that descended to the Earth from the satellite was still charged for a while with lunar force and rejected the attraction of our world. Even I, big and heavy as I was: every time I had been up there, I took a while to get used to the Earth's up and its down, and the others would have to grab my arms and hold me, clinging in a bunch in the swaying boat while I still had my head hanging and my legs stretching up toward the sky.

"Hold on! Hold on to us!" they shouted at me, and in all that groping, sometimes I ended up by seizing one of Mrs. Vhd Vhd's breasts, which were round and firm, and the contact was good and secure and had an attraction as strong as the Moon's or even stronger, especially if I managed, as I plunged down, to put my other arm around her hips, and with this I passed back into our world and fell with a thud into the bottom of the boat, where Captain Vhd Vhd brought me around, throwing a bucket of water in my face.

This is how the story of my love for the Captain's wife began, and my suffering. Because it didn't take me long to realize whom the lady kept looking at insistently: when my cousin's hands clasped the satellite, I watched Mrs. Vhd Vhd, and in her eyes I could read the thoughts that the deaf man's familiarity with the Moon were arousing in her; and when he disappeared in his mysterious lunar explorations, I saw her become restless, as if on pins and needles, and then it was all clear to me, how Mrs. Vhd Vhd was becoming jealous of the Moon and I was jealous of my cousin. Her eyes were made of diamonds, Mrs. Vhd Vhd's; they flared when she looked at the Moon, almost challengingly, as if she were saying: "You shan't have him!" And I felt like an outsider.

The one who least understood all of this was my deaf cousin. When we helped him down, pulling him—as I explained to you—by his legs, Mrs. Vhd Vhd lost all her self-control, doing everything she could to take his weight against her own body, folding her long silvery arms around him; I felt a pang in my heart (the times I clung to her, her body was soft and kind, but not thrust forward, the way it was with my cousin), while he was indifferent, still lost in his lunar bliss.

I looked at the Captain, wondering if he also noticed his wife's behavior; but there was never a trace of any expression on that face of his, eaten by brine, marked with tarry wrinkles. Since the Deaf One was always the last to break away from the Moon, his return was the signal for the boats to move off. Then, with an unusually polite gesture, Vhd Vhd picked up the harp from the bottom of the boat and handed it to his wife. She was obliged to take it and play a few notes. Nothing could separate her more from the Deaf One than the sound of the harp. I took to singing in a low voice that sad song that goes: "Every shiny fish is floating, floating; and every dark fish is at the bottom, at the bottom of the sea..." and all the others, except my cousin, echoed my words.

Every month, once the satellite had moved on, the Deaf One returned to his solitary detachment from the things of the world; only the approach of the full Moon aroused him again. That time I had arranged things so it wasn't my turn to go up, I could stay in the boat with the Captain's wife. But then, as soon as my cousin had climbed the ladder, Mrs. Vhd Vhd said: "This time I want to go up there, too!"

This had never happened before; the Captain's wife had never gone up on the Moon. But Vhd Vhd made no objection, in fact he almost pushed her up the ladder bodily, exclaiming: "Go ahead then!," and we all started helping her, and I held her from behind, felt her round and soft on my arms, and to hold her up I began to press my face and the palms of my hands against her, and when I felt her rising into the Moon's sphere I was heartsick at that lost contact, so I started to rush after her, saying: "I'm going to go up for a while, too, to help out!"

I was held back as if in a vise. "You stay here; you have work to do later," the Captain commanded, without raising his voice.

At that moment each one's intentions were already clear. And yet I couldn't figure things out; even now I'm not sure I've interpreted it all correctly. Certainly the Captain's wife had for a long time been cherishing the desire to go off privately with my cousin up there (or at least to prevent him from going off along with the Moon), but probably she had a still more ambitious plan, one that would have to be carried out in agreement with the Deaf One: she wanted the two of them to hide up there together and stay on the Moon for a month. But perhaps my cousin, deaf as he was, hadn't understood anything of what she had tried to explain to him, or perhaps he hadn't even realized that he was the object of the lady's desires. And the Captain? He wanted nothing better than to be rid of his wife; in fact, as soon as she was confined up there, we saw him give free rein to his inclinations and plunge into vice, and then we understood why he had done nothing to hold her back. But had he known from the beginning that the Moon's orbit was widening?

None of us could have suspected it. The Deaf One perhaps, but only he: in the shadowy way he knew things, he may have had a presentiment that he would be forced to bid the Moon farewell that night. This is why he hid in his secret places and reappeared only when it was time to come back down on board. It was no use for the Captain's wife to try to follow him: we saw her cross the scaly zone various times, length and breadth, then suddenly she stopped, looking at us in the boat, as if about to ask us whether we had seen him.

Surely there was something strange about that night. The sea's surface, instead of being taut as it was during the full Moon, or even arched a bit toward the sky, now seemed limp, sagging, as if the lunar magnet no longer exercised its full power. And the light, too, wasn't the same as the light of other full Moons; the night's shadows seemed somehow to have thickened. Our friends up there must have realized what was happening; in fact, they looked up at us with frightened eyes. And from their mouths and ours, at the same moment, came a cry: "The Moon's going away!"

The cry hadn't died out when my cousin appeared on the Moon, running. He didn't seem frightened, or even amazed: he placed his hands on the terrain, flinging himself into his usual somersault, but this time after he had hurled himself into the air he remained suspended, as little Xlthlx had. He hovered a moment between Moon and Earth, upside down, they laboriously moving his arms, like someone swimming against a current, he headed with unusual slowness toward our planet.

From the Moon the other sailors hastened to follow his example. Nobody gave a thought to getting the Moon-milk that had been collected into the boats, nor did the Captain scold them for this. They had already waited too long, the distance was difficult to cross by now; when they tried to imitate my cousin's leap or his swimming, they remained there groping, suspended in midair. "Cling together! Idiots! Cling together!" the Captain yelled. At this command, the sailors tried to form a group, a mass, to push all together until they reached the zone of the Earth's attraction: all of a sudden a cascade of bodies plunged into the sea with a loud splash.

The boats were now rowing to pick them up. "Wait! The Captain's wife is missing!" I shouted. The Captain's wife had also tried to jump, but she was still floating only a few yards from the Moon, slowly moving her long, silvery arms in the air. I climbed up the ladder, and in a vain attempt to give her something to grasp I held the harp out toward her. "I can't reach her! We have to go after her!" and I started to jump up, brandishing the harp. Above me the enormous lunar disk no longer seemed the same as before: it had become much smaller, it kept contracting, as if my gaze were driving it away, and the emptied sky gaped like an abyss where, at the bottom, the stars had begun multiplying, and the night poured a river of emptiness over me, drowned me in dizziness and alarm.

"I'm afraid," I thought. "I'm too afraid to jump. I'm a coward!" and at that moment I jumped. I swam furiously through the sky, and held the harp out to her, and instead of coming toward me she rolled over and over, showing me first her impassive face and then her backside.

"Hold tight to me!" I shouted, and I was already overtaking her, entwining my limbs with hers. "If we cling together we can go down!" and I was concentrating all my strength on uniting myself more closely with her, and I concentrated my sensations as I enjoyed the fullness of that embrace. I was so absorbed I didn't realize at first that I was, indeed, tearing her from her weightless condition, but was making her fall back on the Moon. Didn't I realize it? Or had that been my intention from the very beginning? Before I could think properly, a cry was already bursting from my throat. "I'll be the one to stay with you for a month!" Or rather, "On you!" I shouted, in my excitement: "On you for a month!" and at that moment our embrace was broken by our fall to the Moon's surface, where we rolled away from each other among those cold scales.

I raised my eyes as I did every time I touched the Moon's crust, sure that I would see above me the native sea like an endless ceiling, and I saw it, yes, I saw it this time, too, but much higher, and much more narrow, bound by its borders of coasts and cliffs and promontories, and how small the boats seemed, and how unfamiliar my friends' faces and how weak their cries! A sound reached me from nearby: Mrs. Vhd Vhd had discovered her harp and was caressing it, sketching out a chord as sad as weeping.

A long month began. The Moon turned slowly around the Earth. On the suspended globe we no longer saw our familiar shore, but the passage of oceans as deep as abysses and deserts of glowing lapilli, and continents of ice, and forests writhing with reptiles, and the rocky walls of mountain chains gashed by swift rivers, and swampy cities, and stone graveyards, and empires of clay and mud. The distance spread a uniform color over everything: the alien perspectives made every image alien; herds of elephants and swarms of locusts ran over the plains, so evenly vast and dense and thickly grown that there was no difference among them.

I should have been happy: as I had dreamed, I was alone with her, that intimacy with the Moon I had so often envied my cousin and with Mrs. Vhd Vhd was now my exclusive prerogative, a month of days and lunar nights stretched uninterrupted before us, the crust of the satellite nourished us with its milk, whose tart flavor was familiar to us, we raised our eyes up, up to the world where we had been born, finally traversed in all its various expanse, explored landscapes no Earth-being had ever seen, or else we contemplated the stars beyond the Moon, big as pieces of fruit, made of light, ripened on the curved branches of the sky, and everything exceeded my most luminous hopes, and yet, and yet, it was, instead, exile.

I thought only of the Earth. It was the Earth that caused each of us to be that someone he was rather than someone else; up there, wrested from the Earth, it was as if I were no longer that I, nor she that She, for me. I was eager to return to the Earth, and I trembled at the fear of having lost it. The fulfillment of my dream of love had lasted only that instant when we had been united, spinning between Earth and Moon; torn from its earthly soil, my love now knew only the heart-rending nostalgia for what it lacked: a where, a surrounding, a before, an after.

This is what I was feeling. But she? As I asked myself, I was torn by my fears. Because if she also thought only of the Earth, this could be a good sign, a sign that she had finally come to understand me, but it could also mean that everything had been useless, that her longings were directed still and only toward my deaf cousin. Instead, she felt nothing. She never raised her eyes to the old planet, she went off, pale, among those wastelands, mumbling dirges and stroking her harp, as if completely identified with her temporary (as I thought) lunar state. Did this mean I had won out over my rival? No; I had lost: a hopeless defeat. Because she had finally realized that my cousin loved only the Moon, and the only thing she wanted now was to become the Moon, to be assimilated into the object of that extrahuman love.

When the Moon had completed its circling of the planet, there we were again over the Zinc Cliffs. I recognized them with dismay: not even in my darkest previsions had I thought the distance would have made them so tiny. In that mud puddle of the sea, my friends had set forth again, without the now useless ladders; but from the boats rose a kind of forest of long poles; everybody was brandishing one, with a harpoon or a grappling hook at the end, perhaps in the hope of scraping off a last bit of

Moon-milk or of lending some kind of help to us wretches up there. But it was soon clear that no pole was long enough to reach the Moon; and they dropped back, ridiculously short, humbled, floating on the sea; and in that confusion some of the boats were thrown off balance and overturned. But just then, from another vessel a longer pole, which till then they had dragged along on the water's surface, began to rise: it must have been made of bamboo, of many, many bamboo poles stuck one into the other, and to raise it they had to go slowly because—thin as it was—if they let it sway too much it might break. Therefore, they had to use it with great strength and skill, so that the wholly vertical weight wouldn't rock the boat.

Suddenly it was clear that the tip of that pole would touch the Moon, and we saw it graze, then press against the scaly terrain, rest there a moment, give a kind of little push, or rather a strong push that made it bounce off again, then come back and strike that same spot as if on the rebound, then move away once more. And I recognized, we both—the Captain's wife and I—recognized my cousin: it couldn't have been anyone else, he was playing his last game with the Moon, one of his tricks, with the Moon on the tip of his pole as if he were juggling with her. And we realized that his virtuosity had no purpose, aimed at no practical result, indeed you would have said he was driving the Moon away, that he was helping her departure, that he wanted to show her to her more distant orbit. And this, too, was just like him: he was unable to conceive desires that went against the Moon's nature, the Moon's course and destiny, and if the Moon now tended to go away from him, then he would take delight in this separation just as, till now, he had delighted in the Moon's nearness.

What could Mrs. Vhd Vhd do, in the face of this? It was only at this moment that she proved her passion for the deaf man hadn't been a frivolous whim but an irrevocable vow. If what my cousin now loved was the distant Moon, then she too would remain distant, on the Moon, I sensed this, seeing that she didn't take a step toward the bamboo pole, but simply turned her harp toward the Earth, high in the sky, and plucked the strings. I say I saw her, but to tell the truth I only caught a glimpse of her out of the corner of my eye, because the minute the pole had touched the lunar crust, I had sprung and grasped it, and now, fast as a snake, I was climbing up the bamboo knots, pushing myself along with jerks of my arms and knees, light in the rarefied space, driven by a natural power that ordered me to return to the Earth, oblivious of the motive that had brought me here, or perhaps more aware of it than ever and of its unfortunate outcome; and already my climb up the swaying pole had reached the point where I no longer had to make any effort but could just allow myself to slide, head-first, attracted by the Earth, until in my haste the pole broke into a thousand pieces and I fell into the sea, among the boats.

My return was sweet, my home refound, but my thoughts were filled only with grief at having lost her, and my eyes gazed at the Moon, forever beyond my reach, as I sought her. And I saw her. She was there where I had left her, lying on a beach directly over our heads, and she said nothing. She was the color of the Moon; she held the harp at her side and moved one hand now and then in slow arpeggios. I could distinguish the shape of her bosom, her arms, her thighs, just as I remember them now, just as now, when the Moon has become that flat, remote circle, I still look for her as soon as the first sliver appears in the sky, and the more it waxes, the more clearly I imagine I can see her, her or something of her, but only her, in a hundred, a thousand different vistas, she who makes the Moon the Moon and, whenever she is full, sets the dogs to howling all night long, and me with them.

Translated by William Weaver

Invisible Cities

Italo Calvino

Kublai Khan and Marco Polo

*K*UBLAI KHAN *does not necessarily believe everything Marco Polo says when he describes the cities visited on his expeditions, but the emperor of the Tartars does continue listening to the young Venetian with greater attention and curiosity than he shows any other messenger or explorer of his. In the lives of emperors there is a moment which follows pride in the boundless extension of the territories we have conquered, and the melancholy and relief of knowing we shall soon give up any thought of knowing and understanding them. There is a sense of emptiness that comes over us at evening, with the odor of the elephants after the rain and the sandalwood ashes growing cold in the braziers, a dizziness that makes rivers and mountains tremble on the fallow curves of the planispheres where they are portrayed, and rolls up, one after the other, the despatches announcing to us the collapse of the last enemy troops, from defeat to defeat, and flakes the wax of the seals of obscure kings who beseech our armies' protection, offering in exchange annual tributes of precious metals, tanned hides, and tortoise shell. It is the desperate moment when we discover that this empire, which had seemed to us the sum of all wonders, is an endless, formless ruin, that corruption's gangrene has spread too far to be healed by our scepter, that the triumph over enemy sovereigns has made us the heirs of their long undoing. Only in Marco Polo's accounts was Kublai Khan able to discern, through the walls and*

Excerpt from *Invisible Cities*.

towers destined to crumble, the tracery of a pattern so subtle it could escape the termites' gnawing.

Tamara

You walk for days among trees and among stones. Rarely does the eye light on a thing, and then only when it has recognized that thing as the sign of another thing: a print in the sand indicates the tiger's passage; a marsh announces a vein of water; the hibiscus flower, the end of winter. All the rest is silent and interchangeable; trees and stones are only what they are.

Finally the journey leads to the city of Tamara. You penetrate it along streets thick with signboards jutting from the walls. The eye does not see things but images of things that mean other things: pincers point out the tooth-drawer's house; a tankard, the tavern; halberds, the barracks; scales, the grocer's. Statues and shields depict lions, dolphins, towers, stars: a sign that something—who knows what?—has as its sign a lion or a dolphin or a tower or a star. Other signals warn of what is forbidden in a given place (to enter the alley with wagons, to urinate behind the kiosk, to fish with your pole from the bridge) and what is allowed (watering zebras, playing bowls, burning relatives' corpses). From the doors of the temples the gods' statues are seen, each portrayed with his attributes—the cornucopia, the hourglass, the medusa—so that the worshiper can recognize them and address his prayers correctly. If a building has no signboard or figure, its very form and the position it occupies in the city's order suffice to indicate its function: the palace, the prison, the mint, the Pythagorean school, the brothel. The wares, too, which the vendors display on their stalls are valuable not in themselves but as signs of other things: the embroidered headband stands for elegance; the gilded palanquin, power; the volumes of Averroes, learning; the ankle bracelet, voluptuousness. Your gaze scans the streets as if they were written pages: the city says everything you must think, makes you repeat her discourse, and while you believe you are visiting Tamara you are only recording the names with which she defines herself and all her parts.

However the city may really be, beneath this thick coating of signs, whatever it may contain or conceal, you leave Tamara without having discovered it. Outside, the land stretches, empty, to the horizon; the sky opens, with speeding clouds. In the shape that chance and wind give the clouds, you are already intent on recognizing figures: a sailing ship, a hand, an elephant...

Zobeide

From there, after six days and seven nights, you arrive at Zobeide, the white city, well exposed to the moon, with streets wound about themselves as in a skein. They tell this tale of its foundation: men of various nations had an identical dream. They saw a woman running at night through an unknown city; she was seen from behind, with long hair, and she was naked. They dreamed of pursuing her. As they twisted and turned, each of them lost her. After the dream they set out in search of that city; they never found it, but they found one another; they decided to build a city like the one in the dream. In laying out the streets, each followed the course of his pursuit; at the spot where they had lost the fugitive's trail, they arranged spaces and walls differently from the dream, so she would be unable to escape again.

This was the city of Zobeide, where they settled, waiting for that scene to be repeated one night. None of them, asleep or awake, ever saw the woman again. The city's streets were streets where they went to work every day, with no link any more to the dreamed chase. Which, for that matter, had long been forgotten.

New men arrived from other lands, having had a dream like theirs, and in the city of Zobeide, they recognized something of the streets of the dream, and they changed the positions of arcades and stairways to resemble more closely the path of the pursued woman and so, at the spot where she had vanished, there would remain no avenue of escape.

The first to arrive could not understand what drew these people to Zobeide, this ugly city, this trap.

Octavia

If you choose to believe me, good. Now I will tell how Octavia, the spider-web city, is made. There is a precipice between two steep mountains: the city is over the void, bound to the two crests with ropes and chains and catwalks. You walk on the little wooden ties, careful not to set your foot in the open spaces, or you cling to the hempen strands. Below there is nothing for hundreds and hundreds of feet: a few clouds glide past; farther down you can glimpse the chasm's bed.

This is the foundation of the city: a net which serves as passage and as support. All the rest, instead of rising up, is hung below: rope ladders, hammocks, houses made like sacks, clothes hangers, terraces like gondolas, skins of water, gas jets, spits, baskets on strings, dumb-waiters, showers, trapezes and rings for children's games, cable cars, chandeliers, pots with trailing plants.

Suspended over the abyss, the life of Octavia's inhabitants is less uncertain than in other cities. They know the net will last only so long.

Eusapia

No city is more inclined than Eusapia to enjoy life and flee care. And to make the leap from life to death less abrupt, the inhabitants have constructed an identical copy of their city, underground. All corpses, dried in such a way that the skeleton remains sheathed in yellow skin, are carried down there, to continue their former activities. And, of these activities, it is their carefree moments that take first place: most of the corpses are seated around laden tables, or placed in dancing positions, or made to play little trumpets. But all the trades and professions of the living Eusapia are also at work below ground, or at least those that the living performed with more contentment that irritation: the clock-maker, amid all the stopped clocks of his shop, places his parchment ear against an out-of-tune grandfather's clock; a barber, with dry brush, lathers the cheekbones of an actor learning his role, studying the script with hollow sockets; a girl with a laughing skull milks the carcass of a heifer.

To be sure, many of the living want a fate after death different from their lot in life: the necropolis is crowded with big-game hunters, mezzosopranos, bankers, violinists, duchesses, courtesans, generals— more than the living city ever contained.

The job of accompanying the dead down below and arranging them in the desired place is assigned to a confraternity of hooded brothers. No one else has access to the Eusapia of the dead and everything known about it has been learned from them.

They say that the same confraternity exists among the dead and that it never fails to lend a hand; the hooded brothers, after death, will perform the same job in the other Eusapia; rumor has it that some of them are already dead but continue going up and down. In any case, this confraternity's authority in the Eusapia of the living is vast.

They say that every time they go below they find something changed in the lower Eusapia; the dead make innovations in their city; not many, but surely the fruit of sober reflection, not passing whims. From one year to the next, they say, the Eusapia of the dead becomes unrecognizable. And the living, to keep up with them, also want to do everything that the hooded brothers tell them about the novelties of the dead. So the Eusapia of the living has taken to copying its underground copy.

They say that this has not just now begun to happen: actually it was the dead who built the upper Eusapia, in the image of their city. They say that in the twin cities there is no longer any way of knowing who is alive and who is dead.

Translated by William Weaver

GABRIEL
GARCÍA
MÁRQUEZ

*G*ABRIEL GARCÍA MÁRQUEZ *(born 1928) is quite well-known, particularly since the award of the Nobel Prize for Literature in 1982. A Colombian writer who now makes his home in Mexico, he is famous for his remarkable novel,* One Hundred Years of Solitude *(1968), one of those rare works that achieve the status of a classic as well as great popularity almost upon publication. If there had been some question whether the magical-realist mode could be managed in a novel, this book resolved it. It sustains the difficult mix successfully, using the form of a family chronicle that is also the history of a mythical village, Macondo, modeled on the little town of Aracataca where the author grew up. Faulkner's influence is discernible in García Márquez's convolutions of time-scheme and syntax, but* One Hundred Years of Solitude *is one of those masterpieces, unique and inimitable, that change the course of literature.*

The mastery for which García Márquez is famous in that novel is equally apparent in his novellas and short stories. From the earliest examples to the most recent, his shorter fiction has displayed a willingness to mix the worlds of dream and waking, fable and fact, peasant superstition and civilized sophistication, fueled always by a narrative energy and a fundamental zest for life that transcend categories and conventions. "A Very Old Man With Enormous Wings" *(1968) provides a useful introduction to the way in which García Márquez works. Subtitled* "A Tale for Children," *it is indeed accessible to readers or listeners of all ages. Yet the more one considers its charm, wonder, and narrative force, the more one realizes that it will yield to no one attitude, no one explanation or point of view; it is as simple and mysterious as nature itself. What seems effortless here is more artful in its concealment of the skill of design and the style behind it.*

"Blacamán the Good, Vendor of Miracles" (1968) is one of this author's funniest performances, and its bravura descriptions and lists suggest the range of García Márquez's style; the sardonic eloquence of this story and its sweeping review of a fantastic career and an even more fantastic revenge give it a very different tone and flavor from "Very Old Man."

Readers who are discovering García Márquez through these stories will want to proceed to One Hundred Years, but they will also discover three collections of short stories—No One Writes to the Colonel (1968), Leaf Storm (from which our two selections were taken; 1972), and Innocent Erendira (1978)—and three other novels—The Autumn of the Patriarch (1976), In Evil Hour (an earlier work published in English in 1979), and Chronicle of a Death Foretold (1983). In all of them, García Márquez has been particularly well served by his English translator, Gregory Rabassa.

A Very Old Man
with Enormous
Wings

Gabriel García Márquez

A Tale for Children

O N THE third day of rain they had killed so many crabs inside the
house that Pelayo had to cross his drenched courtyard and
throw them into the sea, because the newborn child had a temperature
all night and they thought it was due to the stench. The world had been
sad since Tuesday. Sea and sky were a single ash-gray thing and the
sands of the beach, which on March nights glimmered like powdered
light, had become a stew of mud and rotten shellfish. The light was so
weak at noon that when Pelayo was coming back to the house after
throwing away the crabs, it was hard for him to see what it was that was
moving and groaning in the rear of the courtyard. He had to go very close
to see that it was an old man, a very old man, lying face down in the mud,
who, in spite of his tremendous efforts, couldn't get up, impeded by his
enormous wings.

Frightened by that nightmare, Pelayo ran to get Elisenda, his wife,
who was putting compresses on the sick child, and he took her to the
rear of the courtyard. They both looked at the fallen body with mute
stupor. He was dressed like a ragpicker. There were only a few faded

hairs left on his bald skull and very few teeth in his mouth, and his pitiful condition of a drenched great-grandfather had taken away any sense of grandeur he might have had. His huge buzzard wings, dirty and half-plucked, were forever entangled in the mud. They looked at him so long and so closely that Pelayo and Elisenda very soon overcame their surprise and in the end found him familiar. Then they dared speak to him, and he answered in an incomprehensible dialect with a strong sailor's voice. That was how they skipped over the inconvenience of the wings and quite intelligently concluded that he was a lonely castaway from some foreign ship wrecked by the storm. And yet, they called in a neighbor woman who knew everything about life and death to see him, and all she needed was one look to show them their mistake.

"He's an angel," she told them. "He must have been coming for the child, but the poor fellow is so old that the rain knocked him down."

On the following day everyone knew that a flesh-and-blood angel was held captive in Pelayo's house. Against the judgment of the wise neighbor woman, for whom angels in those times were the fugitive survivors of a celestial conspiracy, they did not have the heart to club him to death. Pelayo watched over him all afternoon from the kitchen, armed with his bailiff's club, and before going to bed he dragged him out of the mud and locked him up with the hens in the wire chicken coop. In the middle of the night, when the rain stopped, Pelayo and Elisenda were still killing crabs. A short time afterward the child woke up without a fever and with a desire to eat. Then they felt magnanimous and decided to put the angel on a raft with fresh water and provisions for three days and leave him to his fate on the high seas. But when they went out into the courtyard with the first light of dawn, they found the whole neighborhood in front of the chicken coop having fun with the angel, without the slightest reverence, tossing him things to eat through the openings in the wire as if he weren't a supernatural creature but a circus animal.

Father Gonzaga arrived before seven o'clock, alarmed at the strange news. By that time on-lookers less frivolous than those at dawn had already arrived and they were making all kinds of conjectures concerning the captive's future. The simplest among them thought that he should be named mayor of the world. Others of sterner mind felt that he should be promoted to the rank of five-star general in order to win all wars. Some visionaries hoped that he could be put to stud in order to implant on earth a race of winged wise men who could take charge of the universe. But Father Gonzaga, before becoming a priest, had been a robust woodcutter. Standing by the wire, he reviewed his catechism in an instant and asked them to open the door so that he could take a close look at that pitiful man who looked more like a huge decrepit hen among the fascinated chickens. He was lying in a corner drying his open wings in the sunlight among the fruit peels and breakfast leftovers that the early risers had thrown him. Alien to the impertinences of the world, he only lifted his antiquarian eyes and murmured something in his dialect when Father Gonzaga went into the chicken coop and said good morning to him in Latin. The parish priest had his first suspicion of an imposter when he saw that he did not understand the language of God or know how to greet His ministers. Then he noticed that seen close up he was much too human: he had an unbearable smell of the outdoors, the back side of his wings was strewn with parasites and his main feathers had been mistreated by terrestrial winds, and nothing about him measured up to the proud dignity of angels. Then he came out of the chicken coop and in a brief sermon warned the curious against the risks of being ingenuous. He reminded them that the devil had the bad habit of making use of carnival tricks in order to confuse the unwary. He argued that if wings were not the essential element in determining the difference between a hawk and an airplane, they were even less so in the recognition of angels. Nevertheless, he promised to write a letter to his bishop so that the latter would write to his primate so that the latter would write to the Supreme Pontiff in order to get the final verdict from the highest courts.

His prudence fell on sterile hearts. The news of the captive angel spread with such rapidity that after a few hours the courtyard had the bustle of a marketplace and they had to call in troops with fixed bayonets to disperse the mob that was about to knock the house down. Elisenda, her spine all twisted from sweeping up so much marketplace trash, then got the idea of fencing in the yard and charging five cents admission to see the angel.

The curious came from far away. A traveling carnival arrived with a flying acrobat who buzzed over the crowd several times, but no one paid any attention to him because his wings were not those of an angel but, rather, those of a sidereal bat. The most unfortunate invalids on earth came in search of health: a poor woman who since childhood had been counting her heartbeats and had run out of numbers; a Portuguese man who couldn't sleep because the noise of the stars disturbed him; a sleepwalker who got up at night to undo the things he had done while awake; and many others with less serious ailments. In the midst of that shipwreck disorder that made the earth tremble, Pelayo and Elisenda were happy with fatigue, for in less than a week they had crammed their rooms with money and the line of pilgrims waiting their turn to enter still reached beyond the horizon.

The angel was the only one who took no part in his own act. He spent his time trying to get comfortable in his borrowed nest, befuddled by the hellish heat of the oil lamps and sacramental candles that had been placed along the wire. At first they tried to make him eat some mothballs, which, according to the wisdom of the wise neighbor woman, were the food prescribed for angels. But he turned them down, just as he turned down the papal lunches that the penitents brought him, and they never found out whether it was because he was an angel or because he was an old man that in the end he ate nothing but eggplant mush. His only supernatural virtue seemed to be patience. Especially during the first days, when the hens pecked at him, searching for the stellar parasites that proliferated in his wings, and the cripples pulled out feathers to touch their defective parts with, and even the most merciful threw stones at him, trying to get him to rise so they could see him standing. The only time they succeeded in arousing him was when they burned his side with an iron for branding steers, for he had been motionless for so many hours that they thought he was dead. He awoke with a start, ranting in his hermetic language and with tears in his eyes, and he flapped his wings a couple of times, which brought on a whirlwind of chicken dung and lunar dust and a gale of panic that did not seem to be of this world. Although many thought that his reaction had been one not of rage but of pain, from then on they were careful not to annoy him, because the majority understood that his passivity was not that of a hero taking his ease but that of a cataclysm in repose.

Father Gonzaga held back the crowd's frivolity with formulas of maidservant inspiration while awaiting the arrival of a final judgment on the nature of the captive. But the mail from Rome showed no sense of urgency. They spent their time finding out if the prisoner had a navel, if his dialect had any connection with Aramaic, how many times he could fit on the head of a pin, or whether he wasn't just a Norwegian with wings. Those meager letters might have come and gone until the end of time if a providential event had not put an end to the priest's tribulations.

It so happened that during those days, among so many other carnival attractions, there arrived in town the traveling show of the woman who had been changed into a spider for having disobeyed her parents. The admission to see her was not only less than the admission to see the angel, but people were permitted to ask her all manner of questions about her absurd state and to examine her up and down so that no one would ever doubt the truth of her horror. She was a frightful tarantula the size of a ram and with the head of a sad maiden. What was most heart-rending, however, was not her outlandish shape but the sincere affliction with which she recounted the details of her misfortune. While still practically a child she had sneaked out of her parents' house to go to a dance, and while she was coming back through the woods after having danced all night without permission, a fearful thunderclap rent the sky in two and through the crack came the lightning bolt of brimstone that changed her into a spider. Her only nourishment came from the meatballs that charitable souls chose to toss into her mouth. A spectacle like that, full of so much human truth and with such a fearful lesson, was bound to defeat without even trying that of a haughty angel who scarcely deigned to look at mortals. Besides, the few miracles attributed to the angel showed a certain mental disorder, like the blind man who didn't recover his sight but grew three new teeth, or the paralytic who didn't get to walk but almost won the lottery, and the leper whose sores sprouted sunflowers. Those consolation miracles, which were more like mocking fun, had already ruined the angel's reputation when the woman who had been changed into a spider finally crushed him completely. That was how Father Gonzaga was cured forever of his insomnia and Pelayo's courtyard went back to being as empty as during the time it had rained for three days and crabs walked through the bedrooms.

The owners of the house had no reason to lament. With the money they saved they built a two-story mansion with balconies and gardens and high netting so that crabs wouldn't get in during the winter, and with iron bars on the windows so that angels wouldn't get in. Pelayo also set up a rabbit warren close to town and gave up his job as bailiff for good, and Elisenda bought some satin pumps with high heels and many dresses of iridescent silk, the kind worn on Sunday by the most desirable women in those times. The chicken coop was the only thing that didn't receive any attention. If they washed it down with creolin and burned tears of myrrh inside it every so often, it was not in homage to the angel but to drive away the dungheap stench that still hung everywhere like a ghost and was turning the new house into an old one. At first, when the child learned to walk, they were careful that he not get too close to the chicken coop. But then they began to lose their fears and got used to the smell, and before the child got his second teeth he'd gone inside the chicken coop to play, where the wires were falling apart. The angel was no less standoffish with him than with other mortals, but he tolerated the most ingenious infamies with the patience of a dog who had no illusions. They both came down with chicken pox at the same time. The doctor who took care of the child couldn't resist the temptation to listen to the angel's heart, and he found so much whistling in the heart and so many sounds in his kidneys that it seemed impossible for him to be alive. What surprised him most, however, was the logic of his wings. They seemed so natural on that completely human organism that he couldn't understand why other men didn't have them too.

When the child began school it had been some time since the sun and rain had caused the collapse of the chicken coop. The angel went dragging himself about here and there like a stray dying man. They would drive him out of the bedroom with a broom and a moment later find him in the kitchen. He seemed to be in so many places at the same time that they grew to think that he'd been duplicated, that he was reproducing himself all through the house, and the exasperated and unhinged Elisenda shouted that it was awful living in that hell full of angels. He could scarcely eat and his antiquarian eyes had also become so foggy that he went about bumping into posts. All he had left were the bare cannulae of his last feathers. Pelayo threw a blanket over him and extended him the charity of letting him sleep in the shed, and only then did they notice that he had a temperature at night, and was delirious with the tongue twisters of an old Norwegian. That was one of the few times they became alarmed, for they thought he was going to die and not even the wise neighbor woman had been able to tell them what to do with dead angels.

And yet he not only survived his worst winter, but seemed improved with the first sunny days. He remained motionless for several days in the farthest corner of the courtyard, where no one would see him, and at the beginning of December some large, stiff feathers began to grow on his wings, the feathers of a scarecrow, which looked more like another misfortune of decrepitude. But he must have known the reason for those changes, for he was quite careful that no one should notice them, that no one should hear the sea chanteys that he sometimes sang under the stars. One morning Elisenda was cutting some bunches of onions for lunch when a wind that seemed to come from the high seas blew into the kitchen. Then she went to the window and caught the angel in his first attempts at flight. They were so clumsy that his fingernails opened a furrow in the vegetable patch and he was on the point of knocking the shed down with the ungainly flapping that slipped on the light and couldn't get a grip on the air. But he did manage to gain altitude. Elisenda let out a sigh of relief, for herself and for him, when she saw him pass over the last houses, holding himself up in some way with the risky flapping of a senile vulture. She kept watching him even when she was through cutting the onions and she kept on watching until it was no longer possible for her to see him, because then he was no longer an annoyance in her life but an imaginary dot on the horizon of the sea.

Translated by Gregory Rabassa

Blacamán the
Good, Vendor of
Miracles

Gabriel García Márquez

FROM THE FIRST Sunday I saw him he reminded me of a bullring
mule, with his white suspenders that were backstitched with
gold thread, his rings with colored stones on every finger, and his braids
of jingle bells, standing on a table by the docks of Santa María del Darien
in the middle of the flasks of specifics and herbs of consolation that he
prepared himself and hawked through the towns along the Caribbean
with his wounded shout, except that at that time he wasn't trying to sell
any of that Indian mess but was asking him to bring him a real snake so
that he could demonstrate on his own flesh an antidote he had invented,
the only infallible one, ladies and gentlemen, for the bites of serpents,
tarantulas, and centipedes plus all manner of poisonous mammals.
Someone who seemed quite impressed by his determination managed to
get a bushmaster of the worst kind somewhere (the snake that kills by
poisoning the respiration) and brought it to him in a bottle, and he
uncorked it with such eagerness that we all throught he was going to eat
it, but as soon as the creature felt itself free it jumped out of the bottle
and struck him on the neck, leaving him right then and there without any
wind for his oratory and with barely enough time to take the antidote,
and the vest-pocket pharmacist tumbled down into the crowd and rolled

about on the ground, his huge body wasted away as if he had nothing inside of it, but laughing all the while with all of his gold teeth. The hubbub was so great that a cruiser from the north that had been docked there for twenty years on a goodwill mission declared a quarantine so that the snake poison wouldn't get on board, and the people who were sanctifying Palm Sunday came out of church with their blessed palms, because no one wanted to miss the show of the poisoned man, who had already begun to puff up with the air of death and was twice as fat as he'd been before, giving off a froth of gall through his mouth and panting through his pores, but still laughing with so much life that the jingle bells tinkled all over his body. The swelling snapped the laces of his leggings and the seams of his clothes, his fingers grew purple from the pressure of the rings, he turned the color of venison in brine, and from his rear end came a hint of the last moments of death, so that everyone who had seen a person bitten by a snake knew that he was rotting away before dying and that he would be so crumpled up that they'd have to pick him up with a shovel to put him into a sack, but they also thought that even in his sawdust state he'd keep on laughing. It was so incredible that the marines came up on deck to take colored pictures of him with long-distance lenses, but the women who'd come out of church blocked their intentions by covering the dying man with a blanket and laying blessed palms on top of him, some because they didn't want the soldiers to profane the body with their Adventist instruments, others because they were afraid to continue looking at that idolater who was ready to die dying with laughter, and others because in that way perhaps his soul at least would not be poisoned. Everybody had given him up for dead when he pushed aside the palms with one arm, still half-dazed and not completely recovered from the bad moment he'd had, but he set the table up without anyone's help, climbed on it like a crab once more, and there he was again, shouting that his antidote was nothing but the hand of God in a bottle, as we had all seen with our own eyes, but it only cost two cuartillos because he hadn't invented it as an item for sale but for the good of all humanity, and as soon as he said that, ladies and gentlemen, I only ask you not to crowd around, there's enough for everybody.

They crowded around, of course, and they did well to do so, because in the end there wasn't enough for everybody. Even the admiral from the cruiser bought a bottle, convinced by him that it was also good for the poisoned bullets of anarchists, and the sailors weren't satisfied with just taking colored pictures of him up on the table, pictures they had been unable to take of him dead, but they had him signing autographs until his arm was twisted with cramps. It was getting to be night and only the most perplexed of us were left by the docks when with his eyes he searched for someone with the look of an idiot to help him put the bottles away, and naturally he spotted me. It was like the look of destiny, not just mine, but his too, for that was more than a century ago and we both remember it as if it had been last Sunday. What happened was that we were putting his circus drugstore into that trunk with purple straps that looked more like a scholar's casket, when he must have noticed some light inside of me that he hadn't seen in me before, because he asked me in a surly way who are you, and I answered that I was an orphan on both sides whose papa hadn't died, and he gave out with laughter that was louder than what he had given with the poison and then he asked me what do you do for a living, and I answered that I didn't do anything except stay alive, because nothing else was worth the trouble, and still weeping with laughter he asked me what science in the world do you most want to learn, and that was the only time I answered the truth without any fooling, I wanted to be a fortune-teller, and then he didn't laugh again but told me as if thinking out loud that I didn't need much for that because I already had the hardest thing to learn, which was my face of an idiot. That same night he spoke to my father and for one real and two cuartillos and a deck of cards that foretold adultery he bought me forevermore.

That was what Blacamán was like, Blacamán the Bad, because I'm Blacamán the Good. He was capable of convincing an astronomer that the month of February was nothing but a herd of invisible elephants, but when his good luck turned on him he became a heart-deep brute. In his days of glory he had been an embalmer of viceroys, and they say that he gave them faces with such authority that for many years they went on governing better than when they were alive, and that no one dared bury them until he gave them back their dead-man look, but his prestige was ruined by the invention of an endless chess game that drove a chaplain mad and brought on two illustrious suicides, and so he was on the decline, from an interpreter of dreams to a birthday hypnotist, from an extractor of molars by suggestion to a marketplace healer; therefore, at the time we met, people were already looking at him askance, even the freebooters. We drifted along with our trick stand and life was an eternal uncertainty as we tried to sell escape suppositories that turned smugglers transparent, furtive drops that baptized wives threw into the soup to instill the fear of God in Dutch husbands, and anything you might want to buy of your own free will, ladies and gentlemen, because this isn't a command, it's advice, and after all, happiness isn't an obligation either. Nevertheless, as much as we died with laughter at his witticisms, the truth is that it was quite hard for us to manage enough to eat, and his last hope was founded on my vocation as a fortune-teller. He shut me up in the sepulchral trunk disguised as a Japanese and bound with starboard chains so that I could attempt to foretell what I could while he disemboweled the grammar book looking for the best way to convince the world of my new science, and here, ladies and gentlemen, you have this child tormented by Ezequiel's glowworms, and those of you who've been standing there with faces of disbelief, let's see if you dare ask him when you're going to die, but I was never able even to guess what day it was at that time, so he gave up on me as a soothsayer because the drowsiness of digestion disturbs your prediction gland, and after whacking me over the head for good luck, he decided to take me to my father and get his money back. But at that time he happened to find a practical application for the electricity of suffering, and he set about building a sewing machine that ran connected by cupping glasses to the part of the body where there was a pain. Since I spent the night moaning over the whacks he'd given me to conjure away misfortune, he had to keep me on as the one who could test his invention, and so our return was delayed and he was getting back his good humor until the machine worked so well that it not only sewed better than a novice nun but also embroidered birds or astromelias according to the position and intensity of the pain. That was what we were up to, convinced of our triumph over bad luck, when the news reached us that in Philadelphia the commander of the cruiser had tried to repeat the experiment with the antidote and that he'd been changed into a glob of admiral jelly in front of his staff.

He didn't laugh again for a long time. We fled through Indian passes and the more lost we became, the clearer the news reached us that the marines had invaded the country under the pretext of exterminating yellow fever and were going about beheading every inveterate or eventual potter they found in their path, and not only the natives, out of precaution, but also the Chinese, for distraction, the Negroes, from habit, and the Hindus, because they were snake charmers, and then they wiped out the flora and fauna and all the mineral wealth they were able to because their specialists in our affairs had taught them that the people along the Caribbean had the ability to change their nature in order to confuse gringos. I couldn't understand where that fury came from or why we were so frightened until we found ourselves safe and sound in the eternal winds of La Guajira, and only then did he have the courage to confess to me that his antidote was nothing but rhubarb and turpentine and that he'd paid a drifter two cuartillos to bring him that bushmaster with all the poison gone. We stayed in the ruins of a colonial mission, deluded by the hope that some smugglers would pass, because they were men to be trusted and the only ones capable of venturing out under the mercurial sun of those salt flats. At first we ate smoked salamanders and flowers from the ruins and we still had enough spirit to laugh when we tried to eat his boiled leggings, but finally we even ate the water cobwebs from the cisterns and only then did we realize how much we missed the world. Since I didn't know of any recourse against death at that time, I simply lay down to wait for it where it would hurt me least, while he was delirious remembering a woman who was so tender that she could pass through walls just by sighing, but that contrived recollection was also a trick of his genius to fool death with lovesickness. Still, at the moment we should have died, he came to me more alive than ever and spent the whole night watching over my agony, thinking with such great strength that I still haven't been able to tell whether what was whistling through the ruins was the wind or his thoughts, and before dawn he told me with the same voice and the same determination of past times that now he knew the truth, that I was the one who had twisted up his luck again, so get your pants ready, because the same way as you twisted it up for me, you're going to straighten it out.

That was when I lost the little affection I had for him. He took off the last rags I had on, rolled me up in some barbed wire, rubbed rock salt on the sores, put me in brine from my own waters, and hung me by the ankles for the sun to flay me, and he kept on shouting that all that mortification wasn't enough to pacify his persecutors. Finally he threw me to rot in my own misery inside the penance dungeon where the colonial missionaries regenerated heretics, and with the perfidy of a ventriloquist, which he still had more than enough of, he began to imitate the voices of edible animals, the noise of ripe beets, and the sound of fresh springs so as to torture me with illusion that I was dying of indigence in the midst of paradise. When the smugglers finally supplied him, he came down to the dungeon to give me something to eat so that I wouldn't die, but then he made me pay for that charity by pulling out my nails with pliers and filing my teeth down with a grindstone, and my only consolation was the wish that life would give me time and the good fortune to be quit of so much infamy with even worse martyrdoms. I myself was surprised that I could resist the plague of my own putrefaction and he kept throwing the leftovers of his meals onto me and tossed pieces of rotten lizards and hawks into the corners so that the air of the dungeon would end up poisoning me. I don't know how much time had passed when he brought me the carcass of a rabbit in order to show me that he preferred throwing it away to rot rather than giving it to me to eat, but my patience only went so far and all I had left was rancor, so I grabbed the rabbit by the ears and flung it against the wall with the illusion that it was he and not the animal that was going to explode, and then it happened, as if in a dream. The rabbit not only revived with a squeal of fright, but came back to my hands, hopping through the air.

That was how my great life began. Since then I've gone through the world drawing the fever out of malaria victims for two pesos, visioning blind men for four-fifty, draining the water from dropsy victims for eighteen, putting cripples back together for twenty pesos if they were that way from birth, for twenty-two if they were that way because of an accident or a brawl, for twenty-five if they were that way because of wars, earthquakes, infantry landings, or any other kind of public calamity, taking care of the common sick at wholesale according to a special arrangement, madmen according to their theme, children at half price, and idiots out of gratitude, and who dares say that I'm not a philanthropist, ladies and gentlemen, and now, yes, sir, commandant of the twentieth fleet, order your boys to take down the barricades and let suffering humanity pass, lepers to the left, epileptics to the right, cripples where they won't get in the way, and there in the back the least urgent cases, only please don't crowd in on me because then I won't be responsible if the sicknesses get all mixed up and people are cured of what they don't have, and keep the music playing until the brass boils, and the rockets firing until the angels burn, and the liquor flowing until ideas are killed, and bring on the wenches and the acrobats, the butchers and the photographers, and all at my expense, ladies and gentlemen, for here ends the evil fame of the Blacamáns and the universal tumult starts. That's how I go along putting them to sleep with the techniques of a congressman in case my judgment fails and some turn out worse than they were before on me. The only thing I don't do is revive the dead, because as soon as they open their eyes they're murderous with rage at the one who disturbed their state, and when it's all done, those who don't commit suicide die again of disillusionment. At first I was pursued by a group of wise men investigating the legality of my industry, and when they were convinced, they threatened me with the hell of Simon Magus and recommended a life of penitence so that I could get to be a saint, but I answered them, with no disrespect for their authority, that it was precisely along those lines that I had started. The truth is that I'd gain nothing by being a saint after being dead, an artist is what I am, and the only thing I want is to be alive so I can keep going along at donkey level in his six-cylinder touring car I bought from the marines' consul, with this Trinidadian chauffeur who was a baritone in the New Orleans pirates' opera, with my genuine silk shirts, my Oriental lotions, my topaz teeth, my flat straw hat, and my bicolored buttons, sleeping without an alarm clock, dancing with beauty queens, and leaving them hallucinated with my dictionary rhetoric, and with no flutter in my spleen if some Ash Wednesday my faculties wither away, because in order to go on with this life of a minister, all I need is my idiot face, and I have more than enough with the string of shops I own from here to beyond the sunset, where the same tourists who used to go around collecting from us through the admiral, now go stumbling after my autographed pictures, almanacs with my love poetry, medals with my profile, bits of my clothing, and all of that without the glorious plague of spending all day and all night sculpted in equestrian marble and shat on by swallows like the fathers of our country.

It's a pity that Blacamán the Bad can't repeat this story so that people will see that there's nothing invented in it. The last time anyone saw him in this world he'd lost even the studs of his former splendor, and his soul was a shambles and his bones in disorder from the rigors of the desert, but he still had enough jingle bells left to reappear that Sunday on the docks of Santa Maria del Darien with his eternal sepulchral trunk, except that this time he wasn't trying to sell any antidotes, but was asking in a voice cracking with emotion for the marines to shoot him in a public spectacle so that he could demonstrate on his own flesh the life-restoring properties of this supernatural creature, ladies and gentlemen, and even though you have more than enough right not to believe me after suffering so long from my evil tricks as a deceiver and falsifier, I swear on the bones of my mother that this proof today is nothing from the other world, merely the humble truth, and in case you have any doubts left, notice that I'm not laughing now the way I used to, but holding back a desire to cry. How convincing he must have been, unbuttoning his shirt, his eyes drowning with tears, and giving himself mule kicks on his heart to indicate the best place for death, and yet the marines didn't dare shoot, out of fear that the Sunday crowd would discover their loss of prestige. Someone who may not have forgotten the blacamanipulations of past times managed, no one knew how, to get and bring him in a can enough *barbasco* roots to bring to the surface all the corvinas in the Caribbean, and he opened it with great desire, as if he really was going to eat them, and, indeed, he did eat them, ladies and gentlemen, but please don't be moved or pray for the repose of my soul, because this death is nothing but a visit. That time he was so honest that he didn't break into operatic death rattles, but got off the table like a crab, looked on the ground for the most worthy place to lie down after some hesitation, and from there he looked at me as he would have at a mother and exhaled his last breath in his own arms, still holding back his manly tears all twisted up by the tetanus of eternity. That was the only time, of course, that my science failed me. I put him in that trunk of premonitory size where there was room for him laid out. I had a requiem mass sung for him which cost me fifty four-peso doubloons, because the officiant was dressed in gold and there were also three seated bishops. I had the mausoleum of an emperor built for him on a hill exposed to the best seaside weather, with a chapel just for him and an iron plaque on which there was written in Gothic capitals HERE LIES BLACAMÁN THE DEAD, BADLY CALLED THE BAD,DECEIVER OF MARINES AND VICTIM OF SCIENCE, and when those honors were sufficient for me to do justice to his virtues, I began to get my revenge for his infamy, and then I revived him inside the armored tomb and left him there rolling about in horror. That was long before the fire ants devoured Santa María del Darién, but the mausoleum is still intact on the hill in the shadow of the dragons that climb up to sleep in the Atlantic winds, and every time I pass through here I bring him an automobile load of roses and my heart pains with pity for his virtues, but then I put my ear to the plaque to hear him weeping in the ruins of the crumbling trunk, and if by chance he has died again, I bring him back to life once more, for the beauty of the punishment is that he will keep on living in his tomb as long as I'm alive, that is, forever.

Translated by Gregory Rabassa

ROBERT
ESCARPIT

*R*OBERT ESCARPIT *(born 1918), a French writer and educator, is the founder and director of the Institute of Literature and Mass Artistic Techniques at the University of Bordeaux. Escarpit is preoccupied with the theoretical problems of communication; for many years he has tried to establish programs to raise linguistic consciousness in general, specializing in improving methods of worldwide distribution of books. Only two of his more than forty volumes have been translated into English and these happen to be technical, sociological studies on reading. But Escarpit, who is a great admirer of British literature, has also written a good deal of fiction, including two novels in a magical-realist vein, Honorius Pape (1967) and Les Somnanbidules (1971). In addition, he has published a short-story collection, The Cloud Maker (1969), which contains nine magical-realist gems, followed by a manifesto on what Escarpit has called "the fantastic," a term very close to our notion of magical realism.*

Escarpit feels one must investigate foreign territories in order to discover what truly lies at the heart of one's own territory. He favors exploration through revolt, disruption, and disorientation. The fantastic can be reduced, for Escarpit, to a question of perception, so in his stories he concerns himself with all the classic problems of dream versus reality, discussions on space and time, and even the true nature of language in representing one's imaginative processes. He claims that the infinite richness of reality is ready to be viewed if one actively attempts to break out of overly-structured environments and dogmatic systems of thinking. Escarpit gives us some simple instructions for creating magical realism: "Place an object under the assault of your imagination and little by little, it changes its form, without entirely dissolving, and reveals unknown dimensions."

In the title story of The Cloud Maker, which has been specially translated for this anthology, Jean-Marc is torn between the dangerous liberty of his new discoveries and his more conventional, previous existence. The cloud maker is offered a synthetic world, beyond the norms of society, where he becomes enticed by the overwhelming intoxication of a greater reality. Whatever the outcome of his stories, Escarpit allows the reader exhilarating glimpses into fantastic new vistas of perception.

Cloud Maker

Robert Escarpit

YOU ASK me if I knew him, monsieur? Yes, I knew him. He arrived here right after the war in July 1945. Right away, he got interested in making clouds. The factory wasn't as big as it is now, but in those days we worked for the army and work wasn't scarce. We had twenty workers for the orders from the weather bureau alone.

And then it stopped short with the armistice. Old man Bouhut, Monsieur Francois, was getting old and didn't have a son to take over the business. One by one the young men left to work at the cellulose factory, just built on the other side of the Leyre. Soon only four remained, die-hards too simple-minded to know how to do anything else.

"Pierrot," old man Bouhut said to me one day, "I have to close up shop. The fine cloud has seen its time. I don't have any more orders."

Imagine what a blow that was to me. I had worked in the factory for thirty-two years. I had been apprenticed to Léon Bouhut, the grandfather of Monsieur Francois. He had lived to be eighty and used to teach me the names of the clouds with the smoke from his pipe. In two puffs, he made you such a cumulo-nimbus, monsieur, that you could hear the thunder.

"Boss," I said, "you can't do this. Your family has made clouds for five generations. And there was already a workshop here in the times of the kings. Clouds are our life. How can you think of closing?"

"Then I must sell. I can't do it any more. Find me a buyer, Pierrot. I will give him a good price."

"Yes, sir!"

That was easily said. Where could I find someone who would be interested in the business? Cloud making is a calling, and a rare calling.

I'm talking about making clouds by hand like in the old days with the real vapor from the moors. Now, there is a common market. They import the big clouds from Holland or England, and then trim them by machine. To think that just last week, the fog they sent over Bordeaux for the opening of the Fair was all yellow and sticky. It stank like fuel oil, a lady's cigarette, and I don't know what else.

In short, I was fit to be tied. Well, it was that evening that they both arrived. They got off their motor bike in front of the Post Hotel where I was having an aperitif and they asked for a room. They were dressed in pants like mechanic overalls and sweaters with turned-down collars. Hers was canary yellow and looked so good you would have thought she was a model out of "Marie-Claire."

In fact, she was a model, as she explained later. And he was a fashion designer. It seems theirs was a terrible business. People just don't know. When you work not only with your hands but also with your heart, your mind, and your eyes, like us the ancient cloud makers, you exhaust the man in you, believe me.

They took the room by the orchard because it's the quietest. No one knew if they were married, mind you, but they were very much in love, that was obvious.

Danièle—she was Danièle and he was Jean-Marc, Jean-Marc Leblier—was very worried about Jean-Marc's health.

"There's no noise at all? The phone is on the other side of the house? And the newspaper? Above all, no morning paper. I'll go out to get breakfast myself. Don't wake us before. Absolute quiet is necessary, you see. No cares or concerns. The autumn collection killed this man."

It was the following Sunday that I met him fishing. There were a few roaches in the Tuque pond. But that day they weren't biting. After pulling in his line twelve times with no luck, he put his pole beside him, filled a pipe, and just to say something, showed me a small nimbus that flowed in the sky.

"Looks like rain."

"Not a chance," I answered. "It's a specimen from the Sainte-Foy-la-Grande factory. They use the dry method there. Their clouds never drip. If it was one of ours, I wouldn't be able to say. At our factory we use the wet method."

When he learned I was in clouds, it excited him. He didn't even know men make clouds. He thought they were natural. Of couse, there are some natural ones, but they're easy to recognize. They are wild. If everyone ordered clouds from qualified manufacturers, there would be fewer ruined summers and fewer holocausts. But people don't know.

I took out my pipe and showed him the basics. It isn't sorcery, but you must have the knack. And he had it, the son of a gun had it. At the end of an hour, he was making small cumulus clouds pretty as anything, not very successful from a meteorologist's point of view, but with the touch of an artist. Me, I'm only an artisan. My clouds are solid, it's true. You look at them and take out an umbrella. But his, they were poetry.

"Danièle, come see what I am making," he shouted.

"I see," she answered. "You're in the clouds. That's not new."

"Look at how pretty they are."

"Because they are small. Clouds are like cats."

"They don't scratch."

"No, but they make shadows."

He came to the factory the next day. We were just finishing the last order: some Canaletto-style clouds for the Venetian feast in the Hossegor municipality.

"Why Canaletto?" asked Jean-Marc. "Certainly Italian clouds are beautiful enough by themselves. Those from Venice are like schools of flying fish in the sky. Ones from Florence look like cotton flowers. As for Roman clouds, they are plump and bouncy like cherubs' bottoms."

Old man Bouhut laughed wholeheartedly.

"Monsieur Leblier, I'm afraid that your descriptions are not compatible with the norms of the national weather bureau. We generally work for public administrations, you know. In clouds, there's hardly a private clientele."

"And why not? It's a matter of fashion. Don't you think, Danièle? I see it all clearly. The presentation of spring clouds at Megève, the winter collection in Sologne...as for trends, we have all that's necessary: cumulus in cauliflower, in a bobbin, in a ball, in whipped cream...and the colors! We can revolutionize the range of fabrics, if we look for the harmony of the heavens...Calm Morning, a housecoat, a light drapery with the throat of a pigeon and a slate in spangled silk, with the altostratus of daybreak and a tuft of white cirrus clouds."

"And an infarct for you," said Danièle dryly.

"Infarct?" asked old man Bouhut. "That's not the name of a cloud."

"You see, Danièle? There is no danger. It was Paris that was killing me. Here, I would work in the open air, I would work the air itself. It's magnificent! Say, I will make you a dress with this mauve mist that rises from the heath, and from dewdrops disguised as diamonds."

Jean-Marc bought the factory for more than old man Bouhut had hoped to get for it. It wasn't easy in the beginning. The four workers still remained, but we weren't used to this kind of work, and Jean-Marc didn't let us get away with anything. You can't believe how demanding he was. In vain we tried to tell him that clouds weren't tissue, but he made us re-do the same cirro-stratus twelve times, twenty times just because the curve was a half degree too much.

We got along just the same somehow because Danièle with her connections found a little here, a little there, particularly some orders from Americans who wanted to send back a piece of the French sky to Texas or Nevada. We even made a complete storm with cumulo-nimbus clouds at nine thousand meters for an Arabian potentate whose subjects had never seen rain.

Success did not really come until people started traveling after 1950. It started in Spain. We had two models: a Greek sky which Jean-Marc and Danièle had brought back from Toledo, and a seeding of little good-weather clouds, Costa Brava-style. Then there was the famous Italian series, that Jean-Marc had described on his first visit, and then the Greek clouds crushed in white marble, the fogs of Bosphorus, the thick khamsin clouds and the sirocco with built-in heat, the nimbuses that skim the North Sea and the Baltic. Everyone wanted to take their vacation clouds home.

It was at that time that the Lafayette Galleries showed their line of clouds on the eighth floor. They introduced their collection and believe me, they were mobbed.

The factory grew steadily. Most of the old workers returned from the cellulose factory. We also had pattern markers, colorists, weathermen, and engineers. But for the finished product, we always came back to the die-hards.

"Without Pierrot," Jean-Marc used to say, "the clouds would simply be smoke."

"They are smoke," answered Danièle, "and you smoke too much."

She was right. Jean-Marc was overworking. Day and night, he would only leave the assay office to go to the testing ground in the clearing at Boudique or to Paris to negotiate a contract. Danièle used to cry often in secret. I did what I could to cheer her up.

"You mustn't be upset, Madame Danièle, it's just when clouds interest you it's difficult to think of anything else at all, but Monsieur Leblier loves you all the same, listen to old Pierrot."

"What's it to me if he loves me if he's loony over his clouds? In the past when we came here, it was the patterns of the collections that filled his head. He used to design dresses while he was eating, sleeping, dreaming, and making love. I thought that was finished and now it starts all over with his clouds. Like this afternoon I was sunbathing in the garden. I shouted to him to make something to shade my head. He sent a huge black nimbus that burst right over me, soaking me to the bone. It seems it was an experimental model."

"Yes, I know. It's 'Sad Sunday.' It goes with a Lanvin perfume made from the dead leaves of withered flowers. There are some people who love it."

"Well, not me! I like the sun. A cloud here and there is okay, but clouds that hang on the walls of my bedroom, clouds that invade my kitchen and dampen everything we eat, no, no, no, and no! Do you think that it's pleasant to live with a man who always has a fumarole or two over his head? Haven't you noticed?"

Of course, I had noticed but I couldn't tell her what I thought about it. Jean-Marc was slowly intoxicating himself. Clouds are worse than alcohol. A cloud maker who takes a liking to it is like a bartender who has an aperitif with his clients.

When you're worried, when you're tired, you can't imagine how good it is to have your head in the clouds. You feel light, content, unconcerned about everything. But after returning to earth, it's another story. The clouds stick to you, they swell, they freeze, they crush you. You are lucky if the thunder claps and relieves you for a moment. But as soon as the calm returns, you begin all over again to make your clouds.

I often used to surprise Jean-Marc in his office, his face hidden by a shred of fog or his gaze lost in a curl of mist. As soon as he noticed my presence, he would hurriedly start up the fan, but I wasn't fooled.

"Monsieur," I would say to him, "you're in a bad way. Think of Madame Danièle."

"That's just who I am thinking about, Pierrot. I have discovered a wonderful world in clouds, and I'd like to take her there with me."

"Do you think she wants to go?"

"Yes, when I can show her what waits there for both of us. Look at this, Pierrot."

It was an ordinary glass jar like a five-pint bottle, but the light vapor which floated in it resembled nothing I'd ever seen before. Somehow, it had both transparency and thickness, if you can follow me. You couldn't say it had a hue, but things took on different colors through it, more lifelike and at the same time elusive, as if between two hues. The shapes would change too. You recognized the closest object on the other side of the jar, but beyond you guessed rather than saw the lines, shimmering curves very far off, farther than the walls of the office.

"That's a nifty one, monsieur," I said. "What's it made of?"

"To tell the truth, I don't really know. It's made of elements I collected around me. Chemically, it's only air with perhaps a slight ionization."

"Hey, that could be devilishly volatile, that thing-a-ma-jig. You'll have trouble controlling its boundaries."

"I think I've found a way of restricting the expansion, Pierrot. We will test it next Sunday at the Boudique clearing and I'll really find out whether my clouds can delight Danièle."

The following Sunday was a beautiful fall day with a sparkling golden sky, the kind of day you spend hunting wood pigeons, the kind that makes cloud makers want to close up shop. I took the jeep to the factory and loaded up the equipment, without forgetting the respirators. Despite all they say about clouds not being dangerous, you never know what impurities the present-day dealers are capable of sticking in the raw materials.

When I arrived at the Lebliers, they were just finishing breakfast in the garden and right away I felt that something was wrong. You may not believe me, but on this clear morning there was an enormous cloud spreading quickly overhead, already turning into an anvil in the upper layers of the sky. By the time I stopped the car, the tornado burst forth, right at the corner of the garden. Danièle fled into the house crying.

"I don't understand what happened," said Jean-Marc. "When we got up, everything was going well, and I don't know whether it was the smoke from my cigarette or the toast that I burned, but this cloud formed over us so quickly that I couldn't control it. It seemed like every word and gesture made it grow bigger. Danièle was enraged and we got into an argument. It's absurd."

"I told you, monsieur. You shouldn't play with clouds. Do you still insist on your experiment?"

"More than ever, Pierrot. Let's go."

We went to the testing grounds. Two and a half liters of fog isn't much of anything. We decided on a half-acre grove of pine trees. I had framed it well with wind tunnels, but I didn't expect what was going to happen.

So we arrived and Jean-Marc advanced to the middle of the pines, twenty-year-old trees that had just been tapped. The undergrowth was sparse: just a few ferns and a little heather in flower. Jean-Marc looked around smiling, signaled me to start the wind tunnels to isolate the testing ground, and pop, off went the top of the glass jar.

It didn't even take ten seconds! All of a sudden there was the fog invading the copse and wiping it out. . . . I looked and tried to understand what was going on. In front of me I still saw the first row of pines, much clearer than before; I don't know how to tell you this, but everything was transparent, just like in the bottle I saw only fleeing shapes and changing colors. I approached fearfully. I could make out the ferns, but they were huge, bigger than forty-year-old pine trees. In the direction of the heather, I saw giant violet flames, but they were far off, very far off. . . and the copse wasn't even one hundred meters deep. What really frightened me was that I could no longer see Jean-Marc, who was right there before me, within range of my voice. I called:

"Boss, can you hear me?"

Perhaps you don't know the silence of the forest, especially in the fall when the animals hibernate, when each acorn falling from an oak tree, each pine cone dropping, is heard all through the underbrush.

"Boss!" I shouted. "Answer me."

For a single moment, I believe I heard something like a far-off cry, very high, higher than the trees. But suddenly the breeze picked up and the noise it made grazing the peaks of the pines swept away the silence. I also saw something white in the fog like a screech owl hunting with its great wings outspread.

Then I felt panic overcome me and I rushed to the jeep to cut off the wind tunnels. At that moment, Danièle stepped into the clearing from her four-horsepower car. She reached me out of breath.

"Where is Jean-Marc?"

"In the copse, Madame. He can't have gone very far."

I flipped the switch and the wind tunnel stopped. Then the gusts of wind were swallowed up in the undergrowth. The freed fog was diluted, stretched out; in no time it was all around us. Danièle began to run toward the trees, but scarcely had she gone a few steps when she grew dizzy and fell. As for me, I felt I was hallucinating.

Fortunately I had the respirators. I forced hers on and held her to the ground until I thought the danger was passed. She struggled, cried, and scratched, but Old Pierrot held on tight.

It took a half hour for the wind to purify the atmosphere completely. The copse resumed its normal appearance. We ran through it in all directions. Nothing had changed. We even found the jar, but we never found Jean-Marc.

We scoured the woods. For eight days, the police searched with helicopters, firemen with jeeps, the Civil Department of Bridges and Highways with their bulldozers. They drained all the estuaries, sounding all the deep water.

There are some who talk about the swamp of Biganon, but it's twenty kilometers away and you couldn't drown a mongrel there. No, the real truth is that Jean-Marc was devoured by the cloud he had made. This isn't the first time that this had happened, all the cloud makers will tell you that, but perhaps it's the last since there will never be another like Jean-Marc.

Madame Danièle sold the factory to foreigners, a holding company. These men work just for money. Ha! perhaps it will be their money that eats them.

Translated by Keith Hollaman

DONALD
BARTHELME

DONALD BARTHELME (born 1931) is an innovative and influential American writer, who has broken away entirely from traditional realism to concentrate on conveying the complexities of modern life through experimentation with language, pushing it to its limits, creating extraordinary verbal arrangements of parody, comedy, and extended metaphor. As in the case of Milan Kundera, he makes us much more conscious that there is an artist molding and manipulating the work, and to complicate matters even further, Barthelme will at times deliberately obfuscate or muddle the reader's point of reference.

Raised in Texas, Barthelme became a newspaper reporter and later a museum director in Houston. He moved to New York City in 1962, where he now teaches. Although Barthelme has written two novels, his finest work can be found in his short-fiction collections, in which he concocts an amazing variety of bizarre situations through an equally impressive and unexpected range of techniques. Some works are composed entirely of dialogue, others are interspersed with graphics—some pieces have the semblance of a plot line, others are just dazzling but simple strings of word fragments, floating in their own provocative ambiguity.

From his first short-fiction collection called Come Back Dr. Caligari (1962), Barthelme has become one of the most prolific and most imitated writers in America. His subsequent collections include Unspeakable Practices, Unnatural Acts (1968), City Life (1970), Guilty Pleasures (1974), and a selected volume entitled Sixty Stories (1981). In 1972, he won a National Book Award for his children's book, The Slightly Irregular Fire Engine.

"Views of My Father Weeping" is a fascinating selection from the book City Life, which, through Barthelme's bursts of wild creativity, reveals the nightmare of our demented society, overwhelmed by the absurdities of technology. In this piece, a son investigates the accidental death of his father, but there is such a confusion of conflicting reports, unaccountable interchanges between characters, montage-like cuts from one scene to another, sections of preposterous puns, and blatant anachronisms, that the reader is soon as baffled as the son is. The son tries to discover the truth about this incident, but Barthelme mystifies him and the reader not only through contradictions in the action of the story, but also through the strange mixture of styles. When we feel we are finally going to have the real facts of the case come to light, everything is turned on its head, epitomized by the final enigmatic "Etc." This is the essence of Barthelme's groundbreaking work—to prod the reader into questioning all aspects of perception, as well as the traditional obligations of literary form.

Views of My Father Weeping

Donald Barthelme

A N ARISTOCRAT was riding down the street in his carriage. He ran over my father.

After the ceremony I walked back to the city. I was trying to think of the reason my father had died. Then I remembered: he was run over by a carriage.

I telephoned my mother and told her of my father's death. She said she supposed it was the best thing. I too supposed it was the best thing. His enjoyment was diminishing. I wondered if I should attempt to trace the aristocrat whose carriage had run him down. There were said to have been one or two witnesses.

Yes it is possible that it is not my father who sits there in the center of the bed weeping. It may be someone else, the mailman, the man who delivers the groceries, an insurance salesman or tax collector, who knows. However, I must say, it resembles my father. The resemblance is very strong. He is not smiling through his tears but frowning through them. I remember once we were out on the ranch shooting peccadillos (result of a meeting, on the plains of the West, of the collared peccary and the nine-banded armadillo). My father shot and missed. He wept. This weeping resembles that weeping.

483

"Did you see it?" "Yes but only part of it. Part of the time I had my back turned." The witness was a little girl, eleven or twelve. She lived in a very poor quarter and I could not imagine that, were she to testify, anyone would credit her. "Can you recall what the man in the carriage looked like?" "Like an aristocrat," she said.

The first witness declares that the man in the carriage looked "like an artistocrat." But that might be simply the carriage itself. Any man sitting in a handsome carriage with a driver on the box and perhaps one or two footmen up behind tends to look like an aristocrat. I wrote down her name and asked her to call me if she remembered anything else. I gave her some candy.

I stood in the square where my father was killed and asked people passing by if they had seen, or knew of anyone who had seen, the incident. At the same time I felt the effort was wasted. Even if I found the man whose carriage had done the job, what would I say to him? "You killed my father." "Yes," the aristocrat would say, "but he ran right in under the legs of the horses. My man tried to stop but it happened too quickly. There was nothing anyone could do." Then perhaps he would offer me a purse full of money.

The man sitting in the center of the bed looks very much like my father. He is weeping, tears coursing down his cheeks. One can see that he is upset about something. Looking at him I see that something is wrong. He is spewing like a fire hydrant with its lock knocked off. His yammer darts in and out of all the rooms. In a melting mood I lay my paw on my breast and say, "Father." This does not distract him from his plaint, which rises to a shriek, sinks to a pule. His range is great, his ambition commensurate. I say again, "Father," but he ignores me. I don't know whether it is time to flee or will not be time to flee until later. He may suddenly stop, assume a sternness. I have kept the door open and nothing between me and the door, and moreover the screen unlatched, and on top of that the motor running, in the Mustang. But perhaps it is not my father weeping there, but another father: Tom's father, Phil's father, Pat's father, Pete's father, Paul's father. Apply some sort of test, voiceprint reading or

My father throws his ball of knitting up in the air. The orange wool hangs there.

My father regards the tray of pink cupcakes. Then he jams his thumb into each cupcake, into the top. Cupcake by cupcake. A thick smile spreads over the face of each cupcake.

Then a man volunteered that he had heard two other men talking about the accident in a shop. "What shop?" The man pointed it out to me, a draper's shop on the south side of the square. I entered the shop and made inquiries. "It was your father, eh? He was bloody clumsy if you ask me." This was the clerk behind the counter. But another man standing nearby, well-dressed, even elegant, a gold watchchain stretched across his vest, disagreed. "It was the fault of the driver," the second man said. "He could have stopped them if he had cared to." "Nonsense," the clerk said, "not a chance in the world. If your father hadn't been drunk—" "He wasn't drunk," I said. "I arrived on the scene soon after it happened and I smelled no liquor."

This was true. I had been notified by the police, who came to my room and fetched me to the scene of the accident. I bent over my father, whose chest was crushed, and laid my cheek against his. His cheek was cold. I smelled no liquor but blood from his mouth stained the collar of my coat. I asked the people standing there how it had happened. "Run down by a carriage," they said. "Did the driver stop?" "No, he whipped up the horses and went off down the street and then around the corner at the end of the street, toward King's New Square." "You have no idea as to whose carriage..." "None." Then I made the arrangements for the burial. It was not until several days later that the idea of seeking the aristocrat in the carriage came to me.

I had had in my life nothing to do with aristocrats, did not even know in what part of the city they lived, in their great houses. So that even if I located someone who had seen the incident and could identify the particular aristocrat involved, I would be faced with the further task of finding his house and gaining admittance (and even then, might he not be abroad?). "No, the driver was at fault," the man with the gold watchchain said. "Even if your father was drunk—and I can't say about that, one way or another, I have no opinion—even if your father was drunk, the driver could have done more to avoid the accident. He was dragged, you know. The carriage dragged him about forty feet." I had noticed that my father's clothes were torn in a peculiar way. "There was one thing," the clerk said, "don't tell anyone I told you, but I can give you one hint. The driver's livery was blue and green."

It is someone's father. That much is clear. He is fatherly. The gray in the head. The puff in the face. The droop in the shoulders. The flab on the gut. Tears falling. Tears falling. Tears falling. Tears falling. More tears. It seems that he intends to go further along this salty path. The facts suggest that this is his program, weeping. He has something in mind, more weeping. O lud lud! But why remain? Why watch it? Why tarry?

Why not fly? Why subject myself? I could be somewhere else, reading a book, watching the telly, stuffing a big ship into a little bottle, dancing the Pig. I could be out in the streets feeling up eleven-year-old girls in their soldier drag, there are thousands, as alike as pennies, and I could be—Why doesn't he stand up, arrange his clothes, dry his face? He's trying to embarrass us. He wants attention. He's trying to make himself interesting. He wants his brow wrapped in cold cloths perhaps, his hands held perhaps, his back rubbed, his neck kneaded, his wrists patted, his elbows anointed with rare oils, his toenails painted with tiny scenes representing God blessing America. I won't do it.

My father has a red bandana tied around his face covering the nose and mouth. He extends his right hand in which there is a water pistol. "Stick 'em up!" he says.

But blue and green livery is not unusual. A blue coat with green trousers, or the reverse, if I saw a coachman wearing such livery I would take no particular notice. It is true that most livery tends to be blue and buff, or blue and white, or blue and a sort of darker blue (for the trousers). But in these days one often finds a servant aping the more exquisite color combinations affected by his masters. I have even seen them in red trousers although red trousers used to be reserved, by unspoken agreement, for the aristocracy. So that the colors of the driver's livery were not of much consequence. Still it was something. I could now go about in the city, especially in stables and gin shops and such places, keeping a weather eye for the livery of the lackeys who gathered there. It was possible that more than one of the gentry dressed his servants in this blue and green livery, but on the other hand, unlikely that there were as many as half a dozen. So that in fact the draper's clerk had offered a very good clue indeed, had one the energy to pursue it vigorously.

There is my father, standing alongside an extremely large dog, a dog ten hands high at the very least. My father leaps on the dog's back, straddles him. My father kicks the large dog in the ribs with his heels. "Gid-dyap!"

My father has written on the white wall with his crayons.

I was stretched out on my bed when someone knocked at the door. It was the small girl to whom I had given candy when I had first begun searching for the aristocrat. She looked frightened, yet resolute; I could see that she had some information for me. "I know who it was," she said. "I know his name." "What is it?" "First you must give me five crowns." Luckily I had five crowns in my pocket; had she come later in the day, after I had eaten, I would have had nothing to give her. I handed over the money and she said, "Lars Bang." I looked at her in some surprise. "What sort of name is that for an aristocrat?" "His coachman," she said. "The coachman's name is Lars Bang." Then she fled.

When I heard this name, which in its sound and appearance is rude, vulgar, not unlike my own name, I was seized with repugnance, thought of dropping the whole business, although the piece of information she had brought had just cost me five crowns. When I was seeking him and he was yet nameless, the aristocrat and, by extension, his servants, seemed vulnerable: they had, after all, been responsible for a crime, or a sort of crime. My father was dead and they were responsible, or at least involved; and even though they were of the aristocracy or servants of the aristocracy, still common justice might be sought for; they might be required to make reparation, in some measure, for what they had done. Now, having the name of the coachman, and being thus much closer to his master than when I merely had the clue of the blue and green livery, I became afraid. For, after all, the unknown aristocrat must be a very powerful man, not at all accustomed to being called to account by people like me; indeed, his contempt for people like me was so great that, when one of us was so foolish as to stray into the path of his carriage, the aristocrat dashed him down, or permitted his coachman to do so, dragged him along the cobble-stones for as much as forty feet, and then went gaily on his way, toward King's New Square. Such a man, I reasoned, was not very likely to take kindly to what I had to say to him. Very possibly there would be no purse of money at all, not a crown, not an öre; but rather he would, with an abrupt, impatient nod of his head, set his servants upon me. I would be beaten, perhaps killed. Like my father.

But if it is not my father sitting there in the bed weeping, why am I standing before the bed, in an attitude of supplication? Why do I desire with all my heart that this man, my father, cease what he is doing, which is so painful to me? Is it only that my position is a familiar one? That I remember, before, desiring with all my heart that this man, my father, cease what he is doing?

Why!...there's my father!...sitting in the bed there!...and he's *weeping*!...as though his heart would burst!...Father!...how is this?...who has wounded you?...name the man!...why I'll... I'll...here, Father, take this handkerchief!...and this handkerchief! ...and this handkerchief!...I'll run for a towel...for a doctor...for a priest...for a good fairy...is there...can you...can I...a cup of hot tea?...bowl of steaming soup?...shot of Calvados?...a joint?...a red jacket?...a blue jacket?...Father, please!...look at me, Father...who has insulted you?...are you, then, compromised?...ruined?... a slander is going around?...an obloquy?...a traducement?...

'sdeath!...I won't permit it!...I won't abide it!...I'll...move every mountain...climb...every river...etc.

My father is playing with the salt and pepper shakers, and with the sugar bowl. He lifts the cover off the sugar bowl, and shakes pepper into it.

Or: My father thrusts his hand through a window of the doll's house. His hand knocks over the doll's chair, knocks over the doll's chest of drawers, knocks over the doll's bed.

The next day, just before noon, Lars Bang himself came to my room. "I understand that you are looking for me." He was very much of a surprise. I had expected a rather burly, heavy man, of a piece with all of the other coachmen one saw sitting up on the box; Lars Bang was, instead, slight, almost feminine-looking, more the type of the secretary or valet than the coachman. He was not threatening at all, contrary to my fears; he was almost helpful, albeit with the slightest hint of malice in his helpfulness. I stammeringly explained that my father, a good man although subject to certain weaknesses, including a love of the bottle, had been run down by an aristocrat's coach, in the vicinity of King's New Square, not very many days previously; that I had information that the coach had dragged him some forty feet; and that I was eager to establish certain facts about the case. "Well then," Lars Bang said, with a helpful nod, "I'm your man, for it was my coach that was involved. A sorry business! Unfortunately I haven't the time right now to give you the full particulars, but if you will call round at the address written on this card, at six o'clock in the evening, I believe I will be able to satisfy you." So saying, he took himself off, leaving me with the card in my hand.

I spoke to Miranda, quickly sketching what had happened. She asked to see the white card; I gave it to her, for the address meant nothing to me. "Oh my," she said. "17 rue du Bac, that's over by the Vixen Gate—a very special quarter. Only aristocrats of the highest rank live there, and common people are not even allowed into the great park that lies between the houses and the river. If you are found wandering about there at night, you are apt to earn yourself a very severe beating." "But I have an appointment," I said. "An appointment with a coachman!" Miranda cried, "how foolish you are! Do you think the men of the watch will believe that, or even if they believe it (you have an honest enough face) will allow you to prowl that rich quarter, where so many thieves would dearly love to be set free for an hour or so, after dark? Go to!" Then she advised me that I must carry something with me, a pannier of beef or some dozen bottles of wine, so that if apprehended by the watch, I could say that I was delivering to such and such a house, and thus be judged an honest man on an honest errand, and escape a beating. I saw that she was right; and going out, I purchased at the wine merchant's a dozen bottles of a rather good claret (for it would never do to be delivering wine no aristocrat would drink); this cost me thirty crowns, which I had borrowed from Miranda. The bottles we wrapped round with straw, to prevent them banging into one another, and the whole we arranged in a sack, which I could carry on my back. I remember thinking, how they rhymed, fitted together, *sack* and *back*. In this fashion I set off across the city.

There is my father's bed. In it, my father. Attitude of dejection. Graceful as a mule deer once, the same large ears. For a nanosecond, there is a nanosmile. Is he having me on? I remember once we went out on the ups and downs of the West (out past Vulture's Roost) to shoot. First we shot up a lot of old beer cans, then we shot up a lot of old whiskey bottles, better because they shattered. Then we shot up some mesquite bushes and some parts of a Ford pickup somebody'd left lying around. But no animals came to our party (it was noisy, I admit it). A long list of animals failed to arrive, no deer, quail, rabbit, seals, sea lions, condylarths. It was pretty boring shooting up mesquite bushes, so we hunkered down behind some rocks, Father and I, he hunkered down behind his rocks and I hunkered down behind my rocks, and we commenced to shooting at each other. That was interesting.

My father is looking at himself in a mirror. He is wearing a large hat (straw) on which there are a number of blue and yellow plastic jonquils. He says: "How do I look?"

Lars Bang took the sack from me and without asking permission reached inside, withdrawing one of the straw-wrapped bottles of claret. "Here's something!" he exclaimed, reading the label. "A gift for the master, I don't doubt!" Then, regarding me steadily all the while, he took up an awl and lifted the cork. There were two other men seated at the pantry table, dressed in the blue-and-green livery, and with them a dark-haired, beautiful girl, quite young, who said nothing and looked at no one. Lars Bang obtained glasses, kicked a chair in my direction, and poured drinks all round. "To your health!" he said (with what I thought an ironical overtone) and we drank. "This young man," Lars Bang said, nodding to me, "Is here seeking our advice on a very complicated business. A murder, I believe you said?" "I said nothing of the kind. I seek information about an accident." The claret was soon exhausted. Without looking at me, Lars Bang opened a second bottle and set it in the center of the table. The beautiful dark-haired girl ignored me along with all the others. For my part, I felt I had conducted myself rather well thus far. I had not protested when the wine was made free of (after all, they would be accustomed to levying a sort of tax on anything entering through the back door). But also I had not permitted his word "murder" to be used, but instead specified the use of the word "accident." Therefore I was, in general, comfortable sitting at the table drinking the wine, for which I have no better head than had my father. "Well," said Lars Bang, at the length, "I will relate the circumstances of the accident, and you may judge for yourself as to whether myself and my master, the Lensgreve Aklefeldt, were at fault." I absorbed this news with a slight shock. A count! I had selected a man of very high rank indeed to put my question to. In a moment my accumulated self-confidence drained away. A count! Mother of God, have mercy on me.

There is my father, peering through an open door into an empty house. He is accompanied by a dog (small dog; not the same dog as before). He looks into the empty room. He says: "Anybody home?"

There is my father, sitting in his bed, weeping.

"It was a Friday," Lars Bang began, as if he were telling a tavern story. "The hour was close upon noon and my master directed me to drive him to King's New Square, where he had some business. We were proceeding there at a modest easy pace, for he was in no great hurry. Judge of my astonishment when, passing through the drapers quarter, we found ourselves set upon by an elderly man, thoroughly drunk, who flung himself at my lead pair and began cutting at their legs with a switch in the most vicious manner imaginable. The poor dumb brutes reared, of course, in fright and fear, for," Lars Bang said piously, "they are accustomed to the best of care, and never a blow do they receive from me, or from the other coachman, Rik, for the count is especially severe upon this point, that his animals be well-treated. The horses, then, were rearing and plunging; it was all I could do to hold them; I shouted at the man, who fell back for an instant. The count stuck his head out of the window, to inquire as to the nature of the trouble; and I told him that a drunken man had attacked our horses. Your father, in his blindness, being not content with the mischief he had already worked, ran back in again, close to the animals, and began madly cutting at their legs with his stick. At this renewed attack the horses, frightened out of their wits, jerked the reins from my hands, and ran headlong over your father, who fell beneath their hooves. The heavy wheels of the carriage passed over him (I felt two quite distinct thumps), his body caught upon a projection under the boot, and he was dragged some forty feet, over the cobble-stones. I was attempting, with all my might, merely to hang on to the box, for, having taken the bit between their teeth, the horses were in no mood to tarry; nor could any human agency have stopped them. We flew down the street . . ."

My father is attending a class in good behavior.

"Do the men rise when friends greet us while we are sitting in a booth?"

"The men do not rise when they are seated in a booth," he answers, "although they may half-rise and make apologies for not fully rising."

". . . the horses turning into the way that leads to King's New Square; and it was not until we reached that place that they stopped and allowed me to quiet them. I wanted to go back and see what had become of the madman, your father, who had attacked us; but my master, vastly angry and shaken up, forbade it. I have never seen him in so fearful a temper as that day; if your father had survived, and my master got his hands on him, it would have gone ill with your father, that's a certainty. And so, you are now in possession of all the facts. I trust you are satisfied, and will drink another bottle of this quite fair claret you have brought us, and be on your way." Before I had time to frame a reply, the dark-haired girl spoke. "Bang is an absolute bloody liar," she said.

Etc.

MILAN
KUNDERA

MILAN KUNDERA (born 1929) was born in Brno, Czechoslovakia, the son of a
distinguished pianist. A writer of poetry, drama, and fiction, Kundera is best-known
as a novelist. His first novel, The Joke, appeared in English in 1969 and was the basis for a film
Kundera later wrote and directed. The novels that followed include Life Is Elsewhere (1973),
The Farewell Party (1976), and The Book of Laughter and Forgetting (1980), from which
the present selection is taken. Prior to and including these years, Kundera was having his ups and
downs with the Communist party, from which he was expelled (1950), reinstated (1956), and
expelled again (1970). In 1975 he was allowed to immigrate to France, where he now lives and
teaches at the University of Rennes, having recently been granted French citizenship.

Kundera's fiction explores the territory between psychological and social problems. He is
particularly fond of using sexual predicaments as analogies to social problems. His narrative
style, as the selection here suggests, is more self-conscious and meditative than is usually the case
with magical realism, but the way in which he moves around among levels of possibility and
versions of reality is very much in the spirit of the mode, particularly in his newest novel. The
wonderful feature of the selection from The Book of Laughter and Forgetting presented here is
its orchestration of themes and images. It tells a story through a giant metaphor—Tamina's exile
to the island of the children is clearly a kind of political fable of the fate of Czechoslovakia under
Husak—and at the same time it meditates on music, memory, death, and history. It never allows
us to lose ourselves in the story because it wants us to consider the meaning and value—and
music—of the story as we move through it. It is as if the story in itself is not sufficient to express
what needs expressing; it must be accompanied, must be seen not in its uniqueness, but in its
function as a musical variation.

The Angels

Milan Kundera

I

IN FEBRUARY 1948, Communist leader Klement Gottwald stepped out on the balcony of a Baroque palace in Prague to address the hundreds of thousands of his fellow citizens packed into Old Town Square. It was a crucial moment in Czech history. There were snow flurries, it was cold, and Gottwald was bareheaded. The solicitous Clementis took off his fur cap and set it on Gottwald's head.

Neither Gottwald nor Clementis knew that every day for eight years Franz Kafka had climbed the same staircase they had just climbed to get to the balcony. During the days of the Austro-Hungarian Monarchy the building had housed a German secondary school. Another thing they did not know was that on the ground floor of the same building Hermann Kafka, Franz's father, had kept a shop whose sign had a jackdaw painted next to his name, *kafka* being the Czech word for jackdaw.

Gottwald, Clementis, and all the others did not know about Kafka, and Kafka knew they did not know. Prague in his novels is a city without memory. It has even forgotten its name. Nobody there remembers anything, nobody recalls anything. Even Josef K. does not seem to know anything about his previous life. No song is capable of uniting the city's present with its past by recalling the moment of its birth.

Time in Kafka's novel is the time of a humanity that has lost all continuity with humanity, of a humanity that no longer knows anything

Excerpt from *The Book of Laughter and Forgetting*.

nor remembers anything, that lives in nameless cities with nameless streets or streets with names different from the ones they had yesterday, because a name means continuity with the past and people without a past are people without a name.

Prague, as Max Brod used to say, is the city of evil. After the defeat of the Czech Reformation in 1621 the Jesuits tried to reeducate the nation in the true Catholic faith by overwhelming the city with the splendor of Baroque cathedrals. The thousands of stone saints looking out from all sides—threatening you, following you, hypnotizing you—are the raging hordes of occupiers who invaded Bohemia three hundred and fifty years ago to tear the people's faith and language from their hearts.

The street Tamina was born on was called Schwerin. That was during the war, and Prague was occupied by the Germans. Her father was born on Cernokostelecka Avenue—the Avenue of the Black Church. That was during the Austro-Hungarian Monarchy. When her mother married her father and moved there, it bore the name of Marshal Foch. That was after World War I. Tamina spent her childhood on Stalin Avenue, and when her husband came to take her away, he went to Vinohrady—that is, Vineyards—Avenue. And all the time it was the same street; they just kept changing its name, trying to lobotomize it.

There are all kinds of ghosts prowling these confused streets. They are the ghosts of monuments demolished—demolished by the Czech Reformation, demolished by the Austrian Counterreformation, demolished by the Czechoslovak Republic, demolished by the Communists. Even statues of Stalin have been torn down. All over the country, wherever statues were thus destroyed, Lenin statues have sprouted up by the thousands. They grow like weeds on the ruins, like melancholy flowers of forgetting.

II

If Franz Kafka was the prophet of a world without memory, Gustav Husak is its creator. After T. G. Masaryk, who is known as the liberator-president (all his monuments without exception have been demolished), after Benes, Gottwald, Zapotecky, Novotny, and Svoboda, Husak, the seventh president of my country, is known as *the president of forgetting.*

The Russians brought him into power in 1969. Not since 1621 has the history of the Czech people experienced such a massacre of culture and thought. Everybody everywhere assumes that Husak simply tracked down his political opponents. In fact, however, the struggle with the political opposition was merely an excuse, a welcome opportunity the Russians took to use their intermediary for something much more substantial.

I find it highly significant in this connection that Husak dismissed some hundred and forty-five Czech historians from universities and research institutes. (Rumor has it that for each of them—secretly, as in a fairy tale—a new monument to Lenin sprang up.) One of those historians, my all but blind friend Milan Hubl, came to visit me one day in 1971 in my tiny apartment on Bartolomejska Street. We looked out the window at the spires of the Castle and were sad.

"The first step in liquidating a people," said Hubl, "is to erase its memory. Destroy its books, its culture, its history. Then have somebody write new books, manufacture a new culture, invent a new history. Before long the nation will begin to forget what it is and what it was. The world around it will forget even faster."

"What about language?"

"Why would anyone bother to take it from us? It will soon be a matter of folklore and die a natural death."

Was that hyperbole dictated by utter despair?

Or is it true that a nation cannot cross a desert of organized forgetting?

None of us knows what will be. One thing, however, is certain: in moments of clairvoyance the Czech nation can glimpse its own death at close range. Not as an accomplished fact, not as the inevitable future, but as a perfectly concrete possibility. Its death is at its side.

III

Six months later Hubl was arrested and sentenced to many years' imprisonment. My father was dying at the time.

During the last ten years of his life my father gradually lost the power of speech. At first he simply had trouble calling up certain words or would say similar words instead and then immediately laugh at himself. In the end he had only a handful of words left, and all his attempts at saying anything more substantial resulted in one of the last sentences he could articulate: "That's strange."

Whenever he said "That's strange," his eyes would express infinite astonishment at knowing everything and being able to say nothing. Things lost their names and merged into a single, undifferentiated reality. I was the only one who by talking to him could temporarily transform that nameless infinity into the world of clearly named entities.

His unusually large blue eyes still stared out of his handsome old face as intelligently as before. I often took him for walks. We would walk once around the block. That was all he had strength for. He had trouble walking. He took tiny steps, and as soon as he felt the least bit tired, his body would tilt forward, and he would lose his balance. We often had to stop so he could lean his forehead against the wall and rest.

During the walks we talked about music. When Father could speak normally, I hadn't asked him many questions. Now I wanted to make up for it. So we talked about music. It was an unusual conversation. One of the participants knew nothing but a lot of words, the other knew everything but no words.

Through the ten years of his illness Father worked steadily on a long study of Beethoven's sonatas. He wrote somewhat better than he spoke, but even while writing he would suffer more and more memory lapses until finally no one could understand the text—it was made up of words that did not exist.

Once he called me into his room. The variations from the Opus III sonata were open on the piano. "Look," he said, pointing to the music (he had also lost the ability to play the piano), "look." Then, after a prolonged effort, he managed to add, "Now I know!" He kept trying to explain something important to me, but the words he used were completely unintelligible, and seeing that I didn't understand him, he looked at me in amazement and said, "That's strange."

I knew what he wanted to talk about, of course. He had been involved with the topic a long time. Beethoven had felt a sudden attachment to the variation form toward the end of his life. At first glance it might seem the most superficial of forms, a showcase for technique, the type of work better suited to a lacemaker than to Beethoven. But Beethoven made it one of the most distinguished forms (for the first time in the history of music) and imbued it with some of his finest meditations.

True, all that is well known. But what Father wanted to know was what we are to make of it. Why did he choose variations? What lay behind his choice?

That is why he called me into his room, pointed to the music, and said, "Now I know!"

IV

The silence of my father, whom all words eluded, the silence of the hundred and forty-five historians, who have been forbidden to remember, that myriad-voiced silence resounding from all over my country forms the background of the picture against which I paint Tamina.

She went on serving coffee at the café in a small town in Western Europe. But she no longer moved in the aura of friendly civility that used to draw in customers. She no longer had any desire to lend them her ear.

One day when Bibi was sitting at the counter on a bar stool and her baby girl was crawling around on the floor screaming and yelling, Tamina lost her patience. She waited a minute to give Bibi a chance to quiet the child down and then said, "Can't you stop her from making such a racket?"

Bibi took offense. "What makes you hate children so much?"

There is no reason to think that Tamina hated children. Besides, she detected a completely unexpected hostility in Bibi's voice. Without quite knowing how it came about, she stopped seeing her.

Then one morning Tamina did not show up for work. It had never happened before. The owner's wife went to see if anything was wrong. She rang her doorbell, but nobody answered. She went back the next day, and again—no answer. She called the police. When they broke down the door, all they found was a carefully maintained apartment with nothing missing, nothing suspicious.

Tamina did not report to work the next few days either. The police came back on the case, but uncovered nothing new. They filed Tamina away with the Permanently Missing.

V

On the fateful day, a young man in jeans sat down at the counter. Tamina was all alone in the café at the time. The young man ordered a Coke and sipped the liquid slowly. He looked at Tamina; Tamina looked out into space.

Suddenly he said, "Tamina."

If that was meant to impress her, it failed. There was no trick to finding out her name. All the customers in the neighborhood knew it.

"I know you're sad," he went on.

That didn't have the desired effect either. She knew that there were all kinds of ways to make a conquest and that one of the surest roads to a woman's genitals was through her sadness. All the same she looked at him with greater interest than before.

They began talking. What attracted and held Tamina's attention was his questions. Not what he asked, but the fact that he asked anything at all. It had been so long since anyone had asked her about anything. It seemed like an eternity! The only person who had ever really interrogated her was her husband, and that was because love is a constant interrogation. In fact, I don't know a better definition of love.

(Which means that no one loves us better than the police, my friend Hubl would object. Absolutely. Since every apex has its nadir, love has the prying eye of the police. Sometimes people confuse the apex with the nadir, and I wouldn't be surprised if lonely people secretly yearn to be taken in for cross-examination from time to time to give them somebody to talk to about their lives.)

VI

The young man looks into her eyes and listens to what she has to say and then tells her that what she calls remembering is in fact something different, that in fact she is under a spell and watching herself forget.

Tamina nods her head in agreement.

The young man goes on. When she looks back sadly, it is no longer out of fidelity to her husband. She no longer even sees her husband; she simply looks out into space.

Into space? Then what makes it so hard for her to look back?

It's not the memories, explains the young man; it's remorse. Tamina will never forgive herself for forgetting.

"But what can I do?" asks Tamina.

"Forget your forgetting," says the young man.

"Any advice on how to go about it?" Tamina laughs bitterly.

"Haven't you ever felt like getting away from it all?"

"Yes, I have," admits Tamina. "Very much so. But where can I go?"

"How about a place where things are as light as the breeze, where things have no weight, where there is no remorse?"

"Yes," says Tamina in a dreamy voice, "a place where things weigh nothing at all."

And as in a fairy tale, as in a dream (no, it *is* a fairy tale, it *is* a dream!), Tamina walks out from behind the counter where she has spent several years of her life, and leaves the café with the young man. There is a red sports car parked out front. The young man climbs in behind the wheel and offers Tamina the seat next to him.

VII

I understand the remorse Tamina felt. When my father died, I had a bad case of it too. I couldn't forgive myself for asking him so little, for knowing so little about him, for losing him. In fact, it was that very remorse which suddenly made me see what he must have meant to tell me the day he pointed to the Opus III sonata.

Let me try to explain it by means of an analogy. The symphony is a musical epic. We might compare it to a journey leading through the boundless reaches of the external world, on and on, farther and farther. Variations also constitute a journey, but not through the external world. You recall Pascal's *pensée* about how man lives between the abyss of the infinitely large and the infinitely small. The journey of the variation form leads to that *second* infinity, the infinity of internal variety concealed in all things.

What Beethoven discovered in his variations was another space and another direction. In that sense they are a challenge to undertake the journey, another *invitation au voyage*.

The variation form is the form of maximum concentration. It enables the composer to limit himself to the matter at hand, to go straight to the heart of it. The subject matter is a theme, which often consists of no more than sixteen measures. Beethoven goes as deeply into those sixteen measures as if he had gone down a mine to the bowels of the earth.

The journey to the second infinity is no less adventurous than the journey of the epic, and closely parallels the physicist's descent into the wondrous innards of the atom. With every variation Beethoven moves farther and farther from the original theme, which bears no more resemblance to the final variation than a flower to its image under the microscope.

Man knows he cannot embrace the universe with all its suns and stars. But he finds it unbearable to be condemned to lose the second infinity as well, the one so close, so nearly within reach. Tamina lost the infinity of her love, I lost my father, we all lose in whatever we do, because if it is perfection we are after, we must go to the heart of the matter, and we can never quite reach it.

That the external infinity escapes us we accept with equanimity; the guilt over letting the second infinity escape follows us to the grave. While pondering the infinity of the stars, we ignore the infinity of our father.

It is no wonder, then, that the variation form became the passion of the mature Beethoven, who (like Tamina and like me) knew all too well that there is nothing more unbearable than losing a person we have loved—those sixteen measures and the inner universe of their infinite possibilities.

VIII

This entire book is a novel in the form of variations. The individual parts follow each other like individual stretches of a journey leading toward a theme, a thought, a single situation, the sense of which fades into the distance.

It is a novel about Tamina, and whenever Tamina is absent, it is a novel for Tamina. She is its main character and main audience, and all the other stories are variations on her story and come together in her life as in a mirror.

It is a novel about laughter and forgetting, about forgetting and Prague, about Prague and the angels. By the way, it is not the least bit accidental that the name of the young man sitting at the wheel is Raphael.

The countryside gradually turned into a wilderness. The farther they went, the less green there was, the more ocher; the fewer fields and trees, the more sand and clay. Suddenly the car swerved from the highway onto a narrow road that almost immediately came to an end at a steep incline. The young man stopped the car. They got out. Sanding on the edge of the incline, they could see the thin stripe of a clay riverbank about thirty feet below them. The water was murky brown and went on forever.

"Where are we?" asked Tamina with a lump in her throat. She wanted to tell Raphael that she felt like going back, but she didn't dare. She was afraid he would refuse, and if he did, it would only make her more anxious.

There they stood, on the edge of the slope, water in front of them, clay all around them, wet clay with no grass cover, the kind of land good for mining. And in fact there was an abandoned bulldozer not far off.

Suddenly Tamina had a sense of *déjà vu:* this looked exactly like the terrain around where her husband had last worked in Czechoslovakia. After they fired him from his original job, he had found work as a bulldozer operator about seventy-five miles outside of Prague. During the week he lived at the site in a trailer, and since he could come into Prague to see her only on Sundays, she once made the trip out there during the week to visit him. They went for a walk through just this kind of countryside—the ocher and yellow of wet, clayey, grassless, treeless soil beneath them, the low, gray clouds above. They walked side by side in rubber boots that sank into the mud and slipped. They were alone in the world, the two of them, full of anguish, love, and desperate concern for each other.

That same sense of despair now invaded her, and she was glad for the lost fragment from the past it had suddenly, unexpectedly returned to her.

The memory had been completely lost. This was the first time it had come back to her. It occurred to her that she should put it down in her notebook. She even knew the exact year!

Again she felt like telling the young man she wanted to go back. No, he was wrong to tell her that her grief was all form and no content! No, no, her husband was still alive in her grief, just lost, that's all, and it was her job to look for him! Search the whole world over! Yes, yes! Now she understood. Finally! We will never remember anything by sitting in one place waiting for the memories to come back to us of their own accord! Memories are scattered all over the world. We must travel if we want to find them and flush them from their hiding places!

She was about to tell all that to the young man and ask him to drive her back when they suddenly heard a whistling sound down below.

IX

Raphael grabbed Tamina by the hand. He had a strong grip, so there could be no thought of escape. A narrow, slippery path zigzagged down the incline, and he led her along it.

On the shore, where seconds before there had been no trace of anyone, stood a boy of about twelve. He was holding the painter of a rowboat bobbing up and down at the edge of the water. He smiled at Tamina.

She looked around at Raphael. He was smiling too. She looked back and forth from one to the other. Then Raphael began to laugh. The boy followed suit. It was a strange laugh—nothing funny had happened, after all—and yet pleasant and infectious. It was a challenge to Tamina to forget her anxieties, it was a promise of something vague—joy, perhaps, or peace. And since Tamina wanted to shed her misery, she laughed obediently with them.

"You see?" Raphael said to her. "There's nothing to be afraid of."

·When Tamina stepped into the boat, it began to pitch under her. She sat on the seat nearest the stern. It was wet. She was wearing a light summer dress, and the moisture went right through to her bottom. It felt slimy, and again she was overcome by anxiety.

The boy pushed the boat away from the shore and picked up the oars. Tamina turned around. Raphael stood on the shore looking after them and smiling. Tamina thought she detected something unusual in that smile. Yes! Smiling, he shook his head ever so slightly! He shook his head ever so slightly.

X

Why didn't Tamina ask where she was going?

You don't ask where you're going if you don't care about the destination!

She watched the boy sitting across from her, rowing. He looked weak to her. The oars were too heavy for him.

"How about letting me take over for a while?" she suggested, and the boy nodded eagerly and gave up the oars.

They changed places. Now he was sitting in the stern watching Tamina row. He pulled a small tape recorder out from under the seat. The air was suddenly filled with electric guitars and voices. The boy began jerking his body in rhythm. Tamina looked on in disgust. The child was swaying his hips as provocatively as an adult. She found it obscene.

She lowered her eyes so as not to see him. The boy turned up the volume and began singing along softly. When Tamina looked up at him again for a minute, he asked her, "Why aren't you singing?"

"I don't know the song."

"What do you mean, you don't know it?" he asked, still jerking in time to the music. "Everybody knows it."

Tamina began to feel tired. "How about taking over for a while now?" she said.

"No, you keep rowing," he answered, laughing.

But Tamina was really tired. She shipped the oars and took a rest. "Will we be there soon?"

The boy pointed ahead. Tamina turned to look. They were quite close to the shore now. It differed enormously from the landscape they had left behind. It was green—all grass and trees.

In no time the boat had touched bottom. There were ten or so children playing ball on the shore, and they looked over curiously. Tamina and the boy stepped out of the boat. They boy tied it to a stake. Beyond the sandy shore stretched a long double row of plane trees. After a ten-minute walk along the path between the trees they came to a sprawling, low, white building. There were a number of large, strange, colored objects out front—she wondered what they were used for—and several volleyball nets. It struck Tamina that there was something not quite right about them. Yes, they were very close to the ground.

The boy put two fingers into his mouth and whistled.

XI

Out came a girl who could not have been more than nine. She had a charming little face and walked with her stomach coquettishly protruding like the virgins in Gothic paintings. She glanced at Tamina with no special interest and with the look of a woman secure in her beauty and not beneath emphasizing it by a show of indifference to everything not touching her directly.

She opened the door to the white building. They walked directly into a large room full of beds (there was no sort of foyer or hallway). She looked around for a while, apparently counting beds, and then pointed to one. "That's where you sleep."

"You mean I'm going to sleep in a dormitory?" Tamina protested.

"A child doesn't need a room to itself."

"What do you mean? I'm not a child!"

"We're all children here!"

"But there must be some grownups!"

"No, no grownups."

"Then what am I doing here?" Tamina shouted.

The child did not notice her excitement and went back to the door. Just before going out, she turned and said, "I've put you in with the squirrels."

Tamina did not understand.

"I've put you in with the squirrels," repeated the child with the voice of a dissatisfied teacher. "All the children are assigned to groups with animal names."

Tamina refused to talk about the squirrels. She wanted to go back. She asked what had happened to the boy who had brought her over.

The girl made believe she had not heard what Tamina said, and went on with her remarks.

"I don't care about any of that!" shouted Tamina. "I want to go back! Where is that boy?"

"Stop shouting!" No adult could have been more imperious than that beautiful child. "I don't understand you," she went on, shaking her head to show how amazed she was. "Why did you come here if you want to leave?"

"I didn't want to come here!"

"Now, now, Tamina, don't lie. Nobody takes such a long journey without knowing where it ends. You must learn not to lie."

Tamina turned her back to the child and ran out to the tree-lined path. When she reached the shore, she looked for the boat at its mooring, where the boy had tied it an hour before. But the boat was nowhere to be seen—nor the stake, for that matter.

She began to run. She wanted to inspect the entire shore. But the sandy beach soon turned into swampland, and she had to make a detour before coming back to the water. The shoreline followed an even curve, and after about an hour's search (with no trace of the boat or any possible pier), she found herself back at the point where the tree-lined path came out on the beach. She realized she was on an island.

She walked slowly back along the path to the dormitory, where she found a group of ten children—boys and girls between the ages of six and twelve—standing in a circle. When they saw her, they all cried out, "Tamina, come and play with us!"

They opened the circle to let her in.

Just then she remembered Raphael smiling and shaking his head.

She was struck with terror, and ignoring the children, she ran straight into the dormitory and curled up on her bed.

XII

Her husband died in a hospital. She stayed with him as much as she could, but he died in the night, alone. When she arrived the next day and found his bed empty, the old man he had shared the room with said to her, "You should file a complaint. The way they treat the dead!" There was fear in his eyes. He knew he hadn't long to live. "They took him by the legs and dragged him along the floor. They thought I was asleep. I saw his head bump against the threshold."

Death has two faces. One is nonbeing; the other is the terrifying material being that is the corpse.

When Tamina was very young, death would appear to her only in the first form, the form of nothingness, and the fear of death (a rather vague fear, in any case) meant the fear that someday she would cease to be. As she grew older, that fear diminished, almost disappeared (the thought that she would one day stop seeing trees or the sky did not scare her in the least), and she paid more and more attention to the second, material side of death. She was terrified of becoming a corpse.

Being a corpse struck her as an unbearable disgrace. One minute you are a human being protected by modesty—the sanctity of nudity and privacy—and the next you die, and your body is suddenly up for grabs. Anyone can tear your clothes off, rip you open, inspect your insides, and—holding his nose to keep the stink away—stick you into the deepfreeze or the flames. One of the reasons she asked to have her husband cremated and his ashes thrown to the winds was that she did not want to torture herself over the thought of what might become of his dearly beloved body.

And when a few months later she contemplated suicide, she decided to drown herself somewhere far out at sea so that the only witnesses to the disgrace of her dead body would be fish, mute fish.

I have mentioned Thomas Mann's story before. A young man with a mortal illness boards a train and takes rooms in an unknown city. In one room there is a wardrobe, and every night a painfully beautiful naked woman steps out of it and tells him a long bittersweet tale, and the woman and her tale are death.

They are the sweet bluish death of nonbeing. Because nonbeing is infinite emptiness, and empty space is blue, and there is nothing more beautiful and comforting than blue. It is no mere coincidence that Novalis, the poet of death, loved blue and sought it out wherever he went. Death's sweetness is blue.

Granted, the nonbeing of Mann's young hero was beautiful, but what happened to his body? Did they drag him by the legs over the threshold? Did they slit his belly down the middle? Did they toss him into a hole or into the flames?

Mann was twenty-six at the time, and Novalis died before the age of thirty. I am unfortunately older, and unlike them I can't help thinking of what happens to the body. The trouble is, death is not blue, and Tamina knows it as well as I do. Death is terrible drudgery. It took my father several days of high fever to die, and from the way he was sweating I could see he was working hard. Death took all his concentration; it seemed almost beyond his powers. He couldn't even tell I was sitting at his bedside; he had no time to notice. The work he was putting in on death had completely drained him. His concentration was as focused as that of a rider driving his horse to a far-off destination, pressing his final burst of energy.

Yes, he was riding horseback.

Where was he going?

Somewhere far away to hide his body.

No, it is no coincidence that all poems about death depict it as a journey. Mann's young hero boards a train, Tamina climbs into a red sports car. Man has an infinite desire to go off and hide his body. But the journey is in vain. When his ride is done, they find him in bed and bang his head on the threshold.

XIII

Why is Tamina on a children's island? Why is that where I imagine her?

I don't know.

Maybe it's because on the day my father died the air was full of joyful songs sung by children's voices.

Everywhere east of the Elbe, children are banded together in what are called Pioneer organizations. They wear red kerchiefs around their necks, go to meetings like grownups, and now and then sing the "Internationale." They also have a nice custom of tying one of their red kerchiefs around the neck of a very special grownup and giving him the title Honorary Pioneer. The grownups like it very much, and the older the grownup is, the more he enjoys receiving the red kerchief from the children for his coffin.

They've all received one—Lenin, Stalin, Masturbov and Sholokhov, Ulbricht and Brezhnev. And that day Husak was receiving his at a festive ceremony in the Prague Castle.

Father's temperature had gone down a bit. It was May, and I opened the window facing the garden. From the house opposite us a television broadcast of the ceremony made its way through the blossoming branches of the apple trees. We heard the children singing in their high-pitched voices.

The doctor happened to be making his rounds. He bent over Father, who by now was incapable of a single word, and then turned to me and said in a normal tone of voice, "He's in a coma. His brain is decomposing." I saw Father's large blue eyes open even wider.

When the doctor left, I was so embarrassed I wanted to say something, right away, to push the doctor's words out of his mind. So I pointed out the window and said, "Hear that? What a joke! Husak is being named an Honorary Pioneer!"

And Father began to laugh. He laughed to let me know that his brain was alive and I could go on talking and joking with him.

Suddenly Husak's voice came to us through the apple trees. "Children! You are the future!"

And then, "Children! Never look back!"

"Let me close the window," I said. "We've heard enough of him, haven't we?" I gave Father a wink, and looking at me with his infinitely beautiful smile, he nodded his head.

Several hours later his fever shot up again. He mounted his horse and rode it hard the next few days. He never saw me again.

XIV

But what could she do now that she was there among the children? The ferryman had disappeared and taken the boat with him, and she was surrounded by an endless expanse of water.

She would fight.

It's sad, so sad. In the small town in the west of Europe she never lifted a finger. Did she really mean to fight there, among the children (in the world of things without weight)?

And how did she plan to go about it?

On the day she arrived, the day she refused to play and ran off to the impregnable fortress of her bed, she had felt their nascent hostility in the air. It scared her. She wanted to forestall it and decided to try to win them over, which meant she would have to identify with them, accept their language. She would volunteer for all their games, offer them her own ideas and her superior physical strength, and take them by storm with her charm.

To identify with them she had to give up her privacy. That first day she had refused to go into the bathroom with them. She was ashamed to wash with all of them looking on. Now she washed with them every day.

The large, tiled bathroom stood at the center of the children's lives and secret thoughts. Against one wall were ten toilet bowls, on the other ten sinks. While one team turned up its nightgowns and sat on the toilets, another stood naked in front of the sinks. The ones sitting on the toilets watched the naked ones at the sinks, the naked ones at the sinks looked over their shoulders at the ones on the toilets, and the whole room was full of a secret sensuality, which prompted in Tamina a vague memory of something long forgotten.

While Tamina sat on the toilet in her nightgown, the naked tigers standing at the sinks were all eyes. When the toilets flushed, the squirrels would stand up and take off their long nightgowns, and the tigers would leave the sinks for the bedroom, passing the cats on their way to the newly vacated toilets, where they in turn would watch Tamina with her black pubis and large breasts as she and the rest of the squirrels stood at the sinks.

She felt no shame. She felt that her mature sexuality made her a queen among all those whose pubic regions were smooth.

XV

Apparently, then, the journey to the island was not a plot against her, as she had originally thought when she first saw the dormitory and her bed. On the contrary, she felt as though she had finally come to the place she had always longed to be; she had slipped back in time to a point where her husband did not exist in either memory or desire and where consequently she felt neither pressure nor remorse.

She, who had always had such a well-developed sense of modesty (modesty was the faithful shadow of love), now exhibited herself naked to scores of foreign eyes. At first she found it distressing and unpleasant, but she soon grew accustomed to it. Her nakedness was no longer immodest; it had lost all meaning, it had become (or so she thought) drab, mute, dead. A body whose every inch was part of the history of love had lost its meaning, and in that lack of meaning was peace and quiet.

But if her adult sensuality was on the wane, a world of other pleasures had slowly begun to emerge from her distant past. Buried memories were coming to the fore. This, for example (it is no wonder that she had long since forgotten it; Tamina the adult would have found it unbearably improper and grotesque): in her very first year of elementary school she'd had a crush on her beautiful young teacher and dreamed for months on end of being allowed to go to the bathroom with her.

And now here she was, sitting on the toilet, smiling and half-closing her eyes. She imagined herself as the teacher and the little freckled girl sitting beside her and curiously peeking over at her as Tamina the child. She so identified with the sensuous eyes of the little freckled girl that she suddenly felt the shudder of an old half-awakened feeling of arousal in the farthest depths of her memory.

XVI

Thanks to Tamina the squirrels won nearly all the games, and they decided to reward her handsomely. All prizes and penalties were given out in the bathroom, and Tamina's prize was that she be waited on hand and foot there. In fact, she would not be allowed to touch herself. Everything would be done for her by her devoted servants, the squirrels.

Here is how they served her. First, while she was on the toilet they wiped her carefully; next, they stood her up, flushed the toilet, took off her nightgown, and led her over to the sink; then, they all tried to wash her breasts and pubis and see what she looked like between her legs and feel what it was like to touch. Now and then she tried to push them away, but it wasn't easy. She couldn't be mean to a bunch of children who were really just following the rules of their own game and thought they were rewarding her with their services.

Finally they took her back to her bed, where again they found all kinds of nice little excuses to press up against her and stroke her all over. There were so many of them swarming around her that she could not tell whose hand or mouth belonged to whom. She felt their pressing and probing everywhere, but especially in those areas where she differed from them. She closed her eyes and felt her body rocking, slowly rocking, as in a cradle. She was experiencing a strange, gentle sort of climax.

She felt the pleasure of it tugging at the corners of her lips. She opened her eyes again and saw a child's face staring at her mouth and telling another child's face, "Look! Look!" Now there were two faces leaning over her, avidly following the progress of her twitching lips. They might as well have been examining the workings of an open watch or a fly whose wings had been torn off.

But her eyes seemed to see something completely different from what her body felt, and she could not quite make the connection between the children leaning over her and the quiet, cradlelike pleasure she was experiencing. So she closed her eyes again and rejoiced in her body, because for the first time in her life her body was taking pleasure in the absence of the soul, which, imagining nothing and remembering nothing, had quietly left the room.

XVII

This is what my father told me when I was five: a key signature is a king's court in miniature. It is ruled by a king (the first step) and his two right-hand men (steps five and four). They have four other dignitaries at their command, each of whom has his own special relation to the king and his right-hand men. The court houses five additional tones as well, which are known as chromatic. They have important parts to play in other keys, but here they are simply guests.

Since each of the twelve notes has its own job, title, and function, any piece we hear is more than mere sound: it unfolds a certain action before us. Sometimes the events are terribly involved (as in Mahler or—even more—Bartók or Stravinsky): princes from other courts intervene, and before long there is no telling which court tone belongs to and no assurance it isn't working undercover as a double or triple agent. But even then the most naive of listeners can figure out more or less what is going on. The most complex music is still *a language*.

That is what my father told me. What follows is all my own. One day a great man determined that after a thousand years the language of music had worn itself out and could do no more than rehash the same message. Abolishing the hierarchy of tones by revolutionary decree, he made them all equal and subjected them to a strict discipline: none was allowed to occur more often than any other in a piece, and therefore none could lay claim to its former feudal privileges. All courts were permanently abolished, and in their place arose a single empire, founded on equality and called the twelve-tone system.

Perhaps the sonorities were more interesting than they had been, but audiences accustomed to following the courtly intrigues of the keys for a millennium failed to make anything of them. In any case, the empire of the twelve-tone system soon disappeared. After Schönberg came Varèse, and he abolished notes (the tones of the human voice and musical instruments) along with keys, replacing them with an extremely subtle play of sounds which, though fascinating, marks the beginning of the history of something other than music, something based on other principles and another language.

When in my Prague apartment Milan Hubl held forth on the possibility of the Czech nation disappearing into the Russian empire, we both knew that the idea, though legitimate, went beyond us and that we were speaking of the *inconceivable*. Even though man is mortal, he cannot conceive of the end of space or time, of history or a nation: he lives in an illusory infinity.

People fascinated by the idea of progress never suspect that every step forward is also a step on the way to the end and that behind all the joyous "onward and upward" slogans lurks the lascivious voice of death urging us to make haste.

(If the obsession with the word "onward" has become universal nowadays, isn't it largely because death now speaks to us at such close range?)

In the days when Arnold Schönberg founded his twelve-tone empire, music was richer than ever before and intoxicated with its freedom. No one ever dreamed the end was so near. No fatigue. No twilight. Schönberg was audacious as only youth can be. He was legitimately proud of having chosen the only road that led "onward." The history of music came to an end in a burst of daring and desire.

XVIII

If it is true that the history of music has come to an end, what is left of music? Silence?

Not in the least. There is more and more of it, many times more than in its most glorious days. It pours out of outdoor speakers, out of miserable sound systems in apartments and restaurants, out of the transistor radios people carry around the streets.

Schönberg is dead, Ellington is dead, but the guitar is eternal. Stereotyped harmonies, hackneyed melodies, and a beat that gets stronger as it gets duller—that is what's left of music, the eternity of music. Everyone can come together on the basis of those simple combinations of notes. They are life itself proclaiming its jubilant "Here I am!" No sense of communion is more resonant, more unanimous, than the simple sense of communion with life. It can bring Arab and Jew together, Czech and Russian. Bodies pulsing to a common beat, drunk with the consciousness that they exist. No work of Beethoven's has ever elicited greater collective passion than the constant repetitive throb of the guitar.

One day, about a year before my father's death, the two of us were taking a walk around the block, and that music seemed to be following us everywhere. The sadder people are, the louder the speakers blare. They are trying to make an occupied country forget the bitterness of history and devote all its energy to the joys of everyday life. Father stopped and looked up at the device the noise was coming from, and I could tell he had something very important to tell me. Concentrating as hard as he could on putting what was on his mind into words, he finally came out with: "The idiocy of music."

What did he mean? Could he possibly have meant to insult music, the love of his life? No, what I think he wanted to tell me was that there is a certain *primordial state of music,* a state prior to its history, the state before the issue was ever raised, the state before the play of motif and theme was ever conceived or even contemplated. This elementary state of music (music minus thought) reflects the inherent idiocy of human life. It took a monumental effort of heart and mind for music to rise up over this inherent idiocy, and it was this glorious vault arching over centuries of European history that died out at the peak of its flight like a rocket in a fireworks display.

The history of music is mortal, but the idiocy of the guitar is eternal. Music in our time has returned to its primordial state, the state after the last issue has been raised and the last theme contemplated—a state that follows history.

When Karel Gott, the Czech pop singer, went abroad in 1972, Husak got scared. He sat right down and wrote him a personal letter (it was August 1972 and Gott was in Frankfurt). The following is a verbatim quote from it. I have invented nothing.

Dear Karel,.
We are not angry with you. Please come back. We will do everything you ask. We will help you if you help us...

Think it over. Without batting an eyelid Husak let doctors, scholars, astronomers, athletes, directors, cameramen, workers, engineers, architects, historians, journalists, writers, and painters go into emigration, but he could not stand the thought of Karel Gott leaving the country. Because Karel Gott represents music minus memory, the music in which the bones of Beethoven and Ellington, the dust of Palestrina and Schönberg, lie buried.

The president of forgetting and the idiot of music deserve one another. They are working for the same cause. "We will help you if you help us." You can't have one without the other.

XIX

But even in the tower where the wisdom of music reigns supreme we sometimes feel nostalgic for that monotonous, heartless shriek of a beat which comes to us from outside and in which all men are brothers. Keeping exclusive company with Beethoven is dangerous in the way all privileged positions are dangerous.

Tamina was always a little ashamed of admitting she was happy with her husband. She was afraid people would hate her for it.

As a result, she is not quite sure where she stands. First she feels that love is a privilege and all privileges are undeserved and that's why she has to pay. Being here with the children is a form of punishment.

But then she feels something different. The privilege of love may have been heavenly, but it was hellish as well. When she was in love, her life was constant tension, fear, agitation. Being here with the children is a long-awaited rest, a reward.

Until now, her sexuality had been occupied by love (I say "occupied" because sex is not love; it is merely the territory love marks out for itself) and therefore had a dramatic, responsible, serious component to it, something Tamina watched over with anguish. Here with the children in the realm of the insignificant it finally reverted to what it had originally been: a toy for the production of sensual pleasure.

Or to put it another way, sexuality freed from its *diabolical* ties with love had become a joy of *angelic* simplicity.

XX

If the first time the children raped Tamina the act had all sorts of startling undertones, with repetition it quickly lost whatever message it might have had and turned into a routine that became less and less interesting and more and more dirty.

Soon the children started quarreling among themselves. The ones who were excited by the games of love began to hate the ones who were indifferent to them. And among Tamina's lovers there was definite hostility between the ones who felt they were her favorites and the ones who felt rejected. And all these petty resentments began to turn in on Tamina and weigh on her.

Once, when the children were leaning over her naked body (standing by the bed, kneeling on the bed, straddling her body, squatting at her head and between her legs), she felt a sudden sharp pain: one of the children had given her nipple a hard pinch. She let out a scream and went berserk, throwing all the children off the bed and flailing her arms around her.

She realized the pain had been caused by neither chance nor lust;

one of the children hated her and was out to hurt her. She put an end to her amorous encounters with the children.

XXI

All at once the realm where things are light as a breeze knows no peace.

The children are playing hopscotch, jumping from one square to the next, right leg first, then left, then both. Tamina joins in (I can picture her tall body among the small figures of the children, and as she jumps, her hair flies out around her face and her heart is all boredom), and the canaries start shouting that she's stepped on a line.

The squirrels, of course, protest she hasn't, so both teams stoop down over the lines to look for the imprint of Tamina's foot. But lines drawn in sand lose their shape easily, and so does Tamina's footprint. It is a moot point, and the children have been yelling it out for a quarter of an hour and getting more and more involved in the argument.

At one point Tamina gives a fateful wave of the hand and says, "Oh, all right, so I did step on the line."

The squirrels begin shouting at Tamina that it isn't true, she must be crazy, she's lying, she never touched it. But they have lost the argument—their claim, once exposed by Tamina, has no weight—and the canaries let out a whoop of victory.

The squirrels are furious. They scream "Traitor" at her, and one boy gives her a push that nearly topples her. She tries to grab hold of them, and they take that as a signal to pounce on her. She puts up a good defense. She is a grownup, she is strong (and full of hate, oh yes, she pounds away at those children as if they were everything she ever hated in life), and before long there are quite a few bloody noses in the crowd, but then a stone flies out of nowhere and hits her on the forehead, and she staggers a little, clutching her head. It is bleeding, and the children move away from her. Suddenly everything is quiet, and Tamina makes her way back to the dormitory. She stretches out on her bed, determined never to take part in the games again.

XXII

I can see Tamina standing in the middle of the dormitory full of children in bed. She is the center of attention. "Tits, tits," calls out a voice from one corner. Others join in, and soon she is engulfed in a rhythmic "Tits, titties, tits..."

What not so long ago had been her pride and weapon—her black pubic hair, her beautiful breasts—was now the target of their insults. In the eyes of the children the very fact of her adulthood made her grotesque: her breasts were as absurd as tumors, her pubic area monstrously hairy, beastlike.

They began tracking her down, chasing her all over the island, throwing driftwood and stones at her. She tried to hide, run away, but wherever she went she heard them calling out her name: "Tits, titties, tits..."

Nothing is more degrading than the strong running from the weak. But there were so many of them. She ran and was ashamed of running.

Once she set an ambush and caught and beat three of them. One fell down, two started to make a getaway. But she was too fast for them; she grabbed them by the hair.

And then a net slipped down over her, and another and another. That's right, all the volleyball nets which had been stretched out just above the ground in front of the dormitory. They had been waiting for her. The three children she had just beaten were a decoy. And now here she is, imprisoned in a tangle of nets, twisting and turning, thrashing out in all directions, dragged along by the jubilant children.

XXIII

Why are the children so bad?

But they're *not* all that bad. In fact, they're full of good cheer and constantly helping one another. None of them wants Tamina for himself. "Look, look!" they call back and forth. Tamina is imprisoned in a tangle of nets, the ropes tear into her skin, and the children point to her blood, tears, and face contorted with pain. They offer her generously to one another. She has cemented their feelings of brotherhood.

The reason for her misfortune is not that the children are bad, but that she does not belong to their world. No one makes a fuss about calves slaughtered in slaughterhouses. Calves stand outside human law in the same way Tamina stands outside the children's law.

If anyone is full of bitterness and hate, it is Tamina, not the children. Their desire to cause pain is positive, exuberant: it has every right to be called pleasure. Their only motive for causing pain to someone not of their world is to glorify that world and its law.

XXIV

Time takes its toll, and all joys and pleasures lose their luster with repetition. Besides, the children really aren't all that bad. The boy who urinated on her when she lay tangled beneath him in the volleyball nets gave her a beautiful open smile a few days later.

Without a word Tamina began taking part in the games again. Once more she jumps from square, right leg first, then left, then both together. She will never try to enter their world again, but is careful not to find herself beyond it either. She tries to keep right on the borderline.

But the calm, the normality of it all, the *modus vivendi* based on compromise, have all the terrifying earmarks of a permanent arrangement. While Tamina was being tracked down, she forgot about the existence of time and its boundlessness, but now that the violence of the attacks has died down, the desert of time has emerged from the shadows—frightening, oppressive, very like eternity.

Make sure you have this image firmly engraved in your memory. She must jump from square to square, right leg first, then left, then both together, and make a show of caring whether or not she steps on a line. She must go on jumping day after day, bearing the burden of time on her shoulders like a cross that grows heavier from day to day.

Does she still look back? Does she think about her husband and Prague?

No. Not anymore.

XXV

The ghosts of statues long torn down wandered around the podium where the president of forgetting was standing with a red scarf around his neck. The children clapped and called out his name.

Eight years have gone by since then, but I can still hear his words sailing through the blossoming apple trees.

"Children, you are the future," he said, and today I realize he did not mean it the way it sounded. The reason children are the future is not that they will one day be grownups. No, the reason is that mankind is moving more and more in the direction of infancy, and childhood is the image of the future.

"Children, never look back," he cried, and what he meant was that we must never allow the future to collapse under the burden of memory. Children, after all, have no past whatsoever. That alone accounts for the mystery of charmed innocence in their smiles.

History is a succession of ephemeral changes. Eternal values exist outside history. They are immutable and have no need of memory. Husak is president of the eternal, not the ephemeral. He is on the side of children, and children are life, and life is "seeing, hearing, eating, drinking, urinating, defecating, diving into water and observing the firmament, laughing, and crying."

What apparently happened after Husak came to the end of his speech to the children (I had closed the window by then, and Father was about to remount his horse) was that Karel Gott came out onto the podium and sang. Husak was so moved that the tears streamed down his cheeks, and the sunny smiles shining up at him blended with his tears, and a great miracle of a rainbow arched up at that moment over Prague.

The children looked up, saw the rainbow, and began laughing and clapping.

The idiot of music finished his song, and the president of forgetting spread his arms and cried, "Children, life is happiness!"

XXVI

The island resounds with the roar of song and the din of guitars. There is a tape recorder sitting in the open space in front of the dormitory and a boy standing over it. Tamina recognizes him. He is the boy on whose ferry she long ago came to the island. She is very excited. If he is the boy, his ferry can't be far off. She knows she mustn't let this opportunity slip by. Her heart begins to pound, and the only thing she can think of is how to escape.

The boy is staring down at the tape recorder and moving his hips. The children come running to join him. They jerk one shoulder forward, then the other, throw their heads back, wave their arms, point their index fingers as if threatening someone, and shout along with the song coming out of the tape recorder.

Tamina is hiding behind the thick trunk of a plane tree. She does not want them to see her, but cannot tear her eyes from them. They are behaving with the provocative flirtatiousness of the adult world, rolling their hips as if imitating intercourse. The lewdness of the motions superimposed on their children's bodies destroys the dichotomy between obscenity and innocence, purity and corruption. Sensuality loses all its meaning, innocence loses all its meaning, words fall apart, and Tamina feels nauseous, as though her stomach has been hollowed out.

And the idiocy of the guitars keeps booming, the children keep dancing, flirtatiously undulating their little bellies. It is little things of no weight at all that are making Tamina nauseous. In fact, that hollow feeling in her stomach comes from the unbearable absence of weight. And just as one extreme may at any moment turn into its opposite, so this perfect buoyancy has become a terrifying *burden of buoyancy*, and Tamina knows she cannot bear it another instant. She turns and runs.

She runs along the path down to the water.

Now she has reached the water's edge. She looks around. No boat.

She runs all along the shore of the island looking for it, the way she did that first day. She does not see it. Finally she comes back to the spot where the tree-lined path opens onto the beach. The children are running around, all excited.

She stops.

The children notice her and hurl themselves in her direction, shouting.

XXVII

She jumped into the water.

It wasn't because she was frightened. She'd thought it out long before. The ferry to the island hadn't taken that long. Even though she couldn't see the other shore, she wouldn't need superhuman strength to swim across.

Yelling and shouting, the children ran down to the place where she had jumped in, and several stones splashed down near her. But she was a fast swimmer and was soon out of range of their weak arms.

On she swam, feeling well for the first time in ages. She could feel her body, feel its old strength. She had always been an excellent swimmer and enjoyed every stroke. The water was cold, but she welcomed it. She felt it was cleansing her of all the children's dirt, of their saliva and their looks.

She swam for a long time, and the sun began sinking into the water.

And then it got dark, pitch black. There was no moon, no stars, but Tamina tried to keep herself headed in the same direction.

XXVIII

Where was she heading, anyway? Prague?

She did not know if it still existed.

The little town in the west of Europe?

No. She simply wanted to get away.

Does that mean she wanted to die?

No, no, not at all. In fact, she had a great desire for life.

But she must have had some idea about the world she wanted to live in.

Well, she didn't. All she had left was her body and a great desire for life. Those two things and nothing more. She wanted to get them away from the island and save them. Her body and her desire for life.

XXIX

Then it began to get light. She strained her eyes to catch a glimpse of the other shore.

But all she could see was water. She turned and looked back. There, a few hundred feet away, was the shore of the green island.

Could she possibly have swum the whole night in place? She was overcome with despair, and the moment she lost hope her arms and legs seemed to lose their strength, and the water felt unbearably cold. She closed her eyes and tried to keep swimming. She no longer hoped to reach the other side; all she could think of now was how she would die, and she wanted to die somewhere in the midst of the waters, removed from all contact, along with the fish. She must have dozed off for a bit while her eyes were closed, because suddenly there was water in her lungs and she began coughing and choking, and in the middle of it all she heard children's voices.

Splashing and coughing, she looked around. Not far away there was a boat with several children in it. They were shouting. As soon as they noticed she had seen them, they stopped shouting and rowed up to her, staring. She saw how excited they were.

She was afraid they would try to save her and she would have to play with them again. Suddenly she felt a wave of exhaustion come over her. Her arms and legs seemed numb.

The boat was almost upon her, and five children's faces peered eagerly down at her.

She shook her head desperately as if to say, "Let me die. Don't save me."

But she had no reason to be afraid. The children did not budge. No one held out an oar or a hand to her, no one tried to save her. They just kept staring at her, wide-eyed and eager. They were observing her. One of the boys used his oar as a rudder to keep the boat close enough.

Again she inhaled water into her lungs and coughed and thrashed her arms about, feeling she could no longer keep herself afloat. Her legs were getting heavier and heavier. They dragged her down like lead weights.

Her head ducked underwater. By struggling violently, she managed to raise it back up several times, and each time she saw the boat and the children's eyes observing her.

Then she disappeared beneath the surface.

Translated by Michael Henry Heim

CPSIA information can be obtained
at www.ICGtesting.com
Printed in the USA
BVOW09s1500261017
498702BV00005B/9/P